MW00682355

Johann Peter Lange

The Life of The Lord Jesus Christ

The Gospels: Vol. 2

SALZWASSER
VERLAG

Johann Peter Lange

The Life of The Lord Jesus Christ
The Gospels: Vol. 2

Reprint of the original, first published in 1864.

1st Edition 2022 | ISBN: 978-3-75259-157-6

Verlag (Publisher): Salzwasser Verlag GmbH, Zeilweg 44, 60439 Frankfurt, Deutschland
Vertretungsberechtigt (Authorized to represent): E. Roepke, Zeilweg 44, 60439 Frankfurt, Deutschland
Druck (Print): Books on Demand GmbH, In de Tarpen 42, 22848 Norderstedt, Deutschland

THE LIFE

OF

THE LORD JESUS CHRIST:

THE GOSPELS.

TRANSLATED FROM THE GERMAN OF

J. P. LANGE, D.D.

EDITED, WITH ADDITIONAL NOTES,

BY

THE REV. MARCUS DODS, A.M.

IN SIX VOLUMES.

VOL. II.

EDINBURGH

MDCCCLXIV.

THE LIFE

OF

THE LORD JESUS CHRIST:

THE GOSPELS.

TRANSLATED FROM THE GERMAN OF

J. P. LANGE, D.D.,

VOLUME II.

TRANSLATED BY

J. E. RYLAND, M.A

EDINBURGH

MDCCCLXIV.

CONTENTS OF VOL. II.

SECOND BOOK.

PART III.—THE ANNOUNCEMENT AND CHARACTER OF CHRIST'S PUBLIC MINISTRY.

PART IV.—THE PUBLIC APPEARANCE AND ENTHUSIASTIC RECEPTION OF CHRIST.

PART III.

THE ANNOUNCEMENT AND CHARACTER OF CHRIST'S PUBLIC MINISTRY.

SECTION I.

DETERMINATION OF THE DATES.

ACCORDING to the statements of the Evangelist Luke, which appear to us well accredited, John was about half a year older than Jesus. To this difference in their ages, the difference in the time of their first public appearance most exactly corresponds. John had only for a short period entered on the exercise of his vocation, when Jesus arrived at the Jordan to prepare Himself by baptism for assuming His official functions.

It was not to be expected that these two champions of Heaven (*Gotteshelden*) would begin their ministry before the completion of their thirtieth year. Reverence for their national institutions would deter them from committing such a violation of law and custom, which required that mature age for entering on any public office.[1] But as little could it be supposed that

---

[1] See Num. iv. 3, 37, viii. 24 ; 1 Chron. xxiii. 24; 2 Chron. xxxi. 17. In these passages a scale is noticeable from 20 years old to 25, and again to 30. It has been questioned, whether from the legal standard fixed for the Levites in reference to the commencement and term of their service, any conclusion can be drawn relative to the more irregular ministry of the prophets. Here a distinction must be made between prophetical acts and prophetical authority. Prophetical declarations could emanate in Israel from any individual, even from children and women; but prophetical authority would hardly be granted to one who was levitically a minor,

they would delay beyond this highest point of their manly development, past the limits assigned by the law, to enter upon their divine mission. As, on the one hand, they were kept back by the law up to a certain age, and on the other, impelled by the power of the Spirit to lose no time when they had reached that limit, we may believe that they would carefully observe the exact time of entering on their office; just as the racer starts for the goal at the given signal, or a volley is fired at the exact moment. John might perhaps, during the winter season, delay the administration of baptism, but not the commencement of his ministry.[1]

Matthew does not state the exact time of John's first public appearance. 'In those days,' he says, 'came John the Baptist, preaching in the wilderness of Judea' (iii. 1). He does not mean those days in which Jesus first took up His abode at Nazareth, but that later period in which, by having resided there, He was regarded as belonging to that city (ii. 23). Thus much we gather from this statement, that when the Baptist made his first appearance, Jesus was still residing at Nazareth. Luke informs us still more precisely that 'in the fifteenth year of Tiberius Cæsar, Pontius Pilate being governor of Judea, and Herod being tetrarch of Galilee, and his brother Philip tetrarch of Ituræa and of the region of Trachonitis, and Lysanias the tetrarch of Abilene, Annas and Caiaphas being the high priests, the word of God came unto John, the son of Zacharias, in the wilderness; and he came into all the country round about Jordan, preaching the baptism of repentance for the remission of sins' (iii. 1–3).

---

especially if he was commissioned to rebuke the priests. Besides, John the Baptist was in this respect, as a Levite, subject to the Levitical arrangements. But Christ was not only the supreme Prophet, but also the real High Priest, and would avoid most scrupulously every ground of offence which would make His office of questionable validity to the Israelites. But this legal point was in His case connected with the inner motive, namely, to await the completion of His consciousness.

[1] Though we might give the Theocrat credit that for himself he would not hesitate to bathe in the Jordan when swelled by the wintry snow-water of Hermon, since as a Nazarite he had grown up in the desert in the full heroic energy of a life of nature, yet the multitude would hardly be induced to submit to baptism at that time of the year, the rainy season. See Wieseler, *Chronol. Synops.* p. 148.

Luke seems to distinguish the early prophetic ministry of John in the wilderness, from his coming forward at the Jordan as the Baptist.[1] Even Matthew has in his eye a period of certain days, during which the preaching of John served as a preparation for the rite of baptism which he afterwards performed at the Jordan.[2] Mark joins the two points of time in one; for the preaching of John was from the first an announcement that the people were to submit to a baptism of repentance; and John, as to his manner of life and position, was always in the wilderness; the region he occupied as the sphere of the preacher in the wilderness, formed a decided contrast to the region of the temple. Moreover, the wilderness of Judea, which lies between Kedron and the Dead Sea, and in which John first appeared as a preacher of repentance, is in the direction of the wilderness near Jericho, through which the Israelites travelled from Jerusalem to the Jordan, and not far from it.[3] To the inhabitants of Jerusalem the two wildernesses might more easily seem to run into one another, because John probably had his proper residence still in the wilderness, even when he administered baptism. At all events, the greater number of the persons he baptized had to go through the wilderness in order to reach him. But a large district is always distinguished by its predominant character, and especially by the strong impression it makes by means of some one striking figure. And thus John was everywhere the Baptist in the wilderness, both in a symbolical and a literal sense.[4]

Now if John, as we must suppose, from comparing his age with that of Jesus, was thirty years old in the autumn of the

[1] See Neander, Life of Jesus Christ (Bohn's Tr.), p. 50.

[2] See chap. iii. 1–5.

[3] [A description of the scene of John's baptism is given in Stanley's *Sinai and Palestine*, p. 310.—ED.]

[4] But how, the critic asks, can it be said that Jesus went from the wilderness (where John was), into the wilderness (where He Himself was tempted)? This supposed contradiction is nothing but an illusion to which inaccurate persons are liable from the very accuracy of the designations in the Gospel. He who resides only a few hours' distance from the Rhine says, I am going to the Rhine, though he settles only in a place in the vicinity of the Rhine. From that position, he then goes, when he will, still again to the Rhine. So that one may go from the wilderness into the wilderness,— a marvellous thing, unless the critic has some skill in perspective.

year 779, he probably began to preach about that time. Meanwhile the winter set in, and he could not enter on the administration of baptism before the mild spring-weather of 780; by that time a movement had commenced among the people, and the season suitable for their great lustration had arrived. Jesus also, having about this time completed His thirtieth year, presented Himself for baptism. After His baptism He passed forty days in the wilderness; subsequently, He spent short portions of time at Cana, Nazareth, and Capernaum, probably occupied in the first quiet beginnings of His ministry. Then came the spring of the year 781; and now He went up to the Passover at Jerusalem for the first time in the capacity of a prophet, discharged His office in the midst of the people, and effected the purification of the temple.

Two years before the death of Augustus, about the year 765, Tiberius was raised to share the imperial throne;[1] but in in the year 767 Augustus died. As John probably appeared as the Baptist at the Jordan in the summer of 780, after introducing the rite in the autumn and winter of 779, we must suppose that Luke has included in his reckoning the previous regency of Tiberius. On this supposition, the year 779 would be the fifteenth year of Tiberius.[2]

As great numbers had been baptized before Christ pre-

---

[1] See Wieseler, *Chronol. Synopse*, p. 172; Tacit. *Annal.* i. 3; Sueton. *Tiber.* 20, 21.—Kuinoel, *Commentar. in Ev. Luc.* edit. ii. p. 343. Lucas ad designandum Tiberii principatum non adhibuit vocabulum μοναρχία aut βασιλεία sed nomen ἡγεμονία, quod de quovis imperio, de quavis dignitate ac potestate usurpari solet, etc. Nulla idonea proferri potest ratio, cur non licuerit Lucæ initium principatus imperii ab eo tempore derivare, quo factus esset Augusti collega, quum imprimis in provinciis, qualis Judæa fuit, pari dignitate haberetur, atque Augustus. Non improbabile est, Lucam secutum esse morem Scripturæ. In historia enim regum et in Jeremia anni Nabuchodonosoris reges Babyloniæ ab eo tempore numerantur, quo pater filium in societatem imperii recepit.

[2] Wieseler advocates the view, that Luke (iii. 1) speaks not of John's first appearance, but of a second stage of it, involving a course of action which led to his imprisonment. The mention of the fact, that Herod had 'shut up John in prison' (ver. 20), is in favour of it. But, on the other hand, in the same connection the appearance of Christ is represented as future (ver. 16), which it could only have been previous to Christ's public ministry. That Luke should incidentally mention, by anticipation, John's imprisonment, occasions no difficulty.

sented Himself at the Jordan, we may presume that He was not baptized till late in the summer of 780. But when He purified the temple at the Passover, in 781, the Jews asked Him by what sign He could accredit that act. On His answering, ' Destroy this temple, and in three days I will raise it up,' they rejoined, ' Forty-six years was this temple in building, and wilt Thou rear it up in three days ?' The building of Herod's temple was still in progress, though it was begun before the Passover of 735, and as 46 years had passed since that time, the conversation of Christ with the Jews occurred in the year 781.[1]

The ministry of John, who probably changed his first station on the banks of the Jordan for one higher up, lasted most likely to the winter of the year 781. While he was baptizing in Galilee, Christ was occupied in Judea. At the time of John's imprisonment in Galilee, the supreme council at Jerusalem began to watch the rising reputation of Jesus with an unfriendly eye, in consequence of which He left Judea and retired into Galilee.[2]

[1] See Wieseler, p. 166. [Lichtenstein, however, who is a worthy rival of Wieseler in chronological investigations, shows (p. 75, Lebensgeschichte des Herrn Jesu Christi in chronologischer Uebersicht, Erlangen 1856) that the 46th year is 780; and (p. 153) makes it appear probable that Jesus was baptized towards the end of December 779 or beginning of January 780. So also Andrews, Life of our Lord upon the Earth in its chronol. relations, Lond. 1863. Tischendorf (Synops. Evang. xix.) prefers the close of 780.—ED.]

[2] According to John iv. 1, Jesus probably returned to Galilee towards the end of autumn in 781, because the Pharisees had heard that Jesus made and baptized more disciples than John, and because an extraordinary excitement of popular feeling on His behalf in Judea had begun to make Him an object of hostile observation to the Pharisees. We must consider this return of Jesus to Galilee as identical with that mentioned in the synoptic Gospels (Matt. iv. 12; Mark i. 14; Luke iv. 14). When the synoptic Gospels allege as a motive for His return, that Jesus had heard of John's imprisonment, this motive is not sufficient by itself to explain His conduct, since it was by the tetrarch of Galilee that John had been put in confinement. But that event reacted on the Sanhedrim at Jerusalem. The Pharisees might be stirred up to apprehend the second prophet, since Herod had apprehended the first, and since John, whom with his voice of thunder they feared more than Jesus, could no longer protect the latter by his high repute. The reference of the passage in Luke iv. 43, 44, to one and the same event, is also in favour of this opinion. The passage in John iv. 1 does not imply, as Wieseler thinks, that the Baptist was at that time still exercising his ministry. The comparison of the ministry of Jesus with that of John does not involve that they were contemporaneous.

In the spring of the next year, 782, John was still in prison, and it was then he sent the well-known deputation to Christ, which, according to Matt. xi. 1, 2, appears to have been at the close of the first journeying of Christ through Galilee, and therefore before His visit to the feast of Purim, narrated by the Evangelist John. The beheading of John took place not long after, probably between the feast of Purim and the Passover of 782.[1] Christ did not publicly attend the Passover of this year, but the following one, in 783. The first feast-day of this year, which began with eating the Passover the preceding night, was a Friday.[2]

In addition to the chronological datum by which Luke fixes the time of John's ministry, he has given other historical indications,[3] which are contained in the passage quoted above. Of these the first is, that Pontius Pilate was then governor of Judea : he filled that office ten years,—namely, from the end of 778 or the beginning of 779 to the year 789.

In Luke's description, Herod appears as tetrarch of Galilee. This was the Herod Antipas who beheaded John the Baptist. He held this dignity from the death of his father, Herod the Great, till some years after the death of Christ, but lost it in the year 792. In the third place, Philip is named as being then tetrarch of Ituræa and Trachonitis. He reigned from the death of Herod, at the time of the return of the Holy Family from Egypt, to the year 786. Though all these specifications agree with the history of the times as gathered from other sources, yet some critics believe they have detected a great error in the account of the fourth of the Syrian princes, namely, that Lysanias was tetrarch of Abilene. From Josephus (*Antiq.* xv. 4, § 1) and Dio Cassius (xlix. 32) we learn that, sixty years before the time in which the Lysanias of Luke must have lived, a Lysanias of Abilene was assassinated, and that Cleopatra obtained a part of his dominions ; while Josephus says nothing of a Lysanias who

[1] Compare Matt. xiv. 10, 20 with John vi. 1-14. On the locality from which Herod Antipas issued his orders for the execution of the prisoner in the castle of Machærus, see Wieseler, p. 250 : it was Julias or Livias, in that region of Peræa, situated not far from Machærus.

[2] See Wieseler, p. 176.

[3] [On the significance of these as indications of the political condition of the Jews, see some acute remarks by Lichtenstein, *Lebensgeschichte*, etc. Anm. 11 and 12.—ED.]

reigned about the time of Christ. In this case, according to the demands of a noted critic, the silence of the Jewish historian is to be held decisive against the testimony of the Christian; the inference follows directly, that the latter made an error of 60 years in his account, or held the current designation of that province as the Abilene of Lysanias to be a sufficient ground for assuming that Abilene was then governed by a Lysanias.[1] Those who regard the statement, as it stands, as incorrect, and yet think they can escape the consequence that Luke was mistaken, effect their object by reading the passage modified in one way or another. Dr Paulus thinks that the passage is to be read in connection with the preceding clause, thus: 'At that time Philip was tetrarch over Ituræa and Trachonitis, and over the Abilene of the tetrarch Lysanias.' This translation is obtained either by omitting τετραρχοῦντος after Abilene (with Codex L.); or by reading καὶ τῆς Λυσανίου Ἀβιληνῆς τετραρχοῦντος, and construing τετραρχοῦντος with Φιλίππου; or, lastly, by a forced interpretation translating the text as it stands, in the manner specified. But not only the arbitrary liberty taken with the text and its obvious meaning tells against such an expedient, but likewise the circumstance that it is not only destitute of proof, but is in the highest degree improbable, that Philip, besides his own territory, should have obtained Abilene from the Roman power.[2] It is therefore much simpler to leave the district of Abilene to Lysanias, though we know nothing further about him, than to make it over to Philip, to whom the history does not assign it—indeed, from whose tetrarchy it plainly distinguishes that of Lysanias.[3] Moreover, positive considerations present themselves, as Wieseler in his often quoted work has shown,[4] which justify Luke's statement.[5] First of all, it is worthy of notice that, according to Josephus (*Antiq.* xv. 6, § 4), Cleopatra obtained only a part of the possessions of Lysanias. Wieseler infers, that most probably the remainder was left to the heirs of Lysanias, from

[1] Strauss, *Leben Jesu,* p. 343.
[2] Josephus, *Antiq.* xvii. 11, § 4; *De bello Jud.* ii. 6, § 3. Compare Wieseler, *Chron. Synops.* p. 177.
[3] See the passage from Josephus in Wieseler, p. 177.
[4] With a reference to the treatise by Hug, *Gutachten über das Leben Jesu, critically examined by Dr David Strauss. Freiburger Zeitschrift fur Theologie,* Bd. i. Heft 2.
[5] *Chronol. Synops.* 179.

the circumstance that at a later period one Zenodorus appears as farming the inheritance of Lysanias (*Antiq.* xv. 10, § 1). Wieseler concludes that he probably entered into this engagement because the heirs of Lysanias, being minors, were under guardianship. Then, lastly, the territory of Lysanias is mentioned by Josephus as a tetrarchy, which in the year 790 was given, with the tetrarchy of Philip, by the Emperor Caius Caligula, to Agrippa. From these several indications the critic just named concludes, that between the years 734–790 there must have been a younger Lysanias who governed Abilene as a tetrarch.[1] As the earlier Lysanias is not designated a tetrarch, the fact is of importance, that Pococke describes a coin which names on its superscription a tetrarch Lysanias; and the same traveller discovered an inscription in a temple on the summit of the ancient Abila, 15 English miles from Damascus, which also speaks of the tetrarch Lysanias of Abilene. But the notices in Josephus already mentioned are quite sufficient to introduce the historic testimony of Luke.

To the preceding chronological data Luke adds the striking statement, that 'Annas was high priest, and Caiaphas.' It has been supposed that Annas is placed first because he was the Nasi or president of the Sanhedrim, while Caiaphas was the officiating high priest in the matter of sacrifices.[2] But Caiaphas (according to John xviii.) evidently appears as the proper judge of Jesus; but he was His judge, not as high priest, but as president of the Sanhedrim.[3] Moreover, the Romans, who had less to do with the sacrificing priest than with the presidency of the Sanhedrim, would have thought it of no consequence to remove Annas from the high-priesthood, if that measure had not, in fact, mainly dealt with the presidency of the supreme civil tribunal. Luke seems to mark that degradation of the high-priesthood ironically, when he speaks of a high priest (ἀρχιερέως) Annas, and Caiaphas; the one, that is to say, had the influence, the other the office. In like manner Annas appears in John (xviii. 4): not as president of the council, but as father-in-law

---

[1] [Robinson comes to the same conclusion on similar grounds—Biblical Researches in Palestine, iii. 482–4; and compare Ebrard's *Gospel History* (Clark, 1863), p. 143.—ED.]

[2] See Wieseler, Chronol. Synops. p. 183.

[3] [Lichtenstein supposes he may have been vice-president.—ED.]

of Caiaphas, he had the honour of having Jesus first sent to him. Caiaphas is the high priest 'that same year.' At a period when the office of high priest changed hands so often, he figured as the high priest of the year; but in the national feeling the real, permanent high priest was Annas. It was Caiaphas who uttered the official adage, that 'it was expedient one man should die for the people'—an inconsiderate expression, which evinced neither great political wisdom nor a noble disposition, but which in a higher sense might be regarded as an unconscious prophecy of the atonement.[1]

According to the before-named chronological limits of the ministry of John the Baptist, he was probably engaged in it for half a year before he had fully aroused the people and called them to baptism. After that, he was about a year and a half occupied in baptizing them. Finally, his imprisonment appears to have lasted about half a year. A doubt has been expressed, whether it was possible for John, in the short space of time allowed him by the Evangelists, to make so great an impression on his nation. But if we bear in mind that the infinitely superior ministry of Christ was comprised in the space of two years and a half, we shall find it very conceivable that two years sufficed John for his vocation. Indeed, John must already in the first half-year have agitated his nation, in order to appear as the Baptist. But would it require more than half a year to set Israel in motion when the message resounded, 'The kingdom of the Messiah is at hand! Come, purify yourselves, in order to enter it!' The history of the false messiahs shows that the people were easily set in motion by an announcement of the Messiah's advent. But, apart from the wonderful effect of this message on the theocratic nation, we need only look back on the

[1] It appears from John xviii. 24, that there was no change of place, no sending from palace to palace. The temple guards follow the Jewish national instinct: they lead Jesus first before him who was really the high priest in the opinion of the Jews. He submits Jesus to a preliminary examination, and then sends Him bound, to be disposed of by Caiaphas, who was the officiating, titular high priest—the official high priest in the opinion of the Romans, who by their arbitrary appointments converted the high-priesthood into an annual office. The ἀπέστειλεν αὐτὸν δεδεμένον (ver. 24) may be explained according to the analogy of the passage Luke iv. 19, ἀπέσταλκέ με ἐν ἀφέσει. Annas, as the proper deciding hierarch, sent the Lord bound to Caiaphas; by that His fate was already decided.

middle ages, or into the history of Methodism, to be convinced
how speedily a great preacher of repentance, simply as such,
can agitate the popular mind. We may here be reminded how
the theses of Luther spread like wildfire.

En peu d'heure, Dieu labeure, is a French proverb expressive
of the agency of God generally. But this will apply with peculiar force to the agency of God in critical periods of the
world's history.[1] We must regard those minds as ill endowed
who have no perception that God in His kingdom often works
by voices, thunder, and lightnings (Rev. viii. 5). But, in
reference to John, we might wonder that the widely extended
ministry of such a man left behind so slight an effect, if we did
not also recollect that the splendour of his career was lost in
that of Jesus, as the morning star before the sun; while in the
school of 'John's disciples' only the long shadow of the expiring remains of its Jewish restrictedness has been thrown across
the world's history.

John described himself as 'the voice of one crying in the
wilderness, Make straight the way of the Lord.' He exerted an
influence suited to his gifts and destiny, which were intended to
arouse and prepare, not to fulfil and satisfy. 'He was a burning and a shining light,' according to the words of Christ.
Does such a fiery signal at the outset of a great history require
much time? Certainly much time, says the critic.[2] Does the
sharp note of an overture, wherewith one stroke announces the
character of the piece and prepares the audience for it, require
much time? Surely, thinks the questioner, the instruments
take a long time before they are in perfect tune. The world's
history pronounces otherwise, and herein agrees with art. It is
the office of a historical period to tune the instruments for a
new epoch; but when this opens, new operations succeed, stroke
upon stroke like lightning and thunder. Clement of Alexandria calls the Baptist the voice or sound of the Logos. This
expression is ingenious; though we must remark that the Logos
has His own peculiar sound, and John his own special mode of
thought (*sein eigenthümlich Logisches*) proceeding from the life

[1] ['Usefulness and power are not measured by length of life. . . .
Youth has *originated* all the great movements of the world.'—Young's *Christ
of History*, p. 31.—ED.]

[2] See Weisse, *die evang. Geschichte* i. 253.

of the Logos. If we adhere to Clement's figurative language, we may say that John is to be regarded as a clear trumpet-tone in which the Israelitish feeling for the Messiah expressed itself, and His forthcoming manifestation was announced; or as the clear response which the sound of the incarnate eternal Word, in His New Testament fulness, called forth in the last and noblest prophet of the Old Testament dispensation.

NOTES.

1. Abilene, the territory belonging to the town of Abila, was a district of Anti-Lebanon, towards the east of Hermon; it sloped from Anti-Lebanon towards the plain of Damascus.

2. It is as little possible to learn the special tendency of the Baptist from the tendency of the later sect called 'John's Disciples,' as to form a judgment of a believer who is awakened to a new life from the workings of his old sinful nature in his subsequent history. The so-called John's Disciples who formed themselves into a sect hostile to Christianity, represent John's old Adam; they form the great historical shadow of the great Prophet—the cast-off slough of a religious genius, thrown off when he put on Christ, and whose violent death in Galilee prefigured the violent death of Christ in Jerusalem.

SECTION II.

JOHN THE BAPTIST.

John the Baptist, in his manifestation and agency, was like a burning torch; his public life was quite an earthquake—the whole man was a sermon; he might well call himself a voice— 'the voice of one crying in the wilderness, Prepare ye the way of the Lord' (John i. 23).

But if we attempt to seize the characteristic features of this great phenomenon, we shall be able plainly to distinguish the Nazarite, the prophet, and the religious reformer in a more confined sense, although these characteristics are combined in him in a most living expressive unity.

He 'grew and waxed strong' in the virgin solitudes of

nature (Luke i. 80). In his excursions from the hill-country of
Judea, he had become acquainted with the sacred loneliness of
the adjacent desert region,[1] and here the Spirit of the Lord had
spoken to his spirit.[2] In chosen privation as a free son of the
wilderness, he had accustomed himself to the simplest diet;
locusts and wild honey sufficed him. He clothed himself in
raiment of camel's hair, with a leathern girdle about his loins.[3]
Thus the Nazarite assumed the form of the preacher of repentance. But he also knew the significance of his Nazarite
vow; he knew that he had to lead back Israel from the illusions
of their formalized temple-worship into the wilderness, from
which they had at first emerged as the people of the law, that
they might purify themselves in the wilderness for the new
economy of the kingdom of God. The Nazarite is a preacher
of repentance in the deeply earnest tone of his soul, and therefore in the pensive seriousness of his appearance.

It does not, however, in the least follow from this devoted
man's mode of life that he wished to convert others into ascetics
like himself.[4] He was perfectly aware of the singularity of his
position, and knew how, with noble freedom, to appreciate
other modes of life, and especially higher spiritual stages. But
that the persons who became his disciples must have accommodated themselves to his peculiar habits, lies in the very nature of
such a connection. They were his assistants in administering
baptism, and must therefore have complied with the prerequi-
sites of this employment—of this symbolic preaching of repentance.[5]

But the divine commission which constituted him a prophet
was the revelation that the kingdom of God was at hand for His
people; that therefore the Messiah, as the founder of this king-

[1] See Robinson's Researches [and Andrews, p. 128].

[2] We are here reminded of Fox, the founder of the sect of the Quakers,
and of other distinguished characters of world-wide reputation.

[3] See Von Ammon, *die Geschichte des Lebens Jesu* i. 251. [Kitto, Daily
Bible Illust., 32d Week, 3d Day.]

[4] When Strauss imagines that John, as "the gloomy, threatening
preacher of repentance," would have found it difficult to be on terms of
friendship with Jesus, he substitutes for the historical image of John
in the Gospels one very different from that which really belongs to
him.

[5] Exod. xix. 10, 15.

dom, was forthcoming, and that he was destined to prepare the way for Him. The Spirit of God had also assured him, that by a divine sign the individual would be manifested to him whom he would have to point out as the Lord and Founder of this kingdom. He had become familiar with the idea and presentiment of this destination while under his parents' roof; but the absolute conviction which made him a prophet was imparted by the Spirit of the Lord, at the close of his youthful preparation, in the wilderness. First of all, he had the certainty that the Messiah was already living, though unknown, among the people; then at the decisive moment, on the banks of the Jordan, he received a divine disclosure respecting His person. Such, therefore, was the presentiment, the inspiration, the function and divine mission of his life—to announce the advent of the Messiah, and to make a path for Him in the souls of the people. He was, so to speak, the individualized and final prophetic presentiment of the Messiah among His own people. And only thus, as the herald of Christ, is he an organically necessary and historically conceivable phenomenon.[1] But the prophet, from his wide, clear survey of the pilgrimages to Jerusalem, had from early life been cognizant of the moral and religious decay evinced in the temple-righteousness of his people. He saw through the corruption of the Pharisees and scribes with all the indignation of a genuine Israelite. The holy zeal of all the prophets was concentrated in the lofty repugnance of his powerful soul, and made him in a more restricted sense one of those men of zeal who appeared in Israel in critical moments, as restorers of the damaged Theocracy : such were Phinehas (Num. xxv. 7) and Elijah ; and such was Jesus Himself on the occasions when He purified the temple. In this zeal John became an administrator of baptism, or *the Baptist*. The whole nation appeared to him, as they really were, unworthy and incapable of entering the holy kingdom of the New Covenant, but most of all their

[1] That John, on the contrary, the fabrication of antagonistic criticism, the gloomy monk who in his poor enthusiasm would fain be and ought to be a prophet, and yet is so little of a prophet that he has no presentiment of the Messiah when He comes into his immediate vicinity, and much too late arrives in prison at the conjecture that Jesus may be the Messiah—is a historical monster and a caricature of the biblical Baptist, which we may dispose of in a note, in passing.

leaders and representatives. It was to him a certain fact, that a great general declension had taken place from the spirit of true Judaism, and that even the better sort needed first to undergo a great purification to enable them to receive the King of Israel; and that, after all, the winnowing fan of this King would be needed to separate the chaff from the wheat. The leaders of the people appeared to him mostly as serpents and vipers, in their thoroughly hypocritical natures, and the people in general polluted by the unclean beasts of their evil passions; —and thus, according to the law, a great universal purification was required.[1] The theocratic zealot, therefore, preached the baptism of repentance for the reception of the coming One. With unparalleled boldness he met the Israelitish community with the solemn declaration, that the whole camp was unclean, and that they must first undergo a holy ablution before they could enter into the new community. Thus he, in fact, excommunicated the whole nation, and prescribed for it a symbolical repentance, as a preparation for entering the social communion of the Messiah. The application which John, in his theocratic zeal, made of the rite of holy ablution to his polluted nation, accounts for the institution of his baptism. It was among the requirements of the law, that the Jewish proselytes were to undergo this washing when they passed over from the camp of the unclean, the heathen, to the camp of the clean, the Israelites. But John needed not this inducement to practise baptism. As restorer of the Theocracy, he recognised its necessity as soon as to his inspired theocratic wrath the conviction was established, that Israel had become a camp of the unclean. On the other hand, he too well understood the difference between symbolical and real acts, to confound with his own baptism the sprinkling with clean water which the prophets (Ezek. xxxvi. 25; Zech. xiii. 1) had foretold, and which in a figurative manner denoted the Spirit-baptism of Christ itself.[2] But still less could he fail to distinguish that symbolical act of which he was the administrator, from that anointing with oil which in the Old Testament represented the positive bestowment of the Messianic gifts of the Spirit, in distinction from the washing which was the sign of

[1] Lev. xiv. xv.
[2] As, for example, Strauss, *Leben Jesu* i. 351; also Neander, *Life of Jesus Christ*, p. 50.

negative consecration.[1] John was perfectly aware that the true
essential Baptizer was to come, who would first baptize with the
oil of life, with the Holy Ghost, and with fire. It was his own
mission to restore the community as members of the old economy,
in order to present them pure and set apart for the transition
into the kingdom of heaven. What he required of the people
was in perfect accordance with this mission. Each individual
was to purify himself as an Israelite, to change his mind in
earnest repentance, and in consequence to put away the evil of
his life, and to practise the virtues belonging to his national
calling. Thus would he be fitted for receiving the higher baptism, that of Christ, the real participation of His new, heavenly
life.

The prophetic feeling of the Baptist did not deceive him.
By those warnings with which, like a second Elijah, he stood
forth in the wilderness of Judea, he succeeded in arousing and
agitating the nation. The verdict of his zealous spirit, in which
he described the theocratic commonwealth as polluted, and
announced a baptism of purification, was acquiesced in by the
people. They resorted to him at the Jordan in crowds. He
received them with solemn reprimands, and exhorted them to
conversion, and the practice of the neglected duties of mercy,
brotherly love, honesty, and righteousness (Luke iii. 11–14).
But as for those who were borne along with the tide of the
excited multitudes, and only came to submit to the symbolic
rite as a new instrument of ceremonial righteousness, he calls
them 'a generation of vipers' (Luke iii. 7). They were induced
to flee from the wrath to come, not by the Spirit of the Lord,
but compelled by a regard to theocratic forms. Their fleeing
was therefore pretended. They believed themselves, after all,
to be safe from the coming wrath as children of Abraham.
Therefore the prophet exclaimed, 'Depend not on your descent;
from these stones God can raise up children to Abraham.' A
spirit who could so mortify the Israelitish pride, who expressed
in such strong terms the possibility of the call of the Gentiles
into the kingdom of heaven, was no gloomy ascetic, no man of

[1] The same holds good of Christians of the apostolic age. How strictly
the Essenes distinguished the washing from the anointing is acknowledged.
Only within the pale of modern criticism can the Old Testament washing
be confounded with the Old Testament anointing.

mere statutes. His words of rebuke were pointed quite specially at the Pharisees and Sadducees (Matt. iii. 7). Whether they travelled in one caravan to the Jordan, is not known; nor does it follow in the least from the language of the Evangelist. But at all events, to John's spiritual vision they formed, according to their inner motives, a closely connected band, one caravan of hypocritical penitents. These Pharisees, indeed, followed the track of the people in their acknowledgment of John. The first powerful action of the prophet forced them to accommodate themselves to the popular feeling. They were also moved more or less by enthusiastic hopes of the advent of a Messiah according to their own mind. But as soon as the Pharisees stirred in this direction, the Sadducees were obliged to follow in their footsteps, according to their wont, in order to maintain before the people the appearance of orthodoxy.[1] But John understood their real character; and yet he could not refuse to baptize them, since he had to treat them according to their profession, not according to the thoughts of their heart. It was this contrariety which kindled his wrath into a glowing flame, and led him to employ the strongest terms of censure.[2] He could not deny them the possibility of reconciliation, but still felt himself compelled to announce the judgments which the Messiah would inflict on the wicked. In threatening accents he declared that the axe was laid at the root of the trees. With sadness he felt and confessed that he could baptize only with water the people as they stood before him, a mingled throng of persons eager for salvation, and of hypocritical pretenders. But it gave him consolation that he could announce a mightier One, before whose noble, kingly image his soul was humbled in the dust, with whom he dared not to associate himself, as being no better than a menial or a slave, since he had the feeling that he was not worthy of direct communion with Him.[3] 'I baptize you with water,' he said, 'but there cometh one after me who shall baptize you with the Holy Ghost and with fire.' Such was the Messiah

[1] Josephus, *Antiq.* xviii. 2.
[2] We may pass by the decision of Bruno Bauer on these threatening addresses of the Baptist.
[3] Compare Matt. iii. 11 and the parallel passages. In these words we may find an answer to the question, why the Baptist had not personally attached himself to the Lord.

in his sight; and thus was he to sanctify the people that they might become the people of the New Covenant. The baptism of fire must certainly be distinguished in this place from the baptism of the Spirit.[1] This follows plainly from the image, according to which Christ purifies the grain of His threshing-floor with the winnowing fan, and then burns the chaff. But the Messiah, in fact, administers this twofold baptism in His whole career throughout the world's history. The saving effects of His administration through time will be supplemented by the judgments which result from the rejection of His salvation. This law strikingly shows in the destruction of Jerusalem, as well as in many other fire-baptisms of historic notoriety, how judgment impends over those circles in which the baptism of the Spirit is despised; and so it will continue to the end of the world. It also holds good in the inner and outer life of the individual as he comes into contact with Christ—one of the two baptisms will be infallibly his portion. A man, in meeting with the Spirit of Christ, is either inflamed by the gentle glow of this Spirit, which arouses and purifies, renovates and transforms his life in all its depths; or he begins to burn with a lurid flame of antichristian rancour in destructive enmity against the kingdom and word of Christ. But in the more general contemplation, the fire-baptism may without hesitation be identified with the Spirit-baptism of Christ; and so much the more, because no one receives the salvation of the Christian spiritual life without passing through the fire of Christ's judgment.

That John formed a correct estimate of the supporters of the Jewish hierarchy, is proved by the attitude which they afterwards assumed against him. But equally was his confidence justified, that the Messiah was already living among the people. While many Pharisees had submitted to his baptism for the sake of appearance, Christ submitted in true obedience to this divine ordinance, because He thoroughly understood its significance for the people and for Himself.

NOTE.

John's manner of life was not a completely isolated phenomenon. It occurred more frequently as a link between the

[1] Neander, *Life of Jesus Christ*, p. 55 [Bohn].

order of the Nazarites and that of the prophets or the rabbinical vocation, and exhibited what was true in Essenism, namely, an abstemious hermit-life, which in its strictness as contrasted with the general mode of living was dedicated only to the people's good. Such a recluse was Banus, the teacher of Josephus; his manner of life resembled that of John. See *Vita Josephi*, § 2; Neander's *Life of Christ*, § 34. Josephus mentions John the Baptist incidentally, *Antiq.* xviii. 5, § 2 : his account of John's baptism is not at variance with that of the Evangelists. He represents John as requiring the people, in order to gain the divine favour, not merely to put away from them this or that particular sin, but to purify their souls by righteousness, and to join with that the consecration of the body by baptism. The special gist of John's baptism, its relation to the kingdom of the Messiah, Josephus from his stand-point could not understand.[1]

SECTION III.

THE PARTICIPATION OF JESUS IN THE BAPTISM OF JOHN.

The significance of John's baptism, as explained in the preceding section, furnishes the simplest solution of the problem in modern theology, why Jesus submitted to that rite in order to fulfil all righteousness. Antagonist critics have violently assailed the Apologetics of the Church with the question, How could Christ submit Himself to this baptism of repentance ? At length they have distinctly proclaimed the consequence, that Christ, in submitting to John's baptism, presented a confession of His own sinfulness.[2] The explanations of the Church could not be satisfactory as long as the idea of the sacred ablutions of the Old Testament was not clearly understood.

[1] [The chapter on John in Ewald's *Geschichte Christus*' (pp. 146–160) is, as might be expected, one of the most suggestive in the book. The whole position of John is sketched by the hand of a master. His priestly birth and upbringing, his discovery of the urgent need of deliverance for Israel, his praying in the desert for the coming of the Messiah, his apparent resemblance to but real difference from Essenes and Pharisees, all are depicted in the most striking and instructive manner.— ED.]

[2] Strauss, *Leben Jesu* i. 403. Compare Bruno Bauer, *Kritik* i. 207.

According to the Mosaic law, not only the corporeally unclean in Israel, as for example lepers, but also those who had touched unclean animals, or in a similar way had, according to the Levitical typology, defiled themselves, were excommunicated from the camp of the typically pure congregation.[1] Readmission into the congregation could take place only after a given period, as was fitting for a case of uncleanness. But every Israelite whose object it was to recover the communion he had lost, was obliged to undergo the appointed religious ablution.

And not only those who were unclean in their own life, or had directly defiled themselves, but those who came in contact with them, were involved in that exclusion, and a similar ablution preceded their readmission into the congregation.[2]

According to this enactment of the law, Christ also was obliged to submit to John's baptism, as soon as He recognised it to be a purification of the people which John administered as a true prophet by an intimation of the Spirit of God. For He stood in the closest contact with the people who were regarded by the prophet as excommunicated. In God's sight He was pure; but according to the Levitical law, as restored by the theocratic authority of the Baptist, and made by him into a sermon of repentance, He was unclean through His connection with an unclean people. On the principles of the Old Testament righteousness, therefore, His baptism was required.

But the essential significance of the baptism of Jesus was the symbol of an actual relation. By baptism, Jesus was pointed out as the sacrificial Lamb of the world, laden with no other burden than His historical life-communion with the world. Considered in Himself alone, He might have had joy; but His connection with sin-laden humanity was the great reproach of His life, which led to His death. Thus His death became the real completion of the Israelitish baptism, and the foundation of baptism in its New Testament form and significance. John's baptism in its highest point was a typical prophecy of the death of Jesus; Christian baptism, on the other hand, is a sacramental representation of the same event.[3]

[1] Lev. xi. xiv.   [2] Lev. xv. 5, 10, 11, 19, etc.

[3] When Ebrard (*Gospel History*, 194) denies the relation of baptism to the Jewish ablutions, this view of the subject is not confirmed. On the other hand, his remark, which regards baptism as a rite going beyond simple

But when Jesus came to be baptized, John, the theocratic champion lost his lofty bearing. He who had reprimanded the members of the Sanhedrim as ' a generation of vipers,' exclaimed in tones of alarm to the consecrated Nazarene, ' I have need to be baptized of Thee, and comest Thou to me ?' Thus the splendour of the New Testament broke forth from the verge of the Old.[1] But the sternness of the Old Testament flashed across the dawn of the New when Christ said, ' Suffer it to be so now ; for thus it becometh us to fulfil all righteousness.' Here the staves of the Old and New Testament righteousness form a cross. John represents the New Testament in the presence of Jesus ; Jesus represents the Old Testament in the presence of John. The two economies manifest their relationship and unity by this junction of their contiguous links. We might say that the two covenants salute and bless one another in this holy rivalry ; the one glorifies itself in the other, and from the glory of the first emerges the greater glory of the second.

But the determination of Jesus prevailed, for He came not to dissolve the law, but to fulfil it ; and He well knew that this baptism expressed that consecration of death for His people, which was spread over His life. But by this wonderful humility of Jesus, John was prepared to receive the positive revelation, that this was the Lamb of God which taketh away the sins of the world. At that very instant the feeling must have agitated him, that Jesus was necessitated only by communion with His people to submit to the humiliating ordinance of baptism—that He bore the sins of His people.

NOTES.

1. Strauss remarks, that according to Matt. iii. 6, John appears to have required a confession of sins before baptism. Hence it would follow, that Jesus by submitting to baptism ablution, as far as it involves an immersion of the body, altogether confirms it, if only it is borne in mind that this modification must be considered as a prophetic elevation of the legal form of sacred ablution. According to Ebrard, the baptism of John presents a sign ' that man altogether deserves death.' Yet we cannot admit that John baptized with this consciousness, without maintaining that there was in his baptism an anticipation of the Christian. But his baptism was certainly a typical sign of the death of Jesus, and consequently also of mankind's desert of death.

[1] [Ewald calls this ' the birth-hour of Christianity.'—ED.]

favoured the supposition that He was a sinner. The whole difficulty is obviated by the representation given above of the import
of the baptism of Jesus. But, in addition, it is well to observe,
that according to the words of Matthew, baptism and the confession of sins were identical. But the moment of immersion
was naturally not suited to allow the persons immersed to utter
a verbal confession of sins. If, therefore, the persons baptized
were (ἐξομολογούμενοι) confessing at this moment, they were
so in the act. But this confession of sins was, as we have seen,
according to its nature a social and solidaric (*solidarisches*) act,
by which the measure of the guilt or innocence of individuals
was not determined. In the infinite reciprocal action of social
defilement in which individuals in Israel stood before the law,
a separation of the individual from the whole body was imprac-
ticable. So, then, every one confessed in his own manner, indi-
vidualizing and modifying his confession more or less—the collective guilt of Israel. Hardly would so many Pharisees have
consented to an individual confession before John. But Christ's
confession was this : ' So it becomes us to fulfil all righteousness.' Social righteousness drew Him down into the stream.

2. The ideas μετανοία (repentance), ἄφεσις ἁμαρτιῶν (remission of sins), and ἡ βασιλεία τῶν οὐρανῶν (the kingdom of
heaven), stand in reciprocal action to one another. The one is
as deep as the other, and each has always a significance differently determined on the legal, the pharisaical, the prophetic, and
the Christian stand-point. The purely legal stand-point is that
of the typical rendering of satisfaction and of social atonement,
in connection with an unlimited apprehension of the relations of
Being corresponding to this symbolism. The pharisaic standpoint accomplishes the social satisfaction and atonement with a
more decided dependence on outward works, without the perception of a higher righteousness. The prophetic stand-point
deduces from the social satisfaction and atonement the full feeling of the defect of realizing this symbolism in spirit, and of hope
in the Messiah. John pronounces the whole Old Testament
righteousness to be water-baptism. The Christian stand-point
exhibits, in all the points indicated, the fulfilling of the symbol
in full spiritual reality.

SECTION IV.

THE MANIFESTATION OF THE MESSIAH TO THE PEOPLE OF ISRAEL.

(Matt. iv.; Mark i.; Luke iii.; John i.)

Jesus complied with the call of the law when He repaired to the Jordan to be baptized by John.[1] But in the consciousness of His own purity and divine dignity, He must have deeply felt that on this occasion He only bore the burden of His people. An appointment of righteousness like this, which made Him the associate of the self-accusers and penitents who presented themselves before the Baptist, must have appeared to Him very ominous of the grave character of His future career. But His heart was already accustomed to sympathize with the sufferings of Humanity. Even at an earlier period the fact must have become clear to Him, that all the burden of earth fell precisely on His heart, since His heart exhibited the centre and the depths of Humanity. But He also had already learnt to know the exaltation which always follows the sufferings inflicted on a child of God. Hence He must have come to His baptism with great expectations, with the hope of a wonderful declaration by His Father, while He clearly perceived what was humiliating in His baptism, the suffering for His people which it implied. As at a later period He met death with the confident expectation of His resurrection and exaltation to glory with the Father, so also He came to His baptism, which was a prefigurement of His death, with the certain expectation that the Father would testify to His honour in the hour of His ignominy.

That Jesus was certain of the divine mission of John, is shown by the decisiveness with which He offered Himself for baptism at his hands. Lately some have wished to make out that He was a disciple of John.[2] So He was, for a single moment,

---

[1] [Tradition gives us the 6th January as the day of the baptism; and for a description of the place by Arculf, see Bohn's *Early Travels in Palestine*, p. 8.—ED.]

[2] [So Renan, *Vie de Jésus*, p. 107: 'Loin que le Baptiste ait abdiqué devant Jésus, Jésus pendant tout le temps qu'il passa près de lui, le reconnut pour supérieur et ne développa son propre génie que timidement. Il sembla en effet que, malgré sa profonde originalité, Jésus, durant quelques semaines au moins, fut l'imitateur de Jean.'—ED.]

when He allowed John to immerse Him in the stream, and thus recognised John's theocratic commission.

But John did not at once fully apprehend the significance of Christ's person. This is easily explained. He had to testify of one greater than himself with prophetic certainty. Such a task is in itself infinitely difficult, and indeed, without the guidance of God's Spirit, impossible.

That John and Jesus were acquainted in their youth, may be inferred with great probability from the relation in which their families stood to each other. How many times they might see one another at the feasts in Jerusalem, perhaps look on one another with thoughtful interest! On those occasions John might be much assisted by the utterances of Jesus in understanding the nature of the Theocracy, and in estimating the spirit of the existing hierarchy and their method of guiding the religion of the people. But by such intercourse the consciousness must early have been unfolded in both, that though their lives and spheres of action were to be closely linked, yet they were not destined to coincide. Every superior individuality has a strong feeling of an especial sphere of life, by which its outward relation and conduct towards other individuals is determined; and the purer it is, so much the more decidedly does it follow this consciousness in reference to the historic boundaries and position of its life. There is also in the spiritual world a repulsive force as unerring, and even more so than the centrifugal force of the heavenly bodies, which, in connection with the force of attraction, establishes the organism of the universe. It is too agreeable a view, taken from an inferior sphere of life, to imagine that the great champions of God, John and Jesus, had their paths in life ordained by God to be contiguous, and that these, as their strong natures unfolded, so coincided, that they maintained a close private intercourse, or were associated in outward co-operation. Inward fellowship in the kingdom of God does not as a matter of course lead to an outward companionship. Of John we are informed that he was 'in the wilderness' (Luke iii. 2). He was of a profoundly earnest, hermit-like, pensively pious character, the last and worthy representative of the Old Testament. The whole bent of his mind attracted him into the wilderness. The Old Testament economy had its birth-place in the wilderness, and thither with John it returned to die. Probably a modest reverence, as a rule, kept him at a distance from Jesus; and among other things, he might feel a sad and sombre estrangement from the cheerful gracefulness with which Jesus entered on His great conflict with the world—an inability to value at once the power of His refined agency, and fully to enter into His New Testament spirit.

But the reverence he felt for Jesus, the youthful anticipation that in Him bloomed the hope of Israel, and even the blissful presentiment that Jesus was the Messiah, could not, after all, qualify him to be a public witness for Him. As the prophet of the Messiah he knew nothing officially of Jesus; he knew Him not, so long as he was not assured by God. No female influence could ever induce him to be precipitate in this matter, and do violence to his calling; not even the judgment of those eminent women, Elisabeth and Mary. Whoever comprehends the significance of a prophetic, divine certainty, would not desire that John should deliver the reminiscences of his youth to the people in the name of Jehovah, and hastily alarm the land and the people with monstrous hypotheses. When Jesus came to him, he might indicate to Him at once his own expectations. The impression which this exalted friend made upon him had perhaps often overpowered him; at all events, it did so now. His own official dignity fell from him at the feet of Jesus; he started difficulties as to baptizing Him. Still he had not yet that final, objective divine certainty respecting the Messianic dignity of Jesus which he required, in order to bear open testimony to Him; and for this reason, because he had received the assurance that God would accredit the Messiah to him by an infallible sign. This sign was granted him when Jesus came up from His baptism.[1]

---

[1] [The apparent inconsistency between Matt. iii. 14 and John i. 33 has tested the sagacity of interpreters. Alford is of opinion that already John regarded Jesus as the Messiah, and could not but do so from the nature of their relationship, but that he still required the sign from God which would justify him in announcing Him to Israel. Ellicott, in a characteristically cautious note (*Hist. Lect.* p. 107), seems to ascribe too little to John's former acquaintance with, or at least knowledge of our Lord; and Ewald certainly does so (*Geschichte Christus'*, p. 163, cf. 185) when he supposes that John's shrinking was due to what he learnt of Jesus when He came to his baptism, by conversing with Him as he conversed with all who presented themselves for baptism. Riggenbach (*Vorlesungen über das Leben des Herrn*

It must here particularly be borne in mind, that the reporter respecting this wonderful transaction, namely, John, did not stand on the height of a decidedly New Testament view. The miracle must have assumed for him an appearance which was conformable to his power of contemplation. Therefore the miracle at the baptism of Jesus is narrated according to John's phenomenology, and not according to the christological phenomenology. And owing to this, it has been possible for the ancient and modern Ebionites, Socinians, and other advocates of a mutilated Christology, to support their views by the letter of this narrative, and to regard the anointing of Christ with the Holy Ghost sent down from heaven as contradictory to the doctrine of the eternal divinity of Christ, and of His miraculous conception by the Holy Spirit.[1]

As Christologists, we must assert the fundamental position, that there can be no holier place in the universe than the heart of Jesus. For when in our inner contemplation we contrast the Father with the Son, the Father is without time and place, comprehending and filling all things. Hence it belongs to the phenomenology of the Baptist when the representation presupposes a place in heaven over the heart of Christ, whence the Holy Spirit descends upon Him.

Jesus had immersed Himself by the prayer of the heart in the abyss of Deity, even while He was being immersed in the stream. Baptism was His solemn consecration to God and to death. By this great public surrender to the Father, His consciousness as the Messiah was completed, His calling decided. He was infinitely moved by the fulness of the divine Spirit, and in the illumination of this Spirit the certainty of His eternal unity in God, His Sonship, and the evidence of His calling and course of life, were completely disclosed to Him. The rose at last requires only a single sunbeam to complete its unfolding. The unfolding of the Messianic consciousness of Jesus was completed at His baptism; but equally so the public certainty of

Jesu, Basel. 1858, p. 240) here, as frequently elsewhere, follows Lange.—ED.]

[1] [The Gnostics believed that Jesus was one person, Christ another; and that these were united for a time at His baptism, but again separated before His crucifixion. Full information on this point is given in the very learned and careful work of Burton, *An Inquiry into the Heresies of the Apostolic Age* (Oxford 1829), pp. 186 and 469.—ED.]

His Messiahship; for this the Baptist had to advocate before all the people.

As Jesus rose out of the water praying, the divine greeting from the Father, 'Thou art My beloved Son, with whom I am well pleased,' went through His soul with infinite power, fervency, and splendour. This inner voice was the central point of the miracle. But it penetrated the Lord not merely in a spiritual manner, but resounded audibly through His frame: it so filled Him that all the chords of His life, even those of hearing, sounded simultaneously.

According to the law of sympathy, this voice must have echoed in the related but weaker person of John with thrilling power, 'This is My beloved Son, in whom I am well pleased.' He also heard the call, because the voice of God caused his whole life to vibrate. Suddenly he beheld a visible sign. He saw the heavens open, and the Spirit descending in an outward visible form (σωματικῷ εἴδει), like a dove, upon Jesus, and abiding upon Him.

But we must distinguish, as we have already intimated, the essential component parts of this phenomenon from the form which it obtained in John's contemplation of it. Three particular signs compose the one great sign whereby Jesus was pointed out to him by God as the Messiah. The first is the open heaven; the second, the visible appearance over the head of Jesus; the third is the voice. We believe that from the christological stand-point the order must be reversed. The voice was the greeting, and responsive greeting of eternal love in the heart of Christ resounding in the Spirit-world,—the celebration of the perfected revelation of the Father in the Son, of the divine feeling of Christ in His unity with the Father. Now did He begin as a living fountain of the Spirit of God to spread abroad the breath and life of this Spirit; the Spirit emanated from Him as the scent is shed forth from the full blown rose. But this first great life-stream of the Spirit in Him began in a solemn inspiration which flashed and lightened through His whole frame. At this moment the first rays of Christ's glorification broke forth. A mysterious splendour, probably a white mild lustre like the flutter of a white dove on the wing in the sunbeams, hovered above His head. John on his stand-point beheld it gliding downwards. But probably an upward and downward movement of this mild lustre took place; namely, a balancing or adjustment of the life of Christ entering into the phenomenon, with that world of light which lies at the basis of the whole phenomenal world, and as a locality forms the first inheritance of His glory. We understand this balancing or adjustment thus—Christ is the spiritual life-principle of the world, and therefore specially the principle of the renovation of the world of men, and of their sphere the habitable globe. At this moment His human consciousness of God was completed. His inner light-nature broke forth in the feeling of triumph which pervaded Him at this instant. It was the foretokening of His transfiguration on the Mount and at the Ascension, and consequently of the transfiguration of humanity in the new world by His glorification, as well as the transfiguration of the earthly sphere, as that must supervene with the glory of Christian humanity. But when this ray of the world's transfiguration breaks forth from the life of Christ, the discord ceases which existed between this earthly sphere and the heavenly light-sphere, which as an ideal region forms its opposite in the universe, making up its life. Christ Himself in His corporeal nature had a share in this discord, since this nature, although pure and complete as an organ and image of the divine Spirit, yet was incorporated with actual humanity, and by His whole life-communion with it shared in the darkness and heaviness of its corporeity. As therefore the life-fulness of the Spirit streamed forth from the consciousness of Christ, the transforming power of this life broke through the earthly obscuration of His organism, and by this sacred emanation of His ethereal life-power, the relation to that region of light was called forth. A downward streaming of its light met the upward shining of the light-life of Christ. But after the first festive meeting of these lights, the relation was continued in a more quiet form. The assimilation effected, of the nature of Christ with the region of His glory, allowed the reciprocal acting to retire again into the invisible, till a new enhancement of the same relation caused it to come forth at a later period still more powerfully. This adjustment between heaven and Christ may also be simply regarded as an adjustment between heaven and earth, since Christ is the principle of the earth's glorification. And whoever is inclined to the Christian expectation, that the earth must one day be changed into a heavenly world of light by the energy of Christ, that a transformation of it into the imperishable is approaching through the palingenesia which the Spirit of Christ effects—let him so conceive it, that in that moment in which the heart of Christ enjoyed the full unfolding of His heavenly consciousness in conformity to the intimate connection of the spiritual and corporeal, the bloom of this world's glorification glistened on His head. But in the glorification of the world the alternation of day and night will hereafter vanish; the earth will be seen as a star encircled by the great family of stars. In their new light-life the sun will no more quench the radiance of the surrounding stars, while the earth will be free, as a co-enlightening star, from the sun's overpowering light.[1] And therein will also one day appear the signs of the Son of man in heaven (Matt. xxiv. 30); so that, by means of the great transformation of the earth, the stars will begin to be constantly visible to the earth as clearly as sometimes on the high mountain tops the stars blaze like torches on the dark blue expanse of heaven. But it is well known that even now there are moments in the day-time when single stars are visible. Such a moment probably was that, when Jesus and John from their stand-point beheld the great adjustment between heaven and earth. In the undulation of the light-world between the head of Christ and heaven, the depth of heaven was opened. They probably, therefore, saw the stars come forth in the dark blue, and as it were joyously enwreathe the earth, which now, as thus encircled, seemed the holiest spot in the universe. So in this world-historical single moment, that transformation of the world which it establishes and brings about as a principle, was exhibited in a passing but grand foretokening to the actor and the witness of the moment.

We have already noticed on what account John necessarily saw this transaction through an Old Testament medium. But it attests the vivid anticipation of the New Testament life in the soul of this great man, that he compared the Holy Spirit to the image of a gentle dove[2] gliding down from heaven, as he desig-

---

[1] Rev. xxi. 23. See Göschel, *Unterhaltungen zur Schilderung Göthescher Dicht- und Denkweise* iii. 191.

[2] That we are not to think of an actual dove gliding down on the head of Christ, the theologian ought to know from the fact that the Israelites

nated the Son of God by the title of the Lamb. This heavenly power of Christ's infinitely gentle Spirit-life, which John most wanted in his own life, so full of passionate zeal, but yet in the spirit of humility knew how to value in another. It was exactly those features of Christ's life in which he was most decidedly surpassed that filled his soul with the profoundest reverence; he therefore designated Christ 'the Lamb,'[1] and the spirit of His life a 'dove.'

John was now most certainly convinced of the Messiahship of Christ by the testimony of God, and in the blessedness of this new great certainty he could deliberately say, in reference to his former way and manner of contemplating Him, 'I knew Him not.' It was now that he first knew Him as a prophet, so that he could with confidence testify of Him in Israel. But this was decisive in a man whose private life was so perfectly identified with his public calling, and who wished to be only 'a voice' to proclaim the coming Messiah. Filled with astonishment at the glory of this revelation which had been imparted to him, and at the glory of the personage in whom he now realized the hope of his life, he could say with the deepest emphasis, 'I knew Him not.' The conscientiousness and critical judgment of the man were great, like himself,—the last of the old prophets, who spoke not of their own will or opinion, but as they were moved and actuated by the Holy Ghost.

Thus was Jesus now made manifest to the people of Israel as the Son of God and the Messiah. For John represented the theocratic majesty of Israel, the true host of the people. But whether on this occasion the two men of God were surrounded by many witnesses or few, was in this case of no special importance. At all events, the bystanders could only share in

were forbidden to regard the cry of birds as an omen. Lev. xix. 26. [' The form was real' (Ellicott); it was not only the manner of descent, but the descending bodily form which was like that of a dove. It was not a dove which had been before this time living somewhere on earth (Paulus thinks it was a dove accidentally passing by), any more than the human forms of the angels appearing to Abraham were real men, though they exercised the functions of substantial bodies. It was a real appearance assumed (how, we know not) for the time being, like the tongues of fire afterwards chosen to symbolize a special gift of the Holy Ghost.—ED.]

[1] [This, of course, does not exclude the sacrificial significance of the name, as brought out in the preceding section.—ED.]

their experience in proportion as they were qualified by the sympathy of a life and disposition in harmony with John and Christ.

NOTES.

1. The objective truth of the testimony which the Baptist has left behind of the mysterious transaction at the baptism of Jesus, may be inferred from the Old Testament colouring which it must have gained in his contemplation of it, the effect of which has led into error minds that were deficient in New Testament depth or ripeness.

2. The effulgence (*Verklärung*) will come under consideration in the sequel. As to the adjustment (*Ausgleichung*) between the earthly nature of Christ and His light-world (*Lichtwelt*), the idea of such adjustment or equalization already exists in natural philosophy, though it is applied with uncertainty to the mysterious phenomena of nature-life. Thus, for instance, Faraday conjectures that the electrical equilibrium of the earth is restored by the aurora borealis, by its carrying the electricity from the poles to the equator. According to others, the aurora borealis is a streaming of light from the earth to the sun, while the zodiacal light is an opposite current which connects the sun with the earth.

3. On the significance of the dove in the Hebrew symbolic, see Strauss, *Leben Jesu* i. 416. Von Ammon i. 276: 'The dove was universally considered by Jews and heathens to be an emblem of purity and chastity.' Yet John needed not to take the symbol from tradition; he was great enough to form on his own authority a symbol of this kind, especially in allusion to Solomon's Song ii. 14.

4. The voice of God cannot proceed from any particular place, since God is omnipresent. It is a living and definite expression of God; a *special* word of God, which creates its own voice in the sphere wherein it sounds, as the *general* word of God has created its sound and echo in the universe. But this voice has a full reality, since it is an expression and operation of God. It is consistent with this immediateness of the divine voice, that God speaks in the language of the persons to whom His word is addressed. Every one who can conceive the difference between Judaism and Heathenism ought to know that the Hebrews never imagined the divine essence to be confined in a

dwelling-place above the firm vault of heaven. So also the way and manner in which the speech of God is articulated, and becomes the language of a particular country, must be plain to every one who is not disposed to regard the manifestation of God in the flesh as 'monstrous.'

5. The question, whether the manifestation was designed for Jesus, or only for John (see Neander, *Life of Jesus Christ*, p. 70 [Bohn]), loses sight too much of the peculiar life of this singular moment, in which one of the two prophets could receive no revelation without its also being imparted to the other. Jesus was the centre of the miraculous transaction; but John stood most of all in need of this manifestation in order to fulfil his calling.

6. The message which the Baptist sent from his prison to Jesus must, according to Strauss, imply a contradiction to the confidence of the Baptist as here described in reference to the person of Jesus. In the sequel we shall consider the question, whether the human weakness in the life of the prophet can be taken as evidence against his utterance in the elevated hours of his divine assurance.

SECTION V.

THE GOD-MAN.[1]

Christ, from the beginning of His life in His human nature, was one with God, and indeed in the oneness [*Einzigkeit*] of the Son. His oneness in God consisted in this—that His life formed the pure realized centre of all God's counsels, the innermost secret of all His thoughts and ways in the world's history, and that it possessed the infinitely pure and rich nobleness which naturally belonged to the heart of the world. The holy child was the bud in which the world was to open into a divine flower —into a heaven of pure ideal relations which embraced the in-

---

[1] [For an estimate of the author's Christology, reference must be made to the last volume of Dorner on the Person of Christ. And see also his own vindication of himself from the charges of Krummacher, in the Note appended to sec. ix.—ED.]

finite contents of life in the oneness of an absolutely new form,
in the delicacy of a perfected harmony or bloom of all life. But
the oneness of the Son of God was in Him the movement of an
infinitely pure and delicate impulse of development, in which
His nature from the first preserved its identity with the Spirit
of God,—the perfect harmony in the reciprocal action between
His corporeal and spiritual nature and between His soul and the
world. His life's impulse was the impulse of eternal love breaking forth from its envelopement. 'God was in Christ reconciling
the world unto Himself:' 2 Cor. v. 19. The eternal self-consciousness of God came forth in the development of the consciousness of Christ into the midst of the world, and in this
manner became a manifestation of His being.

This manifestation needed first of all to be completed in the
human consciousness of Jesus; but its completion coincided with
the complete development of His inner life. The starting-point
of this unfolding was the refined living joy of a perfectly consecrated, well-organized nature, kept down by the adverse impression of a darkened, deeply disordered world of sinners,
opposing the glory of such a life. Its progress from the indistinct feeling of pure life to the highest living certainty was a
wonderful presage; it was the beautiful dawn of the new world,
the life-poetry of an unfolding consciousness, which in its all-
comprehensive, quiet life passed through all the sights and feelings of the longing, imaginative youth of the world. We have
been made acquainted with one aspect of this beautiful dawn in
the history of Jesus when twelve years old. Through this
blessed longing the terrors of the kingdom of darkness must
have been acting their part in strange nocturnal sights and
shades of horror—such presentiments as Abraham, the father of
the faithful, had in glancing at the future of his people and
spiritual descendants (Gen. xv. 12). But the objective world
of God presented itself to this longing as a pure, divine administration, which increased in lustre from the darkest night (*Aether-
nacht*) to the clearest noon-day.

As long as this richest individual development was burdened
with any of the uncertainty which attaches to a period of growth,
Christ could not come forth and manifest Himself to the people
of Israel as the Messiah. Nor could this development be completed by one-sided human evidence, but only by a wonderful

transaction in which the testimony of the Father in the voice
which blessed Him coincided with the testimony of His inner
life, and the testimony of the ancient Theocracy, which was represented by the Baptist, with the voice of His heart, and finally
the testimony of heaven and earth with that of His previous
history. This singular harmony of His religious, theocratic,
and physical spheres with the expression of His inner life was
the most special significance of the miracle at His baptism. He
was now made manifest in the world as the God-man from
whom it had to expect its salvation.

His own word unveils to us the form of the inner life of
Jesus. He walked in the presence of God, and bore within
Himself the fulness of the Godhead. The pure reality of the
world identified Him with the divine administration ; He knew
Himself to be surrounded, conditioned, penetrated, and determined by God's Spirit. He was therefore in heaven (John iii.
13), in the bosom of the Father (John i. 18), and simply conditioned by the will of the Father (John v. 30). In the looks
with which the Father beheld Him—in the design with which He
upheld Him—in the fatherly love which begat, saluted, and sent
Him, He felt His own oneness, His eternity and divinity. In
this consciousness He regarded His own life as a pure manifestation of the Father (John xiv. 9, 10), as a glorification of His
being (John xvii. 4). It was His life-conviction that the very
Being of God was manifested through Him in the midst of the
world. He thus expressed His divine consciousness—He came
from the Father, and He went to the Father. His going to the
Father was an eternal act of His consciousness. He was perfectly conscious of the infinitely delicate distinctness of His life,
His unique individuality. He felt the singularity of His life
which placed Him in the presence of God's love, as the pure
image of the Father. He exhibited the determination of God
which lay in His divine consciousness, in perfect, free self-determination. His will might appear as distinct from the will of
God, but only in order to be merged in it with freedom. In
His feelings, He could feel Himself forsaken by God in His
objective administration, but only in order to surrender and
sacrifice Himself to Him. In His acting, He could feel Himself excited by the immeasurable activity of the Father through-

out the universe to work Himself, but only to work the works of the Father in and with Him (John v. 17). It was therefore His human consciousness, that He was ever going again to the Father as the pure, perfected Man.

In this relation the divine consciousness in Christ stands to His human consciousness. The two forms of this consciousness, therefore, in accordance with their nature, make up one living unity. Whoever has not found God, has not found Himself; and whoever has not come to Himself, has not come to God. God becomes one with man, and man with God, in the life of the Spirit. Where spirit appears, there freedom appears. Spiritual personality recognises its destiny, which is from God, and determines itself in the most living free experience and firm hold of this destiny. Those who fancy that with the beginning of the spiritual life, God vanishes in the power of their self-consciousness, are ignorant of spirit, and not less so are those who wish to see their life vanish in God. The Spirit glorifies man in God, and God in man. But Christ had the Spirit in its infinite fulness; and for that reason God was the eternally glorious object of contemplation to His inner life, and He was conscious of the eternal peerlessness and singleness of His life in God. Thus His divine consciousness was one with His individual consciousness, and in this living unity the one is precisely distinguished from the other by the Spirit. He lived in an eternal, infinitely intimate, reciprocal action with the Father. This reciprocal action was a perfect, ever pure, and beautiful rhythm. In this rhythm of His life, as it is sustained by His unique nature and destiny, He appears as the God-man.

The blessedness and power of this life never allowed the Lord to withdraw from the consciousness of eternity. Sin from the first must have been detestable as gloom to His brightness, —as nihility to His power of being,—as the dissonant and deformed to the harmony of His life,—as estrangement from God to His fulness of God. The God-man, according to the power of His freedom, could not consent to sin.

And yet it lay in the nature of His being, that He must be more tempted by sin than any other man. Sin as sin was repelled by the divine power of His self-determination; while sin as the old human life continually troubled and agitated, yea, tortured to death, the human delicacy of His nature. Who

could be so sensitive as He to the temptations which lay in the
sympathy and antipathy of a whole disordered world, whose
head and heart He was destined to be? Who could be more
susceptible in his individual feelings than He to the attraction
of the sympathy of the world, which, with an unceasing syren-
song, wished to draw Him down into the depths of its old life?
Who could experience as He did the repulsion of the world's
antipathy to the transition from the kingdom of the darkened
life of nature to the blessed kingdom of the Spirit? In Him
there was the most delicate sense of honour—the concentrated
noble-mindedness of all humanity, infinitely sensitive, confronting all the shocks of worldly contumely—the most excitable and
tender life-feeling confronting all the sharp pangs of death—
the highest capability of suffering belonging to the strongest,
and therefore most thoughtful love, confronting the thousand-
fold forms of human hatred. In one word, we may say that
Christ alone could and must feel the entire temptation of the
world; and He alone, who perfectly understood and experienced
it in the full clearness of His pure feeling and spirit, could completely overcome it. Those that think man becomes acquainted
with temptation only in proportion as he is defiled by it, lay
down a canon by which man throughout eternity would have,
like another Sisyphus, to roll the load of sinfulness in his vain
struggles after righteousness. Their moral world is from the
first only a modest hell for those who are silently condemned.
But every victory of an honest conscience over temptation re-
futes their system. Christ has converted into historical truth
the possibility of the sinless development of humanity, which in
Adam, as ideal, formed the paradise of humanity, and thus has
founded the new heavens of the world's reconciliation.

The power of Christ's life to resist temptation lay in His
ideal nature. But by His historical nature, by His connection
with humanity, He was necessitated to encounter all the temptations of humanity; and His victory over temptation was
effected by realizing His ideal life in His historical life. The
victory lay simply in this realization. For when He, the Chief
of Humanity, came armed on the field of conflict, in order to
rescue it from the corruption into which it had fallen, then the
whole depth of this corruption must unfold itself and confront
Him. The demoniac background which supported this world of

confusion was forced to disclose itself simultaneously when the
heavenly basis of the ideal human world was laid in the incarnation of God. This was a consequence of the antagonistic historical reciprocal action between the kingdom of light and the
kingdom of darkness. In opposition to the God-man, when, as
Redeemer of the world, He was manifested by His baptism in
the Jordan, the Demon-enemy of man, the Tempter, now made
his appearance.

NOTE.

The correct view of the relation between the divine and
human natures of Christ is still obscured by various false assumptions. The first of these is the notion that the divine life was limited by the human, and in consequence could only partially (which
as divine is in that case not at all) enter into human life. On the
contrary, it has been pointed out in the first part of our work, that
the essence of human individuality is to be looked for, not in its
finiteness, but in its *definiteness*. But this definiteness can be no
hindrance to God in His manifestation, since it is a result of His
determination. With this false assumption another is connected,
that the incarnation of the Son of God is considered in itself a
humiliation of His being, while His humiliation only appears in
His entering into a life-communion with historical humanity.
The μορφὴ Θεοῦ which is attributed to Christ in Philip. ii. 6, is
to be regarded probably as the definiteness of the divine nature,
in which Christ has the eternal ideality of His being.[1] To this
essential 'form of God' attributed to Christ, the 'being equal
with God,' τὸ εἶναι ἴσα Θεῷ, corresponds. We can take this
plural ἴσα as altogether definite, and then it will mark the various
forms through which the Logos passed before He became man;
since first of all He was the principle of the creation of the world,
then the principle of humanity, and next of the Theocracy, till
last of all He became the life-principle of Jesus. The expression, 'He thought it not robbery to be equal with God' (οὐχ
ἁρπαγμὸν ἡγήσατο), does not mean He did not eagerly retain
this equality with God, but divested Himself of it; rather, the
ἴσα εἶναι Θεῷ remained His, even when He became man. But

---

[1] [' The Godhead itself, so far as it is exhibited in the brightest manifestations of the grace and majesty of God.' Witsius, de Oratione, cap. i.—
ED.]

His divine consciousness was not the consciousness of a possession
unlawfully gained by force; or more exactly, it was no act of
outrage, as when a robber or a warrior violently seizes his booty
The feeling of His divine dignity was no ecstasy. It was perfectly matured human life; and so also divine in tranquillity,
love, and condescension. His divine life-feeling was the ripest,
most tranquil enjoyment of His inner being, no spirit-robbery.
So little was He disposed to attain His glory by robbery, that He
rather robbed Himself when He assumed the form of a servant,
and was made like the sinful race of men, even to the death of the
cross. This self-robbery can only relate to the manifestation of
life. He robbed Himself when He concealed the divine glory of
His consciousness in the sinner's garb of man, in the servant's
garb of the Jews, in the criminal's garb of the crucified, and
therefore with infinite humility in a threefold dress of the deepest
humiliation.[1]

Another false assumption confounds the identity which is
presented in the spirit-life with the monotony of a physical unity,
and consequently allows man to vanish into God, or God into
man. In both cases spirit is *naturalized*, that is, denied.

As a third assumption, we may specify the hypothesis of the
latest moral philosophy, which makes Evil a necessary point of
transition in the moral development of the spirit. Perhaps this
assumption is taken from the use of cow-pox, which is destined
to put a stop to the ravages of small-pox, and has been transplanted into the doctrine of spiritual freedom. At all events, it
is only at home in the physical department of life.

---

[1] [This interpretation does not seem to bring out the opposition expressed
by ἀλλά with as much distinctness as the ordinary view, which refers μορφῇ
Θεοῦ to the pre-incarnate, and μορφὴ δούλου to the incarnate state of Christ.
Besides the commentaries, some useful hints on this important passage will
be found in Pearson *on the Creed*, p. 179 (ed. 1835), and Moses Stuart's
Letters to Rev. W. E. Channing, p. 81 (ed. 1829). The doctrinal significance of the κένωσις is fully treated in Dorner, II. iii. 250–259; and its discussion is further pursued by Liebner, in the *Jahrb. für D. Theol.* 1858, p.
349. Dorner and Hasse have also papers on the subject in the same year.—
ED.]

SECTION VI.

THE TEMPTER.

No reciprocal action is more delicate, mysterious, and important than that of spiritual forces in the ethical department of life. As long as this reciprocal action is overlooked—as long, therefore, as the doctrine of sympathies and antipathies is not more developed than it has hitherto been, there can be no satisfactory development of the doctrine of good and evil in the world. Every spiritual individual must be regarded as a spiritual power, operating not only by speaking and acting, but by his very existence, presence, and disposition, and especially by his will, and thus influencing other individuals in the elements of social life. But the greater the power of the individual, so much more important will be his agency.

In the human world these silent forces of individual power and disposition are at work incessantly in every direction. Powerful effects proceed from powerful characters, and form greater or smaller nets in which a multitude of weaker characters are caught. There are spirits that rule in the air (Eph. v. 12).

The history of battles will teach us the mighty power of sympathetic relations. The panic which causes the loss of a battle, is entirely a sympathetic fright. When a little group of gallant hearts, who form the flower of a regiment, flinch and give way, the whole regiment may be lost, and with that the whole army. And so, on the other hand, the heroic self-sacrifice of a single man may rally a whole wavering host, and even, flashing like lightning through centuries, may rekindle in a nation the flame of a holy enthusiasm. The pillars of fire of genuine human heroism are the noble lights of history, which make us feel at ease even while sojourning among spectres, and horrors, and graves.

But antipathy is not less powerful than sympathy, and, taken together, they contribute one phenomenon, which may be designated psychical life-communion. Of this phenomenon, sympathy forms the positive and antipathy the negative pole ; and the latter consequently is, in its kind, as powerful as the for-

mer. It is easier to sail against the wind than to withstand
or break through strong antipathies. We call, and there is no
echo. 'My word,' said the Saviour, 'hath no place in you:'
John viii. 37. We address ourselves to human hearts, and it is
like running against heaps of stones. It is a hard matter to be
cheerful, and keep up one's spirits, when soul does not answer soul.
Christ withstood the antipathy of the whole world. This conflict especially was His chief labour in Gethsemane and on Gol-
gotha. He trod the wine-press alone. And since His victory,
the preponderance of His strong heart goes in triumph through
the world, and, amidst fearful reactions of the antipathy of the
old world-nature, it causes, by the thunders and lightnings of
sympathetic action, all things to bow which are in heaven, and
on earth, and under the earth.

It lies in the nature of this relation, that evil as well as good
can enter into the moving power of sympathy, and as the
checking power of an antipathy. Those who have been overcome by the power of evil, strengthen its operation by the attraction of sympathy; but it confronts the good as a magically
obstructive and repressive antipathy. Who has not experienced
the depressing influence of evil in its silent and most secret
operations? In Göthe's Faust, Margaret makes the discovery
that she cannot pray in the presence of Mephistopheles. Every
material spark, however small, has its effect: it glows, it gleams,
it threatens to kindle a fire. But far more powerful is the operation of a spark of evil. Evil in the heart of our neighbour
speaks to us through the mere power of its existence: if he
does not express it in words, it is impressed upon us in some
most occult way, and can make a language for itself, intelligible
to our hearts and imaginations.

But there are some minds so very obtuse, that they are not
sensible of evil unless it comes before them palpably in words
and deeds absolutely immoral. They know no alarm at the
demon-like power of evil. Such persons are in truth very poor
demonologists.

Many others see the boundaries of evil where crime, and
vice, or gross immorality cease in their immediate circle; but
they have no feeling of the power of evil lying at a greater
depth, working in concealment, or acting at a distance. These
likewise are weak demonologists.

But there are also other spirits, purer, deeper, and of greater moral sensibility,—souls liker Cassandra, who feel the action of the curse breaking forth in the misdeeds of domestic life; or like Thecla, who experience an internal horror when a dark spirit goes through their house. These souls are the true moral philosophers, while technical moral philosophy is sometimes in the hands of ethically callous spirits.

Lastly, there are heroes of world-wide reputation with moral feelings of the highest order; souls that can perceive an ethical agency of prodigious power where an ordinary man would scarcely notice anything; souls that would see a conflagration where the latter would hardly detect the smell of fire. Such a distinguished example of moral perception Christ proved Himself to be, when Peter so urgently dissuaded Him from the dangerous journey to Jerusalem (Matt. xvi. 22). But these heroes, as prophets of the ethical depths of the world, have, with their feeling and penetration, discovered that moral corruption has penetrated through the blood and marrow of humanity from generation to generation. In this fearful discovery Moses and Sophocles meet one another. But a thousand little moralists smile over this theory of the curse, and find, forsooth, that such a doctrine is against morality, though founded on a thousand agonies and griefs of profound and faithful souls.

But this pretended morality does not trouble the moral chiefs of the world. In the depths of their ethical life-spirit they listen to the slightest footsteps of seduction in the house of Adam, in Humanity. They gauge the power of the ethical antipathies which counteract their prayers, and vows, and godly deeds. But in this survey they arrive at the disclosure of a vast relation, since the spirit of divine revelation co-operates with their own foreboding. They announce the fact, that evil in the human world has not merely sprung up in human hearts; there are other stranger, stronger agencies of evil in this region of the universe; there is a devil.[1] The doctrine of the devil proceeds, therefore,

---

[1] Schleiermacher, in his *Glaubenslehre* i. 219, believes that the doctrine of the agency of the devil may be deduced from a defective knowledge of sin, in contradiction of the opinion that it owes its origin to the profoundest knowledge of evil. But he has seldom reasoned more weakly than when he begins to argue against this doctrine (p. 209). The sophistry and worthlessness of most of his arguments directly appear when we put them to the

from a prophetic and profound ethical knowledge of the world.
It might be said that the doctrine of evil demons unfolds itself
from the demoniacal depths of ethical foreboding. But it is unfolded with the development of the manifestation of ethical life
in humanity; and those points which may be regarded as arti-
culations in the development of this doctrine coincide with critical
moments in the history of the human race. But those who look
upon this doctrine as a representation derived from Parsism, and
engrafted on the Hebrew faith, have not discerned the difference,
wide asunder as the poles, between the idea of an evil God and
of a fallen created spirit. The evil God is lord over the substance
of half the world—indeed, the proper materiality of the whole
world belongs to him, and the good God is scarcely able to overpower him. The fallen evil spirit, on the contrary, as he makes
his appearance in the book of Job, is a poor Satan, who cannot
call an atom of the material world his own; who everywhere
can only do just so much as power is granted him for by God,
whose supremacy controls him, and who turns all his projects to
everlasting confusion. How can any one confound the idea of
Ahriman with that of Satan—the idea of the wicked one, in
whom evil is one with sin—with that idea in which evil is the
punishment of sin, its annihilation through substantial life?

proof and apply them to the moral relations of men. For example, the first
argument asserts that only such motives can be given for the fall of good
angels as perhaps pride and envy, which presuppose such a fall. This
amounts to saying that the fall of a pure spiritual being is altogether inconceivable. His second argument caricatures the biblical doctrine of the
devil: we shall return to this in the sequel. Further, human evil must be
identical with possession; besides, the doctrine of Satan must declare that
he lost his understanding by the perversion of his will. And 'how is it to
be conceived that some angels have sinned and others have not?' If we
apply this argument to human relations, we shall find that it equally
amounts to nothing. Is it necessary to enter on the proof of this? The
exegesis of biblical passages which relate to the doctrine of the devil is not
much better, in the aforesaid demonstration, than the philosophical discussion
of the question. Besides, the leading assumption is false, that Christ and
His apostles only made use of this representation because it was in vogue
among the people. How could the popular representation necessitate our
Lord to mark such a great mysterious experience of His life as that given
in the history of the temptation, as a temptation of Satan? [Renan (Vie
de Jésus, p. 41) adduces it as an instance in which Jesus was not more enlightened than His countrymen, that 'il croyait au diable, qu'il envisageait
comme une sorte de génie du mal.'—ED.]

Attempts, indeed, have been made to prove that the idea of Satan involves contradictions; but the observations in support of this view have been very wide of the mark—they apply to the conception of Ahriman, not to that of Satan. It is certainly inadmissible that evil can be absolutely identical with a substantial Being, that such an one can become Evil personified, or that 'persevering wickedness should be able to exist with the most distinguished insight.' But whence has the theologian learnt that 'the most distinguished insight' is attributed to the devil in the Bible? Does not true insight presuppose a harmony with the moral order of the world? Thus insight makes its appearance in the Bible. The theologian is unfortunate in his appeal to it; for all insight is denied to the devil by the Bible. He comes forward, indeed, as a great genius, equipped with a power of understanding refined to superlative craftiness; but his demoniacal cunning appears as moral stupidity, and on all points in which he manœuvred against humanity he is decidedly foiled by the action of the divine insight, especially in the history of the fall, in the trial of Job, and in the history of Jesus. As soon as the theologian has freed himself from confounding Parsism with the pure biblical theology, he will find that no conception is more firmly established than that of the devil. We proceed from this point, that, even before the fall of man, a fall had taken place in a spiritual sphere of the world. A host of spirits, belonging to the train and retinue of a powerful spirit of their own kind, fell with him into sin, and apostatized from God. There is nothing contradictory in this fact. The fall of men proves the possibility of the fall of other spirits. But the manner in which great and highly gifted men have fallen most deeply, and even within the life of humanity have been able to exhibit the demoniacal in evil, throws light on the supposition, that in that pre-human disorder in the spirit-world the greatness in the fall of their chief bore some proportion to the original greatness of his nature. But though the notion of such a region of pre-human fallen spirits cannot be impugned, yet it may seem difficult, not to say monstrous, to admit an agency of these spirits on the human world. The representation, that in ancient times a familiar colloquial intercourse existed between men and devils, has always given offence. How should Satan as such be able to come near men? Here is the proper place for pointing out the significance of the doctrine of the great life-operations in the world, which appear in the antagonism of sympathies and antipathies. Just as the cosmical lights from star to star operate through the wide creation, so, but to a greater degree, do the psychical moods of spirits both good and bad. Thus humanity in its primal innocence had to encounter the action of a fallen spirit-sphere, which depressed the inspiration of its undeveloped ethical life-feeling. The moment of its first trial happened at the moment of such a psychical depressing influence of Satan. Thus the trial became a temptation; and in the elements of this temptation the natural allurements which in every trial operated on man, became a colloquial address of the spirit of temptation. We saw above how the influences of pure spirits can become plastic in the human soul—how they create in its inward intuition an appearance, a language, a conversation. The same holds good of the powerful operations of Satan. The more sensitive, tender, and vigorous a man feels, so much the more every evil influence gains over him, as soon as he wavers in his moral standing, a plastic distinctness which it had from the first in its inner nature, and becomes an appearance, or a discourse, or, in fact, a speaking appearance.

The action of the fallen spirit-world on the first human world may be easily explained, even though it be considered as the action of an extra-mundane sphere. But if it be supposed that in Satan's kingdom spiritual traces appear of a shattered earthly spirit-kingdom anterior to man, this hypothesis gains important confirmation from analogous traditions of a physical kind, which send us back to such a shattered pre-human primitive world. We are led by these ruins, in their relation to the doctrine of Satan, to the supposition that that sphere of colossal serpents, lizards, and other monstrous amphibia had been formed round the centre of an ethically free giant-spirit and his associates, and that this spirit constituted the spiritually conscious centre of his insular world, in the same sense as man, in the present organic form of the earth, exists as the life-principle comprehending and glorifying all organisms in conscious spirit-life. According to this construction of that giant-world in which the amphibious type predominated, we understand why the spiritual chief of that sphere after his fall is designated as the Dragon.

According to this, in demonology the complement of the
physical ruins would appear, quite naturally, in a parallel of
ethical ruins. In this connection Satan may be contemplated
as the ethical giant-fossil from the age of the pre-human
earth-formation. The creation of the human earth unfolded
itself out of the judgment that preceded on the demon-earth.
But though that demon-earth has been judged and set aside by
the formation of the human earth, yet as smothered Chaos it
has in various ways an influence on the tone of the present
world's history. From time to time the tones of that insular
antiquity break forth. The billows again roar, and mingle sea
and land, and miasmata are exhaled from the swamps. In
particular juices of nature the traces appear of the potencies of
that far-gone age—poisons, which are, so to speak, the spirit-
sounds of that buried nature, which reverberate in the present.[1]
The amphibia exhibit the animal type which was predominant
in the kingdom of that fallen spirit-chief; and the serpent, in
the forms under which it has come forth in the new earth-sphere,
has become the symbol of his nature and agency. It could formerly pass through the air in various shapes, winged as a
dragon; but under the present economy it is sentenced to crawl
on its belly, and to eat the dust. Its existence, which was prominent in the former economy, and stood near the demon-chief
of the globe, is now degraded to the lowest dust compared with
that of the higher animals; and the regions in which the spirits
of that condemned original population of the earth have taken
their residence, are the wastes, the deserts, and stormy winds,
by which the effects of their former power are symbolized. But
these fallen spirits themselves have, by their sympathetic influence
on young humanity, converted the trial which it had to stand,
into a dangerous temptation which it has not withstood. Since
that time, the continued action and movement of their tones in
the earthly world form the special centre of gravity and demoniacal depth of all evil on the earth. On this account,

[1] See K. Snell, *Philosophische Betrachtungen der Natur*, the Essay on
the occurrence and significance of poisons in nature, p. 23, especially pp.
36–48. 'Prussic acid gives us a representation of a state of matter which
we must call living death, and of which, without it, we could form no conception. This state was certainly at one time general and predominant in
nature.'

according to the view of all God's moral heroes in holy writ, the whole kingdom of sin appears as a kingdom of Satan.

We must not overlook the fact, that the actual effects which proceed from the region of these demons are symbolically conceived and represented in a twofold way. First of all, they are made use of with poetic liveliness to describe all evil. On the one hand, evil is called simply devilish, because human evil has been called forth by devilish evil, though evil is as human as it is devilish, and throughout creaturely, in the definite mode of a fallen creature, or rather the positively worthless and pernicious which makes man a sinner, and the demon a devil. It is also called 'devilish,' as being the most concrete and powerful expression to designate evil. On the other hand, the devilish is called evil, as if Satan were the ideal chief of evil, identical with evil, although he is only in a historical sense the first, most powerful chief of evil. But Satan is designated simply as the evil one, because the religious feeling takes cognisance only of the destructive ethical side of his life, and stands in no immediate relation to his nature-side. This symbolic in its application to the doctrine of Satan should be thoroughly understood, lest, without intending it, we should make an Ahriman of Satan.

The kingdom of Satan naturally stands in constant antagonism to the kingdom of God. It is developed till the completion of its judgment, confronting the kingdom of light. The manifestations of salvation and of the divine life on earth are encountered by the outbreaks and disclosures of the powers of darkness. They come forward in manifold masks, adapted to the circumstances of the times. But the ethical spirit of humanity ever casts a penetrating glance through all disguises, and detects and rejects the old enemy who is a murderer from the beginning. The first man learnt, not in his sin, but in his repentance, that a crafty demoniacal power had ruined him by its temptation. In the last times of the present course of the world, the true Church, in conflict with 'the beast out of the sea,' and with 'the beast out of the earth' which 'had two horns like a lamb,' will discern that it is the dragon who speaks through all the beasts (Rev. xiii.). Christ in the wilderness, after His baptism, had to encounter a great, critical temptation ; He discerned the tempter behind the temptation.

NOTE.

It must here be stated in most explicit terms, that we carefully distinguish between the doctrine of the devil in itself and the view just given, according to which the fall of the devil is regarded as the fall of the moral central being of the pre-Adamite earth. We are desirous not to make this doctrine dependent, in its general form, in the slightest degree on our hypothesis. But it will not escape the unprejudiced reader how very much this hypothesis is fitted to bring about a harmonious religious view of earthly-cosmical relations. Jacob Böhm, in his visionary speculation, seems to have gained an image of this view, but his image was necessarily obscured and distorted by the influence of his gnostic principles. Thus much he saw, that in the present form of the world, a conflict of two forms of the world appeared, and that particularly 'Man is and signifies that other host which God created instead of Lucifer's host expelled from Lucifer's place.'[1] But in this Adam three principles were from the first active—' the kingdom of hell, the kingdom of this world, and the kingdom of paradise,' although originally his life commenced in the paradisaical principle. The passage, Gen. i. 2, is explained by the adherents of Böhm's system in the same way, since it is regarded as a description of the ruined world of Lucifer. But that desolation and void may be regarded as the consecrated fermentation of the world in process of formation, over the dark depths of which the Spirit of God moved with creative energy. If we wished to find the contrast between the purely demoniacal and the Adamic earth in the contrast of the insular and continental type, that pre-Adamite world-history, with its fall of the spirits, would come in between the second and third day's work of creation, Gen. i. 8, 9.

---

[1] Baur, *die christliche Gnosis,* p. 591.

SECTION VII.

THE SPIRITUAL REST AND SPIRITUAL LABOUR OF CHRIST IN THE WILDERNESS—THE TEMPTATION.

(Matt. iv. ; Mark i. ; Luke iv.)

The words of the Evangelist (Matt. iv. 1), ' Then was Jesus led up of the Spirit into the wilderness, to be tempted of the devil,' have been looked upon by modern criticism as a dark hieroglyphic. But they are explained by the simple law, that every ethical nature, according to the measure of its power and the destiny operating in this power, must maintain on earth the conflict with the powers of darkness, in order to gain influence for humanity, and to become a decided reality. The facts of experience correspond to this law, that to every first inspiration of such a power the tempter unawares stands opposite, as if one power had called forth the other from the darkness of the world to the battle-field. In this manner the divine government of the world fulfils its work. By the uncovering of evil in the course of events, over against the manifestations of good, judgment is executed on the absolute nothingness and baseness of evil. Thus there was a world-historical, and indeed a divine reason, why Christ should be led by the Spirit into the wilderness to be tempted by the devil. His spiritual rest was exchanged for a great and severe spiritual task in the wilderness : it had for its sequel a temptation which was consummated in a mysterious historical act. But after the victory over the temptation, the spiritual festivity reappeared with fresh and steady splendour.

In the Jordan the bright side of sinful humanity had blessed the Lord ; in the wilderness He was obliged to endure the action of its dark side,—the tempting operation of its curse.

If we are informed that the Spirit led the Lord into the wilderness after His God-man consciousness had been festively filled with that divine joy of His inner life, yet we at the same time receive the intimation, that the Lord could not immediately enter with these riches of His heart into the congregation of His people, who formed the contrast to the wilderness.

We might indeed look on the forty days which Jesus spent in the wilderness, first of all, as the celebration of the disclosed fulness of His inner glory. He needed to be a long time alone with God, in order to spread before Him the great revelation which had now been completed, to meditate upon it with Him, and to seal it in the quiet consecration of His life.

This celebration was at all events the beginning, the key-note, and aim of His sojourn in solitude. It was the holy mysterious poetry of the completed unfolding of all Heaven's fulness in the heart of humanity, the beautiful blooming time of roses in the soul of the God-man, the still hour of the holy spring night of the New Covenant on which the nightingale of the world sang its first song to its God. But why call this glorious celebration in solitude, so significantly, the temptation in the wilderness ?

Christ, in the celebration of His Spirit-life, could not turn away from humanity. He could not retain this fulness of life as booty for Himself. It belonged to the nature of this inner glory that He regarded it as God's mission to the world—as Heaven's great benediction—as the salvation of the world. The infinite divine joy with which His heart now throbbed, was at the same time unbounded love of man ; and thus it became an indescribably strong impulse to communicate Himself to the world, and especially to the people of Israel. The impulse of His life was to enter without delay into the midst of the congregation of Israel. And the people called Him. They called Him by all the yearnings of their expectations, by all the thoughts and images of their ideal of the Messiah. The world with all its ideals called Him. But the ideals that called Him were poisoned by the revelry and intoxication of humanity. The Messianic image of a sinful world—a clever, but in all points distorted caricature—as the confused, dim, mocking image of a chaotically agitated and serpent-like wily prince of this world—contradicted the pure image of God in the Messianic consciousness of Christ. Therefore, no sooner had He after His baptism turned Himself in Spirit to the world, with the greeting of His love, than He received a counter-greeting in a loud siren-song of all the distorted intoxicated world-ideals. He could not advance a step among His people without meeting the caricatured image of the chief of men ; without coming upon false assumptions, false words, interpretations and fictions of a false chiliasm perverting the history of the world in a thousand forms, and of a fanatical and carnal idealistic world-vertigo.

The contrariety of Christ's Messianic kingdom to the Messianic ideal of the Jews has often been so explained as if Christ wished to establish a merely spiritual kingdom of heaven —as if He had not inserted in His work the tendency to plant the ideal life, and to advance it to its completion in the actual appearance, and by His redemption really to transform the world. But this 'anti-judaical' spiritualism falls itself into the most palpable error, even while intending to correct the error of the Jews. It contradicts the Messianic image of the prophets, who, agreeably to the nature of the case, combine in one view the inner and outer kingdom of heaven; it equally contradicts the Christian doctrine of that transformation of the world which is to be completed at the resurrection; and lastly, it contradicts the most explicit declarations and promises of Christ Himself, who points to His second advent as the transformation of the world. This view also contradicts every well-grounded theory of the world. It belongs to the dualism which splits the world into two halves—so that ideas must form spectres without cor-poreity, and matters of fact mere animal phenomena without spiritual life. In truth, this spiritualism generally falls back into that chiliasm which it professes to shun. For it must always grant or desire some kind of transformation of the world, and for that purpose it requires both principles and organs. But as it has rejected that transformation by the Spirit and life of Christ, it forms for itself other principles, unchristian and antichristian, which are to make up for or to supplement Christian ones, and must seek in false messiahs for the organs of the world's transformation. But for this dualism Christ has given no warrant whatever by His declaration, 'My kingdom is not of this world.' These words rather express the fact, that with the appearance of His kingdom, this world vanishes, and the future becomes manifest. The very fact that He speaks of His kingdom shows that He has founded not merely a school, or a congregation, or a church, but a morally organized com-munity, completing itself in ideal universality. *The* kingdom is *His* kingdom. But He will surrender it into the hands of the Father; therefore Christ has never given up the expectation that His Messianic kingdom will be a kingdom of outward visibility. As the festival of Easter arises out of Good Friday, so His new world arises from the depths of world-renunciation— His kingdom of glory from His kingdom of the cross. But the expectation that it must begin as an outward kingdom, and therefore outward in its constitution, without being founded in God and in the life of the Spirit,—as a secular kingdom brought into existence by means of craft and force, and so an anticipatory counterfeit of the true kingdom, in which every appearance must proceed from the fulness of the Spirit,—this expectation Christ could never have cherished; for it was the very temptation He combated in the wilderness, and truly a temptation of Satan.

The kingdom of darkness can never realize on earth its chaotic tendencies in their naked, wild form. The destruction of human life, to a large world-historical extent, can be effected only when the spirit of the ethical chaos succeeds in wearing the mask of a transformed cosmos. Only in delusive social forms, political and hierarchical, but especially Messianic and chiliastic, can the 'nameless beast' win for itself, and maintain for a while, a great appearance. The history of evil on the earth proves this. It often appears in chiliastic, often in hierarchical forms; but in the one case the chiliasm is headed by a hierarchical power, in the other case the hierarchy is animated by the intoxication of chiliasm. The 'hierarchy that crucified Christ was in reality Jewish chiliasm throughout. In His time it was concentrated in the falsified ideal of the Messiah. Its special sympathetic power was its connection with all carnal, extravagant idealizing *(Idealisterei)*—with all the fantastic, wild fanaticisms in the world. But its deepest principle was the chief of the demoniacal chaos, who readily disguised himself as an angel of light. When the spirit of a people is hostilely excited in an antichristian tendency against the spirit of Christ and the spirit of the true transformation of the world, in this excitement it necessarily forms a sympathetic union with the spirit of the world in its ungodly tendency. In this sympathy its own tendency coincides with all the tendencies of satanic power; and as this is the mightiest power of the whole

CHRIST IN THE WILDERNESS.

community, so it becomes its animating principle. In truth, demoniacal evil can realize its ideal only in forms of light which allow the inward mockery to be seen through them;—only in forms of the Holy through which may be seen the sneer of the internal contradiction;—only in a false scenery of the transformed world, through which the lightnings of the ancient chaos flash in all directions. The Jewish expectation of the Messiah had its ideal realized in the horrible scenes of the Jewish war.

This expectation met the Lord in His way, as soon as He wished to turn to the people. It was the assumption that He must found His kingdom on an ungodly carnal mind, on unspirituality and internal corruption, on craft and force, which always accompany fanatical idealism among mankind. In His pure sympathy for humanity, He felt the drawing of this intense perverted longing in the world. But no sooner did He feel this influence than it excited a powerful repulsion in the Holy Spirit with which He was filled. This repulsion drove Him into the wilderness. That sympathetic influence opposed Him like a wall. The spirit of temptation encountered Him all the way between Jordan and Jerusalem. Christ, with His Messianic consciousness, sought a sure entrance among His people, and seemed to find none. How could He escape being grievously misunderstood by the world, when He appeared in it as the Messiah, the Son of God? The more He was impelled by the love of mankind to hold intercourse with His people, so much the more a holy shyness towards men drove Him into the wilderness. He could not directly manifest to men the Sun of God's fulness which glowed in His heart, without dazzling their weak eyes. An immediate animated disclosure of His inmost soul would have been for them the final judgment. And how could He expose the glorious mystery of His soul to the unutterable profanation which must ensue, if He was willing to disclose His consciousness directly to the people and trust Himself to the world? It was the curse of the world, that the splendour of His inmost soul, unless it were veiled, must destroy the world. He was obliged to secure His sanctuary in the wilderness from the profanation of the temple-goers, His kingly dignity from the insults of the rulers, His Messiahship from the prevalent Messianic delusions, and His love of men from men. Amidst these embarrassments, He concealed Himself in the depths of the desert. He lived among the wild beasts. They alarmed not the Prince of men, and were less dangerous to Him than men. He wandered about, and could not leave the wilderness, because the Spirit always drove Him back into solitude as often as His heart turned towards men; and then temptation again assailed Him with the alluring sympathy of the world. Thus He was withdrawn from the world for forty days. He had taken refuge in concealment, as if in death, from the siren's song of the world's ideal. He tasted no food during this period of intense mental conflict. His sojourn in the wilderness forms an appalling spectacle,—the spectacle of a man prostrated in the deepest sorrow, and harassed with the severest conflict.

And yet, as we have already intimated, it was not exclusively this mental conflict, involving the interests of humanity, which detained Him in the wilderness. Strongly as the love of man, on the one hand, attracted Him, not less strongly, on the other hand, was He attracted by the love of God. The attraction of the one prepared for Him unspeakable sorrow, that of the latter inexpressible joy. There is a blessedness which is plunged in sadness—a delicate, trembling joy, a solemn festival of the soul in which all the joys of heaven meet and salute all the sufferings of humanity. In this state of feeling we find our Lord. He turned Himself to the Father. In the Father's bosom He concealed His kingly sense of God—His holy horror at the drunken idealizing of the world. If His sorrow caused Him to fast, still more was this effect produced by the peace of this super-mundane retirement, in which He could spend forty days as one holy festival in the presence of His Father. This preponderance of the rest of God over human labour in His spirit—this glorification of His sorrow in His blessedness, of His love of men in His love of God, was just the preponderance of His freedom over the sympathies of His life, which resulted in His victory. This peculiar state of mind serves to explain the long fasting of Christ.

Even in the first days of His fasting, criticism begins to be voracious while it accompanies Him with its meagre reflections. Its doubts cannot disturb us. Christ's fasting was not legal, nor a result of enactment. He might have lived, like John, on locusts and wild honey without essentially breaking His fast.[1] But we can find no difficulty if we take the fasting of Christ in the strictest sense. Often deep thinkers,[2] contemplative devotees,[3] sorrowing penitents,[4] ecstatic enthusiasts, or persons under morbid excitement,[5] have fasted for an extraordinary length of time. But Christ is also in this respect the Prince of men, who in the highest heroic measure comprehends the particular possibilities of this class. In Him the power of the deepest contemplation co-operated with the power of the deepest sorrow, and these with the highest inspiration, in order to sustain a disposition so free from wants and so super-mundane, and which was perfected by means of the highest sympathy which His soul now felt for the entire morbid state of His generation. In truth, His fasting, according to its deepest significance, was the specific, redeeming counteraction against the malady of the world, as far as it consisted in a mad, false idealizing. To that insane chiliastic idolizing of the world which would fain have deluded and fettered Him, He opposed the counterpoise of His perfected sober-mindedness, of which the outward form appeared in His fasting. It should never be forgotten that Christianity was born into the world with a plenitude of the Spirit, which showed the freest exaltation above nature in the fasting of Christ. And this characteristic it retains through all time. In this heroic sobriety of soul it overcame and rescued the Roman-Grecian world in that wild debauchery which would have been its ruin. And thus, hereafter, the Church by the power of a spirit-like sobriety will overcome the jovial banqueting of those who will be eating, and drinking, and amusing themselves at the end of the world (Matt. xxiv. 38, 39). But what specially supported our Lord during those days in the energy of His life, was the creative vital power which gave Him copious supplies of nourishment and vigour, and refreshed His inmost soul. He

[1] Of John the Baptist Christ says (Matt. xi. 18) he came neither eating nor drinking, although he lived on locusts and wild honey, the bread of the wilderness. [Meyer, in his thorough, unflinching way, says the fasting here 'is to be understood *absolutely*,' and refers to the convincing passages, Ex. xxxiv. 28, and 1 Kings xix. 8.—ED.]

[2] Spinoza supported himself for several days on four sous.

[3] Niklaus von der Flüe.

[4] Saul, Acts ix. 9.

[5] See W. Hoffman, das Leben Jesu, p. 315. Many examples of this sort have occurred in modern times.

lived by depending on the mouth of God, while He retired with ecstasy into His innermost principle of life.[1]

In the great movements of His exalted consciousness, the forty days might pass away as a single day, or an hour. It has been observed,[2] that in the lives of Moses[3] and Elijah,[4] periods of forty days occur as fast-times in critical junctures; and the narrative of the sojourn of Jesus in the wilderness has brought to mind the forty years' wandering of Israel in the wilderness. Some have made this remark in order to find out traces of fiction in the history; others, in order to comfort themselves with the thought, that the number of forty days is not to be taken too rigidly.[5] But this rhythmical recurrence of forty days in similar junctures of the Theocracy rather points to a more general mysterious law of life. The forty days' fasting of Moses also forms a contrast to the preceding rebellion of the people, who 'eat, and drank, and rose up to play,' and showed their preference for a false religion. Elijah in like manner presented a spiritual antagonism to the hankering of his people after the fantastic pleasure of the worship of Baal. The common labour of man is comprised in the cycle of a week, and his spiritual labour in the cycle of a week multiplied into itself, in a period of about seven weeks of labour. The spiritual labour by which Israel, as a people, were obliged to purify themselves for the temperate enjoyment of the glories of Canaan, required forty years. But why should not the theocratic history, the innermost essence of which is poetry, be carried on, like poetry, in rhythmical relations? In Christ's life also, this law of life must be fulfilled, according to which the psychical relations stand in living affinity to the earthly relations of time.

But when the forty days were fulfilled, then He hungered. He became vividly conscious of His destitution. He hungered not only after bread, but also after man, and after living intercourse with the world. This was the moment in which all the tempting He had withstood was concentrated, and at the same time unfolded, in most distinct single temptations; the moment in which the tempter, whose spiritual influence He had up to

---

[1] Stier, *Words of the Lord Jesus* i. 37 (Clark's Tr.).
[2] Strauss, *Leben Jesu* i. 450.
[3] Exod. xxxiv. 28.   [4] 1 Kings xix. 8.
[5] Neander, *Life of Jesus Christ*, p. 78 (Bohn).

that time experienced, came before Him in a more defined form. We are able to distinguish exactly these two stadia of the temptation: the secret whispers of the tempting spirit during the forty days, and its final concentration in the three assaults at the close. Matthew has condensed the whole temptation of Christ into those final assaults. Mark has simply noticed the temptation in its duration of forty days. Luke has specified the two constituent parts of the temptation. As soon as we have ascertained the significance of the whole transaction, no real contradictions can be imagined. But we must now endeavour to set in a clear light the distinction between the two forms of the temptation.

During the forty days Christ was tempted in this way, that He was met by the Messianic ideal of Israel in its corrupted chiliastic form, sustained by all the morbid fanatical excitement then existing in the world, and by the powers of darkness. But this temptation was probably not an internal process, as it is often represented in order to explain the history of the temptation.[1] Christ could not in an idle manner brood over the possibilities of sin, or imagine them in darkness by spreading out the allurements of the false ideal of the world before His own spirit. On this supposition, one part of His consciousness would have been the tempter, and the other the conqueror.[2] Such a self-tempting of the consciousness can hardly be imagined, without involving sin.[3] The totality of the soul's life will not allow us to separate the voluntary imagination of the tempting evil from an accompanying movement of evil desire. And apart from this psychological law, another law of life forbids our regarding

[1] 'Transient illusions' (Fluchtige Vorspiegelungen) the temptations of Jesus, according to this view, are called by Fleck (die Vertheidigung des Christenthums, p. 225).

[2] Particularly according to the representation of this transaction by Weisse (die evangelische Geschichte ii. 21).

[3] ['I could as soon accept the worst statements of the most degraded form of Arian creed, as believe that this temptation arose from any internal strugglings or solicitations,—I could as soon admit the most repulsive tenet of a dreary Socinianism, as deem that it was enhanced by any self-engendered enticements, or hold that it was aught else than the assault of a desperate and demoniacal malice from without, that recognised in the nature of man a possibility of falling, and that thus far consistently, though impiously, dared even in the person of the Son of man to make proof of its hitherto resistless energies.'—Ellicott's Hist. Lect. p. 111.—ED.]

the temptation of Christ as a fact of His consciousness isolated from His people's life. It belongs to the order and soundness of the inner life to indulge in no idle brooding anticipations of the future. The soul can and should anticipate the outward experience, but only in proportion as it comes in contact with the spiritual prognostics of the experience, as the collision with experience begins to fall upon its ear; as therefore it is congruous with a human life which must be always prepared and led through the inward to the outward, and with its essential superiority to time. But if beyond this necessity it indulges in arbitrary anticipations, it gets out of its historical rhythm. This arbitrary exercise of the imagination would be in itself sinful, even should there be nothing sinful in the nature of its imaginings. But Christ could not disturb the order of His life in a morbid manner. His battle with the evil one was, therefore, not the result of a fiction. It was a genuine historical collision with him, though a spiritual one. The whole soul of Christ stood firm in the absolute rejection of the temptation, which was not in the least degree the offspring of His own fancy. But not the less was His soul moved and agitated by temptation, in consequence of the sympathy which bound Him closely to His own people and to mankind. In the element of this sympathy He beheld all the images of temptation standing clearly before Him—He heard all the tones of its allurements. Christ's living impulse to manifest Himself to His people placed Him incessantly opposite to temptation, which was continually meeting Him in new forms. The repulsion with which He continually put it away from Him was His victory.

In consequence of this repulsion, Christ must always have remained in the wilderness, unless in some particular moments of His conflict the possibility had not been developed and displayed to Him of entering among the people, and thus fulfilling the mission of His life. The struggle of Christ with temptation was at the same time to secure and determine the complete carrying out of His calling in all its distinguishing traits. And since, on the one hand, in the life of His free love the necessity of manifesting Himself to the people moved Him, and, on the other hand, He felt the necessity of concealing and withdrawing Himself from the people, the plan of His Messianic ministry required to be clearly and distinctly unfolded under the painful reciprocal action of this apparent contradiction. At the end of His conflict He had a fully developed solution of the difficult problem, how He could surrender Himself as the true Messiah to the people, who were carried away by a false Messianic image. The completion of this determination of His calling coincided with the completion of His victory over temptation, and therefore with the completion of the festal repose of His spirit.

But it would be contrary to all general and individual experience if we were disposed to admit that the temptation of Christ was ended and completed in a merely spiritual and ideal form. Actual fact shows us that the moral conflicts of man cannot possibly remain spiritualist combats. The tempting opportunity always meets the susceptible disposition, and converts the ideal conflict into a historical one.[1] The solemnity of the divine superintendence demands it, and the thoughtfulness of life and the truth of victory. How many a flaming inspiration of idealist valour has become to 'rude reality a prey!' The victory of Christ over the tempter would not have been perfectly certain if the latter had not appeared to Him in historic reality.

But how did he appear to Christ?[2] We need not explain at length that Satan could not become a man, and assume flesh and blood, like the Son of God. Such a supposition would expose any one to the charge of Manicheism; it would be condemned for its dualism. But if it were imagined that Satan showed himself to the Lord in a spectral appearance, it can hardly be granted that Christ would let Himself be disposed of by such a spectre of hell on the soil of this earth's reality, and be led through the world in all directions.[3] Nothing is gained, if it is attempted to render the supposition easier, by supposing that Satan transformed himself into an angel of light; for never could he appear more detestable and repulsive in Christ's eyes than under this mask. It is perfectly unchristological to regard these temptations as a series of juggling tricks by the

---

[1] [This view seems to receive confirmation especially from our Lord's own experience in His last trial, when He had first to endure the ideal and spiritual conflict alone in the garden, and then the actual historical sufferings and death.—ED.]

[2] Ebrard, in his *Gospel History*, admits a visible appearance of Satan, without any further explanation.

[3] See Ullmann, *The Sinlessness of Jesus*, p. 160 (Clark's Tr., 2d ed.).

arch-sorcerer, since it supposes that he transported the Lord from one scene of temptation to another.[1] Even the pious popular feeling in the legends, which represent the tricks of jugglers as failing in the eyes of innocent children and virtuous maidens, goes beyond this mode of viewing things, which makes the eye of Christ dependent on the illusions of the Prince of Lies. Indeed, if we wished to deal seriously with this supposed illusion, it might be difficult to distinguish it from the beginning of an internal infatuation.

The tempter did not approach the Lord with juggling tricks, but in the dangerous power of historical circumstances. The kingdom of Satan was represented by the false tendency of the kingdom of this world, and this lastly by the perverted tendency of the Jewish hierarchy. But that the Jewish hierarchy about this time were in quest of a Messiah according to their ideal, may easily be proved.

That deputation which the hierarchy sent from Jerusalem to Jordan, for the purpose of obtaining from the Baptist an explanation respecting his own character, must have returned to Jerusalem, according to the dates furnished by the Evangelists, about the time when Christ's forty days' sojourn had really expired. From the account of the Evangelist John (i. 28, 29), it is quite evident that Jesus came back from the solitude of the wilderness just one day after the return of this deputation from Jordan. Now, the Baptist had declared to them in the most explicit terms that he himself was not the Messiah, but at the same time most distinctly announced that the Messiah was come among them without their knowing Him. From a sense of his theocratic duty, he could not content himself on such a subject with simple intimations. If he pointed out the Messiah to his disciples, much more would he mark Him out to the rulers of his people, whatever might be the consequences. If, then, the deputation came to him precisely at the time in which he had recognised the person of the Messiah, he would regard it as an intimation from the Lord to direct the attention of the deputation away from himself to the acknowledged Messiah. If he could not direct them to His place of sojourn in the desert, yet he could so exactly describe His personal appearance, that it

[1] Olshausen, *Commentary on the New Testament* i. 167 (Clark's Tr.). Krabbe, *Vorlesungen über das Leben Jesu*, p. 172.

would be easy for the deputation to find Him on their way home. But, at all events, it would be a very false conception of this politically excited hierarchy, to suppose that they would take home so quietly the announcement from the lips of the Baptist, that the Messiah was in their midst, without making any further inquiries on the matter of fact. The Jewish hierarchy, filled with deep rancour against the Romans, longed for a political Messiah. As to the existence of this longing, we must not be misled by the hypocrisy with which they delivered up the true Messiah to the Romans, professing the highest devotedness to the Emperor; it is sufficiently confirmed by the later Jewish history. These men therefore left the Baptist under the excitement of this longing, and pursued the traces of the Messiah; and all the more readily they would pass near His retreat on their way home, if, according to traditional accounts, He was sojourning in the wilderness near Jericho. It might not be difficult for them to find out the Man they were so anxious to see, since His inner conflicts were now ended, and His course of life or entrance into the world was now clearly marked out; He was therefore on the point of leaving the wilderness on His return to the Baptist. But if they found Him, they would accost Him with all the parade and impatience of their Messianic expectations. They would present him with a Messianic programme diametrically opposite in all essential points to that which had been formed in His own mind.[1]

The same pure divine Prince of spirits who treated Peter as a Satan when he wanted to dissuade from the path that led to the cross, as ordained by His Father—who regarded the ripened thoughts of treachery in Judas as an inspiration of Satan (John xiv. 30)—and, lastly, who beheld in His own death on the cross a judgment on the prince of this world—must have regarded this historical temptation on the part of the Sanhe-

---

[1] That the view of the history of the temptation as a historical fact in a narrower sense has already existed in Rationalist forms (see Strauss, *Leben Jesu*, p. 442), and that it is marked as antiquated in its unmotived outward form, cannot prevent us from presenting it in a new form and on a fresh foundation. We have in this view not the least interest to settle the demonology, but we shall necessarily be led to it by the motives assigned. Those tempting hierarchs form only the historic heads of the whole transaction, and the organs of a temptation which in its deepest ground and connection we regard as altogether satanic.

drim as the culmination and historic completion of that sympathetic temptation of Satan with which He had wrestled in the wilderness.

The hierarchs, accustomed to a life of luxury, must have been astonished beyond measure, when they discovered the supposed instrument of their designs, the great Prince of the world, in the form of a fasting, hungry hermit. The oriental pomp, we might say, the poetry of courtiers, may be detected in the words, ' If Thou be the Son of God, command that these stones be made bread.' As little as John the Baptist could have thought of a literal transformation of stones when he said, ' God is able of these stones to raise up children to Abraham,' so little could the voice of temptation have required here, in a literal sense, that the Lord should change stones into bread. Such a requirement could have been no temptation for Him. In the soul of Christ least of all could the thought arise, of using His miraculous power in so fantastic a manner. Indeed we can hardly impute such an expectation even to the Jewish hierarchs. It is true, they expected a Messiah whose rule should quickly change the desert into a blooming champaign;[1] but in what manner, was a matter of indifference to them. If He had exhibited Himself decidedly in their sense as the Son of God, the wilderness would very soon, by His magical power over spirits, have become an Israelitish camp-scene, in which would have flowed a superabundance of all earthly enjoyments. But still more directly must He have been able, in their opinion, to change the wilderness into a region of delight by the magic art of a world-transforming culture. This, indeed, was the chief element of the temptation, that He should at once begin the desired transformation of the world for appeasing His own hunger, and for the celebration of the commencing worldly pleasure with the transformation of the wilderness in which they and He were then standing.[2] But this proposal was a real temptation for Him, since the actual transformation of the world lay within the scope of His ministry, and since the infinite patience of His spirit was required to wait for that manifestation of the glorious fulness of life which always floated before Him as the

[1] Compare Isa. xxxv. 1.
[2] The fantastic images of abundance in which Jewish tradition depicts the transformation of the world at its close are well known.

slow, late bloom and fruit of all the activity of His spirit. Thousands suffer themselves to be misled by this first speech of the tempter to a deceptive false glorification of the world, colouring and covering the curse of the wilderness. Thus ofttimes, by popular delusion, by robbery, by the subversion of social order, by enormous loans and deceptions of all kinds, the deserts are made glad, and the stones are turned into bread. We detect traces of this sorcery in the chiliastic Zion of the Munster Anabaptists, in Wallenstein's Camp, as well as in many other historical caricatures of the world's transformation. Still the tempter sings this old song,[1] and his magic tones are just now sounding again through the world with a marvellous power of delusion. Christ, therefore, in virtue of that great sympathy with which He, as Prince of men, felt the pulse of Humanity, heard in the address of the tempter the call of all carnal idealizing of hunger, want, and destitution in the world, the lamentation of all false mendicity, the fawning petitions of all chiliast worldlings, the extravagant requirements of all hypocritical and superficial philanthropists : ' O command that these stones be made bread!' The sympathetic rush of all morbid human longings after the enchanted land of an unjust and measureless abundance, and a glory of the flesh overpowering the spirit, broke out in this temptation against His heart, and made Him shudder, since he felt most deeply all the misery of the world— all the glow of its hope, and all the glory of its prospects. Thus He was tempted to create an abundance with the powers of His divine-human life, in contravention of the divine order, and in a self-willed magical manner. But before this delirious excitement He veiled His unique divine-human consciousness. He answered it with a divine word, which had formerly supported the confidence of pious human hearts during their sufferings in the wilderness : ' Man shall not live by bread alone, but by every word that proceedeth out of the mouth of God.'[2] In the name of humanity itself, of necessitous man, He rejected the assumption that man cannot realize the ideal of his spirit unless

---

[1] Göthe has in a masterly manner represented this temptation of Mephistopheles in his Faust, Second Part.

[2] The expression, ἐπὶ παντὶ ῥήματι, is, according to the words in Deut. viii. 3, ' everything that proceedeth out of the mouth of the Lord,' referable to every creative word from the mouth of God—every vital operation.

he is living in the splendour of outward abundance. He asserted to the tempter, the dignity of the personality by which man is elevated above the requirement of mere animal existence. Man lives not by bread alone; but the breath of life from the mouth of God gives him his life in the most special sense.

By His victory over the first temptation Christ laid the foundation for the genuine transformation of the world, and for the establishment of a real abundance upon earth in the blessing of His Spirit. The two miraculous feedings of the people in the wilderness, which He performed at a later period, would represent, as by a wonderful prelude, this transformation of the earth into the superabundance of heaven.

Now began the second temptation. Satan led the Lord to Jerusalem, placed Him on a pinnacle, and said to Him, 'If Thou be the Son of God, cast Thyself down; for it is written, He shall give His angels charge concerning thee, and in their hands they shall bear thee up, lest at any time thou dash thy foot against a stone.'[1] If Christ had really in an outward sense stood on a pinnacle of the temple,[2] Satan would hardly have made the proposal to throw Himself down literally. At least this suggestion would not have been to Him a temptation—a psychical shock. But the actual temptation must have really agitated Him. Probably He was transported in a figurative sense to the summit of the temple-pinnacle by the ostentatious offers of the deputies of the Sanhedrim. No doubt the most flattering prospects awaited His recognition by the Sanhedrim. The most solemn assurances were given. As the prophetic and priestly King, He saw Himself already placed on the summit of the temple. Thence He was to make His entry into Jerusalem with the recognition of the priests. But this mode of manifestation to Israel appeared to Him as a fatal death-leap. It is true the plea was urged, that, according to the word of God, there could be no danger for the Lord's Anointed; He would

[1] Ps. xci. 11.
[2] It was no impossibility to stand on the pinnacle of Solomon's porch, and perhaps on other parts of the temple. See De Wette's Erklärung des Evangelium Matt. p. 40. [Meyer, in a valuable note on this expression, inclines to the opinion that it points to the ridge of the στοὰ βασιλική, on the south side of the temple. For the giddy height of this altitude, see Josephus, Antiq. xv. 11, 5.—Ed.]

be borne by angels, and glide over all obstructions. But Christ foiled the tempter with the words, 'Thou shalt not tempt the Lord thy God.'[1] Thus He opposed a definite word of Scripture, in its true scope, to the false exposition of an indefinite and obscure one. Thou shalt not attempt to draw God into the way of thy self-will, thy pride, or thy enthusiasm. He will not allow Himself to be drawn by thee into a sinful interest; much rather would He let thee fall and drop. If thou wilt tempt Him, the attempt will become a dangerous temptation for thyself. This is the meaning of the command which the Lord held as a shield before His breast, in order to intercept the second dart of the tempter. He rendered the Old Testament precept more pointed, without altering the meaning, by substituting the singular *thou* for the plural *ye*. He thus at the same time brought it home to the tempter, that he tempted God when he tempted Christ. It appeared, therefore, to the Lord a monstrous, fatal venture to trust Himself to the deputies of the Sanhedrim, and to give Himself up to the priesthood of His people. Had this been possible, only the corpse of the true Messiah would have fallen from the pinnacle of the temple among the people; the hierarchy would have made of Him a different character altogether from what He was. Let us imagine ourselves present at the moment when Christ saw the inclination of the fathers of His nation to receive Him according to their notions of the Messiah, with all the allurements of the historical and Israelitish good-will which such an offer must contain,—let us recollect that all the sympathies which tradition, patriotism, and piety form in the world's history must be involved in His temptation to surrender the sanctuary of His inner life to an infatuated foreign power,—and we shall perceive that His heart must have been agitated to its inmost depths when the storm of such influences broke upon Him. How many noble spirits inflamed by patriotic or religious enthusiasm have fallen before the tempter, because they and their vocation have been held in thraldom by criminal, false, historical tendencies, traditions, and authorities! Jesus withstood the temptation in the power of His sober-mindedness, and of that pure fidelity with which He adhered to His Father's ways. His victory laid the foundation for enabling the kingly and priestly

[1] Deut. vi. 16.

people of believers to make Him known as the Messiah to the
nation of Israel, and to all the world.   In His triumphal entrance into Jerusalem at the last Passover, He allowed the first
bloom of that homage to break forth which hereafter is to be
rendered by the whole world.

The deputies from Jerusalem, who, probably in the manner
we have pointed out, had placed the Lord by their theocratic
phrases on a pinnacle of the temple, could easily stand by Him
on a mountain height in the wilderness as they made their last
attempt to persuade Him.[1]   But the mountain on which they
placed Him was a mountain from which they could show Him
all the kingdoms of the world, and their glory; therefore a
'mountain higher than all other mountains' (Isa. ii. 2)—Mount
Zion, according to its spiritual significance, in the last age of
the world.   The tempter displayed to Him the prospect of the
theocratic government of the world.   Probably into this disclosure, plots against the Romans were introduced,—at all events
unspiritual, ungodly plots, by which their object was to be attained.   And Christ was urged to approve of their hierarchical
plan for the conquest of the world.   But to Him this demand
appeared as a temptation to fall down before Satan and worship Him.   And so it was in fact.   If the hierarchical or political conqueror of the world avails himself of evil means for his
supposed good ends, he acts in reality as a vassal of the prince
of darkness, and has bowed the knee to him.   The demand for
an outward bowing of the knee the crafty enemy would not indeed, in the presence of the Lord, have been very ready to make.
But the prospect he opened had an infinite power of sympathetic
influence on the heart of Jesus.   He cast a glance in spirit
over His inheritance—the world.   Countless hearts were bleed-
ing, the noblest spirits were waiting for Him, the promise of
the Father guaranteed Him this inheritance.   All the motives
of compassion, love, and holy zeal seemed to oblige Him to

[1] Tradition has pointed out the mountain Quarantania, situated in the
wilderness, near Jericho, as the mountain of the temptation. 'In one of its
many ravines Jesus must have kept His fast of forty days.' Winer, RWB
ii. 810. ['This tradition, as well as the name Quarantania, appear not to be
older than the age of the Crusades.' Robinson i. 568. See, however, Ellicott (Hist. Lec., p. 109), who conjectures 'the lonely and unexplored chain
of desert mountains, of which Nebo has been thought to form a part.' This
was formerly suggested by Michaelis.—ED.]

CHRIST IN THE WILDERNESS.

hasten to leave no means untried, but at any cost to make Himself forthwith Master of the world. At such a prospect all His feelings for the world must have been aroused and inflamed. But the maxims on which He was to proceed in immediately beginning the conquest of the world, were such as He was obliged to reject. The splendour of the end could in no wise excuse to Him the detestable means of falsehood and unrighteousness. He could not wish to have the beautiful world at the price of homage to Satan. Every representation of the kingdom of God in the world founded on untruthfulness, false appearances, hypocrisy, and force, appeared to Him fraught with most horrible ruin to the world, a most destructive procedure. His wrath against the tempter now flamed high; and with the words, 'Get thee hence, Satan, for it is written, Thou shalt not tempt the Lord thy God, and Him only shalt thou serve,'[1] He drove him from His presence.

By this victory, in which Christ renounced all pretensions to the immediate conquest of the world, He has gained the world in God's sight, and in the depths of His spirit and of His fidelity to God has already begun to take possession of His kingdom. Since He has not sought the government of the world by base expedients, He has been invested with it by the Father. Luke observes, 'that the devil departed from Him for a season.' Though Jesus all through His life was tempted in a general manner, yet He had two great master-temptations to withstand: first, the temptation of all the demon-inspired pleasure and fanaticism in the world, the temptation to self-delusion in egoistic morbid enthusiasm and in intoxicated arrogance; and next, the temptation of all the demoniac dislike and dread in the world, a temptation to faint-heartedness and despair. The second did not immediately make its appearance when the first was over. But after a certain breathing-time, Christ had to fight with Satan's temptations to despair. The instruments of this second temptation were men—the representatives of the Jewish world of spirit, and this circumstance reflects light on the instruments of the first temptation.

The attitude assumed by the hierarchy against Jesus as soon as He appeared, was so hostile, that we can scarcely attri-

[1] Deut. vi. 13.

bute it solely to His rejection of the rabbinical rules about
the Sabbath. It leads us to conjecture, that the determined
conflict between the spirit of Christ and the spirit of this
hierarchy had already begun in secret when Christ publicly
appeared.

If Christ narrated to His disciples the history of His temptation at the beginning of His intercourse with them, we may
easily conceive, that in consideration of their weakness, He
would avoid placing the heads of the nation as the instruments
of Satan in the foreground of His description. Besides, these
personages were properly the mere conveyers of a temptation
which in its general form He had encountered before their appearance, and which seemed to Him, moreover, in its historical
fulfilment, as an act of the element of ungodliness in the world
generally, and in hell itself. Hence the symbolic form of the
narrative may be explained.

When Jesus had gained His great victory, 'angels came
and ministered to Him.' These words express primarily a spiritual and abiding fact. By this victory over the kingdom of
darkness, Jesus was authenticated as the Prince of humanity,
and humanity, which in Him had now withstood the severest
temptations, appeared in fresh splendour. As a consequence of
His moral elevation and the authentication He had received,
Jesus was now the Prince of pure spirits, and in Him humanity
was represented as a kingdom of spirits exalted over the world
of angels. This, Jesus experienced in His own mind: heavenly
sounds of congratulation greeted Him after the severe conflict.
He received impressions from the world of spirits, and the
homage of angels, when, by His victory over all sympathy with
evil desires in the world, He had restored the full reciprocation
with the joy of the pure spirit-world. And especially in this
hour of joyous victory was He able to come into the most intimate spiritual intercourse with angels. But His victory over
spirits became historically manifest by the entrance into His
service of John and Peter, the noblest angels of the New Testament age.

NOTES.

1. The various explanations of the history of the temptation
are of very different values. They prove the difficulty of the

subject by their manifold contrariety; but most of them contain some elements of truth, which in a living historic view of the transaction appear combined in a higher unity. The temptation especially appears in the grandest manner as an operation of Satan, provided Satan does not appear bodily according to the popular representations, but his operation is conceived as the result of the sympathetic co-operation of the designs of the ungodly spirit of the world with the designs of the kingdom of darkness. We cannot admit that Satan could have captivated the eye of Jesus by the immediate influence of delusive appearances. Meanwhile we must not fail to observe, that the great idealist illusions of the spirit of the world may be considered as juggleries of darkness, the power of which Christ must have experienced mediately, since they have mingled with the noblest aspirations and forebodings of mankind. Hitherto, when the temptation has been explained as an internal occurrence, the objection has arisen, that the essence of the temptation was thus treated as consisting in a free exercise of the imagination of Christ on the possibilities of sin. But this objection is disposed of, when the internal temptation is recognised as an attack of the sympathetic action of the spirit of His nation and of the world on His soul, to which it was necessary for Him to give a decisive repulse. The hypothesis that Christ was tempted by a single deputy of the Sanhedrim, a Pharisee, has been in later times most generally rejected; it had been brought into discredit, owing to its rationalistic origin, and the uninteresting manner in which it was propounded and advocated. This does not prevent us from accepting what is true in it, for explaining the history of the temptation. That Christ could regard men as satanic tempters has been shown. The principal thing here (besides the ethical postulate, that every victory over temptation is complete only when it becomes a historical fact) is the chronological hint, that the return of the deputation to the Baptist from the Jordan to Jerusalem must have coincided with the return of Christ from the wilderness to the Jordan; further, the theocratic requirement that John owed to all his hearers, and must have given them, the clearest information respecting the Messiah; lastly, the historical circumstance, that the conflict between Christ and the hierarchy at Jerusalem came on so early in such a decisive manner. That exposition

which would treat the narrative as a parable [1] has been disposed
of by the remark, that in the construction of a parable historical persons are not made use of, and least of all does the maker
of the parable introduce himself in the parable. Now we have
seen, that the temptation, with all its simply defined historical
precision, has an universal world-historical significance, and
hence it is easily explained how it necessarily assumed in the
representation a parabolic hue, as soon as the Lord, for good
reasons, caused the historical elements of the temptation
to retire behind the symbolic features which expressed their
general meaning. (On this symbolism, see Hase, *Leben Jesu*,
pp. 102, 103). That explanation which would turn the whole
transaction into a dream (Meyer, *Stud. und Krit.* 1831, Part 2),
or into a vision (Paulus, *das Leben Jesu* i. 142), we must regard
as peculiarly unfortunate. A dream is not within the province
of moral responsibility; and world-historical battles and spiritual
conflicts are not fought out in the placid repose of a dream (see
Ullmann). The state of ecstasy, too, must be regarded as the
opposite pole to the state of moral wrestling in God's champions,
though it comes under the same category of true spiritual life.
But in the life of Christ the idea of ecstasy is altogether excluded,
since in Him the great antagonism between the inmost life in
the spirit and common existence which rendered possible the
ecstasy of the prophets, is lost in the harmony of perfected life.
The most meagre view of all is indisputably that which regards
the transaction as made up from a number of Old Testament
fragments, as, for example, Elijah's forty days' fast, etc. (Strauss,
Leben Jesu, p. 446). At all events, we do too much honour to
such an exposition, which treats New Testament facts as a piece
of mosaic made up of fragments from the Old Testament, as a
composition of the merest outward similarities, to which also Jewish
tradition must contribute, if we designate it a mythical exposition.
Mythical exposition must throughout first point to the Christian
idea—and then show that from an aversion to the incarnation and
to fact, this idea has turned into the bypath of its spiritualistic
embodiment in the myth. These collectanea of Old Testament
analogies to New Testament facts have, however, served to draw
attention to the rhythmical relations in the theocratic history.[2]

---

[1] Schleiermacher on Luke, p. 54, etc.

[2] [A valuable criticism of the various theories of the temptation will be

2. When the first temptation is designated a temptation to 'the sin of Genius,' to convert the objects of sense into nourishment for the spirit (Weisse, *Die evangel. Geschichte* ii. 22), we may notice the change in the modern spirit of the age, which for some time was for regarding all the pleasures of sense with fanatical untruthfulness as nourishment for the spirit, devotion and worship, but which now has passed into a decided dualism, which goes to the length of regarding as sin the ennobling of the pleasures of sense into nourishment for the spirit.

3. The chronological difficulties which would make the history of the temptation uncertain, can be regarded only as assumed, if it is observed, how plainly John the Baptist (according to John i. 28, 29), at the time when the deputation from Jerusalem left him, represents the divine attestation to Jesus at His baptism as a fact that had previously transpired. The day after the departure of the deputation, Jesus comes to him, and John exclaims : 'Behold the Lamb of God,' etc. This exclamation is a proof that Jesus had been pointed out as the Messiah by that extraordinary event. But even when the deputation came to John, the manifestation of Christ must have taken place; otherwise he could not have said of the Messiah that 'He stood among them,' an expression which presupposes the manifestation of the Messiah for Israel. Now, since the forty days' sojourn of Jesus in the wilderness followed His baptism, and this sojourn was closed just after the return of the deputation, the baptism must have taken place about forty days before their arrival at the Jordan. Negative criticism, in dealing with this chronological difficulty, is just like a man's standing

found in Meyer in loc. ; by whom and by Ellicott (p. 110) the literature of the subject is given. The condemnations in the latter are too indiscriminate. Did he forget that what he calls ' the monstrous opinion that the tempter was human' was adopted by Bengel? (' Videtur tentator sub schemate scribæ apparuisse'). However, it is to be borne in mind, that in the other instances where Satan used human agency we are made distinctly aware of this by the narrative, whereas in the case before us no such intimation is given, and certainly a different impression conveyed. It is therefore mere hypothesis that Satan here acted through hierarchical or other human persons ; and some may be disposed to reject the hypothesis on the score of its needlessness. Besides that the supposition of intervening persons must be suspected of proceeding from and tending towards a disbelief of the power of Satan to act on the soul of man immediately, as spirit on spirit. From this suspicion the author clears himself above.—ED.]

close under a bridge, and complaining that he finds no passage
over, all the while running down the river, and never thinking
of turning upwards. ' The Evangelist does not make the
Baptist speak as if six weeks had intervened between the baptism of Jesus and the narrative he now gives.' Thus Strauss,
Leben Jesu i. 428. This perfectly arbitrary assertion has, not
without reason, met with ironical treatment from Ebrard.

SECTION VIII.

THE PLAN OF JESUS.

It was the blessed result of the temptation which Jesus
passed through in the wilderness, that the whole course, as it
was to be developed in perfect fidelity to God, was shaped
clearly before His eyes, and settled in the choice of His heart.
When he wrestled with the tempter, who wished to take from
Him the attested evidence of His divine mission, the whole
evidence unrolled itself, and He grasped it as a clear plan of
His career. The first man passed beyond his former condition
of life by transgression; the second, by the preservation of His
righteousness. When He rejected the satanic plan in all its
parts, he gained the most definite and perspicuous counterpart
of it, the plan of His future, of His earthly sojourn.

May we be allowed to describe this ideal conception of His
career, which Christ gained by the temptation, as His own PLAN?
The term is at all events easily misunderstood, and at the best is
feeble in relation to the great thought which in this case it must
bear; and yet it is not easy to find a substitute for it. Christ
gained in the wilderness a distinct survey of His real course
through life. But the most powerful, freest self-determination
was connected with this survey, which might, therefore, be regarded as His choice. He had chosen His life's course when He
returned from the wilderness. But this choice was not merely
dynamic, but a deliberate arrangement of various parts—an
internal programme—the ideal delineation of His pilgrimage.
If we seek for the most suitable word to designate this ideal

draught of the career of Jesus, we shall be led back to the word PLAN.[1]

Not only does reflection form plans, but enthusiasm. Plan, indeed, often stands in contrast to the simple, noble frankness of disposition as a product of calculating design. But the discipline of the Spirit which refines the enthusiasm that pours itself forth irregularly, and which leads to clearness of perception respecting its functions, also compels to the formation of a plan. Not only civil concerns, diplomatic negotiations, and political intrigues rest upon definite plans, but still more the glorious works of art. A perfect work of art is, in its essential characteristics, prepared before its actual execution. Now it would be decidedly at variance with Christ's life, if we were to admit that He had reached this ideal formation of His life in His inner man, but proceeded to His work with a blind enthusiasm. The New Testament age begins from the first in a decided consciousness, which is in unison with the highest rapture of inspiration. This is the specific nature of Christianity, that, on the one hand, its enthusiasm is not pathological or pythical, and that, on the other, its clearness of spirit and consciousness is not reflection or enlightening of the finite by the finite. Therefore provision was made that Christ might enter on His career with perfected consciousness and developed distinctness.

We have already seen that Christ's plan could not be that of a political Messiah. Christ would have contradicted His own nature and calling, if He had wished to erect the political transformation of the world on the rotten basis of the corruption, religious and moral, of the ancient world. Even John the Baptist was far above such modern, demagogical ideas, to say nothing of Christ. But if Christ had first of all proceeded in such a false direction, and had been punished in it by failure, and thus thrown into the purely spiritual direction, after such a

[1] Two of the most distinguished theologians of our time hold opposite opinions in reference to the use of this word in the representation of the life of Jesus. Ullmann expresses himself against the word (*On the Sinlessness of Jesus*, p. 92). Neander is in favour of it (*Life of Jesus Christ*, p. 80 [Bohn's ed.]). But Neander does not dispute Ullmann's view as to its meaning. He only claims for the word *plan* a higher sense in this connection. [' The " plan " of our Saviour's ministry is a topic which most of the modern lives of our Lord discuss with a very unbecoming freedom.'—Ellicott, p. 99.— ED.]

check He could not possibly have accomplished the pure ideal work of the world's redemption. We may without any hesitation affirm that this would have been a fatal blow to the doctrine, precluding, that is, its application to moral relations. For a false swing of the pendulum, when it is over, is always followed by a counter vibration which is sure to produce a one-sidedness, even if it does not rebound again into the false. But a one-sidedness, such as might prove an ornament to the life of an Augustin, would form a remediless defect in the life of Jesus.[1] And such a one-sidedness there would have been, if Christ had wished to confine His mission and agency for all ages to the spiritual. The institution of the holy sacrament clearly proves that Christ intended to take possession of the whole phenomenal world. The sacraments represent this taking possession in symbolically significant beginnings. They form the germ of the world's transformation; and since they constitute what belongs to the essence of the Church, we may regard the Church as the seed-corn of Christ's commonwealth.

It was therefore Christ's leading thought in the predetermination of His career, that He wished to lay the foundation of a new world deep in the spiritual life of humanity, by spiritual operations. Since He had descended into the depths of the world's corruption which confronted Him in the temptation, even to the point where He could seize and destroy it in its foundations, He saw clearly that in all-subduing love, in the firmest confidence, in perfect humility, and with the greatest boldness of spirit, He must go down even to hell; that He could find the world's deliverance only in the most awful world's judgment, and even in the deepest death of His own life. Thus was He obliged to lay the foundation of His work deep in the foundations, or rather in the abysses, of the spiritual world. The more He thus measured the spiritual depths of His work, the fainter must have been the prospect of bringing it into manifestation in the days of His earthly pilgrimage; but the more clearly must He have seen before Him the whole world-historical descent into hell, which He, and with Him the Church, had to experience in the world, and the more must the future unfolding of His economy in the world have appeared as the bright

[1] See Ullmann *on the Sinlessness of Jesus.* This theologian has successfully combated the view mentioned above.

image of an unchangeable glory, as an infinitely splendid ascension to heaven. But especially it appeared to the Lord absolutely necessary to veil the consciousness of His divine dignity and Messiahship as a great mystery from the profane mind of His nation. The Jews could not hear of the Messiah without being intoxicated with political fanaticism on His account, or with hierarchical fanaticism, incurring guilt towards Him even to death. And yet it was absolutely needful that men should learn to know Him as the Messiah in order to find salvation in Him. Hence it was Christ's first business to veil or unveil the mystery of His inner life with the clearest foresight of redeeming love, according to the measure of the spiritual necessities of the world. Thus in the wilderness He carefully veiled Himself before the tempter, in the garb of a plain man, a pious Jew. He expressed the glory of His inner life in Scripture passages, in, if we may so say, catechetical words. And when the Jews wished to make Him a king, when the demon of political enthusiasm began to work, He withdrew from the excited multitude and retired apart to pray. When the demoniacs proclaimed the fact of His Messiahship, which they had perhaps become cognisant of by a morbid relation of the soul to His consciousness, He rebuked them. He trusted Himself to no one, for He well knew what was in man (John ii. 24). It is an evidence of the heavenly fervour which His heart maintained under all this caution, that He at once made known His dignity to the Samaritan woman; that almost immediately He told this poor sin-laden female that He was the Messiah (John iv. 26). To her He ventured to reveal His Messianic dignity, for in Samaria there was not the danger connected with this revelation, which in Judea made such a revelation impossible. And herein the power of His self-determination is manifest, which enabled Him to control the ardour of His soul, that He guarded His inner man with so perfect a mastery in humility from the profanation of the Jews. How long did Christ wait before He raised the conviction of the disciples themselves to full certainty that He was the Messiah! But it is a fact of appalling solemnity, that He did not impart the secret of His Messianic glory to the head of the nation, the high priest, till it had been demanded of him as a judicial confession, and the non-recognition of His real dignity had so far prevailed, that this confession was the occasion of His death

(Matt. xxvi. 64). Not till then was His secret fully secured from the boundless chiliastic worldliness which confronted Him, when He divulged it in the most solemn manner before the Sanhedrim of His nation, and not till then was completed the veiling of Christ's life from all the profane spirits and thoughts in the world. With the crown of thorns and the reed sceptre, He came into the midst of the world's history in a form in which He could be manifest only by His Spirit to the best, the elect of men. And still the cloud of Christ's world-historical ignominy ever veils the holy of holies of His nature from the eyes of those who would turn spiritual glory into carnal. But though Christ, at the beginning of His public life, was firmly resolved to use the name of Messiah only with the greatest caution, since the Jews would have cherished a radically false notion of Him, as soon as they received Him under this name; yet, in His divine truthfulness, He could not help designating His unique nature by a corresponding expression. For this purpose He found the phrase THE SON OF MAN, which is employed in the prophecies of Daniel (vii. 13). Jewish expectation had not laid hold of this expression, as of the other Old Testament designations of the Messiah,[1] and yet it was as characteristic as any other. It gave prominence to exactly that side in the nature of Christ which was to form the special redeeming counterpoise to the illusions of the Jews and of the world. The Jews expected in their Messiah, the Son of God. This Son of God was, indeed, to be also a man, but not in the free universality of the human, but in the sense of pharisaic Judaism, and in the sense of a super-human royal dignity—a demon-like Jew of extraordinary power. To this morbid expectation, Christ opposed His humanity and humaneness when He called Himself *the Son of man*. He wished above all things to be known as a true man—as a poor pilgrim (Matt. viii. 20)—as a man of the meanest appearance who might easily be misjudged (Matt. xii. 32)—as a child of man who, like every other, was subject to the eternal decrees of God (Matt. xxvi. 24); yea, as one who was looked down upon contemptuously by mankind, despised and rejected; who was to be the most marked man on the scale of human

---

[1] Neander rightly directs attention to the fact, that this want of familiarity with the meaning of the name 'the Son of man,' among the Jews, may be inferred from John xii. 34.

misery (Mark viii. 31). Already as such a human being, belonging to the human race, in the reality of His life and sufferings the Lord contradicted the fantastic, orientally exaggerated image of a king, by which the Jew celebrated his Messiah as super-humanly prosperous. But also in the sense of humaneness, of free philanthropy, Christ wished to represent mankind. In the forbearance with which He treated His infatuated adversaries (Luke ix. 56); in the universality with which He devoted His saving love to all the lost (Luke xix. 10); in the power, lastly, with which He exercised His humaneness in the heroic service of philanthropy in His redeeming death (Matt. xx. 28),— He presented the bright image of divine humanity as the soul of the life, in opposition to the Jewish pride of ancestry which would have subjected the human race to Judaism, divesting it as far as might be of its proper humanity. But this expressive demonstration of His being man leads to the conviction, that Jesus in a peculiar sense felt as man. He was not a singular particular man, but THE MAN simply as the Prince of men. But He was not only THE MAN simply, but the SON of man, since He was descended from humanity through the Virgin. Humanity had been pregnant with Him in its wrestling after the righteousness of God, in its aspirations it had brought Him forth under the operation of the Spirit. In the power of this descent He represented the second, higher generation of humanity; He is the second man, the man of the Spirit who is from heaven—the wondrous flower which appears as a bright flame of heaven on the top of the old, dark, decaying genealogical tree of earthly humanity (John iii. 13).[1] Christ therefore expressed the perfected spirituality of His natural human life when He came forward with this name. With this He demands of the hierarchy in Israel, of His own nation, and of the whole world, perfect regeneration by His Spirit (John iii. 3). But although Christ adopted the title, *Son of man*, in order to express and carry out the contrariety between His life and the Messianic ex-

[1] See my work, *Ueber den geschichtlichen Character*, etc., p. 68. Weisse, *die evang. Geschichte.* Weisse is mistaken in regarding the view here given as a novel explanation, as any one may be convinced by the preceding quotation. The author of the first work had already obtained this view from another. Weisse's assertion, that this name is placed in the Gospel history in opposition as good as expressed to the name of the Messiah, is certainly novel.

pectation of the Jews, and all the chiliastic worship in the world
of noble birth and genius, yet He did not thereby wish to contradict in the least the true, prophetic Messianic expectation in
Israel. He was perfectly aware that He was announced as the
Son of man by the prophets, and also that this name denoted
the Messiah. The words He uttered in the Sanhedrim—'Hereafter ye shall see the Son of man sitting on the right hand of
power, and coming in the clouds of heaven' (Matt. xxvi. 64)—
very distinctly allude to the designation of the Messiah in the
prophecies of Daniel. Jesus had therefore consciously selected
from among the titles of the Messiah, exactly that which marked
Him as the future Judge of the world. But He chose it on this
account, because, among the various designations of the theocratic Prince, it was the title that seemed suited to preserve or
divulge His incognito among His nation, in proportion as it
might be needful. But at that juncture, when the hierarchy
were on the point of condemning the Messiah, He found it
necessary to bring forward very distinctly the Old Testament
use of this name in reference to the Messiah, and by which He
was accustomed to appear in their midst, in order that they might
not be able to accuse Him of having led them into a mistake
respecting His nature by using a non-theocratic name. He did
this in a declaration respecting the Son of man, which made it
clear that He was the same wonderful Son of man of whom
Daniel had prophesied. In the same degree, therefore, as this
name served for the concealment of His nature, it also served for
unveiling it to all susceptible spirits. It has, in the course of
the world's history, taken under its protection the doctrine of
the incarnation of God against all idealist or gnostic attempts
to explain away the personality of Christ;—the doctrine of the
divine destiny of humanity, against all monkish or materialistic
contempt of human life;—and lastly, the doctrine of the universal call of humanity to salvation, against the perversions of the
doctrine of election;—with strong and powerful efficiency. In
truth, this title of Christ encloses a richness of meaning which
is continually unfolding itself with increasing glory, and can
fully manifest its hidden splendour only when the Son of man
shall summon the world before Him in His judicial glory.[1]
(John v. 27 ; Matt. xxv. 31.)

[1] [For the title itself as found in Daniel, see Hengstenberg's Christology

When therefore the Lord was certain that He must veil
the consciousness of His Messianic glory before the world, and
could only unfold it with the greatest caution,—that the gradual
disclosure of this dignity is the judgment of the world, and that
its completed revelation will coincide with the final judgment,
it was at the same time decided in His soul that He must abide
under the law in Israel until the time of His personal glorification. He was, therefore, consciously 'made under the law'
(Gal iv. 4). He was obedient to human ordinances, as ordinances of God, even unto death, the death of the cross (Phil.
ii. 8), in order to communicate His divine-human life to the life
of the world, to implant it in the world. In the apostle's words
just quoted the progressive stages of this obedience to the lowest
depths are indicated. In the human jurisdiction to which the
Lord was subjected, there appears a definite succession of stages
in the historic exhibition of eternal ideal right in which He
moved, as a peculiar life-element, one with His own life. The
first form of historic right appears in the monotheistic original
laws of the patriarchs (John vii. 22). To these laws He was
already bound by circumcision. Its second form appears in the
theocratic national law of Israel given by Moses. This law also
He acknowledged in His life and conduct (John vii. 23), and
intimated to the Jews that He was placed under it (Mark x.
19). Further, the historic right took a third form in the teachings of the prophets. These also were held sacred by the Lord,
as He plainly showed by submitting to John's baptism, which
He did in order to fulfil all righteousness. These three historical forms of eternal right appeared to Him as the pure lineaments of ideal life—as the several outlines of revelation, which
in His life attained their living realization ; and so far He distinguishes them, taken together as holy writ, or as the law and
the prophets, very distinctly from the later historical stage of
order and right,—that is, from the maxims of the scribes, the
decisions of the hierarchical government, and the administration of political power. The three former stages of right embrace the theocratical forms of historical right ; the three latter,
its hierarchical and political forms. But although in these latter
forms of right He perceived great and serious misrepresentations

iii. 83 (Clark's Tr.) ; and for the reasons of our Lord's adoption of it, see
Dorner on the Person of Christ i. 54 (Tr.).—ED.]

of eternal right, and even flagrant contradictions, yet He valued them as regulations of life, to which He at all times rendered obedience in their limited sphere. We can therefore regard these forms as the second half of the stages of historical right. The ordinances of the elders form, then, the fourth historical unfolding of right: He also declares their national authority in express terms (Matt. xxiii. 2, 3, 23). The ecclesiastical government in Israel forms the fifth region of historical valid right. To this jurisdiction also He submitted with free recognition as an Israelite (Matt. v. 22),[1] even to death (Matt. xxvi. 64). Lastly, the sixth form of historical right is seen in the political authorities that confronted the Lord as an abstract, purely civil power. This power also He acknowledged in its sphere, as a power ordained by God (Matt. xxii. 21) over the property and lives of those under it. He became obedient to this political right, even to the death of the cross, on the accursed tree which the Romans had planted in the land. Thus, from the stage of ideal right, which He specified as 'from the beginning' (Matt. xix. 8), from the first stage of which the right proceeds through all the stages, and which forms with them a cycle of seven stages of right, He descended to the lowest stage, and endured the extremest or most horrible destiny of the lowest stage—the cross, with entire resignation to the will of the Father. This obedience exhibits the historical consummation of the Incarnation, we might say, the historically satisfied consummation. But such an obedience Christ could not have rendered, if it had not been from the first His decided resolution. But the sharpness and decisiveness of His historical fidelity appear in all these spheres of right in the most luminous indications. He withdrew Himself from the people who would have made Him a king; for He felt Himself to be a subject— His kingdom was not of this world: this was His political obedience. On the demand of the Sanhedrim, He made the declaration on oath that He was the Messiah: thus He acted as

---

[1] The words ' *Whosoever shall say to his brother, Raca, shall be in danger of the council,*' are probably not merely figurative. They rather express the sharpest historical right. Whosoever marks his brother as a heretic, encroaches on the province of the Sanhedrim, who have to decide legally on points of doctrine; he must therefore submit himself, with his brother, to the Sanhedrim.

a member of the Jewish commonwealth. He gave a reply to the scribes by answering them out of the Old Testament, and allowed their gnat-straining to pass as long as it did not contradict higher laws. He held the prophetic right sacred, with a strictness which, as we have seen, went beyond that of the Baptist. But He adhered to the Mosaic right with a decisiveness which even curbed 'the first enthusiastic liberalism of the disciples. He clearly saw that He must confine Himself and His ministry, during His earthly pilgrimage, to the lost sheep of the house of Israel (Matt. xv. 24); and it is a very significant fact, that He granted aid to the Canaanitish woman only on the urgent intercession of His disciples. He could not begin His work among the heathen at the risk of destroying His work in Israel—that is, first of all, among His own disciples,—and therefore He let their intercession precede His aid. Just looking at this completeness of the national fidelity, we might assert that He was the most punctilious Jew, the King of the Jews. But He was so, because He was the Christ. His perfected love entered into all the conditions of its revelation and victory, in the whole historic form of a servant, in which alone it could complete its work with heavenly freedom. The Lord in His ministry paid particular attention to the patriarchal right; in His plan for the extension of His kingdom He placed the Samaritans as theocratic Monotheists before the Gentiles (Acts i. 8), and He gave as a reason for visiting Zaccheus the publican, that he also was a son of Abraham (Luke xix. 9). Abstract cosmopolites and legal theorists have no notion of free love in this scrupulous attention to the conditions of historical fidelity.

But this attention to conditions in the life of Christ because it was a perfectly conscious act of pure love, and because it was in unison with His life could appear only as a result of the purest self-limitation and of the freedom of His spirit. He never could render historic obedience, so as to place Himself in contradiction to eternal right, to the divine righteousness, which was His very life. Rather could He only so exhibit His fulfilling of the law, that, by virtue of the ideal feeling of right, He corresponded to the ideal life-point in the historic right itself, to the will of God in Him; and therefore He decidedly rejected every claim in which the historic right contradicted the

ideal, or, which is the same thing, in which the lower right contradicted the higher. Wherefore from the first He could not
allow the semblance to arise, of being in His inner man an unwilling servant of the existing public constitution. He wished
His own historical obedience to be regarded as an act of freedom. Thus He preserved divine freedom even in submission
to Pilate (John xviii. 36), and equally before the disciples
(Matt. xxvi. 53) and before the armed band (ver. 55), and
especially by His dignified silence before the Sanhedrim. With
such an express preservation of His Messianic dignity He observed the Sabbath (Matt. xii. 8) ; He paid the temple-tax
(Matt. xvii. 27) ; and appealed to the testimony of John the
Baptist (John v. 33, 34), to the writings of Moses (John v.
46), and, lastly, to His correspondence with the spiritual vision
of Abraham (John viii. 56, 58). If especially we estimate,
according to their full meaning, the words which He spoke
before the Sanhedrim respecting His judicial glory, they will
strike us as an appeal from their judgment to the tribunal of
God, and as a summons to appear before His own tribunal at
His second coming to judge the world.

These protestations of Jesus ought to secure the world from
the false notion that He was fettered by its ordinances according
to its own want of freedom. But His own life was ensured by
the circumstance that He recognised, in the discharge of His
historical obedience, the completion of His destiny and the fulfilment of Scripture (Matt. xxvi. 54). It was clear to Him that
only in this way of self-renunciation could He attain to the most
complete manifestation of Himself as bringing salvation to the
world. The entire unfolding of the fidelity of His heart, of the
holiness of His spirit, was possible only by means of this most
complete obscuration of His glory. But in this sense He also
fulfilled the law and His own destiny. His life gave a new
shape and meaning to all the forms into which its contents were
poured. By His political obedience He shed a lustre on the
sphere of civil order, as a sphere of the all-powerful governing
righteousness of God ; He thereby made the civil obedience
even of the oppressed free. He caused the suffering of the
oppressed to appear as a suffering of national retribution (John
xix. 11), and the suffering of the innocent as a seed-time of
blessing and honour. In the sphere of political relations, He

always kept the domain of God separate from that of Cæsar; and since by this means he set the spirit and conscience at liberty, He sowed likewise the seeds of civil freedom. But His ecclesiastical obedience to the Sanhedrim must have put the final seal to His Messianic manifestation. The Sanhedrim rendered His cause this service, that it made Him attest His Messiahship on oath before the highest ecclesiastical judicature in the world, and it was chiefly owing to their opposition that the whole riches of His life were unfolded. The disputations of Jesus with the scribes laid the foundation for unveiling the New Testament in the Old, and for distinguishing the New Testament form of revelation from that of the Old. His faithful adherence to the prophets contributed to bring forward several features and stages of His life in all their spiritual depth and world-historical importance. Then, lastly, as to His relation to the law, He could not fail to perceive that the pure theocratic lineaments of the law were the outline of a life infinitely rich, namely, of His own, and that for that reason they must necessarily be transferred into the lines of eternal beauty, of the divine-human life, as soon as He filled them up with the contents of His own life. Under His breath all the buds on the thorn-bush of the Old Testament law must unfold, and the roses of the New Covenant expand in profusion. The law pronounces a curse on the transgressor, at the same time it announces a blessing, the blessedness of the righteous. In its negations it describes all the forms of the sinner; but in its positivity and unity it is the sketch of the holy life of the God-man. But in this deep reference to Christ, the so-called moral law—the civil social law of Moses—did not stand alone; the ceremonial, or ecclesiastical social law, was also included. It was a shadowy representation of the life and sufferings of Christ, so that every form of it acquired in the conduct of Christ a New Testament significance. The pilgrimages of Christ to attend the feasts of the law became the journeyings of free, beneficent love; and from the feast of the Passover bloomed forth the Holy Supper. But the types of this law were sufficient of themselves to reveal to the Lord the grievous termination of His life. If He had not been familiarized with the dark side of His future by the serious portents of His sacrificial death in the history of His

childhood, by so many a bitter experience of His youth, and by
the predictions of the prophets, yet the fearful symbolic language of the sacrificial system would have led to the same
result. For He, in whose spirit the Theocracy was consummated, must certainly have known how to interpret the spirit
of its signs. The same holds good of the theocratic dignities
which were comprehended in the name of the Messiah. He
would not have understood the official title of His own being,
had He not been conscious that in the actual anointing of His
spirit's fulness all the theocratic offices and dignities were united
according to their deepest meaning in His personality, and were
to be realized in His vocation. He must have been perfectly
aware that His being, as the complete revelation of the Father,
was itself prophecy completed ; that in His pure self-surrender
to the Father, the full meaning of the sacerdotal office appeared,
and it became His calling to give Himself for the life of the
world ; that, finally, His Spirit was the true, eternal King of
humanity, and therefore by His Spirit He was to establish His
kingdom in the world. Thus, in the consciousness of His Messianic dignity the chief outlines of His ministry were given.
But these outlines came out more distinctly to His view by
means of the lineaments of the law and the intimations of the
prophets.

It was therefore evident to the Lord at the commencement
of His public life, that He came to fulfil the law and the prophets ; that is, to unfold by His life no less than by His teaching the whole ideal contents of those lineaments of the law and
intimations of the prophets, according to the spirit from which
they emanated. But it belonged to this fulfilment that He interpreted the three theocratic forms of the historic right by the
ideal law, and that by the same law He adjusted the three
hierarchico-political forms of the historic right—that, generally,
He corrected the lower laws by the higher, and thus restored the
true ideal order of ordinances in the exhibition of the supremacy
and subordination of the various rights. The development of
historic right, as it is conducted by the hierarchy or by political
rulers (the civil power), appears oftentimes as a tedious, gradual
inversion of the eternal ordinances of right by which the under-
most becomes changed to the uppermost. The rights of Cæsar
often supplant the rights of God by being made rights of con-

science; ecclesiastical regulations often paralyse the exposition of Scripture by quenching the Spirit; the expositor often obscures the prophets and law of God by false glosses. In this manner a slow and secret revolution is going on in a thousand ways under the surface of the most quiet historic conformity to the law, and an unbounded desolation is effected in the domain of the spiritual life. These insidious revolutions in the history of the world are sure to be done away with by reforming spirits. Thus Christ as a reformer confronted the revolutionary desolation which the hierarchy of His nation especially had caused. Generally, He vindicated in the widest extent the ideal order of the historical relations of right. He held the power of the magistrate sacred as ordained by God, and was subject to it in its sphere; but He would not be fettered by it in the sphere of His prophetic calling. When Herod, His prince, wished to scare Him away by artifice from the scene of His ministry in Galilee, He answered his messengers, 'Go ye and tell that fox, Behold, I cast out devils, and do cures to-day and to-morrow, and the third day I shall be perfected' (Luke xiii. 32). And when the same prince 'hoped to have seen some miracle from Him, and questioned Him in many words, He answered him nothing' (Luke xxiii. 8, 9). To Pilate He spoke of his sin, and stood in his presence as the King in the kingdom of truth. However, He appears to have acknowledged his judicial right, chiefly because He had been delivered to him by the Sanhedrim (John xviii. 34, xix. 11). For, in matters of Jewish ecclesiastical law, He regarded the Sanhedrim as the supreme court. But when the Sanhedrim or Pharisaism wished to obstruct Him in His higher dignity, in His prophetic calling, He gave way not a single step. Collisions on this ground He never shunned in the least: this is shown by the frequent cures He performed on the Sabbath. He pronounced a woe on the scribes and Pharisees because they broke the law of the Sabbath by their traditions (Matt. xxiii.; Mark vii. 13). But He also showed how the law of Moses was subordinate to the fundamental monotheistic law of the patriarchs; and, lastly, how it was subordinate to the ideal original law of humanity (Matt. xii. 8; Mark ii. 27, iii. 4), and how even the patriarchal regulations—for instance, the custom of divorce sanctioned by Moses—ought to be determined according to this primeval law, which was at one with the moral nature of

man and the immediate expression of the divine will (Matt. xix.
9). Indeed, there can be no real contradiction between the
theocratic rights as they proceed from the patriarchs, from Moses
and the prophets, and the eternal primeval laws, but the former
are to be explained by the latter. But Christ could not possibly
have restored the ideal order of right with such exact and dis-
criminating certainty, had He not been animated by the spirit of
the law. In this spirit He could unfold, arrange, and fill up
the law, and therefore change it into spirit and life. The entire
ideal contents of all divine and human rights were taken up into
His very life. Therefore not a tittle of the law perished; every
single declaration of it was found again in His life, in the form
of the Spirit.

It was evident to our Lord at the commencement of His
ministry, that in this manner He must come forward as a reformer of the historical relations of right in His age. The
restoration of the ideal stages of right was therefore an essential
element of His plan. But this consciousness must necessarily
have produced in Him the anticipation of His sufferings, and
indeed of His civil doom. Had He not been conversant with
the predictions of the prophets concerning the sufferings of the
Messiah, and had He come in no other way to this anticipation,
yet He would have reached it with perfect certainty from the
conflict between the divinely firm decisiveness of His heavenly
ideality or holiness, and the petrified rigidity of the hierarchical
statutes and social corruptions. In the necessary consequence
of the system which stood opposed to Him, the entire depth of
suffering which awaited Him might be unfolded to His view.
No sooner was His rejection on the part of the hierarchy certain,
than the certainty must also have been present to His soul, that
they would deliver Him up to the Gentiles. This delivering
up, of which He had already found an announcement in the
prophets (Matt. xxi. 42), was the central point of His anticipations, and a chief ingredient in the grief which always pressed
heavy on His soul. But then the result of this act of the hierarchy could not be concealed from the spirit of Christ. He
foresaw that the Gentiles would reject Him as well as the Jews;
and as He was aware that the severest punishment of the Romans,
the strongest expression of the world's curse, consisted in crucifixion, His spirit would always descry as the last object in the

path of His sufferings, the death of the cross. As often as in spirit He looked down the precipice of the rejection which awaited Him, His eye found no resting-place short of the abyss of misery and shame on the cross. In such an anticipation, the particular features of His suffering would more easily present themselves the more closely they were connected with the nature of this suffering; as, for example, the spitting with excommunication, the scourging with the crucifixion. But it was simply impossible that Christ could look down into the whole abyss of His sufferings and crucifixion, without perceiving with equal clearness the opposite heights of His glorification. This glorification was assured to Him by faith in the Father, in His righteousness and faithfulness, and by the voice of the prophets as well as by the consciousness of being without a parallel, and by the inner power of life and victory which marked His personal being. But as His death was unparalleled, so likewise must His life appear to Him: deep as was the descent, so high would be the ascent; steep as was the precipice of descent, so would the exaltation be sudden and lofty; appalling to an unheard-of degree as was His judgment, so would His vindication be wonderful and glorious. Thus the mystery of His resurrection would be disclosed to the Lord by this distinct foresight of His humiliation. Lastly, in order to mark His foresight most exactly as christological, we must observe that in His death He must have seen the centre and beginning of the final judgment of the world, and therefore in His victory have looked for the principle, the real beginning of the future resurrection, and, of course, the resurrection of individuals.

But not only was His personal glorification present to His soul, but also its world-historical unfolding in the glorification of the Church. His Church must suffer with Him, and be glorified with Him. And as it was impossible to separate His own destiny from that of His Church, it was equally impossible to disjoin the efficacy of His death from the efficacy of His resurrection. Hence His death appeared to Him as the beginning of the glorification of His name and of His work in the world (John iii. 14, xii. 23). With His death the entire ancient period of the world was brought to its completion, especially its law and its prophecy. He became free from the law on the cross, since a distorted representation of the law crucified Him.

Henceforth the entire essence of the law was preserved and enshrined in the life of His spirit; but its whole form, as to its religious importance, was exploded and dissipated. His death, therefore, was purely identical with the abolition of the rights of the Jewish hierarchy, as well as with the annihilation of the ancient value of the temple (John ii. 19). His spirit was now released from all Jewish legal restraints; His new life belonged to Him alone in His free glory, but in His love it belonged to mankind. His Church also was called to 'enter by His death into this communion of His freedom. As Christ's Church, it is essentially free in Him; and when it submits to legal restraints, it does this in the spirit of freedom, in the unfolding of its life for the world, and in its ardent desire to imbue the life of the world with its own life. As a royal and priestly Church, as the bride equal in dignity of birth to Himself (Matt. xxii. 2), the Church, which was to be the reward of His sufferings, stood before His soul.

Christ's foresight could not indeed take the shape of reflection or laborious deduction. But still the threads of the essential relations between the events of His future were the already marked track which must have been lighted up before His eye, when the prophetic spirit in Him, as by flashes of lightning, threw one great illumination after another over the field of His future. And it is necessary that we should most clearly perceive these essential relations, if we would properly estimate the full distinctness, the bold relief, of so many separate features in the future as foreseen by Christ. If, for example, we have recognised the cross as the lowest depth in the region of the ancient curse of the world, we conceive that the Lord with His deepest humiliation was already assured of His death on the cross. But His foresight was matched by His resolution to persist firmly and intrepidly in the path of His Father's guidance—to reject all the enticements to bypaths as satanic voices —in all the sufferings which He was destined to meet on this path, to look only to the Father's regulative will, and in the judgment which this will ordained for the guilt of the world, to welcome the atonement, and with perfect acquiescence in this judgment, to complete the atonement for the world.

But if Christ was so familiar in His spirit with the fearful path of death on which He was to accomplish His work,—and

with the glory which awaited Him on that path,—the question
arises, How, with a clear foresight of the future, could He lead
a genuine human life devoted to the present? In our times
there has been a disposition to find manifold contradictions between the separate elements of such a foresight, and opposite
moods or states of feeling in the life of Jesus. It has been
asked, for instance, if Jesus was certain of His glorification,
how could He be so deeply agonized in Gethsemane? or, if this
suffering of death still stood before Him, how could He triumph
beforehand in His high-priestly prayer? How could He weep
at the grave of Lazarus, when He was on the point of raising
him from the dead? All these questions seem to proceed from
a mode of viewing things, which is more conversant with the
nature of petrifactions than with the nature of the human soul.
The human heart, placed between the infinite and the finite,
and forming the centre of these two departments of life, has a
wonderful facility in evil as well as in good of varying its moods
in quick succession—now in 'heavenly ecstasy,' and anon 'ex-
ceeding sorrowful unto death;' and more or less to lose sight
of the greatest good fortune near at hand in the misfortune of
the present moment, or of the heaviest impending calamity in
the enjoyment of the passing hour. Is not all the cheerfulness
of human life confronted by the certainty of death? Do not
all the tears of the pious flow under the anticipation that a
harvest of joy is awaiting them? In relation to this subject,
modern criticism has framed a category of impossibilities, which
we must regard as a perpetual petrifying of the human heart,
begun under the operation of a philosophic abstraction which
looks with contempt on concrete life. But the more competent
we are to estimate the giant-harp of human emotion and the
quick alternation of its tones, the more able shall we be to
understand that region in which the human soul appears in
heroic proportions, and where the fiercest battle of life is fought
out in the most varied situations, under the liveliest play of the
strongest emotions. In this freshness and power of human
nature, Jesus was also the Prince of His race. It belonged to
the healthy state of His human life, that with a genuine human
bearing and disposition He could reveal heaven, and conquer
hell, and experience in His own mental moods the whole contrast of descent to hell and ascension to heaven. This healthy

state of His life may be compared to a finished musical performance. The life of Jesus is, first of all, to be regarded in its
rhythm as a complete life. He moves in the measure of the
most correct succession of His internal states of feeling; He does
not with His states of feeling lag behind the time or measure
of reality, and as little does He impatiently hasten before it.
Hence His future lies before Him in correct perspective. He
cannot possibly derange the order of His life's course. He
could not, on the one hand, as a dreamer in a literal sense,
anticipate the particular circumstances of His future experience; nor, on the other hand, could He ever live a day without
observing the strict relation of every step to His final aim.
From this fundamental law of His life's course resulted the
rhythmical, that is, measured recurrence in the presentiment of
His death as well as in the presentiment of His glory. This
rhythm of His life was connected with its dynamic perfection.
Christ spent every instant as a moment of eternity. He gave
to every experience its correct intonation. He often allowed
extraordinary phenomena, such as the storm on the lake, to pass
over His soul like mere shadows, while an incident apparently
insignificant, such as that of the Greeks wishing to see Him
(John xii. 20), agitated Him violently. But He so correctly
estimated impressions, that His counteraction of them was perfectly proportional. This delicately adjusted dynamic gives His
life the expressiveness of a vitality and power combining heavenly tenderness and strength : the gentlest tones, the slightest
breathings, alternate with such as are the sharpest, strongest,
and most startling. Hence Christ estimated every event according to its just importance : the signs of His future must
have met Him in all His experiences with constantly increasing
distinctness; for every single moment has the significance of
a symbol for all the moments with which it forms a whole.
Thus to Christ's eye the dark night of His betrayal began to
cast its shadows from the first embezzlement which Judas committed on the common stock. When Peter protested against
His crucifixion, He probably saw at that hour a clear prognostic
that this disciple would afterwards deny Him. And since every
important fact had in the spiritual hearing of Christ the tone of
its precise significance, so the hosannahs of the feast of Palms
could as little efface from His expectations the approaching

crucifixion, as the cry, 'Crucify Him!' could efface the resurrection. If it be asked, how was it possible for the life of Jesus to represent itself in these refined, ideal, dynamic relations, we must seek the solution in its melodious beauty. The life of our Lord had in all its parts a complete lyric elevation and musical euphony, since He apprehended every fact of experience in God, and set forth every fact of activity with divine freedom. His consciousness stript from every experience the fact of evil, as that which was opposed to God and must come to nought, and sent it back to hell, in order to receive the fact itself as a consecrated ordinance from the hand of God. Even His last agony and judgment appeared to Him as a cup in the Father's hand, as a holy cup of the purest gold, which, in spite of the intense bitterness of its contents, He was ready to empty for the health of the world. His life, therefore, was sustained in all its utterances by the beautiful euphony of a bass, in which the pure human heart constantly rested in God's fulness; and the eternal glory of God revealed itself in the sensibility and distinctness of man perfected in beauty. This melody of the life of Jesus allowed no disturbance to spring up in His inner man respecting His future; but, in consequence of the opulence of His soul's life, it must needs unfold itself in the most exquisite harmony. It was in the nature of the case, that the soul of Christ could not be governed or wholly filled by any natural mood (*Naturstimmung*) of human life or by any single exclusive affection. With one pure feeling which moved Him, every other was in unison, as is conformable to life in the spirit. And when one feeling expressed itself as the predominant tone in the highest degree, the other opposite one came forth in the purest harmonic relation. The two deepest feelings of His soul, relative to His future, were the presentiment of His condemnation and the presentiment of His glory. These two secrets, the one most mournful, the other most blessed, were moving jointly and incessantly in His heart. In the captivating form of a blessed sadness, or of a veiled heavenly cheerfulness, which we may regard as the usual mental frame of Jesus, we see the gently moving counterpoise of those fundamental feelings. The weights often oscillated according to the impressions which Christ received; sometimes one scale sank, sometimes the other. But never did the one feeling completely vanish before the other. In Gethsemane Christ appears dissolved in anguish and sorrow, especially in shuddering horror at the wickedness of the world; and with what touching pathos He here craves for human sympathy! and with what sublimity He raises Himself up! The prayer of His deepest agony on the cross, in which He divulges the crushing sense of being forsaken by God, is at the same time the expression of the highest confidence. And as in this manner the related tones of opposite moods are ever sounding together, we understand how it was that ofttimes the occasions of the Lord's greatest joy were exchanged at once for the deepest sadness, as, for example, the jubilation on His entrance into Jerusalem; while inversely His bitterest experiences could indirectly call forth the most glorious outbursts of joy, as was shown in the wonderful elevation of His soul after the traitor had left the company of the disciples. Thus Jesus overcame what was dangerous in every single affection by the free, harmonious, collective feeling of His life. But the perfection of this harmony was shown by His walking in the Spirit, and therefore the riches of His life always harmonized as a united whole in His spiritual life. By this power of His inner life, He resolved His prospects into His presentiments, His presentiments into His fundamental dispositions, and these again into the spirit of His life. The same may also be affirmed of His plan. Notwithstanding the clearness of its leading outlines, and the continual unfolding of its several portions, this plan still necessarily maintained the free, flexible form of the spiritual life in which Christ Himself moved. The words of Christ distinctly indicate that its separate lines always met in the primary thought, that He was going to the Father. From this primary thought the separate parts of His plan would always enter into new combinations, just according to the train of circumstances through which Christ passed. What He saw the Father do, that He also did. He therefore always met the objective universe, in which He beheld the Father's work, with a self-determination in which His own work combined with that of the Father in an act which should issue in the transformation of the world.

Thus, then, the life-plan of Jesus, as it was completed during the temptation in the wilderness, consisted in a self-determination, developed according to its fundamental principles, always unfolding according to its individual traits, and renewing itself in the Spirit,—a self-determination according to which He wished to combine His Messianic life with the life of the world. But as He combined His whole being and its world-historical name in general with the world by a definite unfolding of His life, so this especially holds good of the separate blessings of His life. He combined, that is to say, the power of His life, salvation, with the faith of the world in the form of His miracles. But the light of His life—the truth—He presented to the world under the guise of parables. Lastly, He made the blessedness of His life become the inheritance of the world by founding the kingdom of God. These fundamental forms of the revelation of His life we have now to contemplate.

NOTES.

1. On the unveiling of the Old Testament economy as accomplished by Christ, see Harnack, *Jesus der Christ*, p. 5. 'We must conceive of this " old to be fulfilled," to which Christ refers, as an undivided whole, since He damaged it in no portion, He neither took away nor weakened any essential part. Hence an unprejudiced exegetical survey sees no reason for dividing the ideas of ὁ νόμος and οἱ προφῆται in a connection where their fulfilment is spoken of, but applies it to their full contents. Nor can we understand by what right each single chief division is to be taken for anything else than the whole law, and for the whole prophetic agency, when that designation (as is almost universally allowed) embraces the entire Old Testament, according to the constant phraseology of the New Testament.'—P. 11.

2. In the teaching of Christ a doctrine of right (a law) is contained, which comprises much sharper and more developed distinctions than is commonly admitted. The sphere that rules all positive spheres of right is that of ideal right, which is similar to the eternal in man, or to the essence of the Son of man.—This right has been transplanted into the world in the form of the Gospel. The three spheres in which positive right has its sources, or in which ideal right becomes positive, are the circles of the Patriarchal, the Mosaic, and the Prophetic Right. The patriarchal right has become fixed by tradition under the form of the Noachic ordinances, to which some other precepts

belong. It is the right which forms the world-historical basis of monotheistic culture. Circumcision is the symbol of this sphere; it marks the religious civilisation of the individual. The essential in which the symbol is fulfilled is regeneration, especially the general culture. This stage of right is perpetuated in the general morality of the cultivated world. The Mosaic right is the basis of monotheistic educated society, of which the characteristic is, that every individual is estimated as a person. So especially is the Sabbath made for man—for his personality. In particular, it protects dependent persons in their eternal rights. The essential of the Mosaic right reappears in Christian state-life. Lastly, prophetic right is the development of positive right according to its spiritual nature, in its spiritual infinity; the unfolding of the ideal law in the positive. This sphere has to exhibit the law in life. It is full of blessing and danger. The false prophet must be distinguished from the true. But he is judged according to his relation to the essential principles of the theocratic society, according to the positive divine law. This province of right is perpetuated in the free Church, and in science, art, and literature generally. The three following circles of right, which are exhibited in the maxims of the scribes, in the Sanhedrim, and in political power, are the circles of the interpretation, the application, and the administration of right. The concrete, christianly grounded, and educated state embraces these circles, as well as the theocratic, in living unity. They appear singly in the region of the Academic Faculties, which express themselves by systems and opinions ; in the region of Jurisprudence, according to right as it has been laid down ; and in the region of Government, which carries into effect what has been determined by law. The theocratic idea of the state has its highest point in the right of the sovereign to show mercy ; on the other hand, its lowest point is seen in the police : this restores the theocratic power in reference to the abandoned class.

3. The difficulties which Strauss has mustered against the idea of the Messianic plan (*Leben Jesu*, § 65–69) are summarily disposed of by the representation before us of the plan of Jesus. Thus, for example, the passage in Matt. xix. 28 is said to prove that Jesus designedly nourished expectations of a worldly Messiah in His disciples, because the promise, that in the Palin-

genesia they should be judges of the twelve tribes of Israel, could not merely denote in a figurative sense their participation of glory in that state. If the author, by the christological idea of the transformation of the world, had got beyond the dualism between the abstract present and the abstract future world, he would likewise have got beyond this difficulty. But this idea appears to him, in its concrete fulness, only as a 'monstrous representation,' p. 521. When it is further said (p. 529), that the views of Jesus respecting 'the abrogation of the Mosaic law' are 'so different from those of Paul, that what the former regarded as not ceasing till His glorious advent or second coming to renew the earth, the latter believed he might abrogate in consequence of the first advent of the Messiah on the old earth,' we must here especially distinguish between abrogating or taking away (*Abschaffung*) and raising—a lifting to a higher position (*Aufhebung*); secondly, between a religious and a national raising (*Aufhebung*); thirdly, between the centre and the periphery of the coming æon (αἰὼν μέλλων), if we are to take a correct view of the subject. Christ Himself resolved to know nothing of an abrogation (*Abschaffung*), but only of a raising or elevation (*Aufhebung*) of it—a realization of the typical law in the life of the spirit. Paul also, in this sense, found the Old Testament again in the New, and he, as little as Christ, abrogated the outward law, whose religious validity he impugned, in its national perpetuity. Lastly, as regards the new æon, Christ represented *Himself* as its principle and centre, and could not therefore attribute a religious validity to the law within the New Testament circle of His agency, that is, for the unfolding of this æon. The complete raising (*Aufhebung*) of the ancient legal conditions cannot take place till the future æon has gained its full periphery, which will be at the second coming of Christ. Consequently the passage in Matt. v. 18 may decidedly be understood to mean that the law would continue to exist in all its types, even to an iota (though in many modifications of form), till it should attain in the new world a complete living reality; or the law would eternally remain, and indeed, as far as it has not yet become life, will it remain as law, so that it cannot vanish entirely in the legal form till the perfecting of the life. It is clear, therefore, that no religious validity of the law before the second advent of Christ, and no special abrogation of it after that event, was appointed. Rather must every 'jot and tittle' of the law be eternally realized, according to its original ideality. The relation of Jesus to the heathen must be explained by distinguishing between the economy of His earthly ministry and the economy of His Spirit. The difference in His treatment of the Gentile centurion (Matt. viii. 5) and of the Canaanitish woman (Matt. xv. 24) is sufficiently established. That centurion was (according to Luke vii. 3) a friend of the synagogue, and probably a proselyte of the gate. In his case, therefore, the spiritual conditions were present for the communication of miraculous aid. But in the Canaanitish woman these conditions were very questionable. At all events, it was requisite that the organ of theocratic faith should be fully unfolded in her, before Christ vouchsafed her a miraculous word. Besides, we must not overlook that intercession was made by the Jews when they saw the economical reluctance of Jesus. The history of the ministry of Jesus in Samaria will come later under consideration.

4. Strauss cites (vol. ii. p. 291) the well-known passages in which prophecies of the sufferings of the Messiah are found, and then goes on to affirm, that in these passages nothing whatever is said of Christ's sufferings, and closes with the assertion, ' If Jesus in a supernatural manner, by virtue of His higher nature, had found in these passages a pre-intimation of particular traits of His sufferings,—since such a reference is not the true sense of those passages,—the spirit in Jesus would not have been the spirit of truth, but a lying spirit.' Exactly in the same way he deals with the predictions of the resurrection, and in p. 323 repeats his unfortunate assertion, ' If a supernatural principle in Jesus, a prophetic spirit, had caused Him to find in these passages a pre-intimation of His resurrection,—since in none of them could such a reference really exist,—the spirit in Him could not be the spirit of truth, but must have been a lying spirit.' These assertions need no refutation ; we only adduce them as historical notices. Just so, the tendency of the critic to decide the question according to the popular representations which existed probably in the time of Christ, in reference to the sufferings of the Messiah, whether the Messiah announced His own death beforehand or not. ' If in the lifetime of Jesus it was a Jewish representation that the Messiah

must die a violent death, there is every probability that Jesus would receive this representation into His own convictions, and communicate it to His disciples, etc; on the other hand, if that representation had not been current among His countrymen before His death, it would still be possible,' etc. Lastly, we here class the question, whence did Jesus, if He foresaw His own death, know for certain whether Herod would not anticipate the priests' party, or who could assure Him that the hierarchy would not succeed in one of their tumultuary attempts at murder, and that, without being delivered to the Romans, He would lose His life in some other way than by the Roman punishment of crucifixion? We need not rise to the height on which Jesus stands in order to learn how to estimate the true nature of such questions. Who, for example, gave Napoleon the assurance that he would not die of the plague, when he went to Egypt with a presentiment of his future greatness? What assurance had Julius Cæsar in the storm at sea, that he could utter such bold words of confidence, that he would not perish in the waves? There were at that time no means of insuring against the murderous disposition of a Herod and the stoning by Jewish fanatics; and thus it always remains a mystery in what way great men have been assured.

5. As to the question on the relation between the obscurer predictions of the death of Jesus in John and the more explicit ones in the synoptic Gospels, as Hasert has treated it in his work, *Ueber der Vorhersagungen Jesu von seinem Tode und seiner Auferstehung* (*On the predictions by Jesus of His death and resurrection*), the previous question is of importance, to what times those single predictions belong. As these chronological data must first be distinctly explained in the sequel, we must return to this question respecting the said predictions. The gradual development of the foreseeing as well as of the predicting is indicated by the relation between Mark viii. 31 and x. 33, 34, or Luke ix. 22 and xviii. 32.[1]

---

[1] [The literature of this, as indeed of all the topics connected with the life of Christ, is given by Hase in his *Leben Jesu*. Renan throughout represents Jesus as rather passively moulded by His age than determining His own character and life; and regarding His idea of His work, he says, p. 121: 'Beaucoup de vague restait sans doute dans sa pensée, et un noble sentiment, bien plus qu'un dessein arrêté, le poussait a l' œuvre sub-

SECTION IX.

THE MIRACLES OF JESUS.

We have seen that Christ had decided on a mission in the world which was designed to form a great means of communication (*Vermittelung*) between the mystery of His glorious spiritual life, and the darkened, sickly, disharmonized world, which was not in a state to bear an unconditional unfolding of His glory. As one special form of this intervention for the purpose of incorporating the power of Christ with the world, we have, last of all, pointed out *Miracles*. By this reference of miracle to the means of communication, so as to place it under the same point of view as the evangelical parables and the founding of the New Testament kingdom of God, it is distinctly indicated that we apprehend miracles, first of all, on a side which forms a decided opposite to that in which it gives so much trouble to the critics who represent ' the culture of our age.' The miracles of Jesus appear, indeed, as very great events, extraordinary, unheard-of, and almost incredible, if we compare them with the course of the old dispensation of the world (*alten Weltäon*); and this is the common view. But if we measure them according to their number, appearance, and importance, by the infinite fulness of the power of Christ's life, a saving power which restores the whole sinful world even to the resurrection, we must regard them as indeed small beginnings of the revelation of this living power, in which it comes forth as secretly, modestly, and noiselessly as His doctrine in His parables; and we learn the meaning of Christ's saying, by which he led His disciples to estimate this misunderstood phase of His miracles, ' Ye shall do greater works than these' (John xiv. 12). But Christ's miracles served in manifold ways to reveal His life-power to the world in subdued forms of operation. When Christ in these separate acts displays His agency, He lets Himself down to the sensuous level of the world, which only by these examples of His deepest

lime qui s'est realisée par lui, bien que d'une manière fort différente de celle qu'il imaginait.' Some valuable remarks on the apologetic significance of the plan of Jesus are made by Young in ' *The Christ of History*,' pp. 44 ff., and by Bushnell, *Nature and the Supernatural*, p. 207.—ED.]

universal agency can gain a perception of that agency itself. He places Himself first of all on a line with the wonder-workers, the exorcists of His time, while He has begun the great work of saving the world, and of expelling the evil spirits from the whole world. By healing the feet of a paralytic, He had to prove that He had previously healed his heart by the forgiveness of his sins. By His wonderful, single operations, which powerfully affected the souls of men, He gradually aroused the perception of the susceptible for contemplating the great, eternal miracle which appeared in His own life. But for profane minds the Saviour of the world retired behind the wonder-worker. Often has it been attempted to find in the miracles of Jesus an ostentatious display of Christianity. But a time must come when men will learn to regard them as acts of the humility of Christ. Still, much of the wonderful that is from beneath must be set aside, before the wonderful from above is entirely acknowledged as the first interposition of Christ's eternal life-power for the world. For this power is holy even as the spiritual light of Christ, as His title of Messiah, and as His blessedness in the vision of God; therefore, it veils itself to the captious, while it unveils itself to the susceptible, and even that measure of it which has become manifest in miracle, appears to them as too much. But we must not misapprehend either the one side or the other of the miracles in which this power finds its medium of communication to men.

We might speak of these extraordinary operations of Christ's life without employing the word *miracle* to designate them, and in doing so, clear the way to some extent for those who always imagine that the facts of the kingdom of God are dependent on the designations affixed to them, or on the later definitions of these designations. If, for example, we should call them, in accordance with the phraseology of the Gospels, spiritual primordial powers (δυνάμεις) or religious primordial phenomena (τέρατα or σημεῖα), we should have the advantage of representing them with these names in their relation to their living origin, the originator of the new dispensation (*Aeon*), and so have designated them as the natural, necessary, and perfectly rational expressions of a new power. But these facts are still, as to their specific nature, rightly designated by the word *miracle* (*Wunder*); namely, when the miracle is regarded as a perfectly novel appearance, which as such calls forth a perfectly novel intuition and state of feeling in the beholders—the highest astonishment and wonder. Now if we have to seek for a developed idea of miracle, it must be almost superfluous to remark, that the Protestant scientific contemplation of the extraordinary facts in the Gospel history, to which the term miracle is applied, cannot be restricted to the definitions of the Church dogmatics. It is confessed that in the course of time these definitions have become more and more unwieldy. But while the free examination must be conducted independently of the maxims of dogmatic science, it must equally be set free from the authority of narrow, worn-out assumptions of natural science, as they have been commonly employed by 'critical' theologians against miracles. It is false when dogmatic theology speaks of an absolute removal of the laws of nature, of a sheer suspension of them by miracle;[1] but is equally false when the philosophic culture of the age pretends to a knowledge of absolute laws, which must make a miracle simply impossible.[2] Such laws of nature are to be called physical gods, or rather divinities; they are perfect contradictions throughout. A law is from the first conditioned by the sphere in which it operates. Now, since nature is an infinitely delicate complex of the most different spheres, it is exceedingly difficult to recognise and correctly define a law of nature as conditioned by its sphere. How different, for instance, the law of nature relative to propagation in the class of mammals and in that of reptiles! How very differently does the law of gravitation act in the region of the double stars and in the region of the earth! But as the law is conditioned in its outward appearance by its sphere, by its relation to space, so also it is conditioned by the course of time to which it belongs by its æon. Therefore, in reality, it

[1] Buddeus terms miracles 'operationes, quibus naturæ leges, ad ordinem et conservationem totius hujus universi spectantes, re vera suspenduntur.' See Hahn, *Lehrb. d. chr. Gl.* p. 24.

[2] 'According to Spinoza, God and nature are not two but one; the laws of the latter are the will of the former in its constant realization. Therefore, could anything happen in nature which contradicted its universal laws (as staying the course of the sun, walking on the sea, etc.), this would contradict the nature of God Himself; and to maintain that God does anything against the laws of nature, is the same as maintaining that God acts contrary to His own nature.'—Strauss, *die Christl. Glaubenslehre* i. 229.

is always conditioned by the spirit and mind of the Lawgiver. Consequently we cannot fail to perceive that the laws of nature are conditioned by the omnipotent Spirit of the Creator. The Creator is the Interpreter of the law of nature. But surely it cannot be denied that the Creator has spoken by the laws of nature, and He cannot contradict Himself. With this remark, the opponents of miracle think they have said something that should settle the question. Certainly there can be nothing more conformable to law than the course of nature, since the eternal clearness and consistency of the divine will are expressed in it, since it is an expression of the Spirit, and not the Spirit itself. The life of nature is in fact its conformity to law. If it were not conformable to law, not faithful to its regulations, not inexorably decided in its course, it could not continue in existence, it could not present the sublime counterpart of the Spirit. Its conformity to law is the mirror of the divine freedom. But the Spirit of God would have for ever bound Himself, and been excluded from His own creation, if He had not from the first conditioned its conformity to law with infinite nicety. He Himself would not be God if nature were absolute in its laws—if *it* were God. Nature too would be shifted from her own proper ground if that great miracle, the act of creation, which bears her phenomena so conformable to law, could not break forth in her midst, and manifest the peculiar nature of her being in a miraculous efflorescence.

Nature may be contemplated in a twofold sequence: its phenomena may be traced from above downwards, or from below upwards. If we take the first path, we shall continually advance from the regions of more indefinite laws, of fluctuating freedom-like life, into the regions of rigid conformity to law, since we shall be penetrating further into the region of the primal and most general features of nature. The migrating bird may be on some occasions deceived by its instinct; but the lightning is thoroughly certain of its path, and belongs proportionably to a much lower region of life. But the further we advance into these low tracts of the most rigid conformity to law, the wider also do the circles of law extend, or so much the more do they bind themselves to fixed conditions, or conceal themselves in the delicate exuberance of variable life. Fire, for instance, is inexorable in its conformity to law; for that reason it generally lies imprisoned in steel and stone. But no sooner do we follow the proper tendency of life in nature, and turn to it from below upwards, than it assumes a quite different form. It appears to us indeed as one of its fundamental laws, that in all its conformity to law it still continues to be nature (*Natura*), that it is always bringing forth, raising, and potentiating itself;[1] and thus from stage to stage it elevates its own laws, forms, and phenomena, and converts them into new ones, and struggles towards glorification in the spirit. It is therefore clear that nature in this direction has throughout a supernatural tendency. She meets on her proud way, as a wonder-worker striving upwards, the wonder-struck theologian, who is as far from free as herself, and performs a miracle entirely the reverse; for he sets aside the laws of the spiritual sphere to seal up the laws of nature by his own gross assumption, since he would make nature the consecrated vehicle of the spirit, naturalistic. But nature is also conformable to law, and incessant in the boldness with which she hastens towards the free spirit; she persists in her wonder-working direction. This rests on the simple law, that every power according to its kind can work itself out in nature; that therefore a higher power can break through the sphere of a lower power, set aside its laws, consume its material, and transform life in it. Thus, for example, the lion rushes as a supernatural principle on the gazelle.. It appears, mayhap, an event contrary to nature that so delicate a form of nature should be destroyed and annihilated in its noble conformity to law, whenever the right of this higher power, the lion, is lost sight of. The lion devours the gazelle, but in his deed, in his blood and life, the unnatural act becomes a new nature.

Had the believers in miracles not allowed themselves to be so prejudiced against nature by the appeal made against them to the laws of nature, they must have found the idea of miracle and its future as plainly indicated in nature as the idea and future of man. A grain of corn contains a visible and distinct likeness of a miracle. The grain of corn, in its innermost being, in its germinant power, is a principle of life. This principle of life is brought into operation through nature. But no sooner does it begin to germinate, than it operates as a supernatural power in relation to the substance of the grain of corn. This its

[1] [See a passage in Coleridge's *Aids to Reflection*, p. 199, 7th Ed.—TR.]

supernatural property begins gradually to operate against nature ; it destroys and consumes the natural material which surrounds it, but it removes this old nature-life in order to exhibit it made young again in a new life. Here all the elements of the idea of miracle are present in a symbolic form. Miracle is indeed the well adjusted irruption of a spiritual life-principle into a subordinate life-sphere, an irruption which in its issuing forth as a principle appears *supernatural*, in its decidedness of action is *antinatural*, and in its final issue completes itself in *natural* development.

The image of miracle borrowed from the grain of corn is in one respect imperfect : the seed moves in the circle of a sphere which always remains the same, though at the same time gently rising, while the idea of miracles can be made quite clear only by a succession of life-spheres. We must have heard the spiritual music of the life-spheres, if we would speak of the idea of law, of freedom, and of miracle ; for all these ideas are referable to spherical relations. But as in the religious department, it is said of the righteous man that for him there is no law ; so in the general department of life, the same may be said of the higher life-principles in relation to the lower life-spheres. So the first crystallization is a miracle, since it very decidedly conditions, or in a conditional manner dispenses with, the law of gravitation, which in a lower element-sphere, that of water, prevails unconditioned. The form or law of unconditioned gravity is the globular ; but crystallization makes sport of this first iron rule of gravitation in a thousand ways, when it forms its delicately constructed mathematical figures. The first plant was a miracle which decidedly changed the world in which it grew. And so it has been correctly said of the animal, that it is a miracle for the vegetable world. Lastly, in MAN the whole of subordinate nature is raised and changed into a specifically higher life-form. He himself, therefore, in this relation to the nature that is subordinate to him, is an eternally speaking image of miracle. In him nature has attained her final aim ; she has come in contact with spirit, and in her movements is elevated, consumed, and transformed by his free moral life in conformity with her original destiny.

But now the question arises, whether we have reached the top of the scale of life, when we have reached man simply, man who is of the earth. If there is within humanity only one life-sphere, only one elaboration of one life-principle, there may indeed be always phenomena resembling the miraculous which depend on the difference of powers; but this does not establish the existence of such a region of miracles as the Theocracy and especially Christianity delineates, since the deciding new principle is wanting which must form and support it. But if there is really a succession of stages within humanity—if here again a sphere of specifically higher human life towers above the lower sphere, we must here also expect what meets our eye on all the other stages of life, namely, that the new superior principle breaks through the old sphere with wonderful effect, in order to draw it up into its higher life. But Christianity announces this new higher life-stage not only as *doctrine*, but as *fact*, and in the idea it finds the completest confirmation of its own. The special characteristic of the first human life in its historical appearance, as it was modified by the fall, was the Adamic discord between the spirit and the flesh, and the predominance of the latter over the former. The special characteristic of the second human life in its historical power, that is, in Christ, is the identity of the spirit and the flesh, and the glorification of the flesh under the supremacy of the spirit. The human spirit itself requires this manifestation of the ideal human life in a distinct and decided principle (*Princip*). But it also requires the actings of this principle—its breaking through the sphere of the first human life, therefore its miracles. In these facts must the new life-principle verify itself as the creative organizing power of a new higher world.

When persons are accustomed to regard nature as only one sphere, and to allow the world of men to coincide with this one circle of nature, it excites the conception of a boundless Mongolian steppe, in which nothing more extraordinary can occur than the ever appearing and ever vanishing of the same sights and the same faces. But the more familiar we become with the succession of spheres in nature, and with the heavenly ladder of æons in the history of the world, the more we shall find in the great central miracle—the life of Christ—the necessity established of the several miracles which form its historical periphery. And the more we can estimate the contrast between the heavenly spiritual glory of the life of Christ, and the shattered, old human world, in all its magnitude, the more we shall expect these miracles of Christ to stand forth in bold relief.

Thus, then, the doctrine of the *miracles* of Christ is most intimately connected with the doctrine of His *Person*.[1] Where the
former appears mutilated, we may justly infer a mutilation of
the latter, and the reverse. The truth of this assertion may be
proved from the fact, that the various discrepancies in the doctrine
of miracles can very easily be traced back to corresponding discrepancies in the doctrine of the person of Christ. Whoever decidedly rejects the uniqueness of the person of Christ, will not be
able to recognise the uniqueness of His works. The difficulty
which 'modern culture' has with the miracles of Jesus, is connected
with a decline in the knowledge of the Son of the Virgin. When
the root of the life of Christ is no longer estimated in its wonderful singularity, how can the golden fruit of miracles be sought
for on the top of the tree? In fact, every one-sidedness in Christology is reflected by a one-sidedness in the theory of miracles.
The older orthodox doctrine of Christ did not at all times estimate the full value of His humanity. It often represented His
becoming a man as a humiliation, and at the same time lost sight
of the individuality of His being. Christ's humanity often appeared as an organic form, or the more concrete human approach
to His divinity. One consequence of this view was, that the
miracles were regarded simply as works of divine Omnipotence.
On this supposition faith in miracles was, in appearance, infinitely
easy. The explanation was always at hand—Christ can do all
things because He is God. But not to say that with this view
the presence of God in nature was regarded as the sway of an
absolute will within the circle of the most exact conformity to
law, it was at the same time forgotten that Christ as the Son
was aware that His own agency was throughout conditioned
by that of the Father (John v. 19); moreover, that He communicated to His own disciples the power of working miracles.
According to this view, Christ was not perfectly incorporated
with humanity; and the same might be affirmed of His miracles,
which would thus form only a conservatory of the choicest plants,
transplanted from heaven, and delighting us as images of heaven,
but never naturalized on earth. They would only attest the one
thought that God is omnipotent, and willing to aid us with His
omnipotence.

While a one-sided supranaturalism, therefore, makes an

[1] [See Note 8.]

exotic conservatory of the miracles of Jesus, the rationalist doctrine of Christ metamorphoses them into a bramble-bush. When Jesus is regarded simply as the son of Joseph, who, at the most, manifested the power of God in a peculiar manner, and fulfilled a mission from God, such a personality is not strong enough to concentrate the miracles of the Gospel history into an overpowering unity, and to make them proceed from Himself as the natural manifestations of the power of His wonderful life. But there they stand; and they must spring forth from the soil of the Gospel history as best they can : from the extraordinary power of Christ; from the ordination of Providence; or even from the favour of chance, from the elements of medical science, from magnetism, from popular credulity, from the embellishments of fiction, and lastly, even from the inaccuracies of the New Testament language. It is natural that such a wonderful soil should bear a thicket of miracles into which the rationalist shepherd is unwilling to lead his flock, since he is afraid they should lose their wool in the bushes, and which therefore he passes by himself as best he can. The Spiritualist, alarmed and troubled at the sight of this thicket, warns us with the looks of honest Eckhart, not to lose our way in the dangerous wood, but rather to adopt a logic which sets the outward and the inward, the letter and the spirit, in eternal contrariety.

But if there is a distinct recognition of the great miracle, namely, the uniqueness of the life of Christ, His separate miracles assume altogether a different aspect. They then form so many branches of a lofty, vigorous tree, and appear quite simply as manifestations of His nature, as His works. When we look at the height of the tree, and keep in our eye the strength of its trunk, its branches appear to us, not as the ponderous crown of an oak, but rather as the cheerful, graceful summit of a palm-tree; they seem to us as towering, slender, waving branches sporting in the wind. Should not the tree of life of the new æon be able to bear this crown without breaking down, and put forth the flowers which adorn it from its own internal vital power? Let it not be forgotten how high the tree rises towards heaven, how deep and wide its roots spread through the life of all humanity! When a young alpine stream, under the impulse of its great destiny, hastens down into the wide world, it shows signs in the region of its origin; waterfalls and

passages forced through rocks testify of the original freshness
of its power. But when Christianity rushes down from the
heavenly heights of the God-man into the low-lying tracts of a
human world, nature-enthralled and sunk in misery, and in its
first irruption carries away with it the great stone of the
sepulchre, here, as in the alpine scenery, the second miracle is
not greater than the first; rather is it purely natural in relation
to the first. If the understanding is here disposed to take
offence, the question must be asked, whether it regards the separate miracles as too little or too great in relation to the central
miracle. Many persons who have seen the falls of the Rhine
have said that they found them small in relation to their previous conception. These persons, at all events, ascribe something, though erroneously, to the reality; while there are others
who cannot imagine the half, at all events the full reality.
Everything here depends on the estimate formed of the power
which calls a phenomenon into life. The greater the power
is thought to be, the easier is the conception of the appearance
found to be; but the more highly the appearance is estimated,
the less adequate is the power. We have turned in our contemplation to the power. In the centre of the world's history, the
principle of principles, the light of lights, the life of the living,
and therefore also the power of powers, has appeared to us; the
one miracle, which causes many miracles to appear as the natural
utterances of a new and higher life-power.[1]

The miracle of the life of Jesus is one with the miracle of
the actual vision (*Selbstanschauung*) of God. Whoever would
explain this miracle to us, must be able to give us the assurance
that he is of a pure heart, or that he sees God, or that he sur-
veys the whole world in all its manifoldness as an ideal unity.
The saint who beholds God, sees, in the very act of beholding,
the nature of His essence; to him the opposition of nature and
miracle has become clear in their perfected harmony in God

---

[1] Neander, p. 138. ['Since Jesus was verily an incarnation of the
Godhead, miraculous works in His life were only becoming and natural.'—
Young's *Christ of History*, p. 267. Similarly, and quite logically, almost all
modern defenders of the miracles. This argument is but the more accurate
statement and amplification of one of Augustine's suggestive utterances:
'Mirum non esse debet a Deo factum miraculum; ... magis gaudere
quam mirari debemur.'—In *Joan*. Tract. xvii. 1.—ED.]

Himself. But whoever has not attained to this elevation, must necessarily regard the nature of God predominantly as a miracle, and accordingly must recognise its miraculous operations as the natural expressions of its essence. The same holds good of the works of Christ, in whom the self-revelation of God has appeared to us. Christ is the miraculous in the centre of nature : out of its relation to Him, even nature is miraculous; but in relation to Him, even miracle is natural. The Christian Gospel miracle must always find its 'natural' explanation in the miracle of the life of Christ. Christ Himself exhibits the completed mediation between the unconditioned omnipotence of God and finite conditioned nature—therefore the mediation of miracles.

The possibility of miracles is correctly proved in a twofold way : either by an appeal to the divine omnipotence, or to the idea of an accelerated natural process. On the one hand, it is argued, With God nothing is impossible; on the other, God changes every year water into wine, only by a slower process than at Cana. When, therefore, *miracle* is described as an act of God's omnipotence, we have named its deepest ground, its possibility; but its actual occurrence is not thereby explained. It is not even explained by representing that the will of the performer of the miracle has become one with the will of God. For our will may become one with the will of God even in the most profound resignation. But in the performance of a miracle, not only does man become one with God in the depths of the divine will in general, but God also becomes one with man in the special act in which man performs the miraculous with supernatural power derived from God. When therefore we are confronted by Omnipotence, by the will of the Almighty, and consequently are deeply moved by the infinite great probability of the miracle, the question still returns, Will God perform a miracle which positively encroaches on miraculous nature ? On the other hand, a miracle can as little be regarded as a mere extraordinary operation of the performer upon nature, when we speak of an acceleration of nature. There can be no question, indeed, that as, on the one hand, a miracle is rooted in the omnipotence of God, so, on the other hand, it celebrates its appearance in the accelerated process of nature. If therefore we turn to this conception of the accelerated process of nature, we certainly find that nature in its processes performs pure miracles—that it

changes water into wine, wine into blood, blood into milk; and this
fact shows us how plainly the miracles of the kingdom of God
are reflected in similar national phenomena. These thousandfold
similarities give us, therefore, again a lively impression of the
near possibility of miracles. We think that such a process of
nature needs only to be in some degree accelerated, and a
miracle will be the result.[1] But if it should come to this phenomenon of an accelerated process of nature, we must have at
any rate the principle of the process, its germ. All processes
of nature arise from principles, which in their ultimate grounds
must be regarded as the thoughts and operations of God. If
now every common process of nature presupposes a principle,
much more must such a one exist for an accelerated process:
for a miracle of healing, a decisive healing power; for the
change of water into wine, the factor of the formation of wine,
'the vine with its branches.'[2] Accordingly the idea of an
accelerated process of nature, strictly considered, exhibits only
the course of a miracle when it is already decided in principle,
just as the appeal to the omnipotence of God exhibits only the
general power of the miracle, without deciding that the miracle
shall actually take place.

We are now, therefore, placed between two possibilities of
miracle, and yet not justified in exhibiting these combined as
giving us the actual occurrence of the miracle. Between these
possibilities, rather, the question still arises respecting the living
centre which exhibits the miraculous power of God in the actual
miraculous fact, so that it can pass imperceptibly into the accelerated processes of nature.

This centre we found in the life of Jesus. The miraculous
reality of His life must, in accordance with its nature, express
itself in miraculous operations. In Him the mediation between
God and nature has appeared complete and effulgent; therefore
He exhibits omnipotence operating in the midst of nature without

[1] See Hase, *Leben Jesu*, p. 109 ; Olshausen, *Commentary on the Gospels*,
iii. 368. The latter appeals to the expression of Augustine—Ipse fecit
vinum in nuptiis, qui omni anno hoc facit in vitibus. Illud autem non
miramur, quia omni anno fit; assiduitate amisit admirationem.

[2] Strauss has justly required for the change of the water into wine at
Cana, the factor of the vine ; but when he supposes that this vine must be
a vegetable one, his thoughts wander among the vineyards of the nature-
æon, while here we have to consider the action of the vine in the spirit-æon.

violating nature in its essence, and exhibits what is conformable to nature in the divine life, without obscuring the divine freedom.[1]

This indissoluble union between the miraculous One and His miracles must be verified in a twofold way : first, because we see in Christ, as well as in His wonder-working, all the elements that make up the conception of a miracle realized in` the most powerful form; and also, because in all His miraculous works we plainly find again the christological characteristic, their relation to the life of Christ.

Miracle has above appeared to us as the decided irruption of a mediated (*vermittelten*) principle of a higher life-sphere into the old form of a lower one, with the tendency to take up this lower sphere into the higher. Now, if we fix our eye on Christ as a principle, He appears to us in this relation as the kingly

[1] J. Müller, in his programm *De miraculorum Jesu Christi naturâ et necessitate*, p. 8, etc., impugns the views of the older theologians of the Evangelical Church, according to which the miracles of Christ were deduced from His divine nature. He justly draws attention to the passages in which our Lord appeals to the Father in His performance of miracles in order to impugn the explanation of miracles from a one-sided activity of the omnipotence of God in Christ. But when he remarks, 'neque ad rem quidquam interest horum scriptorum nonnullos humanæ proxime Christi naturæ miracula assignare ; per communicationem idiomatum enim hujus divinæ virtutis participem factam illam esse volunt;' and further, 'quod autem miracula factitavit, id ei certo tempore concessum est singulari dei dono, quo ad provinciam Messianam administrandam instructus est,'—he strikes into another direction which has been successfully pursued by Nitzsch, Twesten, Neander, Ullmann, and others, for the solution of the problem of miracles. See Nitzsch, *System of Christian Doctrine*, p. 83 (Clark) ; Twesten, *Dogmatik*, vol. i. p. 380 ; Neander and Ullmann, in the passages quoted above. Also, might there not be a propriety in receiving with Christ a *singulare Dei donum?* When the author further shows that God stands in presence of nature in absolute majesty and freedom, he has admirably described the principle of miracles ; and it requires only to give prominence to the incarnation of this God, in order to give to the principle described its concrete form. [Scripture gives us to understand that the Spirit is the Agent of all divine operations. When, therefore, it is pressed, as in the present day it is too frequently and exclusively pressed, that the miracles were wrought by the Spirit, it should be kept distinctly in view that this Spirit is the Spirit of Christ Himself, the Spirit proceeding from the Father and from the Son. Correct views of the immediate power by which the miracles of Christ were wrought, introduce into the apologetic argument from miracles a modification which will be felt by any one who undertakes the argument. Very instructive on this point is Owen, *On the Spirit*, ii. 3, 4.—ED.]

principle of all universal principles. Every subordinate principle is, no doubt, an original power, a product of God's creative operation, a marvellous witness of God's nearness; but
Christ as a principle is one with God's manifestation in the
world, with His highest operation, the principle of the creation
of a new world. But this principle is in the highest degree
conformable to nature, for it is mediated with infinite abundance. Every lesser principle is mediated by some corresponding course of nature; but the life of Christ is mediated by the
whole antecedent course of the world. This mediated method
of Christ is His nature. Therefore, since the nature of Christ
was more mediated or prepared for than any other being, we
can discover in His life the genuine stamp of all naturalness, the
highest fulfilling of all nature-life. But by nature, according
to its power and destiny, is simply the glory or the power of the
divine Spirit over all nature-life. His life is therefore so far
supernatural in its essence and its operations. It is essentially His
destiny to operate supernaturally or metaphysically, to free the
creature from vanity, to transform its life of bondage by the life
of the Spirit. For this reason, in that antinaturalness by which
the higher nature takes up the lower nature, He breaks through
the limits of the old course of nature and the world, first of all
with the miracle of His peculiar birth, and afterwards by the
copious operations of His redeeming power. His life puts to
death the life or the nature of the old Adam throughout the
world, and especially in this sense are His operations antinatural.
These operations have seized human and earthly life in its
depths, and in these depths are working out a great regeneration, which is to break forth resplendent from the ashes of the
old world. It was in the nature of the case for these operations
to disclose themselves in direct, immediate forms; in signs symbolical of Christ's general agency; in miracles which appeared
antinatural to men, in proportion as the old form of the world
was held to be the only normal one, and of eternal validity.
But as the life of Christ, notwithstanding its spirituality, or
rather in this very spirituality, appears as a perfected, beautiful
new nature, so it is also with His miraculous operations. They
all issue and complete themselves in quick natural processes,
the results of which appear in new, delightful forms of life.
Thus His breaking through the old world, by which He ad-

vances to the last judgment and the end of the world, will have for its consequences a new world.

All these constituents of the conception of miracle must be more or less prominent in the single miraculous works of Christ. First of all, the constituent of *mediation*. The need of a miracle is a *constituent* corresponding to the principle for performing miracles, and is the occasion when Christ receives an intimation from the Father to work in unity with Him creatively, that is, to perform a miracle. Indeed, the constituent for effecting the great saving miracle of the world's salvation is ever present to the Lord. But the occasions for allowing the fruits of this redemption to make their appearance in special operations, and for the signs of the transforming power of this redemption, the omens of the future glorification of the world, to shine forth, are more rare (Luke iv. 25–27 ; John xi. 4). There are single moments in which a definite form of the world's misery and the world's Redeemer in His historical pilgrimage meet, we might say, one another on so narrow a bridge, and so exactly face to face, that they must fight with one another, or rather the misery must collapse and vanish before the Redeemer.

These constituent elements are therefore mediated equally with the life itself. The most general mediating is the faith of those who need relief. This faith is the peculiar organ of susceptibility for the miraculous power of Christ—the divine token, in fact, by which the occasion of working a miracle is indicated to Him. But if any one is disposed to make this susceptibility the special factor of the relief granted, and thus to account for the miracle by the faith of miracles, in such a case he would ascribe to the sufferer a greater faith and a greater power than to Christ Himself. But faith as such is generally no more than a susceptibility, which is distinguished from fanaticism by its knowing with certainty that it is met by a positive operation of God. If, therefore, it is altogether erroneous to make faith in its isolated position a worker of miracles without the co-operating power of God, it is also perfectly monstrous to pretend that there are believers who beget this miraculous help out of themselves, when they stand supplicating before the Lord, when He answers their confidence, and receives thanks for the help given. Even Christ Himself worked not in an isolated position, though He had within Himself a positive miraculous power, but in conjunction with the Father (John x. 41) directing a look of confidence towards Him. But this mediating of miracles appears to us to vanish when we look at the miracles of Christ performed at a distance; likewise in His healing of demoniacs; but, lastly and chiefly, in His miraculous operations on nature. But even here we see traces of mediation gradually emerging from the darkness, as we direct our eye to the inner relations of the world, and estimate them higher than is commonly done in relation to the outward phenomena. When Christ healed the possessed child of the Canaanitish woman, the channel through which the operation reached the child is plainly traceable : it was one of the disposition, sunk deep in the heart of the supplicating mother. Her agitated soul with one hand laid hold of the Lord, and with the other of her child, and thus formed a living affinity—an electrical conductor by which the lightning of healing flashed from the heart of Christ into the heart of her child. In the world of clairvoyance delicate streams of fire and tracks of light have been seen, which were formed between separated human souls, so that they thought of one another vividly, and have been occupied with one another : these are spiritual bridges which love, anxiety, remembrance, and especially intercessory prayer, have thrown across spaces of outward separation, and traverse. These communications correspond entirely with a delicate estimate of the dynamical relations of the world.

But not to insist on these, we cannot, at all events, doubt of the living movement of the mightiest powers between hearts which stand in the most intimate and vital relation to one another. But this movement suffices us as a spiritual pathway for the healing powers of the Lord when they have to act at a distance. Thus the nobleman at Capernaum became a conductor of Christ's healing power for his son ; and the Gentile centurion, with his strong faith, was a mediating organ for his servant. But when our Lord had to deal with demoniacs, this mediation lay in a power which, in diseased persons of this class, is generally active with a morbid development, and a more intense energy—a power of psychical foreboding. Of the nature of demoniacal suffering we do not here speak. But it is a fact which occurs among the nervous and insane of our own time, as well as in the case of the demoniacs in the Gospel history, that in their intensified power of foreboding, they are capable of

divining the dispositions and intentions which the persons immediately about them entertain. They are in a morbid state of
psychical agitation, and in a closer affinity than healthy persons
to the psychical movements of the bystanders. Especially have
they an extraordinary sensitiveness for states of mind which are
in contrast to their own. As *clairvoyantes* can be disturbed by
the nearness of impure characters, so demoniacs and insane persons often become excited by the approach of saintly characters.
They feel the operation of a power which even at a distance
comes into collision with their state, and presses punitively on
the secret consciousness of the psychical terror with which commonly their state of mental bondage is connected. Thus the
demoniac whom Jesus met with in the synagogue at Capernaum
could not endure His presence (Mark i. 23), but cried out against
Him. That the demoniacs were the first who proclaimed Him as
the Messiah, may be accounted for from the activity and percep-
tive vigour of their intensified power of foreboding; not simply
because this power of foreboding brought them into a peculiar
relation with the consciousness of Christ, but because it also
formed the same relation between them and the secret thoughts
of their times. That Jesus was the Messiah, was the public
secret of His time, from the beginning of His ministry. John's
annunciation of Him had already taken place; His disciples indulged distinct hopes of the manifestation of His Messianic
glory, and the people were agitated by the fluctuations of foreboding that He was the promised One. But the dark antipathy
of the hierarchy hung like a threatening thunder-cloud over
against this dawn in men's minds. No one ventured to commit
himself by the public and decided recognition of Christ. The
insane naturally took the lead; they proclaimed aloud the obscure mystery which they found in the breasts of their contemporaries. Fools and children speak the truth; so here the accla-
mations of the children soon followed the cries of the demoniacs.
In addition to them, Christ was proclaimed by poor mendicants,
who had nothing to lose; and by the people in a mass, who in
masses always feel strongly. When, therefore, the demoniacs
had an excited feeling and foreboding of the dignity of Christ,—
when by their recklessness they anticipated the people in the
publication of His name, a mediation was thus formed for the
miraculous aid of Christ. As borderers on the kingdom of

spirits, they were raised above the ban of the Sanhedrim by the peculiar sacredness of their calamitous state; and as confessors of Jesus, they were peculiarly the objects of His compassion.

. But no such mediation of the miracles of Christ appears at first sight to be given in the case of the dead whom He restored to life; yet, on carefully considering the circumstances, we shall find that there is a mediation, or rather a double one. The three dead persons whom Christ restored, even when dead were held by strong bonds in the vicinity of life;—the daughter of Jairus, by the loud mourning of the parental house; the young man at Nain, by the inconsolable grief of his mother; and lastly, Lazarus, not merely by the ceaseless yearning with which his sisters waited for the Lord, but also by the unsatisfied expectation with which he himself had sunk into the grave. Even though dead, therefore, these three still experienced the strong attraction towards life on this side the grave. But as spirits, they understood the voice of the Prince of spirits. The modes of mediating the miracles of Christ in His operations on external nature are hardest to discover. Here also the connecting links have been lost for the most part, because sufficient account has not been taken of the co-operation of hearts. This applies especially to the miracles of food and drink which Jesus wrought. How very much has it been the practice to pass over, in these . miracles, the mental states of the persons for whom they were wrought! In many a dissertation on the miracle at Cana, the exclamation, ' They have no wine! no wine!' meets us at every turn; and some theological treatises upon it handle the whole question after so grossly material a fashion, so utterly without a surmise of the significance of the spiritual transaction in this history, that one would think they were composed in a tavern, or meant to lay the scene of the narrative in a public-house! But how could these miracles have a New Testament power and significance, if they were not performed in the element of emotional life (*Gemüthsleben*) and of the sphere of faith? We do not intend to enlarge on this remark here, but reserve the development for the sequel. In the stilling of the storm on the Lake of Gennesaret, the mediating consisted in this, that first of all the hearts of the disciples, as the firstlings of the new humanity, were laid at rest before the winds and waves were stilled. The cursing of the fig-tree was mediated by that presentiment of the judgment awaiting Jerusalem and the end of the world, which so deeply moved Christ in His last days.

It will be understood that the supernatural, which is operative in all Christ's miracles, must be always and immediately looked for in His divine life-power. This life-power, in the case where Christ performed a miracle, is identical with the omnipotence of God; for He performed such an act only according to the will of the Father, and in unity with Him. It was the overpowering agency of the sovereign principle which was placed in the centre of the world, in order to destroy its corruption and effect its glorification. But the expressions of the power of Christ, as they differ in different miracles, so also the forms they assume are different. To the leprous Christ presented Himself as positive purity, the absolute power of all purification; to the deaf, as the ear-forming word; and to the dead, as the positive life-giving life. And as Christ in such agency becomes one with the Father, so is the disposition in which He accomplishes His miracle one with Him. His word is the fructifying principle with which the receptive faith takes in the victorious life-power which is destined to effect the miracle in its own life-circle. The believers in miraculous power therefore received, in the moment of the performance of the miracle, by a sympathetic elevation of their disposition, a share in the noble-mindedness of Christ, and in this moment of their highest nearness to heaven the miracle became incorporated with their life.

But in all cases an old naturalness, either a dark form or a fettering limitation, or an evil of the old world which has become nature, is broken through and taken away by the miraculous agency of Christ. At one time, it is the roaring storm; at another time, it is water in the colourless form which it takes as a defect in contrast with the wine; and at a third time, it is the grave. This character of destruction is most prominent in the cursing of the fig-tree.

But, lastly, we also see that all the miracles of Jesus bear the impress of true miracle, because they enter nature with creative, liberating, formative power, and complete themselves as natural processes. The men whom Christ heals or restores to life come forward again, as forms restored to this world, in all their native freshness. To the daughter of Jairus food is given to eat (Mark v. 43). Lazarus soon after his resurrection is found among the guests at a feast. Our Lord causes this subsidence of miracle into natural life to appear even in effecting His own miracles. The blind man whom Christ cured at Bethsaida (Mark viii. 22), after Christ's first operation, exclaimed, 'I see men as trees walking!' Visible objects still appeared before his eyes in indistinct outline, nor did he perfectly recover his sight till Christ had touched his eyes a second time. The Lord seems carefully to have given prominence to this natural side of the cures He effected, and to have drawn, so to speak, a veil round the strictly miraculous operation by availing Himself more or less of natural operations. Even the word by which He usually effected His work, is not in itself alone to be regarded as a mere unsensuous expression of the spirit. As in its meaning it is a divine thought, so outwardly it is a thunderbolt of the soul's life—a powerful psychical act, inflaming the hearts and agitating the organs of the susceptible. Such a word of Christ is, in miniature, an image of the creative universal agency of God by which He created the world—that infinite expression of God, which inwardly was altogether His sunbright thought and will, and outwardly a mysterious, darkly brooding, immeasurably rich fulness of life —that creative basis of the world which now appeared in Him in individual personality. But the nature-side of His miraculous agency was more striking when He touched the sufferers or laid hold of them by the hand. Such contact must have been, in the case of the leprous especially, a revolting operation (Matt. viii. 3). With such an one Christ placed Himself in the relation of defilement. He exposed Himself thereby to the danger, according to the Levitical law, of being excluded from the congregation as an unclean person ; He even hazarded His life for the sake of curing the leprous when He touched them. This moral operation itself, in its living power to touch the soul, was for the diseased like a flash of lightning from heaven. But it is remarkable, that Jesus never went beyond touching. Though, according to the account in Mark's Gospel (vi. 13), the disciples of Jesus often anointed the sick with oil, and thus restored them to health, yet we are not warranted by this circumstance to conclude that Jesus Himself used such means.

The disciples, with their weaker miraculous power, appear to have depended on a more natural act of healing; as, according to the direction of James, the elders of the Church were obliged to do at a later period. In fact, besides touching, imposition of the hands, or laying hold of the hand of the diseased, in which the complete miraculous power of His holy hand was manifested, Christ only employed one physical means repeatedly, one distinctly individual, a natural bodily means—His spittle. The ancients attribute to the saliva a sure healing power, especially for many disorders of the eyes; an opinion which is still held in our own times.[1] But Christ appears to make this means the vehicle of a higher power. If the personality of Christ is regarded according to its peculiar significance as the life-giving life, as positive healthfulness, we may venture to expect that every bodily substance or quality which has proved itself elsewhere in any degree curative, will be found again in His life in the highest potency, and, as an expression of that life, will exhibit the highest healing efficiency. But Jesus applied the same means in different ways. He healed (according to Mark vii. 33) a deaf and dumb man by putting His fingers in his ears, and then, after spitting on His finger, touching his tongue.[2] In the case of the blind man at Bethsaida, the spittle seems to have been directly applied to the eyes of the blind, and followed by the imposition of hands (viii. 22). When He cured the man born blind at Jerusalem (John ix.), He spat on the ground and made a paste, with which He anointed the eyes of the blind, and ordered him to go and wash in the pool of Siloam. We have here again an advanced application of the spittle: the paste which He spread on the eyes of the blind, as something more than a momentary application, and the time spent in going to the pool at Siloam, during which it remained, constituted this advanced use of it. The washing in the pool of Siloam, which the afflicted man had to perform, seems to have been only a symbolical act in which, with his faith, his cure was to be completed. At all events, it was otherwise with

[1] See Fleck, *die Vertheidigung des Christenthums*, p. 150; Tacitus, *Hist.* iv. 81; Suetonius, *Vesp.* vii.

[2] The ears appear to have been touched with one hand and the tongue with the other simultaneously; and this operation seems to mark a peculiar influence.

the spittle. The repetition of its application plainly shows that
it was used as a means; and although its application does not
do away with the miraculous character of the cures in which
Jesus made use of it, yet it shows how He was inclined to conceal, in a degree, His miraculous acts,—to soften the sublime
abruptness of their direct operation by a connection with some
form, more or less known, of the extraordinary art of healing.[1]
It was a little thing, an act of condescension, for Him to perform these single miracles; while the people were astonished at
them as the highest expressions of His life. This induced Him
to make His healing operations approach a natural form, and to
clothe them in poor, flat, and strange forms, in order to bring
the exalted power that revealed itself in Him into communication with the life of the world. Yet He could not have given
His miracles this form, if He had found in it no healing
power whatever. For this very reason, this form of Christ's
miraculous cures, the application of His spittle, was peculiarly
suited to .make what was miraculous in His operations appear
as natural, and what was natural in His life appear as miraculous.[2] This nature-side of His miraculous power meets us most
strikingly in the history of the woman suffering from the issue
of blood, who was healed by the believing touch of His garment.
The Lord had not conversed with her; yet He was aware that
He had been touched, and that by this contact a cure had been
effected, for He declared that 'virtue had gone out' of Him
(Luke viii. 46). Does not the healing power of Christ here
appear almost in a pathological form as a suffering? Offence
has been taken at this narrative. And yet it only manifests
the most delicate feeling for life in a personality most rich in

---

[1] [Ewald (*Christus*, p. 224, 4th ed.) notices in this connection how our
Lord sometimes inquired into ·the symptoms of the bodily disease. All
these forms of 'mediation' prove to his mind 'that His human acting was
bound to the universal laws of the divine order, and that this He would in
no wise arrogantly violate.'—ED.]

[2] Considering the means of cure objectively, we must at all events distinguish between the animal healing power residing in the saliva and the
psychical healing power communicated through the intention of the worker
of the miracle, perhaps through His breath. If the ancients, embracing
both these elements in their concrete unity, contemplated the miraculous
element as the decisive one, it does not follow that they denied the natural
one.

life. The same Master of psychical life, who had a perfectly developed sense for every sympathy and antipathy that approached Him, could not help perceiving the agitation or hurried respiration of a sufferer who touched Him under the highest excitement of pain, and at the same time of confidence, as one needing aid; and when He blessed in His spirit the sufferer without knowing her as an individual, the contact and the miraculous aid perfectly coincided. It is not said that He did not freely part with this healing power, that He had been robbed of it; for as soon as the Lord felt Himself touched by a suffering, He freely entered into it with His sympathy.[1] But when He wished to cause the woman who had been cured to come forward openly on her own account, He rightly declared that virtue had gone out of Him. It was needful to make the matter public: hitherto the cure had been as it were a stolen one, and the woman remained at least suffering from false shame. At all events, Christ's language informs us that the virtue which proceeded from Him, was to be regarded as a virtue connected with the nature of His life. Hence by this passage we are led to consider a question which in modern times has been often agitated, namely, How far the miraculous cures performed by Christ are akin to the cures effected by animal magnetism. Some have attached great importance to this affinity; others have been apprehensive lest by this similarity the agency of Jesus should be brought too near the profane; others, again, have admitted a greater or less analogy between the two methods of healing. Thus much is certain: if in general the power of magnetism belongs to the flesh and blood of human nature, then Christ also has appropriated this power. But if, on the other hand, all flesh and blood has attained in Christ's person its complete spiritualization, this also is true especially of magnetism, and of the application of its power. If we have first learned to estimate the ascending lines of powers (over against

---

[1] This narrative gives no support to the supposition of 'involuntary healings.' The passages which Strauss has adduced (Matt. xiv. 36; Mark iii. 10, vi. 56; Luke vi. 19), with the remark that Jesus in these instances did not expend self-active powers, but must have involuntarily allowed them to have been carried off, *expressly assert the contrary:* 'They besought Him that they might touch if it were but the border of His garment; and as many as touched Him were made whole' (Mark vi. 56).

the descending line of ideas) in the world, and found that these same powers reappear in all the stages of life, but in ever new transformations and higher potencies, then also the relation of Christ's healing power to magnetism must gradually be made clear. The very term Animal Magnetism expresses that gradation; it marks especially the power of the magnet, as it reappears in a more elevated form in the animal kingdom. If we follow the hint which lies in these terms, we shall be led to the contemplation of a scale of magnetic power, of which the lowest degree lies deep in the elements, and the highest must be revealed in the power of Christ's nature. The light of the atmosphere seems to reappear in the earthly elements as electricity. Electricity is no doubt an elevated power in the magnet. Then magnetism comes forward in the animal sphere as a power working soul-like, of which the operations border on magic. Now, when this power appears elevated again in the human region as a peculiar talent in the life of certain individuals, this is no longer mere animal magnetism, but is exalted into the human. But this power experiences a new consecration in the free spiritual activity of a devout worker of miracles, or of a prophet who acts under a sense of the eternal. Lastly, if it comes again to view in Christ, it must appear in His life according to its nature, not only with the greatest fulness, but in perfect unity with the operations of the Divine Spirit. It also appears here altogether as nature, but as completely ideal, as a pure agency, as a perfect vehicle of the Spirit. Thus, then, in Christ the powers of all the stages of nature are elevated and glorified. He is not only in a metaphorical, but also in a dynamic sense, the light of the world; the lightning which hereafter at His appearing will shine from the east even to the west; the unity of those four divergent forms of life or animal images which symbolically represent the great model-forms of life; the Man in whom humanity is concentrated, and therefore in whom every human endowment appears in its fairest bloom; the prophet who stands and acts in the fulness of the powers of God; finally, He Himself, the God-man, who performs a miracle as little as any other man when God has not indicated it, but also then with the complete certainty with which God Himself works it. Thus, then, the healing power with which Christ accomplishes His work is a power related to, and brought into combination with, the innermost life of nature in all its stages, and therefore verifies itself in its operations as the healing power of the diseased human world; and its product is a new nature.

Thus, as on the one hand the genuine miracle is to be recognised in all the works of Christ as well as in His life, so on the other hand the christological stamp is found in all His miracles, and again especially in the miraculous momenta of His life itself.

The miraculous momenta in the life of Jesus present themselves as a pure linked succession of stages in the unfolding of His christological glory. In His wonderful birth of the Virgin, first of all, life existed as a positive life-power, as pure power; that is to say, an individuality which in its flesh and blood exhibits the completed harmony with the universe, which is born of the Spirit and is one with the Spirit, and, as the power of the Spirit, has power over life. His self-comprehension in human development begins this life of power, and reaches at length the climax of perfect spirit-consciousness with the baptism in the Jordan. Here His individual unfolding in spirit was completed. But, after that, the capability of this life unfolds itself in the soul-life of Christ, and the bloom of this festivity of the soul bursts forth at the transfiguration. Lastly, by the fact of the resurrection the corporeity of Christ was borne aloft out of the region of the old nature and the realm of death into the imperishable; the body was borne aloft in the power of the Spirit, and made thoroughly spiritual and spirit-like, while its life-power and vitality is not only maintained, but perfected in its spiritualization. The ascension is, in the first place, not so much a new miracle, as the full verification of the miracle of the resurrection, the highest evidence of glorification or of completed spiritualization to which the life of Christ has been elevated. It becomes a new miracle as it introduces and represents the session of Christ at the right hand of God. But this again manifests itself in three *momenta*, which run parallel with the *momenta* of the individual glorification of Christ while they exhibit His universal glory. With the outpouring of the Holy Spirit, Christ gains a universal consciousness in His Church. This universal power of the Spirit over the earth will one day bring its constantly regenerating operation in the souls of men into festive manifestation, when the Church of Christ attains to the full spiritual beauty of His kingdom. After that, His individual resurrection will unfold itself finally in the glorification of the world which ensues on the world's judgment at the general resurrection. The first moment (*moment*) of this universal unfolding of the glory of Christ consists, therefore, in the revelation of His dominion over the spiritual life of humanity; in the second appears His dominion over the souls of men, the completion of the victory of Christ's sympathy over the sympathy of evil, which is evinced in a great Christian inspiration of humanity; the third moment reveals His power over all flesh.

It is undeniable that all the momenta of miracles in which the life of Christ is unfolded are throughout christological; that is, they perfectly correspond to the conception of the life of Christ and its significance for the world.[1] When, therefore, we have represented the miraculous acts of Christ as the natural emanations of His miraculous nature, it is evident that they must disclose the same christological nature. And so we find it. In fact, they generally present the most distinct correspondences to the separate christological stages in the development of Christ's life. It is our business to point out these correspondences, and to render as conspicuous as possible the general ideas which lie at the basis of the miracles of Jesus.

If now, with this view, we refer the different kinds of Christ's miracles to the different stages of His life's development, it cannot be supposed that Christ performed a peculiar class of miracles only in a particular form of the development of His power; rather it is implied that in every miracle the whole life of Christ was active when we designate them all generally as christological. But the matter in question here is, that we contemplate the general christological nature of the miracles of Jesus in the sharp distinctness of their type, and that we therefore contem-

[1] [This is the idea of Westcott's suggestive little book, *Characteristics of the Gospel Miracles.* 'The miracles of the Gospel are *not* isolated facts; they are *not* vain repetitions. In meaning, as well as in time, they lie between the incarnation and the ascension. . . . Each (kind of miracle) is needful for the complete representation of the life of Christ,' etc., pp. 6-9. The book is full of most valuable aids towards grasping the miracles as a whole, and is pervaded by the sober and reverent spirit which characterizes all the productions of this useful writer.—ED.]

plate them as phenomena belonging to the progressive development of His life and work.

It is a radical evil of the old æon, that nature has circumvented the spirit of man through his guilt, has gained the upper hand, and stands over him like a menacing giant. According to the ideal relations of the world, it ought to be otherwise. In a life of innocence, the spirit would prove its harmony with nature and its power over it. Instinct, like a prophet, announces this mastery of the spirit over nature, as it appears with a beautiful living constancy in animal life. But for a long time fallen man appears to give the lie to these prophecies. The dog falls into the water and swims; but a man falls in and is drowned. But he is drowned, not by his bodily weight, not by the natural relation of his body to the water, but by the consternation which misleads him to sink into destruction by a morbid excitement, instead of balancing himself on the waves in victorious self-possession.

When, therefore, Christ walks on the stormy sea, the quintessence of the miracle consists in the perfect divine equanimity of His spirit. He is, first of all, quite free from that corrupt act of swimming practised by the natural man. But His pure vital courage in the water is connected with the vital feeling of His organism, which is the crown of all human organisms. The relation of bodies to the water is infinitely various. There are some swimmers that sink deep, and others that hold themselves high.

The Prince by birth of land and sea walks through the waves with His whole figure erect above them. But when man once comes into harmonious reciprocal action with an excited element, his movement in it becomes rhythmical. And so a jubilant feeling must have unfolded itself in Christ's heart on the exulting waters; and with this feeling those hidden powers of life must have been disengaged and become active, which also are said to appear in the life of the magnetically excited, so that such persons cannot sink in water, but are borne up by it.[1] But Christ's walking on the water, in the co-working of

[1] 'As often as they wished to bring her (the seeress of Prevorst) in magnetic circumstances to a bath, a most wonderful phenomenon appeared, —all her limbs, with her chest and abdomen, were seized with a peculiar jerking motion, with perfect elasticity, which always raised her out of the

THE MIRACLES OF JESUS.

this perfect consciousness of God and His imperturbable repose
—of this elevation of soul in the feeling of harmony with the
agitated element—and of this rhythmically borne and noblest
corporeity,—exhibits the unity of the new human life in the
spirit as it attains dominion over nature.   In this miracle the
Man of the spirit, in His world-historical importance, is borne
out of the water of nature-life. It is a symbolical fact which
has gained a natural position in an extraordinary rich history
of New Testament operations.   The more man regains the full
consciousness of the sovereignty of his spirit over nature, the
more he regains power over the natural feelings of his life,—
the more does the dread of nature vanish from his path, and he
resumes the full dominion over its forces.

But this discrepancy with nature into which man has fallen
by his guilt, is further manifest in distinct evils with which man
is afflicted, particularly in his infirmities and sicknesses. These
evils are characteristic marks of the deep corruption of the old
æon ; they are united most intimately with sin.   It would indeed be hyper-Jewish if we were disposed to lay as a burden on
the individual, his peculiar infirmity as his desert. Such a view
can be regarded only as a popular superstition.   It is an insult
to the spirit of the Hebrew religion to charge it with maintaining
it. 'And if any one would ascribe it to Christ, it would be in
opposition to His most explicit declarations.[1]   Yet, on the other

water.'—Extract from the 'Seherin von Prevorst.' See Tholuck's Glaub-
würdigkeit der evang. Geschichte, p. 100.

[1] Strauss (ii. 75) finds, first of all, in the expressions of Jesus (Matt.
ix. 1) a reference to the 'Jewish' view, that evil, and especially the sickness of the individual, is the punishment of his sin. His subsequent remark
is at variance with this, that Jesus expressly declared of the case proposed
to Him (John ix. 1, etc.), that 'this special evil was not owing to the criminality of the individual, but was founded on higher divine designs.'
Thus the 'higher educated' author of the fourth Gospel seems to have
allowed Jesus to reject the former view ; yet, on the other hand, according
to John v. 14, 'infirmity as a punishment of sin' is announced to the man
cured at the pool of Bethesda. But this must relate to 'sinning generally,' so
that the meaning of Jesus was, that if that man only sinned again generally,
he would again be afflicted with disease. The passage in Luke xiii. 1 ought
to confirm the view of the connection between sin and misfortune in every
individual (whence it would follow, that the eighteen men on whom the
tower of Siloam fell, according to the Lord's views, were all equally guilty).
Along with this 'vulgar Hebrew' view of sickness and evil, Jesus must have
been burdened with the opposite Essene-ebionitish 'view,' according to

hand, we must also mark it as hyper-heathenish, if the general connection of all sin with all evil, and the general appointment of all evils to be the punishment of all sins, and if, lastly, the spectacle that a thousand times individuals pay for their individual transgressions, should be denied. Only materialism in morals can wish to dissever the bond of connection between sin and punitive evil. Now, among the people of Israel the feeling of this connection was developed in a very high degree, and partially to a morbid excess. They had experienced God's chastisements under the discipline of the law, and often had bowed under His strokes with slavish dread. The miserable mental state of the unfortunate was aggravated by the harshness with which they were condemned by their more fortunate pharisaically-minded brethren. And at the time of Christ's advent almost all the fruits on the tree of human misery in Israel appeared to be ripened. The chronic diseases which are indigenous in Palestine, and countries of a similar climate, such as blindness, leprosy, paralysis, and nervous disorders, were very widely spread. Christ found Himself in the fulness of the Spirit placed in the presence of this misery. He met with many sufferers, who were at once in need of salvation and of bodily healing. By means of the latter, the sense of the former was ripened; and, in their desire for salvation, the state of mind was produced which fitted them for receiving bodily relief, that is, faith in the possibility of miraculous aid. In the fulness of the Spirit and of the peace of God lay the power of Christ to forgive the sins of those who felt their need of salvation, and, by the assurance of the grace of God, to animate their hearts with the glow of a new life. With an impulse of that positive confidence in God which He possessed, He could transport, by His consolations, to a heaven of divine joy those souls that felt themselves cast down to the gates of hell. How could Christ have cherished in His spirit this power to forgive sins in an abstract form; that is, only a power over the spirits of men, and not at the same time a power over their souls and bodily organisms? It was in accordance with His concrete victorious power over evil, that when it met Him in individual cases, He steadily re-

which the righteous in this æon are the suffering, the poor, and the sick. Such are the contradictions which are here cast as reflections on the clear mirror of the ethical consciousness of Jesus.

garded it from the root to the summit. But so also would the diseased, who, under Israelitish discipline, were trained to exercise faith in His aid, expect from Him, according to their entire view of the world, concrete aid both spiritual and bodily.[1] According to the prophetic promises, the Israelite expected in his Messiah a Saviour who would work miracles; therefore the Jew who was anxious for salvation could not have received and retained so firmly the consolation of the forgiveness of sins from the lips of Jesus, if it had not been confirmed to him by bodily aid. It is difficult for the penitent sinner to retain absolution in pure spirituality. The Christian finds the seal of his reconciliation in the renewed peace of his society (Sozietät), especially in the sacrament, by which he becomes one with the Church and with the Lord of the Church. The temporary sacrament with which the contrite Israelite received his absolution from the lips of Jesus, was the miracle. Although this connection between the outward and inward healing was not in all cases equally apparent and marked, yet even in those wherein it was faintest it existed in some measure, so that those who needed bodily aid did homage to the Lord as the Messiah; and Weisse has justly remarked, that faith in the forgiveness of sins, and the effect of it, is to be regarded as a prominent feature of the cures performed by Christ.

The case of the paralytic at Capernaum (Matt. ix. 1) appears to us the most striking example of this agency of Christ. First of all, he received from Christ the assurance of the forgiveness of his sins. But the pharisaical spirits wished to despoil him of this inestimable gift by pronouncing the absolution to be blasphemy; upon which our Lord ratified it with a heavenly sacrament which they could not gainsay, by saying to the sick man, 'Arise, take up thy bed, and go unto thine house!'

The words of Jesus, therefore, penetrated as a ray of vital

---

[1] [So Ewald, while he maintains that Jesus satisfied all the deepest, godliest longing in Israel, says (p. 219 of his Geschichte Christus), 'The kingdom of the perfect, true religion must break the power and the destructive consequences of sin; but all human ills are so connected with sin, that even those which are bodily only through it become thoroughly dangerous and radically obstinate, and therefore even those are the proper objects of the deeds of might of the genuine King.'—Ed.]

power the hearts of those who believed in His miracles, operating with creative energy, and imparting a healthy vitality to every part of the frame. There is a class of diseases which may be regarded as an exhaustion of the fulness and freshness of the organism, namely, hereditary bodily infirmities. Now it lies in the nature of the case, that such infirmities must soonest give way to Christ's vital ray which penetrates the life-root of the infirm through their organism. The cure of a man born blind may appear more difficult within the range of common experience than the cure of one who has become blind, but in relation to the conception of miracle it may be considered as the easier. The sun with its fresh rays can most easily stimulate the stunted growth of a plant. The solar ray, which somehow was wanting to the bodily stunted in the very beginnings of their life, now darts suddenly into the root of their life, and completes their first birth with the beginning of the second. Also the lame and deformed appear to stand in a nearer relation to the psychico-electrical powerful agency, to the lightning flash of the miraculous word of Jesus.[1]

Fevers form another kind of suffering.[2] Their cure shows how positive repose and heavenly tranquillity can be communicated with healing power to the sick; or how the fiery conflict of fever against evil can be instantaneously rendered victorious by the warm stream of life which proceeds from Christ.

The healing of lepers belongs to the most important[3] cures effected by Jesus. The leprosy seemed to seize inexorably on the whole living substance of the sufferer, and to have doomed him to death. But this fearful disease, which in general was so fatal, was sometimes capricious. It would strike out on the surface of the body, and pass off in a white eruption on the skin. This natural process of cure corresponded entirely to Christ's method of cure; His healing operations proceeded from within outwards.

[1] Cures of the blind are mentioned or narrated in Matt. ix. 27, xii. 22, xv. 30, xx. 30, xxi. 14;—of the paralytic, to whom as a particular class the lame and the maimed belong, Matt. iv. 24, viii. 6, ix. 2, xi. 5, xii. 16, xv. 30; Luke vi. 6, xiii. 11; John v. 1;—the healing of the woman with the issue of blood, Matt. ix. 20;—the cure of a man with the dropsy is narrated Luke xiv. 2. Many cures are repeated in the parallel passages.

[2] See Matt. viii. 14; John iv. 52.

[3] Matt. viii. 2; Luke xvii. 12.

The demoniacs of the New Testament history are, on the one hand, classed by the Evangelists with the other sick; but on the other hand, they are distinguished as a peculiar class from the common sick. That first of all they were considered and treated as sick persons, is evident. They appear as such, according to the symptoms of their malady as nervous, epileptic, insane, raving, and the like. Matthew speaks of the sick who were affected with various distempers and plagues, and then divides these into three classes: 'those possessed with devils, and those which were lunatic, and those that had the palsy' (Matt. iv. 24). But they are distinguished again from the common sick. Mark says, 'Jesus healed many that were sick of divers diseases, and cast out many devils' (i. 34). By these distinctions with which, on the one hand, the Evangelists represent the demoniacs as sick, but on the other, as afflicted by a demon, their conception of the mysterious phenomenon goes beyond the opposition between the supernaturalist and the rationalist views. According to the first, it is asserted, these sufferers were possessed by demons, therefore they were not naturally sick. Then on the other side it is said, they were naturally sick, therefore not possessed by demons. The arguing on both sides may be thus represented: One party maintains, the wind blows into the chamber, therefore the window is not open; the other asserts, on the contrary, the window stands open, therefore the wind does not blow into the chamber.

Here we must revert to the doctrine we have stated above, of the infinitely delicate operation of ethical powers. As it is applicable to the doctrine of angels and of devils, so also to that of demons. The popular view of the material, plastic lodgment of one demon or more in the body of a possessed person is sensuously coarse; but hardly so much so as the opposite supposition, that a man is afflicted with a natural nervous disorder, and on that account does not lie under demoniacal influences. There are hereditary nervous disorders, mysterious obstructions of the psychical life; strange dissonances and disturbances enter into the course of life which have this common quality, that they more or less affect the freedom of man's ethical life. If he could be healthy in this want of freedom, he would go back to the pure instinct of animal life. But such a normal human-animal life would be, in its very naturalness, a frightful monstrosity.

Sure enough, man without freedom must become in his untuned, irritable nerve-life, more or less a foot-ball of ethical influences, as necessarily as an Æolian harp placed in a current of air must receive and return every wandering gust of wind. But the irritability of such a morbid nerve-life, according to the nature of this life, must be simply boundless. Fortunately, under the category of those who were afflicted with divers diseases, the lunatics are found between the possessed and the paralytic. The nature of this complaint may give us the key for the solution of the whole problem respecting the demoniacs. The lunatic is so excitable in his nerve-life, that even the influence of the returning moon irritates him and aggravates his malady. He is, in short, possessed by the moon, inasmuch as he is possessed by its influence. We will not here inquire what power the spirit of the earth (*Erdgeist*) exerts over the healthy man in his sleep, but so much is a fact of very ancient experience, that the moon exerts an irritating influence on a certain class of nervous sufferers. With this remark the whole question is in fact already decided. If the moon can exert so strong an influence on these morbidly excitable chords, which in the normal man are designed to return the pure impression of all heaven, we must much more expect that they will be exposed to the strongest influences and invasions of psychical moods, powers, and intentions. The sick youth whom the Lord cured at the foot of the Mount of Transfiguration was at once epileptic, demoniac, and lunatic; therefore, a person disordered in his nerves, disturbed by the influence of the moon as well as by that of demons.

Yet it is a consideration of great weight, that the excitability of these nervous patients was a consequence of a deeply seated discordance, and therefore was a morbid, gloomy excitability. Hence an elective affinity was formed between this susceptibility and the impure influences of impure spirits. The prophets, as the elect of God, were in the highest degree susceptible for the revelations of the world of light; the demoniacs, on the other hand, presented an inverted prophetic order, which attained its disastrous maturity in the days of the deepest degeneracy of the Jewish nation, when their psychical susceptibility for evil influences was complete. And, accordingly, they were pervaded and domineered over by unclean spirits, by the psychically powerful influences of an evil nature—by demons; but, according to their declaration and the popular notion, they were possessed by them. This condition, therefore, has three factors, which must be estimated conjointly: first of all, the natural substratum of possession, the morbid state of the nerves; then the aggregate power of the influences to which the patient is subjected; lastly, and thirdly, his notion of his own sufferings, which was closely connected with the general popular notion of such sufferings. That natural foundation of possession, the morbid state of the nerves in demoniacs, has many forms and stages. We find, for example, one demoniac like a seer, proclaiming the Messiah, while another is unable to utter a word. Sometimes this disorder appears as a stupid frenzy, impelling to self-destruction; the demoniac throws himself now into the fire, now into the water: at another time it is a spectral illusion; the demoniac is so excited, that he believes himself identified with a legion of evil spirits. But as the irritability was constituted, the influences corresponded to it. The Gadarene might, therefore, be really forced in his irritability to exhibit a thousand-fold different operations of evil. These influences, according to their nature, might proceed from spirits of all kinds, as far as they could exercise an overwhelming influence on his psychical life by a powerful psychical influence, by violent approximation, by vigorous attack, by a peculiar affinity between their power and the susceptibility of the sufferer. The demoniac influences might therefore proceed from devilish spirits, from deceased men, or even from living, powerful and sinister characters; for in this case everything depends on the power and nature of the influences. Further, they might differ in their degree: disturbances, superficial, transitory and constant, weak and strong, distant and near, or in absolute contact. If there are fallen devilish spirits, as we have found to be natural, we are led to expect that the lower class among them busy themselves in producing disturbed phenomena in the region of human misery. If, moreover, earthly and worldly-minded deceased persons strive to return to a life on earth, it is by no means inconceivable that they should seek to put themselves again in connection with the world they have lost through the organisms of those who are not free. The Jews generally recoiled with horror from Sheol. This aversion to the kingdom of the dead was especially rife in

the time of Christ, when the chiliast extravagance was at its
height. The degeneracy of the times might show itself also in
this particularly, that the boundary line between this side the
grave and the other had vanished in a most fearful manner,
since the living were in part fallen to the kingdom of the shades,
while the demons swarmed in unsatisfied craving for life about
the hearths of the living, so that a kind of marsh-land was
formed between this world and the next, in which the deformed
of both regions mingled together. The demons, indeed, in
their influence on the sufferers, could traverse from the most
remote distance to the closest proximity. But it is difficult to
determine to what degree the oppression of the sufferers by the
demons might rise. Yet we cannot get rid of all spirits from
the other world, without losing the notion of possession. And
characters of an evil tendency belonging to this world might
operate injuriously on the life of men psychically diseased. But
these evils were carried to their height by the popular superstition. The doctrine of possession was completed in the popular
dread. The consequence was, that those who personally experienced demoniacal influences soon surrendered themselves with
dismay to their power, and then exhibited it plastically with all
the energy of a spectre-haunted soul. If insanity is contemplated in its simplest form, it shows here the characteristic that
the insane person makes his fixed idea the demon of his consciousness, and speaks out, not from his rational consciousness,
but from this demoniacal one. There is no difficulty, therefore,
in conceiving that demoniacs in general speak from the consciousness of the spirits that torment them. But from such a
phenomenon, it by no means follows that the foreign spirit in
them has lodged itself between their own consciousness and
their body, and thus as a stranger speaks out of a strange house.
Rather, we only see that the demoniac has slavishly surrendered
himself to the influence that torments him. As the prophet, in
the most elevated, luminous, and free ecstasy, announces the
word of the Lord, without distinguishing it from his own—probably, not because his own consciousness has vanished, but because it is identical with the Spirit of the Lord, and acts in
subserviency to it—so also is it with the demoniac, in his en-
slaved and gloomy ecstasy. He himself speaks, though he has
made over his *Ego* and his consciousness to the spirits who

rule him. His consciousness has identified itself with the demoniacal influence which he has imbibed from them, and exhibits it plastically and imitatively in a constrained visionary mood. Only from this state of things can the dark but powerful feeling of deranged life be explained, as is shown by the violent excitement of the demoniacs in the presence of Christ. If the consciousness of a demon itself had been fully active in the organism of the demoniac of which it had taken possession, such symptoms could not have been exhibited; and as little could they have been shown if the patient had not really had the feeling, as if a strange spirit stood before the Lord.

It is very evident from the nature of this condition, that it must be distinguished altogether from those cases in which a man gives himself up to evil in conscious and specific acts of his own inner life. The Gospel history marks the distinction in the most decisive manner, since, as we have seen, it treats the demoniacs as sick persons, and even as irresponsible, which is plainly shown, among many other things, by the representation of their irregularities as acts which the demons performed with them. The early Church also made a marked distinction between reckless sinners and possessed persons : the former they excommunicated, for the latter they employed exorcisms. The mingling of these ethical characters, as it appears in the most offensive excess, when exorcism was connected with baptism, and as it still often occurs in theological treatises on the condition of demoniacs, serves most decidedly to obscure our discernment of the ethical deterioration of man into the devilish as well as of demoniacal possession. Olshausen has felt the existence of the distinction, but has not clearly carried it out (*Comment.* i. 269, Ed. Clark). 'The condition of demoniacs must always presuppose a certain degree of moral culpability; yet so that the sin committed by them does not take the form of absolute wickedness (that is, a voluntary consent to the infused evil thoughts), but appears more as predominant sensuality (especially unchastity), which was always indulged with a resistance of the better self.' Nothing can be made of these distinctions. Of the practical offences of the demoniacs we know nothing, and are not in the least justified in charging, for example, the daughter of the Canaanitish woman with sins of that class. Although it cannot be denied that the condition of demoniacs might originate in individuals from personal offences, from irregularities which opened the door for the demon into the psychical life; yet these sick persons, taken at an average, form a poor little group, which in part even from childhood found themselves under a psychical ban. And so it was with the demons by whom they were tormented. They were regarded by the Jews as inferior devils, or impure spirits that had been forfeited to Beelzebub, since they cherished the notion that they might be expelled by the help of Beelzebub. The most different states and characters are also confounded, when the spheres of demoniacal suffering and of demoniacal acting are not kept distinct. But in order to hold fast this distinction, we must take care to observe that many symbolical expressions are found in the Gospel history, which are borrowed from the sphere of demoniacal suffering, to designate purely ethical relations. To this class apparently belongs the language which John uses of Judas, after he had received the sop from Jesus at the Passover, that '*Satan entered into him*' (John xiii. 27). We might also be disposed to adduce here the account given of Mary Magdalene, that the Lord cast seven devils out of her (Mark xvi. 9), since it is not probable that we are to reckon literally seven distinct demoniacal possessions or psychical enthralments, and from such a reckoning draw a precise and definite conclusion. Add to this, the number seven denotes in a significant manner, not only the extreme generally, but also the extreme of self-activity.[1] The seven unclean spirits remind us, by contrast, of the seven spirits of God. And as these spirits denote the one Holy Spirit in His fulness and agency, so the seven devils may denote the impure spirit of the world in its collective power and activity. And as Christ, by having the consecration of the seven spirits, is distinguished as moving freely in the life of the Holy Spirit, so the possession of seven demons might distinguish the ethically culpable, and therefore metaphorical, possession of an erring soul that was completely under the power of the spirit of the world. According to the Evangelist Luke (viii. 2), the Lord was accompanied in His journeys by 'certain women, which had been healed of evil spirits and infirmities, Mary Magdalene, out of whom went seven devils (δαιμόνια ἑπτά), and Joanna the wife of Chuza, Herod's steward, and Susanna, and many others,

[1] Compare Matt. xviii. 21.

which ministered to Him of their substance.' If into such a group of females, containing one, or several, whom Jesus had freed from demoniacal suffering, a convert entered whom Jesus had rescued from the heavy curse of sin, it is very probable that, in accordance with the prevalent Jewish notions, she would express her gratitude by saying that He had cast seven devils out of her.[1] This explanation is confirmed by Christ's parabolic discourse, in which He represents to the Jews the condition in which they were as most perilous, by the phenomena of demoniacal suffering (Matt. xii. 43, compared with Luke xi. 24). 'When the unclean spirit is gone out of a man, he walketh through dry places, seeking rest and finding none. Then he saith, I will return into my house from whence I came out; and when he is come, he findeth it empty, swept, and garnished. Then goeth he, and taketh with himself seven other spirits more wicked than himself, and they enter in and dwell there; and the last state of that man is worse than the first. Even so shall it be also unto this wicked generation.'

This discourse, if we look at the connection, seems to be neither wholly figurative, nor wholly literal. Jesus had just before cast out a demon from a sick man (Matt. xii. 22). But when the Pharisees reproached Him as casting out devils by Beelzebub, that demon seemed to come back with seven others and insolently to confront Him, as if in mockery of His former victory. Jesus found in this an image of His whole ministry in Israel. Everywhere He expelled the single demon of psychical suffering from among the people; but everywhere it returned again with the seven demons of blaspheming unbelief.[2] The

---

[1] Hence tradition has more weighty reason for regarding this Mary as the great sinner (Luke vii. 36-50), than the circumstance that the woman who anointed the Lord at Bethany is also called Mary. According to Winer, the designation of 'the woman who was a sinner' as Mary Magdalene arose from confounding the history in Luke vii. 36 with John xii. 1.

[2] That the Lord, by the words (Luke xi. 23), 'He that is not with Me is against Me,' etc., designed to point out the cures of the common Jewish exorcists as merely apparent, which rather injured than promoted the kingdom of God, as Neander thinks, is not supported by the connection. For Christ had no conflict with the exorcists, but with the blasphemers who stood before Him. These came against Him as His enemies, as sevenfold possessed, who wished to annihilate His work. The Lord also could not well dispute the genuineness of the cures performed by the Jewish exorcists,

demon appears here with the number seven, and therefore as the demon of free conscious culpability, of the vilest depravity. It is highly significant, and quite in accordance with the Gospel history, to represent those direful demoniacal sufferings as sevenfold less than the wretchedness of demoniacal criminality.

From this metaphorical mode of speaking, with which Christ treated of demoniacal relations, it does not follow, that He adopted by way of accommodation the general opinions of His time respecting the true demoniacal nature of the sufferings of the possessed. That He shared in these opinions, His whole treatment and estimate of these phenomena testifies, which always remained the same in the private conversations He held with His disciples respecting them (Matt. xvii. 21). Strauss therefore is quite justified in ascribing these opinions to the Lord (ii. 7). But from this we are not justified in affirming, that Jesus shared in the sensuous representations of the people respecting the corporeal nature of these demoniacal possessions, as the same writer also maintains. The very connection of the phenomena of demoniac suffering with those of demoniac action, as the Lord understood it, proves that in the possessions He had recognised the psychical element, the relation between suffering and ethical self-activity. We may draw, however, the same conclusion in a special manner from His mode of healing.

As far as we can trace and judge of the moral state in the obscure circumstances of the possessed, the chief feature that strikes us is the moral despondency, the abject flinching and trembling before the assailing hostile power, whether this arose from the demoniac fixed ideas of the sufferers, or from individual demoniacal influences. This abject bearing cannot avoid showing itself in some way or other, so as to afford a glimpse of the moral state of the soul, even in cases where the demoniac is born in the soul-slavery of a disordered state of the nerves. At all events, it appears as the first step in healing the demoniacs, that Jesus crushed at a blow this despondency of the demonized consciousness. He crushed it, namely, by the manner in which He addressed the demon. He set spiritual power against spiritual power, the stronger against the weaker. With a lion's spring He made Himself master of His prey. With one divine, deter-

as far as they were viewed in their psychical limitation, at the very instant, when He appealed to them.

mined wrench, He released the captive soul from its thrall. But this, according to the nature of the case, could only take place by the impartation of His own power to it. His power was shed upon the sufferers when He threatened the demons by His crushing rebuke. The style in which Christ addressed men had always a tone of kingly decision; it was the expression of heavenly power and certainty. By the forcible impression which these brief winged words of command uttered by the Lord made on the souls of men, they have fixed themselves in the Gospel tradition with unchangeable freshness. But it is obvious that Christ, in this method of throwing fire with His words into the soul, made a specific difference between the sorrowful and the despairing. The sorrowful He consoled with all the miraculous tone of a heavenly sympathy: the burdened sinner, for example, He consoled with the words, 'My son! thy sins are forgiven thee!' the woman suffering from the issue of blood with, 'Be of good cheer, My daughter!' Mary Magdalene with the exclamation, 'Mary!' and others in different ways. And here it must be remarked, that the modern philanthropic but enervated treatment of souls has made a great mistake, in placing the despairing in the same category with the sorrowful, and attempting to revive them by consolations. They require a very different treatment: they must be roused to regain their self-possession by words of severity; they need the influences and quickening utterances of glowing, impassioned power. The thunder and lightning of a saintly soul, which can rebuke them as with the flames of divine wrath, restores to them that power which feebler addresses could never give. Indeed, only the pure spirit of Christ can properly discharge this office of rebuke.[1] Christ was the Master also in this art of curing souls. Not only did He in this manner restore demoniacs, but all who either temporarily or constantly were unmanned by dejection. Thus He rebukes the disciples when they lost their self-command in the storm; He rebuked the fever of Peter's wife's mother (Luke iv. 39); and exclaimed in the synagogue to the woman bowed down by a spirit of infirmity, 'Woman! thou art loosed from thine infirmity' (Luke xiii. 12),—He dispersed immediately her despondency, the spirit of her weakness, by His word, and then, by lay-

---

[1] [See Isaac Taylor's *Saturday Evening*, Essay xv. *The Power of Rebuke.* —Tr.]

ing His hands on her, healed her bodily infirmity. This last example leads us to consider the manner in which Jesus especially treated demoniacs. How glorious the royal Prince of spirits appears among them with these master-words of rebuking love! 'He cast out the spirits with a word,' says Matthew (viii. 16). 'He straitly charged them' says Mark, 'that they should not make Him known' (iii. 12). To the possessed in the synagogue at Capernaum He cried out, 'Hold thy peace and come out of him.' Probably the command, 'Come out!' was re-echoed in the soul, as the Lord in such cases injected it as a divine power into the consciousness of the sick man, and the first act of his reawakened freedom consisted precisely in this, that he repeated the word in his own soul, 'Come out!' In this state of captivity the possessed was one with the demon, and spoke out of the consciousness of the demon; therefore the Lord also addressed the demon that was in him. But in the moment of his release he became one with the Lord, and the word which the Lord thundered against the demon he himself addressed to him. If we rely on the exactness of the order of the particulars in the account of Mark (v. 7) and of Luke (viii. 29), the memorable case here occurred, that the demoniac was not at once healed after the Lord had spoken the decisive word. Christ had said to him, 'Come out of the man, thou unclean spirit!' The demoniac consciousness in this man was now indeed shaken to its foundations; but as he felt himself possessed by a legion of evil spirits, the demoniacal within him was not quite reached by the address in the singular. Christ saw at once how the cure was to be completed. He asked him for his name. 'What is thy name?' He answered, 'My name is Legion, for we are many.' But from this insolent raving of his demoniac consciousness the contradiction already glanced forth: the prostration of spirit which had shown itself in the very circumstance of his running to meet the Lord. The demons now asked permission to go into a herd of swine, of which we shall speak hereafter. Matthew's word, 'Go!' seems to have been here the authentic and decisive word of the Lord, which echoed in the soul of the possessed, 'Go!' The rebuke with which Christ met the crowd, who were waiting for Him at the foot of the Mount of Transfiguration, is very characteristic. Here was a spiritual battle to be won again, which His disciples had lost from a want of a more rigorous self-discipline in prayer and fasting. The spirit of despondency which had mastered the whole circle by the unexpected failure, was to be expelled. The Lord was sensible of this psychical obstruction, and removed it by a powerful rebuke. He then made a path for the communication of His miraculous power by strengthening the heart of the father of the unfortunate youth. Then followed the healing word of power. In the crisis of such a cure, the most violent change came over the sufferer in an instant. His consciousness sprang up, so to speak, from the abyss to the heights of heaven. It was natural for the cure to end in a final dreadful paroxysm. The sick man at Capernaum cried out aloud when the divine voice of deliverance pealed like thunder through his soul. In the instance before us, the sufferer became fearfully agitated and fell to the earth as dead; a second miracle was needed, which Christ performed when He took him by the hand and lifted him up.

It is scarcely necessary to call attention to the fact, that all these narratives of miraculous cures bear a decided impress of individuality and the noblest stamp of internal truth.

But in what degree these cures were complete, we see from the language of the restored Gadarene. When his countrymen desired Jesus to depart out of their coasts, he requested that he might be allowed to accompany Him. Though a legion of evil spirits had before haunted him, his consciousness was now firmly fixed in free devoted surrender to the one Spirit of light, whose power had rescued him and become master of his soul.

The whole category of the Lord's miraculous cures serves to exhibit the dominion of His Spirit over the flesh, since their effect was to re-establish the dominion of the human spirit over morbid corporeity, and its victory over the influences of the powers of evil. The liberation of human spirits, and their restoration to health by the blessing of the Spirit, as it goes on to the end of the world, and has its basis in the power of Christ's Spirit and in His victory, exhibited its first blossoms in the miraculous cures. But we now enter on a new circle of miracles. We see the first signs of the spiritual glory of Christ, which is to transform the earthly sphere of this lower world. To this class belong, as the clearest and most distinct signs, the great miracles which Christ performed on the mental states of men. As such, we consider most decidedly the miracle at Cana and those of feeding the multitudes. The key to these truly heavenly facts is wanting when the mental state of the guests of Jesus is left unnoticed, and as much attention is lavished on the elements, as if we had merely to do with bread-baskets and wine-jars. When Jesus made provision for a circle of friends, or for thousands of His adherents, the question is of the highest importance, what influence He exerted on their souls. Now we know He was never disposed to gain adherents by violent or over-persuasive urgency. The Son makes those free whom His Spirit takes captive. He could only by slow degrees establish the heavenly kingdom of Christian dispositions, because He mingled His life with the life of the world through the medium of the holiest tenderness, or through the tenderest holiness. But a heavenly kingdom of states of feeling He could at once call forth, by virtue of that captivating spiritual power with which His personality operated on susceptible souls. Such souls, by the power of His divine spirit which inspired them, and by the glow of sympathy which ravished them when once touched, He could raise for some moments to heaven, and transport into a common frame of divine joy, peace, and love, in which life appeared as new, and the world as transformed. Such foretastes of heaven make their appearance throughout the whole Gospel history. But the difference must be lost sight of between transient moods and permanent dispositions, between occasional flights of excited feeling and the constant soaring of the spirit, when it is thought strange that many of those whom Christ had borne upwards in a favourable hour, should relapse into common or even evil tendencies,—that the majority, or even all, at times should fall away. And it would argue ignorance of the spirit of Christ, if we were to expect that He would not venture so boldly to call forth the flowers of the new life, because He knew that these flowers would for a long while have no fruits. But we find sufficient indications of the miraculous elevation of men's souls in events of this kind, and of the connection of these miraculous transactions with these miraculous states of mind. On the occasion of the marriage at Cana, for the first time in the history of the world a Christian assemblage for festive purpose took place in the presence of Christ. The mother of Jesus is full of great and anxious, and yet joyful forebodings; she communicates her state of mind to the servants of the family, who are imbued

with the greatest confidence in the words of Jesus. They fill
the water-pots—they bring the beverage at His bidding with
perfect readiness. Meanwhile the company are so occupied with
their conviviality, that they know not what has transpired outside.
But the wine they are now drinking at the height of the feast
is pronounced even by the governor of the feast to be as good
as, or better than, what had been drunk before. In the element
of a singular state of mind, in which the wedding guests had
become one as branches with the true vine, with Christ as the
principle of the world's transformation, the water becomes
changed for them into wine. We have here to do with the
operations of a higher ethical ecstasy—with the operations of a
very beautiful but extraordinary state of mind, in which the
festive Jews find themselves transported, by the power of Christ's
Spirit, from the beginnings of the world to the heights of the
transformed world. The drink which they quaff in this state
of mind, being blessed to them by the presence of Christ, is to
their taste the choicest wine. Thus they enjoy it not in mere
spiritualistic fancy, but with the most real gust.[1] But how it

[1] We can represent to ourselves Christ's agency which changed water
into wine in successive stages. From the history of Somnambulism, it is
known that in the high degrees of the magnetic *rapport*, all the sensations
and tastes of the magnetizer are repeated in the person who is psychically
affected by him. Now at Cana there was no circle of magnetized persons
assembled round the Lord, but a circle of souls whom His presence had raised
to ecstasy in their festivity. What therefore in the department of magnetism may appear as a fact, might here recur with intensified power, and in
a more vitalized form (as, for example, the constrained morbid clairvoyance of
the somnambulist in the free healthy clairvoyance of the prophet). When
therefore Christ calls forth in Himself the intuition (*Anschauung*) of wine
with fresh creative power, when Christ drinks good wine, the others drink
it also by means of the psychical connection. But the company that surrounds the Lord is not a mere circle of passive, receptive beings. His companions are by faith brought into active harmony with Him. As the
branches do not merely receive the sap which the vine conveys to them, but
form the wine out of it and with it, so these festive guests, at the moment of
their union with the Lord, infused all their plastic life-power in order to
complete the change. This is the first stage of the immediate operation of
Christ. But the second goes into the elements of the beverage which they
enjoy. And here we would call to mind the taste of magnetized water, only
to indicate again how, in a higher life-circle, the same phenomenon may be
repeated in a higher key. ' The taste of magnetized water,' says Fr. Fischer
(*Der Sonambulismus*, p. 235), ' is said to be exceedingly various ; sometimes
bitter, sometimes sweetish, sometimes sourish like Seltzer water, sometimes

was with the supply of wine outside of the highly vitalized sphere
of the feast, would be a question of the same kind as what transformation (Verklärung) remained in the consecrated bread outside the holy sphere of the actual celebration of the Supper.
Also the miracle of feeding a multitude, which, without pre-
judging, we here consider as having occurred twice, was evidently
effected by a state of mind allied to His own in the guests of
Jesus. The confidence with which He announced that He was
about to feed the thousands, and even the thought of this feeding, was so new a revelation of the kingdom of love and confidence, that the souls of those who had once followed Him as
His adherents into the wilderness, were elevated by this event
far above their ordinary state of feeling. They sat down at His
word, and their doing so indicated an exceedingly high and
powerful elevation of their feelings. But it is an acknowledged
fact, that impassioned expectation and joy can be propagated
electrically and with augmented force among thousands. After
the first miracle of feeding, those who had partaken of the
food wished to make the Lord king,—a proof that they had
celebrated a feast in the highest pitch of theocratic enthusiasm.
In those moments the heavenly power of Christ could feed its
thousands miraculously. His word alone had already strength-
ened them afresh, to say nothing of the word in connection with
the natural means. Thus the feeding so as to satisfy them is
explained,—but not the overplus, the baskets-full of fragments.
On this point it makes a great difference, whether we are inclined to see an Old Testament feast of loving omnipotence, or
a New Testament one of omnipotent love. This remark requires
further explanation. That among the guests of Jesus many
were destitute of food, is certain, and the whole multitude were
in danger of suffering the pains of hunger. But it appears incredible, if we take into account the Jewish method of travelling
and making pilgrimages, that many of these pilgrims should not
have carried with them a supply of provisions, greater or less.
On these supplies, indeed, the Lord would not wish first of all
to reckon. The miracle of feeding and of satisfying which He
undertook, was quite independent of such supplies. But it could

strong and vinous, sometimes burning, sometimes tart like sulphur and ink,
sometimes saltish. But it shows a certain constancy in one and the same
magnetizer.'

as little on that account be His concern to fill a multitude of
baskets with fragments, over and above what was eaten. Now
if such provisions are presupposed, we may be inclined to take
the following view of the transaction. Christ feeds the thousands exclusively with the substance of His own bread. But
those among these thousands who really had provisions, would
hold them absolutely in reserve for themselves. Their hearts
therefore remained closed, their private property remained like
a fixture by their side ; while Christ gives up everything, and the
poor among them take their share of the distributed bread. Even
in collecting the fragments, their gifts in bread do not add to the
amount. Evidently, on such a supposition, the power of Christ
is glorified at the cost of the operation of His love ; and the dark
miracle of the unheard-of, selfish reserve of the multitude hanging
on the lips of Jesus, confronts the direct, exalted miracle of benevolent omnipotence. But if we are desirous of commemorating
the founding of a New Testament feast, a heavenly bloom of
social life, in the miraculous feeding, we must above all things
feel how the hearts of the guests of Jesus thawed under His
festive invitation and thanksgiving—how they were rendered
great, warm, free, and brotherly, so that no one would keep his
bread for himself, while he enjoyed likewise that of his brother.
Thus we gain two splendid miracles of omnipotent love, which
in the warmth of the moment form one—Christ feeds thousands
with His little stock by an operation of heavenly power.[1] But
this feeding, as an operation of love, opens their hearts, and forms
a pre-celebration of the final transformation of the world in the
blessedness of Christian brotherly love—a pre-celebration of the
Christian voluntary community of goods ; and thus the second
miracle takes place, the miracle of superabundance among the
thousands of the poor people in the wilderness.

[1] It will be evident that the explanation of the miracle here given, refers
to the natural explanation which Dr Paulus has given (*Leben Jesu* ii. 162).
But those who rightly apprehend our explanation, cannot fail to perceive
the difference between it and the natural explanation. We regard the
miracle of feeding and satisfying in its whole integrity as an operation of
the power of Christ, which converts the existing means of feeding into the
medium of a divine living power. In that case, the secondary miracle of the
overplus is kept in view, and explained as above. We shall notice in the
sequel the expressions in the Gospels which, according to Strauss (*Leben
Jesu* ii. 197), militate against this view.

It has been justly observed, that in these miracles we may
descry a foreshadowing of the Holy Supper. Certainly the
guests of Jesus were communicants as to the state of their
feelings, though not in developed and ripened Christian insight.
In the communion, wine is always poured out for those who
partake of it, which has the power and significance of His blood,
and bread is broken, which is received and experienced as the
life and action of His body. But in the consecrated circle of
the communion a thousand mysterious experiences occur, experiences of strengthening and refreshment, and even of exaltation to heaven, which are intimately allied to those miracles of
the Lord which affected men's states of mind, and allied not
merely in reference to their special origin, the living power of
Christ's heart, but also in reference to their final aim, the
transformation of the world. Those miracles, as well as the
permanent blessings of Christ in the Holy Supper, may be regarded as foreshadowings of the coming transformation of the
world.

Attempts have been made to throw suspicions on the miracle
at Cana by designating it 'a miracle of luxury.' Criticism
resolves to do anything for the sake of gaining its object, even
to put on pietist airs. But the spirit of Christ is perfectly self-
consistent when it treats the higher modes of want—as, for
example, the worrying perplexity of a new-married couple,
whose wedding is likely to end in ridicule and vexation for
lack of wine—with the same sympathy as the lower modes.
The anointing which Mary performed at Bethany in honour
of the Lord, of whose departure she had a presentiment, also
appeared a work of luxury; but the Lord protected His female
disciple against the attacks of those disciples who thought that
the cost of the ointment should rather be given to the poor.
Christianity will never allow itself to be changed into a mere
hospital or alms-house, but in its spirit and aim always tends to
the pure luxury of freeing and transforming the life, apart from
the beautiful festive ideal manifestation of the spirit. A sickly
spiritualism can accommodate itself only to the coarse natural
constitution of the present phenomenal world; the entire new
world, on the other hand, which is to bloom forth from the
living power of Christianity, and more especially the resurrection of the dead, appears to it as an extravagant luxury of Chris-

tian hope. But the Christian spirit cannot despair of the
eternal unity between the idea and the life, and therefore expects
that all Christian principles will one day celebrate their appearance in the reality, in the full splendour of the idea; and it
descries the foreshadowings of this future transformation in the
'miracles of luxury,' as they meet it, not merely in the marriage
feast at Cana, or in the miraculous feeding of the multitude,
but also in that quelling of the storm which Jesus effected, and
in the miraculous draught of fishes which He caused.

In the history of the kingdom of God there is one class of
miracles which may be called miracles of theocratic parallelism,
—those, namely, in which the inner relation between the life of
the earth and the life of humanity is exhibited in the most striking manner. Those persons who have not perceived, or who
deny, this parallelism in the development of the corporeal and
spiritual side of the current æon, and the coincidence of the
great phases of development both inward and outward, should
not venture to say anything about the supremacy of the idea, and
about the ideality of the world. The Theocracy corrects their
dualism. The majority of the miracles in the Old Testament
history belong to this class of parallel miracles. A great phase
in the history of the earth or the universe coincides with a great
phase in the history of the kingdom of God; and indeed the
former is subservient to the latter, just as reasonably as the
earth is subservient to man, or as the history of the universe is
subservient to the history of spiritual life. Thus, for example,
the plagues of Egypt coincide with the event of the redemption
of Israel from Egyptian bondage; and the moment in which
Israel, pursued by Pharaoh, reached the shores of the Red Sea,
was the same in which a singular natural phenomenon dried
the bed of the sea. The theocratic spirit justly explains the
coincidence of these events as proceeding from God's ordination; it marks it in true dignity of spirit as an operation, a fruit
and consequence of its faith. But like the prophetic spirit,
before the moment of the miracle arrived in which 'the stars
in their courses fought' for Israel, it had an inspired presentiment of it, and therefore announced it beforehand. It need
not in the least perplex us when those miracles of parallelism
come forward in giant forms. Nature always confronts man
as a giant power, and yet bends before his spirit and becomes

subservient to him with all her powers. It is a tacit, eternal
miracle, that man, this naked, defenceless creature, bound to
the earth, shivering in the blast, trembling in the water, dissolving in the heat, standing defenceless amidst a thousand armed
warlike hosts of the brute creation,—this child that 'plays on
the hole of the asp, and puts his hand on the cockatrice's den'
(Isa. xi. 8),—this Daniel in the lions' den,—that he in the
power of the spirit gains even a more decided ascendancy over
nature, even releases it from its own captivity, since he brings
its essence to light, and compels its action into the service of the
spirit. This silent miracle has its great festive hours—world-
historical Sundays—on which the giant spirit of Nature comes
in a critical moment to the aid of the embarrassed divine man
as an elephant to its master's child,—when the course of Nature
unfolds the consecrated, holy tendency of its movements, its
silent concurrence with the course of the kingdom of God, in
clear, grand signs. It is the triumph of Revelation that it has
explained these signs, and with their explanation has declared
the unity of the course of the world in its successive æons in the
life of Nature and of man. These parallel miracles also reappear more strikingly in the history of the apostles; the young
Church needed the service of the giantess, Nature, who recognised in the former the beginning and pledge of her own glorification. In the history of the life of Jesus the parallel miracles
are less conspicuous, because in Him perfected life was manifested, and therefore the glorification of Nature by the Spirit;
the elevation of the parallelism between the life of Nature and
the life of the Spirit into a living unity. Besides the wonderful
events at the death and resurrection of Jesus, which we shall
notice in the sequel, we may regard the stilling of the storm on
the Sea of Galilee as a miracle in which that parallelism appears
and finds its solution. We cannot estimate too highly the world-
historical importance of that hour, when the whole New Testament Church in its embryo life, the entire living power and
spiritual quintessence of the Old Testament theocracy, after
being rescued from a thousand perils by great miracles—in which
therefore the hopes of humanity were enclosed in a paltry fishing-
boat on the Galilean sea—were in the greatest danger of being
swallowed up by the waves. Here also Nature seems to have
presented her dark side—she seemed to rave like a demon savage,

and to aim at swallowing up the noblest life—life absolute. But Christ did not take the storm on this side : the awful agitation alarmed Him not ; it rocked Him to sleep. And when the alarm awoke Him, He found it necessary, first of all, to rebuke the storm in the hearts of His disciples.[1] Storm against storm : He rebuked them till they were ashamed; deeply calmed in spirit, they looked on the storm with new eyes. With this alteration in the state of their minds, the storm must at once have seemed to them greatly to abate its fury. Then He rebuked the wind and the sea. But the wind and the waves are not hostile spiritual powers in His presence; so that what He uttered was not so much an address as a prophetic annunciation, and a mysterious symbolic act. The proximate cause of the stilling of the wind and waves lay in the atmosphere ; and so far was the miracle a parallel one, and the rebuking word of Jesus prophetic. But the ultimate cause of the extraordinary hushing of the elements lay in the life and·feelings of the God-man. To Him it was certain that the apparently monstrous independence thus confronting the human spirit exhibited only an apparent outbreak, in which the actual outbreak of man was reflected and punished ; that therefore this independence of Nature must be abolished in His spirit-life, and must be abolished for the world. This abolition He carried into effect by a symbolical act, the essence of which is a mystery of His deepest life. From the depths of His divine consciousness, of His eternity, He caused the fact to come forth in a miracle, that the spirit of solemn repose in His life put an end to the morbid agitations of Nature. He represented in a symbolical act this quiet operation of the Christian life of humanity, the ripe product of which is to be unfolded in the sabbatical peace of the new world.[2] The mira-

[1] The Evangelist Matthew seems to us to have reported the event in the correct succession of its several parts, since he places the rebuking of the disciples before the stilling of the storm. Mark and Luke adopt the reverse order.

[2] Strauss finds in the scene of Jesus sleeping in the storm so remarkable a picture, that he thinks, ' If it be so, that what in one instance perhaps really happened, in nine instances must be formed from legends, we must be prepared more rationally for the possibility, that we have here one of these nine instead of that one instance.' We should not venture nine to one in order to gain a mere ' possibility' of winning. And yet the

culous draughts of fish which the disciples made twice by the
direction of the Lord (Luke v. 11 and John xxi. 1-11), presuppose in them neither an omniscience on the part of Christ,
nor a universal sciolism (*allwisserei*) disturbing the divine unity
of His life. The means of putting into exercise the extraordinary knowledge which He displayed on these occasions, lay in
the hearts of the men who were attached to Him. Would He
not notice from a distance the deep, bitter dejection which darkened their souls on account of the total failure of their night's
toil? Nothing in the world could more deeply interest Him
than the state of those souls in which He was desirous of im-
planting His own heavenly life. But when, full of sympathy,
He saw (as it were) through their eyes, and sought after the
fish, he was certainly a sagacious fisherman who could detect the
traces of the fishes in the play of shadows on the watery mirror,
or by similar signs, if we are not disposed to admit that He became aware of their existence by the electrical action of an
immense living shoal crowded together. A modern poet expresses the thought, that if man ever corresponded to his idea,
the birds of heaven would fly to him in flocks. Did the poet
fetch this thought from the Gospels, and only believe that he
must change the fishes to birds? That fishes are less intelligent
than birds, does not incapacitate them for experiencing influences
which are beyond our calculation; rather, indeed, for that very
reason they are taken more readily by the slightest impression,
especially as their life has less of individuality. So there are,
for example, kinds which are enticed and taken at night by the
shining of a light. The myth of the effect of the harp of Arion
on the dolphin points, at all events, to some actual fact,—to an
extraordinary movement of fish which was occasioned by the
magic of human influence. Yet we are not going to start the
question, whether perhaps, in both the instances to which we
refer, the fish had made an irregular movement towards the
shore on which Christ was standing. At all events, the Lord
was certain of His word when He staked His whole authority
with these men on the one draught which they were to make;

game is a scanty one; the evangelical view can be played without imprudence; a thousand to one may be hazarded for the conviction, that here
that which is full of meaning (*das Sinnvolle*) is not legendary but reality;
for Christ is unique among millions.

and the less clearly we can understand whence He obtained this certainty, the more sublime do the life-depths appear of the man, as He must be, the God-man, 'under whose feet (according to Ps. viii.) were placed the fishes of the sea.'

Among the facts recorded in the Gospels which especially harmonize with the transformation of the world by Christ, must be reckoned the capture of the fish which Peter had to make in order to satisfy the persons who demanded the temple-tax of Jesus and himself.[1] The account of this miracle has been considered the most perplexing in the whole Gospel history. Some have imagined that they have detected the narrator in a palpable contradiction, when they have asked how the fish could bite the hook with a stater in its mouth. Criticism, in raptures at this discovery, has bitten more daringly than usual the hook of this narrative; no temple-tax in its mouth has made it too difficult. Though, according to the structure of a fish's mouth, the difficulty in question is not so very great, yet it is not said that Peter would find the stater exactly between the teeth in the mouth of the fish. The opening of the mouth may here be supposed to signify the means of getting down to the lower part of the throat. For a fish to have a piece of money in its mouth is by no means wonderful; for "there are accounts elsewhere of finding fishes that had coins and other valuables in their body."[2] Nor would it be wonderful if Peter had accidentally taken such a fish with a stater in its body. The wonder (or miracle) lies in this, that Jesus distinctly assured Peter beforehand of such a fortunate capture. We need not call to mind the powerful action of metals as experienced by *clairvoyants*, in order to render this miracle in some measure conceivable with all its obscurity; and in order to conjecture how Jesus knew this epicure of a fish that gulped down gold, and was so ready to take the bait. When

---

[1] According to Ex. xxx. 13, every Israelite was to give a half-shekel for the support of the tabernacle. According to Winer, this half-shekel originally (according to the standard of the sanctuary) was not quite four groschen. Josephus in his time valued the whole shekel at four drachms (above 21 groschen). The half-shekel is demanded in the Gospel as a double drachm; and two persons would therefore have to pay four drachms, or one stater. [About three shillings and threepence of English money, according to Smith's *Dict. of Antiq.*; but, according to Jahn, two shillings and sevenpence.]

[2] Strauss, *Leben Jesu* ii. 182.

Jesus found Himself reduced to the sheerest necessity, and when a stater was needed to fulfil an obligation, He learned in the mirror of God's Spirit where it was to be found. He needed only to feel in the depths of the sea in order to obtain the requisite piece of money. But here also too much attention has been paid to the outside of the miracle, and so an obscurity has been cast on the motive. The Lord was reminded by the officers of the temple, through Peter, of the temple-tax. This demand seemed likely to produce a collision, as we may infer from the conversation of Jesus with Peter. According to His essential relation to the temple, He was identical with the spiritual meaning of it; the temple was only a faint outline of that habitation of God which His life exhibited. Or, according to the Israelitish law, the temple was God's fortress, the palace of His Father, and He was the child of the palace. But as His Father's child, He was, of course, free from the tribute which the liege-subjects had to pay to His residence. If, then, Christ paid the temple-tax, He would not only deny the consciousness of His right relation to the temple, but He might confirm these Israelites in the false assumption that He owed tribute to the temple like a Jew who needed the Levitical sacrifice and atonement. Yet, if He did not pay the tribute, He might seem to the officers as if He slighted the law; thus they might either be set against Him or against the law, to their own injury. Therefore they would be offended not only by the non-payment of the tax, but even if Jesus had paid it without hesitation. Neither on this occasion was a loan or a borrowing of friends to be thought of.[1] It is said, 'Lest we should offend them, go thou to the sea,' and then further directions are given; as if it had been said, Let us

---

[1] It can hardly be imagined that in the whole circle of the friends of Jesus at Capernaum so small a sum could be wanting; and if it were there, it would no doubt be at His service without the necessity of borrowing. It is below the dignity of New Testament life when one expositor protests that it would be unbecoming our Lord to borrow the amount from His friends, and when another thinks that there is no difficulty in admitting such a thing. It is the same poverty-struck region which a third has before his eyes, who supposes that Christ took possession of the twelve baskets of fragments as His own private property. What a picture! On the one side, the disciples go off with twelve full bread-baskets, and the Master at their head; and, on the other side, the satisfied people depart without carrying away a fragment of the miraculous meal.

adopt this expedient. Now the stater, in a literal sense, was neither more nor less than a stater though found in the jaws of a fish. The moral effect of the payment would be just the same. But even this Jesus seemed desirous of avoiding. This inner motive of the history is as it were its soul, and must determine its interpretation. Jesus wished, then, to discharge the temple-tax in a shape which allowed its payment to appear as a purely voluntary act. This He attained by presenting a natural object to the tax-gatherers, which with wonderful certainty He had caused to be taken fresh from the sea. According to this view, the expression, 'As soon as thou openest the mouth of the fish, thou shalt find a stater,' may be poetical, and mean, 'As soon as thou hast taken the fish off the hook, thou shalt obtain for it the amount which they expect for Me and thee.' This interpreta-tion would be quite impossible if it were said, 'Thou shalt find a stater in its mouth.' These, however, are not the words. But though this interpretation is possible, it is very forced, since the expression of opening the fish's mouth is a singular one, if it only means taking it off the hook. Moreover, it is said, 'When thou hast opened its mouth, thou shalt *find* a stater.' At all events, thus much is clear, that Jesus could not have intended that Peter was to catch as many fish as would fetch a stater in the market, and then give the amount to the tax-gatherers.[1] The disciple, with the first fish he caught, was to have the value of a stater; it might consist in catching a very large fish, or a rare and valuable one, or, lastly, one with a coin in its mouth. In either case the miracle remains the same. It was precisely the design of Jesus to exhibit His free power by the miraculous form of the deed. It was needful, therefore, for this form to appear to the tax-gatherers as a miracle, which it would if Peter informed them in what an extraordinary manner he obtained the stater. But the transaction would be more striking and free if he gave them a fish that was worth a stater, and informed them that he had drawn it out of the sea for them at the Lord's com-mand. The serene energy and the miraculous insight with which Jesus instantly unravelled a complication of legal and

[1] As Dr Paulus explains the passage (*Leben Jesu* I. ii. 17), the ex-position of the words, 'As soon as thou openest the mouth of the fish, thou shalt find a stater,' as he has given it, might be accepted without denying the miracle.

moral difficulties—the majesty with which He laid His hand on
the great treasury of Nature, that in voluntary love He might
pay a tax—make this 'fabulous specimen of stories about the sea'
appear as the brightest, most delightful gleam of a world of love,
of the most peaceful and calm adjustments, and of the richest
blessings,—of a world such as Christ found by His Spirit, and
as it is destined to appear in the transformation of the earth.

But as the first glorification of Christ was connected with
the prospect of His crucifixion, so the first glorification of the
earth must precede the judgment of the world. We therefore now inquire after that miraculous sign by which the judicial power of Christ's Spirit was directly made known. But
though for all the other constituents of His universal agency
we find a multitude of signs, yet for this great and awful constituent only one is given—*the cursing of the fig-tree.* We need
not say a word to show that it could never enter the Lord's
thoughts to punish a fig-tree, or to vent His displeasure upon it.
The Evangelists, also, were so far from entertaining such a
thought, that it could as little occur to them to guard their account against the misrepresentations of a criticism which would
rather find here the anger of an undisciplined child than the
symbolical significant act of the Saviour of the world. That
the act must have had a symbolical meaning, cannot fail to strike
us. W. Hoffman justly remarks, 'Let us read in Matthew
and Mark what subject chiefly occupied Jesus at that time—
what He said in the temple on the very day of the miracle: it
was an announcement of the final destruction of the Jews, who
had remained an unfruitful tree. Whether or not Jesus had
already spoken of it on the way, the cursing in any case remains
a symbolic act. It signified that, as certainly as the green, leafy
tree withered at the word of the Lord, so certainly would all the
divine threatenings against Israel be fulfilled, though it appeared
at that time to stand in such luxuriant growth.'[1] In those days
Jesus foretold unheard-of judgments—how they would come

[1] ['Not in the display of arbitrary power, for He had silenced the solicitations of the tempter; not in the pressure of personal need, for this was
forgotten at the well-side of Samaria; but in terrible justice He spoke
the words of condemnation. As He entered into Jerusalem, parable and
miracle were combined in one work of judgment.' Westcott, *Miracles*, p.
24.—ED.]

on Jerusalem, on the land of Judea, and indeed on the whóle earth—how they would come in His name, in retribution of their wanton rejection of Him, but also as a necessary purification of the world before the event of the resurrection. As the Prophet of judgment, He walked with profound sorrow among His disciples, filled with the thoughts of the coming judgments, while they could not give up the expectation of a transformation of the world without the preliminary terrors and sentences of judgment. They needed, therefore, a sign. Elijah might have devoted for the purpose part of the city of Jerusalem; Christ selected a tree. Criticism in vain assumes here the air of a forester or a gardener, and declaims about the injury done to the tree. With equal right the Lord might be made accountable for the destruction of Jerusalem. No curse is fulfilled without the co-operation of the sovereign God with the foretelling prophet. The Lord was hungry, and the tree seemed to invite Him by its abundant foliage. He went up to it, if perchance He might find some fruit, if only a single fig, upon it; but in vain: there was nothing but leaves. *For it was not a good year for figs.*[1] Then Jesus uttered the words, 'Let no fruit grow on thee henceforth for ever.' The next day the tree was found withered. This miracle was a prognostic of that melancholy drought through the land which began some ten years after, during which the palm-trees disappeared, the fig-trees withered, and the springs were dried up. But how did Christ effect this miracle? When, at a later period, Peter's rebuke fell on Ananias like a flash of lightning, the explanation is obvious—that it struck the conscience of Ananias with deadly energy. But by what medium could this word of Christ pass through the tree and blast it in all its parts? In order to form

---

[1] 'Of figs, which were an important article of food, three kinds were known in the East: (i.) the early fig, which was ripe at the end of June (perhaps still earlier about Jerusalem); (ii.) the summer-fig (Kermoos), which ripens in August; (iii.) the winter-fig, a late Kermoos, which ripens after the tree has shed its leaves, and in mild weather hangs till the spring.' —Winer, *R.W.B.* Mark's expression, οὐ γὰρ ἦν καιρὸς συκῶν, may mean either, it was not the time of the year for figs, or, it was not a favourable year for figs. Taken in the former sense, it perhaps intimated not—there was no reason to expect figs on the tree, but—it was hardly to be expected. At all events, the second construction gives a better sense. Symbolically, all bad trees were punished in this one bad tree, and even the bad season.

a correct view on this point, we must bring before our minds the general judgment in all its significance. In the general judgment the æonian administration of the Father coincides with the result of the æonian agency of the Son ; in other words, the ripeness of the present world for judgment, the ripeness of the earth for the harvest, coincides with the ripeness of the Church. For this reason the Father retains in His own power the time and hour of the end of the world ; and as He is now controlling the cosmical side of the end of the world as He judged Judea, especially in its relation to the history of the world, so here also He brought to view the first phenomenon of the incipient withering of the glory of Judea. God Himself, therefore, caused the tree to wither ; but this was done with a reference to the judgment of Christ, His life and His language. The Father and the Son, therefore, performed this symbolical act in the most living unity. The word of Christ killed the tree, since, having been uttered by the operation of God, it appealed to God's operation, and accordingly with that penetrated destructively through the nature-sphere of the tree. It was a word from the eternal depths of Christ's life, in which the Son felt Himself altogether one with the Father. That lightning which will one day blaze from the east to the west, and set on fire all the old world, here blasted a perversely pretentious, barren tree, and in its withering formed a prognostic of the final judgment. But to the disciples—who in the future could meet with no greater destruction than the outward, secularized Mount Zion, the barren pretentious Judaism—it gave the promise, that at their word of faith 'this mountain' (at all events, a mountain to which He pointed) 'should be removed, and cast into the sea.' The Lord, by a symbolical prognostic on a small scale, brought before their eyes that great judgment which was impending over Israel, when its national glory would be broken up and scattered among the nations (like the mountain cast into the sea). The disciples were thus taught that God met their faith in His judicial glory, and by His wonderful judgments would prepare the way for them as His own people to the glory that would be completed at the resurrection. Besides this miracle of the fig-tree, the darkening of the sun at the crucifixion, and the earthquake at the death of Christ, served to reveal the nature-side of the future judgment in awful omens. It was perfectly in keeping with the relation of Christ to the sphere of nature in the old world, that this sphere should be convulsed and darkened by the first presentiment of its future transformation at the hour when He sank in death. As all the operations of Christ first appeared in distinct single miracles, and then expanded their life in great and deep mediations, and finally were consummated in world-historical miracles, so was it with these miraculous signs which announced the last judgment. Their mediation lies in an operation of the Spirit of Righteousness upon the earth, during which more critical phenomena of the last world's curse are continually appearing; we might say, during which the combustibleness of the earth, and the fermentation in the depths of its life, are evermore unfolding their adaptation for a metamorphosis.

But here we are contemplating the judgment of the world only as an introduction to the resurrection, with which it is closely connected, just as the individual resurrection of Christ was introduced by His death, in which He had experienced the judgment of the world in Himself. The final aim of Christ's work is the resurrection—the introduction of the whole Church of God into an incorruptible and manifested life, penetrated from eternity by the Spirit (1 Cor. xv.). That resurrection finds its deepest ground, the principle which makes it an organic certainty, in the individual resurrection of Christ. This resurrection of the Lord is unceasingly perpetuated in the Church as a living energy. The life of Christ operates according to its nature in the world, awakening, invigorating, healing, and restoring, since it is essentially eternal life, or positive vivifying life. It is therefore not to be thought something merely figurative, and to refer simply to spiritual awakenings, when the resurrection of Christ is regarded as an awakening of humanity victoriously continued and pervading the history of the world. In the same real comprehensive manner in which He combats sin, He combats death; and with the same superiority which He displays in conquering sin, He completes His victory over death. He vivifies life, since He restores to it its intensive value; He conserves life, since He weakens the powers of death; He lengthens life, since He draws it always nearer the tree of life—nearer to a state conformable to the Spirit and to nature; He renews life, since He imparts to the inner man the power of the resurrection. Now, where do

we find the first blossoms of this immeasurable agency of Christ?
We find them in the three miracles which He performed, of restoring the dead to life.

The restoring of the dead to life is in itself so difficult a
miracle, that we cannot receive the instances of it unhesitatingly
unless we are previously satisfied about the resurrection of
Christ. If we are certain of Christ's resurrection, we have
gained the superior principle, of which these miracles are to be
regarded as easy developments.

In the miracle of restoring the dead to life we must hold fast
as the principal point, that Christ, as the Prince of life, rules
dynamically over the kingdom of the dead—that His voice can
reach and penetrate the departing spirit in the slumber of its
transition to another world, in the obscure depth of life through
which it falls into the bosom of God. We experience every day
the enigma, the apparent contradiction, that a person asleep, and
so far not a hearer, can hear a person calling, and we know that
he hears quickest when his own name is called. Sharper voices
and sounds of alarm can even exert an awakening power on
those who are soundly asleep or quite stupified. But no human
lamentation awakens the dead. But how intensely powerful,
how deeply penetrating and all-pervading, Christ's awakening
voice must be, measured by the uniqueness of His person, by
the decidedness of His will, by the certainty of His trust in God,
and by the relationship of His life to the innermost life of the
deceased! But where do we find the organic medium through
which Christ's voice reaches the spirit of the dead? Thus much
is clear, that the body of the deceased in its first state is very
different from a mummy or mouldering corpse. There is, so to
speak, a fresh-paved way between the corpse and the spirit that
has forsaken it. Science also has already arrived at the conjecture, that the last tones of life in the corpse die away much
more slowly than has been commonly represented. The corpse
is still full of the remembrance of life; hence also, in general,
the features of the deceased re-appear in plastic beauty, the reflection, so to speak, of that healthfulness which strove against
the crisis of disease, and gained the victory at the cost of sacrificing the life, a prognostic of the future life. But when so
obscure a track seems to show itself on which Christ reaches the
dead with His voice, the question arises, How can the departed

return into the dead organism? But the power with which the spirit returns, with which it flies back into the organism in its unity with the power of Christ's word that called it, is to be regarded as the ray of life which again restores the organism. We must also here recollect that Christ did not resuscitate many dead persons without distinction in this miraculous manner, but only the individuals whose resuscitation was indicated to Him by the Father. Those who have supposed that Christ could not resuscitate the dead without regarding them as means for other objects, and encroaching on their already decided destiny, seem to have proceeded on the assumption that He performed His miracles without reference to the will of His Father. In this case the same remark might be made respecting His miraculous cures of the sick. But it was included in the destiny of the sick, that they were to be cured by Him (John ix. 3); so also it belonged to the destiny of the dead, that He was to resuscitate them (John xi. 4). In the successive steps by which these resuscitations of the dead follow one another, the power of Christ appears progressively more exalted.[1] First of all, He restores the maiden on her death-bed; then the young man on the bier; and lastly, Lazarus in the sepulchre.

But we see how in all these cases the Lord first of all combats the lamentations for the dead made by those who were around them,—how He quells the psychical desponding mood which surrounded the dead as if to ward off the approach of life, and then makes His way clear to the spirit of the deceased. 'Fear not! only believe!' He says to Jairus, the ruler of the synagogue. Then He makes a selection of those persons who were to be present at the resuscitation, namely, the disciples Peter, James, and John, and the parents of the child. Then He enters the house of mourning, and says to the people who were lamenting the dead, 'Why make ye this ado, and weep? the damsel is not dead, but sleepeth (Mark v. 39). And they laughed Him to scorn.' But He put them all out; and thus by alarming the living, made the field free from the alarm of death. The call, 'Damsel, arise!' impressed itself so suddenly in its original form, Ταλιθὰ κοῦμι, on the disciples, that Mark, who had a keen sense of the exciting, could not help inserting it in his

[1] [Ewald sees something of the same progress in all Christ's works.— *Christus*, 226.—ED.]

Gospel. At the resuscitation of the young man at Nain, this preliminary combat of the life-restorer was shown by two signs. ' Weep not !' He said to the mourning mother, and thus not merely consoled, but raised her into the bright circle of His own state of mind. Then He came nearer and laid hold of the bier,[1] and the bearers stood still (Luke vii. 14). This demonstration, of which the energy is reflected in the narrative, stopped the advancing procession of the mourners ; and then followed the joyful resuscitation. At the resurrection of Lazarus, Jesus sought first of all to raise the dejected heart of Martha. But when Mary and the Jews (the friends of the family) met Him weeping, ' He groaned in spirit, and was troubled.'[2] With mighty indignation He set Himself against the waves of despondency which beat upon her breast ; and without delay betook Himself to the grave. Once more there was a strong internal movement of His soul to repel a fresh attack of despondency. All the words which He uttered afterwards had the same design, to prostrate death first in the hearts of the bystanders. This striving serves to explain the form of the prayer which Jesus offered at the grave, and which some have thought strange and repulsive, because they have not taken notice of the internal conflict which of necessity preceded the act of resuscitation, and occasioned the Lord's uttering aloud His address to the Father. The moment is difficult, serious, and decisive. Jesus cries with a loud voice, ' Lazarus, come forth !' The Evangelist, with the most vivid remembrance of the scene, selects the strongest terms, in order to exhibit the striking effect of that awakening call of Christ.

Although the Lord recalled the dead whom He resuscitated to the present life without transporting them to an imperishable life, yet these restorations constitute the miracles by which He most decidedly displayed His majesty. In significance they are of the same order as His own resurrection, and with the future resurrection of the dead. They reveal the power of the Prince of life to abolish death, that is, to bear aloft all individual life

---

[1] ῞Ηψατο τῆς σοροῦ : He seized, took possession of the bier.

[2] From the close connection in which Christ's state of mind appeared to be with that of the mourners, the meaning of these words (John xi. 33) can be more precisely explained, than would be possible without a reference to this connection.

THE MIRACLES OF JESUS.

according to its innermost nature and destiny from the depths
of nature-life into His own ideality, and to exhibit it in that.
For as far as the tide of death breaks over individuality with
the appearance of destruction, death seems to pollute man in his
sacred individuality.   Wherefore it is said, ' Thou wilt not suffer
Thy Holy One to see corruption,' and the resurrection of Christians is one with His own glorification.   In the miracles of raising the dead, Christ unfolds the boundlessness of His might over
individuals, and of individuals over the change to dust ; they are
the crown of His miracles.

Besides the miraculous acts of Jesus reported by the Evangelists, He appears generally,[1] and especially at Capernaum,[2] to have
performed many other wonderful works.   But yet He was very
far from allowing His miracles to appear with the profusion of
everyday events.   He decidedly set Himself against the craving
for miracles.   The opinion so commouly entertained, about the
fondness of that age for miracles, has little to support it.   Had
it been prevalent in Israel, the people would hardly have reve-
renced as a great prophet,[3] a man without the gift of miracles,
John the Baptist.   But as to their conduct towards Jesus, the
case was different.   As soon as the Jews believed that they had
discovered in Him Messianic features, as soon as He gave any
sign whatever, the craving for miracles which had faintly glim-
mered in their breasts burst forth into a flame, and they were
ever longing for new and greater signs.   The modern shyness
for miracles has sought with great eagerness after those expressions of Jesus in which He checked the craving for miracles, in
order to prove from them that He wrought no miracles, or at
least that He regarded them as of little importance.   But such
a forced interpretation of the words of Jesus may be safely left
to the impression it gives of its utter worthlessness.   It is very
clear from the Gospel history, that the Lord shaped His conduct in the spirit with a constant reference to the belief in
miracles prevailing in His time, that is, He treated every particular case according to its peculiar character.   But in this un-
restricted diversity of treatment, three methods are distinctly
prominent in His conduct.   In those cases in which He could
reckon on unlimited confidence in the persons who needed His

[1] John xxi. 25.   [2] Luke iv. 23.
[3] Neander, *Life of Christ*, p. 140 [Bohn].

help, He rendered aid without any hesitation; indeed, He often brought them aid quite unexpectedly. But when He found that they were in danger of apprehending the miracle superstitiously, of losing sight of His own personality in the astonishment excited by the fact, or of seeking the miracle only as a common outward help, then He kept Himself aloof, and blamed them. 'Except ye see signs and wonders, ye will not believe' (John iv. 48). But if this tendency to bring His miracles into the service of selfishness was decidedly apparent, He entirely refused to gratify such expectations. He would not allow Himself to be taken for a bread-king (John vi. 26), nor a court performer of miracles (Luke xxiii. 8); and as little would He satisfy the chiliastic Pharisees when they demanded of Him a miraculous sign in accordance with their views of the world. It was in the spirit of diametric opposition between His christological world and theirs, when to meet their desire, that He would accredit His mission by a chiliastic sign of the Messiah suited to their notions, He made a reference to the sign of His death (John ii. 18, 19). The sign with which His Messianic kingdom was to come into the world, was His cross; while they were under the delusion, that the Messiah must immediately begin His universal sovereignty under a cosmical sign.[1] He always pointed to this sign of His death whenever they demanded from Him the cosmical sign of the new æon.[2] He declared that only one sign should be given them, the sign of the prophet Jonah. From this declaration it cannot follow in the least, that He had done no miracle, or that His adversaries had never been present at such an act; for the question about which He was treating was the sign which, according to the Jewish chiliastic preconceptions, must at once satisfy the nation that the Messiah was come. The Evangelist Mark explains this declaration of Christ as equivalent to: there shall no sign at all be given them. On the other hand, in Luke, Jonah himself, with his preaching, is regarded as the true sign for the Ninevites. But Matthew gives the *thought* in full. 'For as Jonah was three days and three nights in the whale's belly, so shall the Son of man be three days and three

---

[1] The greatness and importance of this contrast leads to the correct interpretation of John ii. 18, 19, that is, it confirms John's exposition.

[2] Compare Matt. xii. 38-42; Luke xi. 29-31; Matt. xvi. 1-4; Mark viii. 12.

nights in the heart of the earth' (Matt. xii. 40). The three Evangelists have preserved the different sides of the interpretation of a mysterious saying. Mark gives prominence to the negative in the language of Jesus: He would grant no sign to His adversaries in the sense they attached to it. Luke specifies the reason: they ignored the great sign from heaven that was continually exhibited before their eyes in His life; although the heathen Ninevites were awakened to repentance by Jonah, a poor foreigner; and although an Arabian queen was attracted from a distance to Jerusalem by the wisdom of Solomon. But Matthew has preserved the words which occasioned our Lord to speak precisely of the sign of Jonah. Jonah was three days and three nights in the belly of the fish, apparently beyond recall, and lost to Nineveh and the world: so also shall it be with the Son of man. The Jews required a sign from heaven, but a sign from quite an opposite quarter was to be given them: one rising from the depths of the earth, from suffering and death, from reproach and neglect; first of all in the history of Jesus Himself, then in the world-historical course of His Church. This is the sign of the Christian æon, the crucifixion of Christ, as through the resurrection it has been proclaimed to the world. But this sign is to be a critical one for the world—to many, a sign of death, and to many, a sign of life and redemption. The crucifixion of Christ in connection with His resurrection has become the great sign of the new Christian æon; a sign before which all single miracles appear inconsiderable, like the hillocks at the foot of a lofty mountain. As soon as we are certain of the fact of Christ's resurrection, we find in all miracles only a gentle prelude to this great hymn of ideal reality. Hence it is evident that we who find ourselves under the living operation of the resurrection, in the midst of the life-stream proceeding from it, in the natural unfolding and expansion of the greatest of all miracles, cannot possibly expect to witness such miracles in detail as Christ performed before His resurrection. Since the Spirit of Christ is in the most vigorous action, making all the blind to see, and removing bodily blindness in its root, He can no longer expend His power in performing a few single miracles of this kind. And so it is with the other miracles of Christ. In the miracle of the reconciliation of the world, which He accomplishes, He lays the foundation for its resurrection. From what has been said, it is also evident that everywhere on the border territory where Christianity comes into sharp conflict with the pre-Christian earthly life, events resembling miracles, or actually miraculous, may make their appearance. Thus the disciples received from the Lord the gift of performing miracles; this gift consisted in a preponderance of the Christian spirit, especially of the confidence of faith, which raised them above the despondency and bondage to nature belonging to their times. By His blessing their faith, He placed them in such a relation to His own miraculous power, that they could cast out demons in His name (Matt. x. 1; Luke x. 17). By their miraculous deeds, they extended the circle of the first direct operation of Christ upon the world. Also, in the vast extension of Christianity in the middle ages, not merely extraordinary, but even miraculous operations of Christian power, made their appearance, though not invested with the glory of the original Christian spiritual life. And so also the miracles of Christ must return, when the passage of the new Christian æon through the old is completed with the final outburst of the spirit at the end of the days. Then too Christ will give His adversaries the Messianic sign from heaven which they formerly demanded; but at the sight of it, all the tribes of the earth shall mourn. But in proportion as the great miracle of the new world unfolds itself as the effect of Christ's life, it must become manifest, that His single miracles, not only as immediate evangelical facts, but as the subjects of evangelical announcement, were only single, gentle modes of bringing His divine power into communication with the life of the world.

NOTES.

1. A distinct progression in the dogmatic development of the conception of miracle may be observed, which appears accompanied by an increasing obscuration of it. The biblical designations, σημεῖα, δυνάμεις, τέρατα, and ἔργα, jointly rest on the most living, most immediate contemplation, and the most correct estimate of the facts. Miracles as σημεῖα point to the one fundamental power of the principle from which they proceed, and they are referable to it, because they are mediated by a higher nature—a higher spirit-life—a divine revelation of which they testify. But since they extend themselves as δυνάμεις, as so many rays of the original δύναμις from which they are pro-

duced, they appear as overpowering, supernatural principles, which, in conformity to their power, display themselves in their irruption through a lower sphere of nature. But this irruption is effected by breaking through the wonted limits, circles, and presuppositions of the old nature-life as τέρατα, as agitating, unheard-of events. But by their course, their operation and results, they prove themselves to be the noblest works of the Spirit, or of pure love. Every miracle has all these sides and designations; but, according to the varieties of susceptibility, some persons see more of one side, and some of another. The heathenish, superstitious mind stops short at the τέρας; the strangeness of the miracle frightens him, and when he begins to doubt, the relative anti-naturalism irritates him. The believing Israelitish mind sees in a miracle the σημεῖον, the mediated sign of the forthcoming kingdom of God. The firmly established Christian mind beholds in these miracles the powers that unfold themselves from the divine power of Christ, δυνάμεις, as they begin overpoweringly in their first vigorous operations to form a new world in the old; the perfected Christian mind (like John) sees in them simply the works of Christ, the ἔργα, as they appear to him perfectly natural, and the life-manifestations of Christ's glory, transforming nature. In Augustin's times, the opinion that miracles were contrary to nature already existed, but was impugned by Augustin. To him all things were a miracle as far as they proceeded from God's omnipotence, and all things were nature as far as they were constituted by the will of God, who created nature. But he distinguishes in life itself between miracle and nature, since he contrasts the extraordinary with ordinary nature. ' Omnia portenta contra naturam dicimus esse, sed non sunt. Quomodo est enim contra naturam quod Dei fit voluntate, quum voluntas tanti utique conditoris conditæ rei cujusque natura sit. Portentum ergo fit non contra naturam, sed contra quam est nota natura—quamvis et ipsa quæ in rerum natura omnibus nota sunt, non minus mira sint essentque stupenda considerantibus cunctis, si solerent homines mirari nisi rara.'—*De Civit. Dei* xxi. 8. Augustin has at the same time a distinct feeling of the mediation by which miracle is effected, namely, the resurrection and ascension of Christ. ' Legebantur enim præconia præce-

dentia prophetarum, concurrebant ostenta virtutum, et persua-
debatur veritas nova consuetudini, non contraria rationi, donec
orbis terræ, qui persequebatur furore, sequeretur fide.'—*De
Civit. Dei* xxii. 7. The schoolmen elevated the conception of
miracle, since they distinguish between *mirabilia* and *miracula*.
By a miracle, properly so called, Thomas Aquinas understood
what goes beyond the order of all created nature, in which sense
God alone performs a miracle. In this definition the supernatural in miracle is brought to its strongest expression, but yet
the conception is not overstrained; it only wants the satisfying
mediation. Aquinas gives, indeed, a kind of mediation, by connecting the contemplation of *mirabilia* with the definition of
miracula. 'Non sufficit ad rationem miraculi, si aliquid fiat
præter ordinem alicujus naturæ particularis, sic enim aliquis miraculum faceret lapidem sursum projiciendo; ex hoc autem aliquid dicitur miraculum, quod fit præter ordinem totius naturæ
creatæ quo sensu solus deus facit miracula. Nobis non est
omnis virtus naturæ creatæ nota, cum ergo fit aliquid præter
ordinem naturæ creatæ nobis notæ per virtutem creatam nobis
ignotam, est quidem miraculum quoad nos, sed non simpliciter'
(*Summa Theol.* lib. i. qu. 110, art. 4). On these definitions,
through which the ideal contemplation of the object, though
obscure, is sufficiently discernible, the Lutheran theologians
especially proceeded at a later period, when they raised the relative anti-naturalism of a miracle to absolute anti-naturalism, and
then made this overstrained *moment* the only definition of the
conception of a miracle. Besides the definition quoted from
Buddeus, that from Quenstedt may prove this : ' Miracula vera
et proprie dicta sunt, quæ contra vim rebus naturalibus a deo
inditam, cursumque naturalem, sive per extraordinariam dei
potentiam efficiuntur' (*Systema Theol.* p. 471. Compare Hase,
p. 202 ; Hahn, *Lehrbuch des chr. Glaubens,* p. 23). To this
view the philosophy of Leibnitz forms a counterpoise, since it
defines a miracle as ' aliquid cursui naturæ ordinario non autem
essentiæ illius entis, in quo contingit (quoniam absolute impossi-
bilia fieri nequeunt) contrarium' (*Dissert. prælim. ad Theodic.*
etc. § 2, 3. Compare Rixner, *Handbuch der Geschichte der Phi-
losophie* iii. 179). In modern times, some Church theologians
have attempted to maintain the conception of miracle by drop-
ping the strictly *miraculum* and retaining only the *mirabile.*

Among these, J. Müller especially reckons Schleiermacher. Certainly Schleiermacher, in his *Glaubenslehre*, § 47, has made the assertion, that every absolute miracle must disturb the whole framework of nature; on the other hand, he also remarks, that ' since our knowledge of created nature is contained in its *progressive manifestation*, we have the less right to hold anything whatever to be impossible.' The tortuous and obscure expressions of Schleiermacher on this subject proceed from this—that, on the one hand, he recognised Christ as ' the summit of miraculous agency,' while, on the other hand, the Spinozist or naturalistic conception of the monotonous, rigid sphere of nature confronted him. What Schleiermacher has advanced with special cogency, is the entrance of miracle into nature—its appearance in a natural course; and this is a decided gain, for by it the last element of the conception of miracle is firmly fixed. And if we look back, we find in its history the actual unfolding of all its component parts, though charged with one-sidedness and extravagance in the views taken of it. Augustin advocates the *mediation* of miracle; Aquinas its supernaturalness; Quenstedt its anti-naturalness; and, lastly, Schleiermacher its new nature. Weisse (i. 369) makes a distinction between *wonders* and *miracles*, and understands by the former, exertions of Christ's power which ' may be referred to the conception of a peculiar organic endowment,' and by the latter, such acts of which the conception would be ' the purely negative of going beyond the common course of nature, of breaking through the laws of this course of nature.' These miracles—for example, those of feeding the multitudes—must have arisen from a mere misunderstanding of the parabolic discourses of the Lord. This view rests on the ignoring of the new æon, which we have already sufficiently characterized.[1]

2. Göthe has contemplated and exhibited with the greatest admiration the ascending scale which is presented in the life of

---

[1] [Upwards of forty definitions of miracle by the highest authorities are collected in the Appendix to Alexander's *Christ and Christianity*. More recently the subject has been taken up by Baden Powell (*Essays and Reviews*); and in answer to him, from different points of view, by Mansel, Heurtley, Lee, and Davies. On the interruption of the regular course of nature by a power extraneous to it, see Mill's *Mythical Interpretation*, p. 81, and Bushnell's *Nature and the Supernatural*.—ED.]

nature, though he wished also to recognise the scientific designation of nature in an ascending movement; as the passage
quoted by Tholuck from Göthe's *Doctrine of Colours* expresses
it : ' As on the one hand experience is boundless, since it can
always discover something new, so are the maxims throughout,
since they cannot stiffen nor lose the capability of expanding
and embracing a plurality, and even of consuming and losing
themselves in a higher view.'

3. As the attenuation of the conception of miracle is connected on the one hand with the attenuation of the doctrine of
the person of Christ, so is it on the other hand with the attenuation of the eschatology. Those who, from their narrow dogmatic system, which has been contracted under the influence of
philosophy, have rejected the æonian yonder world of space and
time, the heavens and the new world—to whom, therefore, the
idea of the future transformation of the world is wanting—have
with it lost the general Christian view of the universe which
alone is suited to prepare the way for the conception of miracle.

4. The human hand is the twofold organ of those activities
of the spirit which are exercised and developed in the sphere of
ordinary life, and of its dynamico-mysterious activities. It acts
as an organ of the psychico-somatic operations of this kind in
the function of the magnetizer; as an organ of pneumatico-
psychical operations in ordination; lastly, as an organ of the
pneumatico-psychical-somatic operations in the whole energy of
the life of the God-man in Christian miracles. The physical
basis of these operations has in all probability become known
by a new discovery. In a work entitled, *Ueber die Pacinischen
Körperchen an den Nerven des Menschen und der Säugethiere
von J. Henle und A. Kölliker*, Zurich, bei Meyer und Zeller,
1844 (*On the Pacinian Corpuscles in the Nerves of Man and
the Mammalia*, by J. Henle and A. Kölliker), the important
discovery made by Pacini, a physician of Pistola, almost con-
temporaneously with others, is described and scientifically examined. Pacini discovered first of all, in the sensible nerves of
the hand, small elliptical whitish corpuscles; also in the nerves
of the soles of the feet. He began to prosecute the discovery
in the animal kingdom ; but found none in the dromedary, and
few in the ox. So far as the discovery has been followed out
by the editors of the above-mentioned work, these corpuscles are

found (besides in men) in all the domestic mammalia hitherto examined; they are wanting in all birds, amphibia, and fishes. In particular cases some of these corpuscles are found in men, scattered in the nerves of the arms and legs, and in the region of the abdomen. They are found in the greatest number and with the most regular recurrence in the human extremities, and in cats in the diaphragm. In the human extremities, according to the drawing, they adorn the ramifications of the nerves of the skin, as fruit the branches of a tree. This is not the place for a more minute description of the corpuscles. From their general appearance, Pacini has been induced to compare them to the electrical organs of the torpedo, and to describe them as animal magneto-motors, and to refer them as organs to the phenomena of animal magnetism. The authors of the work above quoted make the following remark on Pacini's discoveries: 'It must not surprise us if the adherents of animal magnetism, who are not altogether extinct with us, seize hold of these statements with eagerness and turn them to account. Only let us beg them to extend their manipulations to the epigastric region of cats, which, by reason of their ample magnetic apparatus, promise very interesting facts.' But we need only to recollect the difference between the flesh of cats and human flesh to perceive that this remark is only a joke. This distinction has indeed been firmly maintained in the mediæval fantastic relation between cats and witches, and the new discovery may perhaps contribute to its explanation. It is perfectly natural that the magnetism of the cat should be there for the sphere of the feline vocation, and perhaps serves for the purpose of its holding the magic-bound mouse outside its hole and playing with it. How far below the cat is the torpedo, since with its electricity it immediately strikes and benumbs its victim! This is indeed the rudest first trace of animal magnetism. The magnetizer, on the contrary, stands in the dignity of humanity incalculably higher than the cat in the application of his power, though even in his case the operation on the susceptible is obscure and magical, and the connection of the magnetized with him remains more or less a case of natural attraction (*Gebundenheit*). Magnetic connections of this kind are indeed, under the more general form, present in life in a thousand different modes, and may form themselves, especially in particular circumstances.

But when the same power appears again in the prophetic region, it is transformed by the consecration of the ethical spirit, and operates only as a heavenly power, not disposing to sleep, but awakening,—not bewitching, but setting at liberty. The elementary flash, which even in the life's manifestation of the torpedo leads to death, is here changed throughout into a vivifying operation of life.. The authors of the above-mentioned works find themselves induced to regard these corpuscles ' as a kind of electrical organs.' But it is obvious in such a case, that the human electrical organs, in their nature and operation, must contain and exhibit the specifically human in its whole extent. It is in this respect to be carefully noted, that these corpuscles are not found in all individuals in equal number and strength. This diversity in their allotment may indeed be considered as the foundation of the most different endowments. As to what concerns furnishing the sole of the human foot with these electrical organs, we are reminded by them not merely of the rhythmical structure of the human body, especially the feet, and the ecstatic dances as they occur among enthusiasts, of the not sinking of somnambulists in water, or of their ability to use the soles of their feet as organs of perception, but also of the ancient miraculous art of healing by means of the soles of the feet. Tacitus, after mentioning the fact that the Emperor Vespasian was applied to by a blind man in Alexandria to cure him by means of his spittle, reports that another sick person (prompted like the former by the god Serapis) requested that he might cure his diseased hand by contact with the sole of his foot; and so it really came to pass. It is unquestionably of great significance that these corpuscles, which have been compared to the Voltaic pile, have been discovered exactly in those parts of the human organism which, from a remote age, have been regarded as the life-points of a mysterious magical power.

5. In reference to the Demonology of the ancients, we have to make the following remarks. The conception of δαίμων or of δαιμόνιον (a word in which the impersonal, substituted for the demon, the demoniacal influence is indicated) embraces generally the representation of spirits belonging to the other world, as far as they make themselves known in this world by operations, fatalities, appearances, and living forms (while altogether opposite, the genius seems to denote the light-image of

the other world, the ideal, life-image reflecting itself in the style
of the other world, of an appearance of this world, of a man or
a place). Also, the peculiar innermost nature of man can consequently come forward demoniacally when it exhibits itself in a
dark power which breaks through its everyday life-form, so that
the man himself in these moments stands there as a stranger.
But when the ideal of his life comes so powerfully into visible
manifestation, in this case the conception of demon and genius
coincide; although here the genius maintains a peculiar relation
to the Spirit of God sending or placing him; the demon, on the
contrary, holds a special relation to the breaking of the innermost life through the form of the common life. Now it is
not altogether a correct assertion, that the Greeks reckoned
among the demons generally only departed human spirits,
manes, lemures, and the like. The Greeks had also a super-
human dark kingdom of demons. Göthe has brought this
forward in the second part of his *Faust*, and at the same time
given the reason ·why the Grecian spirit placed these dark
spirits, the Lamiæ and Gorgons, in the background of its
mythology—'Phœbus, beauty's friend, drives away into holes
these births of night, or restrains them.' As this is the manner
of the sunny day, so it was also of the Grecian sense of the
Beautiful. Yet certainly the Greeks, 'especially when they
spoke of possessions, connected the notion of departed human
souls with the words δαίμων and δαιμόνιον.' (See Riegler,
Leben Jesus Christus i. 836). As with the Greeks departed
souls predominated among the demons, though superhuman
demons were not wanting; so with the Jews the fallen angels
predominated among the demons, though there was an intermixture of departed souls. That merely the souls of the giants,
which probably from the narrative in Gen. vi. have been considered as the children of fallen angels, and the great trans-
gressors before and immediately after the flood, were in this
manner numbered with the angel-demons (see Strauss, *Leben
Jesu* ii. 12), cannot be admitted, since among the Jews the
doctrine of the kingdom of the dead (Isa. xiv. 9), the injunction not to interrogate the dead (Deut. xviii. 11), and the
assumption of the possibility of their return, were expressed
without that limitation (1 Sam. xxviii. 8; Isa. xxix. 4; Matt.
xiv. 2). That Josephus in his views attached himself to what

predominated in the Grecian view, since he speaks of (*De bello Jud.* vii. 6, 3) the demons as the spirits of wicked men, proves, at all events, that this theory did not in the least contradict the Jewish consciousness. The opinion that they were the souls of deceased men, has also been expressed by the earliest fathers who have treated of the subject of demons, namely, Justin Martyr and Athenagoras. 'Tertullian appears to have been the first who took a different view, since he maintained that fallen spirits or devils falsely pretended in possessed persons that they were the souls of men deceased.' Since among the Greeks it was the popular opinion that 'the souls of those who died a violent death were demons,' so Chrysostom endeavoured, especially in order to redeem the honour of the martyrs, to destroy the old popular representation. (See Riegler, i. 850.) The New Testament does not express itself more precisely respecting the nature of demons. That they are considered as belonging to the household of Satan (Matt. xii. 25), does not in the least decide that it does not include the souls of deceased wicked men among the demons. At all events, according to John viii. 44, the children of the devil belong as such to his household although they were found among living men. If we carefully examine the Old Testament view, as it precedes the New Testament and that of the early Church as connected with it, it is in the highest degree improbable that the Evangelists could mean by demons, exclusively either evil angels, or wicked deceased men.

6. When the cures of demoniacs as effected by Christ are termed 'conjurations,' the difference has not been observed between the agency of a master-mind who effects the expulsion of demons by the energy of his nature with fresh and free words of life, and the agency of a contracted exorcist who is bound to a traditionary hypothesis, to the expectation of the co-operation of higher spirits, and to an unbending formula. Between conjuration and the Christian casting out of devils there is a similar difference, wide as the poles asunder, as between a common anecdote and the facts of the Gospel history.

7. Strauss (ii. 181) collects the outward similarities in the miracles of the sea that are so characteristically different, called by him sea-anecdotes. 'After they are set in order, each one is connected with the following by a common feature. The narrative of the calling of the fishers of men (Matt. iv. 18) opens

the series; with this the narrative of Peter's draught of fishes has in common the saying respecting fishers of men, but the fact of the draught of fishes is peculiar to it. This latter recurs in John xxi., where, in addition, there is the standing of Jesus on the shore, and the swimming to it of Peter. This standing and swimming appear parallel to the walking on the sea (Matt. xiv. 22, etc.).' The author has forborne to complete his explanation of the significance of these similarities, as the connection of his work required. A gigantic sea-myth seems to have floated before him—a real sea-serpent—which perhaps was not delineated, because the Galilean sea seemed too small for such a mythic monster of the ocean.

8.[1] Mainly with reference to Dr F. Krummacher's review in his *Palm-blättern* (March 1845) has it become imperatively necessary to discuss the question, whether, according to the rigid supernaturalism of the present day, Christ's human nature must be regarded as amalgamated with and lost in His divine nature, or whether the modern free-believing theology has a right to assert the distinction of the two natures in Christ, and is justified in indicating the human element as co-operating with the divine in His miracles. Krummacher seems from the first to proceed entirely on the monophysite theory, though quite unconsciously and without any heterodox design. When I speak of the accompaniment of a magnetic fluid (more correctly, a super-magnetic power), a spiritual-corporeal affinity (*Rapport*), and of a plastic human spirit in the miraculous works of Jesus, Krummacher asserts that the immediate and creatively interfering power of God must be entirely passed by. It would be as logically inferred that, by admitting that the Son of God is come in the flesh, the divinity of Christ is denied. Dare we and should we speak of the reality of His flesh and blood, yea, of eating His flesh and blood? It is at least our right, and indeed, even more, our duty, to keep in view the distinctive qualities of His human nature in their union with the great self-determinations of His divine creative power as they appear in the miracles. Or must the article of our faith, that the Word became flesh, remain for all time unopened, undeveloped? Must the human with the divine form a contradiction even in the life of Christ the God-man?

[1] [This note forms the larger portion of the preface to the third volume of the original.—ED.]

Krummacher is disposed indeed to gather from my representation of the gradual unfolding of Christ's human nature, that I do not acknowledge His eternal divinity. The way and manner in which he arrives at this result I will here expose, in order to give a sample of his critical report on my theology, and with that I shall here close the discussion. I believe that in my work I have shown that the incarnation of God which was historically fulfilled in Christ Jesus was an eternal one, of which the future completion in Christ was revealed and objectively presented to the Old Testament seers in the Angel of the Presence. From this Krummacher draws the conclusion (p. 155) : ' Lange's Christ existed before the foundation of the world only as an idea in God, not as a person with God.' And further on he identifies this Christ with the Son of God, that he may then say, ' He knows nothing of the Son of God begotten before all time, as the personal image of God.' Krummacher is very confident in this assertion, for he goes on to say, ' The expression of our Lord Himself, " Before Abraham was, I am," is then to be explained in the following manner : " I was before I was an I (ein Ich) already regarded as the Son of man in God, as becoming the Son of God in the ardent longing of men." ' In passing, I must here beg the reviewer to be on his guard against the thoughtless use of marks of quotation. Every reader who is familiar with their use would believe that the reviewer, with the words ' I was before I was an I,' etc., had quoted an assertion of mine ; but he would be quite mistaken. I beg the courteous reader to read my explanation of the passage quoted by Krummacher, John viii. 58—an explanation which had been in print long before I had seen the exposition thrust upon me by the reviewer—and then judge how far he proves himself to be a trustworthy reporter of the meaning of my Christology. In my Dogmatics I teach most decidedly the essential Trinity in opposition to the economical and Sabellian. Krummacher himself derives his information from passages in which the eternity of the Son is plainly enough taught (i. 37, ii. 45, etc.). How comes he then to maintain that I know nothing of the eternal Son of God ? I regret to say it : it is because he does not distinguish between the idea of the historical, or, generally speaking, of the personal Christ, and the idea of the Son of God. In all my writings I teach and assume the eternity of the Son of

God; but with that I do not teach that the personal Christ has existed from all eternity as such. For He it is who in the fulness of time appeared as the God-man, or the Son of man anointed with the fulness of the Godhead. But Krummacher thinks that I must teach this in order to be orthodox, and does not surmise that in doing so I must go further in heterodoxy than the ancient Archimandrite Eutyches. Indeed, in speaking of a personal Christ, any one would be mistaken if he were inclined to designate the pre-historical Christ, who certainly is ideal, as *merely* ideal, and ignore His substantial existence. This would be sheer Nestorianism, from which I know that I am most decidedly free. Krummacher indeed asserts, that what stands written in John xvii. 5 of the glory of the Lord must be taken, according to my view, in an ideal and not in an ontological sense. But from this he absolves me on the next page by the remark, that the unfolding (*werden*) of the christological life under the Old Covenant was, according to me, not merely formal, but at the same time substantial. Or what difference should there still exist between the ontological and the substantial sense, in opposition to the conception of the merely ideal on the one hand, and of the historical on the other? It is only needful to be tolerably familiar with my christological view to find that I speak of the ideal Christ as contradistinguished from the historical; but that I hold the eternal ontological being of Christ with a totally different emphasis from that of those theologians who, after the fashion of the older Dogmatic, see in the Angel of the Presence simply a super-earthly peculiar individuality in which the predicates *Angel* and Uncreated Essence are to be connected in a mysterious manner. But if Krummacher was not familiar with the distinctions between the *substantial* and the *historical* Christ, and between the conceptions *Christ* and *Son of God*, he must, as a reporter respecting christological investigations of the present day, fall into misunderstandings and misrepresentations. It is to be wished that he had spared himself the pain which must result from such public unfairness. The details I must reserve for a special answer to his attack. In the meantime I consider him responsible for all the scandal which may arise from the controversy thus forced upon me. I do not mean that I was troubled by his announcement, that he would assist the reader to determine whether 'Lange's book is to be deemed a step forwards or backwards in theology.' I could wish with all calmness, for his sake and my own, and more than all for the sake of the subject which the book advocates in a defective manner, that he would clear up this question. But the conflict in which I find myself engaged with a genial, bold, and long-loved preacher of the Gospel, pains me much, not only on personal considerations, but such as relate to the Church. Yet perhaps this controversy is one of the preliminary skirmishes, occurring here and there, of that warfare which the believing, scientific theology must wage with the mass of monophysitic (abstract supranaturalistic) representations in our Church before the way of the future is again quite cleared for the confession of the Church. May our warfare be carried on christianly and nobly under the inspection of the Lord, and lead to a blessed result.

SECTION X.

THE TEACHINGS OF CHRIST, ESPECIALLY THE PARABLES.

Christ stood in the world with the pure heart, and so with the pure, simple vision, of the Man from heaven. Therefore He beheld God in spirit, His own Father. His course of life was in the perfect light of God, which was concentrated in Him and made Him the Light of the world. The divine decree shone upon His soul like the clear daylight. But He beheld men in the world erring and perplexed, enchanted in ruinous delusion through the dazzling lights and shadows which sin forms from the light of the eternal train of beings in the universe, and through the spirit and world-destroying influence of selfishness (*Egoismus*). He saw them lost and walking in darkness; therefore He was continually striving to enlighten them by the light of His Spirit. And since the light easily becomes to those in darkness 'a deeper night,' it was always His task to mediate the life of His Spirit, as the light of the world, with the life of the world's thoughts.

When truth takes the form of mediating, it becomes teaching (doctrine). The teacher as such is a mediator between the light that is entrusted to him and the eyes of the spirit which he has to illuminate with this light. He must construct a bridge between the heights of knowledge and the low level of germinating thought. But as Christ is generally the Mediator between God and humanity, so is He also specially, as a teacher, the Mediator between the divine counsels and human thought. He is the Teacher: this is involved in His whole character; this He proves by His ministry and operations.

In discharging His office of Teacher, He employs various forms of teaching, as they suited the various relations in which He stood to His hearers, and the inner constitution of these hearers themselves.

When He first of all met with men who had not yet entered into close discipleship with Him, the form of His teaching is dialogue, a distinct interchange with those around Him in accordance with social life. In this dialogical interchange He particularly engaged when He had to do with adversaries. Hence it is evident why this form predominates in the Gospel of John; for John made it his special task to exhibit the most important conflicts between the Prince of Light and the children of darkness. The dialogical words of Christ were in the highest degree important, full of life, and therefore abounding in similitudes. But if the men who heard Him entered into more definite intercourse with Him, He proceeded to the use of other modes of teaching. He then spoke to them in parables, in adages or maxims, or in the free spiritual form of thought, in the form of didactic discourse.

The relation between the thought and its sensible representation is always different in these three forms of teaching. In the parable the sensible representation decidedly predominates, and the thought retires into the background, although for thoughtful hearers it speaks through the powerful imagery of the parable. In the adage (*Gnome*) the image appears in living unity with the thought, the one penetrated by the other. Lastly, in didactic discourse the thought predominates, yet figurative allusions sparkle throughout the whole current of the discourse, in a manner suitable to the most living and richest spiritual utterances. We should now have to consider these three forms of teaching in the order stated, if it were not our business to dwell some time longer on the symbols. This will lead us to consider, in the first place, the two latter forms of teaching. Their contrast to the first decides this arrangement. We first of all see by what mode of teaching Christ mediated the truth among the consecrated and initiated, and then how He mediated it among the uninitiated.

In the circle of those hearers who had a peculiar suscepti- bility for His doctrine, and followed Him with personal regard to the lonely mountain district, whom He therefore could regard as consecrated, Jesus taught many times in adages or religious maxims, in apophthegms which presented great truths in sharp, fresh, luminous forms, which oftentimes are more or less sym- bolic.[1] The adage forms a sentence enclosed in itself and rounded off, the form of which is expressed with the sharpness and freshness of life like an accomplished human individu- ality, and its thought profoundly ideal and rich like the essence of a human personality, and in which this deep thought consti- tutes with this beautiful form a living unity like soul and body in an animated, speaking human countenance. The entire adage is form, and yet again it is altogether thought; a thought in luminous freshness; as in a precious stone the matter, the form, and the light appear in noble unity. With such jewels or pearls Christ presented the consecrated among His hearers.

But to the initiated who had become His friends, Christ spoke in the free form of religious, spiritual expression, in the living dialectic style of instruction. As the spirit is exalted above nature, so is the pure, free utterance of the spirit exalted above the symbolic form. But the living spirit in its energy does not break away from nature in order to indulge in abstract thinking, but takes it into its life, transforms it, and causes it to bear witness of its own essence. And thus the Spirit of Christ shows itself in His teachings; they are intermixed with parables and apophthegms. But these parables rise immedi- ately into the light of the great living thoughts by which they are illuminated and sustained. Thus Christ acted towards the children of the spirit.

But He pursued quite a different course with the uninitiated. To such hearers, who were attracted by the power of His per-

[1] When the adage is correctly apprehended in relation to the thoughtful combination of the sensible and the spiritual, it will be difficult to find in Luke's Sermon on the Mount the Ebionitish, vapid beatitude of the simply temporal poor.

THE TEACHINGS OF CHRIST, ESPECIALLY THE PARABLES. 175

sonality, or outwardly were for a long time attached to Him, but in whom a disposition of coarse worldliness and an impure interest more or less prevailed, He spoke in parables.   Crowds of such men, might gather round Him on the sea-shore from among the fishermen and publicans at Capernaum.   But, especially at a later period, His adversaries at Jerusalem confronted Him with such dispositions as induced Him to teach in the form of parables.

But on what account the Lord taught in parables before such uninitiated men, we shall learn from the very conception of a parable, as well as from His own distinct explanation. We shall also learn it from the effects which the parables continually produced.

The parable is a figurative form of representation in discourse, which we must distinguish from other forms that have an affinity to it.   All figurative forms rest upon the infinite abundance of comparisons which arise from the similarity and relationship of all phenomena, or rather from the unity of the spirit, which establishes all these similarities.   All things are reflected in all things, since they are all allied to one another by their relation to the common basis on which they rest, and to the one object which they aim at, and to the one creative Spirit in whom they live (Rom. xi. 36).   But the special mirror of the whole world is man, since the world appears concentrated in him ; and the world is the counter-mirror of man, since his spirit's inheritance extends throughout its immensity.   Hence all comparisons are crowded into human life as their focus. Hence it comes to pass that man surrounds himself, by means of discourse and art, with images ; in this manner he surrounds himself with signs of the ideality of the universe and of his own being.   But the comparisons which man forms in his discourse may be exhibited in a well-defined series.

First of all we are met by the similitude of fleeting appearance, or rather accord, that is, Metaphor.   It is formed from the endless play of similarities, from the harmonious relations of the harp of the universe.   It proceeds from the intimate relationship of the fundamental tones of life; but the most delicate glances and flashes of similarity are sufficient to produce it. Metaphors are the flowers of speech, the butterflies on the field of the spirit.   Their number is legion ; for as many million

times as the heavens are reflected in the sea, all things are reflected in all, and especially in the spirit of man. Further, we
meet with similitudes of a related form of life, namely, Allegories. Allegory represents one thing by another, another by
another, in a definite, marked formation.[1] But it connects the
image and the object not in a purely arbitrary manner, but is
conditioned by the similarity of the forms of life. Thus the
four horsemen in the apocalyptic vision (vi.) riding on their
four horses, one after another, are allegorical figures closely corresponding to the different forms of the course of the world.
But if we go beyond the phenomena of life to contemplate the
similitudes of the inner man, first of all similitudes of the natural
or also of the moral sense come under our notice. They are
represented by Fable. Fable is fond especially of representing
the reverse side of the ideal, the accidental, the arbitrary and
perverted. But how can evil find its like in nature since the
substance of all things is good? Evil is certainly in itself null,
dark as night, and only like itself. But evil is in the human
world in nature-life, and assumes the form of nature-life, and
also as disease assumes organic forms and modes in the human
organism. By this likeness to nature which evil gains in man,
it gains also its similitudes, and these exist most abundantly in
the animal creation. In the animal creation very numerous
reflections are to be found of human virtues and vices. Hence
it is that fable often exhibits unideal human life in idealized
animal life, or the animal similarities of man in the human
similarities of the animal. When man loses the spirit and becomes like the animal, it is fair that the animal when it represents him should gain his faculty of speech. When Balaam
lost the spirit, his ass gained the language of reproof, which
represented his overborne conscience. Fable has indeed a
wider range than the one we have noticed, but it is its constant
peculiarity to exhibit the manifestations of the natural disposition of man. It lies in the nature of the case, that it seizes this
disposition in its salient points, in its characteristic traits, and
exhibits it with a touch of irony and with a moralizing tendency. It therefore frequently aims at improving the distorted
side of the spiritual by the light side of the natural. For, as

[1] 'Oratio qua quis ἄλλο μὲν ἀγορεύει, ἄλλο δὲ νοεῖ.'—Wilke, Neutest.
Rhetorik, p. 108.

similitude, it aims at the adjustment of the disposition it represents with the whole world besides. But the ideal value is wanting to it, inasmuch as it wants the nature of man, the self-will, the moral obliquity, or even the moral principle. This value announces itself in the similitude of the ideal being, in symbol. The world in its state of rest, or as pure creation, is a system of divine ideas which proceed from the highest idea, the revelation of God in His Son, to branch themselves out and descend into the phenomenal world in definite ideal characteristics of life. On this truth rests the essence of symbol. Every phenomenon, namely, is necessarily a copy and sign of all ideal life which lies upon the same line with it in the direction of the Invisible. When, therefore, such a phenomenon is combined with the ideal being of which it forms an offshoot in the phenomenal world, a symbol is formed.[1] If once a conception of this heavenly ladder has been formed, it will be easy to trace the lines of many phenomena into the Eternal. So a rock in its earthly appearance presents a firm front against the swelling sea, and is an image of firmness against the flood of human instability. In the apostolic rock-man (Peter), and in the Lord, who is a Rock, the ideal essence of it is found again. But the glorification and life's fulness of this firmness appears in another symbolical application of stone, since it proceeds from stone to precious stone, and from this to the heavenly splendour of the mystic precious stones (Rev. xxi.). But the flowing sea is not only found again in the billows of the heathen nations (Ps. xciii. 4; Rev. xiii. 1), but also in the sanctified human life of the world, in the infinitely strong and wave-like sympathy of those who unfold their power only in the spirit of the Christian community (Rev. xix. 6). The dew-drop, the tear of the earth, points upwards to the pearl, the pearl to human tears, and these to the pearls on the gates of the eternal city of God; glorified sorrow forms the entrance to the residence of eternal joy (Rev. xxi. 21). But in the same way of symbolic we may go from above downwards, when, setting out from the primary ideas of life, we descend and seek out the phenomena in which they are copied. Thus, for example, we can proceed from the four pri-

---

[1] From this συμβάλλειν proceeds the σύμβολον.

mary forms of the divine life of Christ in the world to the four
Evangelists, and from these to the four cherubic life-images.
So clearly and powerfully do those ideal primary lines go
through the world; so distinctly does the Divine everywhere
resound in significant symbols of the phenomenal world. The
grain of wheat, the dove, the vine, and the marriage feast, are
symbols of eternal verities in the kingdom of God. But since
that Word in which the fulness of God is expressed, became
flesh in Christ, so He is necessarily the symbol of all symbols,
and surrounded by a garland of most expressive single symbols
in which His own being is reflected. These symbolical relations
are revealed by the world in its state of rest. But when contemplated in motion, it appears as the theatre of spiritual facts.
These also are represented in figurative forms, and their similitude is the parable. This, therefore, is a form of discourse
which represents in a sensible manner an universal, world-historical, religious and spiritual fact, by the exhibition of a special,
related, or similar fact.[1] Such are the parables of the Pharisee
and publican, of the good Samaritan, and other similitudes,
which exhibit in single pictures never to be forgotten the
greatest and most general religious and ethical facts. But in
general the parable is formed in a situation, in which a single
figure meets the teacher wherein he beholds that image of
the moral world; and it is expressly designed to display to his
hearers their whole spiritual position in the world as in a reflected image. The parable is therefore a practical view, by
which the teacher causes his hearers to look into their entire
spirit-world and its relation to opposite modes of spiritual life; and
it may on this account be called a parable, because it suddenly
places before the hearer, or circle of hearers, the living image of
the world in which he may view himself. The parable constitutes the highest form of figurative similitudes in discourse.

These similitudes, therefore, are seen by us in an ascending
line. But here, as everywhere, it is in conformity to an ascending line that the elements of the lower form occur again in the
higher, that therefore they are more or less prominent in it.
Thus, especially the symbolical element in some similitudes of

[1] The παραβολή is formed by the παραβάλλειν, the combination of the
general spiritual fact which is to be rendered visible to the hearer with a
well-defined individual image of it.

Christ is almost exclusively prominent, and some features of the parable are always allegorical. The message which Christ sent to the Galilean prince Herod, who wanted to frighten Him from his country, is almost in the form of a fable. The fox wished to scare the Lion, and to chase Him from his haunts.

From the nature of the parable, it is evident for what reason the Lord chose this form of teaching for His discourses, which was already familiar to the Hebrew mind, but which in Him attained to perfection. The parable, according to its nature, exhibits truth in a coloured light, which becomes indulgence to the weak, excitement to the sensuous, invigoration for purer eyes —which therefore, in every case, mediates the light of truth according to the varieties of mental vision.

According to an opinion prevalent in modern times, which may be regarded as the modern view of the design of the parable, it seems exclusively to render the truth intelligible to the understandings of a sensuous people. According to this popular theology, parables are only a popular mode of instruction, illustrations which form a sort of picture-gospel for a docile, childlike, and sensuous people. But our Lord's own statements respecting the design of parables (Matt. xiii. 13, etc.; Mark iv. 11, etc.; Luke viii. 10, etc.) go a long way beyond these pædagogical school views of the subject; even to the length of an awful reference to the judgment of God. According to the Evangelist Matthew, in answer to the disciples' question, 'Why speakest Thou unto them in parables?' He said, 'Because it is given unto you to know the mysteries of the kingdom of heaven, but to them it is not given. For whosoever hath, to him shall be given, and he shall have more abundance; but whosoever hath not, from him shall be taken away even that he hath. Therefore speak I to them in parables, because ($\delta\tau\iota$) they seeing see not, and hearing they hear not, neither do they understand. And in them is fulfilled the prophecy of Esaias, which saith, By hearing ye shall hear, and shall not understand; and seeing ye shall see, and not perceive. For this people's heart is waxed gross, and their ears are dull of hearing, and their eyes they have closed; lest at any time they should see with their eyes, and hear with their ears, and should understand with their hearts, and should be converted, and I should heal them.' Jesus therefore applies the language in which the prophet Isaiah (vi.) had

described the obduracy of his contemporaries to the Jewish people
of his own time.   It was evident to the prophet in a former age,
by divine illumination, that his preaching would have the effect
of increasing the obduracy of his people ; as this is always the
effect of preaching if it does not make men better.   But he saw
at the same time that by this effect the design of his preaching
was not frustrated, but that in an awful manner God's design
was fulfilled, and that for many persons that would be a judicial
decree of God.   Such a judicial decree Simeon also found in
the advent of Christ (Luke ii. 25), and not less so Christ Himself (John iii. 19).   He was aware of the decisive effect of His
preaching, and knew that it would become a judgment—a savour
of death unto death—through their own criminality.   He sought,
therefore, in His mercy to diminish as much as possible this
danger in the effect of His preaching, by veiling the truth He
announced to the people in parables, which gave to every one an
impression of the truth according to the measure of his spiritual
and moral power of comprehension, without driving him at once
to extremities.   Therefore Christ had not the design which the
modern view attributes to Him, of imparting the truth to the
people by parables in the clearest and plainest form possible.[1]
And on the other hand, still less could it be His design to pro-
pound parables in order to occupy His hearers with purely un-
intelligible discourses, or positively to contribute to hardening
them.   Had such a false predestinarian design influenced Him,
the parables could not have had an enlightening effect, they
would not have been preserved in the Gospels as a perpetual
treasury of knowledge for the Church.   According to the words
of the Evangelist Mark (iv. 33), Jesus propounded the truth to
the people very simply in parables, because it was only so they
would hear it—that is, not merely apprehend, but apprehend and
hear it ; for which purpose this was the most suitable form.
Hence He might have mentioned this reason simply to His
disciples.   Or He might have especially put forward the compassion with which He sought, by adopting this form of teaching, to
ward off the hardening of the people.   But this motive the disciples of themselves could more or less have recognised.   On the
other hand, they would not be so likely to be sensible of the
divine judgment, which lay in the fact, that Jesus was under

[1] See Hase, *das Leben Jesu*, p. 144.

the necessity of treating the majority of His people as 'standing without,' and only by means of parable to instruct them in the mysteries of the kingdom of heaven. But this fact especially occupied His thoughts. It was His greatest sorrow that He could not lay open His whole heart to His people—that He was obliged to communicate the message of salvation with a caution similar to what a physician would use in administering a remedy to a person in extreme danger of death. When, therefore, He was obliged to treat the greater part of the Jews, who ought to have been prepared to receive in a devout spirit all the mysteries of the kingdom of God, just like heathens, or even as enemies of the true sanctuary, who were prepared to profane the Most Holy (Matt. vii. 6); when He felt with deepest anguish the awfulness of the divine retribution in this necessity of veiling from their view His divine treasures, and clearly perceived how close at hand was the judgment of the rejection of this people, it was natural that He should exhibit to the disciples this tragical side of His parabolic teaching, which they could not so easily discern. And when He explained to them more fully His motives for adopting this mode of teaching, we can easily conceive that the disciples would preserve in the most lively recollection the judicial divine motive, which He confidentially imparted to them, because it affected them most deeply, and because it was of the greatest service in explaining to them the later judgments that fell upon Israel. Evidently this reference of the Lord to the judgment of God was present to the minds of all the three Evangelists who report this explanation of Jesus. Nevertheless, their accounts seem almost to divide among them the different elements of the Lord's declaration. Matthew's report brings forward most plainly *the design of Christ's condescension* to the capacity of His hearers, His didactic accommodation. In Luke's brief account, *the preventive motive*, the design of repressing what was dangerous in the effect of the word, is most conspicuous (viii. 10): 'but to others in parables, that seeing they might not see (*ἵνα*), and hearing they might not understand.' Lastly, Mark in his account sets forth *the judicial sentence of God* in the strongest terms. He has so condensed the declaration of Jesus as it is found in Matthew, that the words with which Jesus explains His parabolic form of teaching, and the word which He adduces in illustration from the prophet Isaiah, exactly coincide. This representation is at all events inexact. But in essential points it does not affect the thoughts of Jesus. For the judicial design ·of God must ever have been present to the spirit of Jesus in some form or other, without disparagement to His own compassion; as indeed in God His judicial determinations are not at variance with His love. Therefore we can only inquire how the awful strictness of God's judicial administration expressed itself in the spirit and parabolic teaching of Jesus? The solution is given in the words by which He marked the Jews as 'them that are without.' He was obliged to veil Himself before them as before strangers or profane persons. This, the spirit of truth required. And though He thus veiled Himself before them with the most vehement sorrow, yet He did it at the same time with the holiest decision, conscious and free. His language on this occasion harmonized with those decisive words (Matt. vii. 23), which, with the declaration of the completed estrangement with which the wicked appear before Him, must also express the completed doom. Those persons who are accustomed to regard the parable merely as an idyllic, agreeable mode of conveying instruction to innocent children, of younger or older growth, must be startled at the awful seriousness of this explanation which Jesus gave respecting His parabolic style of teaching. And we must add, that not only is this painful seriousness shown in the choice of the parables, but also in the circumstance that He propounded them without explaining them to the people, and that it was particularly the doctrine of the kingdom of God which He was led to veil in this manner (Matt. xiii. 11).[1] And the doctrine of the kingdom of God was exactly that in which Jesus differed most widely from the views of His nation. On that point He could not but disappoint their expectations. He therefore was obliged to use the greatest caution in His communications to the people on this subject. His crucifixion is a proof that He had not gone too far in His caution; and the destruction of Jerusalem proves that the people were no longer capable of receiving instruction respecting the true nature of the kingdom of God.

We can explain the design of the Gospel parables by the effects which they produce in history. They serve to bring the highest and most glorious mysteries of the kingdom of God

[1] See Hoffmann, *Weissagung und Erfullung*, Part ii. p. 98.

as near as possible to the sensually-enthralled human race—to represent in pleasant, attractive enigmas, forms of character never to be forgotten, and yet to guard them as much as possible from the profanation which would bring destruction on profane spirits. They operate, therefore, on a small scale, exactly as the world from which they are taken does on a larger. The whole world in its state of repose is to be regarded as a symbol, but in its state of motion as a parable of the divine essence. And as the Gospel parables have in reference to individuals a twofold operation, so also has the world on mankind collectively. It serves to conceal the essence of God from all impure eyes; and this concealment has its gradations continually increasing, so that the most impure eyes and the most profane dispositions lose God behind the world or in it, and sink down into Atheism. But this same world serves to unveil God to the gaze of the devout, so that they see the traces of His omnipresence shining forth with ever increasing lustre; and hereafter their purified hearts shall behold Him in perfection as all in all. Both operations of the world are great, extending over all ages, and designed by God. And yet they are not the effect of a double meaning belonging to the world, but rather proceed from its complete, pure simplicity. The eternal heavenly harmony of the world, ever like itself, is the cause of its producing an effect on every man in conformity to his own character. Thus it was with the parables of Christ—those special world-pictures which were destined to represent special spiritual facts relating to the kingdom of God.

From this mediation results the mode in which Jesus accommodated Himself to the people. The rationalist theory of accommodation—namely, the hypothesis that Jesus, in order to gain the people, countenanced their erroneous notions—is shown by the majesty of His truthfulness and by the fact of His crucifixion to be a worthless and degrading view. That theory savours of Jesuitism and a dread of the Cross, and therefore of selfish considerations, to which Jesus was a stranger.[1] But, on the other hand, if by the accommodation attributed to Him is understood that perfect wisdom in teaching with which He let Himself down to the popular mind, it is evident that, exactly in this pædagogical accommodation, His skill as a teacher, or, we may

[1] Neander, *Life of Christ*, p. 119.

say, His special incarnation in the art of teaching, is exhibited. Here it is proper to remark, that Jesus could not feel Himself obliged to correct the popular notions which did not belong to the sphere of revelation, but merely related to unessential historical matters. It would even contradict the organic completeness of His ministry and teaching, if He had taught details that were extraneous to the connection of His work and the exigencies of His position—if, for example, He had been disposed to make disclosures respecting the world of spirits. So He complied with the more or less arbitrary, conventional assumptions and designations which belonged to the popular language, and without which He could not have discoursed intelligibly. But His inclination to substitute more significant terms for such as were conventional proved that He tested the most social types of tradition in His eternal spirit; and, with such an ever fresh consciousness of His truthfulness, it cannot be admitted that He allowed base coins to go through His hands, or false assumptions through His lips.

Discourse in parables served first of all to exhibit the eternal in the temporal, and this was for a long time the predominant effect of it. But the more the nature of parables is thoroughly understood, the more will the impression be removed, that we have in them to do with arbitrary comparisons of things essentially different; we shall evermore recognise the essential relation between the similitude and its ideal world. But when the parable in general is viewed in this light, according to the sentence of the poet, 'everything transitory is only a similitude,' particular parables then also serve to glorify the temporal in the eternal, as before they glorified the eternal in the temporal. So, for example, in the picture of the woman who searched for the lost piece of money, we see the divine valuation of the valuable, how it goes in anxious quest of it through all the world. In the hand of this careful housekeeper we shall see a ray of that sun beaming forth which seeks the lost. In the conduct of the faithful shepherd, who seeks for the lost sheep in the wilderness, and hazards his own life to recover it, we shall recognise the divine foolishness of that love which sacrificed the most glorious life in order to rescue sinners; which therefore does not calculate, and is not rational according to the notions of the earthly world, but whose irrationality is nothing else than the sublimity of the highest reason, which always goes hand in hand with love. Thus therefore the main features of the ideality of the world appear in the parables as it has its principle in Christ, and is to become manifest by the operation of His Spirit; or the first clearest signs of the parabolic character of the world, the primitive forms of the great world-parable in which God unfolds the riches of His Spirit and life.[1]

It lies in the nature of a parable that it can be contracted or enlarged, and that it is sufficiently flexible to allow sometimes one side and sometimes another to be prominent. So we find again in the Gospels several parables with various modifications.[2] But these modifications cannot be regarded as fresh constructions of the same parable without displacing the proper point of view for judging of the parable. For in its formation we have to do, not with a beautiful, elaborated fiction, but with a life-image of the truth. When, therefore, a parable of Jesus corresponds to this object in its first draught, its later enlargement cannot be considered as a completion of it, but only as a modification which is designed to exhibit the truth pointed out in a new relation, in a fresh light. As little can it be admitted that tradition has remodelled the parables. They were impressed too powerfully in the remembrance of the apostolic Church as organic totalities for that to be possible. Yet we may conclude from the free individuality of the Gospels, that each Evangelist, according to the whole spirit of his conception, might allow some integral parts of a parable to retire, and place others more prominently in the foreground.[3]

[1] The Evangelist Matthew appears to have indicated this side of the parable very thoughtfully in the remark in which he applies the words of Asaph (Ps. lxxviii. 2), in a free citation, to the parables of Christ; namely, with the words, ἐρεύξομαι κεκρυμμένα ἀπὸ καταβολῆς κόσμου, ' I will utter things which have been kept secret from the foundation of the world' (Matt. xiii. 35).

[2] So, for instance, the parables, Mark iv. 2 compared with iv. 26; Luke xiv. 15 compared with Matt. xxii. 1–14.

[3] Thus Luke, in the parable of the marriage supper (xiv. 15), according to the connection in which he introduces it, and his own kindly predisposition, gives peculiar prominence to the compassion of the Lord (ver. 21); and, on the other hand, withdraws the element of judgment which is forcibly presented by Matthew (xxii. 7). Luke also omits the second instance of judgment in Matt. xxii. 13. Matthew, on the contrary, gives less prominence to the element of compassion, since he introduces the parable in a

The relationship of the parabolic form of teaching to unfigurative, didactic discourse appears in the parabolic discourses. We must not confound these with the parables properly so called. They are characterized by having the parabolic element mingled with the explanation in the flow of a continued discourse. The parable is therefore not given in its pure, exclusive form, detached from other matter ; but its essential elements, its single images, form the leading thoughts of the discourse. This form of discourse embraces all single forms of imagery in living unity : flashing metaphors, ornate allegories, touches of fable, magnificent symbols, and parabolic figures form the splendour of the beautiful banks through which flows the deep thought-stream of parabolic discourse, and are reflected in its depths with all their colours and forms. And so this form is a copy of the great combination between the images of the divine in the world and the world-transforming thoughts of the Spirit of God.

If we now look back and compare the parables of Jesus with His miracles, they will appear to us like those, as forms of the communication of His divine fulness to the poverty of the world, as mediating forms. But they are related to one another, not only according to their destiny, but according to their nature. The miracles of Jesus are visibly great single similitudes of His universal agency—similitudes in facts. His similitudes, on the other hand, disclose themselves as miracles of His word, when we recognise in them the ideal relation of essence between the eternal and the temporal. The miracle is a fact which comes from the word, and becomes the word. The similitude is a word which comes from the fact, and impresses itself in the fact. The common birth-place of these ideal twin-forms is therefore the world-creative and world-transforming Word.—At the close of this examination we had to give a distinct representation of the parables according to their living connection. But the doctrine of the kingdom of God, which Christ announced and founded, forms this connection ; and since we have to discuss this doctrine in the next section, we shall form the most correct estimate of the parables, if we contemplate them under the point of view

connection in which the idea of the future judgment predominates. But we have here to do with modifications formed by Jesus Himself, so that only the selection of the precise parables can be referred to the individuality of the Evangelists.

just named, in their organic connection as similitudes relating to
the founding of the kingdom of God.

NOTES.

1. Neander also has treated of the parables separately, with
a reference to the thought that forms their basis, the founding
of the kingdom of God.

2. Since art has to do with the ideal contemplation and representation of life, so imagery, as the reflex of the ideal in discourse, must be related to art. But in this relation metaphor
reminds us of music, allegory of painting and the plastic art,
fable of the drama (which by the ancients was also distinguished
as fable), symbol of lyric poetry, and, lastly, parable of epic
poetry and tales. Music is the image simply; it elicits from
objective life the spiritual music of its infinitely powerful relationship to the heart. The plastic arts allegorize throughout;
they exhibit ideal appearances in which homogeneous appearances in life are reflected. The drama is not only related to
fable in this respect, that it causes the characters it exhibits to
operate and exhibit themselves by speech, but also in this, that it
allows their reciprocal action in general to come forth from the
noble or ignoble nature-side of their life not yet elevated into
the spirit. In lyric poetry, on the other hand, the meditating
spirit always exhibits symbolically an ideal image of the world
and of human dispositions; the lyrical element rises above the
complexity of the drama. Epic poetry and tales, lastly, exhibit
spiritual life-images in their practical movements like the parable.
But the two lines of representation are distinguished in this
respect, that the didactic images serve the practical object of discourse, while the artistical images represent life in a state of
rest and enjoyment.

SECTION XI.

THE KINGDOM OF GOD.

As we have already remarked, it is an absolutely false assumption, that Christ entirely rejected the Jewish expectations

of the reign of the Messiah; or at least that He designed to establish a merely spiritual kingdom. In contrast to this notion, we must point to the fact that the spirit of the Gospels throughout favours the promise which was given to Mary, that the Messiah should rule for ever as a king on the throne of David (Luke i. 32, 33), and similar expectations (i. 69). The announcement with which John opened his ministry, that the kingdom of heaven was at hand (Matt. iii. 2), was immediately repeated by Jesus (Matt. iv. 17).[1] And we cannot overlook the circumstance, that all the disciples of Jesus entered into His communion on the distinct understanding that He was about to found a kingdom (Matt. xviii. 1).

But had Christ really purposed to found only a spiritual kingdom—in other words, not a kingdom, but a school—He could hardly with truthfulness have induced the men who came to Him with that expectation to join themselves to Him. Still less could He have yielded His assent to their supposition, as He really did (Matt. xix. 28).[2] Rather, He was conscious of being in the strictest sense the King of humanity, and of founding a kingdom, that is, a realm of God, to come hereafter into actual appearance, and completing itself in a visible community. Only in relation to the founding, the spirit, and the nature of this kingdom, He was obliged to hold Himself aloof from the expectation of the Jews. But it is indeed a false notion to imagine that all the Jews cherished a fully developed, carnalized, equally rude and low expectation of this kingdom. The expectation was originally a religious one, and therefore more spiritual or carnal according as the persons who cherished it had a higher or lower standpoint. Probably it was as multiform as in Christendom the idea of the nature of the Church. There could be no devout man in Israel who did not possess, in the Jewish shell of his idea of the kingdom, a christological kernel. Only thus

---

[1] Glosses have been made, without reason, on this repetition of the words of the Baptist in the lips of Jesus. The Evangelist reports the announcements of both, not in their original extent, but in a condensed form, as is his wont. Moreover, these two great preachers of the kingdom were no rhetoricians, who might have made it their business to describe the one great fact which they announced in embellished variations.

[2] It is very important that Christ calls the revelation of His kingdom *The Regeneration* (παλιγγενεσία); indicating that it must be founded wholly and entirely on regeneration.

was it possible for the Lord to engage the disciples as heralds of His kingdom (Matt. x. 7). He needed not to annihilate their expectation, but only to purify and transform it by the fire of regeneration. In this process of purification all were obliged to go through a great fire, and a Judas through his own criminality became dross; all the rest incurred the greatest risk. But they bore uninjured the certainty that Christ founded the kingdom, though fully purified by the flames. After the resurrection (Acts i. 6) and ascension (Acts iii. 20, 21) of the Lord, the confidence of the disciples bloomed afresh, that He would establish His eternal kingdom by their means; it was imperishable. Nevertheless the doctrine of Christ concerning His kingdom differed, as we have said, so far from the prevalent conceptions of His people, that He saw Himself obliged to bring it near to them under the veil of parables. We can plainly distinguish a threefold cyclus of such parables. The first exhibits the kingdom of God in general, in its development. In the second and third, the essential forms of activity by which God completes His kingdom are pointed out. The second cyclus, namely, includes the parables respecting the mercy which founds and fills up the kingdom of God; the third contains the parables of the judgment, by means of which it is completed in its purity.

Jesus delivered the parables respecting the kingdom of God in general, for the most part, to the multitudes on the shores of the Galilean sea; not all at once, but on different occasions.[1]

The first of these parables describes the sower scattering his seed on land consisting of very different kinds of soil, and of which the crop is regulated by the quality of the soil on which the seed is cast (Matt. xiii. 1–23; Mark iv. 1–20; Luke viii. 4–15). The general groundwork of the parable is the truth, that the culture of heaven is reflected in the culture of earth. God's corn-field, mankind, is reflected as to its chief relations in the corn-field of mankind, the earth. The sower who makes his appearance in this parable is not some petty husbandman who cultivates a small enclosed piece of ground; his field is large, of various quality—an image of the earth, or rather of humanity. So we see that humanity is as distinctly and comprehensively cultivated by its sower, as the earth by man 'The word of the kingdom' is everywhere expressed in its most general form.

[1] Compare Mark iv. 10; Matt. xiii. 10, ver. 36.

This is the first leading thought: the whole of humanity is God's corn-field. But the second thought shows how God treats mankind justly and equally in the distribution of His seed. The seed of the word falls everywhere; the same seed falls on the stony ground and on the wayside that falls on the good ground. But the soil is very different. Even in a smaller piece of ground the difference exists. Besides the good ground, there are corners of the field trodden down—places where there is a want of soil above the rock, and places where there is a rank growth of thorns. On these differences the produce of the sowing depends. Only on the good ground does the seed thrive for the harvest. These relations are exhibited more fully on a large scale. Many cultivated tracts of the earth are trodden down, spoilt, gone wild; and there are in proportion only a few choice districts and cultivated grounds. And so it is in humanity, both on the great and small scale. In this lies the third leading thought of the parable. On the largest scale we see the different soils in the different religions. In Heathendom we see the trodden wayside: the seed of God which falls on this ground is immediately—since the heathen do not understand it ($\mu\grave{\eta}$ $\sigma\upsilon\nu\iota\acute{\epsilon}\nu\tau\sigma\varsigma$)—taken away by the fowls of heaven, by the wicked one. Corrupted Judaism exhibits the stony ground: here the seed sprang up quickly, but withered under the sun of tribulation, under the rays of the Cross. The ground where the good seed is choked by the thorns of worldly lusts, is the Mohammedan world. The good ground is Christendom. But even within the pale of Christendom there are again the same varieties of susceptibility; hearts which have been hardened by the repeated tread of evil, so that the seed of the word not received only rests on it outwardly, and is taken away by the first temptation of the evil one;—superficial souls, who receive the word with a sudden enthusiasm, but remain unchanged in their radical disposition, and therefore easily fall away;—souls which are deeply involved in the cares and pleasures of the world, and therefore cannot surrender themselves to the highest. On these soils the seed thrives not. But yet the husbandman gains a clear profit from his sowing, a joyful harvest. The earth yields its increase, and so does humanity. God obtains His harvest from the good ground in humanity. The plan of the parable might easily have led to conceive of these differences of susceptibility in a fatalist sense. But this is not the Lord's design. First of all, He obviates such a mis-interpretation by changing men of different soils into men of different fallings of the seed. He speaks of that which is sown on the wayside, instead of the wayside on which it is sown; of that which is sown on the stony ground; and so on. According to this construction, men are the seed in various states; there is a life in them, and a human life according to the kind of men. Then it is said of the man of the good ground, ' This is he that heareth the word and understandeth it;' the activity of his spirit is rendered prominent. And when it is said, in conclusion, that the good ground bore thirty, sixty, or a hundred-fold, not merely the difference of the natural capacity, but likewise the free ap-propriation and application of the word is pointed out. In the definiteness of these numbers are represented the definiteness and harmony of the blessings, the living powers, of the kingdom of God.—Thus God obtains His world-historical harvest in humanity on the good ground of chosen and faithful hearts. He therefore conquers the negative hindrances to His kingdom, those of the manifold defective and blunted human suscepti-bility.

But His kingdom has also positive hindrances to overcome. This is shown by the parable of the tares among the wheat (Matt. xiii. 24–30, 36–43). The general symbolic of this parable con-sists in the delineation of the positive tendency to degeneracy and running wild which is shown in the life of the earth, and presents hindrances to its culture; and just so in the life of humanity. As in the ground, the noxious plants threaten to choke the noble cultivated plants; so in the life of humanity, the seed of corruption threatens the seed of salvation. Three leading thoughts proceed from this truth. This is first evident: the heavenly sower is opposed by a dark sower, his enemy; a noxious seed is placed in opposition to the good seed and threatens to choke it. Thus, therefore, not merely human weakness, unsusceptibility, and culpable defect are opposed to the kingdom of God, as in the first parable, but a kingdom of conscious wickedness whose point of unity is Satan, as the enemy of Christ, as the life-principle of all Antichristianity. His sowing time is the night, when people are asleep. Under the protection of human weakness, the work of devilish wicked-ness flourishes. The seed which the enemy sows in the consecrated field, in which the wheat has already been sown, is darnel, a weed resembling wheat, but a positive weed, since it grows up between the wheat and endangers it. ' The good seed are the children of the kingdom ; but the bad seed are the children of the wicked one.' Not men as men form the contrast, for Satan is no Ahriman who can form men, but men as they are become identical with the *spiritual seed* received into their inmost being. The wicked, therefore, are here described as the weeds as far as they are identical with the ' offences' (τὰ σκάνδαλα, Matt. xiii. 41) which check the growth of Christ's good seed. Evidently these offences are the religious and moral heresies in the Church. They have in common a life-germ of demoniac origin, and an antichristian bias. They are collectively and separately the wheat-like darnel. The element of truth which in them is decomposed into falsehood, the form of doctrine which they assume, and the enthusiasm with which they are carried away—all this makes them have the semblance of the wheat of pure doctrine, and of the Christian life that is the product of that doctrine. But this darnel owes all its vital power to the fact, that men identify themselves with it until they exhibit it themselves, and therefore realize the antinomian principle (ἀνόμια) which lies in heresy. The greatest danger in the appearance of the darnel arises from its not springing up merely in one patch of ground, but going through the whole corn-field, scattered in every part. In this manner it apparently threatens to destroy the whole crop, and this it is which so alarms the servants of the proprietor. Then we are introduced to the second leading thought of the parable. The servants wish to pull up the noxious plants ; but their master orders them to let them grow with the wheat till harvest. The excitement of the servants proceeds first of all from their anger at the wickedness of the enemy : they wish to punish him by destroying his crop ; and next, their zeal is roused for the cleanly state of the field, that it may be throughout free from blemish. Lastly, their fears are excited lest the darnel should choke the wheat, or even adhere to it and change it into darnel. But the master is superior to their excitement, for he sees that these zealous servants would be as dangerous to his crop of wheat as the enemy. In their passionate zeal they are not in a state to distinguish stalk for stalk between darnel and wheat, particularly as in the green shoots

they are so much alike, the less they are developed. There is
therefore great danger of their doing great damage to the crop
of wheat in their attempt to weed it. But their master knew of
a certainty that the wheat would remain wheat, and in time
overtop the darnel; and the nearer the harvest approached, the
more distinctly it would contrast with it, so that at last the
wheat would be most easily separated from the darnel. In this
feature of the parable the great thoughts of the Lord respecting
His kingdom are contained. The servants of the sower have in
history proved it a thousand times by the fact, that the darnel
and the wheat cannot be distinguished with sufficient exactness.
How often have the purest doctrines been execrated as noxious
weeds; how often have the children of the kingdom been condemned as darnel and committed to the flames! In such cases
the servants have assisted the enemy himself: their hatred of
men has been kindled by his; his unbelief has inflamed the
unbelief in them which imagined that the seed of Christ could
be destroyed; they had lost the repose of spirit and the clearness
of vision which beheld the glory and righteousness of their Lord.
These zealots in the wheat-field commit violence, contrary to the
express commands of their Lord. He knows that the false heart
will always form false doctrine, and false doctrine will always
find a congenial soil in false hearts, which assimilate themselves
to it, and thus the noxious plant must complete its history. It
must ripen till harvest,—then the entire worthlessness and noxi-
ousness of its seed will be discovered. How otherwise could it
be perfectly judged at the last judgment? But to the Lord it
is equally certain that pure doctrine will always find true hearts;
that it will be ever retained and flourish in congenial dispositions
till the day of harvest, when the whole crop will be ripened in
the life of the children of the kingdom. The precious seed and
its precious operations, and the precious souls,—that is, the precious seed of Christ in the Gospel, the precious seed of the Spirit
in the Church, and the precious seed of the Father in the creation,—will ever meet together and form a wheat-field, which,
though outwardly intermixed with darnel, yet remains true to
its destiny, and will certainly reach it. There is one more consideration which the parable could less definitely express. That
seed of light and the opposite seed of darkness both find a sus-

ceptible soil in humanity. But it does not follow that some hearts have originally only a disposition for the darnel and others for the wheat. In this relation the most numerous intermixtures, fluctuations, and transitions take place, and it is not well to pass a final judgment during this stormy season of development. Even erroneous doctrine and the truth itself, during this intervening period, are found in such an intermixture, not in themselves, but in the heads and opinions of men, that even in doctrine the wheat and the noxious plants cannot be perfectly and in all their parts separated from each other till the end. The harvest-time is here that terminus where heresies have set themselves as completed scandals, as principles of destruction against the truths of the Gospel, the principles of salvation, and where men who advocate the contrary to these principles have at length become identified with them, so that judgment must follow. From this significance of the final judgment, we may understand in what sense Christ has required His servants to tolerate the darnel-crop during the present life. In the law of the Old Testament theocracy the punishment of death was inflicted on false prophets. Religious zeal might erroneously transplant this law and apply it in a manner most detrimental to the very essence of this economy, by concentrating all the elements of this theocratic typical process against the false prophets. This took place when such zeal placed on an equal footing mistaken opinion with erroneous teaching, and erroneous teaching with fixed heretical dogma, and this with actual social outrage, and outrage with a capital offence, and this with the offending soul; and, accordingly, at one stroke instructed, refuted, excommunicated, tried, condemned, and everlastingly damned the real or supposed heretic. In this way, forsooth, has the Old Testament typical law been expounded and practically enforced by the hierarchy of the Christian Church. In opposition to the horrible judicial arrogance of such servants, whose minds have been darkened by the fear of the devil and the hatred of men, the Lord requires the toleration of the darnel in His wheat-field. But this toleration cannot signify an absolute impunity to evil; but only a holy keeping apart of the *momenta* we have mentioned. The passing error should only be corrected, for it is sufficiently ripe for that (Jas. v. 19). Distinct erroneous doctrine should be refuted, and its teachers punished by admonition; for this purpose are the angels of the Church there (1 Tim. iv. 1–6). Fixed antichristian dogma must be excluded from the Church, with its promulgators, for it has become a scandal to the consciousness of the Church (Gal. i. 9). The offender against the laws of social order must be judged (Rom. xiii. 4), and he who is chargeable with a capital crime must atone for it with his life (Matt. xxvi. 52). But no one must be condemned and rooted out of the Church as a noxious plant; for only at the last judgment can this judgment be passed by holy beings, by the impartial angels, and the judgment of Christ Himself. Thus Christ wills toleration as an infinite energy of patience, which must come forth for ever new in His congregation, from the purest reciprocal action between the spirit of righteousness and the spirit of mercy; and with this, the last principle of this parable is announced. There is coming such a complete separation of all impure and pure elements, of all that is Christian and antichristian in humanity, as certainly as harvest-time follows seed-time; and that harvest-time comes as a sudden great epoch at the completion of the development of the seed. Then will men be treated in judgment like the principles with which they have identified themselves. This identification on the part of the good is a complete one, for a man can become altogether one with the light; but with dark-ness he cannot altogether become one, for identification with evil, in which evil men become individual scandals, is an incom-plete, a crying contradiction, an internal laceration, and fiery torment, which in itself is a judgment, and to which, as an out-ward judgment, the fire of hellish relations corresponds, into which the wicked will be thrown, and in which they will burn. That the noxious plants are gathered into bundles before they are burnt, points to the bringing together of the bad by their separation from the good, as it forms one part of their judgment. But the good form a wheat-harvest, in which all will become living-bread for all, a world of ideality, in which all will be up-held and borne by all in the eternal brightness of life—the pure produce of the development of humanity. One great fact of the kingdom of God is here depicted, when it is said, that after the separation of the darnel from the wheat, the righteous shall shine forth as the sun. The release of the pure Church from the pressure which, by the mixture of its members with the anta-

gonist members, weighs down their souls, must have the effect of
giving them an infinitely powerful and delightful elevation. The
Lord adds to this promise the words which always arouse the
attention to an important communication, ' Whoso hath ears to
hear, let him hear.'

The third parable (Mark iv. 26–29) represents in a very
striking manner the gradual development of the kingdom of
God in time. This kingdom is bound to a rhythm, the succession in time of the development of nature. No sooner is
the seed sown, than the growth proceeds of itself agreeably to
nature, without incessant toil and anxiety on the part of the husbandman. He cannot bring on the harvest before its appointed
time; he must quietly wait, and so it certainly comes to him.
But it comes when the seed has gone through all its forms of
existence, till it appears in the last stage of ripened corn. First
the green blade shoots forth, then the ear, after that the full
corn in the ear, and last of all the ripe grain. This beautiful
parable shows that the kingdom of God, not only in its widest
extent, but in the individual soul, requires time and patience
for its development, and that the seed of God grows quietly
and surely, day and night, wherever it is in the right soil. At
the same time the important thought is presented, that we
ought rightly to estimate all the forms of development in the
kingdom of God—the green field of hope in its youthfulness,
as well as the time when the Gothic spires rise towards heaven
as do the high-pointed, but not yet full ears; and the time when
the stalks become heavier, and the heads droop, as the time of
harvest, when all is shining in the golden light of joy.

After the development of the kingdom of God in time, its
development in space, its spread in the world, is depicted in the
parable of the grain of mustard-seed (Matt. xiii. 31, 32; Mark
iv. 30–32; Luke xiii. 18, 19). The kingdom of God in its beginning is the smallest of all seeds; but in its unfolding it is
the greatest of herbs, a real tree, so that the birds of heaven
come and make their nests in its branches. In its beginning,
therefore, it is remarkably small; in its development, remarkably large—its extension in space is wonderful. And thus the
kingdom of God has actually been extended. The earthly
appearance of Jesus was the wonderful small grain of mustard-
seed; but the plant which sprung from this germ is ever spread-

THE KINGDOM OF GOD.

ing itself throughout the whole world. The same thing is true of the seed of the kingdom of God in the breast of the individual: a single word of God, which lies, as it were, buried in the depths of the soul, spreads itself by degrees as a tree of life through his whole inward and outward life.

This certainty and power of expansion belonging to the kingdom of God indicates also a preponderance of power by which it overcomes all earthly opposition. This specific preponderance of the life of Christ over the whole natural life of the world, is expressed in the parable of the leaven (Matt. xiii. 33; Luke xiii. 20, 21). The leaven is simply and invariably a match for the dough. Let only a small quantity of it be mixed in three measures of meal, and as it were buried deep in it, yet it will penetrate and leaven the whole heap, and change its nature into its own nature. With the same certainty Christianity gains the mastery over the natural life of humanity, as it is buried both in the nature-fulness of the world and in the nature of a single individual whose inner man is affected by it. This perfectly certain, victorious power of the Christian principle is here depicted; not merely its imperceptible, quiet, gradual operation, though this quiet, imperceptible delicacy of its action is contained in the parable. But at the same time the parable declares the circumstance, that Christianity with this preponderance must christianize humanity. As, on the one hand, the leaven is different from the dough, so is Christianity from the natural life of men. Therefore it cannot allow this life to retain its old character. And as, on the other hand, the leaven bears an intimate relation to the dough, so does Christianity to the essential life of man, and therefore can and must mingle with it. But that is a higher potency of the dough. On the certainty of this fact rests the confidence of the woman who kneads the leaven into the meal; she knows that owing to its superior power it must transform the dough into its own nature. In like manner Christianity is a higher potency of humanity, and on that rests the confidence of the Church, which, with its weak hand, performs the same office in spiritual things as the woman in earthly things, when it infuses the life-power of Christ into the blood and life of humanity.[1]

[1] Olshausen believes that the reference of the three measures of meal to the sanctification of the three powers (*Potenzen*) of human nature by means

But this preponderance of the Church is no natural necessity for individuals in the world, so that they would become Christians without knowing how. They may be outwardly christianized by that leavening influence of Christianity without becoming Christians in their individual inward life. For individuals in the world, Christianity remains continually a mysterious, hidden treasure. At the best, they are aware of its existence as a hidden, far-distant treasure, celebrated by report. Whoever finds it may esteem himself fortunate in the highest degree; for in this discovery God's highest freedom co-operates with the highest free agency of man. When a man has found this treasure, he recognises it as the highest good of his life; he gives up everything in order to gain the divine good of individual, vital Christianity. Thus the world-historical Christianity becomes individual. These relations are pointed out by the treasure hid in the field (Matt. xiii. 44) and by the pearl of great price (ver. 45). The two parables resemble one another in this point, that they show how Christianity must be first found by the individual; how it becomes his portion in concentrated unity as the highest good of life, and desired as an absolute, new, and heavenly life-treasure, so that the man is ready with joy to resign his ancient life-treasure, in whatever imaginary good it might consist, and at the same time his own self-will, with which he clung to that treasure. This surrender is represented under the image of purchase-money, in part allegorically, and in part symbolically. It is only allegory when it is said that man gains the pearl of great price by the surrender of his earthly comforts; for this surrender cannot be considered as the payment of the purchase-money, but only as the removal of obstacles, as the fulfilment of conditions: yet the description is, in its internal sense, symbolical; when man surrenders himself and his old life-image to God in faith, he gains, in the vital exchange of love, a participation of the life of God. He gains Christ, the treasure hid in the field, the pearl of great price; and if he possesses the most precious pearl in its unity, he no longer seeks the inferior pearls in their multiplicity, which, compared with that pearl, are valueless. But though no one re-

of Christianity, is not to be unceremoniously rejected. But then we must also bring in the three powers which Christianity spiritualizes in its totality; and as such we may regard the Church, the State, and the cosmical Globe.

ceives the treasure of Christianity otherwise than on the condition of a pure surrender, yet there is a great difference in the way and manner by which individuals obtain it. In one case the superintendence of grace which makes a man the happy finder is conspicuous in all its nobleness. Most suddenly he lights upon the treasure in the field, and from a poor day-labourer becomes a wealthy man.[1] In the other case his discovery is the final result of a long, conscious striving. He was a merchant whose attention was directed to precious pearls, and who gladly laid out his property on the choicest goods of life; who perhaps sought his satisfaction in the pleasure resulting from high morality, the cultivation of the fine arts, of literature, and of science. He was seeking for goodly pearls; he finds the one pearl of great price. This merchant is also a finder to whom the highest blessing of Heaven, grace, is propitious. But his long seeking, the mediation of finding by a higher striving, is made more conspicuous. On the other hand, the favour of Heaven came suddenly on the first finder, although he was unconsciously a seeker, a man who was digging the field for the sake of bread. As the free saving agency of the grace of God in the reconciliation of man is set forth in the parable of the treasure hid in the field, so is the noblest striving of man in it by the parable of the pearl of great price.[2]

The last parable in this cyclus is that of the net cast into the sea, and enclosing all kinds of fish (Matt. xiii. 47–50). When full, it is drawn on shore. The fishermen sit down and gather the good into vessels, but cast the bad away. The explanation of this parable shows, that the judgment is represented under a new point of view. The judgment had already been spoken of in the parable of the darnel and the wheat; but the leading thought of that parable was the necessity of tolerating heretical

---

[1] The contrivance which this man employed to make the field his own, must, as Olshausen justly remarks, be explained on the same principle as the parable of the unjust steward.—[See Trench, *Notes on the Parables*, p. 126. —Tr.]

[2] To the same class, according to Neander, belong the passages in Luke xiv. 28 and 31, about the man who built a tower and counted the cost, and the king who was about to make war and consulted respecting his forces; but these passages rather belong to parabolic discourses, since the comparisons are only incidentally made.—[Neander, *Life of Christ*, § 208, p. 342. —Tr.]

spirits; and the judgment itself appeared principally as a separation of offences and their perpetrators. But here the distinction between the good and the bad, the elect of humanity and its refuse, is represented unconditionally in the contrast of the good and the bad fish. The net is the Church in its widest extent, as the institution which, in its consummated operation at the end of the world (ἐν τῇ συντελείᾳ τοῦ αἰῶνος), embraces the whole world, and has continually embraced it according to its ideal significance as the glory of Christ's kingdom. The judgment here appears from the point of view which regards the correct estimate of the essential worth of individuals. The righteous form collectively an essential heaven; the wicked, an essential hell; and the separation is made accordingly. Here also the judgment of the wicked is marked by their being cast into the fire where is wailing and gnashing of teeth.[1]

All the parables in this cycle show to what extent Christ deviated from the Jewish representations of the Messianic kingdom, and combated them. According to the Jewish preconception, the heavenly sower had cultivated and sown only a small field in the wilderness of the world, the people of Israel, who bore the best fruits in the fidelity of their observances. This corn-field, according to the false notion of the Jews, was pure enough; but all round there grew a crop of noxious plants, the heathen world. At the most, there appeared in those opposed to the one Jewish sect but one kind of noxious plants; but when this appeared distinctly in the shape of individual opinion, they inflicted stoning in order to exterminate it. Neither the meta-

---

[1] The fiery furnace into which at the revelation of the new æon the ungodly will be thrown, is a counterpart of the fiery furnace into which, while the old æon flourished, the godly were thrown (Dan. iii.). In that furnace ' the song of the three men in the fire' resounded as a great song of praise; in the other furnace will be heard the howl of anguish and pain, and the teeth-gnashing of wrath and wickedness (see Rev. ix. 2). By the fiery trial of the pious, heaven was rendered visible in humanity; the fiery heat which the wicked endure, brings to light the inward hell in humanity. So also the outer darkness in which there will be weeping and gnashing of teeth (Matt. viii. 12, xxii. 13), is thus pointed out in contrast to the holy darkness in which God dwells (Exod. xx. 21; 1 Kings viii. 12), among the praises of Israel (Ps. xxii. 3), and the darkness of the tribulation of the pious, which, by the blessing of their inward peace, shall be as clear as noonday (Isa. lviii. 10). These contrasts plainly indicate that it is the wicked who make hell, hell.

morphoses of the kingdom of God as depicted in the third parable, nor its extension, as in the fourth, suited their system. The doctrine of the vital operation of the kingdom of heaven as portrayed in the parable of the leaven, agreed not with their system of traditions; still less could they admit, in their self-righteousness, that each one among them must enter the kingdom of heaven through a special act of grace in his individual experience. The judgment, they imagined, would consist in the exaltation of the Jews and the punishment of the Gentiles; this momentous separation was, in their opinion, completed long before outwardly. Thus, in one word, the whole difference was decidedly exhibited between the completely pure original Christianity and totally decayed Judaism in all these doctrines of the kingdom. It was only in parables that the people could endure such severe Christian truths.

By means of the three last parables of the first cycle, the two following cycles are already announced. If here, in the parables relating to the agency of mercy, the traits of judicial righteousness come forth at first gently, but afterwards more powerfully; and if again, in the parables relating to judgment, the traits of redeeming grace and love are constantly to be found, we are not to be surprised. For these fundamental forms of the divine administration are not antagonistic to one another. Rather we may affirm, that one is a necessary complement of the other, and that they build up the divine kingdom in living co-operation. This twofold aspect of the parables we are about to consider, may in some instances make it doubtful whether we are to place them in the second or in the third group; in such cases, we must pay particular attention to the leading thought of the parable.

It accords with Luke's peculiar predilection, that he has collected most of the parables that illustrate the administration of mercy. These parables the Lord was especially induced to bring forward, when, towards the close of His ministry, He came into frequent collision with the Pharisees, and had to censure their unloving disposition.

The first of these parables is a noble portraiture of mercy, which very properly opens this cycle; namely, the parable of the good Samaritan (Luke x. 30–37). By means of this parable, Jesus explained to the scribe, who wished to tempt Him, who was his neighbour. The man who, according to our Lord's representation, falls among thieves between Jerusalem and Jericho, is a Jew from the metropolis. His neighbours in the Jewish sense are the priest and the Levite, who heartlessly hurry by him as he lies half-dead. The Samaritan who travels the same way is, according to the Jewish prejudice, not his neighbour, and he dare not promise himself any help from him. But generous pity moves his breast as he sees the Jew lying there half-dead. The latter must be glad, that in such a plight a Samaritan salutes him, lifts him up, binds his wounds, and pours in oil and wine. He readily consents to be placed on the beast of the reputed unclean stranger, and to be taken by him to the inn. He must acknowledge such a deliverer to be his neighbour, and, ashamed and overcome by his noble-mindedness, must also become the neighbour of his deliverer. With wonderful skill Christ has so put the case, that no choice is left to the scribe, but he must himself condemn his Jewish prejudice. No feature of the parable is impossible. An orthodox Jew from Jerusalem might fall among thieves. There are priests and Levites who would be heartless enough to pass by him without sympathy; it is very possible that a Samaritan might pity and help him. And such traits of character are frequently to be found in real life. But the reality is always a judgment on that hatred of heretics which eradicates universal philanthropy and the love of our neighbour. It is not a Samaritan whom the priest allows to be in his blood, but a Jew. The priest, with cold selfishness, is conscious of his elevation above this layman, although he was of the same confession. The Levite also prides himself too much on his peculiar temple-purity. Even the Jewish innkeeper is not altogether free from the charge of heartlessness, for he allows the Samaritan to pay for his Jewish brother. How striking and how awfully true are these traits of inhumanity, as it begins to operate in regions where fanaticism leads to the hatred of those of a different faith! Such fanatics cannot be content with striking down the Samaritan, and leaving him in his blood. They rob one another, and strike one another half-dead; and their very priests and Levites leave the unhappy man who has been attacked by robbers lying in his blood; and all this within the circle of one and the same fanatically excited confession. Thus the Jewish nation, in the last war before the destruction of Jerusalem, was overrun by robbers and fanatics, the same persons being often both. No consecrated institution holds men together any longer, where love has grown cold, and is even regarded as a sin. In the circle of such heartlessness, every person is an obscure separatist, and every family a sect in opposition to the great universal Church of grace and mercy, and scarcely is the nearest, to say nothing of those at a distance, regarded as a neighbour. But calamity comes forth, on the one hand, with giant steps, and plunges the fanatic into misery; on the other hand, mercy conducts the differently minded, and makes him an angel of deliverance for him. Thus the holy, inalienable humanity of benevolence and compassion breaks down those bariers of religious and national animosity, by which man in his selfishness can fancy that he does honour to God by his nation or his creed, while he has become worse than a heathen in his disposition. And as far as this humanity exerts its influence, and establishes a higher intercourse between calamity and mercy— as far as this pure unselfish human love reaches, it is manifest that man, simply as such, is neighbour to man, as far as he is man, as far as he can receive and return love. The good Samaritan is in all his features an image of the freest and richest mercy; and this has given occasion to find in this parable an allegory of the love of Christ. Christ too was, in the eyes of the pharisaical Jews, an unclean person, a heretic; and He it was who rescued prostrate, half-dead humanity from sin, while the priests and Levites never vouchsafed a glance at the deep wounds of their race. Thus the first parable delineates the mercy of love in its most general form, embracing all opposites, and overcoming all obstacles.

The parable of the man who made a wedding feast, in the first form in which Luke presents it (xiv. 16-24, compared with Matt. xxii. 1, etc.), is also, as we have already mentioned, predominantly a parable of mercy. The insulting behaviour of the persons who were first invited, who betrayed by their paltry excuses their contempt of the invitation, called forth, of course, the anger of the householder. But this anger revealed itself again as the ardour of an invincible love: he was angry, and sent forth his servants to invite other guests, till his house should be full of the poorest and meanest. And he resolved, in accordance with justice and honour, that 'none of the men that were bidden shall taste of my supper.' The banquet of this noble-minded personage represents the blessedness of the Christian spiritual life. Jehovah is the giver of the banquet. He had long before invited guests. The Israelites had been prepared for the great banquet, and had been invited to it. But the latter summonses must be distinguished from the first invitation; now the feast was ready. These summonses coincide with the advent and ministry of Christ. But now the invited, as if preconcerted from the first, began to make excuse. The excuses of these persons are excused in a foolish manner,[1] contradictory to the spirit of the parable, when the text is explained thus: that the first and second wished to settle their purchases; and when, as to the third, it is observed that the newly married Israelites, according to the law, were free for a year from military service (Deut. xxiv. 5). These excuses must from the first appear as worthless, and indeed contain their own refutation. For temporal and worldly business does not in itself prevent man from being a guest in the kingdom of heaven, but bondage of the will, the tumult of the passions by which he is impelled, and the confusion of a worldly mind, as it appears in all imaginable forms. This confusion is shown in this, that the two first, having made their purchases, wished to inspect them at night-time, when all field-boundaries are obscure, and all cattle are black; and that the third has been made a vassal by his wife, which means more in the East than in the West. The earthly mind in its various forms makes men unsusceptible for the spiritual life of the kingdom of heaven; particularly as delight in earthly possessions, represented here by 'the piece of ground,' and in the love of power is symbolized by brandishing the goad over five yoke of oxen; and lastly, as slavish sensuality and surrender to men in love and fear, perversities which the hindrance arising from marrying represents. The subtle forms of opposition to the Gospel as they met the Lord in Pharisaism and Sadducaism are everywhere animated by these various elements of the worldly mind. The offence against the giver of the feast consisted in breaking the word of promise made to him, and that his kindness was treated with contempt by worthless excuses precisely at the most joyous event in his life. But yet he gratified his ardent

[1] Very often, exegetical pedants labour to make reasonable what in the Gospels is represented as foolish.

desire to make a festival. We cannot hesitate to understand by ' the poor, the maimed, the halt, and the blind,' whom he caused to be invited in haste from the streets and lanes of the city, in the first place, the 'publicans and sinners' in contrast to the Pharisees. And when the servant is sent out of the city to invite the people who were lying about in the highways and hedges, this must apply to the Samaritans and heathens in contrast to the Jews in general. The hedges may refer to the extreme borders of Judaism, and to its being fenced in, as it were, from the Gentiles who were situated on the borders of the Israelitish territory. But here again, in the outward contrast an inner one is reflected. The Pharisees and Jews are in this case only the representatives of the worldly happy and the worldly-minded throughout the world; the publicans, Samaritans, and heathen, on the other hand, represent the poor in this world, the souls who are longing for the blessings of the kingdom of heaven. These poor persons, who could scarcely conceive of so high an invitation, the giver of the feast causes to be earnestly invited, yea, compelled to come in. Yet we must not impute to them a spirit of resistance against entering the house of the Church, which is to be overcome by force, as fanaticism has interpreted the passage; but simply the hesitation of joyful surprise in humble minds, who deem themselves unworthy of such an invitation. Thus the house of the divine liberality is filled with guests who can celebrate the feast of love and of the spirit; the worldly happy remain without.

The love, generosity, and mercy which are depicted in this parable are shown in the next place as redeeming grace, which is not only applied to the suffering and the poor, but equally to the lost. It is thus exhibited in the parables of the lost sheep, the lost piece of money, and the prodigal son. In all the three parables, that overflowing, wonderful, self-sacrificing inspiration of love is delineated, which to the earthly mind must appear as foolishness. The shepherd risks the ninety and nine sheep in the wilderness, and even his own life, in order to rescue and recover the lost sheep; and his rejoicing on having found it far exceeds the pecuniary value of the sheep. And the very pains with which the woman who had ten pieces of silver seeks to recover the lost piece, and the joy with which she tells her neighbours of its fortunate recovery, goes far beyond the bare value of the coin. But the father, who sees his lost son returned, prepares a feast such as he had never prepared for the elder son who had remained at home with him. So wonderful, even to the miraculous, is love, that even the angels of God, in all their number and glory, can 'rejoice over one sinner that repenteth.' Yet is this apparently foolish love, divinely wise grace. Mercy also acts with all the motives of wisdom. It came, in the person of the Son of man, to seek what was lost. When anything that God has made is lost in His world, a violation of the divine order is involved, against which not only love but also wisdom enters the lists. The beautiful completeness of his flock is lost to the shepherd, to make up the number one hundred; and the woman also dwells upon the round number of her savings— that she had exactly ten pieces of silver. The deficiency is so painful, especially in the father's house where one of two sons is wanting.[1]

Therefore the consideration of the whole guides mercy when it seeks for the single lost one. The divine regard for the symmetry and beauty of the eternal temple causes the divine love to exert itself about this or that stone in the structure. But there is also consideration of the individual, of its life and value. A lost sheep is indeed, as lost, a very poor creature; but the shepherd values it as a sheep of his flock; he gives it not up to the wolf; he pities its unhappy life in its wanderings and distress. The lost piece of money lies in the dirt, tarnished and useless; but still it is a coin composed of a noble metal, and stamped with the image of a prince. But the value of the lost son which remains to him in all his degradation, consists in his being the nearest relative of his father, that his being is derived from his father's being. Thus grace seeks to deliver the lost sinner, partly on account of the relation in which, according to the divine destiny, he stands to God and to the eternal family of God; but also on his own account, because he is an unhappy being, because in his nature (*Substanz*) he has an unchangeable

[1] To the shepherd one of a hundred sheep is wanting,—to the woman, one of ten pieces of silver,—to the father, one of two sons, while in the other he can no longer have any real satisfaction. In a bolder form, but with profound evangelical insight, Angelus Silesius expresses the longing of God after the reconciliation of man by the words, 'I am of as much consequence to Him, as He is to me.'

value, and because he is originally of divine descent. The parable of the lost son is a gospel in the Gospel. It has been said, that here is reconciliation without mediation through Christ, and so it has been erroneously assumed that every parable must exhibit the whole rule of faith; the parable of the lost sheep and its shepherd is already forgotten; and in this of the lost son, it is not understood what is meant by the father's running to meet him with agitated heart, and falling on his neck and kissing him. The divine salutation in the heart of the returning sinner, the first blessed feeling of grace, is here exhibited in the most beautiful manner.[1] Every stroke is to the life. The youngest son loses his inheritance, by separating through mere selfishness his own property from his father's, withdrawing from his father into the paths of worldly pleasures, and squandering his property in the indulgence of sensual lusts. He is punished by famine, by the want of the peace of God in the land of vanity, and by the lowest degradation, that he, an Israelite, must prolong his life in a most dishonourable existence, as swine-herd of a heathen, a most servile and disgusting occupation—till at last he must vainly wish to live upon the swine's fodder, and therefore sank into a depth of misery, which made the lot of the most unclean animals an object of envy. But by these means his awakening is brought about. This is expressed with admirable beauty: 'he came to himself' ($\epsilon\iota\varsigma$ $\dot{\epsilon}\alpha\nu\tau\grave{o}\nu$ $\delta\dot{\epsilon}$ $\dot{\epsilon}\lambda\theta\acute{\omega}\nu$). He reflected on the happy lot of the *hired servants* at his father's, and resolves, 'I will arise and go to my father, and will say unto him, Father, I have sinned against heaven, and before thee, and am no more worthy to be called thy son; make me as one of thy hired servants!' The hired servants were not the offspring of his father. If we are not disposed to consider them as merely allegorical figures, which is precluded by the fact that their happy condition made so deep an impression on the prodigal, their tranquillity denotes the tranquillity of creation, particularly of the irrational creatures, which formed so lively a contrast to the miserable state of the distracted sinner, and admonished him to turn from his evil courses. The confession, 'I have sinned against heaven,' is very significant; by every sin a heavenly nature is

[1] Olshausen remarks, that in the parable of the prodigal son human activity in the work of conversion is delineated. But the divine activity also is not wanting in this parable.

violated and disturbed. Compassionate grace could not be depicted in a more striking manner than is shown in the conduct of the father. The lost son brings the confession of his guilt before him; but grace has expelled the gloomy element in his repentance; the petition, 'Make me as one of thy hired servants,' has died in his heart. He cannot affront the father with this monkish or slavish sigh of distrust. But the father reinstates him joyfully in his filial dignity; orders his servants to put on him the best robe, and a ring on his hand, and shoes on his feet: he must be seen again in the full array of sonship. Then he commands them to kill the fatted calf, and to prepare a feast, because this son who was dead, is alive again; he was lost, and is found.[1] He therefore prepared for him a feast of restoration with the highest joy, devotion, and distinction. The elder son forms a difficult element of this parable. It seems a contradiction that he should be contrasted with the lost son as remaining at home, and should yet be irritated with his father for showing compassion to his brother. But if we closely look at it, traces of the same lost condition will gradually show themselves in the secret recesses of his soul, with which he upbraided his younger brother. In his legal good conduct he is outwardly unblameable, but inwardly he is not more in harmony with his father. He is not of one mind with him in mercy; he no longer knows his father's property to be his own; he is not dutiful to him; he even refuses to go into his father's house, where the feast for the return of his brother is celebrated, so much is he offended at the festive sound of the music and at the dancing. How strikingly is this feature apparent in the conduct of the Jews when the Gentiles became Christians! They went with heathenish rancour out of their Father's house in which grace celebrated their redemption-feast. And for a long time the elder son cherished a secret embittered feeling against the Father; for he fancied that he had served Him so many years, and never

---

[1] If we attempt to explain the particulars of the description, the best robe may denote the rejoicing of the son with the father, the reconciliation. But the seal-ring (δακτύλιος) is not equivalent to the seal or sealing; it rather denotes the filial right to act and seal in the father's name. The sandals are a sign that the reformed one can go in and out freely. The fatted calf, in the singular, indicates that the father spared no expense, but provided what was of most value.

transgressed His commandment, but the Father had never yet estimated his conduct according to its merits. It is evident that he had no inward delight and joy from his morose external correctness of deportment. A fearful truth lies in the words, ' Thou hast killed for him the fatted calf; yet thou never gavest me a kid, that I should make merry with my friends.' He never found a real feast of soul in his legality. But, in truth, he fain would have made merry without idea and occasion, as his brother had done in a foreign land; this now comes out with his chagrin. With a feast of the spirit he had nothing to do; this is proved by his ill feeling towards the feast for his brother. His last words are full of bitterness and falsehood. ' But as soon as this thy son was come, which hath devoured thy living with harlots, thou hast killed for him the fatted calf' (ver. 30). He was unwilling to call the returned prodigal his brother, though obliged to recognise him as his father's son. He exaggerates and misrepresents his irregularities, and describes the expense of the feast as an excessive indulgence of the prodigal, and wastefulness. He even depreciates his father's character; and his own degeneracy, which had been hitherto concealed under outward propriety of conduct, now comes to a head. Thus mere outward righteousness is always brought to shame when it sees the feast of grace. It cannot endure the sight of sinners being saved by grace. In the tumult of envy which this spectacle arouses, all the selfishness, coarseness, and depravity which had been hitherto concealed, break forth. The history of the Jews in the days of the Apostle Paul proves this; and the history of the hierarchy in Luther's time on the large scale, while on the small scale it has been repeated a thousand times. Thus, for example, a feeling of chagrin may be observed in many sanctimonious rationalist writings respecting the conversion of Augustin, and his high reputation in the Christian Church. The elder son is a character that perpetually recurs in the history of the kingdom of God. But it was not within the scope of the parable to narrate the sequel of his history. His fall first became visible when that of his brother was retrieved by grace. This grace also calmly confronted his perversity with soothing and admonitory words. The divine mercy is as much illustrated by the closing words of the father, with which he admonished the elder son, as by the joy with which he hastened to meet the younger.

The parable of the prodigal son is plainly reflected in the parable of the Pharisee and publican (Luke xviii. 9–14). The two forms which stand in presence of the grace of God in such different frames of mind, again make their appearance. But the elder son here developes himself fully in his self-righteousness, and the younger stands before us in the attitude of ripened repentance. This advance, however, is not the only difference of the two parables; for a turning-point is here introduced, since a man is depicted as praying with such complete success as to obtain the redeeming grace of God. We must here connect several parables with one another as representations of the life of prayer, by which man becomes sure of the grace of God and of all its aids. The parable already mentioned forms the beginning. From the connection we gather that the publican is the principal person in it, as is also shown by the structure of the conclusion. Christ spoke this parable ' to certain which trusted in themselves that they were righteous, and despised others.' It has been remarked, that, since a Pharisee is introduced in this parable, Christ could not have addressed it to the Pharisees, for in that case the form would have been unsuitable. But on this hypothesis, no publican could have ventured to be present at its delivery, nor any priest or Levite at that of the parable of the good Samaritan. Since the figure of the Pharisee was not chosen to put into the shade any individual of that sect, or the sect itself, the question appears to be unimportant, whether the Pharisees were present or not at the delivery of this parable. The parable recognises, indeed, that the Pharisee had the pre-eminence of dignity and conformity to the law, before the publican : he is with propriety placed first. It is not his zeal for the law in itself that brings him into a disadvantageous position, but the delusion that by this zeal he was righteous in God's sight. With emphasis it is said that he stood thus in the temple and prayed *by himself*.[1] He thanked God that he was not as other men are, extortioners, unjust, adulterers, or even as this publican ; and then he tells what he really is—

---

[1] πρὸς ἑαυτόν. Perhaps he did not venture to utter aloud so offensive a prayer. Taken literally, the words would mean that he did not really address himself to God, but in vain self-idolatry had only himself before his eyes, though ostensibly praying to God.

he fasts twice a week, and gives tithes of all that he has.   This shocking poverty of the feeling of life, which would make out of two useless excesses of a religious and civil legality the true riches of life, and even a righteousness before God, shows his character.   The key-note of his prayer is contempt of other people ; and the worst thing in it is, that he condemns the pub- lican personally while celebrating his own reconciliation with God. The publican was an Israelite as well as he, and had an equal right to enter the temple.   But, bowed down by the consciousness of his sinfulness, he did not venture to go far into the sanctuary. The sanctuary reproved him as the visible majesty of God, and perhaps the Pharisee himself appeared to him as a cherub who threatened to hinder his entrance into paradise.   He would not so much as lift up his eyes to heaven, not even his hands, but smote upon his breast, saying, ' God be merciful to me a sinner !' The judgment of Christ follows this contrast : ' I tell you, this man went down to his house justified, rather than the other; for every one that exalteth himself shall be abased, and he that humbleth himself shall be exalted.'   Thus, then, man obtains grace in the way of sincere humiliation before God, and of be- lieving prayer; not in the way of legal performances.   But, owing to his spiritual slothfulness no less than to his pride, he is always inclined to enter the path of self-righteousness, and thus to estrange himself from the grace of God and from true spiritual life.   This striving of man to realize righteousness in his religious and civil performances sinks him a thousand times into the most unspiritual Pharisaism, which sharpens his performances in mere external things, while spiritual death gives the most ghastly signs of its having seized on the inner man.   And a thousand times the poor publican stands agitated by the feeling of his guilt, and burdened by the condemnatory sentence of the Pharisee, and in the internal sentence that he passes on his own soul, sees the day-spring of God's grace.   Thus both the Pharisee and the publican are world-historical forms ; they walk immortal through all ages of the theocracy and of the Christian Church.

While this parable shows how the sinner obtains grace by means of prayer, the parable of the unjust judge (Luke xviii. 1–8) represents how Christians who are in a state of acceptance with God obtain at last, in times of severe trial, His merciful aid by means of persevering prayer.   Here, therefore, the unjust judge represents the image of God, as in another parable the unjust steward denotes the pious man. In both cases these delineations are manifestly to be regarded as allegorical, in distinction from symbolical ones. God can only according to outward appearance seem like the unjust judge when He allows the pious to suffer long under the oppression of the world and the attacks of the evil one, when, as in the instance of the sufferings of Christ, He seems to continue inexorable in the deepest sufferings of the innocent. But, according to His nature, He is always the merciful One. Parables in which such bold allegorical strokes occur, peculiarly require an explanation, such as is given here and at the close of the parable of the unjust steward. Olshausen has justly referred to the often-recurring outward appearance of the inexorability of God, in which He only expresses His own unsearchableness in order to explain the figure of the unjust judge. According to him, the oppressed widow is to be regarded as an image of the persecuted Church ; and her adversary who oppressed her, an image of the princes of this world. The explanation which Jesus appends to the parable favours this interpretation. He calls attention to the words of the unjust judge. As the poor widow was always importuning him to extend to her the protection of the law against her adversary, he said to her, 'Though I fear not God nor regard man, yet because this widow troubleth me I will avenge her, lest by her continual coming she weary me.'[1] 'Hear,' said Christ, 'what the unjust judge saith. And shall not God avenge His own elect, which cry day and night unto Him, though He acts towards them with lofty reserve,[2] and therefore inscrutably ? I tell you that He will avenge them speedily.' The closing words, 'Nevertheless, when the Son of man cometh, will He find faith on the earth ?' express the same thought in the strongest manner. God will not only respond to the prayers of His elect, but will so far surpass them, that the appearance of the Son of man, with which the redress of their wrongs will take place, will be incredible to the majority. In this parable, therefore, the whole praying life of the Church is marked as the con-

---

[1] μὴ ὑπωπιάζῃ με, lest she strike me under the eye, or clench her fist at me.

[2] So, I believe, we must translate καὶ μακροθυμῶν ἐπ' αὐτοῖς, according to the connection and the literal sense of the words.

dition on which the entire mercy which God cherishes for His
Church in His Spirit will be manifested. The appearance of
not hearing, of unmercifulness for a long time, confronts the
supplications of the Church; but when the hearing comes, the
unfolding of the mercy will be so glorious, that it will be met by
the appearance of unbelief in those who had implored it.[1] But
though this parable, according to its precise interpretation, is a
living image of the Church in all ages, it is equally an image of
individual believers. The destitute soul is reminded of the full
power of constant access which God grants it in the privilege of
prayer. In the way of prayer it can be certain of the super-
abundant unfolding at a future time of God's mercy.

A kindred parable, but presented in the form of a parabolic
conversation, we find in Luke xi. 5–8. Here the Lord describes
a person who knocks in the middle of the night at his friend's
door, to seek his assistance on a pressing occasion. Another
friend, travelling by night, has turned in for a lodging, and he
wants three loaves to entertain him; so he comes to his friend
with a request to lend them to him. Will this friend, in such a
case, call to him from within,[2] 'Trouble me not; the door is
now shut, and my children are with me in bed?' 'I say unto
you,' says Christ, 'though he will not rise and give him because
he is his friend, yet because of his importunity he will arise[3]
and give him as many as he needeth.' Both friends have excellent motives, which clash with one another. The one entreats
under the pressure of a sacred obligation which friendship, and
indeed hospitality, had imposed upon him in a most urgent form.
For the other, it is hard to disturb his little ones in their sweet
sleep so suddenly and alarmingly, especially by the opening of
the house-door. But still he does not consider it well to set his
own motive against that of his friend. The unabashed urgency

[1] Compare Ps. cxxvi. 1, 'When the Lord turned again the captivity of
Zion, we were like them that dream.'

[2] It is in accordance with the connection and the harmonic construction
of this parabolic discourse to take ver. 7 as an inference, so that the question involves a negation, and is such as the following: 'Who will have a
friend who should give such an answer (even though he well might)?'
Probably the recollection of the parable of the unjust judge has contributed
to alter the interpretation of this parable.

[3] The ἐγερθείς would be quite superfluous if it were not significantly used
in reference to the preceding ἀναστάς.

to which his friend is impelled by the requirements of love forms an exciting power which overpowers him and makes him quite alert to render aid. And if he were not his friend, yet he could hardly withstand him. How much more, then, will God, in His deep, heavenly repose, faithfully and graciously hearken to the supplication of man in his midnight distresses—that supplication which in its purity always proceeds from the holiest solicitude of love, honour, and duty!

The experience of God's great clemency which redeems and rescues the sinner, can only be completed when the life of love again awakens in his breast and begins to gush forth. It will therefore express itself in reciprocal love and gratitude, and in their preservation. This truth the Lord exhibits in the short parable of the two debtors (Luke vii. 41, 42). Both were in debt to the same creditor. The one owed him five hundred pence, and the other fifty; and since they could not pay him, he frankly forgave them both. Simon the Pharisee, to whom Jesus had addressed this parable, was obliged himself to decide, that he to whom the creditor forgave most would love him most. Jesus then declared to him, that the sins of the woman who had occasioned this conversation were forgiven, since she had given proof of greater love; ' but to whom little is forgiven, the same loveth little.' It plainly follows from the connection of the parable, that the forgiveness of sins is to be considered not as the consequence, but as the ground of love to the Lord. But the leading thought of the parable is this, that from the fulness and power of a man's proofs of love we must draw conclusions respecting his love, and through that, respecting the reconciliation from which alone it can proceed. Where the love is great, the reconciliation is great; where there is little love, the reconciliation is slight; that is, the reconciliation scarcely exists, or is not yet begun. And the more the love of man unfolds itself, so much more deeply he enters into the blessed kingdom of love and mercy. But the more he gives himself up to an unloving disposition, the more he loses the right state of mind for mercy and the hope of it.

Christ shows in three great parables, that if men would obtain mercy, they must exercise mercy. In the first, the parable of the unjust steward (Luke xvi. 1–8), we see the blessing of mercy; on the other hand, in the two others, the parable of the rich man and Lazarus, and of the servant who owed ten thousand talents (Matt. xviii. 23, 35), the curse of unmercifulness is depicted. In the exposition of the first parable, we must, above all things, not overlook the key which the Lord has given, since this parable is more difficult than the others. This remark applies particularly to the words, ' The children of this world are in their generation wiser than the children of light.' The unfaithful steward must be regarded as one of the children of this world, since he deceives his lord. And the debtors are, at all events, people who live in the same worldly element as the steward ; they become parties at once to his unfaithfulness. Of his master we know nothing that sets him above the region of the children of this world. It strikingly indicates his worldly mode of viewing things, when we are told, in ver. 8, that he actually commended his unfaithful servant. It is true, he praised him only for his cleverness—that by the exercise of a great though unrighteous liberality he had made provision for his own maintenance. Now thus the children of light ought to be wise in their way, in accordance with their own character. Money is almost an imperishable idol, the Mammon whose worship will not vanish even among Monotheists ;[1] for which reason Christ calls money by the name of the idol. But He calls it still more definitely the Mammon of unrighteousness ; not only because it passes through so many unrighteous hands, but because it never purely corresponds to its proper destiny, an ideal standard of value for worldly things and relations. Money (Geld) should express the essential value (Geltung), and thus secure righteousness in commercial transactions ; but in its actual use it is often a caricature of its destiny—a false standard of value, and therefore a medium on which a thousand false estimates and returns, and therefore deeds of unrighteousness, depend.

[1] Mammon is probably not a mythological divinity, but in the Syrian and Phœnician commercial life has been transformed into an idol, just as is now often done in a half-jocose, half-serious·manner. Bretschneider : ' Μαμωνᾶς. Heb. ממון, fortasse significat id cui confiditur ut LXX. אמנה, Jer. xxxiii. 6, θησαυρούς ; Ps. xxxvii. 3, πλοῦτον, reddiderunt ; vel est ut multi putant nomen idoli Syrorum et Pœnorum, divitiarum præsidis, i.q. Pluto Græcorum.' Olshausen : ' Augustin remarks on this passage—congruit et punicum nomen, nam lucrum punice Mammon dicitur. Gold appears in contrast with God, as a person, an idol, a sort of Plutus, without its being proved that an idol of this kind was worshipped ' (i. 231).

But the children of light should always feel about money as if something alien and unsuitable belonged to it, and therefore should devote it most willingly to making friends with it—friends who may receive them, if they now suffer want, into everlasting habitations. It would not be consonant to the spirit of Christ's doctrine, if we were so to understand these words, as if the pious could by works of mercy purchase a reception into everlasting habitations, or that this reception is dependent on the generosity of the perfected in the other world. In this parable we find ourselves placed in the kingdom of free mercy. According to this view, the leading thought is: Sanctify temporal possessions, which generally become a burden to men; make them an organ of blessing by your liberality; make them the channels of your mercy. If you so devote the temporal to mercy, you will make friends for yourselves, who will give you in exchange the eternal for the temporal, and receive you into their everlasting habitations. Here in the everlasting habitations of the Church, and in the other world in the everlasting habitations of the perfected kingdom, you will be welcomed as belonging to the family. Whoever devotes his powers to mercy, living and dying, he will fall into the arms of mercy. Olshausen has developed the leading thoughts of the parable in an ingenious manner, so that all the parts obtain a definite meaning. The rich man is the world, or the prince of this world. Opposite to him stands another, the true Lord,—God as the representative of those who receive the destitute into everlasting habitations. The steward stands in the middle between the two. ' He labours with the property of the one for the objects of the other.' We are here reminded of the better sort of publicans, who had an entirely different position from that of the Pharisees. They were outwardly, indeed, very much mixed up with the world, but their inner man was inflamed with a longing after the divine. The Pharisees, on the contrary, were ' outwardly in close conjunction with the divine, as the representatives by birth of the theocracy; but their inner life was attached to the world, and they made use of their spiritual character for temporal objects.' But the parable, by certain definite features, requires the exposition of Olshausen to be in some degree modified. According to ver. 13, the rich man is Mammon himself—the allegorical Plutus—the spirit of gain, or the worldly mind so far as it amasses wealth

in the spirit of selfishness. Every man of wealth or property is
a steward in the kingdom of this Mammon. But the pious man
of wealth does not serve him faithfully; he embezzles, according
to worldly notions, the treasures which he ought strictly to employ for self-interest, since he employs them in the spirit of
liberality and sympathy. Lastly, he is too much for the calculating genius of gain, who purposes to dismiss him from his
service; that is, the steward by his liberality puts himself in a
wrong position to the spirit of gain in the world; he is in danger
of being reduced to poverty. But this knowledge of his situation does not frighten him back into worldly covetousness. He
wishes, indeed, not to starve, nor would he like, in order to live,
to be a bungler in a trade that he had not learnt, or to practise
the fawning servility of a mendicant. So he goes confidently
and boldly forward in his way; he takes still bolder steps in
disregarding his lord's interests, for he contributes to the kingdom of love and mercy. The parable makes it manifest, how in
the Christian Church the rigidity of selfish acquisition ever more
becomes relaxed in the service of love, and how the Christian
spirit contributes to a brotherly communion in the enjoyment of
goods.[1] The practical application made by Jesus calls this unfaithfulness of the pious against Mammon, faithfulness in little,
the least that can be required of a Christian. ' If ye have not
been faithful in the unrighteous Mammon, who will commit to
your trust the true [riches]? If ye have not been faithful
in that which is another man's, who shall give you that which
is your own?' Here the thought is more decidedly brought
forward, that money is not to be managed according to the
mind of the wealthy world of Mammon, but according to the

[1] It is scarcely necessary to remind the reader here, that the Christian
community of goods is an ideal community realizing itself with the perfecting of the Church, and resting on the principle of freedom, holiness, and
love, while modern communism would make a profane realistic community
by a forced method on the principle of self-interest. The way and manner
in which Christ lets the unjust steward set aside the requirements of his
lord, points to the living mediation between the kingdom of private property and that of the Christian community. The circumspection of the
mediation is shown in this, that, in the first instance, he lowers the demand
from a hundred to fifty; in the second, only to eighty. But the praise bestowed by the idol of wealth on the steward might be referred to the com-
munistic ideas of the worldly mind.

Spirit of God. Lucre is dangerous as well as unessential for the Christian. If he succumbs to the spirit of the world in this little thing, the true riches cannot be entrusted to him, and he cannot come into the possession of the eternal goods intended for him. This saying struck the Pharisees, and was designed to strike them; but we are not at liberty to suppose that this parable was a mere allegory on the Pharisees and publicans.

The rich man in the next parable, at whose gate poor Lazarus was laid, forms a counterpart to the unfaithful steward. Recently some have attempted to maintain that this parable is founded on Ebionitish views. We are not to suppose that the rich man had to atone in eternity for his sins in the present life; nothing of this sort is to be found in the Gospel. It is not said that he had not given relief to Lazarus; rather, he was punished because he was rich and had lived prosperously in the present world. On the other hand, nothing is known of the good conduct of Lazarus; rather, he was admitted into heaven simply because he had been poor in this life. To the rich man special praise has been awarded, because he wished to send a messenger to his brethren who were yet alive from the kingdom of the dead, that they might be warned by his fate. This last circumstance tells against the preceding remarks. The rich man, at all events, admits that he might have escaped the place of torment if he had been suitably warned, and that his brethren might yet escape it. Did it ever enter his thoughts, that they must divest themselves of their wealth? He says nothing of the sort, but rather that they must repent (ver. 30).[1] Criticism has indeed not altogether overlooked this circumstance; just so the description that the rich man ' was clothed in purple and fine linen, and fared sumptuously every day.' It is indicated with sufficient clearness that Lazarus had not to rejoice in any sympathy on the part of the rich voluptuary. He lay at his door ('laid at his gate'), covered with sores, and *desiring* (ἐπιθυμῶν) to be fed with the crumbs which fell from the rich man's table. Yea, even the dogs which came licked his sores. The expression ἀλλὰ καὶ, 'but also,' with which the mention of the dogs is introduced, makes them appear not as friends, but as sorry rivals of the destitute. The dogs here spoken of are such as in the East run at large in the

[1] See Neander, *Life of Christ*, § 219, p. 354.

towns and greedily seize whatever food they can find. The abundant fragments of the rich man's luxurious table attracted them in great numbers. They gathered round Lazarus and licked his sores. He was obliged to share his scanty fare with these greedy dogs, among whom it was his lot to be thrown.[1] Lazarus dies; so also does the rich man. The funeral procession of the former was a guard of honour from the other world: the angels carry him into Abraham's bosom.[2] The interment of the latter was an earthly ceremonial; with emphasis it is said, 'he was buried.' The rich man had charged his memory with the name of Lazarus.[3] He was surprised in the other world, in Hades,[4] to see this man in Abraham's bosom, while he was tormented in the flame. And this is exactly the finest, keenest master-stroke of the parable, that the rich man is disposed to treat Lazarus with an unconscious continuation of his earthly arrogance even here, and with contempt. Lazarus must come down to him into the fire, and cool his tongue by applying the moistened tip of his finger; perhaps only in this slight manner, because he had seen the poor man in the impurity of his sores. Lazarus must undertake the errand to his father's house, and convey information to his brethren as an apparition from the other world. Lazarus here, Lazarus there. Thus he regards him with the same eyes as before, and with the same estimate. Lazarus must be his errand-boy. The arrogance with which he intrudes into Heaven from Hades he foolishly grounds in part, even in the presence of Lazarus, on his descent from Father Abraham. But even in Abraham's presence he is not teachable. He contradicts his assurance that Moses and the

---

[1] See Olshausen, *Commentary* iii. 63. Some are fond of finding here an important feature, by regarding the dogs as belonging to the rich man, and explaining their licking the sores of Lazarus as sympathy. In applying this view, it is said that the rich man's dogs showed more pity to the poor man than himself. Yet we must here take into account the habits of dogs in the East.

[2] [See the beautiful sentences of Augustin (*De Civ. Dei* i. 12) on this, beginning, 'pompa exequiarum magis sunt vivorum solatia, quam subsidia mortuorum.'—Ed.]

[3] 'Probably symbolical—עָזְרִי לֹא the helpless, the forsaken.'—Olshausen.

[4] Olshausen justly remarks that we are not to confound Hades, the kingdom of the unblessed dead before the last judgment, with Gehenna, in a stricter sense the abode of the unblessed after the last judgment.

prophets gave sufficient instruction about time and eternity for men who are willing to hear. 'Nay, Father Abraham, but if one went to them from the dead, they will repent.' His anxiety for his brethren's house implies a covert censure of Moses and the prophets, that they were not sufficient to bring persons to repentance; and a bitter reproach of the divine economy, that it neglected him in his religious need, and had suffered him to perish unwarned. The declaration with which Abraham closes the conversation is justified by the events that followed. Even the resurrection of Christ made no impression on the hearts of those who had not been willing to learn the awful importance of eternity from Moses and the prophets. Lazarus throughout the whole parable does not utter a word. Hence it has been inferred that we know nothing of his disposition, and that, according to the Evangelist, he was transported to heaven on account of his former sufferings. But not to say that, as Neander remarks, he is not the principal person in the parable, and that from his relation to Abraham we may conclude that he bore his sufferings with pious resignation, his silence in his present situation must be regarded as most impressive. He is silent before the gate of the rich man, where he calmly lies, a beggar of princely pride and unblemished honour. He is silent also in Abraham's bosom (whence the rich man would recall him for his service in hell), a humble, blessed child of God, without self-exaltation, in the bosom of glory. If we duly estimate the great virtues of silence, we shall see that of Lazarus come forth conspicuously. This parable would have been better understood if the powerful impression of a transaction between the spirits of heaven and those of hell had not led men's minds away from the leading thought. Olshausen justly remarks, that this conversation is to be regarded only as a living reciprocal action between the two domains of life. His remark is also worthy of notice, that the description here given relates not to eternal salvation and damnation, but to the intermediate state of departed souls from death to the resurrection. 'In our parable, therefore, nothing can be said of the everlasting condemnation of the rich man, inasmuch as the germ of love, and of faith in love, is clearly expressed in his words.' We cannot indeed but acknowledge in him the feeling of sympathy for his brethren; but, in the whole form which it takes, there is a mix-

ture of the most impure elements, namely, of ill-will and unbelief, and even of superstition. The disclosures which Olshausen
finds here respecting the relations of the intermediate state,
must be admitted; namely, ' (1) That departed souls are con-
gregated in one place; (2) that they are separated according to
the basis of their character into the good and the wicked; (3)
that after death a transition from the good to the wicked, or the
reverse, is impossible.' But, as we have already remarked, information respecting the detail of things in the other world is
not the essential design of the parable. The key to it lies in the
declaration of Father Abraham: 'Thou in thy life-time receivedst
(ἀπέλαβες) thy good things, and likewise Lazarus evil things;
but now he is comforted, and thou art tormented.' Of the mere
life-position of the rich man in this world on the one hand, and
of the poor man on the other, nothing is said, even remotely;
but of the way and manner in which the rich man conducted
himself in his prosperity, and the poor man in his adversity.
The one had enjoyed his good things.[1] He had seized upon
them as his felicity, and by this enormous delusion had laid the
foundation for his future sinking into the fiery torment of un-
quenchable desires and ever-devouring circumstances. The
other received his evil things, his grievous lot; and by his resignation to the divinely decreed suffering, he became capable of
blessedness. Reposing in Abraham's bosom, he could find a
heaven in that calm retreat; while the other, in his fearful agitation, would fain have set heaven and earth in commotion.
These destinies, so distinctly marked, considered in their parallelism, would show the judgment of the Gospel to be far exalted
above the reproach of Ebionitism. But these destinies inter-
sect one another, and for this reason,—because the rich man
kept his earthly goods for himself, without mercy towards the
poor man; because he turned that abundance itself into a curse
which should have been a blessing to the other; and because the
poor man in his indigence had borne with resignation the misery
of the world together with the misery of the rich man. The
true poor man is merciful in the manner in which he bears un-

---

[1] And this is a more severe reproach than that which is popularly expressed, 'He had taken an excess of good things.' According to Strauss
(i. 633), the latter only is to be regarded as a reproach, and not the
former.

enviously and quietly in God the burden of the world, its dis-
cordancy; wherefore he will obtain mercy. The false rich man,
who receives his property as booty for his sensual indulgence, is
without mercy by the very manner of his luxurious living;
retributive justice confronts him in eternity with its punishments.   Dives and Lazarus are world-historical personages.

The rich man, by worldly luxury, allowed himself to be
seduced into unmercifulness, and thus incurred heavier guilt,
since he had experienced the liberality of God in his abundant
possessions, and was therefore bound to exercise liberality.   But
much heavier is the guilt of him, who in the spiritual life experiences the mercy of God, and after such an experience treats
his neighbour in spiritual relations with unmercifulness.   This
criminality is depicted in the parable of the unmerciful servant.
The king who would take account of his servants (Matt. xviii.
23–35) is evidently an image of God in the administration of
His strict justice.   When he begins to reckon, there is one who
owes him ten thousand talents.   In the presence of eternal recti-
tude, the very best servant of God is a sinner burdened with
an immeasurable debt.   The servant is unable to pay.   So man
cannot possibly wipe away his own sin.   His lord threatens the
debtor to sell him with all his family, according to the ancient
law of debt, in order to recover as much as possible.   Thus
the punishment which strikes the sinner, falls also on those who
belong to him.   But the debtor, in his terror, pleads for a respite;
and his lord yields to his prayer, takes compassion on his family,
and remits the whole debt.   It deserves special notice, that the
debtor asked for a respite; it did not amount to a frank admission of his insolvency; he could not leave the legal standpoint.
He shows the same temper also in his conduct immediately after
towards his fellow-servant, who owed him a hundred pence : ' He
took him by the throat, saying, Pay me what thou owest;'[1]
and without being softened by his entreaties, ' cast him into
prison till he should pay the debt.'   His hard-heartedness is represented in sharp, bold strokes.   This took place on his going
out from the chamber in which his lord had just forgiven him

---

[1] The reading εἴ τι, preferred by Lachmann [Tischendorf and Tregelles],
gives certainly a much more expressive, sharper sense than ὅ, τι. The personal violence preceded the demand for payment, and the claim was not
substantiated.

his immense debt. As he had thrown himself at his lord's feet, just so his fellow-servant fell at his, and in the same words as he had used to his lord, besought a respite. And the claim was so trifling. By these traits is depicted the legal harsh demeanour of a member of the theocracy, or of the Christian Church, towards his brethren who are in debt to him. His fellow-servants were sorely grieved at such conduct, and told their lord. They plainly recognised another higher right—the right of mercy. Their lord now called the unmerciful servant into his presence and reproached him for his baseness. He handed him over in wrath to the tormentors, and to a painful imprisonment, till he had discharged his whole debt. But how could he exact from him the debt which he had already remitted? According to our civil law, to revoke the remission of a debt is not permissible. But in the legal relation in which this king stood to his servants or slaves, it was allowable for him to impose a heavy fine, or to exact the debt he had remitted. He had remitted the debt because he besought him (ἐπεὶ παρεκάλεσάς με). But the real suppliant gives the assurance that he believes in mercy, and therefore that the spark of mercy is in his own heart. If this debtor had supplicated in truth, he would have given a guarantee that he also practised mercy. His having been the recipient of an act of mercy, bound him to the exercise of mercy. This his lord plainly reminded him of, in the words, 'Shouldst not thou also have had compassion on thy fellow-servant, even as I had pity on thee?' Therefore the act of remission was nullified by his own fault. If the old debt had been remitted, he had now incurred another, greater one; had he incurred no new debt, the old one remained. According to this law which he had set up against his fellow-servant, the law of inexorable legality, he is now handed over to justice. His lord first treated him according to the law of justice, for the sake of the truth of justice. Then he treated him according to the law of mercy, or of supplication; for supplication as an expression of faith in mercy is a prophecy of mercy, and so its germ. But since he had practically repudiated this law, his lord returns with him to the first law, and holds him a prisoner in this stern hard world of exacting, avenging, inexorable justice, until he has paid all—for ever, if he does not learn to believe in the kingdom of mercy. The latter proviso we must make, for his lord had not changed his own nature in itself; but towards him he is the strict judge, not only for the sake of justice, but of truth; and this conduct is at the same time concealed mercy.—We are not to suppose from the particular traits here given, that a pardoned sinner in the stricter sense is depicted, who by his decidedly unmerciful conduct towards his fellow-men again falls back into his old state of condemnation. Christ distinctly assumes that he to whom much is forgiven, also loves much. But the possibility is certainly expressed in the parable, that a man may lose the beginnings of a life in grace by unmercifulness, or that he may decidedly disturb and obscure the continuance of his life in reconciliation with God, by more or less rash single acts of natural or legal hardness. And in this reference, the parable is a solemn warning. But if we keep in view the meaning of the words, that the lord took account of his servant, and remitted his debt, the whole life in Christianity is marked as a life in the kingdom of mercy, and therefore mercy as the highest duty. The Christian has, by his profession, from the first acknowledged himself to be a heavy laden debtor to God;—the central point of his prayers is supplication for forgiveness—his whole faith is grounded on the remission of sins; therefore his duty to show mercy to all who need mercy, and are susceptible of it, is expressed as the great and prime duty of his life. But it has happened a thousand times that the professed servant of God has come from his Lord's presence in the ordinance of the Church, after absolution, and immediately, according to another rule of action, the purely legal, has treated his fellow-servant with the greatest harshness while the absolution was still sounding in his ears and should have found an echo in his heart. And thus he often comes from baptism, or from the communion, or from prayers; and a thousand times he is in danger, as he comes out, of forgetting the remission of his own great debt, and of seizing his neighbour by the throat for a small one. And if he falls into this temptation, it proves that his supplication was not of the right kind, and therefore that he has not really obtained absolution. His whole transaction with the merciful Lord was rendered nugatory, because his supplication was no real reflex and witness of eternal mercy. We need only take a glance at the history of the Church, or even at our own lives, in order to see what a fearfully clear and reproving mirror of a thousand instances of spiritual unmercifulness, under the banner of eternal mercy, is held up in this parable. And as in the rich man the unmerciful practices of men of the world are condemned, so in the parable of the two debtors the unmercifulness of professed Christians is condemned. And as the former suffered torment because in his unmerciful selfishness he had extinguished in himself the true capacity of enjoyment, so the latter came under the tormentors of the legal world, in the gloomy circumstances of self-tormenting both in this world and the next, and of endless quarrelling with humanity, because he did not thoroughly believe in forgiveness, and therefore could not forgive. This law is distinctly expressed in Christ's closing words (ver. 35). But the unmercifulness of the latter is the greatest. The former closed against his neighbour the treasures of temporal means; the latter closed against his own heart the treasures of mercy.

Thus we see in a succession of pictures the agency of the love of God, which has its central point in Christ, as it establishes and extends the kingdom of God in its two great forms of life, in the glory of grace, and in the fervour of mercy. Every parable is a special world-image of this agency of love; each one exhibits a new revelation of its spirit and operation, as it is reflected in a new glorification of the world; and so the representation of the widest circle of its agency stretches forward to the most decided manifestations of its world-glorifying operation. In this series we see grace constantly approaching the fulfilment of the time when it will change itself into the form of judicial righteousness, in order to complete the erection of the kingdom of God, or in order to free the finished structure of ideal humanity from the rubbish and scaffolding which surround it.

The world of the merciful Samaritan is the world of merciful love in its widest extent. It embraces heaven and earth, the good and the evil. Hence it oversteps all the limits of nationalities and confessions, and chooses the strangest instruments among foreigners, dissidents, and heterodox, in order to put to shame and to conquer the unlovingness of national and confessional pride. It operates in a thousand forms on earth. Children and women, even heathens and savages, are active in its service. It is the healing balsam which streams forth from human hearts in their philanthropy and sympathy. Its symbolic representative is the good Samaritan; its real chief in its quiet world of wonders is the Crucified. If we see in this image the great labour of love, the second world-scene shows us the festival of love; we are taught its special object. It has prepared a great feast for humanity. Men are to assemble in its hall for an eternal feast—a feast of the highest divine communion, spiritual joy, and blessedness. The feast is announced in the morning of the world against the world's evening; the first invitations have already been issued. And the glory of this love is most of all verified in not allowing itself to be perplexed by the despisers of its feast among the invited—that even in its wrath towards them it remains true to itself: it sends out messengers and seeks new guests among the poorest and most forlorn. And throughout all ages of the world this is the boldness of love, that it still makes efforts for winning hearts for the spiritual life of heaven, notwithstanding that the most honourable, consecrated, and dignified administrators of its outward ordinances often appear estranged from this life, and even in a state of awful death. But not without labour does love convert into guests of heaven those who ofttimes would fain have appeased their hunger with the food of swine. A new world opens. We see grace go forth on its sacred errands to seek out the lost. The great history of reconciliation is unfolded before our eyes in the parables of the lost sheep, the lost piece of money, and the prodigal son. The anxiety of the good shepherd, who is ready to lay down his life for his sheep, shows us the impassioned, self-sacrificing, uncalculating devotedness of the love of the Redeemer. The painstaking housewife is the lively image of a whole world of beautiful redeeming solicitudes in the heart of Christ and His Church. The restoration of the prodigal son, which the father celebrates by a feast in his house, is the history of numberless experiences of grace, and of its welcomes in the hearts of believing penitents, and an image of every evangelical jubilation in Christendom which sounds forth from time into eternity. But the life of Christ in us must verify itself under trial. The parts are shifted. Before, man was for a long time irresponsive to the call of his God; now, God appears to be irresponsive to reconciled men. We see humanity in its genuine christological life of prayer turned towards salvation: the work of God's faithfulness in the trial and distress of His

people, the glowing operation of His purifying power in their
earnest supplications, is unveiled to us. The innermost life of
humanity is disclosed; its wrestling after the righteousness of
God and the completion of His kingdom, in the praying publican, in the persistently supplicating widow, and in the friend
made over-importunate by necessity. Then, in the parable of
the thankful debtor, we see the community of believers in the
overflow of their love; they love much because many sins have
been forgiven them. We see how humanity in its choicest spe-
cimens gratefully gathers round its Redeemer. And now the
Christian spirit begins to transform the old world of selfish acquisition, the ice-bound kingdom of Mammon, into a new genial
world of brotherly kindness, of benevolence, and of the common
enjoyment of God's blessings. But we see how, against this
bright side of the new world, a dark night-side is presented; the
world of secular and spiritual unmercifulness that constantly
becomes more intense, represented by the rich man and the unmerciful servant. With these parables we approach the representation of the judgment as it is given in the third cycle of
parables. Already, in the earlier parables, our attention has
been directed to the judgment by single traits; as by the priest
and Levite, by the despisers of the great feast, and by the elder
brother of the prodigal son. But as the kingdom of God in its
absolute power and glory embraces the whole world, those persons who reject His mercy are still within the range of His
government, and fall into the hands of His justice. Yet,
while His justice visits them with its judgments, it remains one
with His mercy. But as it is the office of mercy to found and
to build the kingdom of God, so it is the office of justice to
purify and to complete it.

The parable of the day-labourers who each received one
penny, notwithstanding the unequal times of their labour in the
vineyard (Matt. xx. 1–16), must stand at the head of the parables
of this group; for it shows how the justice of God exercises a
rewarding retribution which is wholly animated by the muni-
ficence of grace. Grace determines and gives a brilliancy to the
hire of these labourers, and equalizes it. The parable shows us,
therefore, how the administration of God's justice is perfectly one
with that of His love. A proprietor hires labourers for his vineyard: the first, about six o'clock in the morning, at the begin-

ning of the day; others, at nine o'clock (about the third hour)—
people whom he finds standing in the market-place, detained
there by the attraction of earthly things, loungers in the region
of worldliness; others, again, about noon; a fresh set, about
three in the afternoon; the last, an hour before sunset, or about
the eleventh hour. These latter answer to his inquiry, 'Why
stand ye here all the day idle?' 'Because no man hath hired us;'
and at his bidding they go immediately into the vineyard. Here,
then, we have a series of conversions exhibited according to the
measure of their earlier and later temporal beginning. Some
of these labourers have grown up in a life of piety, and from the
first have been active in it; others have been called later; many
have stood all day idle in the market-place, and enter the Lord's
service not till the evening of life. Now, according to the relations of earthly justice and rewards, it would be natural to
expect that the payment of these labourers would be reckoned
according to the term of their labour. So the Jews probably
expected that the heathen who should be converted in the world's
evening, would receive a smaller reward than themselves. Also
in modern times it has been maintained by rationalist theologians, that the neglected opportunities of the sinner in the time
before his conversion can never be repaired—that the loss of
time follows the converted man himself into eternity in an irre-
parable shortening of his felicity. But this parable seems to
have been specially constructed to explode such an erroneous
opinion. It belongs to the majesty of grace, that from the bosom
of its eternity it can restore the otherwise irretrievably lost time.
Hence also the circumstance is explained, that God could allow
the heathen to go on in their own way thousands of years without losing sight of them, and similar mysteries. The power of
grace shows itself in the reward of the labourers as the parable
depicts it. The proprietor agrees with the earliest labourers for
one penny; to the next he made the indefinite promise, that
'whatsoever was right, that they should receive;' and with the
last he appears scarcely to have made even this condition.[1] And
when evening was come, the lord of the vineyard desired his
steward to call the labourers and give them their hire, in such
order, that he began with the last and ended with the first. Now

---

[1] The words, καὶ ὃ ἐὰν ᾖ δίκαιον, λήψεσθε, in the 7th verse are omitted
by Lachmann, [Tischendorf, and Tregelles.]

when the labourers who were hired in the early part of the morning saw that those who were hired at the eleventh hour received a penny, they expected much more, and murmured when they also received only a penny. Manifestly the parable expresses first of all the equal position of the earlier and later converted in the state of blessedness. But if the parable merely represented this truth, that salvation would at last be equal for all the converted, although they entered at different times into the service of the kingdom of God (as Neander thinks), the most striking features of the parable would be to no purpose. Rather it is clear, that the labourers hired last enjoyed the distinction of being first paid. And since in proportion to their time of labour they could not expect much, one penny was for them extraordinary good fortune. The first labourers, on the other hand, not only received their penny last of all, but embittered their own joy in it by expecting more. The outward equality of their pay, therefore, became an inward inequality in favour of the labourers who were last hired. How are we to explain this circumstance? Manifestly we must regard the labourers who were first hired as saved persons. For the one equal payment denotes the salvation to be imparted equally to all. But there is originally a difference in men's capacity for salvation, and in proportion the fulness of salvation must be different to different persons. Now these first labourers appear to be delineated as more legal, calculating natures, whose capacity for salvation was not of great extent. They bargained with the proprietor for a penny. Labouring in his vineyard had become irksome to them—the chief point in the recollection of their labour is the burden and heat of the day. And they think it strange, that the others should be placed on an equality with them in point of wages. Since they ground their complaint on the principles of daily wages, the proprietor points out to them, that even on these principles they had received what was due to them. As to the last hired, on the other hand, the lord of the vineyard appears to take into account that they had not the opportunity till late of entering into his vineyard, and possibly they had a battle with themselves to exchange towards evening their indolent mode of life for hard work, and yet went briskly to their task without a stipulated reward. At all events, they appear now as, in proportion, the more richly rewarded, for this reason, that the amount of the reward must have surprised them. Thus a great fact in the kingdom of God seems to be reflected in their relation to the labourers who were first hired. The kingdom of God is the kingdom of spirit, in which the power of time and the relations of nature are abolished—in which a thousand years are as one day, and one day as a thousand years. In this kingdom it can be, then, of no decisive importance, in what outward temporal extent any one has lived for the kingdom of God, in what number and measure he has accomplished laudable works in its service. Rather the point of importance is, with what energy he can surrender himself to eternal love, and in what abundance he is able to receive it. And it is frequently found that the spiritual service of one convert forms a strong contrast in its energy to the formal service of another in its outward extent; as, for example, the conversion of the woman who was a sinner contrasted with the religiousness of Simon. In this contrast, one hour of human conversion and of divine reconciliation may have greater weight in their spiritual importance, than many years of life which have been spent under the reciprocal action of a well-considered human piety, and a proportional scanty flow of divine blessings. The differences of the measures of blessedness in the kingdom of God are adjusted, therefore, not according to the calculations of a mercenary disposition, or according to the outward measure of religious service, or according to the rules of human industry, but according to the relations of power and energy in the spiritual life. But viewed under these relations, it may be asserted as a maxim, that a man's capacity for spiritual blessedness is smaller in proportion as he is more disposed to make stipulations with God, and greater in proportion as he is bold and large-hearted in joyful surrender to the free love of God. According to these relations of the energy of love, the determination of the dynamic inequalities is regulated, which allows the justice of God to enter into the circle of equality which embraces all the saved as saved. The justice of God is, according to its nature, not an outward forensic justice, deciding according to outward laws,—but it is a spirit, and therefore decides spiritually ; it is one with free grace, and therefore gives to man in proportion as he can apprehend it as this free power of love. The parable expresses this truth in the words which the lord of the vineyard addressed to one of the dissatisfied labourers : 'Friend, I do thee no wrong; didst not thou agree with me for a penny ? Take that thine is, and go thy way. It is my will to give unto this last (θέλω δοῦναι) even as unto thee. Is it not lawful for me to do what I will with my own ? Is thine eye evil because I am good ?' The concluding words are also explained by the intention of the parable : 'So the last shall be first, and the first last ; for many are called, but few chosen.' According to Neander[1] and others, this addition does not suit the parable, but is only outwardly attached to it, since the parable should express simply the equalization of all the converted in heavenly felicity. But we have seen how the parable also gives prominence to the dynamic inequalities within this equalization, and how deeply they enter into its main scope. According to this view, the parable terminates quite naturally with the words just quoted. It is a fact, that many of those who were called early into the kingdom of God were last in what related to spiritual fulness, and that many of those who were later called, appeared in this respect the first. But how can this relative fact be expressed in one sentence which states the matter quite unconditionally—The first will be last, and the last first—since Abraham and the elect of the Old Covenant generally belong to the early called, and, on the contrary, among the later called even the majority will present themselves as the inferior organs of glory ? First of all we have to answer, that it belongs to the nature of an apophthegm to express a manifold conditioned thought in an unconditional form, since it must influence by the paradoxical emphatic expression of its chief element. But the warrant for this lies in the symbolical nature of the apophthegm ; and so in this instance, the last which will be first are those who appear before the Lord with the slightest pretensions ; while inversely, the first are those who by their undue pretensions became the last. This sentence was most strikingly fulfilled in the time of Christ : the Jews, who were the first in their pretensions, became the last ; while the last, the Gentiles, advanced to the rank of the first. But even among the Gentile Christians the same phenomenon was repeated, and the ultimate reason is, that many are called, but few chosen. Even because only a few are chosen, so, many of the early called, as they grow up from childhood, in all confessions, according

[1] *Life of Christ*, § 240, p. 385 (Bohn).

232 ANNOUNCEMENT AND CHARACTER OF CHRIST'S PUBLIC MINISTRY.

to their internal capacity for salvation, occupy of themselves decidedly a subordinate situation in the organism of the kingdom of God. But the few chosen also enter into their high position although their calling in time reached them later; for they meet the infinite energy of the love of God with a corresponding energy of a yearning and trustful disposition. Thus the kingdom of royal love obtains its organization, because the relations of eternity, or of the spirit, overcome the relations of time. Those who find love in justice, move towards the centre; on the contrary, those who only see justice predominating in love, move towards the circumference. But the circle of equal blessedness encloses them all; each receives his penny.

In the parable we have just now considered, the administration of God's justice is exhibited in its refined and lofty spirituality, in its peculiar glory. This contemplation is continued in the parable of the ten servants among whom the ten pounds were divided (Luke xix. 11–28). The former parable shows us how the divine justice requites labour outwardly unequal with an equal reward. In the latter, we see how the faithful employment of an equal number of pounds, on the part of different servants, is followed by an unequal success, and consequently by an unequal reward. But in the former case an internal dynamic inequality was plainly apparent, notwithstanding the equality of the reward; and in the latter we see how this inequality, which is here exhibited in its full extent, is equalized by every labourer's receiving a reward which exactly agreed with his gains. And this constitutes the peculiarity by which the divine justice is infinitely exalted above the human, that it can exhibit the essential life in law, and equally in law the essential life; that it does not do away the great inequalities of life in the equality of right; and that it faithfully preserves the pure equality of right in the inequalities of life—that it can be justice and grace at the same time, in the one majesty of its administration.

As to what relates to the form, it has been thought that in this representation the Evangelist has committed the mistake of confounding two parables together, and that to restore their integrity they must be separated, so that one depicts the relation of a king to his rebellious subjects (vers. 12, 14, 27), and the other the relation of a rich lord to his servants.[1] But the blending of these two parts into one living unity constitutes the very pith of the parable. The kingdom of Christ is a realm which first of all was imperilled by a rebellion of its legitimate citizens, the theocratic nation; and its Ruler must gain the kingly power by travelling to a distant land which would place Him in a position to assume it on His return. Now, what was the first duty of His faithful servants whom He had left behind among the rebellious citizens? Should they take arms in order to make an attempt to gain possession of the kingdom for their Lord?[2] But this is precisely what this prince was obliged to forbid his servants. In this critical interval they were to administer his property in a perfectly peaceful agency, to make use of their abilities, and to employ the time in promoting his interests. Could our Lord have more impressively told His disciples that in the interval between the ascension and His second advent they were not to think of a worldly exhibition of His kingdom, or of vindicating His royal dignity and identifying His word with the laws of social life, but that they were only faithfully to administer the real goods, namely, the spiritual, which He had left behind, in their unassuming evangelical offices, in order to form a basis for the outward appearing of His kingdom by means of its spiritual riches? But at a future time, when He returns with kingly power, they will also surround Him in royal splendour—be placed over the cities of His kingdom, and assist Him as warriors to execute judgment on the rebellious. Such being the leading thought of the parable, we can understand why the Lord delivered it to His disciples exactly at the time when He was going with them to Jerusalem, and they were expecting that the kingdom of God would directly appear. Luke takes particular notice of the close connection of this discourse with the occasion of its delivery (ver. 28): 'And when He had thus spoken, He went before, ascending up to Jerusalem.' Now, if we look at the several particulars of the parable, we meet with traits of great signifi-

---

[1] See Strauss, *Leben Jesu* i. 636.

[2] 'Instead of a capital for trading, he ought rather to have sent them arms.' Modern criticism often proposes emendations of this sort in the Gospel history. We have here a specimen how, without intending it, it can inflict a wound on the very vitals of a biblical passage.

cance. The certain man to whom the parable relates is a nobleman, a person of high birth; namely, Christ the chief of humanity. But as in that age Jewish persons of rank frequently resorted to the Emperor at Rome in order to get themselves invested with princely dignity in Palestine, so this noble personage went into a distant land in order to obtain a kingdom and to return home; an evident reference to His ascension, and His return at a future time for the manifestation of His kingdom.

The nobleman, before setting out, calls his ten servants, commits to their care ten pounds,[1] and says to them, ' Occupy till I come !' The great number of his servants indicates the dignity of his house; the number ten is the round number of the world's course. Each servant receives only one pound: by the equality as well as the smallness of the amount, we are led to think not of the gifts of grace entrusted to them considered in themselves, but of the official calling in which they find their expression. Every disciple of Christ is like the rest in his calling; and such a calling appears very mean in contrast with the splendour of the world. But his citizens hated this nobleman, and sent a message after him with the declaration, ' We will not have this man to reign over us.' We are here reminded of the embassy which the Jews sent to Rome to remonstrate against the government of Archelaus ;[2] and we are thus shown how Christ, in the contemplation of His theocratic claims to the throne of David in the sense of eternal duration, might wish to bring it into comparison with the way and manner in which the partisans of Herod at Rome canvassed for the earthly throne in Israel. The fulfilment of this part of the parable was first of all shown by the refusal of the Jews to receive the tidings of Christ's glorification after His ascension and the day of Pentecost. But in a wider sense all unbelievers in the whole course of time belong to these rebels. When the nobleman returned, invested with kingly authority, he commanded the servants to whom he had given the money to be called before him, that he might know how much each had

---

[1] The Attic mina (Μνᾶ), equal to rather more than L.4. (Smith's *Dict. of Ant.*)

[2] Josephus, *Antiq.* xvii. 11, § 1. Compare De Wette, *Exegetisches Handbuch*, on the passage.

gained by trading. The first came forward and said, 'Lord, thy pound hath gained ten pounds.' And he said unto him, 'Well, thou good servant, because thou hast been faithful in a very little, have thou authority over ten cities.' The second came forward and said that he had gained five pounds. He was put over five cities. In this description the gain is first of all to be estimated. With the pounds are gained pounds; that is, from a few messengers and witnesses many others are made; His people, who are called to testify of Him, become numerous. But next, the difference in the gains of the different servants is strikingly exhibited. With one pound one had gained ten pounds; another, only five. If this difference lay entirely in the difference of industry, the servant would scarcely pass muster with the gain of only five pounds; but other causes appear to have co-operated, namely, the diversity of talent, and especially the talent of energy, in order to account for such a difference in the result. Then the recompense comes under consideration. Since the kingdom of Christ has now become a monarchy, His faithful servants become royal governors over its cities, and according to the measure in which they have gained with the sums entrusted to them. In the success of their activity in the kingdom of the Cross, they had developed their qualification for their activity in the kingdom of glory, and the measure of it was fixed. The juxtaposition of the two faithful servants is sufficient to illustrate these truths. But another comes, saying, 'Lord, behold, here is thy pound, which I have kept laid up in a napkin; for I feared thee, because thou art an austere man; thou takest up that thou layedst not down, and reapest that thou didst not sow. And he saith unto him, Out of thine own mouth will I judge thee, thou wicked servant. Thou knewest that I was an austere man, taking up that I laid not down, and reaping that I did not sow: Wherefore then gavest not thou my money into the bank, that at my coming I might have required my own with usury?' Now follows the sentence: 'Take from him the pound, and give it to him that hath ten pounds.' The servants object, he has already so much; but their lord answers, 'Unto every one that hath shall be given; and from him that hath not, even that he hath shall be taken away from him.' The wicked servant allowed the pound entrusted to him to lie unemployed. It is characteristic, that he had laid it aside wrapped up in his napkin; he had used neither his pound nor his napkin; in cold indolence he had neglected, concealed, and denied his calling. From the reason he alleges, it is evident that he had no attachment to his lord, that he could not regard his master's business as his own. We cannot, as Olshausen has done, look upon his excuse as indicating a noble nature, which was merely held back by the timidity and scrupulosity of the legal standpoint from putting out his pound to interest. Christ reproaches him as a wicked servant, and condemns him out of his own mouth. His excuse was therefore hypocritical. Devotion to his lord was wanting. He stood on the egoistic, and hence on the slavish standpoint. He undervalued his calling and the talent entrusted to him as a matter of insignificance, which, as he thought, was not worth considering whether he could gain or lose by using it. Trading with the sum entrusted to him seemed everything; the sum itself as nothing; and accordingly he reasoned thus: If I gain large profits with the pound entrusted to me, I shall gain no advantage from it—my lord will take it all; but if I suffer loss, I shall be made responsible for it without mercy. Hence it will be best for me to lay the pound by for him, and take care of myself. Thus the man of a slavish spirit calculates in the Lord's service. He feels not how great the gift of his calling is; for surrender to the love that has called him is wanting. He thinks that everything in religion depends on his working. But he is afraid of becoming a saint, since he cannot regard as his own gain what he is to gain for God. On the other hand, he is so very much afraid of failures in Christian endeavour, and on that account postpones his conversion, as many Christians in ancient times deferred their baptism. Wherever a slothful servant of Christ looks upon his calling in relation to the harvest of the world, which Christ will expect from him, as a troublesome, contemptible sowing, and on that account neglects it, this parable obtains its fulfilment. But Christ passes sentence on the servant according to his own showing. Exactly because he expects great things from the improvement of every gift and calling entrusted to man, must every one make the best use he can of his pound. The very least which the slothful servant could have done, would have been to put his pound in the bank;

without any great exertion on his own part, he would then have
secured at least the usual interest of the money. He might
give back his calling to the Church, who would then transfer it
to some one else (place the pound in another person's hands for
trading with), and the Lord would then receive the profits
which He might expect from a faithful application of it.[1] Instead of this, he retained the calling, but neglected it, and
thereby inflicted an injury on his lord's affairs. As a punishment, his pound is taken from him and given to him who had
ten pounds. All the rights of the Christian calling which the
unfaithful neglect, will one day revert in the world of perfect
reality to those who have been faithful in their calling; and
precisely those who have the richest blessing of power and
fidelity will obtain the richest reversion. This expectation is
thoroughly certain, since it is a settled matter that the correct
relations of power and being in the kingdom of God, and therefore the relations of rank in those who sustain them, must one
day appear in a perfect, clearly expressed organism. Whoever
has the reality, to him also will be imparted the glory of the appearance; but whoever is destitute of real life in the calling of
Christ, from him will be taken away the outward calling to
exhibit it. After this sentence passed on the slothful servant,
sentence is also passed on the rebels. They are already defeated
by the glorious return of the lord; he now causes them to be
brought and slain before his eyes. In this is contained the announcement, that the sentence of condemnation on the enemies
of Christ will take place at His return before His throne.

The parable of the talents (Matt. xxv. 14–30) has such an
affinity to the preceding, that by critics of different schools[2] it has
been regarded as only another recension of it, or as the original

[1] In the parable of the pounds in Luke, the lord tells the unfaithful servant that he ought to have given his money into the bank (ἐπὶ τὴν τράπε-
ζαν) ; on the other hand, in the similar parable of the talents, Matt. xxv.,
it is said, ' Thou oughtest to have put my money to the exchangers (τοῖς
τραπεζίταις): this difference corresponds to the different character of the
parables. The offices are returned to the Church ; but the gifts of grace,
which are in danger of being injured, are to be rendered productive by
their possessors connecting themselves with the most active leaders of the
Church.

[2] Strauss, *Leben Jesu* i. 634; Olshausen, iii. 283. On the other hand,
Schleiermacher, *Ueber die Schriften des Lukas*, p. 239.

from which the other is taken. But notwithstanding the affinity
of its leading features and thoughts, it is distinguished from it by a
marked peculiarity. As to its position, it is connected with the
parable of the ten virgins, which immediately precedes it, by
the thought that the delay of Christ's return is a probation for
His disciples, and at last will suddenly come upon them with a
dangerous surprise; and by this same thought it is clearly distinguished from the parable of the pounds. In both parables,
Christ's servants are individually tried by the great distance
which separates Him from them. But in the former it is the
distance of space, here it is the distance of time, which forms
the ground of their trial. *There*, it is questionable whether the
candidate for the throne will return from a distant land invested
with regal power; here, the master of the household is a long
time away from home, and his servants, owing to the uncertainty
whether he will ever return, and the long destitution of his personal appearance, are tempted to slothfulness and the neglect of
what is entrusted to their care. According to this view of the
parable, the first thing that strikes us is the relation of the lord
of the servants to the kingdom. He is not described as a person
of high birth, but simply as 'a man travelling into a far country.'
He has three servants. If in the number of ten servants the
relation of the disciples of Jesus to the whole course of the
world is made apparent, here the three servants mark the work
of the Spirit which is committed to the circle of the disciples
on earth; for three is the number of the Spirit. And if in the
one pound the equal discipleship of all Christians, in its humble
aspect in the eyes of the world, is represented, so here the trust
committed to the disciples appears to us rather in its essential
importance.[1] According to this proportion, one of these servants
had a sum three hundred times greater than in the former parable.
Poverty-struck as the calling of the apostles and evangelists may
appear on the secular side, thus splendid is its inward spiritual
side; however faint the outward lustre of the calling, great are
its golden contents, the gifts of grace; for we can understand by
the talents nothing else than the gifts of grace bestowed on the
disciples. The calling of the disciples is equal: each has only
one pound. But the gifts of grace are various: to one servant

[1] The talent (Τάλαντον) contained 60 minæ, worth about L.243, 15s. of
our money.

five talents are entrusted; to another, two; to another, one.   On
this rest the inner differences of Christian discipleship, and hence
it is explained that one with his pound could gain ten pounds,
while another gained only five. This diversity in the gifts of
grace which Christ dispenses in the kingdom of redemption is
regulated by the diversity of natural gifts which God has dealt
out in the kingdom of creation. The master, on his leaving, fixed
for each of his servants the number of talents according to their
' *several ability* ' (κατὰ τὴν ἰδίαν δύναμιν), it is said in the parable.
What in the domain of human natural life was intellectual power,
in the kingdom of Christ, when purified and consecrated by
grace, becomes wisdom and knowledge ; what in the former was
a power of the soul, here becomes a holy flame of love; and thus
every gift, from being a mental natural talent, is converted into
a spiritual talent of the kingdom.   After the distribution of these
gifts of grace, the master straightway departs (ver. 15).   The
ascension and Pentecost nearly coincide, and, according to the
inner nature of things, the outpouring of the Holy Spirit is the
immediate consequence of Christ's ascension.   Now a long
period elapses; a dangerous term of probation for the servants.
The reckoning takes place at the final return of their lord, and
it then appears that the two first servants have dealt faithfully
with their talents.   Each of them has gained as much as was
entrusted to him; consequently the spiritual capital entrusted to
the believer is exactly doubled by its faithful application.   But
why only doubled, while the capital of the calling, the pound, has
realized ten times its own amount?   The calling operates on the
broad, wide world, where an apostle in fulfilling his vocation
might gain half the world, or bring a whole generation under his
power.   But the gift of the Spirit operates within the kingdom
of the Spirit; hence it will gain just so much life as is specifically
related to it.   For every positive power of the kingdom of God,
a proportionate receptive power exists in the spirit-life of the
world destined for the kingdom of God.   Outwardly this simple
gain of the essential gift of the Spirit may appear less than
the tenfold gain of the official calling; but according to the
scale of importance in the kingdom of God, it stands perfectly
equal to it.   For the mental gift, in its faithful application, is
exactly that which imparts to the calling its destined productiveness.   In truth, it is the greatest gain when it is granted to a

Christian to reclaim five talents of human mental gifts from their
wild growth and perversion for the life of the kingdom of God;
hence an abundance of new offices of life arises. The reward,
also, which is here granted to the faithful servants, points to the
profoundest relations of the kingdom of God. They were faithful over a little;[1] now they are placed over much. And this
exaltation is thus expressed—the rewarding Lord says to each,
'Enter thou into the joy of thy Lord!' He admits them into
the fellowship of His own life of joy—the fellowship of His perfected rest. The former parable makes the reward of God's
servants for their fidelity in their temporal calling to consist in
the glory of their heavenly calling: they were placed over many
cities. Here, their fidelity in their human spirit-life, as it was
peculiarly conditioned and diversified, is rewarded by their being
raised to the sabbatical rest of the unconditioned spirit-life of
their Lord. There, they received their reward in a new, heavenly
investiture; here, their temporal striving is rewarded with the
most entire rest from toil. There, heavenly labour is the blessing
on fidelity to their earthly calling; here, heavenly repose of spirit
is the consequence of temporal activity of spirit in divine things.
In the former case, those who had maintained their fidelity become God's vicegerents; in the latter, they become members of
His family. Thus one parable describes the outward side of
their inheritance; the other parable, the inner side. But the
servant who had received only the one pound appears very
similar to the slothful servant in the former parable. He calls
his lord a hard man, reaping where he had not sown; and says, that
for fear of him he hid his talent in the earth. He returns it to
him unimproved. Manifestly he also was induced by an under-
valuation of his gift to hide it in the earth. That in this manner
he gradually lost the life of the divine Spirit and sunk the life
of his own spirit deep in the earth, the parable could only express
by showing how he never properly made the entrusted talent his
own, since he brings it again to his lord as *his* ('Lo, there thou
hast that is thine'), with which he had nothing to do. But his
lord rebukes him as a 'wicked and slothful servant.' His condemnation is then expressed as in the former parable. His talent
is taken from him and given to him who had ten talents. This
is designed to teach, that the faithlessness and apostasy of God's

---

[1] It is said ἐπὶ ὀλίγα, not ἐν ἐλαχίστῳ as in the former parable.

wicked servants produces on His faithful servants a most salutary
reaction, a stimulating effect, by which their life acquires an extraordinary elevation.[1] But the unprofitable servant is here not
merely punished by being deprived of his pound. He is cast
into outer darkness, where is wailing and gnashing of teeth.[2]
When he kept back a gift of the Spirit from the kingdom of
God, after he was pledged to employ it, the necessary consequence was, that he became an enemy of this kingdom; hence
the severest punishment was inflicted upon him. Finally, if we
notice the circumstance that the servant was guilty of this unfaithfulness with the smallest sum, we shall see, on the one hand,
the connection of the religious self-determination of man with
his gift. This servant had, in proportion, the least religious
capital. But on the other hand, we also see the full manifestation of freedom in the unfaithfulness of the servant; for he too
had his talent, and could have gained a second with it. It was
therefore his guilt that he so conducted himself as if he had no
vocation for the kingdom of God, and by this guilt he incurred
his condemnation.

Thus we see how the three parables, which exhibit the rewarding justice of the Lord in such great acts of allegiance, by
degrees bring forward more distinctly its punitive administration. This punitive administration gradually comes forth in
the following parables in all its majesty. Especially we find
parables which announce beforehand this punitive justice; we
might designate them parables of warning and threatening
justice.

The constant nearness of the divine judgment is continually
announced to men by the prevalence of death. The nearness
of death, when it makes itself perceptible to sinners, is everywhere an omen of threatening judgment. This is shown in the
parable of the foolish landholder (Luke xii. 16–21). This

[1] Compare Acts v. 11, 12.

[2] 'The βασιλεία is viewed as the region of light, which is encircled by
darkness. In reference to this point, the metaphorical language of Scripture is very exact in the choice of expressions. Concerning the children of
light who are unfaithful to their vocation, it is said that they are cast into
the σκότος; but respecting the children of darkness, we are told that they
are consigned to the πῦρ αἰώνιον; so that each one is punished in the opposite
element.'—Olshausen, iii. 287.

242 ANNOUNCEMENT AND CHARACTER OF CHRIST'S PUBLIC MINISTRY.

man was rich; his fields were crowned with an abundant and
splendid harvest. He found that his barns were too small,
and resolved to build greater, in order to stow in safety his
fruits and his goods. And then he would 'delude his soul'[1] to
look upon this store for many years, to eat, drink, and be
merry. Here God Himself makes His appearance in the
parable. 'Thou fool!' He said, 'this night thy soul shall be
required of thee; then whose shall those things be which thou
hast provided? So is he that layeth up treasure for himself,
and is not rich towards God.' Judgment overtook him. The
death of such a man is in itself a judgment, because it exhibits
with one blow all his labour as vain, his whole calculation as
false, his striving as folly, and meets his self-will with an inexorable counter-working fate, but especially by the result, that it
places him in his nakedness and destitution before God. Thus
God's judgments incessantly proceed through the whole world
in the most appalling forms and visitations. But the threatening omens go before the judgments themselves in all the signs of
death. In these circumstances, in which death stands for judgment, he is the antipodes of the good Samaritan. He likewise
knows no limitations of confessions or nationalities. As the former (the good Samaritan) restored the half-dead to life, so the
latter hurries them to the grave. The administration of salutary
severity stands as a complement over against the administration
of salutary kindness; and the ministers of justice join themselves to the ministers of mercy.

But the same man, who is threatened by the impending
judgment because his heart is set on earthly things, calls also
for punitive retribution, since by this vain striving he becomes
an unfruitful tree for the kingdom of God. This truth is exhibited in the parable of the barren fig-tree (Luke xiii. 6–9).
This fig-tree was in a very favourable position. It stood in its
owner's vineyard, under the care of a faithful gardener. And

---

[1] 'In this case neither $\sigma\tilde{\omega}\mu\alpha$ nor $\pi\nu\epsilon\tilde{\upsilon}\mu\alpha$ could have been employed.
According to the divine ordinance, nourishment is required by the body, but
the $\pi\nu\epsilon\tilde{\upsilon}\mu\alpha$ has relation to nobler than sensuous blessings and food. The
$\psi\upsilon\chi\acute{\eta}$, as being capable of education and development, can refer as well to
the lower region of the $\sigma\acute{\alpha}\rho\xi$ as to the higher one of the $\pi\nu\epsilon\tilde{\upsilon}\mu\alpha$. In this
very thing consequently does the point of the thought before us lie, that
he gave up to the $\sigma\alpha\rho\kappa\iota\kappa\sigma\tilde{\iota}\varsigma$ that $\psi\upsilon\chi\acute{\eta}$, which he should have consecrated
to the $\pi\nu\epsilon\upsilon\mu\alpha\tau\iota\kappa\sigma\tilde{\iota}\varsigma$.'—Olshausen, ii. 300.

yet, for three years in succession, it brought forth no fruit. Then the owner said to the vinedresser, 'Cut it down, why should it impoverish[1] the ground on which it stands!' But the vinedresser interceded for the tree on which sentence had been passed. 'Lord, let it alone this year also, till I shall dig about it and dung it: if it bear fruit, well; and if not, after that thou shalt cut it down!' In the theocratic symbolic, the people of Israel, in consequence of its early awakening to the knowledge of the true God, were in its prime the early fig-tree among the nations (Hos. ix. 10). But now, in consequence of its being stiffened in the unspiritual observance of traditions, it had become an unfruitful fig-tree. Its unfruitfulness was the more unnatural, because it enjoyed such distinguished care in the garden of God. Already, at the first appearance of Christ, a judgment had been manifested on the people, for they were not capable of receiving Him. But He, whom the faithful vinedresser resembled in spirit, implored a respite for them. This respite took place in the time of Christ's ministry, and was then on the point of expiring, without the fig-tree's promising to reward the last labour bestowed upon it. Therefore the doom that had already been pronounced by the Judge was coming on with hasty steps. But the Christian Church was also such a fig-tree in the garden of God in its outward form, and in a wider sense the whole human race, and indeed, in the most varied appearances, every Christian and every individual man. The spirit of justice which presides over the earth, continually presses forward the developments of human life with accelerated speed, to judgment. But the spirit of mercy exerts a force in an opposite direction, and is ever keeping back the threatening judgments.[2] This makes the time of salvation always more precious and more momentous. Long-suffering counts the days of the granted respite, and the greatest facts in which the power of Christ's love and the monitions of His Spirit are manifested, announce most of all as warning prognostics that judgment is nigh.

But at last the threatened judgments make their appearance. Man can suffer them. This is shown in the following

[1] [More than the ἄχθος ἀρούρης of the Greeks, for which see *Plat. Apol.* p. 28.—ED.]
[2] 2 Pet. iii. 9.

parables, especially the parable of the marriage of the king's son
(Matt. xxii. 1–14). Here that feast appears, which was before
exhibited in its relation to mercy, in its opposite relation to
judgment. The greatest blessing of earthly life is, that man is
invited in it to the feast of God's felicity; and it is his
heaviest loss in life, if he has neglected this invitation. But
his punishment does not consist in mere destitution. The destitution of essential life, of life in life, must, according to its
very nature, become a tormenting fire in the centre of life—a
death in life. A king makes a great feast to celebrate the
nuptials of his son; the guests invited are his subjects. Evidently the king is God Himself, and his son is Christ, as He
is on the point of uniting Himself with His bride the Church.
That the persons invited, if they accept the invitation, belong
themselves to the life-form of the bride, is not a point for consideration; for Christ is perfectly certain of His Church as a
whole, although individuals of the invited guests should be
wanting. Indeed, believers themselves, in their individual
capacity, are to be regarded only as wedding guests who partake of one joy with the Bridegroom. Since the guests are the
king's subjects, they would be obliged to comply with the invitation, although he had summoned them to compulsory service.
Thus motives of the highest honour, of the highest love and
joy, and of the highest duty, combined to induce the persons
invited to appear in the most joyful manner at the great festival. Their refusal is, therefore, something quite monstrous,
and in its threefold aggravation is to be regarded as a rebellion.
To the first invitation they gave a simple refusal, without
alleging any reasons for it: 'they *would* not come.' Their
lord condescends to request them by a second set of messengers. He represents the abundance of the feast, the embarrassment of his household if the oxen and fatlings should be killed
in vain, and that all things were ready. How strikingly in
these traits is the earnestness, the ardour of love in the preaching of the Gospel, depicted! But the persons invited turn
away with contempt, and go their way to their usual avocations.
Some even proceed so far as to insult and kill the servants
who invited them. The king hears of this, and is wroth; he
sends forth his armies and destroys those murderers, and burns
their city. This is the first act of retributive justice. It has

been said that no reason has been given why some of these ungrateful guests killed the servants of their prince who invited them.[1] Certainly no motive is alleged for their conduct; nor can any be given, any more than for the fact in the department of spiritual life, that the indifferentism with which the earthly-minded man refuses the invitation to the blessed feast of reconciliation with God, can change itself into a positive demoniac hatred against that invitation and its bearers. It is, indeed, an awful thing, that by the guilt of those who were invited, an avenging sword and a dismal conflagration must proceed from the marriage feast of the King of humanity, by which the despisers of the feast perish with their city,—that therefore the greatest gift of God to humanity is rejected by many with a rebellious spirit which can only be put down by the most fearful judgments. In the description of the burning city, there is certainly an obscure allusion to the destruction of Jerusalem; yet we must not overlook the fact, that all the features are symbolical in the most comprehensive sense, so that, for example, the burning city may reappear in Constantinople taken by the Turks, and often in the history of the world; last of all, in the mysterious conflagration which will accompany the last judgment. The parable now more distinctly falls in with the representation in the similar parable contained in Luke. We see that the marriage feast of the king's son cannot be rendered nugatory. 'The wedding is ready, but they which were bidden were not worthy,' the king says to his servants. He therefore sends them into the highways with a commission to invite whomsoever they can find. The servants execute their errand in the most comprehensive manner; they invite good and bad, and thus the house is filled with guests. We here see how powerfully the preaching of the Gospel is carried on in the world according to the will of the Lord, and how the free invitation addressed by Him to all is at special times more strongly urged by His servants.

The most righteous in their ecclesiastical and civil relations are too bad (οὐκ ἄξιοι) if they are self-righteous; the most unworthy, on the other hand, are good enough if they seek righteousness in redemption. Grace, indeed, would not be grace in its divine majesty if it could not redeem, and wished not to redeem,

[1] Strauss, *Leben Jesu* i. 688.

the most unworthy. Therefore the contrast of good and bad which was formed in the old-world æon makes no difference, if only the good acknowledge with penitence the evil in their lives, and the bad lay hold of goodness in Christ as the destiny of their life. But the emphasis with which this majesty of grace must be announced, in order to put an end to all doubt and despondency, may be badly managed by some servants, as soon as they carry it on in an antinomian spirit—as soon as they accommodate the doctrine of faith to the earthly mind, and grant admission into the Church or absolution with undue facility. In a similar manner, false hearts may misinterpret the Gospel by falsely hearing it, and wish to unite the service of sin with assurance of salvation. But with this a new fall of man is originated worse than the first, just as in the case when unbelief rejects the Gospel. Wherefore the judgment of God pervades the kingdom of grace, and with more intense severity, because the conscious service of sin which will find its way into this kingdom is of all offences the most heinous. Men cannot indeed unite the peace of reconciliation with sin, but they may make the attempt both in doctrine and life; and then always, as an outrage against the holy pure spirit of mercy, must call forth the greatest judgments. The parable exhibits this fact in the king's going in to take a view of the guests, and finding one among them who had not on a wedding garment. This image has been explained by a reference to the Oriental custom of furnishing a splendid garment for the guest who came to the feast of a man of rank.[1] On the other hand, it has been remarked that it is not certain that this custom was prevalent in the time of Jesus.[2] Then again it has been urged, that Oriental customs are characterized by their constancy;[3] and as a proof, the narrative of Samson's wedding feast has been adduced (Judg. xiv. 11-13). Samson promised to his thirty companions, whom the Philistines managed to bring with an evil intent to his wedding, thirty sheets and thirty change of garments, on the condition of their explaining his riddle. He might not like to make such a present to the perfidious guests; but since established custom seemed to require

[1] 'Allusion is made to the Eastern custom observed at feasts, of distributing costly garments.'—Olshausen, iii. 176.

[2] Strauss, Leben Jesu i. 639.

Neander, Life of Christ, § 255, p. 409.

it, he imposed on them the task of earning the gift by his riddle. But in our parable a king is speaking before a multitude of poor people, whom he had most graciously invited. It is therefore presupposed that he would not let them want the festive garment.[1] Therefore this man, in the imagery of the parable, is a vulgar, coarse-minded being, who knew not how to value the king's kindness, or to enter into the spirit of the feast—who did not esteem the master of the feast nor the occasion, nor even respected himself. But according to the spiritual meaning this guest cannot be considered as a self-righteous person, ignorant of the righteousness of faith; for this class has already been sentenced under the image of those who ungratefully refused the invitation. That this man appears among the guests in the house of mercy, marks him as one of those who assented like the rest to the doctrine of justification by faith, and tried to regard the consolations of salvation as belonging to himself. But his delinquency consisted in his not entering into the spirit of the feast, into the holy and sanctifying import of reconciliation. As far as he was concerned, the wedding feast would become a coarse carousal, the Gospel would be mere absolution, and Christian orthodoxy a cloak for sin. But the king's glance detected him even among the genuine guests. He asks him, 'Friend, how comest thou in hither, not having a wedding garment?' And he was speechless. The king commands the servants to bind him hand and foot, and to cast him into outer darkness, where shall be weeping and gnashing of teeth. Thus the parable becomes once more a parable of judgment. The judgment is first of all to be regarded as an internal one. A greater self-delusion cannot exist, than when a man attempts to confound the experiences of grace, of which the essence is to eradicate sin, with the actings and thoughts of sin. This wicked course has for its consequence the most mischievous derangement of the life of the soul. But an outward judgment follows the inward. First of all a fearful repulsion arises between the pure spirit of the Church of Christ and the impure spirit of the hypocrites, and often the latter, when suddenly unveiled, retire as the most mischievous adversaries into outer darkness. But then the special

---

[1] This trait in the parable would occasion no difficulty if there had been no trace of the custom to which we have alluded. The poorest person provides his own dress, if as a mark of favour he be invited to court.

punishment attends them : the servants bind their hands and feet. In their actions and course of conduct they are much more completely ruined than other reprobates. So deeply diseased and prostrated are they, that they have destroyed in themselves the capability of self-respect, and in the Church the possibility of believing in their return ; and moreover, by the worst entanglement in the curse, they have utterly deprived themselves of the free movement of their life in the world. Here again the saying holds good, Many are called, but few chosen. Even in the body of professed believers in the righteousness by faith, individuals are to be found who are destitute of the fidelity of the chosen.

The chief contrast of this parable, as exhibited in the despisers and guests of the marriage feast, is shown on a small scale in the parable of the two sons whom their father wished to send into his vineyard (Matt. xxi. 28–31). The first answered to his father's command to go and work in his vineyard, 'I will not,' but afterwards repented of his refusal and went. The other replied to the same injunction, 'I go, sir,' and went not. The Lord propounded this parable to the members of the Supreme Council at Jerusalem, who questioned His authority for purifying the temple, and called on them to decide which of the two sons did the will of their father. They answered, The first. Upon this they were obliged to listen to the denunciation, 'Verily I say unto you, that the publicans and harlots go into the kingdom of God before you.' The publicans and harlots had first of all renounced the service of God, the one by their position in life, the other by their sinful course. But the spirit of repentance which moved many of them in the time of Christ, was a proof that they repented of their inconsiderate haste. Many of these erring ones became labourers in the vineyard of the Lord. On the other hand, the heads of the Jewish people appeared, by their whole bearing, to be giving a constant assent to the call of God ; while their conduct towards the Messiah was a constant decisive negative, which was consummated in the crucifixion. In this parable also, notwithstanding its definite immediate application, we cannot fail to perceive its general symbolical nature.

The high priests and elders might indeed have reminded the Lord that the people of Israel were God's true vineyard, and it

cannot be disputed that they as official labourers continued to
work in it. To this representation Christ assents: He causes
them to appear in a new parable (Matt. xxi. 33–41; Mark xii.
1-9; Luke xx. 9–16) as labourers in the Lord's vineyard.
Here therefore the vineyard is an image of the kingdom of
God in its universal theocratic form,[1] while in the former
parable He described the kingdom of New Testament life
breaking out of the shell of Judaism.

The owner of the vineyard is God. He has completed the
whole according to the ideal of a vineyard. The vines are
planted; a hedge surrounds the plantation; and it is furnished
with a wine-press and a watch-tower. The word of God, as the
principle of consecrated life, forms the plantation; the social
communion as the exclusion of those who are not members of
the kingdom (under the Old Covenant represented by circumcision and the Passover, under the new by baptism and the
supper) forms the hedge;[2] the wine-press denotes the holy suffering by which the spiritual wine is pressed from the grapes;
and the tower, the sacred discipline, the office of watching and
punishing, in the Church. This vineyard the owner let out to
vinedressers and went into a distant country. In the fruit-
season he sent his servants to receive the rent. But these
servants were ill-treated by them. According to Mark, one
servant was sent first of all, whom they beat and sent empty
away; then another, whom they stoned and wounded in the
head, and handled him shamefully; last of all, one whom they
killed outright.[3] The owner then sent a greater number of
servants, whom they maltreated in the same way. These vinedressers are manifestly the rulers of the Jewish nation, as far
as they represent generally the prevailing tendency of the
people in general. At their hands the Lord might expect to
receive the proceeds of His capital, the genuine fruits of repentance. But they shamefully maltreated His prophets, and

[1] Compare Isa. v. 1–7.
[2] We cannot understand this hedge to mean the Mosaic law. Nor can
we help noticing, that at the close of the parable the vineyard is transferred
to other husbandmen. The kingdom of God passes into the New Testament
form. But how is it possible to regard the Mosaic law as hedging in the
New Testament kingdom?
[3] According to Luke, they cast him out wounded.

killed some of them. Christ makes two divisions of these messengers, in order that the sending of the son may appear more suitable as the third and last. The owner last of all sends his own (his only, his beloved) son to them, saying, They will reverence my son. He still wished to regard them not as rebels and robbers, but only as misguided men. But when the son came, they said, This is the heir! This expression is highly significant. By employing it, Christ reproaches His enemies as well knowing that He came from the Father, and was filled with the life of God. The vinedressers were perfectly aware that to Him the vineyard really belonged, and on that account resolved to kill Him in order to get possession of His inheritance. 'And they took him and killed him, and cast him out of the vineyard' (Mark xii. 8; Matt. xxi. 39). The meaning of these words strikes us at once. They were fulfilled to the letter. These Jews slew the Messiah before the vineyard. They put Him to death as an excommunicated person by the hands of the Gentiles. Jesus again caused the Jews to pass sentence on themselves. To the question, 'When the lord of the vineyard cometh, what will he do unto these husbandmen?' they say to Him, 'He will miserably destroy these wicked men, and will let out his vineyard to other husbandmen, which shall render him the fruits in their seasons' (Matt. xxi. 40, 41).[1]

Thus the judgment on the wicked administrators of the Old Testament theocracy is announced. But the same spirit of judgment which presides there, pervades also the New Testament theocracy, and executes also in it the decisions of eternal righteousness. But its judgments will come forth especially at the close of the New Testament economy. Then all false, unspiritual Christians will be rejected, while the faithful will enter into the kingdom of perfection. This is shown in the parable of the wise and foolish virgins (Matt. xxv. 1–13). But especially will all faithless overseers of the Christian Church experi-

---

[1] Mark condenses the narrative, since he represents the Lord Himself as uttering this judgment. According to Luke, Christ's adversaries answered this address of the Lord by saying, God forbid! If the Pharisees, according to Matthew, passed this judgment themselves—on the supposition that they rightly understood the meaning of Jesus—this feigned impartiality certainly meant that it would be far from them to slay the true heir of God.

ence a heavy sentence; this is taught by the parable of the wicked servant (Matt. xxiv. 45–51; Luke xii. 42–46).

There are times of darkness in the history of the kingdom of God, times which are full of severe temptation for believers. Such a time was that of Christ's crucifixion (Luke xxii. 53). The Lord has particularly illustrated the characteristics of a midnight of this kind by the parable of the ten virgins, which is constructed on the Jewish mode of celebrating weddings. The bridegroom went out at eventide in nuptial array, and with great pomp, to fetch his bride from her parents' house and bring her home to his father's. The bride watched for him, surrounded by the bridal virgins, who were provided with festive lamps, in which oil nourished the burning wick, and which were often carried on a wooden pole, so that they resembled equally torches and lamps. It was the office of these virgins to go out and meet the bridegroom on his approach, to congratulate him, and then to accompany him in a joyous procession with their lamps to his father's house, where the wedding was celebrated. On these occasions the bridegroom sometimes kept them waiting till late in the evening, and thus the bridal virgins were subjected to a trial. Their lamps might burn out if they were only scantily supplied with oil, so that they would suffer disgrace, especially if they fell asleep, and thus did not notice early enough the deficiency of oil in their lamps. The characteristic of this nocturnal trial, which the Lord has also exhibited in another parabolic discourse, consists in this: that the waiting virgins lost the festive disposition and earnest attention; that they did not continue in that watchful and joyous state of feeling which the occasion itself and the near approach of the bridegroom ought to have inspired. The significance of this danger is obvious. It is midnight for the Church of Christ when the diffusion of a worldly spirit has so gained the ascendancy as to produce the appearance as if the history of the Church were subject to the common course of the world and nature; as if the kingdom of heaven would not be completed at the judgment and the transformation of the world; as if Christ would not come again. Believers at such a time would be more than ever tempted to lose the feeling of being in the midst of the development of the wedding of the Christian reconciliation and purification of the world, and gradually to renounce their calling of contributing to the festivity of the work of their Lord. But more than once in the midnight of the progress of Christianity the cry is made, 'The Bridegroom cometh.' Heavy judgments and great awakenings testify the near approach of the Lord, and His spiritual advent expresses in continually stronger manifestations the approach of His glorified personality, as it takes place at an equal ratio with the transformation of the earth. But the members of the Church of Christ, through spiritual slothfulness, may sink into a state in which every great incident in Christ's approach will become a heavy judgment. Such a judgment is exhibited to us in the fate of the foolish virgins. The ten virgins, taken all together, do not form merely some part of the Church, as Olshausen thinks, but the whole Church, as indeed is indicated by the number ten. But they signify the Church in one peculiar relation, namely, as it ought to exhibit the glory of the bride with her abundant splendour; the Church, therefore, in its destiny, as full of spiritual joy and blessedness, waiting with the full brightness of her Lord's inner life, to maintain His honour in His absence, and to meet Him triumphantly at His advent. The sleeping in this parable is indeed a questionable thing; but it is not the special point of criminality, otherwise the wise virgins would not be represented as sleeping at the same time as the foolish ones. It is distinctly said of all of them, 'While the bridegroom tarried they all slumbered and slept.' For a while they lost the consciousness of the importance of their position, and of the commencement of the wedding. But this situation was critical, especially since they could not notice whether. the oil in their lamps was too quickly consumed. The point of importance in this parable is the oil, the spirit of the inner life.[1] The foolish virgins awaken, as well as the wise, at the cry raised by the most wakeful spirits in the Church, 'The Bridegroom cometh!' They also are provided with lamps, and begin, like

---

[1] De Wette remarks on the passage: 'The oil which they have in store is not (according to a current devotional interpretation) precisely the Holy Spirit, possibly because *anointing* is, in Scripture language, equivalent to being under the Spirit's influence (*Inspiration*). It denotes the internal persistency in watchfulness, and, so far, internal spiritual power.' This remark depends on the distinction between the anointing of the Spirit, and the internal spiritual power in the Christian life.

the others, to trim them, that they may burn clear. But now
it is found that oil is wanting to their lamps; they are gone
out. The wise, on the contrary, are provided with a sufficiency
of oil; and in this consists the essential difference. The parable therefore exhibits the contrast between the unspiritual,
dead members of the Christian Church, and those who are
spiritually alive. This difference exists at all times. But it
always becomes more important as time advances, and at last
appears in all its fearfulness, and is the basis of an essential
decision and separation, in the judgment which awaits the
Church. All the members will wish, at last, to take a part
in the imperial glory of the Church. They all have lamps—
the forms of faith, the confession of the Church, and their
outward position in it. But then the question will be, whether
this form speaks the truth, or deceives; whether it is filled
by the eternal contents of the Spirit of Christ or not. The
foolish virgins have not the Spirit of Christ; they want the
burning lamps, the proofs of love and the songs of praise.
But it belongs to the more allegorical finish of the parable,
when the foolish virgins say to the wise, 'Give us of your
oil, for our lamps are gone out;' and when these answer,
'Not so; lest there be not enough for us and you; but go ye
rather to them that sell, and buy for yourselves.' On the one
hand, the earnest longing after the communication of the Spirit
is the first beginning of the spiritual life itself; and on the
other, the spiritual fulness of one Christian cannot be diminished
by impartation to another. Nevertheless, this representation
has also symbolical features. The feeling of a deficiency is
now awakened in the foolish virgins, and yet they wish to retard
the completion of the wise. But these must now attend to their
calling, to begin the festive life of the kingdom in the communion of their Lord. The separation is come to maturity.
Still a prospect seems to open to them of reaching their destination, since the advice is given them, 'Go to them that sell, and
buy for yourselves;' since the wise ones counselled them to seek
for the spiritual life in the regular way of Christian meditation
and of Christian endeavour; in the faithful employment of the
instituted means of grace. But while the foolish virgins went
to buy, the bridegroom comes. The wise virgins become par-
takers of the feast, and the door of the festive hall is closed.

At last the foolish virgins come and cry out at the door, 'Lord, Lord, open to us!' They receive the answer, 'Verily I say unto you, I know you not!' This is manifestly a judicial sentence. Olshausen maintains, that from the connection it results that the sentence, 'I know you not,' cannot mark eternal condemnation. 'Rather,' he says, 'the foolish virgins were only excluded from the marriage supper of the Lamb' (Rev. xix. 7). But it is very uncertain, when Olshausen says, 'These virgins had the universal condition of salvation, faith (from their calling κύριε, κύριε, ἄνοιξον ἡμῖν, ver. 11), but they wanted the requisite for the kingdom of God which proceeds from faith, sanctification (Heb. xii. 14).' The objective fact which he has here in his eye is the difference between the first and second resurrection—between the preliminary judgment of the world which is to be succeeded by the glorification of the Church of Christ on earth, and the last judgment, which will be followed by its transformation into a heavenly state of existence. But this constitutes no reason for seeing in the parable only the preliminary judgment. That the foolish virgins said, 'Lord! Lord!' and craved an entrance to the feast, did not qualify them as believers. Had they been believers, they would also have been welcome guests. Even the rejected at the last judgment will excuse themselves, according to Matt. xxv. Yet it is not to be lost sight of, that there is a difference between the description of the judgment as it affects the foolish virgins, and as it affects the finally rejected. Therefore, although no particular preliminary judgment is here spoken of, yet the thought of a transient judgment seems to predominate. According to the whole structure of the parable, we may venture to see in it all the preliminary judgments of the Lord, even to the last judgment. And such is the actual fact. As often as the Lord comes to His Church in a new manifestation of His Spirit, a separation is made between the dead and the living members of the Church. Only the children of the Spirit form a joyous procession with Him to His marriage supper. This was the case for the first time, when at Pentecost the Lord returned to His Church by His Spirit. The wise in Israel went in with Him to His feast; the foolish remained without. This will one day be signally verified when the palmiest times of the Church begin, her true glorification in the world. The unspiritual, perfectly dead part of Christendom then set themselves, in some form or other, in marked opposition to the glorified Church. The final judgment was not yet passed upon them; but it is not said that they would necessarily be restored in that judgment. That will depend upon how the last judgment will find them.

As to what relates to this judgment which will come on the Church, the Lord finally has expressed in the most striking manner the climax of evil in the Church, by the parable, already mentioned, of the wicked servant. It is remarkable, that it was Peter who gave the Lord occasion to deliver it. The Lord exhorts the disciples to watch (Luke xii. 35, 36) like servants who wait for their lord when he returns from the wedding. They are to have their loins girt and their lamps burning. They must wait in earnest expectation of their coming Lord, and not incur His displeasure by self-indulgence, and by allowing, like dark spirits, their lights to become dim and go out. Christ closed this exhortation with the words, ' If he shall come in the second watch, or come in the third watch, and find them so, blessed are those servants' (ver. 38). But then this cheerful earnest image is changed into a threatening one: ' And this know, that if the good-man of the house had known what hour the thief would come, he would have watched, and not have suffered his house to be broken through. Be ye therefore ready also: for the Son of man cometh at an hour when ye think not.' The thief easily deceives the householder in the night, if he does not know at what hour he will come. If he only knew this, nothing would be easier than to hinder the thief. Therefore the uncertainty of the hour of the coming of Jesus Christ is the great danger which always threatens the careless among His disciples; and the more they surrender themselves to their carelessness, so much the more dangerous and obnoxious to them will be the coming of Jesus Christ, as to a householder the breaking in of a thief.[1] This parabolic representation contains two most important thoughts. The Christian must indeed consider, that the very next moment may put him in a fearfully difficult position, which will urge him to a decision for his life, and become a judgment for him, if he has not carefully watched beforehand, so as to understand the meaning of this hour when it comes. Christ's language, which He so often repeats, respect-

[1] See Olshausen's *Commentary* ii. 307.

ing the uncertainty of that hour, shows us most clearly how distinctly the certainty was present to His mind, that after the tardy course of the periodic time of the Church's æon, the final catastrophe which is to introduce a new epoch will come with fearful and startling rapidity. Peter having asked the Lord whether He had uttered this parable in reference to them, the disciples alone, or to all, the parable we have mentioned follows (Luke xii. 41–48). It appears at first not in parabolic compactness, but in a discourse which gradually assumes a distinctly parabolic form. The Lord said, ' Who then is that faithful and wise steward, whom his lord shall make ruler over his household, to give them their portion of meat in due season ? ' This question distinguishes in their spiritual importance between the class of spiritual stewards and those whom they provide for in the Church. But who is the servant ? The decision is difficult, but it is given in the following words : ' Blessed is that servant whom his lord, when he cometh, shall find so doing.' Whoever, therefore, at His coming is occupied in dispensing spiritual food to the household, as it becomes him, the doctrines, the consolations, and the encouragements of the Gospel, him his Lord will mark as the servant originally called by Him, and will attest him to be such by placing him over all His goods, and thus making him a prince in the kingdom of the Spirit. But if that servant, who in his real character was distinctly present to his mind as evil (' *that evil servant,*' Matt. xxiv. 48), should say in his heart, My lord delayeth his coming, and should begin to beat the menservants and maidens, the younger members of the household, and to eat and drink, and give himself up to inebriety, and therefore changing his calling to furnish food to his fellow-servants into the standpoint of a despotic judicial taskmaster in the house, the lord of that servant will come in a day when he looketh not for him, and at an hour when he is not aware, and will pass upon him the sentence of theocratic zeal; he will cut him in sunder,[1] and will appoint him his portion with the unbelievers, or with the hypocrites. And thus will he make it evident that he was not his true and accredited servant; for in the kingdom of Christ, according to its essential spirituality, the office must coincide with the interior life and the conduct. The general rule by which the Lord inflicts those severe punishments is

[1] Compare 1 Sam. xv. 33.

next given. The servant who knew his lord's will and prepared
not himself, neither did according to his will, will suffer many
stripes. But he that knew not, and did commit things worthy of
stripes, shall suffer few stripes. For every man has an immediate
feeling of the will of his heavenly Lord, which he ought to culti-
vate; and as punishment is due even when a servant does not
know what his lord wills, so in a like sense is a man punishable
when he does not know what God wills.[1] But the punishment of
the servant who wilfully transgresses his Lord's will, will be great.
By this rule a greater punishment will be inflicted on a bad Christian than on a bad heathen, and a greater still on a bad clergyman;
and so the scale rises up to a bad bishop, and that servant who
holds the highest position in the Church with the greatest unfaithfulness, will on that account be punished most severely.
The punishment of being ' cut in sunder,' expresses the fearful
contrast which is formed between the greatest, most careless,
judicial arrogance, and the sudden endurance of the most horrible doom. Such a doom falls everywhere on the clerical office,
where it falls asunder by a schism into dead parts, where by
divisions it loses its authority and power. But as to what concerns the despotic functionary in the Church of Christ, his punishment is more precisely determined in Luke : ' his portion is
appointed with unbelievers.' He was an unbeliever who made
himself a lord of the Church, because he did not thoroughly believe with his heart in the return of his Lord, and therefore neglected and ill-treated his fellow-servants, and gave himself up to
a life of self-indulgence. But, according to Matthew, he receives
the punishment of the hypocrites, since in his unbelief he
assumed the credit of the greatest and most ardent zeal, while
he maltreated his fellow-servants. The punishment of the ' evil
servant' is therefore this, that he is cast into the abode of the
lost, where there is weeping and gnashing of teeth.

The two last parables distinctly point to the great representation of the last judgment, which Jesus has given, not in a parable,
but in a discourse pervaded by parabolic traits (Matt. xxv. 31–
46). We have seen how the parables relating to the kingdom
of God rise in one straight stem, and then branch out into
parables of mercy and of judgment. Last of all, the lofty summit

[1] Compare Olshausen, iii. 1.

of this parabolic system appears in the parabolic representation already mentioned of the last judgment. And here, in the crown of the system, we see the blossom of the parable fully expand, and the resplendent flower break forth of a clear representation of the appearance of the kingdom of God in its New Testament glory; while, by the abundance of its symbolical traits, it shows that it forms the crown of the parabolic system. Nor will the circumstance that this representation is destitute of the compact parabolic form, prevent us from considering it, since it forms the natural organic head of the cycle of parables; in fact, it is the key by which Christ teaches us to unfold what is hidden and veiled in all the parables of the kingdom.

We see here, how mercy is to form the decisive rule by which the Lord will pass sentence, and consummate His kingdom. The Son of man appears in His glory, and all His angels with Him, and He sits on the throne of His glory. Thus is the revelation of Christ's consummated kingdom of glory depicted. All nations are assembled before Him.[1] All men come under the judgment of the Christian rule of life; and as a shepherd divides the sheep from the goats, so Christ divides men. He places the sheep on His right, and the goats on His left. Therefore on that day the human race is so matured in the works of separating contrast, that it needs only the coming forth of Christ, only a signal from Him, to complete the separation which had matured in life. Now the merciful are saluted by Christ as the blessed of His Father. In His judgment they have brought the required aid to Him in all His sufferings: they have fed the hungry, given drink to the thirsty, taken in the stranger, clothed the naked, visited the sick, sought out the prisoner. But these merciful ones are also the humble; they cannot recollect that they have acted as such angels of mercy on earth. And these humble ones are also the truly Christ-like. For what they have done to the least among them whom Christ calls His brethren, they have done, in His judgment, to Himself. They had, therefore, in their eye not merely the physical in the sufferers, with an unspiritual sensu-

---

[1] Olshausen, without reason, would find in this representation only the delineation of a final judgment on unbelievers. Unbelievers, as such, would indeed not be yet ripe for judgment. Besides, this judgment is too decidedly represented as a judgment on all nations.

ous sympathy; but they cherished and raised the inner man in them, their Christian destiny and christological dignity. The noble marks of the divine lineage in the unfortunate have attracted and moved them as a life related to their own, and by their charity they have brought them nearer to Christ. 'Inherit the kingdom,' Christ says, announcing their reward, 'prepared for you from the foundation of the world.' They enter into eternal life, as the blessed of the Father, as those who were pervaded by the blessing of the Father. The kingdom of a chosen humanity perfected in the Spirit of Christ, in humility and love, and raised above death, has been founded in them from the beginning, and its completion will be carried on among them in the development of the world, and above them in the administration of the Father. Now this inheritance exists in its bloom, and receives them as the phenomenal world, corresponding to its inner nature. But the wicked will be rejected as the unmerciful, who, in all the relations of misery, have no heart for the destitute. But they reveal themselves, moreover, as the self-righteous, since they are not disposed to convict themselves of negligence in the duty of mercy. But lastly, it contributes to their severest reproach, that they entirely ignored the golden threads of the christological relation which go through all human life, that they have not regarded in man the calling to Christ, and therefore not Christ in humanity. Christ sends them away from Himself as accursed. The word here is no mere term of reproach, but the description of a reality. They are pervaded by the curse as a petrifaction by the stony material (κατηρα-μένοι). Therefore they will be thrown into the æonian fire, prepared for the devil and his angels; and they will be sent into the æonian punishment. The æonian fire began from the fall of Satan to develop itself in him and in his associates; and in this development a great spiritual torment, a great community of destruction, ripened in humanity. This must separate itself under the sentence of the Lord in the last crisis of the Christian world, as a tormenting fire-æon, from the blessed light-æon of perfected humanity. The Christian development of the world, according to its whole epic course, cannot pass over into a heavenly nature in an idyllic continuity, but must close with a catastrophe —must complete itself in a fiery paroxysm of world-historic magnitude. As, in a man with a mortal disease, the departing life at last breaks loose from the stiffening body in a fiery conflict, so at last the world of light will separate itself from the world of the curse—the kingdom of the new humanity perfected in love, from the æon of fierce discord, and of an old humanity devouring itself in the doom of *egoism,* which falls back into the pre-human spirit-regions of the demons. This will take place when the kingdom of Christ in this world has, in its last development, most nearly approached to the kingdom of Christ in the other world, and when, in consequence of reciprocal attraction, this world passes over into the other, and the other into this, so that the barrier falls, and Christ appears in the midst of His people *here,* or His people appear before His glorious throne *there;* both in one and the same event.

The cycle of the parables of judgment forms also a succession of world-historical pictures, in which retributive justice exhibits the successive great acts of its administration. The parables of the labourers in the vineyard, each of whom receives a penny, of the pounds, and of the talents, reveal the administration of rewarding retribution, and at the same time show how punitive retribution accompanies it as its complement. The first world-picture shows us the action of the energy of the Spirit in the founding of the kingdom of God. The divine justice appears in its unity with grace, since it is altogether spirit; therefore it does not miss its reward, according to the external mode of valuing human work. Human conversion corresponds to it in its spirituality; it raises itself above the loss of time, and can receive and experience from God the blotting out of the guilt of this loss. The second world-picture shows us how the external might of the offices of the kingdom appointed by God gains the world. The nobleman in his appearance is poor, and his servants are poor; but he gains the whole kingdom and puts down the rebellion; while they gain for him the single component parts of his kingdom, according to the measure of the internal energy of the life of their calling. The third world-picture shows us how recompensing justice gives every servant of God a spiritual gain in the kingdom of God, and how it corresponds exactly to the faithful application of His spiritual gifts. But we see punitive justice by the side of the remunerative acting in a threefold manner: the servants of a mercenary, outwardly calculated mechanical service were punished by the disappointment of their outward expectation; the servants of spiritual sloth, by being deprived of their gifts; and the actual rebels against the government of a prince who is identical with grace, by the severe punishments which their own unmercifulness demanded. Then the scenes of judicial justice, in its predominant agency, are announced by the phenomena of its menaces and warnings. We see Death as the messenger of Judgment stalking through the world, and hear in all the paths of mortality the footsteps of the approaching retribution. A whole world of manifestations of divine grace is further shown us in the history of the respited fig-tree, as a numerous group of revelations of long-suffering, in which already the most alarming omens of judgment are disclosed. Then follow the images of the judgment itself. We see how first of all judgment strikes man in general when he despises the invitation of God to the spiritual feast of the divine life in His kingdom, and likewise when he would profane this spiritual feast, and change it into the common carousal of a sinful life. These crimes of despising and desecrating the Eternal appear in an aggravated form as crimes of dishonesty. The unchristian changes into the antichristian, and calls forth a judgment of the rejection of whole communities, as is represented in the parable of the criminal vinedressers. These special acts of penal justice point to the general judgment as they come forth more distinctly at the end of time. Judgment begins first of all at the house of God. We see in the parable of the foolish virgins, how the dead part of the theocracy, as well as of the Christian Church, is shut out from the festive communion of living believers; and in the parable of the wicked servant, how the hardened individuals among the overseers of the Church must suffer the heaviest retribution. Out of this judgment of the Lord on the Church the judgment on all nations finally unfolds itself. But as rewarding justice is always complemented by punitive justice, so this again is also accompanied by the former, which is constantly unfolding the divine affluence of its grace. For God changes not towards man, but man changes towards Him; and in this change a separation according to their opposite tendencies is produced, which is constantly widening, till at last a separation which reaches to the bottomless pit is consummated in the last judgment. Hence the completed condemnation of the ungodly is the completed redemption of the godly. The separation of the æon of light and the æon of the curse in the last crisis of the history of humanity, forms therefore the completion of the Christian kingdom of God.

In this manner Christ has delivered to His people the doctrine of the founding of the kingdom of God, in parables which form themselves into a system with wonderful fulness and distinctness.

The very name of this institution characterizes its nature. It is the kingdom of God[1] in opposition to the kingdom of this world—the completed theocracy. While the ancient theocracy exhibited itself in the individual inspired flashes of the prophets, and thus its peculiar function consisted in momentary flowings forth of eternity into time, this kingdom of God is a firmly established kingdom of human spirits, in which God Himself rules as King, and His Spirit as the supreme law of life, and the union of human hearts with God in His royal supreme will is its peculiar life-element. This kingdom is also, according to its nature, equally the kingdom of heaven;[2] an ideal state, or a state of ideality, of the purest distinctness and action of all relations in the unity of a heavenly, consecrated life. That which makes heaven to be heaven is the perfect elevation of all its phenomena into its idea, or its ideality. But its idea is its consecration to God. In that, therefore, consists the holiness of heaven, that it rises into this divine consecration. The kingdom of heaven is consequently an institution pure and consecrated as heaven itself. Hence the Lord can recognise the kingdom of heaven in no state of inferior purity. But this institution is also termed ' the kingdom' simply (Matt. xiii. 19, etc.), because in it the perfected human society, the eternal organism, is realized in the essential relations of humanity. This organism culminates, and has its point of unity, in a head animating all the members, that is, in Christ, and hence this kingdom is also called the kingdom of Christ (Matt. xiii. 41; John xviii. 36, etc.). But since this kingdom has been prepared by the theocratic plan of the entire world-history, and since, according to this great historical development, it has appeared first of all in a prefigurative form in the Old Testament consecrated kingdom, it has been also named after that typical kingdom in its

---

[1] Ἡ βασιλεία τοῦ Θεοῦ. Mark i. 15, etc.

[2] Ἡ βασιλεία τῶν οὐρανῶν. Matt. xiii. etc.

greatest splendour, and thus is called the kingdom of David
(Mark xi. 10). The head of this kingdom is also its principle.
Its first, unrecognised appearance in the world, is the person of
Christ Himself. This kingdom flourishes in His heart, in His
Spirit, and begins to unfold itself in His works. The King of
truth is the soul of the kingdom of truth; therefore on His
appearance the proclamation is made, 'The kingdom of heaven
is at hand!'

But the historic goal of this kingdom is the completion of
the Christian æon, the appearance of the glory of Christ in
the perfected manifestation of the glory of His Church, and the
glorification of the Church by the appearance of the Lord.
The leading outlines of that completion of the ancient æon,
upon which the new æon of the kingdom makes its appearance,
are the following. The life of Christ, as the vital principle of
humanity, has completed its regeneration. The palingenesia is
effected in the core of humanity to such a degree that a new
humanity exhibits itself in perfect beauty as a splendid organism
which shines forth in eternity, and from which the image of
God is reflected (Matt. xix. 28). The earth itself is drawn upwards in this palingenesia. Its ethereal light-image has become complete with the new humanity, and issues forth as a
heavenly star from the cloud of its humiliation (Matt. v. 14;
Luke xii. 49).[1] The appearance of Christ is accomplished in
this way, that the interval between this world and the next is
removed by the completed victory of the Christian spirit
(Matt. xxiv. 14).

The kingdom of God, therefore, is in constant development
between these two points of its life—between its principle, the
invisible life of Christ, resting in the depths of heaven and of
humanity, and between that glorious appearance of the transformed human world resting in the depths of the future. The
question now presents itself, by what means is the life of Christ
changed into the life of humanity?

The first means by which the life of Christ becomes the
life of the world, is the word of Christ, the Gospel (Matt. xiii.
3, 19). It is secured to the world by a perpetual ordinance of
Christ in the evangelical office of teaching.[2] But the teaching

[1] Christ kindles the earth itself with His fire.
[2] John xx. 21.

of Christ is from the first quite identical with His life, and therefore His life exhibits itself in a second means, in His collective heavenly doings (John ii. 18). But His course of conduct and His works are secured to His Church by the calling of His witnesses (Acts i. 8). But Christ's doings are completed only in His sufferings and death. His death is the redemption of the world (Matt. xxvi. 28). And His death is continually incorporated with the world by the confession of His people (Matt. xvi. 24, 25). And as Christ has completed His work in His own eternal Spirit, so also it can be completed in the hearts of His people only by the same Spirit (John xvi. 7). With His Spirit, His life and sufferings first become a peculiar possession of His people in their unity, power, and depth, as a full divine work, and by the life of His Spirit they become His Church. By His Church, then, the life of Christ is transplanted into the world (John xvii. 18). But how is His Church to be recognised? In this way, that they exhibit His life in their life (John xiii. 35); that they miss His visible presence with consciousness and earnest longing, and hope with firm confidence for His return (John xiv. 27, 28); and that, in the certainty of His spiritual presence, they express this intermediate state by celebrating the communion according to His institution— the present and future communion by the rite of holy baptism, the past communion by partaking of the holy supper (Matt. xxviii. 19; Luke xxii. 19). In the holy sacraments the Church comprehends all the means, as given by the Lord, by which the kingdom of God in it and by it is established in the world— the word, the doing, and the suffering of Christ, His Spirit and His future appearance. In the moments of true communion the Church for an instant enters into that appearance, it shines in an anticipated lustre of the kingdom (Mark xiv. 24, 25; Luke xxii. 29, 30).

By the continual use of these means the Church is constantly advancing towards its manifestation, urged on by the power of Christ's life; and this movement is healthful in proportion as the means co-operate in living unity, and as it is carried on with a reference to both points. Consequently, the progress of the Christian palingenesia is always arrested where the sacraments are administered without the living word, or where the word is proclaimed without the exhibition of its power of manifestation in the sacraments, or where the word and the sacraments are administered disconnectedly because the spirit that unites the two elements is not sought by prayer. But if, on the one hand, the manifestation of the kingdom of Christ is prematurely exhibited in a State where the ecclesiastical power is supreme, this is a too active manifestation that goes beyond the truth and loses itself in illusions, in which the vital principle of the palingenesia must more and more be lost. And if, on the other hand, the word of Christ should be made a mere scholastic term, so that the sense of the need of communion, to say nothing of longing after the manifestation of Christ and His glory in humanity, is continually diminishing,—this is a spiritualism which cannot be recognised as the spiritual life of the Word made flesh, and is not capable in the least of effecting the regeneration of the world.

Therefore, where there is no well-developed Christian communion, no guarantee can exist that the Christian life will be active in its vital principle; and where the communion goes beyond its destination, and is changed into a State organism, it is a sure sign that it operates no longer deeply and with perfect fidelity as the spirit of regeneration. The communion in its ideal form, is therefore the constant living medium between the throne of the invisible Christ and His future appearing. And thus through Christian fellowship His life mingles itself in its separate elements with the life of the world. His word is the law of the kingdom and of life to it. Were it governed by an inferior law, it would not be the communion of Christ. But it makes His word not immediately the political life-law of the world. If it attempted this, it would change Christ into a Moses, and Christianity into Judaism, instead of being the medium of imparting His life to the world. But it feels that the latter object is its vocation, and proves it, since by ingrafting Christ's words on the morals and laws of the world, it constantly keeps in view its final aim that the world may become the kingdom of Christ. And in the same way it imparts the mysteries of its doctrine, as well as its whole life. If it were to subtract anything from the original fulness of Christianity, it would damage the institution which it was appointed to maintain, and evermore adulterate it with the heathenism of the natural worldly mind. If, on the other hand, it were disposed to make this institution predominant in the world at the cost of human freedom, it would change Christianity into Judaism. Rightly to bring the institution of Christ into harmony with the freedom of the human mind and conscience, is a task infinitely difficult, and yet blessed in itself and in its consequences.

It results from the magnitude of this task, that the kingdom of God can only by slow degrees attain the maturity of its manifestation in the world, and that the exact time of its future cannot be computed (Mark xiii. 32). Further, it results from its free spiritual character, that the kingdom of God cannot be exhibited prematurely in heavenly purity (Matt. xiii. 30), but that, nevertheless, its sanctification must be aspired after, according to the measure of its vital principle, its spirit, and its aim.

Hence the firm planting of the kingdom of God is effected by a continual movement, which, on the one hand, always exhibits the entire fulness of the divine mercy, in the reception of all who stand in need of salvation (Matt. xviii. 21-35), and on the other hand, the entire severity of the divine judgment, in the constant exclusion of all by the ecclesiastical discipline, who would bring scandals into the Church. On the other hand, this movement has not its full energy, or rather it is depressed by hindrances in the same proportion as admission is effected with carnal rigour or facility; or as the exclusion, with similar carnality, is carried to the length of political persecution, or is neglected to the loss of the social sense of honour in the members of the Church.

But all defects in the progress of the Church, between the manifestation of mercy and of judgment, will be corrected and rendered complete by the great administration of mercy and of justice by the Lord over the Church. They will be rectified: the Lord receives the merciful Samaritan in a thousand forms into the communion of His people, and ejects the guest without the wedding garment, as well as the evil servant, with a fearful doom from the communion. They will be rendered complete: the Church itself, like the world, is an object of the completed judgments and mercies of the Lord; and in a mysterious reciprocal action between the formation of the Church for the world, and the world for the Church, the time advances, when with mighty throes the epoch of the final decision suddenly comes. On the one hand, mercy celebrates its manifestation in the living images which are filled by it, and become its perfected organ, its everlasting feast in the kingdom of love. Then, on the other hand, justice celebrates its glorification, since the condemned exhibit its administration, and must justify it in their own persons in the kingdom of inflexible wrath and vengeance. But justice and mercy are never separated, although their æons, when completed, separate from one another in humanity. Justice reveals itself to the Church of the saved in the holiness of love. But the multitude of the reprobate is involved in the darkness of a corresponding æon, by a compassion which has veiled itself in punitive justice. But the kingdom of God is then completed, when in this manner Christ has communicated His blessedness to the new humanity. The Church is united to Him as His bride. It is therefore wholly participant of His life, and enters into the inheritance of His glory. And if a region is situated opposite this Church, in which the despising of His life is punished by an æonian spiritual agony, it is shown by this how men are struck in its depths by His rays, and shaken to bow the knee in His name, and in the relation of their life to Him, to occupy the right position in the kingdom of spirits (Phil. ii. 10, 11).

PART IV.

THE PUBLIC APPEARANCE AND ENTHUSIASTIC RECEPTION OF CHRIST.

SECTION I.

THE PUBLIC TESTIMONY OF THE BAPTIST TO CHRIST BEFORE THE JEWISH RULERS.

WHILE Jesus was fighting in the wilderness with the temptation which met Him under the form of the distorted Messianic hopes of His age, and in this victorious conflict developed the course of His Messianic work, the same hopes induced the Sanhedrim at Jerusalem to send a deputation to John the Baptist. John had made a powerful impression, not only on the people in general, but also on their leaders, the Pharisees, many of whom, as we have already noticed, were so carried away by the popular enthusiasm as to submit to his baptism. Gradually a more distinct judgment had been formed in the Sanhedrim respecting the unquestionable importance of so extraordinary a theocratic undertaking. They had arrived at the conviction, that a man who, on good grounds, could venture to subject the nation to such a purification, which implied a previous excommunication, must be either the Messiah Himself, or one of His forerunners, who was announced as Elias by the prophets, or the prophet promised by Moses (Deut. xviii. 15; John i. 25). But if the Baptist, by his course of action, set forth such extraordinary claims, it was an official duty on the part of the Sanhedrim to take cognizance of it, and to come to a clear understanding with him. Accordingly this body resolved on sending a deputation to him, which consisted, as a matter of course,[1] of priests and Levites. To the priests was entrusted the sanctioning of reli-

---

[1] [Lampe quotes from Maimonides: 'Synedriorum pars maxima ex Sacerdotibus constitit et Levitis.'—ED.]

gious purification, which included the observance of the laws relative to ablutions,[1] so that those who were sent on this occasion might be regarded as duly qualified commissioners.   They were very properly accompanied by Levites, who served in part as an honourable escort, and in part to act, if need be, as a hierarchical police force, should John not be prepared to show his credentials.[2]   And now, if the deputation accomplish their object, the Baptist must be recognised as one of the great prophets of the Messianic advent, or exposed as a false prophet.— But the Jewish national spirit in the high council would be completely misunderstood, and its members would be turned, against their own will, into Roman senators, if we supposed that they were averse to the announcement of the Messiah under every condition.   Yet such a judgment has been rashly formed, from the circumstance that, at a later period, the Baptist was not acknowledged by them, and that Jesus was absolutely rejected; while it should be borne in mind that it was precisely by chiliastic-political motives that the Sanhedrim were determined to this course of conduct (see p. 59).   It could not therefore be the primary aim of this deputation to dispute the claims of the Baptist; it may rather be supposed that they were actuated by chiliastic excitement.[3]

From the account of the Evangelist John, we see that the deputation must have intimated to the Baptist that he would very likely announce himself as the Messiah.   The Sanhedrim, as we have seen, must have regarded his baptism as a phenomenon of the commencing Messianic æon, and in a character who spiritually moved and carried with him the whole nation, they might find a claimant to the Messianic dignity.[4]   Now it is evident that a question which assumed the possibility that the

---

[1] Lev. xiii. and xv.

[2] The ground of suspicion which Weisse has taken against the truth of the narrative from the phrase ' priests and Levites,' is changed by a clear view of Israelitish relations into a ground of credence.   This point has already been satisfactorily settled by Lücke and Ebrard, and barely deserves a passing notice.

[3] [' Nulla adsunt vestigia, quæ ex mera invidia aut impediendi studio prognatam esse legationem suadeant. Honorifica per se erat.' Lampe in Joan. i. 407.—ED.]

[4] This disposes of what Strauss has remarked (i. 388) against the probability of such an inquiry.

Baptist might be the Messiah was a great temptation to him.
And thus John was tempted at the same time as Jesus. The
Evangelist has indicated the force of the temptation by the
words, 'He confessed, and denied not, but confessed, I am not
the Christ' (John i. 20).[1]

But the Baptist likewise gave a negative to the question
whether he was Elias.   How could he do that, since it was
undeniable that Malachi had announced the forerunner of the
Messiah under this designation ?   This declaration of the Baptist seems also to clash with the language of Christ, who at a
later period told His disciples that in the person of the Baptist
they might see that Elias who was to precede the Messiah
(Matt. xi. 14, xvii. 10–13).   But Zacharias, the father of John,
distinctly understood by the revelation of the angel that this
identification of Christ's forerunner with Elias was to be taken
in a spiritual sense (Luke i. 17).   And in the knowledge of this
fact lay the reason of the Baptist's negative to the question. He
was actuated, doubtless, by the same motives as those which
induced the Lord in the wilderness to reject the Messianic programme of His time as it was presented to Him.   In the same
proportion as the image of the Messiah or of the King was distorted into a carnal one, would be the image of His forerunner ;
or even in a still higher degree, inasmuch as this misrepresentation was carried to the length of expecting the return literally of
the ancient prophet Elias.   When, therefore, the Jews asked
him, Art thou the Elias of the Messianic advent ? the question probably meant, Art thou that Elias who was translated to
heaven, returning at the founding of a new æon ?   And taking
it in this sense, John answered, 'No!' and in saying that, he
did not deny that he was the Lord's forerunner in the spirit and
power of Elias, for that was testified by his whole life, by his
daily ministry.   Under similar circumstances, Christ expressed
Himself even with more caution and reserve.   He avoided the
misinterpretation of His Messianic calling, without the risk of
fostering the opposite error, that He disowned all claim to be
regarded as the Messiah.[2]

[1] [On which Augustin says: 'In eo probata est humilitas ejus, quia
dixit se non esse, cum posset credi esse.' *Tract. in Joan.* iv. 8.—ED.]

[2] Among other passages, that in John xviii. 34 proves how carefully the
Lord avoided all misinterpretation relative to the Messianic title.

Lastly, the Baptist answered in the negative the inquiry of the deputation, whether he was 'The Prophet' (ὁ προφήτης), namely, that particular prophet whom the Jews, according to the promise of Moses, expected before the beginning of the new era. For this he had still greater reason, because such a representation of this Prophet had not become a general definite expectation among his nation. The genuine children of the theocratic spirit referred the passage to the Messiah Himself (Acts iii. 22). Now, if the Baptist also received this exposition, as must be admitted, the question in this sense would be a repetition of the first question, which he had already met with a negative. But others expected, according to the same passage, that one day Jeremiah would return and take part in the renovation of the theocracy. By others, again, Joshua was pointed out as the person to be expected.[1] It is quite plain that John could not give assent to preconceptions of this kind. But though some persons in Israel had regarded the Prophet simply as the forerunner of Christ, John could not admit that this was the meaning of the official inquiry addressed to him; hence he gave a most decided negative also to this question. Thus, then, John repelled three tempting questions, which were animated by the same spirit as the three temptations which Christ conquered in the wilderness.

It has been thought surprising that the deputation asked the Baptist whether he was '*the Prophet*,' after putting the question to him, whether he was the Christ or Elias. If it were possible to consider the Prophet as identical with Christ, or with Elias, in both cases the question had already been settled. But probably the deputation already entertained one of those views which were developed more distinctly in the later Jewish traditions; probably they understood Jeremiah by '*the Prophet*,' and in that case the question was perfectly necessary. But even on the opposite supposition, if they held '*the Prophet*' to be identical with Elias or with the Christ, still they knew not what the Baptist on his part thought on this point. Hence this third question was unavoidable, and its insertion marks the diplomatic exactness of the authorities, and indirectly the historical fidelity of the whole narrative. But if we view the series of questions in relation to their final object, we shall find that they are very carefully arranged. Was John, for instance, the Messiah, then

[1] See Lücke's *Commentar über das Evang. des Johannes* i. 386.

his warrant for baptizing was placed beyond all doubt; was he the second Elias, it would stand equally firm; was he, lastly, ' the Prophet,' still its validity would be allowed.

When the deputies from the Sanhedrim pressed the Baptist to declare at last who he was, he answered them : ' I am the voice of one crying in the wilderness, Make straight the way of the Lord, as said the prophet Esaias ' (xl. 3). As Christ veiled His Messianic call in the most spiritual designation, which was diametrically opposed to the carnal enthusiasm of His nation, by calling Himself the Son of Man, so the Baptist chose the most delicate and spiritual characteristic of the forerunner, as he found it in the prophet Isaiah. That voice of one crying in the wilderness was primarily the theocratic presentiment, incorporating itself in prophecy, of the return of Israel from exile, as it would be accomplished under the spiritual guidance of Jehovah. But the Baptist rightly saw the highest fulfilment of that passage in the Israelitish presentiment of the advent of the Messiah, which had formed itself into a voice in his person.[1] Yet the Jewish mind was not in a state to discover the deeper and more spiritual references of the Old Testament Scriptures, and on that account this interpretation was not received in the schools of the scribes. Hence the deputation took no notice of the positive declaration of the Baptist, and now asked him in the form of a reprimand, ' Why baptizest thou then ? ' This ministration appeared to them an unallowable undertaking if he could not substantiate his claim to either of the titles adduced.[2] But John felt his ground; he answered firmly, ' I baptize ; ' but when he added, ' with water,' he passed a judgment on his baptism which he set in opposition to the judgment of the Sanhedrim. To them, this ritual observance appeared of extraordinary importance; to him, on the contrary, it appeared of extraordinary insignificance, because the vastly superior agency which the Messiah would shortly exert was always present to his thoughts. But while he depreciated his own baptism, he also justified its use, by announcing to the deputation that the Messiah was already nigh at hand.

---

[1] This passage is the first proof that references to typical prophecy in the Old Testament occur in John as well as in Matthew.

[2] [Τοιαύτας εἶχον παρὰ τῶν διδασκάλων ἑαυτῶν παραδόσεις, ὡς μόνοις ἐκείνοις ἐξῆν βαπτίζειν, i.e., to the Christ, Elias, and that prophet. Ammonius in Catena.—ED.]

Even now He is in your midst, and ye know Him not—even Him who cometh after me, and yet was before me.[1] So mysteriously and yet so distinctly did the Baptist speak of the Messiah, while he also had a feeling of the discrepancy between the expectations of his people and the character of Him who was about to appear. The Messiah had become a public character for His people, and therefore had come into their midst, when He accredited Himself to the person who was appointed by God to announce His appearance. But when the Baptist designates the personage who was to come after him as 'He'who was before him,' he expresses the essential priority or princely dignity of Christ, His essential precedence to himself in the kingdom of God. Such a twofold relation exists even in the case of a common herald. The herald outwardly hastens on before the prince, but the prince possessed his dignity before him, and made him a herald, and, according to the privilege of his rank, the prince preceded him. The herald is the outward forerunner of the prince, but the prince is the spiritual forerunner of the herald. But if the Baptist had the full .impression that in his calling he was entirely regulated by the higher calling of Christ, that his dignity was derived from Christ's dignity, and if he declared that Christ had this priority in the theocracy, he expressed at the same time the essential priority of Christ in the eternity of God; for the one is not without the other. We have not here to examine how clearly and comprehensively he thus developed, theologically, the eternal existence of Christ. But without doubt he was already more certain of the eternal existence of his own inferior personality in God, than many theologians are certain of the eternal existence of Christ.

John knew that Christ in His spiritual essence had exerted His agency throughout the Old Testament dispensation, and was undoubtedly the King of Israel. Hence he declared that he was

[1] The words ὃς ἔμπροσθέν μου γέγονεν are wanting in several manuscripts. Lücke conjectures that they were taken from the parallel passages, vers. 15, 30. Lachmann considers the reading as doubtful; the connection of the passage favours their retention. To the mysterious assertion, 'He is in your midst, and ye know Him not,' the other corresponds: 'He cometh after me, and yet was before me.' The unknown and manifested One of the people is the follower and predecessor of the Baptist. [Tischendorf, Meyer, Tholuck, and Alford reject the words.]

not worthy to loosen His shoe-latchet. He was willing to vanish, with all his works, before the glory of the Lord, and with this feeling he dismissed the deputation from Jerusalem, who were so destitute of the fitting presentiments as to regard his water-baptism as the greatest event of the times.

We have already seen how extremely improbable it is, that the deputation should not be anxious to have an exact descrip-tion of the outward appearance of a personage whom the Baptist had thus magnified, and how much it accorded with the duty of the Baptist to give them such a description. Hence we may confidently assume that the deputation returned with highly raised expectations, after receiving such an account of the person and presence of the Messiah. It is an important circumstance, that this conference took place at Bethany, on the other side Jordan, where John was then baptizing; so that the deputation must needs return home through the wilderness, in which John was tarrying.

In the meantime, it was quite a matter of uncertainty what judgment the Sanhedrim would form in the sequel respecting John. That judgment would now depend on the question, what relation the Sanhedrim would assume towards Jesus. As soon, therefore, as a collision took place between the spirit of that body and the spirit of Christ, as, according to the view we have taken, must have happened at the close of Christ's tempta-tion in the wilderness, the Jewish authorities would come to a rupture with the Baptist. But since the people, and even many members of their own body, had already done him homage, it suited their policy to conduct themselves towards him, and to express their opinion respecting him, with the greatest reserve. Yet they were not able to conceal the contradiction which existed between their earlier personal homage and their later official reserve. The Lord could reproach with unbelief towards John, men who at one time resorted to the Jordan (Luke vii. 33). If, therefore, the Evangelists appear to contradict one another when in one place they report (Matt. iii. 7) that many Pharisees came to John, and in another that the Pharisees and scribes were not baptized of him (Luke vii. 30), a real and striking fact is exhibited in a very characteristic manner. The ambiguous position which the Jewish rulers occupied in relation to the question whether John was a prophet, was founded on the

constant embarrassment they felt, owing, on the one hand, to
John's decisive testimony to Christ, and, on the other, to the
decisive opinion of the people in favour of John.   Hence
Christ, towards the close of His career, when they questioned
His authority, probably to execute the purification of the
temple, with the most wonderful sagacity proposed to them a
counter-question, and showed that He saw into the very depths
of their evil conscience,—the question whether the baptism of
John rested on divine authority, or was an arbitrary human
institution (Matt. xxi. 24).   They confessed their inability to
answer the question—a confession most disgraceful to the tribunal
they formed—rather than they would express a decision either for
or against the Baptist; a proof how completely they were non-
plussed by the question of Jesus.   The fact that the Jewish
rulers never ventured to form an official judgment respecting
the Baptist, confirms in a very significant manner the account
of the Evangelist John, that the Baptist had, by a solemn testimony, directed the people through their rulers to Christ, and
that Christ expressly appealed to this testimony (John v. 33,
etc.).   But since John testified so publicly of Christ, he linked
His fate with his own; and Herod Antipas probably considered
the outrage he committed on the stern preacher of repentance
as greatly favoured by the circumstance that his authority had
not been supported by the Sanhedrim.

NOTES.

1. Von Ammon in his *Geschichte des Lebens Jesu* (i. 261)
remarks, 'Full freedom of opinion and of public speaking prevailed among the Israelites as long as the fundamental doctrines
of the law were not endangered, as we find also among Christians in the time of Paul at Corinth (1 Cor. xiv. 29).   If, on
the other hand, a Chakam or Rabbi indulged in attacks on the
Mosaic theocratic constitution, the Lesser or Greater Sanhedrim,
and the high-priestly board especially, was authorized to inter-
fere constitutionally, and to call the innovating teacher to account respecting his authority for such proceedings (Vitringa,
De Synagoga vetere, p. 866).   This was done by the Great
Sanhedrim in the case of Jesus, and previously in reference to
the Baptist.'

2. The fact of the testimony of the Baptist to Jesus is dis-

puted by the latest critics. Weisse even thinks that true faith in the divine revelation in Christ requires most peremptorily a deviation from the letter of the Gospel narrative in reference to this testimony. Strauss adduces a series of reasons for setting aside this testimony. First of all, the later sending of the Baptist to Christ. This we shall consider in its proper place. A real difficulty brought forward also by others is the question, why the Baptist still continued to baptize, and why he did not rather join himself to Jesus? But this question has weight only as long as the significance of John's baptism is not clearly understood. John could not venture to cease purifying the old Israelitish congregation for the Church of the Messiah, as long as any unbaptized persons resorted to him. His attachment to Christ, therefore, was evinced by remaining at his post, and by fulfilling the vocation given him by God as the labour of his life. As all the other Israelites who were believers in Christ were not called to join themselves to Him as disciples in the more special sense, so neither was this the case with John. Rather would he have been unfaithful to his christological calling, had he relinquished his baptismal office. It is further alleged that John, on his 'contracted standpoint,' was unable to form a conception of that higher one which Jesus occupied (i. 377). Here again the author constructs a psychology at his own hand. This time he sets out on an assumption of ethical pitifulness, owing to which men on lower standpoints cannot help making mistakes when they look up to a man who stands higher than themselves. We are here reminded of the self-denial with which Farel implored Calvin to remain at Geneva,[1] and the earlier judgments of Erasmus on Luther, and other similar facts. Even Bodmer's behaviour towards Klopstock and Wieland's judgment on Göthe (Weisse i. 271, and Ebrard) may be here adduced. In the history of modern philosophy, the author might indeed believe he could find vouchers for his canon. But the assumption was quite false, that the ethical ability of humanity is to be estimated according to that individual philosopher. Further on we meet with the well-known quick evolutions of sophistical dexterity (p. 379). 'According to Matt. xi. 2 and Luke vii. 18, John sends two disciples to Christ with the doubting inquiry

---

[1] [See Kirchhofer's *Life of Farel* (Religious Tract Society, 1837), p. 136; Henry's *Leben Johann Calvins*, Hamburg, 1835, i. 161.—TR.]

whether He was the ἐρχόμενος, while according to the fourth Gospel he directed likewise two disciples to Him, but with the definite assertion that Jesus was the ἀμνὸς Θεοῦ, etc.' The reader can supply the *et cetera* in the well-known style of this writer. As to the relation of the Baptist to Jesus generally, Strauss defines it in a manner which has drawn forth the following remark from Kuhn (*das Leben Jesu* i. 223) :—'In order to convict the synoptical representation of a legendary character, it is assumed that the Baptist and Jesus were not acquainted with one another at an early period; in order to set aside St John's representation as unhistorical, the very opposite is assumed, that the two men were well acquainted with one another in early life. This I call a splendid specimen of critical art, which (as Lichtenberg playfully tells Philadelphia), to speak without bragging, goes far beyond the miraculous; indeed, so to speak, is absolutely impossible!' As to the supposition that the Baptist and Jesus were early acquainted with one another, Strauss thus expresses himself : 'John allows the Baptist to make rather the opposite assertion, but only because another interest, the one just noticed, preponderated in his mind.'

3. Bethany on the other side Jordan is to be distinguished from the Bethany not far from Jerusalem. Origen, as Lücke remarks, has altered it to Bethabara, against all, or almost all, the manuscript authorities.[1] 'It may be admitted that the place, as was often the case, had two names of similar meaning— Beth-abara, בֵּית עֲבָרָה Passage-house or Ford-house, and Bethany, perhaps from בֵּית אֳנִיָּה Ship-house.'[2] Lücke, *Commentar* i. 391-395. We may be allowed to conjecture that the name Bethany, *Ship-house*, which belonged to the palmiest days of Israel, had fallen into disuse when a boat to ferry passengers over was no longer employed, and persons were obliged to wade through, which in favourable seasons was possible in several places, and so the name was changed to Bethabara or *Passage-house*. This latter designation might perhaps be founded on the recollection, that the place in former days, when likewise there was no ferry, was called Bethbarah (Judg. vii. 24), as it is supposed that this

---

[1] [Alford gives Origen's defence of the alteration, and exposes its weakness. Stanley, however, follows Origen (*Sinai and Palestine*).—ED.]

[2] [As Meyer remarks, however, this etymology will scarcely do for Bethany on the Mount of Olives.—ED.]

was only a contraction of Bethabara (see Robinson's *Palestine* i.
536; Von Raumer's *Palestina*, p. 250).

SECTION II.

THE TESTIMONY OF JOHN TO THE DIGNITY OF CHRIST,
UTTERED TO HIS DISCIPLES.

The day after John's temptation Jesus returned to him from
the wilderness, where He also had overcome the last and most
violent onset of His great temptation. Both were animated
by a lively feeling of victory; and John more than ever was in
a state of mind to understand the suffering Messiah, since his
own soul was now enjoying the blessedness of a verified renunciation of the world. But a presentiment of His victory on the
cross seemed to glorify the whole being of Christ. In this state
of mind, and in the beauty of the priestly spirit, He came to the
Baptist. How He greeted him—what He announced to him—
and in general what passed between them, the Evangelist does
not inform us.

But he narrates the impression which Jesus at that time
made on the Baptist, and which the latter probably communicated, in whole or in part, to his disciples in the presence of
Jesus. With deep emotion he exclaimed, 'Behold the Lamb of
God, that taketh away the sins of the world!' The same prophet who, in the voice of one crying in the wilderness, as spoken
of by the prophet Isaiah, recognised the serious image of his
own life, now beheld with equal clearness the tragical image of
the Messiah's life, in the suffering Lamb of God bearing the
sins of men, as spoken of by the same prophet. The recognition of the one is closely connected with that of the other. The
Baptist might indeed have thought, when he used this expression,
of the sacrificial lamb in the Israelitish worship, as it must have
been present to the prophet's mind. But no doubt his expression is founded immediately on the language of the prophet.
As he had derived from the prophet the information respecting
himself—that he was to be heard as a voice in the wilderness—
so he had learned respecting Christ, that He was the Lamb of

God described by the prophet, ordained by God, and consecrated
to God, and therefore that He must accomplish His redemptive
work by unparalleled endurance. At all events the presentiment of atonement flashed through his soul in this expression.
Those who feel themselves placed in a dilemma by this language,
—who say, either the Baptist must have propounded a doctrine of atonement dogmatically defined; or he must, at the most,
have intended to say that Christ as the meek One would remove
the sins of the world;[1] or, forsooth, with this critic, he could not
have uttered the sentence had he not spoken as a dogmatic,[2]—such
persons fail to understand the whole type of prophetic knowledge
and illumination. We must, first of all, survey in general the
region of the spiritual dawnings of great spirits, if we would distinguish between the momentary flashes of illumination vouchsafed to the prophets and their average knowledge. Respecting
the nature of such a difference as it is exhibited in the department
of general intellectual life, some great poets of modern times can
certainly give us information. They would inform the critic how
very often the pregnant language of a man of genius exceeds his
everyday insight. Of a prophet this is doubly true; and if John
was ever to be the complete herald of Jesus, and therefore the
herald of His sufferings, which he was to be, the moment must
contribute to it in which he met the Messiah in the identical mood
of triumphant renunciation of the world.[3]

Under these circumstances, the Baptist developed his testimony. 'This,' said he, 'is He of whom I said, After me cometh
a Man who is preferred before me, for He was before me.' In
these words he declared that Jesus was identical with the Messiah, whom he had designated in similar terms to the deputation
from the Sanhedrim.

The words just mentioned form, accordingly, the official
testimony of the Baptist, which is found in its original form in
his address to the deputation (ver. 26), while here He repeats it
before his disciples. But what the Evangelist John had already
communicated respecting this testimony, was his own account
respecting this second declaration.[4]

[1] Hug, *Gutachten über das Leben Jesu* 184.   [2] Strauss, i. 368.
[3] Comp. W. Hoffmann, *das Leben Jesu* 292.
[4] That is, on the testimony in ver. 26 the reference in ver. 30 is founded,
and on this the statement in ver. 15.

Then he tells his disciples how he arrived at the knowledge
of this most important fact. 'And I knew Him not; but that
He should be made manifest to Israel, therefore came I baptizing with water.' He next utters his testimony respecting the
extraordinary event on which his knowledge of the Messiahship
of Jesus rested. 'I saw the Spirit descending from heaven like
a dove, and it abode upon Him. And I' (he again affirmed)
'knew Him not till then.' Whatever he might at any time have
otherwise known of Him as a relation or a friend—all *that* constituted no prophetic certainty, no divine assurance, of the Messiahship of Jesus. But now he says that he was certain of it;
that is, so certain of it, that as a prophet he could testify of Him
in Israel.[1] For the same Being who had sent him had also
given him this sign, that He on whom he should see the Spirit
descending and remain would be another Baptizer—One who
would baptize with the Holy Ghost. This sign was therefore
given him in the same prophetic state of mind in which he had
received his own commission. So that, in the same ecstasy in
which he had received the divine assurance that he should be
the forerunner of the Messiah, he received also the certainty
that the want of the fulness of the Spirit marked the difference
between himself and the Messiah, and that the Messiah would
be manifested to him by the fulness of the Spirit resting upon
Him as the real divine baptism. This sign appeared to him
over the person of Jesus; wherefore he was now made divinely
certain as a prophet. 'And since I have seen this (the Baptist
concludes his declaration), I am decidedly convinced that this
is the Son of God.' In these words he expressed in what sense
he announced the priority of Jesus to the deputation from the
Sanhedrim.

On that day he must have expressed himself publicly with
the most elevated feelings concerning Jesus. In recollection of
that event, the Evangelist writes (ver. 15), 'John testified of
Him (continually). He exclaimed aloud, This was He of whom

[1] On the strange supposition of the well-known critic, that he ought to
have announced the faith of his mother publicly as a prophet, see the preface to the first volume of this work. In the declaration of the Baptist
there lies as little a contradiction to Matt. iii. 14, 15 (as Lücke i. 417 supposes); for though the Baptist felt the highest reverence for the person of
Jesus, yet this did not amount to objective certainty.

I spoke : He that cometh after me is preferred before me ; for
He was before me.'

1. Strauss justly asserts (i. 367) that, according to the fourth
Gospel, the Messianic idea of the Baptist has the marks of atoning suffering and of a heavenly pre-existence. But the first
objection raised against the truthfulness of such a representation
amounts to this—that such a view of the Messiah was foreign
to the current opinion. The prophet, therefore, is made dependent on the current opinion, which, moreover, in relation to the
Messiah, differed as much in Israel as in Christendom. The
second difficulty is presented in the question, If the Baptist
knew the mystery of the suffering Messiah, which the disciples
of Jesus never knew, how could Jesus declare that he stood low
among the citizens of the kingdom of heaven? (Matt. xi. 11.)
But the greatness of John was the greatness of his personal
elevation on the Old Testament standpoint ; the greatness of the
least in the kingdom of heaven was a generic greatness, or a
general elevation on the New Testament standpoint. The least
Christian was so far above John and exalted over him as his
standpoint was higher—he stood, as we may say, on his shoulders.
But it is well to observe, with Hoffmann, that, on the one hand,
in John the glimpses of his higher knowledge were not a ripened
and developed insight, and that, on the other hand, the disciples
of Christ, before His ascension, could not be considered as decided citizens of the kingdom of heaven in its New Testament
spiritual glory. Christ discerned the littleness of the great
John in this, that, in his Old Testament zeal, he was in danger
of being perplexed at his own quiet spiritual working without
violent action, while the greatness of the least Christian consisted in understanding this course of Christ in the spirit, and
exhibiting it in his own life.

If John, as is admitted, in his reference to the Lamb of
God, was supported by the passage in Isa. liii., his word is a
voucher that this passage was referred to the Messiah by the
enlightened Israelites of his time. On the meaning of that
passage, let the reader consult the admirable discussion by
Lücke, *Commentar* i. 401–415. The expedients which have
been adopted to make the passage in question non-Messianic

are at once rendered nugatory, if the principle be first settled, that every prophetic expression in the Old Testament must find its ultimate aim in the Messiah and His kingdom. But this principle results from the whole constitution of the Old Testament prophecy, and nowhere does the Messianic character appear more conspicuous than in the prophecies of Isaiah, without any distinction of the different parts of the book. If we apply this principle to our passage, the sufferings of the servants of God must, at all events, according to the spirit of the prophet, find their highest fulfilment in the person of the Messiah—even should the prophet set out in his contemplation from his own person, or from the elect portion of the theocratic people, or from any historical type whatever of the Messiah.

3. That the πρῶτός μου ἦν (vers. 30, 15) must denote no mere abstract pre-existence of Christ, results indeed, first of all, from the religious weakness of this conception; secondly, from this, that this earlier existence could be no sufficient ground for the earlier authority of Christ in Israel. Rather the predicates, 'the earliest' and 'the only one,' are always identical when Christ's priority is spoken of. Christ was before John in Israel, because He was above him in eternity; He had the precedence in rank, because He was his essential Chief (*First*). Hence this testimony of John finds a distinct correspondence in Mal. iii. 1, as Hengstenberg has shown in his *Christology* (iv. 186), and probably there was a conscious reference to it. But, after all, John found the reason for his assertion in the entire Messianic character of the Old Testament. The Messiah as a spiritual form was 'before' him in Israel, precisely on account of His eternal glory in God.

SECTION III.

THE FIRST DISCIPLES OF JESUS.

On the next day after the Baptist and Jesus had again met and greeted one another, the former took his station, as usual, on the banks of the Jordan, with two of his disciples by his side. He saw Jesus, as He was walking about, on the point of taking

His departure. The Baptist understood His intentions, and fixed his eye upon Him wistfully.[1] As the best singers may utter their first notes tremulously,—as a Cicero turned pale when he ascended the rostrum,—as the sun descends with blushes; so it might harmonize with the exquisitely delicate human feelings of the Shepherd of men, to begin His vocation of collecting men around Him with the most tender, virgin-like modesty. John understood the heart of Jesus. Hitherto none of his disciples had been moved by the inspired testimony of the preceding day to attach themselves to Him; the faithful harbinger of the Messiah was therefore induced to repeat the solemn words, 'Behold the Lamb of God!' He felt in the delicacy of Christ's personality all its capability of suffering, and its suffering destiny. But this time his words forcibly struck the two disciples who stood by his side, and they followed Jesus. Jesus understood the sound of their footsteps, and turning round, He said to them, 'What seek ye?' This brief expression depicts their eagerness and His clear perception. They ask Him, 'Teacher, where dwellest Thou? where is Thy abode to-day?' From this we may infer that the way on which they stopped Him was the first part of His road—a part which, towards evening, He would leave behind. 'Come and see!' said the Lord. They came and saw where He dwelt, and abode that day with Him. Thus the simplest conventional intercourse led to the most important results. Of infinite significance was the question of the sympathetic traveller, 'What seek ye?' How full of feeling and promise the question in return, 'Where dwellest Thou?' uttered in a tone of earnest longing; as much as to say, We too would fain abide there. And lastly, the answer so rich in promise, 'Come and see!' It was about the tenth hour, according to the Jewish reckoning, or four o'clock in the afternoon. The narrator tells us that Andrew, Simon Peter's brother, was one of the two who heard John and followed Jesus. By this form of expression, he leads us to guess who the other was. From the earliest times it has been admitted that it was John himself. It is quite in his style to suppress his own name, or to use a periphrasis.[2] Moreover, the conference of the

---

[1] Καὶ ἐμβλέψας τῷ Ἰησοῦ περιπατοῦντι.

[2] ['Mos evangelistæ nostri, ut ex modestia, ubi de seipso scribit, nomen suum omittat.'—Lampe In Joan. Proleg. i. 2, where four other reasons are given for supposing the unnamed disciple to be John.—Ed.]

two with Jesus is so vividly in his recollection in its minutest
particulars : how they saluted Him by the title of Rabbi, their
decisive interlocution, and the hour of their visit to Him—all was
indelibly impressed on his memory.

They abode with Him that day ; but not without going out
in order to fetch Simon Peter, the brother of one, and friend of
the other.[1]   Andrew first found him, and announced to him,
' We have found the Messiah !'   The expectation of the Messiah
prevailed generally among the people; but the circle of John's
disciples, to which Peter belonged, lived in the expectation of
His speedy advent.   They were certain of His very speedy appearance, and lived in a state of intense listening and watching
for the signs of it.   Therefore, after announcing the Messiah,
Andrew led his brother to Jesus.   No sooner did Jesus behold
him, than He said, ' Thou are· Simon, the son of Jonas (the
Dove), thou shalt be called Cephas (the Rock).'[2]   For the Hebrew, who knew the relation between the dove and the rocks, in
which the dove in Judea loved to build her nest, and between
the chosen people and the dove,[3] which might appear as its symbol,
these words contain a great contrast full of promise.   Thou
art now the son of the shy dove of the rock ; in future thou shalt
be called the protecting rock of the dove.[4]   Jesus might know

[1] From the circumstance that the Evangelist enumerates the separate
days from the return of Jesus out of the wilderness to the marriage at Cana,
without assigning a particular fresh day for this particular event, we may
conclude that it belongs to the very day on which Jesus met with the first
disciples.

[2] 'This act of giving a name is founded on the very ancient Jewish custom of giving significant names or surnames from peculiar events or traits
of character : Gen. xvii. 5, 41, 45 ; Dan. i. 7.'—Lücke, *Commentar* i. 448.
[To change the name was the prerogative of one in authority, Gen. xli. 45 ;
Dan. i. 7 ; and peculiarly, therefore, the prerogative of the Lord, who alone
can give and maintain the new character indicated by the new name, and
prevent it from becoming a mockery and reproach.   The second Adam is in
the new creation something more than the first Adam in the old, Gen. ii. 19.
—Ed.]

[3] Cantic. ii. 14, compare Jer. xlviii. 28.

[4] According to Lampe the antithesis would be : Thou hearer [Gen. xxix.
33] (Simon) and Son of Grace (of Jonas, contracted for Jochanan) shalt be
called Rock.   But the reading 'Ιωάνου, 'Ιωάννου, or 'Ιωάννεο is supported by
very few manuscripts and translations.   According to Dr Paulus the antithesis means, Thou son of weakness shalt be called Rock.   But he takes
יוֹנֶה to signify *weakness* on insufficient grounds.   See Lücke, i. 450.

many things about Peter the Galilean fisherman through John the Baptist and the two first disciples, but His own first piercing glance would decide the judgment He passed upon him; and the name which He now gave him He might afterwards confirm, as it was confirmed in the sequel by history.[1]

On the following day, when Jesus was about to leave the Perean valley of the Jordan in order to go into Galilee,[2] He found Philip. The circumstance that he was from Bethsaida on the Galilean Sea, and a fellow-countryman of Andrew and Peter, brought him into the society of Jesus, and at His call he became His disciple.

On their way to Galilee—at what place the Evangelist does not tell us—Peter found Nathanael. It has been assumed that this meeting occurred in the neighbourhood of Cana, since Nathanael, according to John xxi. 2, belonged to that place. We should certainly imagine that the mysterious scene under the fig-tree to which Jesus alludes, points us to the home of Philip, since the Jews were fond of reposing under the fig-trees which adorned their homesteads,[3] or resorted to them for meditation and prayer; and since it is most natural to regard the spiritual vision with which Jesus looked on that scene as a consequence of His coming within the immediate sphere of Nathanael's life. But yet there is no certainty on either point. Or Nathanael, while walking under a fig-tree in a lonely path,[4] might indulge in such musings as our Lord would regard as a token of his deep Israelitish sincerity. But how far the feeling and mental eye of Christ, particularly at this time, when He was collecting His first disciples, reached into the distance and discerned states of mind, which, as earnest longings after the Messiah, indicated a germinant discipleship, and formed a second sight for His own spirit, we cannot at all determine. No sooner had Philip found Nathanael than he announced to him his new good fortune, the salvation of Israel: 'We have found Him of whom Moses in the law, and the prophets, did write, Jesus the son of Joseph, the man of Nazareth' (John i. 45). Philip himself seems to have felt the contrast he announced; but it does not trouble him. He brings

---

[1] Matt. xvi. 17. There the name is presupposed.
[2] ἠθέλησεν ἐξελθεῖν εἰς τὴν Γαλιλαίαν.
[3] Compare Micah iv. 4; Zech. iii. 10.
[4] Fig-trees especially stood in the paths and highways.

it forward; he lays an emphasis upon it; and is astonished that the Messiah, the son of Joseph, is the man of Nazareth.[1] Nathanael at once sceptically seizes on the contrast, and asks, ' Can any good thing come out of Nazareth?' Nazareth was therefore, at all events to the man of Cana—who in these words passed so severe a judgment on his neighbours in the mountain district of Galilee—too insignificant, it stood spiritually too low to expect that from it would come forth the great Prince of his people. It cannot be maintained that Nathanael gave his answer in a proverb. But the proverb which has been formed from these words, from the history of its origin, has become ironical, and means: Out of Nazareth the best thing can come unexpectedly. But as Nathanael was prompt in his judgment and doubt, he was equally prompt in willingness to put his judgment to the test, and to correct it. ' Come and see!' Philip replies. Nathanael knew what was due to the vivid conviction of his friend, and to God, who performs the greatest miracles. He therefore goes with Philip in order to see with his own mental eye. And as he approached, Jesus said to those around Him, ' Behold an Israelite indeed, in whom is no guile!' An ' Israelite indeed' means, therefore, a truthful Jew. Every noble nation finds the firmest foundation of its nationality in truthfulness and fidelity.[2] But the Jew, before all others, is entitled to this, since in Christ is the deepest life of his nation.[3] Nathanael does not disown the eulogium; he affects no false modesty; but he cannot account for its being bestowed, and asks the Lord, ' Whence knowest Thou me?' Then the Lord utters a word that startles and agitates him: ' Before Philip called thee, when thou wast under the fig-tree, I saw thee.'

[1] If we take the words of Philip in their literal meaning, we shall see what stress he laid on bringing forward the predicate of meanness, which made the discovery of the Messiah in such a place so extraordinary. In this sense, the mention of His father Joseph served to point out His civil advent, but by no means His bodily descent, which latter it was not necessary for Philip to be acquainted with. What has been urged from this passage against the miraculous conception is perfectly trivial.

[2] A ' German indeed,' or a ' true German,' is a specially true, honourable German; and the praise of the uprightness of the Frank is uttered in the expression—He is *Frank*.

[3] It signifies nothing if ' nothing is heard elsewhere of this national virtue of the Jews.' The kernel of the Israelitish people is the ' faithful witness' ' in whose mouth was found no guile.'

Nathanael now felt that Jesus had beheld a secret of his soul, probably his Israelitish longing after the Messianic kingdom, or after his spiritual reconciliation, such as no man could have detected with his bodily eye—a process of his inner life, in which the faithful Israelitish disposition had been exercised. But by this divine master-glance Jesus had been verified to him as the Messiah. 'This is an Israelite indeed,' Jesus had said of him. Nathanael now offers Him homage in a truly graceful manner, by making the acknowledgment—'Rabbi! Thou art the Son of God! Thou art the King of Israel!' that is, Thou art the King of the Israelites who are without guile; Thou art my King! Nathanael had believed in Him on account of the sign which Jesus had given him. But Jesus promised him still greater signs in the future, which he expressed with great certainty and solemnity: 'Verily, verily, I say unto you, from this time ye shall see the heaven open, and the angels of God ascending and descending upon the Son of man.'[1] It is not improbable that this remarkable form of the promise of Jesus has a relation to the state of mind which rendered Nathanael noticeable to Him when under the fig-tree. If he had been praying in those words of the prophet, 'Oh that Thou wouldest rend the heavens, that Thou wouldest come down' (Isa. lxiv. 1)!.give me a sign—send me an angel;—this form of the promise of Jesus would be clearly explained. We leave this point undetermined, but certainly the language of Jesus had a reference to Nathanael's state of mind.[2] In these words the Lord cannot possibly refer to the special angelic appearances which occurred in His own life. Rather His language is apparently symbolical. The promise begins to be fulfilled from the time then present (ἀπ' ἄρτι). The open heaven is the revelation of the fulness of the Godhead disclosed in Himself. And as Jacob in a dream saw the heavens open, and the angels of God ascending and descending

[1] It is no Hysteron-proteron that ἀναβαίνοντας is here placed first.

[2] [Whatever was the special petition of Nathanael, the form of the promise was particularly suitable to every 'Israelite indeed;' referring him back as it did to God's appearance to Israel himself at Bethel. Nathanael was waiting for the fulfilment of all that had then been promised to Jacob; this attitude of mind had become his characteristic; and to tell him that the symbolic and prophetic appearances of patriarchal times were now to be realized, was the simplest way to tell him that the hope of his heart would be satisfied—that the Messiah had now come.—ED.]

on the ladder which connected heaven and earth, so now must the real angels of God become manifest in the life of Christ, and exhibit an everlasting movement of mediation, reconciliation, and reunion between heaven and earth. The prayers, the intercession, the works of Christ, and His sacrifice ascend; the visitations, the blessings, the miraculous gifts, the helps, and assurances of peace from God descend. Thus all the longings of Nathanael and his associates must be fulfilled.

Nathanael's name does not occur in the later complete lists of the apostles. But in these, generally Bartholomew[1] appears next to Philip. Hence it has been conjectured that Nathanael appears again among the apostles in the person of Bartholomew; and since the name Bartholomew is properly only a surname, and means the son of Tholmai, the conjecture is thereby confirmed. At all events, it is not probable that so distinguished a character as this Nathanael, whose call John has narrated with so much interest, should not be admitted among the apostles; and the circumstance is very conclusive, that in the days immediately succeeding the resurrection we find Nathanael among the most confidential disciples of Jesus (John xxi. 2).

John the Baptist, as a faithful forerunner, rendered the Lord the most essential service, by preparing for Him disciples of such worth as John, Andrew, and Peter, and by inducing them, directly or indirectly, to join themselves to Him. But we see how the Lord displays the hand of a master in attracting souls, in winning over to His spiritual communion and enlisting in His service the choicest spirits, while He is regulated by what the Father works for Him in the minds and hearts of men, and by the opportunities presented in His working for the Father. With a quick eagle-eye He recognises the spirits that are destined for Him; while these hasten to Him with all the decisiveness of satisfied longing, in proportion as they understand the call of their much-loved King in His word. They spread abroad the tidings of His advent among those who are like-minded, with the joyful exclamation, We have found the Messiah! This corresponds to the morning hour of the New Covenant, since all its spiritual conditions are silently matured. It is like a mutual agreement of long standing, ripened in the profoundest depths

[1] In Matt. x. 3, Mark iii. 18, Luke vi. 14, Bartholomew stands next to Philip; in Acts i. 13, Thomas.

of the life, of which vulgar souls (*Philister*) have no conception, that the Lord so quickly recognises His noblest disciples, and that they attach themselves so soon to Him with the most cordial self-surrender.

NOTES.

1. The opinion that by the tenth hour (John i. 40), according to the Jewish mode of reckoning, we are to understand four o'clock in the afternoon, has been called in question by Rettig in his *exeg. Analekten*, in the *Theol. Studien und Kritiken*, 1830, Part i. According to Rettig, John here, as well as in the passages iv. 6, xix. 14, employed the Roman computation of time, which begins at midnight, so that the tenth hour would mean ten o'clock in the forenoon. Lücke has invalidated this view by the remark, that John could have no reason for adopting the Roman computation instead of that with which he was familiar, since the Asiatic churches, for whom he wrote, used, in common with the Jews, the Babylonian mode of reckoning, namely, the natural day from sunrise to sunset divided into twelve equal parts. As to the passage in John iv. 6, A. Schweizer, to obviate the remark that it was not customary to go to the wells at noon, has justly observed, that the woman could hardly have been with Jesus alone so long if the common time for drawing water (six o'clock morning or evening) had been intended. Besides, it may be easily admitted, that a woman of such a character would avoid meeting with other females. The discrepancy that Mark xv. 25 gives the third hour as the beginning of the crucifixion, while according to John the sentence of crucifixion was 'about the sixth hour' (John xix. 14), may be explained, apart from unimportant various readings, by supposing that John made use here of the Roman mode of computation.

2. The first connection of Jesus with Andrew, John, and Peter, which is here narrated, forms no contradiction whatever to the account given by the synoptic Gospels of the later calling of the two pair of brothers, Andrew and Peter, John and James, to a more definite following of Jesus (Matt. iv. 18; [Mark i. 16, 19]). In the relations of the disciples of Jesus, according to the Gospels, there appears very distinctly an internal and essential gradation, which finds its expression also in their outward calling. The believing disciples of the Lord, as such, were not always

called to be His constant associates and messengers, and these, again, were not destined to be apostles in the strict sense. Twelve such apostles Jesus chose: besides these, He had a circle of seventy messengers; but the collective body of disciples at the time of His ascension contained at least one hundred and twenty men (Acts i. 15). It is therefore in perfect correspondence with this gradation, if the first calling is distinguished from the first delegation, and this again from the setting apart of the twelve apostles. And even in this latter circle we find again a special selection, that of the three most confidential witnesses of Jesus. Strauss (i. 549) is justified in finding in the words of Christ, ἀκολούθει μοι, 'the junction of a permanent relation;' but he has not taken into account that the junction of a *permanent* relation is to be distinguished from the junction of a *peculiar* relation. And the circumstance that the first disciples were in constant attendance on Jesus did not make them His evangelists, any more than the female disciples became evangelists, though they constantly accompanied Him.

<hr>

SECTION IV.

THE MARRIAGE AT CANA.

(John ii. 1–11.)

On the third day, says the Evangelist, without defining the time more exactly, there was a marriage at Cana. We cannot well find this more exact definition in the nearest preceding datum, because one such special reference has to be given. The general statement, 'on the third day,' leads us to expect that the first and second have been enumerated. And so, in fact, we find it. The Evangelist reckons from the day when Jesus returned from the wilderness to the Baptist, which followed the day on which John the Baptist at the Jordan had borne that great testimony to Jesus. At that time Jesus was still concealed, although He stood in the midst of Israel. But from this time, the Evangelist wishes us to understand, He became manifest in a quick succession of mighty works of the revelation and recognition of His glory.

On the next day after the testimony of the Baptist, Jesus returned from the wilderness, and the Baptist publicly and solemnly pointed to Him as the Messiah of Israel (ver. 29). The following day John repeated this demonstration, which induced Andrew, John, and Peter to join themselves to Jesus as His first disciples (ver. 35). But on the third day the spiritual power of the Lord gained two new followers of importance, Philip and Nathanael (ver. 44). This is reckoned the third day since the return of Christ from the wilderness, and the same day on which the marriage feast at Cana in Galilee began, which soon led to a fresh glorification of Jesus.[1]

On the day, therefore, when this marriage feast began, Jesus set out from the first travelling station in the Jordan valley, in order to go to Galilee. As it took Him two days to reach Cana, the marriage feast when He arrived had already lasted two days. The men of Galilee who had now become His disciples, and had no more to do with John in Perea, were naturally His fellow-travellers, not only as disciples and friends, but as going homewards. They came with Him to Nazareth, where they did not find the mother of Jesus, as she was now at Cana beyond Nazareth, at the marriage feast with her friends.[2] Thither Jesus was now invited with His disciples.[3]

[1] There is no reason for breaking through so definite a succession of dates from the first to the third day by an intercalation of days which rests on mere conjecture. It does not follow from ver. 40 that Peter was not brought to Christ till the day following. If the question, 'Where abidest Thou?' meant, 'Where dost Thou pass the night?' then, by the words, 'They abode with Him that day,' the fact is indicated that they passed the night at His lodgings. [Meyer, Lichtenstein, and most recent expositors count from the beginning of the journey into Galilee, ver. 43, which is certainly the most natural interpretation. Luthardt, without any distortion of the narrative, arranges a succession of seven well-defined days, so that the Lord's ministry begins, as it ends, with seven days whose events are specifically mentioned. See Andrews' *Life of our Lord*, p. 135.—ED.]

[2] Compare Robinson's *Palestine* ii. 346, and Helmuth's Map of Palestine after Robinson. But it is a question, whether, according to Tholuck's Commentary on this passage, p. 98 (Clark's Tr. 1860), the road for Jesus to Capernaum and Bethsaida went through Cana; also, whether Mary had arrived there from Capernaum. ᐧ [See also Robinson's pithy reply (iii. 109, note) to De Saulcy, who advances the claims of Kefr Kenna. Compare Thomson's *Land and Book* 425. Ewald (*Christus*, p. 170, note) agrees with Robinson in supposing that Kana el Jelil is not only identical in name with the village of the narrative, but is also identical in position. It lies about 12 miles north-west of Nazareth.—ED.]

[3] A clear passage is obscured when it is fancied that it can be made

The mother of Jesus was certainly well aware of the significance of her Son's visit to the Baptist, and met His return
home with joyful anticipation. Doubtless the family circle at
Cana, where the marriage feast was held, shared in the same
sentiments. It so happened that the duration of the feast had
been prolonged,[1] and that the bridegroom, in the glow of excitement, had suddenly issued invitations for an additional number
of guests—invitations which were totally unconnected with the
first formal arrangements of the feast, and which as a bold out-
gush of Christian presentiment went far beyond the calculations
of the Jewish mind. But soon the true friend of Mary and of
the Lord had to repent of this open-heartedness as an act of
imprudence. The wine began to run short; and with the
approaching deficiency the festive mood of the worthy couple
seemed likely to be extinguished. The Jewish mind, which also
regulated conduct in the strictest legal manner, caused those
who were thus depressed to feel their perplexity as a fearful
burden. The mother of Jesus was initiated into the domestic
trouble.

'They have no wine!' Thus Mary deplored confidentially
to her Son the distress of the family. Some explain the words
as meaning that Mary meant to call upon the Lord to perform
a miracle at once. Others imagine that she wished to intimate
that it was time for Him and His disciples to take their departure.[2] Sagacious expositors! Might not a religious disposition generally, to say nothing of female tenderness, lead her to
lament to the benevolent Lord a want of her own or of others,
without prescribing to Him the way and manner of rendering
help? And in this, indeed, Mary's female excellence was conspicuous, that she vented her sorrow in such a spirit, resigned
and not prescribing.

The Lord answered her, 'That is My concern, not thine,

clearer by taking the aorist ἐκλήθη in the sense of the pluperfect. It was
now that Jesus was invited, when the marriage feast had already begun.
The singular indicates that the invitation of His disciples was only a consequence of His own invitation. Compare Adalb. Meier's *Commentar über das
Evang. Johannes* i. 247.

[1] The marriage feast commonly lasted seven days, but among the poorer
classes three, or even one day. See Winer, *R.W.B.*, article 'Hochzeit;'
Maier, *Commentar*, p. 248.

[2] Compare Lücke, *Commentar* i. 469. [So Bengel.]

O woman !' Or, in other words, Let Me alone, leave that to Me, thou troubled, tender-hearted one !¹

He added, 'My hour is not yet come.' His hour was His own time, as the Father determined it, for acting or suffering by the occasion and in His own mind, in opposition to the hour which was marked out for Him by the approval of men.² Therefore this reference to His hour was a consolatory assurance to His mother that He was certain of the right moment for the right result. Hence also Mary could intimate to the servants, who knew that the wine was running short, and in their position would be most of all uneasy, that they had only to do whatever Jesus told them. This language by no means implied the promise of a miracle, of which she herself knew nothing yet, but the tranquillizing power of an unshaken confidence, which expected that at the right time He would certainly obviate the difficulty as a trustworthy adviser and helper. Now there were standing in the house six water-pots of stone, containing two or three baths³ apiece. They were set apart for the purpose of the Jewish rites

---

¹ That this is the meaning of this much-discussed, difficult passage [on which no fewer than eight separate treatises have been written—ED.], may be inferred from the connection as well as from distinct analogies. First of all the doubtful exclamation מַה־לִּי וָלָךְ is to be explained by the connection. It occurs in 2 Sam. xvi. 10, in an address of David, evidently quite friendly to the sons of Zeruiah. (Thus Maier on the passage) Ebrard (p. 215) translates the passage thus: 'That is My concern; or, Leave that to Me.' The appellation γύναι, Woman! was used by Jesus on the cross to His mother, according to John xix. 26. There it might be translated, Poor, tender-hearted one! Similar was the address of Jesus to Mary Magdalene, John xx. 15. In the same manner Augustus addressed Cleopatra, in Dio Cassius, Hist. li. 12 (quoted by Tholuck): θάρσει ὦ γύναι, καὶ θυμὸν ἴσχε ἀγαθόν.

² Compare John vii. 6; Luke xxii. 53.

³ Probably John understood by this measure the Attic metretes, which was equal to the Hebrew bath, 2 Chron. iv. 5. The Attic metretes made about one and a half Roman amphoræ: the Roman amphora was equal to five gallons. But the Roman amphora was also called metretes; and if this were intended, the total quantity would be much less. On the other hand, the Babylonian and Syrian metretes was equal to one and two-thirds of the Attic metretes, or 120 sextarii. Yet neither of the latter measures is intended, but the Attic; for most of the Greeks used the Attic measure— Galen, de mensur. c. 9—and also the Jews, after the Greeks obtained the supremacy in Asia. So Maier on the passage. According to Von Ammon's reckoning, the gift of wine was much smaller.

of cleansing. These vessels Jesus commanded the attendants to fill with water, and then to draw the liquor from them and take it to the governor[1] of the feast. They did so. But their doing so leads us to infer the existence of a wonderfully elevated tone of feeling in the whole household. If even the servants exhibited such unreserved confidence in the words of Jesus, we may admit that the festive feeling had resolved itself into a deep devotion to His person, and a blessed experience of the fulness of His Spirit and His love. The whole company were now gradually raised above their ordinary state of feeling, as at a later period the three disciples on the Mount of Transfiguration. In the element of this state of feeling Christ changed the water into wine.[2] The governor of the feast tasted the new beverage without knowing whence it came. It was another, more generous wine than that which he had drunk at first, as he testified to the bridegroom with unfeigned pleasure. Thou hast reversed the ordinary custom, he said to him : every man at the beginning sets forth good wine, and when they have drunk enough, that which is inferior ; but thou hast kept the good wine till now.[3] We cannot suppose that the governor of the feast wished to find fault openly with the earlier wine which had been furnished by the bridegroom. When, therefore, he praised the new wine as the good, he bore testimony to it as a peculiar and most generous kind of wine, and to the elevation of feeling with which he drank it. Thus Christ transported a circle of pious and devoted men to heaven, and gave them to drink from the mysterious fountain of His highest life-power. He showed how in His kingdom want vanishes in the riches of His love—water

---

[1] The ἀρχιτρίκλινος, who gave orders to the servants, is to be distinguished from the συμποσιάρχης, who, according to the custom of the Greeks and Romans, was chosen by the guests, and presided over the entertainment. But if the superintendent of the servants was here intended, probably the command of Christ relative to drawing the wine reached him first of all.

[2] [Tholuck and others have represented the author as maintaining that the elevated frame of mind on the part of the guests caused them to taste the water as wine. This is scarcely fair. The miracles required a certain state of mind in those on whom and for whom they were wrought, but neither consisted in nor were caused by this state of mind. The author seems distinctly to maintain the objective miracle, as well as and in combination with the frame of those who were blessed by it.—ED.]

[3] See De Wette, *Commentar* on this passage.

in the wine of His wonder-working divine power—the common
pleasure of conviviality in the intoxication of delight which is
connected with the first enjoyment of the vision of His glory.
It was no nectar, but a divine beverage, into which the water
was changed. The *work*, therefore, was the signal of His
world-transforming heart-power; and thus the beginning of His
miracles, the first sign by which He manifested His glory. His
disciples were already devoted to Him by faith; but now their
faith gained such a new impulse, that John could describe it as
a new era in their life of faith in the words, 'And His disciples
believed on Him' (John ii. 11).[1]

NOTES.

1. According to Wieseler (*Chronol. Synops.* 252), the beginning of the Passover (the 15th of Nisan in the year 781)[2] which
Jesus, according to John ii. 12, attended a few days after the
marriage at Cana, fell on the 30th of March. If now, Wieseler
remarks, He came, according to the Jewish custom, on the 10th
of Nisan to Jerusalem, and if we reckon three or four days for
the journey thither, He must have set out from Capernaum not
later than March 21. Moreover, some days must be reckoned
backwards, which He spent at Capernaum. Add to this the
undetermined sojourn of Christ at Cana; but which was probably only one day, at the most two days; and then, lastly, the
three glorious days of the first victory of Christ after His return
from the wilderness. It is, indeed, not necessary to suppose,
with Wieseler, that His stay at Capernaum occupied the remainder of March. Let us also reckon some days after the return
of Christ from the wilderness to the marriage at Cana, as the
aforesaid critic has done (see Wieseler, p. 252). Thus we need

[1] [The author might perhaps have noticed the appropriateness of the
first miracle being a work of creation, thereby showing that He who came
to be the Restorer was the Creator of all. This is also in keeping with the
form of this Gospel, which (though there be nothing in the analogy between
its opening words and the opening words of Genesis) introduces the Redeemer as the Creator coming to 'His own.' In proving that He is the
Creator, He effectually grounds His claim to become the Restorer.—ED.]

[2] [On this date see above, p. 5; see also Greswell's fourth and fifth Disser-
tations, where this Passover is determined to have been 9th April 780. A
very useful table of Jewish feasts for several years is given by Greswell,
vol. i. 331.—ED.]

not go beyond March into February in order to reach the moment when Nathanael probably was reposing under the shade of the fig-tree. Probably the deputation to John was planned in the Sanhedrim, in consequence of the fresh influx of pilgrims for baptism, which commenced in the spring of the year 781.

2. From the *History of the Life of Jesus* by Von Ammon, we learn many interesting particulars respecting the wines of the ancients, especially those of the Hebrews. One fact especially is brought forward, that the Jews had inspissated and spiced liqueur-wines, like the Greeks and Romans,—vinous substances which required to be mixed with a large quantity of water. After these preliminary observations, Von Ammon remarks, that Jesus changed these water-pots into wine-vessels, in order to show ' a delicate attention to the newly married couple.' The wine He presented to them was better and stronger than the weak and diluted liquor which in their straitened circumstances they had previously offered their guests, yet not unmixed, but less abundantly watered ; on account of its agreeable and superior vinous quality, it found great favour with the master of the feast. ' But what happened in the interval, whether the water-pots were empty and soon filled up to the brim, we do not know, etc.' Such theology as this veils from our inquisitive gaze the mysteries of a public-house, but leaves us with strange forebodings.

3. According to Dr Von Baur, in his essay on the composition and character of John's Gospel, in Zeller's *Theol. Jahrbücher*, the history of the marriage at Cana is to be viewed as an allegory, in which the relation of Christ to John is represented. ' Why should this not be granted, if water with perfect propriety is to be taken as the element and symbol of the Baptist, that by the wine is to be understood the high pre-eminence of the Messiah above His forerunner, and by the change of water into wine the transition and advance from the preparatory stage of the Baptist to the Messianic agency and glory ?' On the mental prejudice, which is not in a state to grasp the historic reality of evangelic ideas, see the First Book of this work, vol. i. p. 139. Certainly the allegorists understand things after a very peculiar fashion, who regard reality as so trivial that history will vanish at once from their view wherever they can see a conceit glimmering, while they perform a splendid counter-miracle to

that of Cana, namely, that of changing the wine of evangelical reality into the water of vapid conceit.[1]

4. Among other things, it has been objected to the miracle at Cana: ' Moreover, miracles are always beneficial because they remove a natural defect; but what the Lord is said to have done at Cana did not aim at the removal of a natural evil, but only to reanimate an interrupted pleasure' (Strauss, ii. 211). Maier in his commentary on this passage (John ii.) justly points out, that the same critics bring into comparison the other miraculous narratives in the Gospels, of which they deny collectively the objective truth; therefore they assume a point of comparison which on their standpoint does not exist. This belongs to the long catalogue of those self-contradictions of the critics, who put us in mind of the history of Susanna.

SECTION V.

THE FIRST MESSIANIC ATTENDANCE OF JESUS ON THE PASSOVER, AND THE PURIFICATION OF THE TEMPLE.

(John ii. 12–25.)

From Cana Jesus directed His course to Capernaum, accompanied by His mother, His brethren, and His disciples. There were various reasons for going down from the mountain district to the sea-shore. Most of the new friends of Jesus lived near the sea; and as they had not yet given up their wonted occupation, their presence at home might be required not only by their families, but by their business. Thus, for instance, Peter was a

---

[1] [This, of course, does not hinder us from attaching an allegorical significance to the miracle, so long as we maintain its historic reality. To the Baptist's disciples it can scarcely have failed to be significant, that out of the water-pots for the *purifying of the Jews*, their new Master drew wine for the inward cheering and strengthening of man. And it is difficult to remove from our minds the idea, that in this first manifestation of His glory, when He provided wine for the marriage festivity, there is a symbol of the consummation of His glory, when He shed that blood which purchased and cleansed His bride, and furnished everlasting refreshment to them that have entered into the joy of the Bridegroom.—ED.]

householder in Capernaum (Matt. viii. 14). It was natural that the Lord should give His company to His friends, as they had accompanied Him, when they had to leave their own home. At Cana a fellowship had been formed between His first natural family and the new spiritual family which now belonged to Him. This fellowship was celebrated by their travelling together, when the Lord's spiritual associates surrounded Him full of admiration and hope. But the approach of the Passover formed a special reason why Jesus and His followers should go to Capernaum. Probably a large company of pilgrims set out from that place, and already pilgrims began to flock thither. And as it would be a point of consequence to Him to move in a circle which would give full scope for His exertions, He would greatly prefer going up to Jerusalem in the centre of such a caravan.

Though Jesus stayed only a few days in Capernaum, this time was sufficient for an opportunity of manifesting His Messianic spirit and calling. Among the excited crowds in that city, whose attention must have been directed towards Him by the testimony of His devoted adherents in the first festive joy of their faith, He must have performed a succession of miracles. For when, after a longer stay in Judea, He first of all visited Nazareth, the people there were disposed to blame Him for bestowing His blessings on Capernaum in preference to His own town, and therefore more eagerly expected from Him miraculous performances (Luke iv. 23). Those miracles have not been reported in detail. The chief narrators of the synoptical accounts were not yet among the followers of Jesus, and the few disciples whom He had already gained were probably very much taken up with household matters in the short interval between the two great journeys. This was probably the cause that no more distinct testimonies have been given of these events.

The most memorable act of Jesus in Jerusalem at this time was the purifying of the temple. John relates it at once, in order to indicate that by this act the Lord had entered on His public ministry in the very centre of the theocracy. He found in the temple—that is, in the precincts of the sanctuary, in the court of the Gentiles[1]—the dealers in oxen, sheep, and doves, as well as the money-changers sitting at their tables. These malpractices had gradually arisen from the wants, usages, and

_____
[1] See Lücke, *Commentar* i. 479, [or Tholuck, p. 105.]

THE PURIFICATION OF THE TEMPLE.

notions of the Jewish nation. Those persons who attended the
festivals, or generally the Israelites who offered sacrifices, required animals for that purpose ; and thus a cattle market was
held. Besides this, according to Exod. xxx. 13, the Jews paid a
temple-tax, and in the temple coinage, a half-shekel according
to the shekel of the sanctuary ; hence the money-changers
were needed.[1] Probably this temple-market was originally in
the neighbourhood of the outer court, and gradually brought
within it. But how can the circumstance be explained, that the
strict pharisaical Jews in the time of Jesus could allow such a
desecration of the temple to creep in ?

This circumstance may be explained from the spirit of
Pharisaism ; and we must first enter into its meaning, in order
fully to understand the indignation of Jesus. In the same degree in which Pharisaism looked with increasing contempt on
the Gentiles, it valued the sacrificial animals, since they had a
relation to the temple, more highly, and at last esteemed them
as the nobler of the two ; for, according to the later Jewish theology, an Israelite might be defiled by intercourse with Gentiles
(see Acts x. 12, etc.). They stood, in this respect, on a level
with unclean beasts, while the sacrificial beasts served for purification. It was, therefore, quite in accordance with the spirit
of Pharisaism when these animals were allowed to expel the
Gentiles from their court. But, on the other hand, it was quite
in accordance with the spirit of Christ when His zeal was roused
against such a disorderly proceeding. He combated the false
temple-service in the temple itself, because it desecrated the
temple and marred its most peculiar design.

His mode of proceeding is remarkable. He makes 'a scourge
of small cords.' This scourge He wields, not against the men,
but against the oxen and sheep, and against these animals
naturally, not merely symbolically.[2] It is a mark of His superiority that He drives the cattle out directly, as if they had run
of their own accord into the temple.[3] In the same way He

---

[1] This tax might be paid out of Jerusalem, Matt. xvii. 24 ; but persons
who attended the feast generally preferred paying it in Jerusalem.

[2] See Ebrard, *Gospel History* 219 ; also Maier's commentary on the
passage.

[3] In this, as it appears to me, consists the peculiar legality of the act.
Jesus drove out the cattle with the scourge, both sheep and oxen—πάντα;—

overturns the tables of the money-changers quite simply, since He proceeds in a straightforward manner, and takes for granted that no tables ought to stand there, and thus scatters about the money of the exchangers. But He did not like to overturn the dove-cages, because they contained living creatures; nor could He scare the doves away, because they sat in the cages ;[1] so He commanded their owners, 'Take these things hence,' and then gives the cause of His zeal both in reference to them and the rest: 'Make not My Father's house an house of merchandise.' When Jesus had accomplished this act of zeal, His disciples remembered that it was written, The zeal of Thine house hath eaten me up.[2]

The Jews[3] could not deny the theocratic fitness of Christ's act; they must have allowed it to be a purification of the temple. But they desired to know what authority He had for performing it. Certainly, every Jew might come forward as a zealot against illegal abuses in the national life.[4] But the greatest zealots generally justified their proceedings as prophets and workers of miracles.[5] And in the present case the Jews believed that they were bound to make peculiarly strong demands, since the Lord by His act had rebuked the whole nation, and the Sanhedrim itself. They demanded, therefore, a sign to legitimate His proceeding.

Jesus replied to them, 'Destroy this temple, and in three

as if they were a shepherdless multitude which had run into the temple. The sellers would, of course,.rush out with the cattle, and quite as naturally the buyers with the sellers.

[1] See Rosenmüller's *Scholia* on the passage. Also Schweizer, *das Evang. Johan.* p. 135. It would be strange to admit that those that sold doves had a greater right than the rest to desecrate the temple, on the ground that the doves were intended for the poor, or, according to Stier, because Jesus saw in them an emblem of the Holy Spirit.

[2] Ps. lxix. 9, compared with John xv. 25, xix. 28, 30 ; Acts i. 20.

[3] As ' the Jews' here, for the first time, meet the Lord in this hostile manner, we may remark once for all, that John uses the expression neither in the sense of national distinction, as a designation of the Jews in a narrower sense, nor as a designation of the members of the Sanhedrim. The Jews, in John's Gospel, are rather Hebrews who judaized in opposition to Christianity, whether in Galilee or in Judea, whether they belonged to the people or to the Sanhedrim. The passage in John v. 41 favours this view. See vol. i. p. 216 of this work.

[4] Num. xxv. 7.   [5] 1 Kings xviii. 23.

days I will raise it up again.' The Jews understood His words of their visible temple, as their answer proves : ' Forty and six years was this temple in building, and wilt Thou rear it up in three days ?'[1] John repudiates this interpretation with the explanation, 'Jesus spake of the temple of His body.' This explanation was not immediately disclosed to the disciples, but first became clear to them at the resurrection of Jesus ; and this fulfilment of so remarkable a prophecy contributed to strengthen their faith.

In modern times, it has been thought needful to correct the exegesis of John, or of the disciples generally, in the explanation of this passage, by remarking that the destruction of the temple must mark the destruction of the theocracy which the Jews merited, but its rebuilding, the higher restoration of the theocracy by the work of Christ ; and it is supposed that the three days may be regarded as the concrete designation of a short time.[2]

It ought, at the same time, to have been perceived, that the Old Testament theocracy could be really destroyed, and was destroyed, only by the rejection and crucifixion of Christ, and that His resurrection founded the real restoration of a new and higher theocratic order, a higher temple.[3] The exposition of the Evangelist is distinguished from the aforesaid modern one in this, that he seizes the fact in question, of the destruction and rebuilding of the true theocracy, clearly on its innermost substance, in its special life-principle ; while the same fact floats so dimly in its outward extent before the modern exposition, that it never succeeds in estimating the substance of the fact in its real significance, and in comprehending it in its unity with this outward extension. The saying of the Lord was certainly not easy to be understood by the Jews ; with their judaizing disposition,

[1] ' They evidently mean the building of the temple by Herod, the rebuilding of the temple erected by Zerubbabel after the captivity, and reckon the forty-six years from the beginning of the building in the eighteenth or fifteenth year of Herod, including the interruptions. The building was completed under Herod Antipas.'—Lücke, *Commentar* i. 487.

[2] The treatises on this subject have been fully noticed by Lücke, *Commentar* i. 489.

[3] Compare Ebrard, p. 220 ; and Stier, *Words of the Lord Jesus* i. 71. The author of this work has not overlooked (vol. i. p. 211) that Ebrard had already found the solution of the ancient problem.

they persisted in supposing that He meant the material temple on Mount Zion. From this carnal conception there was only a single step to the slanderous misrepresentation which we find again in the mouth of the false witnesses at the judicial examination of Christ. But for Christ the temple had from the first its spiritual existence in the theocracy ; and that He referred to this, the better disposed must have surmised. But the best disposed also found in the fulfilment of this surmise that His personal life was the quintessence of this theocracy, and therefore His body was properly the temple.

The three first Evangelists narrate another perfectly similar purification of the temple, which the Lord performed on the last Passover He attended. In the present day, it is generally assumed that this event could not have happened twice. But for this assumption there is no sufficient reason. Rather there is great probability in favour of the opposite supposition, which adheres to the account in the Gospels. It is difficult to suppose that Jesus would allow so crying an abuse to exist without animadversion up to the time of His last visit. He combated it at once. But let it be supposed that He combated it with permanent success, and we must admit such a single great result of His agency in the Israelitish cultus as could not easily fall to His lot according to the whole remaining bearing of the Jewish theocracy towards Him.[1] If, then, the old irregular practice soon revived, the question would be, whether Christ could have endured the repeated observation of a public scandal, peradventure for the reason that His first denunciation of it had been of so little avail. It is, we allow, possible that the one remembrance of the disciples might have added to the one act of Jesus some traits taken from other similar acts.[2] Yet the difference of the two accounts is not to be mistaken. The act in both cases is the same ; only that, on the second purification, Jesus, according to Mark (xi. 16), would not allow the vessels to be carried through the temple. But the saying with which He accompanied His act

---

[1] See Ebrard, *Gospel History*, p. 378.

[2] [This is barely consistent even with what the author has already said of the 'sacred remembrance' of the life of our Lord by His disciples, and does certainly not allow for a more than ordinary distinctness of remembrance. Neander is of opinion there was but one cleansing of the temple ; but this idea seems to be now very generally given up as untenable.—ED.]

in the two cases is wholly different. The tone of the saying in
John is quite mild: 'Make not My Father's house a house of
merchandise.' The second saying in the synoptic Gospels is
marked by great severity. 'It is written, My house shall be
called a house of prayer, but ye have made it a den of thieves.'
This sentence is a vigorous blending of two prophetic passages,
Isa. lvi. 7 and Jer. vii. 11. 'Is this house, which is called by
My name, become a den ' robbers in your eyes?' the Lord asks
His people by Jeremiah, for this reason, that the people came to
His house in an ungodly state of mind, many of them murderers
and adulterers. Jesus availed Himself of this language in its
freest application. On the other hand, in Isa. lvi. the an-
nouncement is made, that the Gentiles should be fellow-wor-
shippers with Israel in the temple; and in this sense it is said,
'My house shall be called a house of prayer for all people.'
This was the design of the court of the Gentiles, to represent the
living germ of Universalism in the Old Testament religion and
Church quite palpably and visibly in the arrangements of the
material temple. Hence Mark reports the words of Jesus most
correctly in their full extent: 'My house shall be called of *all
nations* a house of prayer.' And it was quite in keeping with
the whole character of the transaction, that Jesus should bring
home to the pharisaic spirit, at the second and more unsparing
purification of the temple, the ultimate ground of His conduct.
He now declared, without reserve, that He meant to advocate
the right of the nations, of the Gentiles, to the temple, against
the pharisaic spirit, which would have dislodged the Gentiles
from their lawful position by the pressure of their sacrificial
traffic. The consequences of the two acts were also essentially
different. At the first purification, the Jewish party left it still
undecided whether the proceeding was right or not; Jesus only
justified His zeal by a sign of prophetic spiritual power and
authority. At the second purification, matters took quite a different turn. The space which had been left free by the expulsion of the cattle was occupied by the blind and the lame whom
Jesus healed, and by pious children who chanted their hosannas
in His praise; while, on the other hand, the chief priests and
scribes retired with renewed animosity to conspire against His
life.

Thus the first great public act of Jesus was one of the most beautiful zeal, of reverence, and love; it was an act of inspired wrath, in which He contended for the divine honour and the spirit of devotion against the profane disposition that desecrated the sanctuary, and by which, at the same time, He asserted the rights of humanity against the spiritual arrogance which treated with contempt the claims of the Gentiles, who, though still at a distance, were called to salvation. He came as the Lord to His temple, according to the prophecy of Malachi (iii. 1); the out-ward, special purification of the temple was an emblem of the great universal temple-purification which He accomplished by His whole work of redemption.

This act was miraculous in its religious, moral, and psychical operation; only the physical element, which completes a miracle in the stricter sense, was wanting. It was a miracle, as an act of extraordinary spiritual illumination and power, as an act of religious and moral majesty which operated on the people with irresistible power,[1] alarmed the traffickers, paralysed adversaries, agitated the popular mind, and elevated the souls of the pious, though it filled them with anxious forebodings. Such a fore-boding seized the souls of the disciples of Jesus, and brought to their recollection that solemn expression in the Psalms which represented zeal for God's house as a consuming fire terminating in death.

John does not relate the other miracles which Jesus per-formed in Jerusalem at the Passover. But he alludes to them when he says, 'Many believed in His name, when they saw the signs (σημεῖα) which He did' (John ii. 22). But Jesus was too deeply conversant with the essential quality of human nature in its sinfulness and weakness, to be able to trust Himself to those men, who in the first fervour of their emotions had de-clared themselves for Him. He knew them all, that is, He knew the Adamic type of man fundamentally, so that He needed not that any one should give Him information respecting the peculiar character of the generation among whom He lived. This collec-tive body stood before Him as one man; and what was in man He already knew, He was aware of it, He saw through him. And owing to the inconstancy of the Adamic man in his noblest flights and aspirations, it was evident to Him that He could not immediately reveal and trust Himself to His admirers without

.   [1] [Πράγμα πολλῆς αὐθεντίας γέμον.—Cramer's *Catena* in loc.—ED.]

being unfaithful to Himself and His cause. For the sake of their salvation, He was obliged meanwhile to conceal Himself in many ways, and to impart and trust Himself to them under the laws of the holiest reserve. This important feature in the plan of Jesus appears in John as well as in the three first Evangelists.

NOTES.

1. If, in accordance with the Gospel tradition, we admit the repetition of the purification of the temple, it will be easily understood that the second must be by far the most important for the synoptists, since it was witnessed by all the disciples, and therefore occupied a conspicuous place in the Gospel tradition. But then John found that the first only required yet to be reported, and he reported it in preference to the other, since according to the whole composition of his Gospel the admission of the second was more out of his way.

2. Against the reference of Christ's words, 'Destroy this temple,' etc., to His death and resurrection, several remarks have been made, which may all be settled by one answer. It has been forgotten that the terms employed first of all ought to sound as if Jesus meant only to say, 'Demolish this material temple, and in three days I will rebuild it,' since He wished to intimate something deeper under the covering of this paradoxical expression. Hence (1) He must say λύσατε, though this was not a proper expression for the crucifixion of His body; hence (2) He says τὸν ναὸν τοῦτον with a reference to the temple, though He had in His mind the theocracy, and His own body as the organ of the theocracy; hence (3) He says ἐγερῶ, though in a strict sense He did not raise Himself, but was raised by the Father (yet so, that His resurrection was at the same time an act of His own life, according to John x. 18). Also, the remarks, that the Jews had as yet done nothing which indicated the design of putting Jesus to death, and that they could not have understood such an intimation as that given by Jesus, may be obviated by the rejoinder, that here the most distinct relation exists between the outer and the inner, the general and individual relations of the theocracy;—first of all between the temple, the body of Christ, and the theocracy;—then between the desecration of the temple, the crucifixion of Christ, and the

destruction of the ancient theocracy;—lastly and thirdly, between the purification of the temple, the resurrection of Christ, and the establishment of the New Covenant. To this we must add, in conclusion, the relations of time. The Lord required only a few moments to cleanse the temple—He required three days for the resurrection—He required a short time in order to exhibit the new temple in His pentecostal Church. Therefore Bruno Bauer's requirement (*Kritik der evang. Geschichte des Joh.* p. 82) is satisfied; the second, deeper meaning of Christ's words lies really in *the direction* of the first meaning. That three days may signify a short space of time, Hos. vi. 2 has been adduced to prove; and it has been justly remarked, that the expression generally has something proverbial, since Jesus did not remain three days in the grave in a strict sense, but rose again on the third day.

3. 'This multitude of persons, who might be certain of the protection of the priesthood, would not let themselves be ejected from the temple by a single man, without any ado.' This dictum belongs to the well-known standing canon of a critical foregone conclusion, which always treats as improbable the manifestations and operations of spiritual majesty.

SECTION VI.

THE CONVERSATION BY NIGHT WITH NICODEMUS.

(John iii. 1-21.)

Among the many men in Jerusalem who received the first impulses to faith through the miracles of Jesus, were already some persons of distinction, Pharisees, and even members of the Sanhedrim. Nicodemus is a representative of these friends of Jesus, and his visit by night to the Lord is a proof how much reason Jesus had not altogether to trust Himself to believers at this stage.

As the noblest mystics proceeded from the monks of the Catholic Church, from the Dominicans especially, and the great Reformer Luther from the Augustinians, so two great witnesses of the most living Christian faith, Paul and Nicodemus, were supplied to the kingdom of God by the Pharisees, a party noted for their sanctimoniousness and bondage to the letter. In the person of Nicodemus, Christ at the very outset of His ministry conquered not only a Pharisee, but a ruler of the Jews, a member of the Sanhedrim. It has been a very common hypothesis in schools of theology, but without any foundation, to regard him as a spy, who at first came to Jesus with a sinister design. The sincerity of His inclination towards Jesus is, from the first, decided; a genuine germ of faith already begins to combat his own pretensions and prejudices; otherwise he, an old man, could not resort to a young man, and, though a distinguished member of the council, ask questions of the Galilean Rabbi as a scholar, thus putting his whole reputation in peril. We also see how this germ gradually increased in power, till perfected in the ripe fruit of faith, after passing in its development through distinct stages. But that the germ in its first form was feeble, Nicodemus plainly indicates, not only by his coming to Jesus by night, to which, no doubt, considerations of fear determined him, but also by the tenor of his language.

In general, it has been assumed that John has not fully reported the conversation of Christ with Nicodemus. But if we grant this, it cannot be admitted that he has given only a fragmentary abstract, so that we cannot fully depend on the connection of the separate parts. The abstract must preserve the connection equally as well as the discourse in its full extent.

Nicodemus salutes the Lord in terms of reverence which seem to include, and which in a certain sense do include, a perfect recognition of His divine mission and prophetic dignity. ' Rabbi, we know that Thou art a teacher came from God; for no man can do these miracles that Thou dost, except God be with him.' This salutation appears altogether so suited to form a point of connection for the teaching of Christ, that it has often excited astonishment that Christ's answer so entirely passes it over, or rather appears to treat it as quite unsatisfactory. With powerful pathos the Lord replies to this courteous and honest salutation by the momentous declaration, which has become the fundamental maxim of His Church, ' Verily, verily, I say unto thee, Except a man be born from above,[1] he cannot see the kingdom of God.'

[1] It is a much agitated question, whether ἄνωθεν is to be translated *from above* or *again*. Compare especially Lücke, i. 516, and Tholuck, p. 114.

Between the salutation of the guest and this counter-salutation of the Lord there is evidently a chasm ;—but the chasm is obviously an original one, it is an element of the transaction. This absolute contrariety is indeed the most important feature of our history, positively designed by Jesus, and of decided efficiency.

Nicodemus met Him with a homage in which the consciousness of his high position was not concealed, so that it almost assumed a patronizing character. 'Rabbi, we know what we have to think of Thee,' he said, as if he wished to assure Him of the favour of a powerful party. But, along with this patronizing language, which lay in the indefinite plural 'we know,' the acknowledgment seemed to be uttered in a lower key, 'Thou art a teacher come from God.' But this conviction Nicodemus grounded altogether on an inference from the Old Testament orthodoxy—Thy great miracles are the proof of Thy higher mission. And how feeble the conviction was that was so grounded, but which Nicodemus seemed to regard as a great acknowledgment, is proved by the choice of night for his visit. There was an unconscious contradiction between the pathos of his recognition and the expressions of reflection and fear which alternated with it.

The great Master of the human heart saw at once that He

Lücke urges that John uses ἄνωθεν elsewhere only in iii. 31 and xix. 11, 23, and in the two first passages unquestionably for ἐκ τοῦ οὐρανοῦ, or ἐκ τοῦ Θεοῦ, and in the last, in the sense of *from above* or *from the top*,—never therefore for πάλιν. Moreover John, the same writer remarks, never speaks of *being born again*, but of *being born of God*: chap. i. 13 ; 1 John ii. 29, iii. 9, iv. 7. He declares himself therefore in favour of the first interpretation, and understands it as more exactly expressed by—*born of God*. Tholuck, on the other hand, draws attention to the expression in the rejoinder of Nicodemus, δεύτερον γεννηθῆναι, and to the phrases ἀναγεννηθῆναι, 1 Peter i. 3, 23 ; παλιγγενεσία, Titus iii. 5 ; καινὴ κτίσις, Gal. vi. 15 ; and accordingly adopts the second interpretation, yet so that ἄνωθεν is not exactly equivalent to πάλιν, but denotes *anew, afresh*. But it is more accordant with hermeneutics to interpret (with Lücke) a word in John's Gospel from John's usual phraseology, than (with Tholuck) from that of Peter and Paul. But, taken strictly, it is wrong to discuss the word ἄνωθεν merely for itself. Let the phrase ἄνωθεν γεννηθῆναι be considered as a contrast to ἐκ τῆς γῆς γεννηθῆναι, and with the idea, born *from above*, there will arise the idea, *born again*; the word comprehends the rich thought—*to be first rightly born from renovating heavenly principles*.

could not win this aged man, who by honours and dignities, by the views and habit of his outward and inward religious life, was firmly rooted in the soil of legal worldliness, by the tedious method of theological controversy; but that he must be won by the shattering stroke of His first rejoinder—that He must loosen him by a wrench in his position, though not pull him from it compulsorily. Nicodemus presented himself to Him, as if he were a trustworthy member of the kingdom of heaven. He wished already to know who Christ was, and the design of His mission. His theology of the new age was, as he imagined, complete in the main outlines, and with it the commencement of the new age itself. And thus he was willing to guarantee for many that they were already adherents of Jesus. This disclosure of his views made the Lord feel the deep contrast between the old world-view of Nicodemus and the fundamental principles of His own new world, and He suddenly placed this contrast before the mind of the theologian. With a solemn asseveration, He gave him the assurance that the new world He announced, the Messianic kingdom, was a completely hidden mystery for all who were not thoroughly transformed, new-born again from above; that no one was in a condition even to see this kingdom, to say nothing of entering it, unless such a new birth had given him new eyes for this new world. The Lord knew that He must risk and could risk the future of Nicodemus on the agitating operation of this announcement.

The answer of Nicodemus proved that the words of Jesus had, in fact, moved him in his inmost soul. Nicodemus knew indeed the language of the prophets respecting circumcision and the renewal of the heart;[1] he might also be familiar with the circumcision of the Jewish proselytes as new-born children.[2] This, therefore, was certainly clear to him, that Jesus, by His requirement, could not literally mean a second bodily birth. But it was also evident from the words of Jesus, that He did not recognise the being a Jew or the passing over to Judaism as a new birth; nor even the pharisaic righteousness by which Nicodemus assuredly believed he had gained the renewal of the heart, like thousands on his legal standpoint. And since Nicodemus could not at once sacrifice his distinguished position in

---

[1] Deut. x. 16, xxx. 6; Jer. iv. 4; Ezek. xi. 19, 20, xxxvi. 27, 28.

[2] Compare Lücke, i. 520.

life and his honoured old age to the assurance that they contributed nothing to his understanding the kingdom of God, that he
needed a new birth, therefore he could not or would not admit
that Christ's words could have for him an allowable spiritual
meaning. He therefore wilfully took them in a literal sense,
not from contractedness of mind,[1] but from irritated sensibility.
In order, by a manœuvre of rabbinical logomachy, to hold up
Christ's requirement as extravagant, he answered, 'How can a
man be born when he is old? can he enter a second time into
his mother's womb and be born?' Christ would not allow Himself to be moved from the composure of His sacerdotal dignity.
He repeated the solemn asseveration, and set a second time the
might of His heart against the rabbinical dialectics of the aged
man. But He at once wrests from him the objection he had
made, by the distinct requirement, 'Except a man be born of
water and of the Spirit, he cannot enter into the kingdom of
God.' It is evident that Jesus here opposes as the second birth,
the birth of the Spirit, to the first natural birth of the human
mother. When in this sense He joins water with Spirit, we are
led to think of the connection, so frequent in the Gospel, of
water-baptism with Spirit-baptism. John met the Pharisees
with the condition, 'If ye would enter the kingdom of heaven,
after submitting to my water-baptism, ye must also receive the
Spirit-baptism of the Messiah.' Christ again insists on this
condition; with the necessity of His Spirit-baptism He also
asserts that of John, or at least of the water-baptism introduced
by John. But this requirement has been thought strange in
the mouth of Jesus, since it has been supposed that His Spirit-
baptism would be sufficient. In order to remove this impression,
water-baptism must be regarded as the symbol of repentance,
while Spirit-baptism represents the life of faith.[2] But the water
signifies not only individual, but also social repentance,—the
entrance into the true theocratic society. And this society was
constituted by Christ to be the historical foundation and main

---

[1] Compare Schweizer, *d. Ev. Joh.* p. 32.

[2] [Alford asserts that it is mere doctrinal prejudice which has determined Calvin's interpretation of these words: 'Spiritum qui nos repurgat,'
and Grotius' 'Spiritum aquæ instar emundantem.' But Matt. iii. 11 speaks
strongly for this interpretation; and we were not aware that, among the
very numerous and diverse doctrinal prejudices ascribed to Calvin, a low

condition of the operations of His Spirit. Thus, as the first natural world was formed under the movement of the Spirit which hovered over the waters, so also must the second world, that of the new life, emerge from the water of baptism to repentance, which forms the new sacred community, and from the administration of the Spirit in this Church. No one is born again simply of the Spirit, for the Spirit presupposes in His operation the historical community which has been collected round the name of Christ, acknowledges His word, and is distinguished from the impure world by its public common repentance or purification. A man must first become a historical Christian before he can become a spiritual Christian. With his entrance into the new society by baptism, he dies to the old world and renounces its worldly mind, devotes his old life to death, and enters into the historical conditions which must confirm the new life in him. Thus he is born of water. But this birth is not a special birth *per se;* it is not completed till he becomes a new man in his whole inward being and life-principle, through the Holy Spirit, who is the life-element of the new community; he becomes a child of God because the life of Christ becomes his own, a free fountain of life in his breast. But the reason why this renewal must be a total, and therefore a new birth, Christ explains by the canon, ' That which is born of the flesh is flesh, and that which is born of the Spirit is spirit.' Kind never ceases to be kind. (*Art lässt nicht von Art.*) From the stock of the old humanity, whose life has the predominant characteristic of carnality, the preponderance of sensuousness and of carnal desires above the free life of the Spirit, in which all the affections of the senses should rise up pure, only carnally-disposed men can proceed—only such in whom the dark nature-side of life predominates in a destructive manner, morbidly, and contrary to their destiny, over the luminous Spirit-side. Therefore, if the adamically constituted man is to be truly a new creature, he must become new in his kind of life, and be born of the Spirit.

sacramentarian theory could find place. In consistency with what Alford says on this passage, we might have expected his remarks on John vi. 51 to be somewhat different. The sacrament is quite as easily found in the one place as in the other. The doctrinal bearing of the expression is shown by Turrettin, loc. xix. quæst. 13, 19. He too interprets it, 'Spiritus lavans et mundans corda.'—ED.]

Since Christ represents this new birth as indispensable, in doing so He marks the relation in which the man who is not yet filled with the life of Christ stands to the kingdom of God. He attains it not by his theological science, nor by his logical deductions; he has it not in his religious energy. It is a new creation from heaven, which must bury his old life in its consecrated stream in order to give him a new life—a mystery of life, in which he must become a subject of the formative power of divine grace, like an unborn child. The more he anticipates this creative power, yearns for it, and humbly receives it into his life, so much nearer is he to the kingdom of God.

After the requirement has been positively laid down, the Lord proceeds to explain the possibility of its fulfilment by an analogy. Wind is akin to spirit—a natural symbol of its existence and action. And perhaps at that very time, while they were thus conversing together, the night-wind might be making itself perceptible by its murmurs. At all events, the Lord took His comparison most appropriately from the nearest, freshest life. ' Marvel not,' He therefore said to him, ' that I said unto thee, Ye must be born from above. The wind bloweth where it listeth, and thou hearest the sound thereof, but canst not tell whence it cometh and whither it goeth!' Here, then, is a powerful, actual life, which goes beyond your knowledge. Thou canst not deny the existence of the wind, nor its irresistible action, nor its omnipresent movement round the globe. For it rushes sometimes here, sometimes there; it makes itself known to thee by its loud tone, its voice. And yet it is to thee a twofold mystery,—first in its origin, then in its movements. ' So is it,' said the Lord, ' with every one who is born of the Spirit.' He might have said, ' So is it with the Spirit;' but since he who is born of the Spirit is one with the life of the Spirit, the expression actually chosen is equally correct, while at the same time it is more full of meaning.[1] The life of the Spirit comes out from a depth, and length, and height which human intelligence cannot fathom; and thus, even in the man whom it apprehends, it appears as a holy, divine mystery! The same life of the Spirit goes to an immeasurable distance over land and sea; and so is the child of the Spirit with his destiny. His way goes up-

---

[1] The same remark is applicable to the parables, Matt. xiii. 20, ' He that received the seed into stony places,' etc.

wards (Prov. xv. 24).   But however full of mystery is the life
of the Spirit and the spiritual life, it makes itself known in the
most powerful facts, and its attributes are—*Freedom ; manifestation of power in all degrees, even to irresistible might ; infinite
fulness; and vivifying operation.*   The wind everywhere is begotten from a life full of mystery, as if from itself ; so is the
Spirit, it is free.   The Holy Spirit also begins its operations
with the gentlest whisper ; but this can become the mightiest
tempest.   But in its fulness it is as immeasurable as the atmosphere, for it is the life of God moving itself.   And as the wind
is an indispensable principle of life in the material world, so is
the Spirit in the spiritual world.   The moving winds form the
vital element of the globe; the moving currents of the Spirit
are the vital element of the kingdom of God.   But as the wind
places itself in opposition to the water, in order to form a world,
and as without the antagonism of a solid world it would only be
an enormous hurricane; so the Spirit manifests itself in living reciprocal action with man's definite life, and with the divine word
as the life of history ; and those persons who turn history into
unsubstantial shadows, make the Spirit to be *No-spirit* (*Ungeist*).

Nicodemus indeed had at first doubted the necessity of his
new birth ; but now he had received an obscure impression that
so it must be.   Christ's first address had impressed upon him
the difference between the legal righteousness of one outwardly
circumcised and the new life of one born again from heaven,
and his own capability for the kingdom of heaven.   The delineation of that glorious spiritual life brings gradually to his consciousness his own painful deficiency, which moves him as an
obscure aspiration has distinguished him from the common
Pharisees, and driven him to Jesus.   But he trembles at the
thought, whether it be possible that such a spring-storm of an
awakening spiritual life could pass through his aged breast, and
exclaims, 'How can these things be ?'   Then Christ answers
him, 'Art thou a teacher of Israel, and knowest not these
things ?'   He was not only *a* teacher in Israel, but *the* teacher
of Israel, since he now wished to instruct Israel respecting the
divine mission of Christ, and placed himself at the head of those
who were cognizant of the Messiah.[1]   He wished to know the

[1] According to Scholl (see Lücke, i. 527), three persons stood at the
head of the Sanhedrim: (i.) the *President* (הַנָּשִׂיא) ; (ii.) the *Vice-President*,

fundamental relations of the kingdom of God; and now it became evident that he did not even know the doctrine of regeneration, and therefore not thoroughly the spiritual meaning of
circumcision. Now Christ confronts the bewilderment of Nicodemus with His own divine certainty; the right relation between
Himself and Nicodemus is firmly settled. The solemn asservera-
tion, 'Verily, verily, I say unto thee,' is repeated a third time,
and then follows the declaration, 'We speak that we do know,
and testify that we have seen, and ye receive not our witness.'
The plural of Christ is opposed to the plural of Nicodemus; He
also has those who share in His knowledge. Perhaps He had in
His thoughts not merely John the Baptist, but rather His disciples and the whole world of future believers.[1] Nicodemus
stands answerable for a visible party, which subsequently was
for the most part dissolved; Christ for an invisible party, which
is ever coming more powerfully into life. And with Him and
those who belong to Him it is not a matter merely of intellectual
knowledge, but of spiritual intuition, of experience; therefore
they are not merely speakers concerning eternal things, but witnesses out of eternity. This certainty with which we meet you,
and which you must feel in our testimony, will you deny it?
Thus Christ introduces the disclosures which He wishes to make
to him respecting the kingdom of God. He continues His
gentle censure with an expression which probably means, If I
have told you truths already naturalized on earth (in the Israelitish community), and ye believe Me not, how will ye believe if

or *pater domus judicii sive Synedrii* (אֲבִי בֵית דִּין); and (iii.) sitting on the
left, next to the President, a distinguished member of the Sanhedrim called
the *wise man*, חָכָם. Scholl supposes that Nicodemus occupied the place of
the last mentioned, and hence is called *the teacher of Israel*. But, apart
from the fact that these official distinctions are doubtful, the designations
wise man and *teacher of Israel* are not synonymous. According to Lücke,
the explanation of Erasmus is the true one, that the definite article is used
rhetorically,—*Ille doctor, cujus tam celebris est opinio.* According to our
view, the expression is not rhetorical, but sharply definite.

[1] [It will be remembered, however, that the use of the plural by one
person addressing is by no means so uncommon that it requires special explanation of this kind. The Greek interpreter in Cramer's *Catena*, after
conjecturing of whom the plural can be used, concludes, ' ἢ περὶ ἑαυτοῦ
μόνον.' Alford's explanation, ' a proverbial saying,' is also quite admissible,
and probably the best.—ED.]

I tell you the new revelations of heaven?[1] The doctrine of
regeneration is a truth which, as we have seen, was brought
forward with sufficient distinctness in the Old Testament to be
regarded as one already naturalized in this world; it is, besides,
a mystery that concerns the earth, for regeneration has to do
with earthly-minded men, with earthly humanity and earth.
And this a heathen ought painfully to surmise—not to say that
a teacher in Israel ought to know, at least believe when it is
announced to him. But if he will not believe when it is announced most solemnly by an acknowledged Prophet, how can
he receive those heavenly mysteries embracing earth, but not
yet naturalized on earth, which become first intelligible in the
light of regeneration, since they are the causes and effects of
regeneration? How can he become acquainted with the concealed side of the spiritual life, the ultimate *whence* and *whither*
of the spiritual wind, when he will not understand the manifest
side of the same life, the sound of that wind? This reproof of
Christ excites the curiosity of His aged scholar for the announcement which He has yet to make to him. To these heavenly
doctrines belongs, first of all, the doctrine of the Son of God;
next, that of atonement; then that of redemption; and, lastly,
that of the judgment.

'No one hath ascended up to heaven but He that (continually)
cometh down from heaven, the Son of man, who is at home in
heaven (*as His native place*).' These mysterious words express
the divine glory of Christ as it is exhibited in His threefold
relation to heaven. But these relations are spoken of because
He wishes to announce to Nicodemus those heavenly things
which no one else can announce to him. And the reason why
no one else can announce them is, because Jesus alone has
attained the heavenly standpoint and range of vision, the elevation required for looking into all the depths of the divine
counsels. But He has attained it, because in heavenly love and
condescension He continually descends from the heaven of His
divine blessedness and glory, into all the depths of human misery,
and even goes down into hell. By His descending in love He
has His heavenly elevation in knowledge. And thus His Spirit

---

[1] Lücke understands τὰ ἐπίγεια, like Wisd. x. 16, τὰ ἐπὶ γῆς, to be
synonymous with τὰ ἐν χερσὶν, things intelligible and close at hand; and by
τὰ ἐν οὐρανοῖς, things unsearchable, at a distance, and concealed from man.

floats upwards and downwards between heaven and earth, since
according to His heavenly nature and His consciousness He is
continually in heaven, and since in the identity of His consciousness of God and of the world He has the eternal consciousness of
heaven.[1] The first clause, therefore, marks His heavenly intuition and knowledge; the second, His heavenly loving, suffering,
and doing; the third, His heavenly being and inner life. His
heavenly being is an eternal present;[2] His heavenly loving,
suffering, and doing, is a constant constructing and administrat-
ing[3] throughout His whole history; His heavenly intuition is a
decided acquisition, resulting from that life and administration.[4]
This was the first profound heavenly truth of the New Covenant which Nicodemus needed to learn: that the fulness of
divine revelation and knowledge is laid up in Jesus; that it proceeds from His divine existence, and His heavenly self-sacrifice
and work; and that He is the Christ. The second great truth had
been already announced by the declaration that Christ descended
from heaven. It is the doctrine of His atoning sufferings.

'And as Moses lifted up the serpent in the wilderness, even
so must the Son of man be lifted up, that whosoever believeth
in Him should not perish, but have eternal life.' Under this
image He represents the atonement, since it strikingly marks
the nature of the atonement, in the mysterious lifting up ($\dot{v}\psi\omega$-
$\theta\tilde{\eta}\nu\alpha\iota$) represents the descending and ascending of the heavenly
Lord in their unity.[5] Moses, by Jehovah's command, erected a

[1] Lücke and Tholuck are mistaken in regarding these expressions as
metaphorical or figurative. Rather, the inner life of Christ in heaven is
altogether literal and real. ['To explain such expressions as mere *Hebrew
metaphors*, is no more than saying that Hebrew metaphors are founded on
deep insight into divine truth.'—Alford. Augustin says on these words,
'Ecce hic erat, et in coelo erat: hic erat carne, in coelo erat divinitate.'
Calvin, with greater exactness, remarks that the 'being in heaven' is pre-
dicated of the humanity also, by the communicatio idiomatum.—ED.]

[2] Hence the present $\dot{o}$ $\ddot{\omega}\nu$. It is characteristic that since Erasmus it has
been the practice to change $\dot{o}$ $\ddot{\omega}\nu$ into $\dot{o}\varsigma$ $\ddot{\eta}\nu$. If generally one part of exegesis
consists in rendering shallow the deep meaning of Scripture, this is gene-
rally most conspicuous in reference to passages like this, of unfathomable
depth.

[3] Hence the aorist $\dot{o}$ $\kappa\alpha\tau\alpha\beta\dot{\alpha}\varsigma$.

[4] Hence the perfect $\dot{\alpha}\nu\alpha\beta\dot{\iota}\beta\eta\kappa\epsilon\nu$. This tense is decisive against those
who would refer the word to the ascension.

[5] John viii. 28, xii. 32, 34. In the first passage, in the same expression

sign of deliverance for the Israelites who had been bitten in their march through the wilderness by poisonous serpents.[1] It is remarkable that the sign of deliverance was the serpent itself; the brazen image of a serpent, hung upon a pole. The looking at this serpent, which was no real serpent, but one without life, and yet lifted up on high, saved the terror-struck people.[2] Thus the human race are to be saved. It has been troubled by poisonous serpents, harassed to death by seducers, slanderers, corrupters. But it must be saved by beholding the elevated image of that spiritual serpent, by the operation of the great transgressor nailed to the tree, the Crucified, whom the world has cast out as the curse, or even as the evil demon himself. That serpent-image was no serpent, but the reverse of all serpents, the banner of sanctification. So is this image of a transgressor no transgressor, not the demon of the curse, but living salvation against all the destructive and satanic existences on earth, the Saviour. With the believing contemplation of the brazen serpent, the terror-struck lost all their fatal alarm, became death-defying and calm in spirit. By the contemplation of the Crucified, men are freed from the fatal dread of death and are ready to surrender themselves to the judgment of God. But with the surrender to judgment, faith in the atonement is gained. There, the serpent-image was to express the fact, that God, by the faith of Moses, destroyed the rage of the serpent's brood; here, the image of the Crucified expresses the truth, that God in His death has cancelled the sins of the world. And as there God's help had descended so low as to operate under the form of a poisonous rep-

the reference to the crucifixion apparently predominates, and in the second, to the glorification, although here the reference to His death is not wanting. Lücke would only allow a reference to the crucifixion (i. 535). Yet the symbolic serpent-image was so far glorified as to be made an image of salvation.

[1] Num. xxi. 4–9.

[2] The closer consideration of that Old Testament history does not belong to this place. On the different explanation, see Winer's *R.W.B.* The religious gist of that miraculous cure consisted in this, that the image of the deadly evil was changed into the image of the restorative salvation—a divine institution which by its boldness awakened the highest confidence. With the horror of those who looked on the serpent-image as an image of salvation, the fear vanished which in a thousand ways the serpents themselves excited, and raised the effect of the serpent's bite into a deadly terror in the host.

tile, so here everlasting salvation had condescended to reconcile
the world under the most accursed form, that of the Crucified.
And this is indeed the central point of the type.   The Israelite
bitten by the serpent obtained, by the contemplation of the
sanative serpent-image, a presage of the deliverance which the
glory of God provided from the deadly evil, and thereby gained
a miraculous vital energy; the man bitten by the serpent of sin
and of satanic evil, obtained, by the contemplation of the redeeming holy image of the transgressor, the confidence that God
condemns sin through sin, and in its condemnation establishes
deliverance and reconciliation.   So rich are the relations between
the brazen serpent and the crucified Saviour.   Nicodemus was,
indeed, by no means in a condition to understand clearly the
language of Christ; but this language might convey to him a
strong intimation, that Christ could only bring the salvation to
the people which he expected from Him under a form of dreadful suffering.

Thus he received in an obscure form, but more exciting to
his reflection, the second revelation of heaven.   We learn in the
next place how the atonement is exhibited in its more general
form as redemption.   'For God so loved the world that He
gave His only-begotten Son, that whosoever believeth in Him
should not perish, but have everlasting life.   For God sent not
His Son into the world to condemn the world, but that the
world through Him might be saved.'   Thus the whole work of
atonement appears in the light of redeeming love;—God as the
most Merciful One in His love; Christ as the given and self-
surrendering Redeemer; the world as the object of love to be
purchased at the highest price; the believer as one who is redeemed for the blessedness of love, and who in believing gains
the principle of an imperishable, blessed life.   By means of this
third revelation of heavenly things, Nicodemus would learn
the extent of redemption : how it proceeds from a love of God
embracing the whole world; that it embraces all men, and not
merely the Jews, as the pharisaic spirit might imagine.

But as redemption does not reject believing Gentiles, so
judgment does not spare unbelieving Jews.   Judgment makes
no difference between Jews and Gentiles, but between believers
and unbelievers.   This is the last great heavenly truth which
he has to learn.

Christ therefore came into the world, not to condemn the world, at least not in the sense in which the Jews expected Him to be a rigorous judge of the Gentile world. Rather the world is to be saved by Him; and whosoever truly believes in Him is not condemned. He has in Christ received the life of righteousness, and incorporated it in his inmost soul; therefore sin is ever more condemned in him and expelled, while he himself is purified and redeemed in his own being. But a man can refuse to believe in Christ; and if he does so, judgment has already been passed upon him in his unbelief. In its principle, the unfolding of his condemnation has already begun, since he has excluded himself from the kingdom of light, love, and reconciliation. *He has not believed;*—that means, in the solemn perfect form: he has chosen, he has made up his mind. But he has not believed in the name of the only-begotten Son of God, that is, not in the highest perfect revelation of God to the human race,—not in the highest act of love,—not in the light principle of the ideality and glorification of the whole world, and of the ideality of his own being, nor in the expression of the eternal personality of God and of humanity, in that personality which makes heaven and earth one.

Therefore this faith, as well as this unbelief, is throughout of an ethical nature, determining the worth of a man in God's sight. Faith in Christ has the worth of righteousness in judgment, because it consists in the surrender to righteousness which verifies itself in judgment. Unbelief towards Christ, on the other hand, is the judgment of man respecting himself, that he cannot lay hold of and accept the heavenly moral system in its clearest expression and principle in the life of Christ. By it a man rejects his citizenship in the ideal world of Christ, and adjudges himself to an entirely opposite system full of condemnation. Hence unbelief has the demerit of all the bad qualities which it contains dynamically in itself and can originate. But how can this fearful decision be formed in a man? It is at all events the result of a persistence in evil-doing. Thus there arises 'the condemnation, that light is come into the world, and men loved darkness rather than light, because their deeds were evil.' Condemnation therefore proceeds from aversion to the light, and this is perfectly identical with aversion to Christ. It is an aversion to the ideal clearness of the intuition of the world

(*Weltanschauung*), to the apprehension of life in its pure eternal relations. Now light is this ideality of the world, and Christ is the light, because in Him the world discloses itself as the kingdom of spirit. This aversion could not be formed in man if he did not really hold fast the darkness, the confusion of the world in his consciousness and of consciousness in the world,—if he did not seek in religious and moral self-bewilderment a protection for his evil works, his outward deeds, and the deeds of his heart. This therefore is the condemnation : it is already there; its commencement has been made. But all men do not prefer the darkness to the light. Respecting this contrast, the Lord finally lays down a general canon : ' Every one that doeth evil hateth the light, neither cometh to the light, lest his deeds should be reproved. But he that doeth truth cometh to the light, that his deeds may be made manifest, that they are wrought in God.' He who does evil is bewildered himself and bewilders others, and therefore cannot love the principle which would extricate him, that is, the light. So when the clearness of the light meets him, his life appears in its criminality as a perversion of life. Thus the light punishes him ; therefore he hates the light, and chooses darkness. But it is altogether different with the man who does the truth as it manifests itself to his inmost soul. He follows the impulse of eternal clearness, and therefore cannot help coming to the light. His works are children of the light; they must enter into their element, into the light. Good is itself a part of eternal revelation : it is done in God; therefore it cannot remain hid, it must become manifest. This close is thoroughly suited to form the last words with which Jesus dismissed Nicodemus. If we imagine that the Lord went with Nicodemus to the door when he left, and uttered these last words to him under the darkness of the evening sky, we shall probably feel what a striking, powerful, and admonitory farewell they contain. Nicodemus by his nocturnal visit had apparently ranked himself with those who, with an evil conscience, seek the darkness for their evil deeds. For this the Lord rebuked him; but He also blessed the thirst of his upright soul for light, and therefore dismissed him with words of most distinct hope and promise, as if He had said to him, ' Thou art nevertheless a child of the light, and wilt surely be led into the light by the impulse of thy uprightness. Yes, thy present act of feeble faith which the night

conceals, shall become manifest in the light, because it is wrought
in God, when thou thyself shalt one day come to the light, both
in the clear day of the Spirit, of revelation, and in the clear day
of the world, of publicity. We shall meet again in the light!'

When at a later period Christ hung on the cross, Nicodemus
with his faith and work of faith came decidedly to the light.
Christ's promise then obtained its complete fulfilment. But
here Nicodemus, on his leaving, took it with him as a fruitful
seed-corn in his heart.

NOTES.

1. 'The whole scene with Nicodemus is treated by Strauss
as a fiction which owed its origin to the reproach that the success of the Gospel was confined to the lower classes, which left
a sting behind in the souls of the first Christians. But Neander
has shown, with historical as well as Christian penetration, that
the Christians of that first age rather gloried in the fact that
the common people were exalted to such dignity by Christ.'
Thus Tholuck, p. 124. The explanation of Strauss (i. 661)
belongs to his peculiar view of the poverty-stricken character
of man, and especially of the Christian, and proceeds on the
assumption that the poor primitive Church, which was unable to
win any proselytes from the higher classes, created imaginary
proselytes, though certainly on a less noble principle than that
which instigated the poor schoolmaster, in Jean Paul, to write a
Klopstock's *Messiah* because he was too poor to buy one. The
only place where one really misses the mention of Nicodemus is
Matt. xxvii. 57. Why, it is asked, is not Nicodemus mentioned
here as the helper of Joseph of Arimathea? But it is at once
evident that the reason of this special mention of Joseph alone
is, that it was he who begged the body of Jesus from Pilate,
and he who had made ready the tomb for its reception.

2. According to Baur, in his *Essay on the Composition and
Character of John's Gospel,* Nicodemus is to be regarded as the
representative of unbelieving Judaism even in his faith, and on
the other hand, the woman of Samaria as the representative of
such Gentiles as were susceptible of faith. A person must read
this statement of Baur's, to be convinced how far the passion for
making an allegorical scheme out of the living reality of the

Gospel history can lead to the most unfortunate distortions of that history.   Not to say that we are here offered nothing but the moonshine of spiritualistic fictions for the sunshine of the highest ideal reality, the allegorist never once reaches the pure realization of the living poetical contents of these evangelic representations, but covers them all over with his stiff rationalist constructions, with much the same effect as covering a beautiful painting with large dull patches of one colour.   We do not meet with even the ordinary freshness of colouring of the simplest kind on the tablet of Nicodemus, but only a dirty grey.   'Faith on account of σημεῖα, such as is ascribed to Nicodemus, it is said, is related to true faith as the outward to the inward, or the carnal to the spiritual ; and hence it is nothing but a further description of the faith that relies on σημεῖα, when Nicodemus, however fairly we may estimate his want of understanding, appears as a teacher in Israel, to whom, in his incapacity of rising above sensuous experience to spiritual conceptions, ·all susceptibility for true faith in Jesus was wanting.'   Here at last the author of the fourth Gospel must be allowed to justify himself.   He unquestionably places Nicodemus among the friends of light ; our critic places him on the side of darkness.   On the other hand, the poor Samaritan woman is to represent the whole Gentile world, though she refers to 'our father Jacob ;' and moreover is to exemplify the susceptibility for faith which asks not after signs, though her faith originates entirely from the wonderful insight of the Lord into her life.

3. The section from vers. 16–21 has been considered, after the example of Erasmus, by most theologians in modern times as a carrying out of the conversation of Jesus with Nicodemus, which we are to ascribe to the Evangelist himself (compare Lücke, i. 543 ; Tholuck, p. 123 ; Adalb. Maier, p. 302).   In the first place, it favours this view, that the conversational style is entirely dropped from ver. 16.   Moreover, the expression μονογενής occurs only in discourse that is strictly John's own—for example, i. 14, 18,—not in the discourses of Jesus.   Besides, many expressions betray the later consciousness of the writer which look back to the completed history of Jesus ; such as the past tenses, and among these, especially ἠγάπησαν and ἦν, ver. 19. But the first reason alleged would lead to the supposition, that the conversation communicated by John must be artistically

carried out, but could not merge into an explicatory discourse of
the Lord. But this assumption would be arbitrary and false, since
it is rather in accordance with the character of Christ's ministry
for vivid developments of His teaching to arise out of conversations immediately preceding. As to the expression μονογενής,
and the Evangelist's colouring of the representation, there is no
reason for denying that this expression might have been formed
by the apostle in reporting his recollections. Yet neither is it
inconceivable that John might have taken this expression as
originally used by Christ on this occasion, and incorporated it
with his theology. The passage in ver. 19, apparently, may be
referred most decidedly to a later standpoint. According to
the common conception of the evangelic history, it seems as if
at the time of this conversation no such decision, involving condemnation, as Christ here characterizes it, had taken place. But
if we contemplate the history of the temptation according to
our view of it, and likewise take into account the unfavourable
attitude which a part of the Sanhedrim must have already taken
openly in reference to Jesus—since only such an attitude can
explain the visit by night of Nicodemus,—the condemnation had
already begun. The light had already manifested itself in the
world; it had already called forth a decision and a separation,
though at first only as germinant. On the one hand, the majority of the Jewish rulers, who as the deciding authorities are
called οἱ ἄνθρωποι, had already chosen the darkness. On the
other hand, the upright had begun, although timidly like Nicodemus, to come to the light. Christ could therefore point to the
condemnation as a fact already existing. Therefore the reasons
on account of which some would separate this section from the
conversation itself, are not decisive ; while we, on the contrary,
have cogent reasons for maintaining the unity of the two parts.
Lücke remarks, that everything is wanting by which the transition from the conversation to John's own reflections would be
outwardly marked ; on the other hand, the γὰρ (ver. 16) seems
to mark most distinctly the continuation of the conversation.
Besides, it is to be observed that the conversation would be in its
structure a fragment if it ended with ver. 15, and that it would
break off just where it had begun, and announced an important
conclusion. The ἐπουράνια, namely, which are announced in ver.
12, are partially communicated in vers. 13 and 14 ; the continua-

tion follows from ver. 16 to the close. This *complement* belongs, therefore, altogether to the conversation. But one most decisive circumstance has been altogether overlooked. In the 15th verse there is no special reference to Nicodemus—no farewell; it is all general. On the other hand, vers. 20 and 21 contain a most touching farewell, which marks distinctly the relation of this man to Jesus, as we have already noticed above; since Jesus rebukes with a gentle censure his coming *by night*, and invites him to come to Him for the future in clear daylight.

SECTION VII.

THE LAST PUBLIC TESTIMONY OF THE BAPTIST TO JESUS.

(John iii. 22-36.)

From Jerusalem Jesus betook Himself with His disciples to a district in the land of Judea, which is not more distinctly specified. Here He tarried with them and baptized. On this latter point the Evangelist explains himself more particularly in chap. iv. 2, and remarks that Jesus Himself baptized not, but His disciples. Therefore they baptized by His authority.[1] John the Baptist was at the same time still discharging his office. But he was baptizing at Enon, near Salim; 'because there was much water there,' says the Evangelist. According to the old geographical tradition which we find in Eusebius and Jerome, this town was situated in the Samaritan territory.[2] But the circum-

---

[1] [' Semper is dicitur facere, cui præministratur. . . . Itaque tinguebant discipuli ejus, ut ministri.'—Tertullian, *de baptismo*, c. 11. Similarly Bengel *in loc.*—Alford aptly compares the case of Paul, 1 Cor. i. 14. Lampe objects to all the reasons commonly assigned, and concludes 'res non adeo plana est.'—ED.]

[2] Compare Lücke, *Commentar* i. 553; and Winer, *R. W.B.*, art. *Aenon* and *Salem;* Robinson, ii. 279 [also iii. 298]. The Sâlim which Robinson found not far from Nabulus lies at such a distance from the Jordan, that it is not very probable that Enon was on the banks of that river. Probably it was, according to Lücke, only a place of fountains. עינון is derived from עין a fountain. On the form, see Tholuck, p. 127. But if Enon was situated near the Jordan, the expression 'there was much water there' would not be used without a reason—not so ridiculous as some would wish to make it, for every boy knows that it is not every part of a river's banks which is suited for bathing

stance that the Baptist should baptize on Samaritan ground has
appeared so strange, that it has been preferred to place these
towns lower down, within the bounds of Judea, or to consider
places with names of a similar sound—Silchim[1] or Seleim, and
Ain, which, according to Josh. xv. 32, lay on the most southern
border of Judea—as those which are here specified. But Silchim
is not convertible with Salim, though we might allow Ain to be
used for Enon.   Besides, it is improbable that John, so short a
time before his imprisonment, should have stayed here in the south
of Judea.   We must therefore turn to those places fixed by.
tradition, if we would know anything more exactly about Enon.
But if we were induced to give up the site of Enon, as stated in
Jerome, by remarking that there might be, and actually were,
places in different parts of Palestine which were called 'Fountains' or 'at the pools,' yet it must be observed that here in the
text, as in Jerome, Enon and Salim are closely connected.
When therefore ancient tradition points out two places which
are quite contiguous, as the Gospel history asserts of two like-
named places, and when that tradition maintains that these places
are the same which are here mentioned, we must let the matter
rest.   And in this instance it is nothing to the purpose to remove
the place into the Jewish territory, in order to make the representation more readily explicable, that John baptized there.   The
view must be justified rather on the ground of the judaizing mind
of the Baptist.   That large-hearted theocrat who addressed to
the Pharisees that bold word of Universalism, 'God can of these
stones raise up children unto Abraham,' was able as a prophet
to occupy a standpoint on which he could regard the Samaritans
as a part of the Israelitish family.   It would be committing a
great mistake to confound his theocratic strictness with Jewish
narrow-heartedness, and evince a blunted sensibility to the mental
elevation of that ardent strictness.   How could that mightiest
thunderer in Israel, Elijah, be an inmate so long with a Phœnician widow, if in that zealous spirit there had not been lodged
the germ of the most wide-hearted humanity?   Thus Jonah
was sent to preach repentance to the heathen Ninevites.   But
our text appears to contain several indications that John was now
baptizing in the Samaritan territory.   Probably the Evangelist

---

[1] שָׁלְחִים, or Σιλειμ according to the Cod. Alex. of the Septuagint.

had this contrast in his thoughts when he wrote the singular
clause, 'Jesus came' (from Jerusalem, in the centre of Judea)
'into the land of Judea,' and baptized there. He also assigns
a reason for the remarkable choice of a place by the Baptist, in
the words, 'because there was much water there;' and when he
goes on to say, 'and they came and were baptized,' it seems
as if he meant—'it succeeded, though it seemed hazardous,—
persons presented themselves for baptism even here.'   Also,
the fact, that a Jew[1] disputed with some disciples of John
about the baptism of purification,[2] appears to indicate that this
Jew had some objection to make to the validity of the rite administered by the Baptist. Probably he gave the preference to
the rite which the disciples of Jesus administered, because it
was performed in the land of Judea. But lastly, it might
naturally be expected that the man who was destined to devote
his life to God as the forerunner of Christ, the great restorer of
all Israelities, and in truth of all nations, would at least take the
first steps in his office, to pass beyond the bounds of an exclusive
Judaism. But if any one made objections to this bold enlargement of his sphere, he would probably answer, in a tone of rebuke, I find much water here, and much water I require for the
purification of this people.

Thus, then, Jesus and John for a short time were occupied
near one another in the administration of baptism. The Evangelist adds to his account the explanatory observation, 'John
was not yet cast into prison.' This at least determines the correct chronological relation between the beginning of the history
of the ministry of Jesus, according to John, and the first occur-
rences in the same ministry which are narrated in the synoptic
Gospels.   It has been already remarked, that the synoptists
pass over the beginning of it. But it has been thought surprising that Jesus and John should thus stay and baptize in each
other's vicinity. It may be here asked, especially, why John
did not enrol himself among the disciples of Jesus? This has
already been answered. In this case, John would have relin-

---

[1] 'The preponderating majority of the most important authorities have
'Ιουδαίου instead of 'Ιουδαίων.'—Lücke, i. 555. [So Lachmann, Tischendorf,
Alford, and Wordsworth.]

[2] The expression περὶ καθαρισμοῦ plainly shows that baptism was regarded in its connection with the Jewish symbolic ablutions.

quished the Messianic service which had been specially assigned to him. This must have made him certain, in his position, that Jesus did not require him to be an outward follower. But the other question is more difficult, Why did Jesus allow His disciples to baptize close by John? At the first glance it might seem as if the great act of purifying was thereby divided. But this act was of such significance, that possibly ten zealous theocrats might have administered it in different parts of the land, without breaking up its unity; just as now it is administered by thousands of the clergy throughout the world, and everywhere has the same meaning of incorporation into the Church of Christ. Besides, we cannot but suppose that the disciples who here surround the Lord, and probably consisted of some of John's disciples, whose numbers might be increased by Jewish adherents of Jesus, were accustomed to adopt this method of preparing the way for the kingdom of Christ. And it might be important to them to perform their old work with new joy and mental elevation in the presence of Christ and under His authority.

The relation of the baptism of John to the baptism of Jesus has been often discussed. Tholuck[1] distinguishes the baptism of John from this first baptism of Jesus, and this again from the baptism of the Christian Church, which Jesus instituted before His ascension, and which began after the outpouring of the Holy Spirit. According to Tholuck, the first baptism was into the future Messiah; the second, into the Messiah who had actually come; the third, again, had a character of its own. We may certainly speak of different forms of baptism; but it is not practicable to see in them, at the same time, different kinds of

---

[1] See his *Commentary*, p. 125. [Robert Hall, *Terms of Communion* (postscript), Works ii. 170; also his *Essential Difference between Christian Baptism and the Baptism of John*, Works ii. 175–232.—Tr. Calvin (*Instit.* iv. 15, 18), Turretin (*Instit.* xix. 16), and Witsius (*De Œcon. Fed.* iv. 16, 9) agree in maintaining that the baptism of John agreed with that of Jesus in essentials, but differed in circumstances, and especially in the smaller gift of the Spirit which accompanied that of John. The Council of Trent says summarily (Sess. vii. Can. 1), ' Si quis dixerit, Baptismum Johannis habuisse eandem vim cum baptismo Christi, anathema sit.' Tertullian has been quoted on the other side (*De Baptismo*, c. 4),—' Nec quicquam refert inter eos, quos Joannes in Jordane et quos Petrus in Tiberi tinxit;' but this he said only to show that there was no special sanctity in any particular water. In chap. 11 of the same treatise he takes up the above question. Burnett (*On the Thirty-nine Articles*, Art. 27) also treats it, but is not satisfactory.—Ed.]

baptism, It is here of the first importance to determine the peculiar significance of baptism. The essential character of baptism lies not in its various relations to the appearance of the Messiah, but in its symbolically representing the purification (the καθαρισμός) of the defiled for the pure host, the community or society of the Messiah. Hence there is only one proper baptismal rite from the beginning of the tabernacle to the end of the world—the water-baptism of the theocratic community, as a symbol of the Spirit-baptism by which this community is converted from a typical into a real community of God. The Spirit-baptism of Christ is, after all, the only proper baptism, when we speak of the essence of baptism and not of the rite. On the other hand, water-baptism is the only proper baptism, when we speak of the rite and not of its essential significance. Hence Lücke[1] is justified in maintaining ‘the essential identity of John's baptism with Christ's water-baptism;’ only it easily creates a misconception to designate the latter baptism as water-baptism. The relation of symbolical to essential baptism is represented in a threefold manner. On the one hand stands the baptism of John—water-baptism connected with the promise of Spirit-baptism. On the other hand stands the proper baptism of Christ—the Spirit-baptism connected with the sacramental sealing by means of water-baptism. Between these two appears the third form of baptism, the transitional form—a water-baptism which was supplemented by the beginning of the Spirit-baptism. The baptism of the Christian Church may appear in all these forms.[2] That water-baptism which some disciples of Jesus administered for a while under His inspection in Judea, may be regarded as a transitional form. Christ permitted His disciples this kind of ministry, while He supplemented it by His own.

But why, then, did the disciples suddenly abandon their administration of baptism? For this we must suppose, since, till the founding of the Christian Church at Pentecost, we hear no more of baptism. On this striking fact Lücke makes the following remark (*Commentar* i. 559) : ‘Must not the reason of this have been, that definite faith in Jesus the Christ, as involved in baptism, appeared so seldom in the lifetime of Jesus,

[1] *Commentar* i. 551.

[2] In compulsory baptism it sinks below John's baptism ; for compulsory baptism is, properly speaking, no baptism.

THE LAST PUBLIC TESTIMONY OF THE BAPTIST TO JESUS.

and so much the less, as Christ, in reference to His adherents, attended more to their selection than to increasing their number?' But yet, during the whole period of Christ's ministry, individual confessors of His Messiahship were always coming forward, who, according to Lücke's supposition, must have submitted to baptism. This difficulty can only be explained from the far too little understood social significance of baptism. Baptism constituted a distinct contrast between the old impure, and the new purified community. As long as the Baptist and Christ were not checked in their ministry, the Israelitish social body (*Societät*) might be regarded as a community making a transition from impurity to purity. But no sooner was the Baptist, the primary organ of purification, imprisoned, and the guilt of his execution laid on the tetrarch of Galilee, and mediately on the whole land, than the state of the case was altered. Whither should the baptized in Galilee be directed and conducted? The circumstance that the baptism of Jesus was questioned in the Sanhedrim (iv. 1), might render doubtful the admissibility of further baptisms. The nation, as a nation, could no longer be baptized when the representatives of the nation gave positive indications that this act appeared to them objectionable or suspicious. But as Jesus not long after was treated by the Sanhedrim as an excommunicated person (John ix. 22), it would have been in the highest degree against the truth and social sense of honour, if He had introduced baptized persons into that social body which had excommunicated Him. But as little was it the time when, in contrast to the impure host, He could have formed a pure one into an outward Christian society. He must now go out of that camp bearing His reproach (Heb. xiii. 13), and, by the baptism of blood which He endured, a people were collected who were ready to go with Him out of that camp and to present themselves opposite to it as His Church. Hence baptism was now soon suspended till the completion of His work.

Through the ministry of Christ, the baptism of His disciples gained a fuller meaning and made a more powerful impression than the baptism of John. For it so happened that the confluence of the people to Jesus became greater, while that to the Baptist declined. This mortified John's disciples; and, moreover, at last the reproaches which that Jew mentioned by the Evangelist seems to have cast upon them, aroused their jealousy.

So they hasten to him and vent their complaints. 'Rabbi, He that was with thee beyond Jordan, to whom thou barest witness, behold, the same baptizeth, and all men come to Him.' They avoid mentioning the name of Jesus—a suspicious sign! They seem to wish to suggest to their master, that Jesus, on the other side Jordan, had allowed Himself to be reckoned as one of his disciples. At all events, they would fasten upon Him an abuse of the witness borne to Him by John : now that He has the attestation, they mean to say, He requites the Baptist by commencing His own ministry, and renouncing his acquaintance. Undeniably an envious thought of this kind oozes out in their discourse. And now the full greatness of the Baptist is shown in contrast with the littleness of his disciples : in them only the most superficial of his once flourishing school were left to him, while he had dismissed the best to the school of Jesus. Solemnly, and with an inspired sacerdotal presentiment of his approaching tragical exit, and of the incipient glorification of Jesus, he yet once more bears his testimony to Him : 'A man can receive nothing except it be given him from heaven.' Ye yourselves bear me witness that I said, I am not the Christ, but that I am sent before Him.' He then describes the glorious position of Jesus. 'He that hath the bride, is the bridegroom.' To Him belongs the Church of God in its noble first-fruits as well as in all its future members, the community of those who are susceptible of life from God; in Him it recognises its beloved Lord who brings to it the life of God. Since the Church of God hastens to Him as a bride, it marks Him as the bridegroom. But the friend of the bridegroom is free from envy; rather he rejoices with cordial sympathy. The happy and jubilant tone of the bridegroom's voice moves his friend's soul to greater joy. 'This my joy,' the Baptist says with unconscious dignity to his little disciples, who in their poverty of soul would importune him not to give up his reputation unenviously to his greater successor—'is now fulfilled. He must increase, but I must decrease.' His eye then brightens into prophetic clearness, that he may once more behold and announce the Messianic glory of Jesus. 'He that cometh from above is above all,' he exclaims. 'He that is of the earth, is earthly, and speaketh of the earth. He that cometh from heaven is above all.' How the one, the Adamic man, rises out of the poor earth. He is in his origin earthly-minded, and cannot perfectly rise above himself. Even his illumination, and the very expressions of his rapture, are still affected with earthly obscurity, in contrast to the clear intuition of Him who comes from heaven in the royal perfection of the new life, and who is decidedly above all. Conformably to this inspired hymn, in which he expresses with the deepest humility the whole contrast between the Adamic and the Christian æon—between the men who are of the earth, among whom he reckons himself, in contrast to Christ, and the man from heaven—he turns to his disciples in their littleness with the admonitory declaration, 'And what He who cometh from heaven hath seen and heard, that He testifieth. But though He announces heavenly things with an intuition clear as heaven itself, no man receiveth His testimony.' The critic here reminds us, with annoying literality, that this contradicts the preceding account (ver. 26): 'all men come to Him.' This is indeed a contradiction, but it is a contradiction of the noble-minded master against his little-minded disciples. For them it was far too much—they saw all men run to Jesus; for him it was far too little. Manifestly he would have gladly sent them also to Jesus; and if they were not willing to go, he would gladly have got rid of them. 'He that receiveth His testimony,' he then adds by way of encouragement, 'hath set to his seal that God is true.' From what follows, it is evident that the Baptist uttered these highly important words in the most original sense. For thus he proves his own expression: 'He whom God hath sent, speaketh the words of God.' He speaks the words of God simply; that is, all God's words, which the various prophets had spoken in parts, He utters together in the living unity of His word, in complete revelation. 'For God giveth not the Spirit in limited measure,' since He now gives it to Him in its perfected clearness. Christ has it in its fulness. Whoever therefore repairs to Christ, proves that he recognises His words as the words of God—that therefore all the words of Christ agree with all the words of all the prophets; but not merely with these, but also with all the exigencies of his spiritual life produced by God. And herein lies the strongest confirmation of the truthfulness of God in its highest manifestation, which consists exactly in the agreement of all His words and operations. It is a beautiful verification of the truthfulness of God, that the leaf of the plant agrees with its flower, and the flower with man's sense of the beautiful. But the highest glorification of the divine truthfulness is revealed in this—that the positive revelation of God in Christ agrees with the word of God in faithful hearts, with the faith of the elect. But this agreement of faithful hearts with the words of Christ must be quite perfect, since He has the fulness of the Spirit, so that no deficiency of the Spirit can form breaches and divisions between Him and His people. 'Yea, the Father loveth the Son' (the seer proceeded to say), 'and hath given all things into His hand.'

Thus the Baptist crowns his Messianic knowledge with the most luminous recognition, and then closes his exhortation as the forerunner with a sentence which is altogether worthy of the great zealot. 'He that believeth on the Son hath everlasting life; and he that *obeyeth not* (ἀπειθῶν) the Son shall not see life, (no, not from afar,) but the wrath of God abideth on him.' Such a man refuses to conduct himself aright towards the principle of life, and central point in which the whole world finds life, light, love, and salvation, and gains its pure ideality; and thus he takes a disturbing, hostile, false position against this Prince of life, against God, against the world and his own life. Wherefore the whole government of God must reveal itself to him as an overpowering, destructive, and fiery reaction of the righteousness of God; the wrath of God remains over him, its weight evermore pressing on him more powerfully and crushingly. This denunciation of the Baptist may be regarded as the last utterance of the Old Testament—the final peal of thunder from Sinai in the New Testament.

NOTES.

1. Schneckenburger, in his very learned work on the *Antiquity of the Jewish Proselyte Baptism and its connection with the Baptism of John and Christian Baptism (Ueber das Alter der jüdischen Proselytentaufe und deren Zusammenhang mit dem Johanneischen und christlichen Ritus*), combats the view which deduces John's baptism from a baptism of proselytes before the Christian era. His view is as follows (p. 184): '(i.) The regular admission of strangers into Judaism, as long as the temple stood, was by circumcision and sacrifice. A lustration followed the former and preceded the latter, like every other sacrifice, which, like all the other lustrations, was esteemed merely as a Levitical purification. (ii.) This lustration was not distinguished

in outward form from the ordinary lustrations, but was performed like those, merely by the proselytes on themselves. (iii.) This lustration by degrees, yet not demonstrably before the end of the third century, took the place of the sacrifices which had been discontinued, etc.' The above-named learned writer has laid too great stress on the difference, that the proselyte did not undergo the lustration by means of another person, but performed it himself. Even in John's baptism of the persons to be purified, the Baptist did not dispense with the self-purification, but on the one hand, before baptism, represented the excommunicating, and on the other hand, after baptism, the receiving Church.[1] The fundamental idea in which all the lustrations were one—namely, that they were intended to purify men symbolically for their entrance into the fellowship of the pure community—ought to have been placed in the foreground of the disquisition. If the people of Israel were obliged to wash their clothes at Sinai (Exod. xix. 10); if Aaron and his sons, before putting on their priestly vestments, were to wash themselves before the door of the tabernacle (Exod. xxix. 4); they were obliged to undergo, as to its symbolical meaning, the same purification as the leper when he was purified. But that purification the person to be purified performs on himself, because it relates to the merely probable, or to the daily leper defilements which would not necessitate the defiled to a sojourn without the camp, to which a number of leper defilements belonged (compare Lev. xv., xvii., etc.). This, on the contrary, the priest performed before the camp, since he sprinkled upon the leper seven times with water (Lev. xiv. 7). We have here also a lustration which the priest performed on a Jew in order to his being received again into the congregation; and therefore, even according to Schneckenburger's distinction, a kind of baptism. It is a very remarkable fact, that the Jews who (according to Num. xxxi. 19) had, in fighting with the Midianites, come in contact with the corpses of the slaughtered Gentiles, were obliged to remain without the camp seven days, and to be purified by being sprinkled with water. In the same manner, they were

---

[1] [So it was appointed by rabbinical law that proselyte baptism should be administered in presence of three wise and trustworthy Israelites, who should see that all was duly performed. Witsius thinks there is a reference to this in the three witnesses of 1 John v. 7.—ED.]

obliged to purify their captives whom they kept as slaves, and
also their boooty; they were even to pass through fire whatever
could bear it, such as gold and silver, and other metals. Moreover, the passages are to be noticed which relate to the reception
of Gentiles into Israel (Josh. vi. 23, ix. 28; Ruth. iii. 3), as well
as the seven times washing in Jordan prescribed to the Gentile
leper Naaman (2 Kings v. 10), which corresponded to the sevenfold sprinkling of the Israelitish lepers. Also the washing of
Judith (Jud. xii. 8) may here be noticed. Thus much is evident from the Old Testament, that the Jews themselves who had
come in contact with Gentiles, to say nothing of the Gentiles,
were obliged to undergo a lustration. For this reason the
sprinkling of the Gentiles promised by the prophets (Isa. lii. 15)
denotes their solemn and actual reception into the theocratic
community.   From this significance of the Old Testament lustration, we can understand why Peter regarded the deluge as a
baptism of purification for the human race preserved in the
family of Noah (1 Peter iii. 21), and why Paul also looked
upon the passage of the Israelites through the Red Sea as a
baptism (purifying them from contact with the Egyptians),
1 Cor. x. 1, compared with Heb. x. 22. As to the Jewish
testimonies on this subject from the times of Christ, Schneckenburger (p. 103) quotes a passage from Philo (*ed. Mang.* ii. 658),
on which he decides as on another: In these passages reception
into Judaism is spoken of; so it appears that no doubt respecting the existence of proselyte baptism can any longer be entertained. But, in fact, Philo here appears to characterize the three
conditions of reception into Judaism—circumcision, ablutions or
baptism, and sacrifice—in descriptions for the uninitiated, in the
same manner as the ancient Christians in the *disciplina arcani*
treated and described the Christian forms of consecration as
mysteries. Accordingly, ὁσιότης would be a periphrasis for
circumcision, καθάρσεις for baptism, and ἐνέχυρον for sacrifice.
The passages which the author (p. 79) quotes from Arrian [1] and

---

[1] [The quotation from Arrian referred to (*Epictet.* ii. 9) which speaks of
Jews as baptized, is rendered invalid by the great probability that Arrian
might confound Jews with Christians. Cyprian is too late to be of any use
as a witness, for long before his day there was a manifest tendency among
the Jews to baptize. As early as Justin Martyr there was a Jewish sect
known as the Baptizers (*Dial. c. Tryph.* 307).—ED.]

(p. 127) from Cyprian, obtain their full significance only if, as has been remarked, the various Jewish lustrations are viewed in their common significance; and in connection with this discussion, the talmudic and rabbinical accounts which have been adduced, appear as witnesses that those ablutions which the proselytes had to undergo, after the time of Christ, certainly gained an increased consideration, yet without becoming for the first time a rite of consecration.[1]

2. In modern times the section vers. 31–36 has been held to be a further simplification by the Evangelist, in which he has developed the testimony of the Baptist. As to the supposed contradiction between ver. 26 and ver. 32, which has been urged in favour of this view, the explanation already given is sufficient. When, further, doubts are entertained about attributing to the Baptist the profound christological expressions that follow, it appears to be overlooked, in reference to this passage, as in other cases, that we have to recognise in the Baptist not merely an expounder of the Old Testament, not merely a zealous preacher of repentance, but a prophet, who, like Isaiah and Ezekiel, in inspired utterances could express profound insight into the nature of the Messiah, which far transcended his common matured views. And it is well to bear in mind that we have here before us his last testimony to the glory of Jesus. But the close of the discourse is altogether conformable to the Old Testament standpoint of the Baptist; the wrath of God is denounced on the unbelieving. The circumstance that the Baptist speaks in the present tense, as Lücke remarks, favours the opinion that the Baptist is here continuing his own discourse. Lücke admits that the Evangelist mingles his own train of thought with the discourse of the Baptist. But we believe that in this section there exists the unmixed stream of thought of one in a state of mental transport. No doubt the Evangelist's phraseology has contributed to the form of the representation. But if here John the Baptist speaks like the Evangelist, it is

---

[1] [The English reader who desires to pursue this subject will find all the material for doing so in Selden, *De Jure Naturæ et Gent.* ii. 2 ; Lightfoot, *Hor. Heb.* on Matt. iii. 6; or Wall's *History of Infant Baptism* (Introd.), where the passages from Jewish writers are given in detail and commented upon. Gale's 9th and 10th Letters in reply to Wall ought also to be considered, though much of what he adduces is quite beside the point.—Ed.]

right to recollect that possibly the Evangelist might, in some measure, learn from his former teacher to express himself like John the Baptist. The hypothesis that this section originated in the desire of the author of the fourth Gospel to exhibit a more favourable testimony of the Baptist to Christ than history furnished, in order to make an impression on John's disciples, is, to say the least, in the highest degree unworthy of him; and it is almost needless to remark, that a Christian, apart from inclination, could hardly be so simple as to hope that by such a fiction he could make the disciples of John uncertain of their own tradition.

SECTION VIII.

THE CONVERSATION OF JESUS WITH THE SAMARITAN WOMAN.

(John iv. 1–42.)

Jesus had carried on His ministry in Judea with success probably for more than half a year, when suddenly the hostile feeling of the pharisaical party compelled Him to quit the region that had been so highly favoured. The Evangelist only slightly hints at the cause of this interruption. The Lord had been informed, and indeed was well aware (ἔγνω), that 'the Pharisees had heard that Jesus[1] made and baptized more disciples than John.' He had been denounced, and the denunciation had taken effect. But as soon as the ill-will of the Sanhedrim offered opposition to His ministry in this theocratic form, He withdrew, as we have seen, for the sake of social order and truth. But that He at once left Judea, was a consequence of His now modified position. Not only the foresight with which He avoided hazarding His life till the decisive moment, but also the holiness of His consciousness, which abhorred all intermingling of the kingdom of heaven with a corrupt hierarchy, drove Him from the public scene of action in Judea. And there was besides an-

[1] That the name of Jesus is introduced here instead of the pronoun, makes the sentence appear as a report,—as *the* report of those who had first stated the fact to the Pharisees.

other serious motive.[1] John was just about this time cast into prison by Herod (Matt. iv. 12; Mark i. 14). This imprisonment was, it is true, the act of the ruler of Galilee, but it gave, most probably, great satisfaction to the Sanhedrim. To that body the disturber of their repose seemed now put out of the way. But there appeared immediately, as they thought, a greater one in his place (John iv. 1).[2] Hence by the imprisonment of John the Sanhedrim appeared to be excited, and inclined to remove the second hated preacher of repentance, of whom they knew that He did not suit their plans.

Jesus had gone up to the feast at Jerusalem in the month of March. When He returned it was about seed-time, as may be inferred with probability from ver. 35, and therefore in November or December.[3] He took His way directly through Samaria, as He often did, without troubling Himself about the scruples of the Jews, who preferred making the journey between Judea and Galilee through Perea. But this time He had a special reason for going through Samaria: because He was probably already near the Samaritan border.[4] He must (ἔδει) therefore, under the circumstances, take this route.

A place in Samaria, in which He stayed a short time, claims our attention on three accounts: for its name; for its local and historical relations; and for a memorable relic of former times, Jacob's well. It has been generally supposed that the city of Sichem[5] was the place where Jesus sojourned, but it is remarkable that the Evangelist calls it Sychar. According to different derivations, the place obtained the nickname of *the town of the drunken,* or, *the town of falsehood.*[6] But a third derivation

---

[1] See Maier's *Commentar,* p. 327.

[2] On Wieseler's chronological view in his *Chronol. Syn.* p. 224, compare what has been said above, p. 4.

[3] Wieseler adopts the latest terminus, since he puts off the journey to January 782. [Meyer, Lichtenstein, and Ellicott prefer December. Alford thinks that ver. 35 does not afford a safe chronological datum.—ED.]

[4] Maier, *Commentar,* p. 328.

[5] שְׁכֶם, Συχὲμ, Σίκιμα (Acts vii. 16), afterwards *Flavia Neapolis,* in honour of the Emperor Vespasian—the modern Nablûs.

[6] The derivation is 'either from שֶׁקֶר, a lie, the lying city, alluding to the Samaritan worship on Mount Gerizim, at the foot of which Sichem lay; or from שִׁכֹּר, *drunken,* with a reference to Isa. xxviii. 1, where Samaria is

makes the name a title of honour, *the town of the sepulchre;*[1] and
since this designation has the support of Jewish tradition,[2] it is
to be preferred to the former, which rests on mere conjecture.
If John had wished to intimate that Jesus was not ashamed to
connect Himself with the citizens of that centre of Samaritan
life, which by the Jews was called the abode of drunkenness or
falsehood, he would have brought it forward more distinctly.
But indeed he could without difficulty make use of a more significant designation, deviating from the common appellation, if
it were already known, since he was fond of significant names.
Yet it was also possible that the Sychar of the Evangelist was
distinguished from Sichem proper as a suburb.   According to
Schubert's route,[3] travellers come first to Jacob's well, where ' a
few houses are standing close ;' then they reach Joseph's grave,
' in a hollow of Mount Gerizim;' and then, ' farther westward in
the valley, the modern Sichem.'   The city of Sychar, as fixed
by the Evangelist, lay near the parcel of ground that Jacob, as
the Israelitish tradition reports, according to Josh. xxiv. 32, gave
to his son Joseph.   The district in which the modern Sychem is
situated, is, according to K. v. Raumer,[4] compared by Clarke to
the country about Heidelberg.

called " the crown of pride to the drunkards of Ephraim."   In Sirach l. 26
it is said, καὶ ὁ λαὸς μωρὸς ὁ κατοικῶν ἐν Σικίμοις.'—Lücke, i. 577.

[1] So Hug in his *Einleitung*, iii. 218, derives the word from סובר, remarking that it denotes the burial-place where the bones of Joseph (Josh. xxiv.
32) and, according to a report common in the times of Jesus, the bodies of the
twelve patriarchs of the people of Israel were deposited (Acts vii. 15, 16).

[2] In the Talmud, the name of a place עין סובר occurs.   Wieseler finds in
this (p. 256) a designation of the city of Sychar, since he translates the
words *the fountain of Sychar*.   Apart from this, the appellation of *the fountain of the sepulchre* might connect for the Israelites, in a very significant
manner, the hallowed well of Jacob with the hallowed sepulchre, and thus
the name Sychar might originate.

[3] It is worthy of notice, that according to both Schubert and Robinson,
the ancient Sichem was situated nearer Jacob's well than the modern town.
Besides this, it is to be observed, that in the days of Eusebius, Sychar and
Sichem were regarded as two places; a view to which Eusebius himself
assents (*Onomast.* art. Sichar, Sichem).   Robinson would find in this tradition confusion and inconsistency, but does not give his reasons (ii. 292).
But if Jerome treated the reading Sychar in the Gospel of John as false,
this at least is important, that in his treating of the *Onomasticon* of Eusebius
he passes over his view of it in silence.

[4] *Palästina*, p. 159.

'The city of Nábulus' (the former Sichem), says Robinson,[1] 'is long and narrow, stretching close along the north-east base of Mount Gerizim, in this small, deep valley, half-an-hour distant from the great eastern plain. The streets are narrow; the houses high, and in general well built, all, of stone, with domes upon the roofs as at Jerusalem. The valley itself, from the foot of Gerizim to that of Ebal, is here not more than some 500 yards wide, extending from south-east to north-west. . . . Mounts Gerizim and Ebal rise in steep, rocky precipices immediately from the valley on each side, apparently some 800 feet in height. The sides of both these mountains, as here seen, were to our eyes equally naked and sterile; although some travellers have chosen to describe Gerizim as fertile, and confine the sterility to Ebal. The only exception in favour of the former, so far as we could perceive, is a small ravine coming down opposite the west end of the town, which indeed is full of fountains and trees; in other respects, both mountains, as here seen, are desolate, except that a few olive-trees are scattered upon them.'[2]

The same travellers found the noted Jacob's well, 35 minutes distance from the town. The well had evident marks of antiquity, but was now dry and forsaken. According to Maundrell, the well was dug in a hard rock, was about nine feet in diameter and 105 feet in depth. It was full of water to the height of 15 feet. But, according to Robinson, the old town probably lay nearer this well than the present. Yet he remarks this could not have been the proper well of the town, since there was no public machinery for drawing water. As the woman came hither and drew water, we must suppose that either she lived near the well, or that the inhabitants attached a particular value to the water of this ancient Jacob's well, and now and then took the trouble to go and draw from it.

The well was held in great veneration from the tradition connected with it; the Samaritans were proud of this inherit-

[1] *Biblical Researches* ii. 275.

[2] It must not be forgotten that Robinson saw Gerizim in the middle of June. But in the hot season many tracts of the warm south lose the ornament of grass and other kinds of vegetation which they possess in another part of the year. Von Schubert saw Gerizim in April, yet he speaks only of the foot of the mountain, which he describes as fertile compared with Ebal. In the same way it may be explained that Robinson found Jacob's well dry. Schubert, on the contrary, tasted its 'refreshing water.'

ance of the patriarch Jacob. Jesus was weary with travelling when He reached it, and so sat down at the edge of the well. It was about mid-day. The disciples were gone into the city to buy food. Jesus therefore accustomed them to combat and lay aside their Jewish prejudices. There came a Samaritan woman to draw water. Jesus said to her, 'Give Me to drink!' These few words were of infinite significance and efficacy. It was the beginning of that agency of Christ's Spirit which broke down the ancient partition-wall of grudge and hatred between the Jews and Samaritans, who afterwards were to enter the Church of Christ. It shows how an inoffensive, humble request does wonders. But not only that the Lord made His request to a Samaritan woman, and to a woman alone, but lastly, and more especially, to a sinful, erring woman, exhibits Him in the full freedom and grandeur of His love. For, as to the first point, it would have been an offence to any Jew, for the Jews avoided all intercourse with the Samaritans; as to the second point, every Rabbi would have taken offence, since, especially for Rabbis, it was unbecoming to converse alone with foreign women; and, thirdly, it would have been an offence to every Pharisee, for it was a pharisaical maxim that the fallen were to be treated with severity. Thus, then, this brief request of the Lord at one and the same time displayed His spiritual glory in three directions. The woman was at once struck with the extraordinary character of this address. She recognised in the language, or in the dress and in the whole bearing of the Man, to what nation He belonged, and could not forbear expressing her astonishment: 'How is it that Thou, being a Jew, askest drink of me, which am a woman of Samaria?'

Although the woman might vaguely be sensible of the condescension of this wonderful Jew, yet she seemed disposed to gratify her national feeling at His need of help. She lays great stress on the circumstance, that He, the supposed proud Jew, is the petitioner, that in His need He is now depending on her benevolence. Her tone leads the Lord to bring forward the opposite relation: that she is the needy person, and that He is the possessor of the true fountain of satisfaction. Oh! hadst thou known to value the gift of God, this singular opportunity, and who it is that offers thee to drink, thou wouldst have asked of Him, and not in vain: He would have given thee living water, water gushing from the fountain. He shows that her answer was quite beside the mark. She made a difficulty of granting the smallest request; He wished from the first to be bountiful to her in granting the highest object of desire. Thus the way of salvation is opened for the heart of a poor creature lost in vanity, but, as it appears, impelled by a deep, ardent longing. The woman takes the figurative language literally : ' Sir,' she says, ' Thou hast nothing to draw with, and the well is deep; from whence, then, hast Thou that living water ? Art Thou greater than our father Jacob, which gave us the well, and drank thereof himself, and his children, and his cattle ?' Still she would persuade herself that He is the needy person, although she cannot get rid of the impression that He is no ordinary man. But since she fancies that He presents Himself to her in Jewish pride as ready to confer a favour, her national feeling rises still higher; she stands before Him as a daughter of Jacob, and will not allow Him to depreciate her Jacob's well. If one on this occasion spoke to her of superior living water or spring-water, she first of all assumed that he must draw it from the depths of this well. But since Jesus had no vessel for drawing, He seemed disposed to extol perhaps some fountain in the neighbourhood, in preference to the water of this well. But for that He was bound to show a higher authority than that of their father Jacob. Probably it belonged to the orthodoxy of the Samaritans, that the water of this well was superior to that of the neighbouring fountains, and they fortified themselves in this opinion by the authority of the family of Jacob. However sinful the woman was, she strictly adhered to the preservation of the tradition. But Jesus now brought her to institute a comparison between His fountain and her well. ' Whosoever drinketh of this water shall thirst again ; but whosoever drinketh of the water that I shall give him, shall never thirst ; but the water that I shall give him shall be in him a well of water, springing up into everlasting life.' This is again in the Lord's wonted manner; it is the decisive word, uttered with the greatest confidence, and rousing the soul of the hearer from its lowest depths. She cannot deny that the water of Jacob's well, however excellent, cannot quench the thirst for ever. But now she requests the Lord to give her a draught of that water which will quench her thirst for ever. This promise must surely have awakened in her a misgiving

feeling of her wants—of the wants of her eternity! Still more
the promise, that this mysterious water would be converted in
the person who partook of it into a fountain from which streams
would flow in rich abundance throughout eternity. The critics
make the remark, that in John's Gospel the Lord always speaks
so high, everywhere too high for the understandings of His
hearers. It is true He everywhere speaks equally high, down
out of high heaven itself, as the Baptist says. And how could
He speak lower? But it is manifest that He speaks here as
clearly as possible. Nicodemus receives the promise of the
Spirit under the image of the blowing wind, of the fresh vital-
izing wind which brings the fresh vernal life; the Samaritan
woman receives it under the image of a wonderful fountain
flowing for ever through an eternal world, and able to quench
all her thirst, even her deep, obscure longings. And they both
hear Him with a successful result; as all do who hear Him with
susceptibility. To this promise the woman answered, 'Sir, give
me this water, that I thirst not, neither come hither to draw.'
She can now no longer suppose that He is speaking of earthly
water, though she has no clear perception of the heavenly water.
At all events, the presentiment of a wonderful satisfying of her
unsatisfied life is awakened in her. It is indeed strange that she
says, 'Give me that water, that I come not hither to draw!'
But perhaps the visits of the woman to Jacob's well were connected with the impression of a meritorious sanctity in them as
a kind of religious service. At least, according to Robinson,
there must have been wells at Sichem which lay nearer the
town. In that case she might easily surmise that her journeys
would come to an end as soon as she obtained such satisfaction.
At all events, her answer is not to be understood as said in ridicule; it rather seems to express the awakening of an unlimited
confidence in this wonderful personage.

The answer of the Lord has been thought strange. Suddenly breaking off from what He had been conversing upon, He
commands her, 'Go, call thy husband, and come hither!' This
apparent digression in the discourse has been thus explained:
The woman now required to be led back to her own life—to be
conducted to self-knowledge and repentance. And as it was
necessary for Nicodemus to get an insight into his entire spiritual
ignorance before he could be benefited by higher communica-

tions, particularly respecting the person of Jesus, so this woman needed to be made sensible of her own unworthiness. But although the Lord had this result in view, yet He might not have used the requirement, 'Call thy husband!' as a pretext in order to lead her to a confession of her criminal course of life. Rather a second motive was combined with that first, and caused Him to ask for her husband. It has been remarked, that it was a rule laid down by the Rabbis, that no man should converse for any length of time with a female, particularly with a stranger, and that Christ had this rule in His eye. Lücke, on the contrary, starts the question, 'If He had any regard for this, why did He not earlier break off the conversation, or indeed why did He enter upon it at all?' Certainly Christ, according to rabbinical notions, would not have ventured to enter on such a conversation with the woman. But at this moment a turn occurred in the conversation which made the presence of the husband imperative according to a right superior to the rabbinical, when the wife stood (generally speaking) under the rightful authority of a husband. Hitherto the conversation had been the free intercourse of persons brought transiently into each other's company, and as such raised above the exactions of a punctilious casuistry or scrupulous conventionality. But now, since the woman had shown herself disposed to become a disciple of Jesus, to enter into a nearer relation to Him, it was proper that her husband should now be present. According to Jewish regulations, a wife was not permitted to receive special religious instruction from a Rabbi without the sanction of her husband; indeed, such a condition is involved in the very nature of the marriage relation. The Lord therefore at this moment required, according to the highest, most exact social rights, that the woman should call her husband, though He already knew that she was not living in lawful wedlock.[1] The woman replied,

[1] [The author has been censured for this interpretation, on the ground that, in the case of this woman, who had but a paramour and no husband, there was no 'social right' existing which our Lord could meet. On the other hand, it is difficult to believe that our Lord had no meaning in His order, save to convince of sin; that He did not intend that, first of all, His order should be executed. 'Nugas sane meras hic agunt Patres, quando ea de causa id postulatum esse putant, quod non satis honestum videretur, nuptæ mulieri quicquam donari inscio marito. . . . Neque tamen etiam illis adscendo, qui simulato solum Jesum id jussisse volunt, ut scilicet tan-

'I have no husband.' Upon that the Lord rejoins, and surely with a penetrating look, 'Thou hast well said, I have no husband; for thou hast had five husbands, and he whom thou now hast is not thy husband; in that saidst thou (too) truly.' Confounded, the woman replied, 'Sir, I perceive that Thou art a prophet.' She admitted that He had hit the mark; that He had by one stroke depicted her life. And that she had been conscience-struck by the words of Jesus, is plain from the sequel; she declared to the people in the city, that Christ had told her all things that ever she did.

We pass over the trivial remarks, by which this wonderful insight of Christ has been accounted for as merely accidental, or represented as a glance of absolute omniscience, and impossible. For it is obvious that we have here to do with the insight of the God-man's deep knowledge of the soul and of life. That a woman has a husband, or is not a virgin, or that a woman is living in a criminal connection—this might perhaps be found out by any other person well versed in the study of human nature. But Christ could read the whole guilty history of the woman in her appearance. And as the forester concludes respecting the age of a tree from the rings in the wood, so Jesus found the different impressions of the psychical influence of the men with whom the woman had stood transiently in connection, again in her appearance. For it must be granted that every life-relation of this kind will leave a trace behind that is discernible by the eye of the highest intelligence. But especially must the images of these men have been strongly reflected in the psychical life of a woman who had been involved so deeply in the sexual relation. Perhaps, also, she had acquired from one a bigoted, from another a fickle disposition, and from another, again, other traits of character which were distinctly apparent.[1] It was sufficient, however, that Jesus read the

tum viam ad sequens colloquium idoneam sterneret' (Lampe, i. 729). If, then, our Lord wished the woman to bring her husband, what was the reason of this? May it not have been that, in the presence of him with whom she had sinned, she might be shown the evil of her sin; and that, with the reality of her guilty life thus distinctly brought to view, she might receive that 'living water' she had asked for? Otherwise, she might have thought it a gift that bore no relation to her present guilt and future character.—ED.]

[1] [Yet if such insight as this is not to be ascribed to the divinity of

history of her life in her being, in her soul. He expressed her guilt, but also her misery. She had probably passed through a succession of divorces, of which, at all events, she had shared the criminality, and now lived in an immoral relation, either because her last marriage had not yet been dissolved, or because she had disengaged herself from the obligations of social morality. She was a great sinner, but also unhappy; in spite of all the confused restlessness of her soul in which she had been connected with so many husbands one after another, she had no husband. The words of Jesus had struck her conscience. She admitted her guilt in a dexterous manner, by making the admission to the Lord that He now spoke like a prophet. 'But great is in her the impression of prophetic knowledge.' It appears, in fact, that she comes to the following question not merely to ward off Christ's reproof, but in the earnest spirit of religious inquiry.

She brings forward the most decided point of controversy between the Jews and Samaritans, on which she wished to learn the prophet's judgment: 'Our fathers worshipped in this mountain.' In these words she referred to the adjacent mountain Gerizim, on which the Samaritans formerly, in the time of Nehemiah, had erected a temple, and on which they even now offered their prayers, though about the year 129 John Hyrcanus destroyed the temple. 'But ye say,' she continued, 'that Jerusalem is the place where men ought to worship.' That was the point in dispute. But Jesus shows her the reconciliation in the distance which would consist in a decided elevation of both parties above the ancient antagonism: 'Woman, believe Me, the hour cometh, when ye shall neither on this mountain nor yet at Jerusalem worship the Father.' Then this division will be made up in a higher union. But in the meantime He de-

Christ's person, it is difficult to select or suppose any case in which His divinity may be said to be operative. If it is not to be kept in the background throughout His life, and conceived of as a mere inoperative constituent of His person, as the necessary condition or substratum of perfect humanity, then surely this is an instance of which we may say, Divinity is here directly in exercise. We would not, as is too commonly done, separate what God has so joined that they never exist in separation; we would not say, Up to this point humanity is in exercise, and here divinity comes into action; but we would point to such cases as that before us, and say confidently, *There* is something more than mere human faculty.—ED.]

clares that the Jews were in the right in opposition to the
Samaritans. 'Ye worship,' He says, 'ye know not what;' that
is, the object of your worship, your God, is no longer an object
of true knowledge for you, since you have given up the continuance of His revelations, the constant guidance of His Spirit
until the appearing of salvation. 'But we,' He adds, 'know
what we worship; for salvation is of the Jews.' The true Jews
worship the God of a continued revelation. The proof lies in
this, that salvation comes forth from Judaism. Therein it is
shown that their worship, in the best part of the nation, in their
chosen, is clear, true knowledge. This knowledge is matured in
the life-power and form of salvation. But now He leads the
woman beyond the difference between the Jews and Samaritans,
after He had humbled the proud Samaritan in her, as a little
before He had humbled the sinner. He announces to her a
new religion, the commencement of which already existed in
the true worshippers. Spirit and Truth are the holy mountains
of worship for them, the temples in which they stand to offer
prayer. And such worshippers God seeks; His Spirit forms
them; and with them alone He enters into an everlasting living
communion. And this in conformity to His nature. Since He
is spirit, the infinitely free, conscious, omnipresent life, so the
worshipper only reaches Him when he worships God in spirit,
in the inward self-movement of his own life in God, in the
eternity which is exalted above space and time. Only this
worshipping in the spirit is real worship at all, the worshipping
in truth; a worship in which man so becomes one with God in
His all-comprehending life, that Gerizim and Moriah and all
the mountain heights of the world are embraced by His prayer,
as the being of God embraces them. And as life in the Spirit
in union with God makes praying in truth the highest act of
life, so on their side this energy of worship, in which man consciously comes before God as the eternal conscious Spirit, leads
to life in the Spirit.

The woman begins to reflect on the profound words of the
Lord, which affect her whole Samaritan view of the world, and
dart the first rays of spiritual life into the murky twilight of
her bigotry. Should she give her full confidence to the noble
stranger? The question is now respecting the highest spiritual
surrender, which she can make only to the Messiah, the expecta-

tion of whom is now become alive in her soul with the excitement of her deepest feelings and anticipations. The true-hearted one turns again to the subject with earnestness of spirit. 'I know,' she says, 'that Messiah cometh; and when He is come, He will reveal all things to us.' Adalbert Maier justly remarks, 'If the Messianic hope of the Samaritans, who received only the Pentateuch, was founded on Deut. xviii. 15, they must have expected in the Messiah principally a divine teacher who would, like Moses, announce to them the divine will and lead them into truths hitherto concealed.' He adds, it is in accordance with this that the woman says, when Messiah comes, He will tell us all things; also, the appellation of the Messiah which has been common among the Samaritans, that of *the converter* (חַשֵּׁב, חַתָּאֵב), accords with this expectation.

We know not what anticipations might move the woman in the last words. At all events, it must have been a feeling of noble longing with which she sighed for the advent of the Messiah, for the Lord surprised her with the declaration, 'I that speak unto thee am He.' He was able to announce Himself as the Messiah, in the outlying world of Samaria, because their minds were not pre-occupied with the proud Messianic conceptions of the Jews. The woman longed after the Revealer of heavenly truth; and now the Converter stood before her!

Meanwhile the disciples returned from the city, and marvelled that He talked with the woman. But they maintained a reverential silence; no one asked what He sought of her, or why He talked with her. But she left her water-pot, hastened to the city, and eagerly said to the people, 'Come, see a man which told me all things that ever I did; is not this the Messiah?' She publicly proclaims her discovery, and the people are excited;—a multitude hasten from the city to Jesus. But neither the water-pot which stands at the well as a witness of the mental emotion of the woman, who had left it in such haste, nor the elevated mood of their Lord, can draw the disciples' attention to the spiritual transaction; they urge Him to eat. To them it seems the time for taking their repast. Then He says, 'I have meat to eat that ye know not of!' And now they express to one another the conjecture, that some one had brought Him food. By this sensuous perplexity they occasioned the utterance of that beautiful saying, 'My meat is to do the will of Him that sent Me, and to finish His work!' That was His pleasure, His life, His food!

Thus a glorious noonday scene is exhibited to our sight. The disciples bring earthly food, and wished to arrange the meal. But their Master has forgotten thirst, and forgotten hunger, in order to save the soul of a poor woman. And the woman herself has already experienced the mighty influence of His Spirit; she has forgotten Jacob's holy well and her water-pot, and shyness before the people, and even the inclination to palliate her course of life, and hastens to the city to spread the knowledge of Him. Jesus goes on to address the disciples: 'Say ye not, There are yet four months,[1] and then cometh harvest? Behold, I say unto you, Lift up your eyes and look on the fields, for they are white already to harvest.'· They saw the Samaritans coming: that was the harvest which their Master saw commencing, and hailed. Then follows the general remark, that in the spiritual field, the sower and the reaper rejoice together;— the reaper, for he receives his reward, and gains the precious fruit, the souls of men; but also the sower, for the reaper brings the fruit into eternal life, so that in the world of everlasting life the sower can celebrate with him the common spiritual harvest feast. And so it must be, the Lord means to say; for in this relation the proverb, One soweth, and another reapeth, first obtains its full essential verification. The expression is primarily used in reference to earthly relations, to signify the fact, that often one must labour by way of preparation for another, or labour vigorously without his seeing himself the fruit of his labours. But that is in a higher measure true in the spiritual field. Here,

---

[1] If Jesus had not uttered this saying to the disciples nearly about the time of sowing, He must either have used it as a proverb, or probably must have said: Do not you generally say about seed-time, There are four months to harvest, etc.? (see Wieseler, p. 216). The seed-time in Palestine lasted altogether from the end of October to the beginning of February. 'The harvest began on the plains generally in the middle of April (in the month of Abib), but it was formally opened on the second day of the Passover, therefore on the 16th of Nisan, and lasted till Pentecost. The first reaping was the barley, sown perhaps in November and December, or in part still later, in January. Here the proverb would apply, if they reckoned the intervening months in the gross.'—Lücke, i. 605. 'The proverbial expression of four months for the time from sowing to harvest is stated from the Jews by Lightfoot and Wetstein, and from Varro by Wetstein.'—Baumgarten-Crusius, p. 166.

very often the sowers go very far before the reapers, and die
without seeing any fruit. These are the noblest and severest
sorrows on earth; herein the whole bitterness of that saying is
felt, ' One soweth, another reapeth.' But the rich eternity, the
world of eternal life, equalizes this disproportion. And thus in
our case the word is true in the highest sense, He would further
say: 'I have sent you to reap that whereon ye bestowed no
labour; other men have laboured, and ye are entered into their
labours.' Taken in their connection, we cannot consider these
words as having any reference to the later conversions at Samaria (Acts viii. 5); and perhaps some would understand them in
the sense that the Lord was now sowing the seed, and that they
would one day reap the harvest. But this exposition is not admissible, because Christ would in that case mix two images together—one in which He now was reaping the harvest with His
disciples, and the other according to which He, as the sower,
preceded them, the reapers. But it is evident, and conformably
to the Lord, that He gathers in His harvest with the disciples
in living unity. Evidently He is speaking of a harvest to be
gathered at the time then present, and His disciples must here
regard themselves as generally, after the commission they had received, as the reapers. For these reapers the earlier sources of the
seed must now be sought. A sowing certainly had taken place
in Samaria, first by means of Moses, whose Pentateuch was in
constant use among the people, then by the Jewish priests who
had converted the heathen population in Samaria to the rudi-
ments of Judaism; but perhaps, last of all, by John the Baptist,
who had baptized at Enon near Salim, at all events not far
from this region. If we assume that John the Baptist had
kindled afresh in Samaria the expectation of the Messiah, we
must regard the expression of Jesus as one of mournful recollection. He who had sown the seed would be rejoicing among
the reapers in the eternal life of the other world. This mournful consolation was probable, for John had been apprehended
a short time before in this district. But if we refer the words
of Jesus to those oldest sowers of the divine seed in Samaria,
they will appear to us in all their sublimity. Jesus is struck with
amazment, that that ancient divine seed in Samaria, of which
the sowers were hardly known, which seemed to be lost and
buried in half-heathenish superstition, should now spring up

suddenly for the harvest; and it testifies to the singular depth, we might say the exalted gratitude, as well as the love of His heart, that at this hour He is mindful of those ancient sowers, and rejoices in their joy to eternal life. In this state of feeling He says, 'More than ever in the present case is that proverb verified.'

The Evangelist informs us that many people of that city believed on Jesus, in consequence of what the woman had communicated to them; how He had exposed to her what she had done; how He had laid before her the register of her criminal life. Hence these persons invited Him to tarry with them, and He abode there two days. For the disciples, this tended decidedly to promote their general philanthropy; it was a preparation for their future universal apostolic ministry. But now many more Samaritans believed on Jesus, and with a very different decisiveness, for they heard His own word; and they declared to the woman that their faith no longer stood on her report, which now seemed to them as insignificant (as λαλιά) compared with what they heard from Jesus Himself. They themselves had now heard Him, and knew that this was in truth the Messiah, the Saviour of the world. A quiet blessing rested on that harvest, which the Lord with His disciples had reaped in Samaria. It did not extend over the whole country. Hatred against the Jews formed too great an obstacle (Luke ix. 51). Nor was it the design of Jesus to include Samaria generally in His ministry, since in doing so He might have seriously injured or ruined His ministry in Judea [1] (Matt. x. 5). But the harvest was at the same time a sowing which, after the day of Pentecost, ripened into a fresh harvest, and from Sichem came forth one

---

[1] Strauss (i. 537) finds a contradiction between the command excluding the Samaritans in the instructions given by Jesus to His disciples, and His own journey to the Samaritans previously to giving those instructions. But if this connection with the Samaritans be properly estimated, it will rather tend to confirm those instructions. We find that Jesus, in travelling through, only concerned Himself with the Samaritans in consequence of being in their vicinity; that He spent only two days with them, while He devoted the whole time of His ministry to Judea, Galilee, and Perea. Hence it follows that His plan, which His disciples were to follow literally, required the temporary exclusion of Samaria from His ministry, while His spirit contemplated them as called with the rest; and accordingly He attended to the Samaritans when an occasion offered, and in preference to the Gentiles.

of the most distinguished apologists of the ancient Church, Justin Martyr.[1]

NOTES.

1. Jacob's 'parcel of ground' is situated on a plain to the east of Sichem (Robinson's *Biblical Researches* ii. 287). In going from Judea to Galilee this plain is passed through from south to north, and the valley of the city of Sichem, which runs between the mountains Gerizim and Ebal in a north-western direction, is on the left (Robinson, ii. 274). Hence Christ might send His disciples in that direction to the city, and wait for them at the well: by so doing He would remain meanwhile in the ordinary travelling route. This 'parcel of ground' was a constant possession of the children of Israel in North Palestine from the days of Jacob. According to Gen. xxxiii. 19, the patriarch bought it of the children of Hamor. At a later period (Gen. xxxiv.) Simeon and Levi took possession by force of the valley and Sichem, the city of Sichem the son of Hamor. To this event probably the expression in Gen. xlviii. 22 refers, which the Septuagint distinctly explains of Sichem.[2] But perhaps the language of the patriarch is figurative, and means, 'I gained the parcel of ground which I gave to Joseph by *my* sword and bow;' that is, by fair purchase, not by the sword and bow of his violent sons. According to Josh. xxiv. 32, the bones of Joseph were buried here on the conquest of Canaan, and the ground became the inheritance of the sons of Joseph. Abraham himself made the first acquisition of the theocratic race in Canaan, when he purchased the field of Ephron, with the cave in Hebron, for a burial-place (Gen. xxiii.). This was the first possession of Israel in the southern part of the land.

2. On the history of the hatred between the Jews and Samaritans, see Robinson, ii. 289. The religious archives of the Samaritans consist of a peculiar text of the Pentateuch,[3] and ' a

---

[1] [See Semisch's monograph *on the Life, Writings, and Opinions of Justin Martyr*, translated by J. E. Ryland, 2 vols. Edinburgh, 1844: in Clark's *Biblical Cabinet*.]

[2] ' I have given thee one *portion* (שְׁכֶם) above thy brethren.'—A. V.
'Εγὼ δὲ δίδωμί σοι Σίκιμα ἐξαίρετον ὑπὲρ τοὺς ἀδελφούς σου.—LXX.

[3] [On the Samaritan Pentateuch, see Hävernick's *Introd. to the Pentateuch* 431.—Ed.]

sort of chronicle extending from Moses to the time of Alexander Severus, and which, in the period parallel to the book of
Joshua, has a strong affinity with that book;' besides ' a curious
collection of hymns, discovered by Gesenius in a Samaritan
manuscript in England' (Robinson, ii. 299). A knowledge of
the religious opinions of the modern Samaritans has been derived
from Samaritan letters, which, since the year 1589, have been
received at various times in a correspondence carried on between
the Samaritans and European scholars. Since the Samaritan
religion was only a stagnant form of the ancient Mosaism in
traditionary ordinances, which wanted, together with the living
spirit of Mosaism, the formative power, the ability of advancing
through prophecy to the New Testament, it is not surprising
that the expectation of the Messiah among the Samaritans
appears only as a stunted copy of its first Mosaic form. With
this remark we may set aside what Bruno Bauer (*Kritik der
evang. Geschichte der Johannes*, p. 415) has inferred from the
Samaritan letter against the existence of a Messianic expectation
among the Samaritans. In the Hatthaheb, whom they designated as their messiah, they could only have expected the appearance of the Deity returning to them. But the hope of an
appearance of the Deity, or the transient revelation of an ' arch-
angel,' must never be confounded with the theocratical expectation of a revelation of the Deity transforming the historical
relations of the people. It is in favour of the originality of the
Messianic expectation of the Samaritans, that they gave the
Messiah a peculiar name. Robinson's Samaritan guide showed
him and his fellow-travellers on Mount Gerizim twelve stones,
which he said were brought out of Jordan by the Israelites, and
added, ' And there they will remain until el-Muhdy (the Guide)
shall appear. This,' he said, ' and not the Messiah, is the name
they give to the expected Saviour' (ii. 278). Baumgarten-
Crusius, in his *Commentary on John* (p. 162), remarks, that he
could cite it as the last word of Gesenius on this subject, that
he had explained this Messianic name el-Muhdy, *the leader*, as
equivalent to the earlier name Hathaf or Tahef, which, according to the explanation of Gesenius, denotes the restorer of the
people in a spiritual and moral sense. In this question, as Von
Ammon[1] justly remarks, the fact is of great importance, that

[1] *Die Geschichte des Lebens Jesu* i. 354.

Dositheus,[1] in the first century of the Christian era, could act the part of a false Messiah among the Samaritans, and likewise the influence which in a similar manner Simon Magus managed to gain among them when he represented himself as the great power of God (Acts viii. 9, 10). In addition to the above-named, Baumgarten-Crusius mentions also Menander. Very important is the fact brought forward by the last-named theologian, that the apostles (according to Acts viii.) found so early an entrance into Samaria on the ground of the Messianic faith. It was indeed very possible that the Samaritan woman at Jacob's well made use of another term for designating the Messiah; but the term here given may be referred to the presumed ministry of the Baptist in Samaria.[2]

3. The coincidence noticed by Hengstenberg and others, of the five husbands of the Samaritan woman with the fivefold idolatrous worship which, according to 2 Kings xvii. 24, was practised by the five nations from Assyria, and the relation of the sixth husband, who was not the legal husband of the woman, to the mixed *Jehovah*-worship of the Samaritans, is an ingenious combination of the 'coincidence of the history of this woman with the political history of the Samaritan people,' which, according to Baumgarten-Crusius (*Commentar z. Joh.* 153), 'is so striking, that we might be disposed to find in this language a Jewish proverb respecting the Samaritans applied to an individual of the nation.' But thus much is clear in the simple historical construction of the Gospel, that Jesus makes the remark to the woman in a literal sense respecting the husbands whom she formerly had and the one whom she then had. For, had He wished to upbraid the national guilt of the Samaritans by an allegorical proverb, He could not have made use of the accidental turn which the conversation took by the guilty consciousness of the woman in order to appear as a prophet; but He would have felt Himself still more bound to have further developed the obscure proverb. Add to this, the Samaritan

---

[1] [Neander's *Church History* ii. 123 (Bohn's Tr.); Dr Lange, *Die Apostolische Zeitalter* ii. 103, 104, Braunschweig 1854; Gieseler, *Lehrbuch der Kirchengeschichte* i. 63.—Tr.]

[2] [On the Samaritan expectation of a Messiah, see Hengstenberg's *Christology* i. 75 (2d edit. Clark), and the references there.—Ed.]

people practised the five modes of idolatrous worship and the
service of Jehovah simultaneously, while this parallel is wanting
in the history of the woman. At all events, an allegorical
representation of the relation must have treated quite differently
those historical relations. According to prophetic analogies, it
must have been said inversely, Thou hast lived at the same
time with five paramours, and now thou hast not returned to thy
lawful husband; thou dost not yet fully belong to him. But
allowing the simple fact of the narrative to remain intact, there
lies in the aforenamed reference of it certainly no more than
a significant, striking correspondency of the relations of this
woman to the religious relations of her nation.

SECTION IX.

THE PROPHET IN HIS OWN CITY OF NAZARETH.

(John iv. 43, 44; Luke iv. 14–30; Matt. iv. 12, 13; Mark i. 14;
Matt. xiii. 53–58; Mark vi. 1–6.)

The land of Galilee has received its name from a district on the
northern borders of Palestine, in the tribe of Naphtali, which was
very early so called.[1] This circumstance, that the whole land of
Galilee received its name from that region which latterly was distinguished as Upper Galilee from Lower Galilee, is of importance
for this section, as well as for other passages in the Gospels. Probably the original Galilee, in the mouth of the Jewish people,
was emphatically called Galilee; and according to the Israelitish mode of expression, persons might go from Lower Galilee to

----

[1] Compare Josh. xx. 7, xxi. 32. גָּלִיל originally denoted a circle, hence a
boundary, the environs of a country. Thus, in Josh. xiii. 2 and Joel iii. 4,
the ' borders' or ' coasts,' גְּלִילוֹת of the Philistines, are spoken of. In Josh.
xx. 11 we read of the ' borders'—Geliloth—of Jordan. But in a more definite sense, the district round the mountain heights of Naphtali appear to
have been designated as Galilee. This Galilee was more distinctly described
as Galilee of the Gentiles (Isa. ix. 1), since there probably the Jewish and
Gentile towns lay together in a district which exhibited a geographical
unity.

Galilee, as any one might go from Geneva to Switzerland, or from Berlin to Prussia.[1]

According to Josephus,[2] Lower Galilee was divided from Upper Galilee by a frontier which went from Tiberias to Zabulon. According to the direction of this boundary line, Nazareth belongs to the province of Lower Galilee, while the Cana designated Kana el Jelil by Robinson as our New Testament Kana most probably belongs to the province of Upper Galilee.[3] Most decidedly Capernaum is situated within the borders of Upper Galilee.

From what has been said, it may be explained how Matthew could write that Jesus, 'leaving Nazareth, came and dwelt at Capernaum,' and that then was fulfilled what was prophesied by Isaiah of the Messianic visitation of Galilee of the Gentiles.[4]

In the same way the difficulty may be disposed of which is found in the Evangelist John, when he writes, that Jesus, after spending two days at Sychar, 'departed thence and went into Galilee,'—to Galilee, for He himself had testified, 'that a prophet hath no honour in his own country;' and when the Evangelist, notwithstanding these words immediately preceding, observes, that Jesus was very well received by the Galileans.[5]

---

[1] ' By " Galilee of the Gentiles" is commonly understood the northern part of the land, or Upper Galilee.'—Forbiger, *Handbuch der Alten Geographie* ii. 689.

[2] *De Bello Jud.* iii. 3, § 1.

[3] In the exegesis of John's Gospel a counterpart has been sought to the Cana in Galilee ; see Lücke's *Commentar* i. 468. Since Kefr Kenna, which tradition has pointed out as the Galilean Cana, lies in a southern district, so this might be in the province of Lower Galilee, and, according to our supposition, that Upper Galilee was pre-eminently called Galilee, might form the counterpart, especially since the two places were not far from one another. The denomination might be used to distinguish it from Cana in the tribe of Asher ; for it also belonged to the politically defined Upper Galilee, though it was not situated in the original Galilean circuit.

[4] With this a difficulty is solved, which Bruno Bauer (*Kritik der Evang. Geschichte* i. 23) has urged with a self-complacent prolixity,—when he remarks that the Evangelist knew not that Nazareth was a city of Galilee. We saw before, in opposition to the above-named critic, how a person might go from the wilderness into the wilderness : we see here how it was possible to go from Galilee to Galilee. The expression in Luke iv. 31, He came from Nazareth to Capernaum, a city of Galilee, is also to be explained in the same way.

[5] Even at Capernaum itself the district of Cana seems to have been re-

From Samaria Jesus turned His steps to Nazareth, His wonted residence, where His mother still lived with His relations. But here He found, even from the first, no very agreeable reception, and a momentary admiration of His personality (Matt. xiii. 54) soon gave place to a decided aversion. They rejected Him, and Jesus then uttered these words, which have become a perpetual proverb : 'No prophet is accepted in his own country' (Luke iv. 24).

The Evangelist John, according to the plan of his work, might not narrate the incident; yet he slightly hints at it, since he has assigned the cause why Jesus did not take up His abode at Nazareth, but went to Galilee Proper (Old Galilee), in his own words.

Matthew also at first only mentions the circumstance (iv. 12, 13), that Jesus left Nazareth and settled in Capernaum. But afterwards he recurs to the incident which occasioned the Lord's making this change in His residence. That this is the same incident which we find related much earlier in Luke, can admit of no doubt. Matthew was induced by his peculiar arrangement to bring it in so late. He has formed no connection of events which forces us to consider his narrative as referring to a later period.

Mark does not mention the change of residence; but he also narrates the same incident which is reported by Matthew (vi. 1), in a combination of events, indeed, which is to be taken as an indefinite connection.

But the Evangelist Luke gives to the history its correct chronological arrangement, if we except the inexactness already spoken of, which we find in all the synoptic Gospels; namely, that the return of Jesus from the wilderness is not distinctly separated from His later return from Judea. Luke is obviously occupied with this latter return. According to Matthew and Mark (iv. 12 ; Mark i. 14), it was caused by John's being cast

garded as Galilee in the strictest sense, as appears from John iv. 47. Hence the conjecture may be hazarded, that that district on which Cana lay, adjacent to a round mountain, had been the original circuit, the Galil, from which the province takes its name (Robinson). Accordingly John's mode of expression might be regarded as a provincialism,—as when, for example, a Zuricher says, I am not going to Hutli but to Albis. To any other Zuricher this would be intelligible, since on the spot Albis is distinguished from Hutli ; but not by a distant geographer, since he would join Hutli with Albis.

into prison ; according to John, there was this in addition, that Jesus could not carry on His work uninterruptedly in Judea.

That the synoptists could not mean the return of Jesus from the wilderness, is plain from the circumstance that John was not then cast into prison. But they might also not mean the second return of Jesus from Jerusalem, which John vi. 1 presupposes; for this time He soon hastened over the Galilean sea, near the east coast, while the former time, according to the three first Evangelists, He spent a longer time on the west coast. John, too, about this time had been already put to death. The synoptists therefore have reported the same return of which John gives us an account in the fourth chapter.

On the way to Nazareth Jesus everywhere appeared as a teacher in the synagogues of Lower Galilee, and His fame always went before Him[1] (Luke iv. 14, 15). Accompanied by the disciples He had already gained, He entered His own town. Here He laid His hands on a few sick persons and healed them, as Mark tells us. But he immediately remarks, that the unbelief of His countrymen constantly counteracted and repressed the joyfulness of His spirit, so that, according to the truth and delicacy of His divine life, He could not do many miracles in this spiritual sphere. Thus, already troubled in spirit by their obtuseness, He entered on the following Sabbath into their synagogue.[2] Here He gave an address. 'After the custom of the ancient synagogue, persons in whom confidence was placed,

[1] [Fame, and whatever depends on the communication of man with man, varies with the density of the population. The description of Galilee by Josephus (*Bell. Jud.* iii. 3) gives one the idea of a fat, prolific land, swarming with inhabitants. 'The cities,' he says, 'lie close together, and the multitude of villages everywhere through the land are so populous that the smallest contains upwards of 15,000 inhabitants.' The distinction between cities and villages given by Lightfoot (*Hor. Heb.* Matt. iv. 23) is in itself interesting, as giving us a glimpse into the civilisation of the Jews, and, in connection with this section, useful. 'What is a great city? That in which were ten men of leisure. If there be less than this number, behold, it is a village.'—ED.]

[2] ' The κατὰ τὸ εἰωθὸς αὐτῷ,' says Olshausen, ' does not refer to an earlier time.' Why not, since Jesus had already been engaged above half a year in His public ministry? Indeed, why should not the expression refer to the simple attendance on the Sabbath, to which Jesus had been accustomed from His youth? Bruno Bauer (i. 255) ascribes to the narrative of Luke the intention of relating the first appearance of Jesus, that he may raise a contradiction out of the expression : ' as His custom was.'

even though they were not Rabbis, might give addresses in the
synagogue. They stood while reading the word of God. The
servant of the synagogue presented the roll, and then the reader,
when he finished the section, gave an address. A passage from
the prophets was joined to a section from the books of Moses.[1]
Jesus therefore stood up to read the prophetic section which
was in order, according to the synagogue-service. This happened to be the prophet Isaiah; and for this Sabbath the section
which He found on opening the roll was the remarkable prophecy of the Spirit's anointing of the Messiah, Isa. lx. 1. Thus it
came to pass that, according to the regulations of the synagogue,
He was obliged to read the words, which He certainly could
not have read by an evasion of these regulations, without arousing the displeasure of those old acquaintances who already undervalued Him [2]—'The Spirit of the Lord is in and upon me:
hence He has anointed me (and officially appointed me). He has
sent me to announce glad tidings to the poor, to heal the broken-
hearted[3]—to announce deliverance to the captives, and sight to
the blind; to set at liberty them that are bruised—to proclaim
the acceptable (the beautiful, great jubilee) year of the Lord.'[4]

---

[1] Olshausen, *Commentary* ii. 148. [Lightfoot (*Horæ Hebr.* on Matt. iv.
23) is very full on the customs of the synagogues. In conclusion he says,
' By what right was Christ permitted by the rulers of the synagogue to
preach, being the son of a carpenter, and of no learned education? Was it
allowed any illiterate person, or mechanic, to preach in the synagogues, if
he had the confidence himself to do it? By no means. But two things gave
Christ admission,—the fame of His miracles, and that he gave Himself out
the head of a religious sect.' Lightfoot should be consulted also on Luke iv.
16, where he illustrates the reverence shown for the law by the standing pos-
ture of the reader.—ED.]

[2] This is contrary to Olshausen's remark: he thinks that Jesus was
guided by the Spirit in finding this passage, with a deviation from the order
of the synagogue. [But Lightfoot shows that, while in the reading of the
law no deviation from the established order was allowed, it was permitted
to *select* a passage from the prophets.—ED.]

[3] The words ἰάσασθαι τοὺς συντετριμμένους τὴν καρδίαν are wanting in
many manuscripts and versions; [and are omitted by Tischendorf and
Alford.]

[4] The Evangelist has given the passage freely according to the Septuagint—we have altered the common punctuation according to Breitinger's
edition of the Septuagint. The Evangelist has introduced the words ἀποσ-
τεῖλαι τεθραυσμένους ἐν ἀφέσει from Isa. lviii. 6; for καλέσαι he has chosen
the more pregnant term κηρύξαι. On the relation of this mode of quotation

After the solemn delivery of these words, which He not only read from the roll, but also uttered from the depths of His inner life, He rolled up the book, gave it to the servant, and sat down. Everything that He said and did made so powerful an impression on the hearts of the persons present, that all eyes in the synagogue were fastened upon Him. And He began to speak to them respecting the glad tidings. This day, He said, is this Scripture fulfilled in your ears. His compassion flowed forth to them with the holy words of Scripture and in His exposition of them, for they appeared to Him as those poor, and blind, and bound, and bruised ones to whom He was sent. And it seemed for a while as if their cold hearts would be thawed. They began to testify to the power of His Spirit, and wondered at the gracious words that streamed from His lips.

But the ignoble feelings that mastered them soon produced a reaction against the salutary impression, and destroyed it. The unconscious self-contempt in which the earthly-minded man moves in his state of torpidity, does not allow him easily to arrive at the joyful belief, that close by his side, out of his own circle and the poor materials of his present condition, a higher life may possibly break forth, and even a heavenly messenger proceed. He is therefore tempted to put down the highest experience of this kind by the mean, the common, to disown the prophet, although he feels his spiritual power, because he appears in the form of a peasant, to whom he can as little attribute spiritual life as to himself. To this temptation the inhabitants of Nazareth succumbed. The first indication of altered feeling was shown in their beginning to look upon His peculiar gushing spiritual life as a strange, far-fetched scholastic learning, and initiation into the qualifications for miracle-working. They asked, Whence hath this man all these things? What is this wisdom (what school) which has been given to Him? and whence

to the doctrine of inspiration, see Olshausen on the passage. [Olshausen has no ground from these quotations for saying that the inspired writers ' confused passages and mistook words.' At the most they show that they quoted from the LXX., and freely amalgamated similar passages so as to bring out a new meaning, which is surely consistent with the strictest theory of inspiration. Had the writers of the New Testament not been conscious of the sacredness of their task and the infallibility of their guidance, they would probably have shown themselves more scrupulous in their dealings with the Old Testament.—ED.]

is it that such mighty works are performed by His hands? Is
He not the carpenter, son of Joseph the carpenter? We know
quite well how His mother is called, they would again go on to
say, asking in jest, Is she not called Mary? And then they
would proceed to count His brothers on their fingers—James,
and Joses, and Simon, and Judas; and even His sisters they
cannot leave out in the reckoning. In this manner they were
scandalized at Him; that is, they took an offence at His parent-
age which was fatal to them.

As soon as Jesus remarked this change He said to them,
'Surely ye will repeat to Me the proverb, "Physician, heal thyself!"' He explained His meaning. They seemed at first to
desire to see such deeds as, according to the generally spread
report, He had performed at Capernaum; they seemed to expect
that He would unfold all His powers of healing in His own city,
and thus as it were heal Himself in the persons of His countrymen, in order to induce them to do Him homage more decidedly; in fact, He ought first of all to free Himself from the
meanness of His own family relationships, if He expected them
to regard Him as the Saviour of the nation.[1] But He specified
to them plainly the obstacle that withheld Him from working
miracles there; namely, the sad fact that a prophet was held in
no esteem in his own country, among his own kin, and in his
own house (Mark vi. 4). And then He justified His reserve by
great examples in the Old Testament. The first example was
this: there were many widows in Israel during the great famine
in the time of Elias, when the heaven was shut up for three
years and six months;[2] but to none of them was Elias sent as a

[1] See Olshausen, ii. 155.

[2] In Jas. v. 17 the time is also given as three years and six months.
On the contrary, in 1 Kings xviii. 1 a time is fixed which reaches only to
the third year. Olshausen remarks (p. 156), that the difficulty is removed
if the time is reckoned, not from the ceasing of the rain, but from Elijah's
flight, as Benson has proposed (compare what De Wette says on the other
hand, p. 36). The case seems to be thus explained: If the Jews reckoned
according to the circumstances of their country, how long the drought must
have begun before the beginning of the famine, which would not begin immediately with the drought, they would probably be obliged to add a year
to the time of the famine in order to determine the time of the drought.
But Elijah appears to have gone to the brook Cherith at the beginning of
the famine (1 Kings xvii. 3), and the date in chap. xviii. seems to refer
itself to the symbolic moment of the beginning of the famine.

preserver but to a Gentile, the Sidonian woman at Sarepta. The
second example was the miraculous cure of the Syrian captain,
Naaman. There were indeed many lepers in Israel in the time
of the prophet Elisha, but none of them were healed by the prophet, excepting the Syrian. So far the Jews had already in
ancient times rejected the salvation which their prophets would
have brought to them, and left it to strangers. The people of
Nazareth must have felt the force of these examples. But they
seemed·to regard it as intolerable that He should compare them
to the unsusceptible and the neglected, and even to idolaters
among the Jews of former days, and that He should compare
Himself with those great prophets. They were also offended at
His taking histories from the Old Testament which seemed so
very favourable to the heathen. Thus they gave themselves up
to the ebullitions of an anger which, without their perceiving it,
confirmed most completely the judgment He had expressed. In
a paroxysm of rage they expelled Him from the synagogue,
which amounted to excommunication; they thrust Him out of
the city, which was equivalent to outlawry, the deprivation of
the rights of citizenship. They even wished to deprive Him of
life, and for that purpose led Him to a height on the edge of a
precipice in order to cast Him down headlong. But at the critical moment the Lord displayed an operation of His personal
majesty, which more than once in hazardous circumstances
paralyzed His enemies and preserved His own life. He retired
from among those who had hurried Him before them to that
spot—so suddenly, so quietly, and yet with such dignity, that,
awe-struck, they involuntarily formed a passage for Him. He
therefore walked freely through them.[1] He quitted His beauti-

[1] See Hase, *das Leben Jesu*, p. 117. What Strauss has remarked against
it is unimportant, i. 478. There are several faint analogies of this event;
for example, the well-known history of Marius and of the soldier who was
to have put him to death, etc. [Robinson (ii. 335) says, 'There is here
no intimation that His escape was favoured by the exertion of any miraculous power.' Alford, on the contrary, says, ' Our Lord's passing through the
midst of them is *evidently miraculous.*' Ellicott inclines to the same opinion
(*Hist. Lec.* 160, note). No doubt His escape was due to His being a divine
person; yet there seems no necessity for attributing to Him in this instance
the exercise of a power solely divine, and which is not commonly used
among men, but only the higher exercise of a natural, human power. It is
quite conceivable, and in keeping with other instances in His life, that He

ful home as an outlaw. From its heights He had often surveyed
the rich extent of His inheritance,—towards the magnificent plain
of Esdraelon; towards '.the round top of Tabor,' and the opposite mountains of Samaria—the long line of Carmel; towards
the Mediterranean, first of all to be seen far in the south on the
left of Carmel, then interrupted by that mountain, and again
appearing on its right; towards the beautiful northern plain and
the northern mountains of Galilee, among them the mountains
of Safed overtopping them all, on which that place is seen, ' a
city set upon a hill;' farther towards the right, ' a sea of hills and
mountains' backed by the higher ones beyond the Galilean sea,
and in the north-east by the majestic Hermon with its icy crown.[1]

From this sanctuary of His childhood He was now expelled.
The inhabitants of Nazareth therefore commenced the rejection
of Jesus, which afterwards became almost universal; since Judea,
and even the whole earth on a larger scale, was the home, the
Nazareth of this Prophet, which disowned Him in His poor
human appearance. He was now separated by the ban of His
countrymen from the consecrated home of His noble mother,
to which, during His official life, He was always so glad to return. This probably occasioned His relatives afterwards to
leave Nazareth. But the disfavour of the people of Nazareth
could not prevent the Galileans from receiving Him with great
joy; for the beautiful festive-time of enthusiastic welcome, with
which His people had met Him, was not yet come to an end.

NOTES.

1. Both Neander and Von Ammon place the expulsion of
Jesus from Nazareth after His reception by the Samaritans.
But the ingenious supposition of Von Ammon, that ' the hospi-
table reception given to Jesus by the Samaritans contributed
greatly to His unfriendly reception at Nazareth,' is destitute of
proof.

held His enemies at bay by the dignity of His bearing, until He was beyond
their reach. Surely we 'are not asked to believe that He was rendered for
the time invisible.—ED.]

[1] See the beautiful description of the view from the hill over Nazareth
in Robinson's *Biblical Researches* ii. 336. [More fully described by Dr Wil-
son in his *Lands of the Bible*; and very eloquently by Renan, *Vie de Jesus*
25-8.—ED.]

2. By means of the above distinction between the provincial, and the political and geographical meaning of the name Galilee, the difficulty which expositors have found in John iv. 44 might be obviated. The Evangelist, as well as Matthew (iv. 12), under the strong influence of the provincial mode of expression, presupposes a contrast between the home circuit of Jesus and Galilee, and forms his phraseology in ver. 44 according to this contrast. In this way the different ingenious attempts to explain the passage in question are disposed of. See Lücke's *Commentar* i. 613. That Jesus, by His own country in which He had no honour, could not mean Judea, although He was born in Bethlehem, is sufficiently evident (apart from the favourable reception He met with in the land of Judea) from the matter-of-fact relation which lies at the basis of the declaration of Jesus. It was not because the prophet is born in a certain place, but because he has grown up in it, that his countrymen are accustomed to regard him as their equal, and thus he becomes unimportant to them. Besides, the Jews did not know much about the birth of Jesus at Bethlehem. Tholuck explains the difficulty by considering the γάρ as explanatory of the following clause, and translating it by '*namely.*' J. Chr. Hofmann explains the γάρ in a peculiar manner (*Weissagung und Erfüllung*, p. 88). He supposes that Christ, in consequence of the Sanhedrim's regarding both the Baptist and Himself with the same rancour as if they were one, was induced to avoid, for the present, notoriety and a crowd; and hence it was best that He should go to His own home, for a man whom God has called to a great service is nowhere so little esteemed as in his native place. But had it been possible for this motive to have determined Christ to go into Galilee, His plan, as the text directly shows, would have been altogether defeated.

3. 'The town of Nazareth,' says Robinson, 'lies upon the western side of a narrow oblong basin, extending about from S.S.W. to N.N.E., perhaps twenty minutes in length by eight or ten in breadth' (*Biblical Researches* ii. 333). Hofman remarks (*Weissagung und Erfüllung* ii. 65), that the radical meaning of the word נֵצֶר, according to Isa. xiv. 19 and lx. 21, seems to be a *shoot* or *sapling*, and draws the inference, 'Since Nazareth lies in a basin surrounded by hills, etc., it might have its name from this, since it was placed there like a sapling in a hole.'

Hengstenberg, in his *Christology*, expresses the opinion, that
Nazareth was marked by this name as a weak sapling in contrast to a stately tree. ' There was so much greater inducement to give this name to the place, because the symbol was
before the eye in the vicinity. The limestone hills of Nazareth
are covered with low bushes (see Burckhardt's *Travels* ii. 583).
Therefore the name might mean, the place of shrubs, or a shrub.
Yet, on the other hand, what Schubert says of the vegetation of
the vale of Nazareth (iii. 170) seems to contradict this. As to
the locality where they were about to cast Jesus down, Robinson
remarks: ' From the convent (which is said to cover the spot
where the Virgin lived) we went to the little Maronite Church.
It stands quite in the south-west part of the town, under a precipice of the hill, which here breaks off in a perpendicular wall
forty or fifty feet in height. We noticed several other similar
precipices in the western hill around the village. Some one of
these, perhaps that by the Maronite Church, may well have been
the spot whither the Jews led Jesus that they might cast Him
down headlong. . . The monks have chosen for the scene of this
event, the Mount of the Precipitation, so called ; a precipice overlooking the plain of Esdraelon nearly two miles south by east of
Nazareth. Among all the legends that have been fastened on
the Holy Land, I know of no one more clumsy than this, which
presupposes that in a popular and momentary tumult they should
have had the patience to lead off their victim to an hour's distance, in order to do what there was an equal facility for doing
near at hand' (*Biblical Researches* ii. 335). But it is not to be
denied that the text of the Evangelist allows us to reckon upon
a distance between the city and ' the brow of the hill ' (ὀφρύς).
' They thrust Him out of the city,' it is said, and led Him or
drove Him unto, etc. Then the question is, whether we are to
read ἕως ὀφρύος or ἕως τῆς ὀφρύος. The manuscripts here differ.
Lachmann reads ἕως τῆς. If, in this definite sense, some one
commanding mountain height is sought for in Nazareth, a precipice near the city, appearing similar to many others, would not
suffice. Then it may be asked, whether the vale of Nazareth
is reckoned as belonging to the mountain on which the city was
built, so that the whole mountain range is spoken of, or whether
we are to translate ἐφ' οὗ on which, so that that particular hill is
meant which overhung the city. If we decide in favour of the

first supposition, then that precipice overlooking the plain of Esdraelon belongs to the mountain range of Nazareth. Robinson has shown that the legend in question is of late date as a historical tradition and of no value. It is another question, whether it has not been formed as a hypothesis, and as such is again to be considered. That 'casting down headlong,' which they intended to perpetrate, would at the same time represent the symbolical expulsion from their borders. Now, since He had come thither from Samaria, the men of Nazareth would point Him the way He came if they led Him in the direction of the rock of the legend. That precipice of the legend is, according to K. von Raumer (*Palästina* 134), 80 feet to the first ledge, and to the bottom, 300 feet.

SECTION X.

THE NOBLEMAN OF CAPERNAUM.

(John iv. 45–54.)

When Jesus, under these circumstances, after His expulsion from Nazareth, came to Upper Galilee, the Galileans received Him, having seen all that He did in Jerusalem at the feast. Especially, Jesus met with a favourable reception at Cana, where the miracle by which that place had been distinguished, was held in lively remembrance. In Cana He appears to have remained some time; long enough, at least, for His coming to be known at Capernaum, and for Him to be sought out by one who needed His help in that place. This person was a royal officer (τις βασιλικός), and therefore in the service of Herod Antipas.[1] Anxiety for his son, who was dangerously ill, made him hasten into the hill country; and as soon as he came to Jesus, he besought Him urgently that He would come down to Capernaum in order to heal his son. There was need for the utmost expedition, for his son was at the point of death. But it was totally out of character with the vocation of Jesus, that He

---

[1] [Not necessarily in the *military* service, as may be seen from the examples collected by Krebs (*Observ. e Josepho* 144).—ED.]

should be a bodily helper or physician for any one till a spiritual relation had been developed between the person needing help and Himself; least of all could He be at the bidding of persons of rank, who possibly might believe that they might venture to make use of Him, on an emergency, as a wonder-working physician, without declaring themselves as His adherents, and resigning themselves to His agency. In addition, this royal officer expected that the Lord would leave His fixed circle of operation to effect this cure. But what most of all trenched on the dignity of Jesus, was the importunity of an excitement which would have taken Him away as perforce, or, at least, wished Him to make a hurried journey to Capernaum. But Christ met all excitement of this sort with the greatest placidity and composure; He met it with His strong peace in God, which taught Him that God does not rule over men with confusion and excitement, and that hence man, even under the strongest movements of the soul, ought to preserve the clearness, repose, and dignity of his spirit. The waves of agony must break their force on the rock of his elevated rest in God. In this spirit He answers the father calling for help, in order to put him on the track of confidence: 'If ye do not see signs and astounding miracles,[1] ye will not believe!' This reply has been thought a hard saying; and it has been said, that the man's trustful coming to Jesus makes it appear unreasonable.[2] But it is not borne in mind, that, in general, the dispositions of the persons to whom Jesus was about to render aid, required to be prepared for a genuine corresponding reception of it; and, indeed, often by a conversation which led them to self-knowledge by taking a humiliating turn. But here it was in the highest degree necessary to set the excited royal officer in a right spiritual relation to Jesus. Had Jesus not purified his request, and had He hastened immediately with him over the mountains, He would have made Himself more intelligible to modern criticism; but He would not then have appeared as the chief of men divinely commissioned, but rather as a submissive retainer of the nobleman. Therefore the sharp word of Jesus, which asks the man whether he belonged to the great multitude of those who sought in the divine covenant earthly help and demoniac terror, must test and stimulate his capability of faith. But now Jesus cannot separate his

---

[1] τίρατα. [2] Lately Baur.

faith from his anxiety for his son, and feels that his persistent supplication is an expression of his faith. ' Sir,' he exclaims, ' come down ere my child die !' The father's call for help evinces how close he stood in spirit to his suffering son, and how close at the same time to the helpful spirit of Christ. Now Jesus calls to him in His impressive manner : ' Go thy way !'— Probably there was a pause here which for a moment sunk the man into the abyss, and by the pain of denial and hopelessness made him ripe for the highest exertion of miraculous power which he was to witness. In his own thoughts he must already have gone home unaccompanied by Jesus as a helper. ' Go thy way !' was said first of all ; but then, in his dejection, the heavenly words were heard—' Thy son liveth !'

And in the very same moment in which this life-ray of deliverance darted into the father's heart, it darted to the heart of his distant son. But how near this father was to his son in his internal relation, was known to Jesus alone.

' And the man '—the Evangelist writes with an admiration which is felt in the text—' the man believed the word that Jesus had spoken unto him, and he went his way.'

And as he was now going down, and therefore had not quite reached Capernaum, his servants met him and brought him the news, Thy son liveth—he is restored ! But now he wished not merely to indulge in the joy of the cure, but to be certain that he was indebted for it to Jesus.[1] He therefore inquired of them the hour when his son began to amend ; they answered, ' Yesterday, at the seventh hour, the fever left him.'

Probably the nobleman had left Capernaum in the morning. If we assume that Cana el Jelil, situated in the north-east, was the place to which he travelled, we conceive that it must be late in the afternoon before his interview with Jesus came to a close. But then he could not reach Capernaum on the same day. It is also possible that he started at a different hour of the day. In this way, at all events, De Wette's surprise that he should pass a night on the road is shown to be without reason. Probably his servants met him early in the morning of the following day.

The hour which the servants reported to the father on his way home as the joyful crisis of his son's illness, was the very

[1] See Tholuck on the passage, *Commentary*, p. 146.

hour in which the Lord had given him the assurance, ' Thy
son liveth.' This circumstance made him certain that he had
received the miraculous aid of Jesus, and the faith now developed in him was so powerful that it communicated itself to his
whole house.

And so it came to pass that Jesus a second time, immediately
on His return from Judea to Galilee, performed a miracle.[1]

NOTES.

1. On the relation of this narrative to the history of the
miraculous aid which the centurion at Capernaum obtained,
see the first volume of this work, p. 214. By a more exact
computation of dates, it is proved that the centurion of Capernaum belongs to a quite different period. To this must be
added the other points of difference (see Lücke on this passage,
Commentar i. 626). The leading difference is the great contrast between the mental states of the persons seeking help,
especially between the spiritual physiognomies of the two figures,
while the most dazzling likeness of the narratives for the juve-
nile eye of criticism, as we have already remarked, lies in the
royal dress of the men. See Ebrard, p. 280.[2]

2. By an argument of Baur's, in which he has almost out-
done himself in his own style of demonstration, the following
result is obtained in his Essay, p. 83: 'Because σημεῖα and
τέρατα are related negatively to faith, they lead not to true
internal faith, but to an outward false faith.' One need to be

---

[1] The πάλιν δεύτερον is not to be referred entirely to σημεῖον, so that it
must mean that this was the second miracle performed in Galilee generally,
as Tholuck supposes (p. 146); but it plainly stands in relation to the whole
clause, τοῦτο σημεῖον ἐποίησεν ὁ Ἰησοῦς ἐλθών, and has this meaning: it was
the second time that Jesus on returning from Judea to Galilee performed a
miracle. Origen's doubt, that Jesus did not perform that first miracle on
returning from Judea, is settled, if we bring into account the high probability, that Jesus then, as He came to the marriage at Cana, had stopped
not only in Perea, but also in Judea.

[2] [Ewald declares for the identity of the two incidents, but in favour
of that opinion adds nothing which has not been again and again answered.
It is quite in his style to dismiss the subject with the dictum that 'the
differences, at first sight significant, disappear on closer investigation; and
the essential similarities are so decided, that *no one can doubt* that they
belong to one event.'—(*Geschichte Christus' und seiner Zeit*, p. 277, 2d
ed.)—ED.]

convinced with one's own eyes of the desperate contrivance by which this kind of criticism in such a way prolongs its existence. It is, moreover, false when Baur maintains that Christ uttered so harsh an expression respecting faith in σημεῖα and τέρατα: according to the text, He rather rebuked that unbelief which is first disposed to turn to faith with the requirement of miracles, and which on that account desires to see the σημεῖον as much as possible in the definite form of τέρας. And that He rebukes this unbelief, and yet performs a miracle in His own great, unostentatious manner, perhaps invisibly, contains evidently no contradiction. Baur finds also that there is in the narrative (of which the Evangelist must have taken the historical materials from the synoptic Gospels) no contradiction, for here the ground-idea of miracle has indeed risen to the greatest height; but on this highest stage of its ascension, on which the miracle surpasses itself, it is at war with itself, it turns over into its opposite, it annuls itself. How far? Because here the performance of the miracle is believed before the miracle is seen, and without seeing it. But it is only necessary to be transported into the scene of any Gospel miracle at pleasure, in order to find that on every occasion faith in the word of Jesus precedes the miracle, and that the special miraculous operation is never seen. The question, What value at all could miracles have, if they already presupposed the same faith in the person of Jesus which they must first of all produce? we are willing to leave standing as a snow-mannikin of sophistry in our path, at the risk of those who are children in understanding being frightened at it.

SECTION XI.

THE RESIDENCE OF JESUS AT CAPERNAUM.—THE MAN WITH
AN UNCLEAN SPIRIT IN THE SYNAGOGUE. PETER'S WIFE'S
MOTHER. PETER'S DRAUGHT OF FISHES. THE CALLING
OF THE FIRST APOSTLES.

(Matt. iv. 12–22 ; viii. 14–17.   Mark i. 14–38 ; iii. 9–12.
Luke iv. 31–43 (44) ; v. 1–11.)

Jesus had already proclaimed in the synagogue at Nazareth
the Gospel, the glad tidings, that now the time was fulfilled—the
kingdom of God, the kingdom of heaven, was at hand.   This
announcement He repeated in the synagogues of Galilee, which
He now visited one after another repeatedly, when He required
of His hearers to recognise the importance and the demands of
this great time, to renew their minds, and to receive the tidings
of the new kingdom with the self-devoting heroism of faith.
But He delivered this announcement to His people as a blessed
certainty of His own spirit, filled with the kingdom of heaven.
Never had such words been heard, such sounds of sorrow and
of joy, of love, of peace, and of new life.   All who heard Him
were charmed, if they were tolerably free from prejudice, and
extolled Him.   Everywhere, at this beautiful time, He was
greeted with an enthusiastic welcome, and the gloomy sign that
He had been expelled from Nazareth was withdrawn into the
background.

The joy of greeting the Chief of the new age was in a peculiar degree granted to the city of Capernaum, which lay between
the borders of Zebulon and Naphtali,[1] on the western side of the
Lake of Gennesareth, not far from the entrance of the Jordan
into the lake, and formed a flourishing station on the line of
traffic between Damascus and the Mediterranean Sea.   In this
city Jesus took up His abode, in the sense of making it the centre
of His excursions and journeys.   Hence it is distinguished by
the Evangelists as ' His own city ' (Mark ix. 1).   Here He seems

---

[1] One critic, from the circumstance that ὅρια denotes the border-terri-
tory, has made it a jest, that the Evangelist has placed Capernaum at the
same time in two tribes. On this point see Ebrard.

generally to have resided under Peter's roof. He had no house of His own.[1] Probably His own family at a later period followed Him in this change of residence. The distinction which was by this event conferred on Capernaum reminded the Evangelist Matthew of the prophetic words of Isaiah (ix. 1, 2) : 'The way of the sea beyond Jordan, Galilee of the Gentiles; the people which sat in darkness saw a great light, and to them which sat in the region and shadow of death light is sprung up.'[2] Matthew with his profound insight may possibly oblige those persons to acknowledge the Messianic import of the passages quoted by him, who have no taste for his more delicate apprehension of the 'fulfilment' of the Old Testament references in the New Testament. That district was the most despised in the Jewish land—far from the visible residence of the theocracy, in contact with the Gentiles and mingled with Gentiles—it now became the theatre of the revelation of the glory of the Lord.

Jesus appears to have spent about a week in Cana and the neighbourhood after He had been expelled from Nazareth. There He made His last appearance on a Sabbath. Here we find Him first of all, according to Luke, in the synagogue. Everywhere His word operated powerfully; so it was here. He taught in the might of the full truth of the divine word; not like the scribes, with their lifeless formulas and phraseology.

---

1 Mark i. 29 ; Luke v. 8. Compare Matt. viii. 20.

2 It appears to me that it was not the intention either of the prophet or the Evangelist to mark four particular districts of Northern Palestine, as Chris. K. Hofmann (*Weissag. und Erf.* p. 94) supposes. For such specifications the expression ὁδὸν θαλάσσης would be little suited. Every one of the four designations too much coincides with the other in a geographical relation. But no geographical interest has influence here, but the matter is to designate despised Upper Galilee from the proud standpoint of Judea. And it is then reproached in three ways. First of all, as the land of the profane sea-way, not as the sea-way simply ; hence the accusative ὁδόν. It is evident that not the Sea of Gennesareth, but the Mediterranean, is intended. Then it is called the land—the land beyond Jordan—not according to the contrast of the two banks of the Jordan, but of the consecrated valley of that river and the unconsecrated region which was situated beyond it up the stream. The hyperbole of the language may be illustrated by a hundred analogies ; for example, by Schiller's sentence about the left bank of the Rhine, ' where German fidelity expires.' The third designation makes the two former sufficiently clear.

His individual word was identical with the essential power of the Word,—an emanation of the Logos, and therefore an act of original freshness, creative, transforming, wonder-working. As He was acting with this power in the synagogue at Capernaum, suddenly an extraordinary event occurred. A man in the assembly cried aloud, ' Let us alone ! what have we to do with Thee, Thou Jesus of Nazareth ? Thou art come to destroy us ; I know Thee who Thou art, the Holy One of God !' This raving man was known : he was mastered by the agency of an impure demon ; and since his consciousness was identified with that of the demon, he felt in the holy agency of Jesus, with the most vivid repulsion, an attack on his demoniacal condition, and there-fore, as he now felt himself, an attack on his very existence. The Saviour appeared to him as a destroyer. But Jesus had com-passion on the maniac. He addressed him imperatively with the word of power, ' Hold thy peace and come out of him !' This convulsed the poor man ; he fell down in the midst of the · assembly ; loud shrill tones escaped from him ; but it was the final paroxysm. The demoniacal power let him go ; and the last frightful scene, in which the demon seemed ready to destroy him, inflicted no injury upon him. Universal astonishment seized the spectators. The synagogue was broken up ; the service was abruptly closed in the most animated expressions of praise. They said one to another, and the question runs round, What is this ? Whence has He this word of power, this new doctrine, that with authority He commands the unclean spirits, and they obey Him ? The fame of this miracle spread through all Galilee.

From the synagogue, His disciples—most probably the four, Simon, Andrew, James, and John—accompanied Him to the house which belonged to Simon and Andrew (Mark i. 29). Simon was already married, as we learn from this history ; and it is a remarkable fact, that we are distinctly informed respect-ing this chief of the apostles, that his married state continued during his apostolic ministry (1 Cor. ix. 5). Peter's mother-in-law lay ill in bed of ' a great fever.'[1] From this circumstance

---

[1] [Alford thinks this expression is used by Luke *as a physician*, to distin-guish the *kind* of fever. Would the article not be necessary in this case ? And has it been sufficiently considered, that not the physician, but the fisher-man, was the original reporter of the case ?—ED.]

we infer that Jesus now for the first time entered into Simon's house—not earlier, or He would have cured her. But they inform Him at once of her illness. He went in, stood over her, and uttered the curative, menacing words which thrilled through her life, as if He would have rebuked an evil demon in the fever (ἐπετίμησε τῷ πυρετῷ, Luke iv. 39). He took her by the hand, and she rose up, and was so free from fever, so well, that she could at once minister to Him as her guest. The day was a festival for Simon's house. The family felt that there was not a house in Capernaum so highly favoured and honoured as their own, and she who was restored to health at once proceeded to prepare a festive entertainment for the holy guests who had brought such a blessing on herself and the family.

On that day Capernaum was in a state of wonderful excitement. When the evening came, and the sun was setting,[1] they brought many sick and demoniac persons to Jesus, sufferers, in short, of whatever kind; so that it seemed as if, in the throng of sufferers, and those who accompanied or carried them, or those who were spectators, the whole city was gathered before the door (Mark i. 33). Jesus healed the sick one after another, since He laid His hands on every one of them. But many exciting scenes occurred among the demoniacs whom He cured. They agreed in a psychical intensifying of their power of foreboding, in which the universally spread expectation that Jesus was the Messiah became a certainty; and so, amidst the furious paroxysms that attended their restoration, they cried out and addressed Him as the Son of God. But the Lord would not win the acknowledgment of His people by such signs and witnesses. He who only by compulsion, or rather out of condescension to the weakness of the Jews, appealed to the testimony of John,[2]

---

[1] Not in order to avoid the sun's heat were they brought so late, for it was the winter season. It was perhaps a determination of a delicate feeling, that for a public exposure of humiliating infirmities of all kinds the dusk was chosen. It may be added, that towards evening that commotion reached its highest point. [The general opinion seems to be, that the note of time is given to show that the Sabbath was now past. The Greek interpreter in Cramer's *Catena* (Mark i. 32) says, 'They let the Sabbath be past, because they thought it unlawful to heal on the Sabbath.' Lightfoot (on Matt. viii. 16) says, 'They took care of the canonical hour of the nation.' Ewald (292) adds to this, that it was the cool of the day.—ED.]

[2] John v. 34.

could not support His cause on the testimonies of so morbid, and spectral, and bedimmed a sphere of life. He threatened them, and would not allow them to speak.

On that evening the distresses of the city of Capernaum weighed Him down like a heavy burden. In the representation of this extraordinary scene, the Evangelist Matthew is rightly reminded of the words of Isaiah, ' Himself took our infirmities and bare our sicknesses' (Isa. liii. 4, 5).[1]

A great day of festivity and of labour had thus been passed by the Lord,[2]—a long day of victory in His conflict with the kingdom of sin and death; and His life was put in the greatest commotion. With such emotions of triumph He gladly hastened into solitude; for it was not beneficial to the people to continue in a state of such violent excitement; and for Himself, it was a necessity to refresh Himself in solitude, deep in the heaven of prayer, in communion with His Father. So the Spirit impelled Him early the next morning, when the day had scarcely dawned (πρωὶ, ἔννυχον λίαν, Mark i. 35; γενομένης δὲ ἡμέρας, Luke iv. 42), to retire into a desert place. But with the earliest morning the throng of persons seeking for help and healing again assembled before Simon's house. Jesus was away, but Simon was pressed, and had to seek Him out. In this errand, it seems, not only the household and the disciples of Jesus, but also persons belonging to the crowd, joined him; and when they found Jesus, the disciples declared to Him that He was anxiously sought by all, while the rest entreated Him that He would not leave the city. Thus the citizens at Capernaum acted the opposite part to the men of Nazareth. The latter had thrust Him out; the former wished to detain Him, and, if possible, to confine Him

[1] See Olshausen's *Commentary* i. 255. To speak, with Olshausen, of a spiritual exhaustion of Christ, might be hazardous, if he did not mean a psychical exhaustion. Von Ammon could not find in this instance the propriety of the application of that prophetical passage, because he had no perception of the deep-lying relation between spiritual, psychical, and corporeal sicknesses.

[2] [Ewald (*Christus* 290) says, ' This day's work serves as a specimen of His daily activity during this whole period.' So Ellicott, p. 166 : ' Such a picture does it give us of the actual nature and amount [of His merciful activities], that we may well conceive that the single day, with all its quickly succeeding events, has been thus minutely portrayed to show us what our Redeemer's ministerial life really was, and to justify, if need be, the noble hyperbole of the beloved apostle,' etc.—ED.]

to a constant residence with them. They probably made very urgent appeals, but Jesus would not be fettered by them. 'I must preach the kingdom of God to other cities also,' He declared, 'for therefore am I sent;' and turning to the disciples, He said, 'Let us go into the next towns.' But before He took His departure, which the Evangelists have already mentioned in general (Mark i. 39; Luke iv. 44), Jesus fulfilled the wish of those who had sought Him out, in order once more to grant the blessing of His presence to the expectant multitude.

The Lord directed His course to the sea-shore, probably in order to secure freedom to His movements. Then the people crowded round Him greatly, in their longing to hear the word of God from His lips (Luke v. 1). He was still surrounded by the first most moveable and susceptible hearers; and, as suited such an audience, He preached first of all in the most general sense the Gospel of the coming of the kingdom of God, of the beginning of the great jubilee, and exhorted the people to a true change of mind,[1] the fundamental condition of entrance into His kingdom. But His labours in teaching were interrupted by the over-pressure of those who were themselves afflicted with diseases, or who carried the sick. The Evangelist Mark gives us a very graphic representation of this over-pressure in a passage which doubtless belongs to this period (iii. 9–12). Since the sufferers in the crowd had an interest in being close to the Lord, in order to make known their sufferings, or secretly to touch Him, so an involuntary pressing movement of the whole circle of living beings that surrounded Him, towards Him as the centre, took place; and in this way His discourse was subject to perpetual interruptions by the multitude. Hence the Lord was obliged to restore the equipoise between His working of miracles and His teaching, and to secure the delivery of His discourse, by taking refuge on the water. As the throng was constantly increasing, and with it that popular excitement was created which He always shunned, because it ever tended to a chiliastic vertigo, He looked out for the two ships of His friends, which lay there on the shore. But as soon as they perceived that He wished to get into a vessel with them, they bethought themselves that they might again follow their vocation as fishermen to which they originally belonged: they quickly cleaned their nets in order to cast them

---

[1] μετάνοια.

into the sea. The Evangelists have designedly brought forward
this circumstance. We see how these disciples are still zealously
occupied with their earthly calling; how they did not yet imagine that soon they must decidedly give it up, in order to devote
themselves exclusively to the service of Jesus. But Jesus desired Simon, into whose vessel He had entered, to thrust out a
little from the shore, that He might be at a short distance from
the land. And now He turned again to the people, who were detained on the shore by His spiritual power, as He was detained
by the intense longing of the people after His word. The expectation of the fishermen therefore, who already had taken their
nets in hand, is frustrated by this direction of Christ's spirit, in
a similar manner as at Jacob's well, when 'they prayed Him,
saying, Master, eat.' Seated in the ship, the Lord speaks once
more to His hearers, before He leaves them, of the great kingdom of salvation which had begun. In this style of preaching
we feel the entire living freshness of a heart overflowing with
compassionate love to men. But Jesus also does justice to His
disciples; they must provide for their families. He therefore
commands Peter to launch out into the deep, and to let down
his net for a draught. The disciple had just then no great
expectations of success. 'Master,' he exclaims, 'we have toiled
all the night and have taken nothing; but at Thy word I will
let down the net.' We perceive here a secret trouble in the disciple. After a beautiful day for the city of Capernaum, he had
passed an unfortunate night. His desire to improve the toil of
the night for the concerns of his family was defeated, and defeated when the glory of the preceding day had promised a richer
success than usual. Yet now, at the encouraging words of Christ
his spirits revive. So he throws out the net with confidence, and
soon it swarms with fish; it threatens to break when they would
draw it back again. They beckon to their partners in the other
ship, probably that of James and John, and to their servants
(ver. 10); and these come and help them to make sure of their
draught. And so abundant is the draught that the two ships
are filled with it, so that they began to sink. At this transaction
Peter is overpowered, and he falls on his knees before Jesus,
exclaiming, 'Depart from me, for I am a sinful man, O Lord!'
This draught had filled him and all his companions with astonishment and affright. Peter understands fishing better than the

theological critic who cannot understand the reason of his excitement.[1] He sees something greater in this event than in the
miraculous cures of which he had been previously a witness.
For it allows him to look all at once from the land of toil and
trouble through wide-opened gates into the paradise of a perfect
superabundance. How rich is he suddenly, and how would it
be if Jesus remained near him with this assistance! This
thought thrills him; but while it thrills him, he is in dread, and
feels most keenly that such miraculous success cannot thrive
with him.[2] This is expressed in his petition; the most glorious
feeling in the most unsuitable words: 'Lord! depart from me!'
The divine glory of Christ so deeply humbles him, that the whole
feeling of his sinfulness was aroused in him; and his prosperity
in temporal things so overwhelmed and ashamed him, that he
was alarmed at the thought of its constant enjoyment. Christ
grants the extraordinary petition, not according to the letter but
the spirit of it. He had wished to provide for the families of
His friends richly for a longer time, for they were now to draw
with Him. 'Fear not,' was the consoling word; 'from henceforth thou shalt catch men.' Thus, then, they still wash and
mend their nets. As soon as it is said, Aboard! they thought
only of the fishing, and threw their nets into the sea. Henceforth they must throw their net into humanity. The friends
now know that they can altogether trust their Lord with their
temporal and earthly wants. They feel that they and theirs
are safely provided for in His service. And how great is His
promise, that they should draw men in such miraculous draughts
out of the sea of the world for the kingdom of God, as they

[1] Schleiermacher, *Lukas* 71.

[2] Von Ammon shows himself quite unable to enter into the disposition
of the noble and pious fisherman. On the exclamation of Peter he has
much that is thoroughly beside the point (p. 378). [Ewald does not show
his usual profound spiritual sagacity when he says that the sinner is overwhelmed in presence of the Holy One, 'because he fears that the same power
which now unexpectedly blesses him, may, if he should (perhaps unwittingly)
sin against it, as unexpectedly destroy him' (*Christus* 288). Riggenbach
(*Vorlesungen über das Leben*, etc., 351) follows the author, almost verbally,
yet with spirit, and with one or two good additions. He interprets the
words as the words of the fervid Peter, whose utterance oversteps his real
desire. The comparison of his request with that of the Gadarene demoniac,
verbally agreeing, but really so different, is useful.—ED.]

had now made a miraculous draught in their old calling of fishermen! A greater calling He could not give them. They recognise it as such; and forthwith they are resolved; they bring
their ships to land, forsake all, and follow Him.

It would probably make a great sensation in Capernaum,
when these young men so suddenly gave up their employment,
to which they seemed to be so entirely devoted, though it was still
not forbidden them occasionally to resume their old avocation.
It was known how painful such a sacrifice was to an Israelite.
It was known that these men had just been mending their nets.
And now they suddenly leave everything, in order to go with
Jesus through the land. The astonishment at the power of
Jesus which effected this change, is reflected in the narrative
of the calling of the four first apostolic disciples, as we find it in
Matthew and Mark. Especially might Matthew, although probably already moved by the appearance of Jesus, be struck even
then with the marvellousness of this total change of life, since
a less noble calling, that of a publican, fettered himself. Thus
in him and others this history, in all its peculiarity, has been
distinctly stamped for evangelical tradition as a peculiar history.
It is as if Jesus had now for the first time found those men on
the beach, and as if one word from Him sufficed, with an almighty
irresistible power, to make them become His followers. And, in
truth, this history presents in a new light the relation of Jesus
to these disciples, in the first place, as to their giving up their old
calling, and next, as they were now called by Christ to become
changed into the first fishers of men, or apostles.

NOTES.

1. That the history narrated in Luke v. 1, etc., is identical
with that reported in Matt. iv. 18, etc., and in Mark i. 16, Ebrard
proves (p. 234) briefly and conclusively by the simple remark,
that in both narratives the subject-matter is, how Jesus induced
these disciples to give up their vocation as fishermen, and how
they could not give up a second time their employment, after
they had already given it up. The same theologian has proved
(p. 236) in a masterly manner, that the history narrated in John
i. 41, etc., does not exclude the calling of the four disciples at
the sea-side.

2. As to the situation of Capernaum, see Tholuck, *Exposi-*

tion of the Sermon on the Mount, p. 54. Robinson combines the
various notices of the Evangelists on the landing-place of the
Lord, on that return, when He walked on the sea (Matt. xiv.
34; Mark vi. 45, 53; John vi. 17), and arrives at the conclusion that Capernaum was situated in a tract on the western
coast of the lake, called the land of Gennesareth, and that
Bethsaida, in the vicinity of Capernaum, was probably in the
same tract. This district, from which the lake must naturally
have taken its name, Robinson finds, according to Josephus, *de
bello Jud.* iii. 10, § 8, and other notices in the New Testament
and the Talmud, situated in a fertile plain extending along the
shore, from el-Mejdel on the south, to Khân Minyeh on the
north (*Biblical Researches* ii. 404). According to Josephus,
this district was well watered, particularly by a fountain called
by the inhabitants Capharnaum. 'Josephus here mentions no
town of this name,' says Robinson, 'but the conclusion is irresistible, that the name as applied to the fountain could have
come only from the town, which of course must have been situated at no great distance.' Capernaum, כפר נחום, means, as Winer
remarks, according to Hesychius, Origen, and Jerome, *vicus
consolationis, village of consolation;* perhaps better, *Nahum's
village*, but not *Beautiful village*, as has been also conjectured.
In relation to the mental and religious character of Capernaum,
a remark of Von Ammon may here be quoted, that the place
was inhabited by Jews and Gentiles, and in Jewish writings is
noted as the residence of free-thinkers and heretics. It would
have been a striking contrast, if at that time Tiberias in the
esteem of the Jews had been regarded as a peculiarly holy place,
as was the case after the destruction of Jerusalem.

SECTION XII.

THE FIRST JOURNEY OF JESUS FROM CAPERNAUM THROUGH
GALILEE.   THE SERMONS ON THE MOUNT.   THE HEALING
OF THE LEPER.

(Matt. iv. 23–viii. 4.   Mark i. 31–45 ; iii. 12, 13.   Luke v.
12–16 ; vi. 12–49.)

With His four companions, Jesus travelled from Capernaum
through Galilee, hastening from place to place, from one synagogue to another.   Everywhere He proclaimed the glad tidings
that the kingdom of God had commenced: and He proved the
great announcement by His deeds ; for He healed the sick, and
removed every imfirmity and disorder of the people which met
Him in His progress.   On the bright path of the Prince of Life,
every form of suffering which encountered Him vanished like
a dissolving view.   He became highly celebrated.   His fame
spread far and wide through all Syria at this time, in the first
outburst of joy on account of the great salvation.   A general
impulse was diffused abroad, to bring the sick to Jesus, as if
everything diseased had been tracked and hunted out for the
purpose.   But especially He healed 'many that were possessed,
and those which were lunatic, and those which had the palsy.'
But He had not merely to do with crowds streaming to and fro,
but many groups of travellers followed Him, His Galilean adherents especially, but also those who were well affected towards
Him in Decapolis, in Jerusalem, and Judea generally, as well
as Perea.

The Evangelists have not given us many particulars of this
journey, but only three facts of importance : the Sermon on the
Mount, the sermon on the mountain-plain, and the healing of
a leper.   As to the two sermons, it is in the first place doubtful
whether they are to be distinguished from one another, or identical, and only differing in the manner of being reported : in the
former case, whether they belong to the same period of Christ's
ministry or not ; and lastly, for what reason, if they belong to
one time, they belong to this place according to Matthew, and
not to the beginning of the summer of the year 782, in which
Luke seems to place them.

In our times the two discourses have been generally considered as identical, that is, as two different evangelical reports of one and the same discourse of Jesus;[1] so that, by some Matthew's report,[2] by others that of Luke,[3] has been held as the least authentic; by a third class, no great authenticity has been ascribed to either.[4] It certainly cannot be denied that the similarity of the two discourses in the leading thoughts is so great, that we may be induced to believe that they are to be regarded as the same discourse, only differently reported. Truly the fundamental thought of both is the same : the representation of the exaltation of the depressed and the humble, and the depression of those who are falsely exalted, the self-exalted,— which begins with the year of jubilee. The similarity appears most strikingly as to form in the beatitudes. But in all of them the differences are so great, that they cannot possibly be set to the account of the Evangelists, unless the right can be established, generally to ascribe to them a faded, 'washy' (*verwaschene*) representation of the Lord's evangelical ministry. The number of the beatitudes is not the same in the two discourses, and the construction of single sentences is different. The Evangelist Luke presents a contrast to the beatitudes in a parallel series of woes. The contrast is, indeed, found in Matthew as to the substance, in the delineation of pharisaical righteousness and its consequences, but the form in Luke is totally different. Add to this the difference of the locality and of the auditory which the Evangelists state for each discourse. According to the Evangelist Matthew, Jesus delivered His discourse seated on the top of a mountain ; according to Luke, He came to a level place on the side of a mountain in order to preach to the people. *There*, He, at the sight of the multitude of people, withdrew to the circle of His disciples;[5] *here*, He came down with His disciples from the top of the mountain, and places Himself in the midst of the multitude, in order to speak to them. Thus, therefore, we have evidently two different addresses or discourses, which are formed of the same materials, before us ; and before

[1] See Tholuck's *Commentary on the Sermon on the Mount*, p. 1 (Clark's Tr., 1860).

[2] Olshausen, i. 181.　　　[3] Tholuck, 17.　　　[4] Strauss, i. 614.

[5] This is, at all events, the meaning of the passage Matt. v. 1. Compare Weisse, ii. 27.

we turn to the hypothesis of 'faded representations,' we have
first of all to try our good fortune on the method of estimating
the most living peculiarities of the Gospels.   But here the two
discourses immediately appear to us as highly characteristic.
The Sermon on the Mount (properly so called) manifests
throughout the character of a discourse such as Christ would
not deliver to a promiscuous audience.   This remark applies
particularly to the delineation of the Pharisees and scribes and
their righteousness, and to the description of the striking contrast
between His doctrine and theirs.   He could not have yet spoken
in this manner to the Jewish people in general, without endan-
gering His work to the utmost by a disregard of consequences.
And if in this discourse we also admit that the Evangelist
might give some particular passages in a different connection
than they stood in the original, and have inserted some others,
yet the discourse, in its whole structure, has too original and
harmonious a character for us to ascribe it in essentials to the
Evangelist.[1]   The Sermon on the Mount appears to us, consequently, as a discourse of Christ which has throughout an
esoteric, confidential character.   But in this character it corresponds entirely to the account of the Evangelist respecting
its origin, according to which the Lord delivered it to His
disciples in the mountain solitude, withdrawn from the people ;
though the Evangelist, by the inexact observation at the close,
that the people were 'astonished at His teaching,' which is only
to be referred to the second mountain discourse of Christ, has
in some measure weakened that more exact statement.   In the
Sermon on the Mount, the Lord exhibited to His confidential
disciples the leading doctrines and characteristics of His kingdom, in opposition to the doctrine and religion of its opponents.
But by the disciples we need not necessarily understand only
the four already distinctly called, but rather the circle of
His confidential adherents generally.   Even a Matthew might
properly find himself among them, though his calling to the
apostleship did not take place till a later period.   While this
discourse has a marked esoteric character, on the contrary the
discourse in Luke is throughout popular in its concrete vivacity,
symbolic phraseology, and conciseness ; it has altogether an
exoteric character, and so it exactly corresponds to the connection

[1] Tholuck, 17.

which the Evangelist Luke has given to it. Christ delivers this discourse standing among the multitude, though His eye rests with a blessing on His disciples, who form the choicest part of the audience.

If we now propose the question, in what relation the two discourses stand to one another as to the time of their delivery, from various indications we arrive at the conclusion, that the discourse to the people (*Volkspredigt*) was delivered immediately after that to the disciples (*Gemeindepredigt*). First of all, in reference to the order of time, we may be guided by the history of the centurion at Capernaum. As this in Matthew follows close upon the discourse to the disciples, so in Luke it follows close upon the discourse to the people. Thus the two discourses are brought very near one another; they occur within the same time of one journey of Jesus through Galilee. Let us now add to this, that a multitude of people stand waiting below the mountain while Jesus delivers His first sermon to His disciples, and that when He has come down from the mountain with His disciples, He delivers the latter sermon to the people; and if we thus account for the material resemblance of the two discourses, we gain in this way a perspicuous, comprehensive view of the whole question. We see how Christ, first of all, in the mountain solitude initiates His confidential disciples into the mysteries of His kingdom, and then, on His return to the people, propounds the same doctrine in its leading features, but in a form more suited to the popular apprehension.[1]

We must now examine to which of the Evangelists the preference is to be given in reference to determining the time. In this respect Matthew furnishes important elements for determining the question. First of all, we take into account that the longer discourse so shortly preceded his own calling. It is not at all probable that he would have placed the great events which occurred so close to that calling in a chronologically false position. Add to this, the contents of the second discourse presuppose a circle of hearers for the most part wholly susceptible; a larger than which, Jesus rarely had in His second official summer. But the most significant circumstance is, that the contents of the discourse in both forms very distinctly refer back to the leading

[1] We return, on good grounds, to the hypothesis of Augustin (see Tholuck, p. 1).

thoughts of the first announcement of salvation made by Jesus, namely, to the thought that the great, real jubilee year of God had commenced.

If we would thoroughly apprehend the import of the twofold discourse, we must set out from its relation to the jubilee year in the legislation of the Old Covenant.[1]

The law speaks respecting the year of jubilee as a deeply typical determination of the eternal ideal divine law which is to overrule the historical relations of earthly social rights, including those of person and property. In it is plainly reflected the correct relation of God's proprietorship and that of the holy national community, founded and invested by God, to the proprietorship of the individual, and the personal right of the individual in contrast to the relations or duties of servitude.

The year of jubilee was the *Sabbath* of the holy community; hence it was founded on the sabbatical year which brought about a great Sabbath[2] of the Holy Land, which also was for the advantage of the community. The land was to be once every seven years free from the discipline and coercion of cultivation; it was not, as commonly, to be sown and cleared by reaping, but to produce freely whatever it carried in its bosom as its own genius pleased. It was to be quite as free from the checks on its own luxuriance which the self-interest of the possessor might commonly impose, and to pour forth its abundance as a pure divine property, and be for the common benefit of all, masters and servants, Jews and strangers, man and beast. Every seven years, therefore, the splendour of a theocratic Arcadia, of a glorified paradisaical world, was to shine forth in the Holy Land. But by this rest (or Sabbath) the principle was expressed, that the ground and soil of the earth must ever be a middle property between common property and private possession; that it could never become absolute common property, Church, State, or communal property, but also never absolute private property. So, then, in the seventh year the claim of the community, and especially of the poor in it, also of foreigners, and even of the beasts within their range, to the free abundance of the land, was celebrated. But as nature in seven years completed its cycle through toil to rest, so

---

[1] Lev. xxv. 5; Deut. xv.; Isa. lxi. 2.

[2] שַׁבַּת שַׁבָּתוֹן. Every seventh year was to be *a Sabbath of rest* to the land. Lev. xxv. 4.

the holy national community completed its cycle in seven times
seven years. For society is nature multiplied by itself—nature
elaborating, spiritualizing itself. The fiftieth year (not the
nine-and-fortieth) must therefore be the sabbatical year of the
congregation of Jehovah, the year of jubilee, or trumpet-year.
Its beginning was to be signalized by the great feast of atonement; therefore, from the remission of debt before God must
proceed the remission of debts in society. The opening of this
great festival was to be announced by trumpets; and from this
custom its name is explained.[1] In this year, every inheritance
which an Israelite had sold from necessity reverted again to him,
and upon this reversion the purchase-money was to be calculated.[2] Also, the servitude into which the Israelite, by his
poverty, had been subjected to his brother, a wealthier Israelite,
was to cease with this year;[3] it could never amount to slavery.
Thus with the year of jubilee the bondsman became free, and
he who had lost his inheritance regained it. The ideal fundamental relations of the holy nation, in which the eternal kingdom
of God was reflected, sprang out of the complications and priva-
tions of a severe reality, and the community rested from its own

[1] 'שְׁנַת הַיּוֹבֵל. It has this name from the rams' horns by which it was
announced.'—Winer, R. W. B., art. Jubeljahr. The year of jubilee would
accordingly be designated the year of trumpets. But if, according to the
Chaldee and Hebrew expositors (see Gesenius, Lexicon), the word יוֹבֵל is
interpreted a ram, hence rams' horns, trumpets made of rams' horns, the
choice of these horns would mark a return to the poetic, glorified state of
nature. The jubilee horn was the festive horn of the theocratic Arcadia,
and to be regarded in a distinct relation to similar institutions which have
for their basis the idea of a theocratic festal nature-life, particularly the
feast of Tabernacles and the Nazarite's vow.

[2] 'The voluntary seller of his estate certainly could gain nothing by that
appointment, since, on account of the reference to the year of jubilee (and
the right of reselling), the real purchase-price was reduced, and literally
would only be turned into a rent.'—Winer.

[3] The legal time of service of a Hebrew slave was six years. He became,
therefore, free in the seventh year, according to Exod. xxi. 2, unless the
exception in ver. 5 should occur. This seventh year, or year of release (Deut.
xv.), is not to be identified with the sabbatical year of the land. The latter
was a universal fixed period, contemporaneous for all the people; the year
of release, on the contrary, dated from the time when a Hebrew became the
bondsman of another. He must, therefore, as a rule, serve six years. But
when the year of jubilee came, it made all the Hebrew slaves free.

hardships as the holy congregation of the rich and equally por-
tioned heirs and heiresses of Jehovah.[1]

Thus the Divine Spirit in Israel had withdrawn the three
most essential goods of life from the will, the absolute possession
of the individual, as well as the right of prescription and perpetual exchange—the produce of the field, the holy soil of the
land, and the personal freedom of the individual. These goods
were reserved for the Lord, and hence must always revert to the
holy congregation of God. From the right of goods, a twofold
right of eternal possession was distinguished, both downwards
and upwards.

There was, upwards, an eternal divine possession, or possession of the holy community, which could not become the possession
of individuals. To this belonged the fields of the Levites (Lev.
xxv. 34). But there was also, downwards, a perpetual private
possession, which was not included in the great reversion of the
year of jubilee. To this, without doubt, belonged especially
money[2] and moveable goods, besides the dwelling-house in an
unwalled town, if it was not redeemed within the first year after
the sale. Yet from this the houses in the cities of the Levites
were excepted. They could be sold like the landed property of
other Israelites, but must revert like that, since they were the
landed property of the Levitical individual (Lev. xxv. 29).
Further, the heathen who had become the bondsman of a Jew
was regarded as private property; he might be held in perpetual
slavery. Moveable goods, wealth, are incorporated with the
individual; they belong to his personal dignity. But this slave,
as a heathen in the typical ritual, had not yet attained the enjoyment of personal dignity; yet he was not treated as a thing, as
among the heathen, but as a man theocratically under age.[3]

---

[1] According to the fundamental idea of this right, in the future, at the
expiration of a greater period of debt, Canaan must revert to Israel. The
nations, in their calling to the kingdom of heaven, are the heirs of Jehovah
on the great scale.

[2] Perhaps the passage in Josephus, *Antiq.* iii. 12, § 3, according to which,
debts generally were remitted at the jubilee, is so to be understood as meaning that there was also a cancelling of money-debts. See Winer.

[3] Exod. xxi. 20, 26. The twenty-first verse certainly appears to contradict this, since here the slave is spoken of as property ('for he is his money');
but from the connection it may be inferred that this is to be understood
only in a limited sense.

Lastly, as to the unwalled house in a city, it was separated by the walls from the fields of the country (Lev. xxv. 30, 31), and the individuality was measured by this boundary. The unenclosed house belonged, with the fields, to the divine community and to Jehovah; the house in a walled city fell to the individual, and belonged again, like himself, to the Lord.

In these fundamental distinctions of an ideal right of property, are underlaid, without doubt, the ideas of the eternal right of the kingdom of God. They form the typical ground-plan of the rights and regulations of the Christian social age, the realization of the kingdom of heaven upon earth.[1] They stood so high above the reality, that they could not easily in Israel become a fixed civil usage. But they answered this valuable purpose, that the people, when better disposed, could always use them as a directory. Moses foresaw that the people would not grant the land its Sabbath, and foretold that in the future desolations the land would obtain its rights, and enjoy its Sabbaths (Lev. xxvi. 34, 35). And his prediction was fulfilled first of all, according to 2 Chron. xxxvi. 21, in the misconduct of the people before the Babylonish captivity, and in the punishment which followed. In the last days before that catastrophe, the people, it is true, made an attempt to realize the theocratic rights of persons, but in vain (Jer. xxxiv.). But in proportion as the actual state of things contravened the law, the prophets perceived that the year of jubilee must first of all be exhibited in its spiritual relations, before it could be realized in the earthly ones. They saw in spirit that Jehovah Himself must establish, and would establish, a great year of jubilee,— that He Himself, as the great creditor, must proclaim remission for His debtors, and release His captives, and thus would establish the time of a great general restoration of the children of God. Thus arose the visions of the most delightful longing, hope, and promise, in which the age of the Messiah is depicted

---

[1] Stier has clearly marked the idea of the kingdom of heaven in distinction from the idea of the kingdom of God. The phrase contains 'an indication of real consummation in the future. Hence this idea was developed in the calamitous times of the Jewish theocracy (Dan. ii. 41), when the antagonism between the profane kingdoms of the world and the heavenly kingdom of God, which was hereafter to be realised on earth, was fully grasped by the consciousness of the theocrat.'

as the great jubilee of Jehovah, in which the Messiah appears
as the messenger of God who sounds the trumpet of the jubilee;
as in the passage of Isaiah (lxi. 1, 2) which the Lord read and
expounded in the synagogue at Nazareth.

Just as He there announced the kingdom of heaven as the
beginning of the spiritual and everlasting jubilee, so He appears
to have preached the kingdom of heaven variously in this
figurative representation, which was admirably suited to move
the Israelites in their inmost souls, and was, indeed, from the
first an ideal of the new heavenly age. This is testified by the
last words of the message of Jesus to John—'the poor have the
Gospel preached to them.'[1]

Just so, this equalizing which is to bring the kingdom of
God as a year of jubilee for both poor and rich of the old
world, is a fundamental thought in the two discourses of the
blessedness of the poor in the new world.

On the first great journey of Jesus through Galilee, not only
the groups of His adherents in a narrower sense increased, but
also the multitude of sufferers, and began to press upon Him more
and more. When He saw the crowds thus increasing, He felt
Himself obliged to withdraw from their excessive intrusion,
since He never would expose the holy action of His life to
being overpowered by a host of carnal proselytes and their
mean interests. He went therefore to the mountain, the Evangelists narrate here in the same sense as John on another
occasion; *the* mountain (τὸ ὄρος), namely, in distinction from
the high plains or terraces on which the people stayed.[2] He

[1] According to Wieseler, the year from the autumn of 779 to the
autumn of 780 was a sabbatical year.

[2] In this way may be most easily explained the difficulty which Gfrörer
(h. Sage 138) and Bruno Bauer (Kritik, p. 288) have found in the standing expression τὸ ὄρος in the Gospels. Our explanation, vol. i. p. 215, is
accordingly to be supplemented,—that the sea-shore, which in John vi. 2
forms the contrast to the mountain, is to be regarded as the place where
the people assembled, from which Jesus retired. This is apparent particularly from the words ἀνεχώρησε πάλιν εἰς τὸ ὄρος (ver. 15). Ebrard explains the use of the definite article from a contrast which resulted from
the formation of the Jewish land. It might, indeed, be difficult to consider
the high table-land of Canaan as one mountain—*the* mountain; yet thus
much results from this notice of the character of the Palestinian high table-
land, that we see how the going of Jesus to *the* mountain is favoured by it.
Since the multitude followed the Lord on the beaten roads of the country,

withdrew into the mountain solitude exactly overhanging the encampment of the people.[1] This we gather very distinctly from the representation of Luke (vi. 17).[2]

But into that loneliness He took only His confidential disciples with Him: 'whom He would' (Mark iii. 14). It is very possible that not only the later twelve apostles formed this circle, but that also many others of His more confidential disciples surrounded Him. On that account Mark and Luke might transfer to this place the more distinct separation of the Twelve, which took place somewhat later in their being actually sent out, especially since these Evangelists do not particularly report that later sending. At all events, it was a confidential circle that surrounded the Lord, as is indicated by the significant and historically certain fact, that He stayed and sat down sociably in their midst. On the other hand, surrounded by thousands of people, He could not well preach to them sitting. ' And He opened His mouth,' says the Evangelist. He felt the world-historical importance of this moment, in which Christianity was first expressed in its grand outlines by Christ, and that in contrast to Judaism. It was the moment of breaking open the greatest seal of the world, the moment of the revelation of a new religion, of a religion that transcended Judaism. He opened His mouth and revealed the mystery of this new religion, the Christian in a circle of persons animated with the strongest attachment to Judaism.[3]

This discourse of Christ is called the Sermon on the Mount in a literal sense, but it may be likewise so called in a symbolical sense. Christ stands on the summit of spiritual human life;

so it was easy in a mountainous district for Him, in withdrawing from their place of assembling, to go to the mountain, as in every house where there is a battlement one goes not to *a* battlement, but to *the* battlement.

[1] That the going to the mountain always here means withdrawing from the people, besides the connection here and in Luke, is supported by Mark iii. 13 and John vi. 15.

[2] The Evangelist Mark here relates inaccurately (iii. 13), inasmuch as he confounds together two occasions on which the people thronged around the Lord. But it is an inaccuracy easily explained, if Matthew allow the discourse to the people to be identified with that to the disciples, so that it appears as if the assembled multitude were the auditory who heard the Lord's first discourse.

[3] 'The first word of His mouth is *Blessed!*—and again and again, *Blessed!*'—Stier, i. 98.

His soul is filled with the beatitudes of His holy and perfected divine-human life. From this elevation He addresses poor man in error and confusion, in the depths of an unhappy life, in order to call him up, to lead him, to draw him to His own standpoint; for His word is not only the word of light, but also of power. We may call this discourse the Summit-sermon in order to distinguish it from the following, which was delivered on an elevated plain or lower mountain-terrace, and hence may be designated the Plateau-sermon.

We may contemplate the Summit-sermon as an organic unity which unfolds two principal parts in a most significant contrast, and closes with a third practical part. If we look at it as a unity, the doctrine of Christ appears to us in it in its main outlines, or, more definitely, the representation of the righteousness of Christ as it is unfolded in His disciples, or as the announcement of the spiritual jubilee year, as it consists in rectifying inequalities in the kingdom of God. If we consider it in its two chief component parts, it exhibits the contrariety of the doctrine of Christ to the doctrine of the scribes and Pharisees, or, more definitely, the true righteousness of His disciples in opposition to the false righteousness of His adversaries; or also, the contrasted equalizing which is brought by Christ's jubilee— the exaltation of the poor, and the humiliation of the rich. If, lastly, we fix our attention on the threefold division of the discourse,—the first part depicts the gradual progression of Christian righteous men, how it rises from the depths of poverty of spirit to the summit of blessedness in the vision of God (Matt. v. 1–19); the second part depicts the descent of the pharisaically righteous, how they begin their way of error with deforming the law, and end it by giving that which is holy to the dogs and casting pearls before swine, and in return are torn in pieces by them (Matt. v. 20, vii. 6); the third part gives directions how to avoid the false way down-hill, and to choose the true way up-hill,—it announces, therefore, the true method of the spiritual life. In this threefold division, those distinctions are shown to us, according to which the great equalization is effected which the year of jubilee brings. Especially, therefore, is this discourse to be considered in its unity. We see here the beginning of the New Testament law of life breaking forth from the husk of the Old Testament law. For only by the specially strict law of Jehovah in a narrower sense could the appointed poverty of spirit and the disposition of divine mourning connected with it be produced; the longing after righteousness. We see, then, how in this new legally progressive unfolding the old law celebrates its glorification, since here all its literal appointments are spiritually fulfilled. Then the Lord shows how this new life completely loosens itself from the withered husk of pharisaical maxims by which it was covered, and we are taught the element of Christian practice (*Askese*), of spiritual good conduct, in which this fruit ripens into the complete purity and blessedness of the inner life.

Therefore the Sermon on the Mount in its unity is an organic representation of the appointed forms of life according to Christianity. In this relation it has, not without reason, been compared with the giving of the law on Sinai. As the first comprehensive announcement of the Gospel, it forms the most expressive contrast to the announcement of the law from Sinai. There, the prophet of the Old Covenant received the revelation from the hand of Jehovah by the mediation of angels, therefore with feelings which elevated his life far above the ordinary state; here, the Prophet of the New Covenant utters the revelations of God from the depths of His own innermost life, from the matured moments of His most habitual and yet highest spiritual condition. There, a law is announced which confronts the people with threatenings on tables of stone—accompanied by thunder and lightning, the phenomena of Omnipotence which stands in harmony with the righteousness of God, and therefore accompanied by the signs of armed, threatening, and warning righteousness. *Here*, a law utters its voice, which begins to write the power of the Spirit of Christ in the hearts of men, and whose vivifying power makes itself known in the promises of salvation by which it is accompanied. And while *there*, Moses shattered the first tables of the law in displeasure at the idolatry of the people, and then brings a second, perfectly similar, stern repetition of the law; so *here*, Jesus brings the first form of the Sermon on the Mount, which is only comprehensible by His initiated disciples, in a second concrete and more comprehensible form, out of tender regard to the weakness of the people. But His law remains in all its features a gospel, as His Gospel preserves in all fulness the legal precision. This, therefore, is the

unity of the Sermon on the Mount; it is the Gospel of the law,
or the law of the Gospel. The origin of this law is a human
heart, the holy heart of the Lord; the tables of this law are
human hearts, the susceptible hearts of believers; all its written
characters are life-forms of the real world. If we look at the
Sermon on the Mount according to the antagonism which
animates it, its peculiar theme lies evidently in the twentieth
verse. The righteousness of the disciples of Jesus is delineated
in opposition to the righteousness of the scribes and Pharisees.
The one rise upwards as copartners of the shame and glory of
Christ, till they stand near Him in the light of glorification; the
others descend into the depths of grossness, till they are trampled
under foot by the dogs and swine of the spiritual world. The
close of the discourse shows how men have to walk in one way,
and to avoid the other.

If we let this closing word come forth in its entire significance along with the preceding words, the division of the three
parts is plainly shown, according to which we wish to consider
the discourse in particulars.

The beatitudes form the chief materials of the first part.
These beatitudes are certainly nine, if we number them me-
chanically; but if we keep in view the main point, the successive
steps, it will be seen that the old reckoning of seven beatitudes
is perfectly well founded. While the beatitudes, as far as the
seventh, exhibit a definite succession of steps in the Christian
life, the eighth relates to the pursuit of the Christian after
righteousness in general, and to his holy sufferings arising from
it in the world, as both begin when he takes the first step in the
inner life. He must suffer for righteousness' sake on all the
stages of his development; and this is a blessed suffering. But
that he suffers for righteousness' sake, is identical with suffering
for Christ's sake, which is extolled in the ninth beatitude. Here
only the life which at first was depicted in its general spiritual
form, appears in its concrete Christian distinctness and beauty,
and it is manifest that Christ is the historical, perfected life-
principle of Christian righteousness, and of its unfolding through
all its stages.

As to what regards the relation of this delineation of the
inner life, we have to contemplate it in accordance with its evangelical character, not as an outward legal prescription of the Lord

respecting the conduct of His disciples. Rather His lawgiving is a creative act. When He describes the righteous, He calls them into life by His word; a new world is drawn forth, not from the gloomy fermentation of the elements, but from the night of internal judgments and divine sorrow. This world exists upon His word. We see, therefore, the holy mount surrounded by steps, and all the steps covered by souls rising from the depths to the heights. They *are*, these 'poor in spirit,' these 'mourners;' they live, and that in the spirit. In their unfolding we witness the noiseless formation of the new heavens in the quiet recesses of the hidden world of the affections, and even in the abysses of an unutterable sorrow, by which the Christian life makes its way through the opposition of the old world life.

Life in the spirit is the fundamental character of all Christians. The Christian begins his Christian existence with feeling himself poverty-struck in spirit: he is conscious of an infinite want in his spirit, with an equally powerful craving after satisfaction. But he feels this want so strongly in the spirit, because he lives in the spirit. Without life in the spirit there is no Christianity whatever; no theological science, no moral culture, no church ceremonial, can supply the place of life in the spirit. In spiritual life, that is, in that life in which the spirit of man comes in contact and is united with the Spirit of God, the various stages of righteousness and blessedness are all identical. It lies in the nature of the spirit, that it exhibit itself in the whole circumference of its constituent elements. Therefore the poor in spirit on the first stage must also be in the germ a peacemaker; and in the blessed peacemaker of the seventh stage there is still poverty in spirit in its essential contents, though transformed into a most blessed humility. Nevertheless, the succession of stages is a necessary, organic, and perfectly definite succession. Every step has its own character, controlling and determining the whole inner life, and the Christian in his inner life must experience all these phases of his spirit's constitution to verify their eternal value, and to exhibit them on the summit of his development in perfect unity.

It is the foundation of an organically determined development, that man begins his new life in the spirit in the feeling of his woeful destitution of all the highest goods of the spirit. This poverty embraces the whole new life of the spirit as a germ, and breaks forth in a twofold direction in polar unfolding. In poverty of spirit, man comes to himself, and now he necessarily comprehends in his inmost soul his most intimate relation to God. Then the root of his new life is formed in pure, holy sorrow, which in its nature is a divine sorrow, a mourning on account of separation from God, a pining after home. But in this divine sorrow his relation to other men becomes a new one; the old fierceness and hardness of his natural egoism is stripped off, and the stem of his life is formed under the smooth spiritual control of gentleness with which he now meets his fellow-men. That sorrow is nourished by this gentleness, and, striking its roots deeper, becomes an ardent longing after the righteousness of God. This gentleness, under the holy longing after righteousness and its satisfaction, is developed into tender-heartedness, which recognises his neighbour as miserable, and is interested in positively rescuing him. Lastly, that hungering and thirsting after righteousness before God is satisfied under the exercises of mercifulness and the acts of self-denial which accompany it, and purity of heart is its fruit, the lily-blossom of the perfection of the life turned to God; and so at last this mercifulness ripens to the highest vitality in power to bring the peace of God, and to establish peace upon earth, and therefore in the perfection of the life turned to men. But this double threefold development of the Christian is a conflict against the world for eternal righteousness, and therefore is connected with the severest suffering; it is a suffering for God. But it is equally a suffering for holy man, a suffering for Christ's sake,— indeed a dying with Him on His cross.

These phenomena of the spiritual life consist neither in well-disposed natural states of the affections, nor in imperfect strivings of the will; they are neither moral virtues, nor legal habitual acts of a laborious, striving self-determination. They are rather, as constituents of the proper spiritual life, such dispositions as on the one hand may be contemplated as operations of God, as new states of the spirit, and, on the other, altogether as the ripe, free, ardent, decided acts of human striving; therefore spiritual determinations in which man, striving and free, lays hold of the divine life as he is laid hold of by it.

Now, if the Lord pronounces men blessed in these spiritual

states, it is not merely a promise of blessedness. They are already blessed, although they have not attained the full consciousness of this blessedness. The deepest divine sorrow exists under the influence of the peace of God, and is more blessed than the highest worldly enjoyment. But this blessedness is to be perfected;—the promises express that. To the poor in spirit the whole kingdom of heaven is allotted. Since he is poor in spirit, he is poor in the infinity of the divine life; therefore he is craving, poverty-struck, with a consecrated hungering after the Eternal,[1] and on that account, because the infinite fulness of the Divine Spirit has already enkindled him, and thus he is nobly covetous of the highest, he is become a spiritual mendicant, so that the whole world can no longer satisfy him. In his eager anticipation, that fulness has already touched him and penetrated his inmost life; hereafter the complete effulgence of that fulness shall enter his spirit. But as his poverty in spirit is formed and unfolded before God and the world, so also is his reward, or the inheritance that is promised him. To mourning absolutely—that is, the highest, pure, divine mourning sorrow for destitution of God—corresponds consolation absolutely; therefore, consolation from God in the heavenly refreshment and encouragement of his life. For this mourning proceeds from the disgust man feels with pleasure in vain things: the mourner absolutely is impelled by the presentiment of the eternal, serene, divine life, the peace of God; and hence this peace is to greet him in a spiritual rejuvenescence of life, and will hereafter become altogether his portion. But the disciples of Jesus inherit the earth as the meek. The holy land of the world, now in the course of transformation, and hereafter to be wholly transformed, gains immediately for them a fresh splendour, and will be one day their heritage, the earthly basis for the appearance of their glory,[2] not only because meekness as the mightiest spiritual life must lead to victory over the rude, impassioned men of violence, and because God makes up to the patient his injured rights by abundant recompense, but also

---

[1] 'To translate πτωχοί with perfect exactness, we should use *egeni* and *mendici*, to which it corresponds, as πένης to *pauper*.'—Tholuck, 67. [See Trench's *Synonyms of the New Testament* (First Series), pp. 141-144.—TR.]

[2] 'Then shall the lambs feed after their manner upon their pasture;' Isa. v. 17.—Stier, i. 106.

because the meek is already filled with the ideal of the transformed earth, and therefore cannot eagerly contend about the
provisional forms of the earth and earthly phantoms; since he
has chosen paradise in the earth, while others have chosen in it
the accursed ground, therefore, in fact, only the curse which is
to be withdrawn from the earth.[1]   Here it becomes evident, in
what a rich sense the rights of the Jewish year of jubilee find
their essential realization in the consummation of Christ's kingdom.   Therefore the disciples of Jesus appear as renouncing
their claims in the old world, not because they have no sense of
the beauty of the world, but because the resplendent image of
the pure divine world ravishes and ennobles them, and has raised
them above the lower desires of transitory things.   But above
all things they yearn after the prime fundamental condition of
all divine life—righteousness.   All their longing, every desire of
their life, is tinged and controlled by this highest spiritual aspiration, and is drawn into the ardent revolution of this aspiration; therefore, their very breaking of bread easily becomes the
supper for the remembrance of the death of Jesus, and their
bridal festivity a symbol of Christ's relation to the Church.
But since in all things they long after righteousness, all the
fulness of life to their life's satisfaction is to be given to them
in and with the righteousness of God; they are to be satisfied
absolutely—altogether calmed with the reconciling righteousness first of all, but also with all heaven, which is in its train,
until they are satisfied in their infinite longing, and express it
in never-ending praise.   This satisfaction is already announced
in their hunger and thirst; for the most ardent desire after righteousness is the most ardent motive to be released from the bondage of creature-desire, the cessation of the desire of human
nature-life, by entrance into the Christian ideality of the world,
in which man enjoys everything in the spirit.   The pain suffered for eternal righteousness leads the higher longing of life
into the quiet tribunal in the breast in which earthly wishes die,
there to be examined and tried; and thus it is glorified as the

---

[1] ['The dross of the earth the meek do not inherit; the *damnosa hære-
ditas* of the earth's pomps and vanities descends to others; but all the true
enjoyments, the wisdom, love, peace, and independence, which earth can
bestow, are assured to the meek as in their meekness inherent.'—Henry
Taylor, *Notes from Life*, 29.—ED.]

joy of sorrow, rests in God, comes forth from this tribunal, and in the transformed sorrow of life's deepest depths has recognised its choicest part, the blessedness of the cross. With this divine satisfaction of their life, the disciples of Jesus have become rich in the presence of suffering humanity; and as in these riches they exercise mercy, so also they obtain mercy. In the soothing balm which now streams forth from their benevolent heart into the wounds of their neighbours and of the world, they have gained the sense for the rich, divine balm of healing mercy which streams into their own sick life, their life's wounds, in order to complete their restoration; and in the gentle influence of God's Spirit they feel assured of finding mercy both with God and man—in distress and death—that even after they lose their health and sink strengthless, everything must be transformed for them into a sheltering bosom of God's love—into a holy grave filled with the healing and reviving power of God. The perfection of their life in its upward direction consists in purity of heart. The heart is first pure in positive power, in the firmness of the eternal spirit, when it desires, grasps, and retains nothing worldly as worldly, and nothing of its own as its own; when it seeks and finds all things only in God, and only God in all things. In this state of the perfected spirit no desire disturbs its Christian ideal or holy relation to God and the world; and therefore the heart has become a pure mirror in which the glory of God is expressed most clearly to a spiritual eye that can see God. This seeing of God is to be accomplished as the most intimate knowledge and experience of God's administration and nature, as it is revealed through all the world; therefore it is mediated by the spiritual contemplation of Christ, in whom the organic life-principle of the world is revealed, in whom the image of God has appeared. The possibility of God's being seen is conditioned by this revelation of God (which at the same time is the glorification of the world), by the being of Christ. Moreover the possibility of the heart's becoming pure is conditioned by the believing contemplation of the positive purifying divine purity in him.[1] According to this promise, the heart's becoming pure must be essentially allied to the elevation of the spirit to the sight of God. Hence it follows that the cognitive power of

[1] On the reciprocal relation of seeing God, and likeness to God, compare the admirable remarks of Tholuck, p. 95.

man, his power of spiritual vision, has its innermost nerve in the life of his heart. If he is foolish in his thinking, so is he foolish in his heart,[1] and out of the corruption of his feelings arises the corruption of his thoughts. If a man is wise, he is wise in his heart: the fear of God is the beginning of wisdom. The highest form of knowledge is therefore not the abstract apprehension of philosophizing thought, but the spiritual seeing in which all the faculties (*Qualitäten*) of the spirit discharge their functions, priest-like, in the most living unity—a seeing in which the whole life becomes knowledge, and all knowledge perfect life—the eye one with the heart, and indeed one in the clearest beholding of God, as it proceeds from union with God in the purity of the heart.[2] The human heart was originally consecrated to be a place for the spaceless, a measure of time for the timeless, a uniqueness of the revelation of the eternal God; therefore it can never become a *tabula rasa* of infinite desolation and worthless insensibility; as it has died altogether to the world, it has become alive in the eternal God. Now, since man, according to the measure of this purification becomes a peacemaker and a messenger of peace for the world, an angel of the Gospel, or a Christian genius of the world's peace resting in reconciliation with God,—so he also obtains an inheritance that corresponds to this life. The kings and judges of the earth were from the beginning destined to rule as peacemakers in a higher sense over the earth full of contentions, and to quell the hellish strife of the passions; and in accordance with this destination they are called in a higher sense, children or sons of God.[3] But the kings and judges of the ancient world mostly contradicted their destination, and in the best instances exhibited only more or less strong symbols of the essential heavenly life of their calling that could be first realized in spirit in the life of the disciples of Jesus. These therefore undertook in the most real sense the office to judge and to rule on the earth by the word of God in the spirit of His love; and for this

[1] Ps. xiv. 1. When people are foolish, they are foolish in their heart.

[2] The origin of the spiritual promise of seeing God proceeds from Eastern customs. 'Eastern kings kept themselves aloof from the view of their subjects; hence beholding the countenance of the king was regarded by them as a peculiar favour and distinction.' See Tholuck, p. 91, where what is essential in the spiritual application of this expression is admirably pointed out.

[3] John x. 34; compare Ps. lxxxii. 6.

ever more, as the end of the world approaches, will the honour be awarded them, that they have become the true chiefs of the human race,[1] its perpetual assessors of peace,[2] and the most genuine sons of God in the world's history. They were once the most real, most absolute mendicants,—mendicants emphatically, as the poor in spirit; and to this character it corresponds that they have now become the most special chiefs of humanity, illustrious chiefs in the kingdom of the spirit, sons of God, and are recognised as such.[3] Thus the rewards of the disciples of Jesus rise with their virtues. In their spiritual position before God they were first of all comforted, then filled, lastly illuminated and glorified in the vision of God by His sun-like splendour; but in the presence of the world, they gained the inheritance of the new earth, they experienced the healing of all their life's wounds, and attained those spiritual honours which are the reflection of their inner life and outward conduct in the award of God and the acknowledgment of men. But as that Christian deportment towards God and towards men unfolded itself in a constant polar reciprocal action—so that, for example, mourning before God became meekness towards men, and from mercy towards men came purity of heart before God; so likewise their rewards unfold themselves in this reciprocal action. As the comforted ones, Christians have begun to understand the true enjoyment of the earth, and the images in it of the Eternal; as those who see God, they have gained that power of light which is reflected in their countenances, so that they can overpower the demons of strife on earth. But because on the whole path of this spiritual life they have been persecuted for righteousness' sake, theirs is the kingdom of heaven. But why again the kingdom of heaven, as well as in the case of the poor in spirit? For this reason : the kingdom of heaven is the all-comprehensive expression of the divine requital, and because it developes itself in a distinct contrast from the deepest secrecy as the work of God in the heart to the highest glorification of the life and of the world. As the poor in spirit, they already possess the kingdom of heaven in its foundation, for the work of God has made its beginning in their hearts. But they scarcely know themselves how rich they

---

[1] Rev. i. 6. [2] Matt. xix. 28.

[3] Without doubt Christians in this more definite sense are here called υἱοὶ Θεοῦ.

have become. As the rich in spirit, they have been driven and
persecuted through the world ; but by this means they have become conscious that to them belongs the kingdom of heaven, and
indeed that they exhibit, reveal, and spread it in the world by their
life ; and at last they know perfectly that their life is one and the
same with the kingdom of heaven, and that the kingdom of heaven,
in its complete manifested glory, becomes their inheritance. But
this was the historical, the satisfied form of their holy life, that
they suffered for Christ's sake and with Him. He was the life-
principle of their whole spiritual life and condition; therefore their
inheritance gains the complete historical form; they enter into
the kingdom of Christ's glory, in which they associate themselves
with their predecessors the prophets in one grand choir, and in
the perfected relations of blessedness receive their full reward in
the personal assembly of the redeemed. The spiritual relations
of the kingdom of heaven, therefore, perfectly coincide with its
individual relations; the name of Christ is one with righteousness ; and as the suffering for righteousness was a suffering of
persecution for Christ's sake, so the spiritual gain of the kingdom of heaven is an individual entrance into heaven, and a reception of the reward in the circle of the blessed prophets.

   Thus has the Lord marked out the ascent of His disciples
to the summit of their felicity. This heavenly way forms a contrast to the world's way of death ; and hence the conflict and
persecution experienced by believers. Therefore they should
not think this experience strange ; they must go through this
necessity of conflict. The Lord points this out to them by two
similitudes. They are the salt of the earth. Salt, as the most
living mineral substance, as the highest, sharpest life-spirit of
earthy minerals, seasons the earthy nutritious matter, and checks
the corruption of animal substances ; and so the children of the
Spirit of Christ, in the power of this Spirit punishing what is
evil, vivifying and transforming what is naturally good, are the
seasoning, conservative, and transforming life-power of human
society.[1] But since salt is the noblest mineral, which can improve even bread and flesh, vegetable and animal life, it becomes
the least valuable when it is decayed, and loses its seasoning
power ; it then sinks below dead rubbish, and can only serve as
the most worthless mineral, to be cast out of doors to mend the

   [1] On the great value attached to salt by the ancients, see Tholuck, 106.

road. Such deterioration is indeed not possible in pure earthly salt; and as little is it possible in the pure spiritual salt, the life of Christ. But as there is in nature an imperfect salt, which, on account of its earthy mixture, can decay and become worthless,[1] so it is also possible with the spiritual salt which the disciples exhibit before the world. Just as Christ calls them the light of the world on account of the illumination which they receive from Him, although much that is dark in their minds requires to be removed; so here He calls them the salt of the earth because the sharp, spiritual power that He imparts to them must form the governing principle of their life, although still much that is earthly is in their spiritual nature, by which they may be again corrupted, and then most awfully be cast away. The disciples therefore are to preserve their salt-power and sharpness before the world. And while as the salt of the earth they are to preserve the world from moral corruption and hellish ruin, they must likewise plant in it the highest, heavenly life as the light of the world. They are not to imagine that they can remain hidden any more than a city that is set upon a hill.[2] Still less should they aim at concealing their luminous spiritual life. A lamp is lighted, not to be put under a corn-measure,[3] but on a stand, that it may give light to all that are in the house. So should they confidently let their light, of which the first ray is poverty in spirit, and therefore humility, shine before men; and if people at first revile in them the mystic source of their light, the name of Christ, yet they will at last learn to value the beneficial effects of their light, their good works, and glorify the Father in heaven. This is the practical close of the discourse on the beatitudes.

[1] Compare the quotation in Tholuck from *Maundrell's Travels*. 'In the valley of salt at Dachebal, some 16 miles from Aleppo, there is a declivity of twelve feet high which has been formed by the continual removal of the salt. I broke off a piece where the surface is exposed to the action of the rain, air, and sun; and found that, although it contained the mica and particles of the salt, it had entirely lost the taste of salt. The inner portion, however, which was more joined to the rock, still retained the peculiar taste.'

[2] It has been often supposed that in these words Jesus alluded to the town of Safed; but, according to Robinson, it is doubtful whether Safed was in existence in the time of Jesus. See *Biblical Researches* ii. 425.

[3] See Tholuck, p. 114.

But now the Lord must display to His disciples the world
with which they will come in conflict in its worst form, in the
positive descent from the mountain, from the pure legal standpoint, therefore (so to speak) from the consecrated heights of
Sinai, as it was exhibited in the righteousness of the Pharisees
and scribes. And since His disciples, like the Jews generally,
were wont to identify the law of Moses and the maxims of the
scribes, the hallowing of that law and the righteousness of the
Pharisees according to those maxims; so they were in danger of
being perplexed at the doctrine of Christ as soon as they perceived its contrariety to the maxims of the Pharisees. Hence
Christ first of all determines the relations in which, on the one
hand, He stands with His doctrine to the Old Covenant, and in
which, on the other, the Pharisees and scribes are to the same.

This is the relation of Christ to the Old Covenant. He
came not to destroy the law or the prophets.[1] Generally He
came not to destroy, but to fulfil.[2]

In His institution the perfection of all the legal institutions
and ordinances of the kingdom of God lies in their unity; just
as in the flower, not the half, but the whole substance of the
plant is brought into splendid exhibition. In His life this fulfilling of the Old Testament seed was completed in its chosen
part or centre. But as to its circumference, the unfolding of
this fulfilment continues to the end of the world.[3]

And before heaven and earth or the old world-form are dissolved, not an iota, not a tittle[4] of the law will be dissolved or
destroyed; nothing of it will be destroyed till all which it has
determined has become a reality.[5] Whatever was fixed as law

[1] ἢ τοὺς προφήτας. The ἢ here is not to be taken as equivalent to καί.
Among the Jews there were different ways of annulling the Old Covenant.
The Sadducees annulled the prophets, the Essenes the law, the Pharisees
in reality both the legal and prophetical portions. The 'or' refers to such
contrarieties. Christ held the whole development sacred, and exhibited it
complete on His higher standpoint.

[2] See Tholuck, p. 121. Stier (i. 136) explains this passage in a very
beautiful and striking manner.

[3] See Tholuck, p. 122.

[4] The iota denotes the smallest Hebrew letter, י; but the little point or
tittle, κεραία, denotes a smaller stroke which distinguishes similar letters
from one another, as ד from ר. And so figuratively the smallest part of the
law. See Tholuck, 132.

[5] ἕως ἂν πάντα γίνηται. The law has therefore two termini; one nega-

can only be removed by its being changed into a principle of life by the spirit. But when a false spirit, as Spiritualism, would remove such a legal appointment by a pure negation, without renewing and elevating it into an evangelical appointment, the supposed expunged iota or the misunderstood fragment of the mutilated law will make its appearance again in large or even flaming characters; it will take vengeance on those who in a perverse spirit misinterpreted or rejected it. And thus will the law for ever enforce its claims till every part of it has come to pass or become life—until this mature life-birth of the realized law makes its appearance as a new world, and the enclosing shell of the old world is broken through and destroyed.

Therefore he is not a reformer, but a revolutionist, who relaxes or destructively repeals one of the least enactments of the law, or perverts it by a false interpretation,[1] without restoring or preserving it in an evangelical form. And whoever misleads others to this nullification, such a person will be called least in the kingdom of heaven, because his spirit has the smallest compass, because he cannot come to the life of the law without giving up the fulness of its enactments and confining himself to a few abstract principles. But whoever strives above all things to keep the law in its power and full extent, and teaches accordingly, shall be called great in the kingdom of heaven. This is the greatness of the reformer, that he collects together all the riches of the enactments of the law, and unfolds them in the fully comprehensive, though not directly explicit, enactments of the Gospel.[2] But such revolutionists who disannul the true law we have had to seek for a thousand times in a quarter where we should least suspect them to exist, among the men of prescriptions. The righteousness of the Pharisees and scribes leads not to the kingdom of heaven, but downhill to the abyss. And this

tive, and the other positive. The negative is the destruction of the old world-form; the positive is its realization in the new world-form.

[1] Tholuck says: 'There is a fulfilling of the law which, because it is only a fulfilment of the letter, is really a transgression, according to the profound truth of the saying, Summum jus summa injuria; and, on the other hand, there is a transgression of the letter which is essentially a fulfilment of the law.'

[2] We are here reminded of the contrast between the Peasant War and the Reformation; between the Revolution and the Christian renovation of the world which is still to come.

is shown first of all in their disfiguring the true law. While, therefore, in Christianity the glorification of Sinai, the fulfilling and bloom of the Old Covenant, must be recognised, we see in the righteousness of the Pharisees and scribes a dissolution of this covenant.[1] This heavy charge the Lord establishes in the sequel. From His showing, it appears that the old law might be annulled in different ways.

This annulment had been brought about slowly, by a succession of criminal acts, the offspring of false tradition. We cannot say who did it; it was effected by the general spirit of the interpretation (ἐῤῥέθη); but this tradition was carefully taken up by the ancients, or at least by those who were like-minded (ἀρχαίοις). The first corruption of the law was shown in this, that it was not developed according to its spirit, but was limited to its literal meaning. Thus the Jews had understood the law, *Thou shalt not kill,* by the addition of the civil enactment, *Whosoever shall kill shall be in danger of the judgment,* in stiff literality, without ascertaining its spirit and applying it to the life; therefore they had deprived it of its spirit and annulled it. But the law must be developed if it is to remain true; it operates falsely as soon as it is only enforced according to the letter. This we see in the first example. Christ develops this first law according to its spirit. Whosoever is angry with his brother without a cause[2] shall be in danger[3] of the district court;[4] for he

[1] It will be understood that, in taking a correct view of Christ's words, we are not to think of finding in them a rectification of the Mosaic law. Christ certainly comes forward in contrast to Moses, but in that harmonious contrast which has for its base an organic connection, not in contradiction to him. See Olshausen, i. 199.

[2] We read ὁ ὀργιζόμενος with the addition εἰκῆ, not only because the authorities, according to Griesbach, are stronger for this reading than those which are against it, but especially because the connection appears to require this addition. The εἰκῆ must, at all events, denote a peculiar form, an outbreak of anger, by which it is characterized as being angry for a trifle, extravagantly, at random. It has often been remarked in connection with this passage, that anger in itself may be a holy feeling, as we read of the wrath of God and of the anger of Christ.

[3] ἔνοχος ἔσται. He will be subject to that tribunal. The choice of expressions indicates that he is to be considered as one doomed to the sentence mentioned according to justice, not as really so to be sentenced.

[4] As in ver. 21 mention is made in a definite sense of the Jewish inferior courts or district courts in criminal cases (which was preceded by a

has exalted himself against its right to be judge over him, and thereby made an insolent attack on the rights of this court. But whoever says to his brother, Racha! thou detestable one! thou accursed one![1] he is obnoxious to the judgment of the San-hedrim, since he has designated his brother as one excommuni-cated from the congregation—a judgment which belongs only to the Sanhedrim. But whoever says to him, Thou fool! thou wicked, abandoned reprobate! he is obnoxious to the heaviest divine judgment in Israel, which sentences to be thrown into the hell of fire, to be executed and thrown into the valley of Gehinnom, and to be burnt as a corpse with the corpses that are thrown there,[2] according to the same law, because, without right or reason, he had condemned his brother to this penal court. Therefore the unauthorized judge rightly incurs the same judgment which, contrary to love, he inflicts on his neigh-bour. If he treats him as a criminal, he exposes himself to the criminal court; if he condemns him as a heretic, he is ob-noxious to the tribunal for heresy; and if he gives him up as a reprobate past recovery, he is obnoxious to the highest religious tribunal in which the punishment of damnation is reflected. It

smaller court for civil causes), the expression here must refer to the same tribunal.

[1] Racha is probably not to be derived from ריק, רין in the sense of *stupid*. This word of reproach would probably stand highest in the first category: it describes the brother who belongs as a malefactor to the San-hedrim. We would rather consider as correct the derivation from רקק, *to spit upon*, since it appears to have been a symbolical act to spit on persons who were condemned as heretics. Racha, according to the analogy of the lengthened imperative (see Ewald's *Grammar of the Hebrew Language*, translated by Nicholson, p. 164), may be an interjection (*Spit!*), which might express the sentence of the judge condemning the heretic, which per-mitted the accuser to spit on the condemned.

[2] The Jewish hell (Gehenna, from גיא הנם) is quite different from Sheol, or the kingdom of the dead. It was first of all the place of the exe-cution which would be inflicted on a malefactor when his corpse was thrown into the valley of the sons of Hinnom, where from time to time the pro-scribed corpses were burnt. This punishment marked a rejection continued in the other world, and hence was an image of damnation. In that valley the Hebrews once practised the horrible Moloch-worship (1 Kings xi. 7); hence king Josiah defiled it by causing corpses to be thrown there (2 Kings xxiii. 13, 14). See Tholuck. It is remarkable that the symbolical place of hell proceeded mediately from the Moloch-worship—the place of horror from the place of abomination.

is therefore manifest that Christ does not merely intend to represent an uncharitable disposition as damnable, by an arbitrarily marked hyperbolic punishment: He rather exhibits uncharitableness from the first in its subtle, social offences, as to make it punishable according to the spirit of the law in a social sense. The aggravations of guilt are quite definite, and with the same definiteness the succession of courts of justice to which the person guilty of uncharitableness would be amenable. The meaning of the succession of courts of justice was, in short, this: it is criminal when a man stamps his brother, in unauthorized private passion, arbitrarily as a criminal; it is heretical when he stamps him as a heretic; and damnable when he dooms him to perdition. These sharp distinctions must serve to show how far the law, ' *Thou shalt not kill*,' goes beyond the limited exposition, *the murderer alone falls under the judgment of the criminal court:* how soon the uncharitable would be lost with the first expressions of his uncharitableness, if he were judged by God and man according to the standard which his own uncharitableness has set up.

That severity, therefore, which too hastily judges a brother, always exposes itself to its own sentences, and that according to its own rules. So sharp is the law in its development, since it demands the greatest gentleness of love, the placable spirit which the Lord characterized by a single case. ' If thou bring thy gift to the altar, and there recollectest before God— where the admonitory and punitive Spirit of God looks sharply upon man, and where the pious easily becomes conscious of a hidden fault—that thy brother hath ought against thee, leave there thy gift before the altar, and go thy way, and be reconciled to thy brother, and then come and offer thy gift.' So very much is reconciliation with God conditioned by the spirit of reconcilableness towards man. The point in question is, indeed, not an outward and literal, but a spiritual fulfilment of this rule; as, for example, it was in this sense a custom among the early Christians for the members of a family to beg forgiveness of one another before they went to the holy supper. ' See to it,' the Lord adds, ' that thou agreest with thy adversary who hastens a suit against thee whilst thou art on the way to the judge; quickly come to terms with him, that he may not hand thee over to the judge, and the judge cause thee by his officers to be cast into prison.' If there is the right to bring to judgment, it will operate in the form of judgment; there will be no release till the last farthing is paid, till the debt has been discharged according to law. Thus man must cherish a deep, holy solicitude, lest he should in any way violate love. This spirit of mildness and reconciliation is the spirit of the law, *Thou shalt not kill.*

Also a second command, the law, *Thou shalt not commit adultery*, the Jews had deprived of its due force by not developing it according to its meaning, but, on the contrary, misinterpreting it. The Lord restores this development: *Whoever looketh on a woman with the design to lust after her, he has already committed adultery with her in his heart.*[1] So easily may guilt be contracted if we are not on our guard. The law of marriage requires a holy caution, which shows itself particularly in two respects. A man must pluck out his right eye, if he is seduced by the eye to commit this transgression. This probably is to be understood of the pleasurable gazing on beauty. The pleasure of beholding which leads to ruinous desires must be entirely renounced, though it may be the most ardent enthusiasm, the pleasure of the right eye. And so a man must cut off his right hand, if by this hand he is seduced into transgression. This probably is to be understood of friendly intercourse. It must be entirely given up, if a man cannot overcome and destroy the temptation in it by faith, even though it were the most powerful attachment.[2] But not only had the Jews injured the law of marriage by the want of development, but likewise in another way: that political concession which Moses had annexed to the promulgation of the eternal law itself, in order gradually to

---

[1] We must regard it as decided that πρός designates the inward aim. Tholuck, p. 208. Therefore it is not the unpremeditated feeling that is here spoken of, but the intentional and conscious desire. Although the former is a sin, yet, as Luther expresses himself, it is like an evil thought without consent, not a deadly sin. 'Nevertheless it is a sin, but comprehended in the general forgiveness.' See Tholuck, p. 209. According to the exact grammatical construction of the sentence, the desecration of marriage in conjugal intercourse by the designed excitement of sensual desire might be intended.

[2] Hardly does the eye denote merely 'the organ of ἀκολάστως βλέπειν and the hand that of ἀναισχύντως ἄπτεσθαι;' for if so, why should the *right* eye and the *right* hand be specified?

pave the way for the true sanctification of marriage, they neither recognised nor practised according to its true and holy intent, but had represented it with lightness as a trivial matter. Moses found the practice of divorce, as a natural result of his people's hardness of heart, to be a custom which he could not put a stop to by legislation, because the actual marriage very often did not correspond to the ideal true marriage. As long as the actual marriage was frequently at variance with the idea of marriage, so long it was needful for the concession to continue. But it must be regulated and checked by the law, in order that many marriage-contracts might not be contaminated by the preceding unrestrained divorces, and that the law might promote the continual tending of the actual marriage towards the ideal. Therefore Moses introduced a check on the unrestrained practice of divorce by ordaining ' *a writing of divorcement*.'[1] But instead of seeing a limitation of divorce in this statute, the Jews saw an encouragement of it. Hence Christ pronounced the decision, 'Every divorce which is not occasioned by adultery (whoredom) is itself adultery, inasmuch as the divorced is beguiled to regard herself as free and to marry again; and so also he violates the marriage who espouses the divorced.' Adultery, therefore, is committed when the divorce of the former marriage ends in a new one.

A similar manner of obscuring the law by a misinterpretation of its decisions, is shown in the way the Jews decided on the law of oaths.[2] Moses looked upon the oath in civil matters as an unavoidable instrument of justice.[3] But in general he counterworked the taking an oath. This he did in three ways. In the first place he interdicted the false oath as an abuse of the name of God (Exod. xx. 7; Lev. xix. 12); then he insisted on regarding as sacred, and on fulfilling, a vow made with an oath;[4] and thirdly, he decided that persons were to swear by the name of the Lord.[5] In this way of counterworking the taking of oaths, Christ advances to the full accomplishment; and certainly in opposition to the Jews, who had made out of the Mosaic regulations a very easy theory of oath-taking. Christ forbids the spontaneous swearing of the individual abso-

---

[1] Compare Deut. xxiv. 1; Matt. xix. 8.   [2] Compare Matt. xxiii. 16.
[3] Exod. xxii. 11; compare Heb. vi. 16.
[4] Num. xxx. 3.   [5] Deut. vi. 13.

lutely, that is, asseverations by oath in a literal sense. The person swearing appeals to some object as a witness; he constitutes that object an avenger or a pledge for the truth of his deposition. But in this lies the wrongfulness of the common voluntary adjuration. How can a person constitute anything as a pledge for the truth of his assertions when all things belong to God? If he swears by heaven, he presumes to pledge the throne of God. Just so, he acts against eternal right when he would pledge the earth, which is God's footstool; or Jerusalem, the chief city of Jehovah as the great King of the theocracy; or even his own head, his life, which altogether, even to every hair, in all its several relations, is under the control of God. Only his own consciousness can he pledge. But this is done when he makes his simple assertion in yea and nay serve for an oath, when he strengthens the common Yea or Nay by a solemn Yea! or Nay! and therefore speaks with a collectedness and certainty which may be regarded as the consciousness of one taking an oath who speaks in the presence of God. Whatever goes beyond that, the Lord says, is from the evil one, at all events, proceeds from the corruption of the world. When the State makes a form of. adjuration, because it cannot dispense with it for the sake of the general body, the Christian should then drop his yea and nay, but should know that his yea and nay signify the pledge of his moral person for his word before God; and that of themselves no adjurations can have greater force which do not become him, and which obscure the true essential oath-nature of veracious speech (Jas. v. 12).

It is no contradiction of this statement respecting the law of oaths when Christ admitted the validity of the oath before the Sanhedrim, for He rendered it on His part by the solemn yea, which to Him was always equivalent to an oath. And when the Apostle Paul appeals to the truth of Christ within him (2 Cor. xi. 10), or to his conscience in the Holy Ghost (Rom. ix. 1), or calls God to witness,—in these assurances there appears to us precisely the glorification of the oath, namely, the avowal of his Christian elevated consciousness, in which the truth of Christ, the witness of God and his conscience, are one. For his consciousness is exactly that over which the speaker has power, which he can pledge by his assurance as a witness. From this it may be inferred that the pure oath in God's sight, in the life of the

believer who has united himself with God, is no oath in the
common sense, and hence it was not mentioned by Christ.   But
when it is said, God swore by Himself (Isa. xlv. 23 ; Heb. vi.
13), this is the expression of the perfect self-consciousness of
God, which is one with His personality, and the most solemn
assurance that in the power of His self-consciousness or personality, He makes an everlasting covenant with His children
as personal beings related to Him.

Again, another perversion of the law takes place when it
is falsely applied ; when, for example, *a regulation for public
State life is extended to private life.*   So it was with the strict law
of retaliation (*Lex talionis*), ' *Eye for eye, tooth for tooth.*'[1]   The
Mosaic legislation expressed this law of sheer retaliation most
vividly in these words.   Moses gave this right of retaliation the
form of revenge, in order to intimate that it should set aside
revenge and be a substitute for it.   Indeed, private revenge he
expressly forbids (Lev. xix. 18).   And that legislation itself was
not wanting in the living explanation and application of this
enactment.   The enactment was orally made (Exod. xxi. 26),
when any one smote his servant or maid in the eye, and the eye
perished, or when he smote out a tooth of either, he was to be
punished by letting the injured party go free.   But the Jew
brought this right of retaliation as a right of revenge into his
private life; exactly contrary to the intention of the law, which
was to guard against revenge.   Therefore the Lord developed
the law in His declaration, ' Resist not evil :' you are not to
assert your right by personal individual violence, but by the
greatest patience and forbearance promote the rule of public
justice, appeal to and announce the eternal justice.   This precept the Lord illustrates by concrete specifications which are to
be explained together, not literally, but spiritually : ' Whosoever shall smite thee on the right cheek, offer him also the left :'
let him feel by thy equanimity and willingness to suffer that
thou art not agitated about thy right, but with firm joyfulness
abidest certain of eternal justice, which protects thy dignity.
Let not the civil tribunal be thy highest confidence.   If any
man will sue thee for thy coat, and seek to take it from thee
in that way, let him have thy cloak also, though it may be

---

[1] Exod. xxi. 24; Lev. xxiv. 20.

of greater value.[1] Let him quietly dispute with thee about
thy property, and rather let all go as a poor beggar, than
oppose in court a quarrelsome disposition with the same spirit,
or lose thy Christian equanimity by a false judgment. Do
not continue disputing in an earthly court of judicature, but
give an unequivocal sign that thou art certain of the eternal
court of judicature. And though the supreme earthly power
does thee injustice, when a person more powerful than thyself
compels thee to go a mile as a messenger,[2] outvie the coercion
of this world of violence by the alacrity of a spirit which proclaims the victory of love over force by going two miles with
him. And when, lastly, any one employs the most powerful
weapons against thee, gentle entreaty, as a needy person, or a
borrower, grant him his request. Here in a wonderful manner
culminates the enactment, *Eye for eye, tooth for tooth.* The
highest, strictest justice is, according to its innermost meaning,
this tender love which, in the deep humiliation of a man before
his fellow-man as if he were a king, beholds a claim to which
he must respond by the tenderest compliance.

It is due to one's neighbour, it is due to one's self, to limit
these maxims in actual life, or to apply them with wisdom. But
the preservation of personality which opposes ill-usage must
never become revenge; the preservation of property must never
become a fondness for litigation; the preservation of free self-
determination must never become a fierce wrestling with superior
power; the preservation of domestic economy against beggars and
borrower must never become a heartless 'turning thyself away'
(Matt. v. 42); but in all these cases, the spirit of the highest love
must dictate and animate the protective measures. Thus the
Christian spirit, by cheerful submission to suffering, moderation,
compliance, and willingness to serve others, is to spread abroad
a spirit of life which overcomes the endless litigations of the old
world, which always threaten to become an endless complication of revenge, and allows the bloom of the most rigid public

[1] μὴ κολύσῃς says Luke. He inverts the relation between cloak (ἱμάτιον)
and coat (χιτών), because he had in his eye the violence of the robbery
which must begin first of all with the cloak, while the litigious man would
begin with the least valuable, and therefore lays claim to the coat.
[2] On the meaning of the word ἀγγαρεύειν, see Tholuck, p. 273; [De
Wette, *Exeg. Handbuch.*]

retribution to appear in the manifestation of the free kingdom
of love.   But how these precepts are to be fulfilled, in the spirit,
not in the letter, that was shown by the Lord, when before the
Sanhedrim one of the officers smote Him with the palm of his
hand (John xviii. 22).   The calm reprimand which He gave to
the man, showed that He was not afraid of a second blow, and
perhaps was the occasion of His being smitten still more (Matt.
xxvi. 67).

The last obscuration of the law is the worst, namely, *the
positive falsification and perversion of a legal enactment*.   The
bigoted pharisaical spirit had referred the Mosaic command,
Thou shalt love thy neighbour,[1] exclusively to the Jews, and then
deduced from it the poisonous false converse, *and hate thy enemy*.
To this vile perversion (Lev. xxiv. 22) the Saviour opposes the
true development of the law of love to our neighbour.   Our
enemy is exactly so far our neighbour, that he more than any
one else agitates and occupies our thoughts; therefore he is
especially commended to our love.   Precisely on those who curse
us, must we more urgently invoke, than upon others, the blessings
of illumination and mercy, if their curse is not to kindle in us the
curse of hatred.   Towards them that hate us, we have most of
all to take pains not to damage, but to benefit the bedimmed
human life in them; and lastly, for those who slander, threaten,
and actively injure us,[2] our intercessions are especially demanded,
since they are constantly giving us fresh impressions of their
unhappy state.   These are the mournful images in which our
neighbour must always continue to be commended to our love.
It is God's plan so to rule over His enemies with sunshine and
rain: the children of His spirit must imitate Him in this love of
enemies.   This is the special test of the spiritual life of a genuine
believer.   But if we merely love our friends, and kindly salute
our brethren, this is merely an exercise of the natural affections
as they are found among publicans and heathens, without any
self-conquest; no victory and no blessed fruit of the spiritual
life.

After the Lord had shown how His Jewish opponents had

---

[1] Lev. xix. 18.

[2] That more private and contemptible persecution which is carried on by
threats and slander is probably intended by ἐπηρεάζειν, and the more violent
and public by διωχειν.

deformed and relaxed the law of God[1] by their maxims, He points out how they corrupted religious life by their sanctimoniousness and hypocrisy, and precisely ' in the three chief modes of practical religion, in the performance of which the arrogance of pharisaic piety was pre-eminently displayed, and which the Church of Rome has specially comprehended under the name of good works, almsgiving, fasting, and prayer.'[2] Pharisaism imagined that it rendered the highest obedience in these principal relations of religious life, which ought to exhibit the right demeanour of a good man towards his neighbour, towards God, and towards his own life, while in reality, by forced service and false appearances, it corrupted these works, and sank down to the poorest and grossest unreality of the heathen.

These hypocrites, first of all, made out of righteousness[3] a dead mechanical service of almsgiving, and out of this mechanical service a parade of pretended holiness. When they gave alms, they caused trumpets to be sounded before them in the synagogues and public places. The trumpets which the Lord refers to were probably the loud and shrill beggars' litanies, which are always the offspring of mendicity wherever pharisaic beneficence carries on its operations; and so they have their reward—the foolish praise of blind admirers. But the Christian ought to give his alms with the greatest quietness and absence of parade. His left hand is not to know what his right hand doeth (Matt. vi. 3). No scrupulous counting out of one hand into the other is permitted before the almsgiving, and no vainglorious clapping of hands after it. The deed is performed as a pure impulse of the heart by the beneficent hand under the protection of its inward truthfulness, and never is it published to the bystanders. Whoever thus performs his good works in secret is seen by his Father in heaven; and in the public blessing which He causes to come upon him, it is manifest that He has recognised and rewarded his liberality.

Equally did these pretended religionists desecrate prayer. Since the Jew everywhere performed his prescribed devotions, as soon as the appointed hour of prayer arrived, wherever he

---

[1] See Stier, vol. i. p. 194. .   [2] Tholuck, 293.

[3] According to the reading δικαιοσύνη, vii. 1. In the Old Testament, alms-giving, ἐλημοσύνη, proceeds from justice; in the New Testament it proceeds from love, the practical charité, from the believing charitas.

might be, 'the hypocrite could so contrive that exactly at that time he should be in the streets.'[1] In such public situations these men preferred to pray in order to be seen by the people. But in return, this show was their only gain. The Christian, on the contrary, prays according to another rule. He prays in his chamber[2] with closed doors; for he has to do with his Father, who Himself acts in secret, and from His secrecy beholds him who is praying in secret. And this prayer, this most secret of secret things, as it were lost in invisibility, is blessed by God as a living spiritual work, and becomes manifest in the most glorious open effects.

But not only by their hypocritical pretensions and gloomy slave-like service did the hypocrites desecrate their prayers, like the heathen, they made them, in their delusion, mere babbling: the more words, forms, litanies of devotion, so much greater merit and acceptance with God. The Christian dare not and cannot so pray; for he knows that He to whom he speaks, who already knows all that he has to say, and whose Spirit meets the words in his own spirit, anticipates his wishes, and changes his prayer to praise.

The Lord now points out to His disciples how they ought to pray, by communicating to them what we call *the Lord's Prayer*. This does not appear to stand here in its right place, since it interrupts the progressive delineation of pharisaic corruption. At all events, Luke has specified a more suitable occasion for it. He narrates (xi. 2) that the disciples had seen their Lord praying in private, and that at the close of the prayer one of them availed himself of the opportunity to request Him that He would teach them to pray, as John had taught his disciples. It has been supposed that the time when the Lord communicated the prayer to His disciples is more correctly given by Luke than by Matthew.[3] But since Luke does not everywhere keep to the

---

[1] Tholuck, 305.

[2] Although this is said of a chamber in a general sense, yet there may be a special reference to the upper apartment in a Hebrew house, the Alijah. See Tholuck, 306.

[3] See Schleiermacher, *Lukas* 172; Olshausen, *Commentary* i. 217. Tholuck, p. 315, and Stier, i. 214, in an ingenious manner, give a twofold origin to the prayer,—that Christ the first time exhibited the prayer to the people as an example how men should pray without vain repetitions; and at another time gave it to the disciples, at their request, as a form

exact order of events, since particularly he gives this history in a connection that rests on no exact chronological datum, we may well admit that the placè where the disciples saw the Lord praying was the top of the mountain, the summit, where He first honoured them to live in the most cordial intercourse with Him, and so to see Him praying; and as soon as we make that point clear, this occurrence becomes very probable. The most distinguished of these disciples were themselves of the school of John, and prayed in forms which John had taught them, and which probably referred to the kingdom of the Messiah and the baptism of the Spirit as future divine institutions. As soon, therefore, as in this confidential intercourse they saw the Lord's method of prayer, it occurred to them that in their method of prayer they were still the disciples of John, and now the forms of prayer they had received from him must appear to them as unsatisfactory, perhaps as quite unsuitable. Hence the boldest in their circle was induced to represent this circumstance to the Lord, with the wish that now, as they had become His disciples, they might be taught to pray according to His method.

Here, therefore, the request of the disciples is clearly accounted for. If, on the other hand, we suppose it was made by them half a year later, perhaps in the summer of 782, the time to which the general position of the prayer in Luke may point, it might then appear as rather too late; and the exact reference of the disciples to the circumstance that John also taught his disciples to pray, would be without any adequate reason, since Jesus, in a great variety of ways, had already explained His relation to John.

But if the Lord's Prayer was dictated in the manner we have specified on that Galilean mountain-top, in all probability it originally preceded the Sermon on the Mount. It formed the transition, so to speak, to the instructions which Jesus here imparted to His disciples. But the Evangelist, who wished to exhibit the whole discourse of Jesus in uninterrupted connection, placed it here, where the subject under consideration was the right method of praying, in opposition to the pharisaical.

John the Baptist, in accordance with his general character,

of prayer. That the disciples, before the Sermon on the Mount, requested the Lord to give them a form of prayer, other expositors also have supposed.

would attach much greater weight than Jesus to training his disciples in outwardly fixed religious exercises, since he could not impart to them what constitutes the life of all true exercises of devotion, the baptism of the Spirit. Christ, on the contrary, taught His disciples to pray from the first by a different method, since He carried them on imperceptibly in the way of evangelical guidance to life in the spirit. He taught them, in truth, to pray without ceasing. Yet He did not deny their pious request, and so they received, at their little but living request, which itself was a beginning of most spiritual praying, that great, infinitely deep prayer, the form of prayer which they preserved as an invaluable jewel, and have handed down to the Church. We may regard this prayer as the most concentrated form of all Christian spiritual life. Just as the eternal Word, generally, was made flesh in Christ, or as the whole æthereal fire which animates our planetary system has found its expression in the sun; just as in the diamond all the elements, particularly water and light, seem to sparkle in concentrated unity; so is this prayer a form in which all the elements of the Christian spiritual life are united. First, all the doctrines of the fundamental relations of the Christian life, and of the correct order and sequence of its component parts, are to be found in it. Then it is also a compendium of all the divine promises which invite man to Christianity, and lead him to find in it his complete redemption. On the other hand, it presents the arranged pure expression of all true human prayers as they issue from the flames of all human sighs, from the purified glow of all human aspirations.[1] Therefore it is, at the same time, the combination of all Christian vows, in which the promises of God have become one with human sighs, and the work of the regeneration of the Christian completed. And as this whole Christian life rests on the life of Christ, so at the same time we may see in it a regular series of the redeeming facts of Christ's life. Lastly, the course of the Christian's life, and, in fact, the world-historical development of the Church, is expressed in it ; for the Christian's pilgrimage begins with calling on the Father, and closes with redemption from death. The Church of God is born into the world with calling on the name of God, and the general judgment at last brings its complete redemption.

[1] 'All the cries of the human heart, which ascend from earth to heaven, meet here in their fundamental notes.'—Stier, i. 213.

The invocation of the prayer manifests the pure and perfect spirit of prayer, which is one with the spirit of perfect religion, and with the spirit of the highest knowledge. *Father*, prays the Christian in the spirit of a child. But this child-spirit is not without the feeling of humanity and brotherhood, in truth a fraternizing with all good spirits; therefore it is said, *Our Father* —Father of us all. And great as the Father and as the praying family is the Father's house: the spirit of devout Christian Theism, in its elevation above all Polytheism, Pantheism, and Deism, expresses this by the addition, *Who art in heaven!* Present in all heavens, not merely, according to the meagre representation of modern Pantheists, superintending the earth, or rather only struggling into consciousness Himself; transforming all worlds into heavens, not, according to the representation of the more profound ancient Pantheism, inundated and darkened by all worlds; in all heavens ONE, not, according to the erroneous fancy of Polytheists, divided into numberless powers. In all heavens comprehending also the earth, not, according to the false notion of the Deists, withdrawn into a heaven beyond the visible universe; He Himself is in all heavens; the supreme consciousness, the perfect personality, the Father who hears His praying child when he calls upon Him. So is He *our Father in the heavens!*

After the invocation follow seven petitions, in which the primary relations of the kingdom of God, as well as of the Christian life, appear in orderly sequence and in the most living form. In seven spiritual acts and priestly dedications of life the child of God consummates the one spiritual act by which he calls down his Father with His heaven to earth, but which causes him to be drawn upwards by the Father out of all distresses, sins, and evils, into heaven.

But this is the order of the spiritual life and of prayer: first of all, man must bear in his heart the cause of God, then the concerns of his own life and heart in God. If he merely, or first and chiefly, directs his regards to himself, then he loses God, or shrivels his sense of God into Pietism. In this case he is more conscious of his own devoutness than of his God. But were he to lose himself in God, and not also apprehend his own life in God, then would he not recognise God with a pure, childlike feeling, as the Father who loves and protects His child; he would give himself up as a Pantheist to the illusion of a Deity absorbing his life, or at all events allow his life to dissolve in Mysticism. In the life of a healthy piety, man apprehends God in himself and himself in God, by the Eternal Spirit which is given him in Christ; but he puts the life of God before his own life, for by the beholding of God in Christ must his own life be glorified.

The Father Himself is the true heaven of all heavens; He therefore must come upon earth, in order that earth may become heaven. The faith of the child of God sees Him coming; but he also sees what is disposed to obstruct His advent, and stands ready to meet it with dark threatenings, though powerless. Therefore the most ardent longing is unfolded, and hastens its flight towards Him. It calls to the Father that He would come with His heaven, in the three first great petitions. God is indeed on earth already, as in heaven, with His essential presence and superintendence, but not in the knowledge and acknowledgment of men—not with His name. The essence of God cannot be desecrated, but His name may be desecrated; just as the sun itself cannot be darkened, but the clear image of the sun in the earthly water-mirror, since it is broken and vanishes when the wind agitates the stream and obscures its clearness by the mud of its bed. In the turbid religions of earth the name of God is desecrated. In the true religion, which in its concentration is one with the person of Christ, the reflection of God's glory, the express image of His essence, this name must become glorified to humanity, that it may confess to the Heaven of heavens, *Hallowed be Thy name!*

But in proportion as humanity acknowledges and hallows this name in the reception of the right knowledge of God through Christ, this heaven lowers itself to earth. The kingdom of God which is in the heart of Christ is unfolded in the life of a holy community in which the perfect kingdom of God is exhibited—a kingdom in which the domain, the laws, the Ruler, and His administration, make up together one spiritual life, in which the King has His throne in every heart, and every heart has in its King its most glorious inheritance. This kingdom is in progress, but is confronted by the resistance of a kingdom of darkness. God must prepare its way, and the Christian will prepare its way in God. '*Thy kingdom come!*'

But if heaven descends to earth, then must earth become heaven. How will it become heaven? Not by satisfaction being given to the millions of morbid human desires and all the false aspirations of sinful human hearts, which would be doing the will of the world: by having everything removed which strives against and withstands the will of God, so that every heart is offered to Him, all life becomes subject to Him. Thus will the earth become a beautiful heaven when humanity in its life shall be entirely one with the life of God's Spirit. *Thy will be done, as in heaven so on earth!*

Thus the Christian in praying has given glory to God. The name of God has so cast its rays upon him, that he has forgotten his own name; the kingdom of God has overwhelmed him with its fulness, and humbled him, so that his own glory has become nothing; the will of God has seized him like the glowing last day, and has consumed him as a burnt-offering with the innermost part of his own life—his self-will. Thus he has given God His due, but he himself seems vanished from the scene. The world itself appears a sacred pile of ashes under this devouring fire of the will of God, seizing and penetrating all things. Yet the God of the Christian does not consume his sacrifices, but transforms them, by consuming the evil in them. Thus then the believer comes forth purified from the divine fire, and now brings his own concerns to God. In the three first petitions, zeal was perfected for the honour of God, for the heavenly name of the Father, for the kingdom of the Son, for the perfected will of the Holy Spirit. In the four last petitions, on the other hand, the blessedness of the Christian is completed which proceeds from the view of this honour done to God, the higher world-life of men wherein they stand before God as eternal individuals. Three is the number of the Spirit; four is the number of the world-life. The man who rightly sinks himself in God, finds himself again in Him as a God-loved child, with his whole life borne and sustained by Him by means of his daily bread. Daily bread appears to him as the noble central point in that great operation of God's hand which always preserves him. But what preserves and animates him? The whole divine agency appears to him as daily bread, a single agency in all, whatever promotes his outer and inner life. It is not, therefore, simply earthly bread, such as a mortal father provides for his mortal child, that is here spoken of, but the bread of God with which the eternal Father daily nourishes the life of His eternal child and satisfies his heart, as this bread consists of bread and wine, light and air, men and solitude, friendship and love, God's word and light, according to the varying needs of every soul. For the Christian daily bread becomes a nourishment of the spirit by thanksgiving, and the nourishment of the spirit becomes daily bread by the intensity of the enjoyment; the two always becoming more one by the unity of his outer and inner life.[1] And in this spirit he feels all his own peculiar wants, he understands human necessity, and the divine provision for his trusting brethren, and the morbid indigence of the starving world. But with a bold soaring of filial confidence he sets himself free from all the infinite anxiety of his own heart and of the world by taking refuge with the Father. *Our Bread*—the essential (or what corresponds to our nature as the essential nourishment of life), the super-substantial, the bread of heaven, the bread of men and Christians[2]—*give us to-day*. Thus first of all his present time is glorified.

But in the next place, not the future but the past troubles him. The Christian cares first of all for yesterday, then for to-morrow. It is true he stands, in general, already in faith in the atonement; of the blotting out of his transgressions he is assured, and absolved from the sentence of final condemnation. But he well knows that he has been infinitely indebted to God with his sins and shortcomings, and will ever be indebted, and with him all his brethren.[3] His own past casts a dark shadow over his life. The longer he stands before God, with so much greater force all his own debt affects him; the debts also of his

---

[1] Comp. Stier, i. 227.

[2] So probably may the obscure word ἐπιούσιος be explained: what corresponds to our nature, with a special reference to the super- substantial, therefore to the subjective, to the ideal bread of heaven;—an exposition which, after the example of Jerome, is plainly given by Zwingli in his comment on Matthew, p. 236: ' Dum vero corpora nostra alimento quotidiano cibat, non satis esse putemus; sed animum intendamus altius et epiusion, hoc est super-substantialem petamus, plus de animæ cibo quam corporis solliciti.' On the various interpretations, see Tholuck, p. 341.

[3] Stier, 231.

brethren press upon him as well as his own sins.[1] And even the
sins by which his brethren had injured him, he now feels as his
own trouble before God. The spirit of reconciliation in its
unity with the spirit of reconcilableness agitates his soul, and
his readiness to forgive his neighbour is to him a sign of the
grace which will forgive him much more. On this point it
cannot be supposed that 'our reconcilableness gives a measure
for the divine,' still less that it can be a meritorious means of
obtaining it. But reconciliation is reconciliation once for all;
it is a spirit moving in every direction. If the offerer of the
petition does not find the moving of the spirit of reconcilableness
in his own breast, he cannot comfort himself with the divine
reconciliation. What, then, he feels and performs in this
respect is to him a sacramental sign of the great reconciliation
in God. Thus he lays down forgiveness for his neighbour,
which his neighbour perhaps cannot yet understand, on the
altar of God. He really pledges himself in the most solemn
manner to forgive all offenders, as he feels that he needs forgiveness; so that his prayer would be an imprecation on his
own life, if it were not the most certain dedication of it in
commemoration of the general atonement. He therefore seeks
the transformation of his whole past, and of the past of all
men, through grace. *Forgive us our debts as we forgive our
debtors!*

And now he turns confidently to the future, with heavenly
composure, but also with the holiest earnestness. His heart
still trembles at the recollection, how a thousand times he has
grievously transgressed through light-mindedness. He now
knows the whole danger of the past, and has an impression that
the path of his future will be haunted by the spirits of darkness.
It has become evident to him that man tempts God a thousand
times by his pride, and that, according to God's justice, the
temptation which he has practised must be abandoned, if he is
to be humbled. He sees that, according to the everlasting right,

---

[1] If it is remarked that Christ could only communicate this petition
to His disciples didactically, but could not offer it Himself (compare Tholuck, p. 353), yet it must not be overlooked that no one could feel as
He did the sins of humanity, by means of the human sympathy in His
heart, and pray for their forgiveness as the debt of the universal family of
man.

most men under the effect of the old curse-destiny enter a
tragical course in some peculiar sentence of temptation, or even
of death; thereby they come to the real redemption from the
curse which oppresses their life.   And in the life of the Lord, the
certainty makes him tremble that they might be led into such
courses in the deepest temptation, not merely for themselves,
but also for others, since in the tragical or retributive leading of
Providence, everywhere men with men—the most innocent with
the most guilty—are swallowed up in one catastrophe.   But it
is for him a most awful phenomenon, that many men mar again
their tragical course to redemption in the catastrophe, and so
get another fall under great temptation, and plunge into deeper
ruin.   This danger, which threatens his own life and that of all
his associates, terrifies him.   It cannot indeed surprise a Christian, that throughout his whole life he should meet with a succession of temptations; and this general character of his pilgrimage he cannot wish altered, since only thus he fights out the battle
of his life so as to test it.   But he knows that the most inconsiderable temptation would be his ruin, unless he took refuge in
God.   And what might be the issue if all the destructive materials of temptation, if all the powers of darkness, were permitted
in a concentrated position to attack him in all his weakness,
and completely to agitate and imperil him?   He knows not what
he may unconsciously have been guilty of in this respect, or what
may impend over him on account of others.   But the mere possibility horrifies him, as the prospect of the crucifixion agonized
the Lord in Gethsemane.   And so, in sympathy with that future
agony of his Lord, and from regard to thousands of his brethren
who all in some way or other are in peril, and to the millions
who still recklessly rush onwards into darkness, an irrepressible
sense of his own and all human weakness rises within him, and
he entreats God, *Impel us not thither; do not, in retribution,*[1]
carry us away into temptation!

A profound sense of the justice of God, which plunges
sinners who tempt God into critical situations, catastrophes,
and judgments, is expressed in this entreaty, Hurry us not away

[1] μὴ εἰσενέγκῃς ἡμᾶς εἰς has at all events this meaning, as not only the
expression and the thought in itself leads to it, but also the antithetical
clause ἀλλὰ ῥῦσαι ἡμᾶς.

into temptation! After this prayer, a profound sense of the mercy of God can discharge itself in the petition,[1] *Rather bear us upward to Thyself in redemption from evil.*[2]

He has confessed all his weakness to God, and entrusted Him with his whole temporal future. He has become assured, in his weakness, of God's redeeming omnipotence, and of its victory which annihilates the domination of all the powers of darkness. Over the evil one, and over evil and all the consequences of evil—all ills, over distress and death, his joy in God now soars aloft. He knows that all present ills are to be changed into angels of redemption, and that with the last ill, death, full redemption must come. Therefore now, with eagle's wings, his hope flies to meet the coming redeeming Lord above all the troubles of time, and transports him in spirit to His own heaven. And in this hope he embraces also the whole still threatened and oppressed community, the entire suffering humanity, in its misery, supported by the promise of Christ, 'And I, when I am lifted up from the earth, will draw all men unto Me' (John xii. 32). And, rejoicing in spirit, he sees how redeeming Omnipotence carries upwards the whole heavenly humanity from the distress and anguish of the old earth and the bonds of darkness, from death and the flames of judgment, in triumph. In this anticipation of blessedness he utters his last petition.[3] Thus the entire present and past, with the temporal and eternal future of the Christian, obtain through the prayer a heavenly transfiguration.

---

[1] The greatness and clearness of this antithesis is decisive for regarding the two clauses as distinct petitions, though in the winged course of the prayer they are joined by the ἀλλά into a living unity. We reckon therefore, with Augustin, seven petitions. The reckoning of six petitions, which has been customary, after Chrysostom, in the Reformed Church, and among the Arminians and Socinians (see Tholuck, pp. 327 and 363), overlooks the great difference and progress which exist between the thought of the sixth and that of the seventh petition.

[2] ῥύομαι, 'properly, to draw a person, namely, out of danger; hence, in the current use of the word, to draw or snatch out of danger, i.e., to rescue, to save.'—Passow.

[3] According to the whole connection of the petition, the expression ἀπό τοῦ πονηροῦ can in fact refer only to the whole sphere of πειρασμοί, of temptations, as Tholuck remarks, p. 364; so that the word is here construed as neuter, and denotes the sum-total of all evil, moral and physical. See Stier, i. 235.

The prayer here loses itself in a solemn silence which in its nature is an inexpressible act of adoration, a glorification of God resounding through the life. The doxology which has been added later[1] to the Lord's Prayer, translates this blessed silence into words which may be regarded as its correct interpretation. The words of this doxology express that the fulness of God, that His majesty, is the basis, the soul, and the aim of the prayer.

The essence of this majesty of God spreads itself out in a threefold manner on the deep foundation of His eternity. The world is His kingdom, for He rules over it with absolute control; and thus everything which the Christian implores must proceed from His fulness and His appointment. The world is His work, for with absolute power He establishes and sustains the world; therefore the petitioner stands in the contemplation of His power. His very prayer is an effect of it, and all which is asked for must be obtained by its operation. Lastly, the world is the theatre of His honour, for with absolute clearness He reveals Himself in the world, and through it in its constantly increasing transfiguration, and all prayers, as well as all the fulfilments of all prayers, tend to His glory. Finally, the Amen is the seal of the prayer, in which the Spirit of God harmonizes with man, and the spirit of man with God; it is the announcement of the fulfilment of the prayer, and therefore a prophecy of the world's transformation.[2]

The Evangelist Matthew appends to the prayer a comment on the fifth petition: 'For if ye forgive men their trespasses, your heavenly Father will also forgive you: but if ye forgive not men their trespasses, neither will your Father forgive your trespasses' (vi. 14, 15). We learn from the Evangelist Mark (xi. 25) the true relation of this explanatory remark to Christ's doctrine concerning prayer. Christ urged in that connection,

[1] The doxology is not only wanting in the parallel passage in Luke, but also in the principal Greek manuscripts as well as in the tradition of the oldest Latin fathers. See Tholuck, p. 365. It is no doubt of later origin, and added for liturgical use. In the Const. Apos. vii. 24, it appears in its first form, ὅτι σου ἐστιν ἡ βασιλεία εἰς αἰῶνας· Ἀμήν. Olshausen, i. 217. For its biblical materials a reference has been made to 1 Chron. xxix. 11. We may find the germ of this liturgical amplification in 2 Tim. iv. 18, which Stier considers as a sign of the originality of the words.

[2] See Stier, i. 240. 'Whenever the Amen of the prayer is uttered, it anticipates the great universal Amen of all creation.'

that the disciples before every prayer, just as before every sacrifice, under the enlightening, purifying effects of God's presence, should call to mind the ill-will which might be in their heart against any offender, and effect a reconciliation in their hearts with him, that the curse of hypocrisy might not fall on their prayer. They were bound to make it clear to the last that the spirit of the need of reconciliation before God was identical with the spirit of reconcilableness towards their neighbour, and to recognise in the absence of the one, the absence of the other, and in the presence of the one, the presence of the other.

The Lord next proceeds to give a representation of the third positive corruption of religious life. It shows itself first in legal, then in hypocritical fasts, and in works of worldly-mindedness which proceed from the operation of worldly sorrow and a false renunciation of the world. The hypocrites put on dismal looks at their fasts; they disfigure their countenances, exchange cheerfulness for gloom, to make a show before other people; their renunciation of the world is therefore in itself false; it is, in fact, a hankering after the praise of the world. But the abstemiousness of a Christian, when he finds it needful for the discipline of his outer and the furtherance of his inner life, ought to be a festival of his soul, and to proceed from the elevation of his soul above the lower necessities of the world; therefore he ought to fast with anointed head and fresh-washed countenance, with cheerful appearance and demeanour.[1] His painful free renunciation remains a mystery to the world, but it is manifest in a rich recompense from God. What the Spirit of God takes from him, it gives him back a hundredfold. From the pain of his renunciations, his higher life acquires fresh vigour.

Upon this follows a longer warning against avarice and worldly anxiety, the connection of which with what goes before has been mistaken by many persons.[2] And yet it might be understood by a glance at the conduct of the Pharisees, which the Lord had described. These men were, on the one hand, persons

---

[1] Compare Stier, i. 243. 'The Lord unsparingly condemns all affectation in its minutest form, and counsels His disciples, in order that they may more securely avoid this danger, to adopt as defence against it, where they have only to do with themselves in the sight of their Father in secret, a certain directly opposite *dissimulation* of face.'

[2] Strauss, i. 601; Tholuck, p. 376.

who fasted with a sad countenance; and on the other hand, such
as were greedy of gain, amassing riches, and even devouring
widows' houses.[1]   Therefore in their hearts that fasting and this
avariciousness must have a most intimate connection, or form a
decided polarity.   The history of monastic life is also an important voucher for the deep-lying connection of these passages.   In
it are seen the intensely dismal looks of a pseudo-Christian un-
worldliness; in the enormous accumulation of wealth and property in monastic institutions, the other pole is shown of the
same perverse tendency.   Discontent with the world (*Weltgroll*)
always turns into eager desire after the world (*Weltgier*), since
from the first it is animated and excited by a hidden germ of it.
And when the monastic spirit has once realized its worldly greed,
it is then pre-eminently a collector of ' treasures upon earth;' it
appropriates a dead estate, and lays upon it its oppressive *dead
hand*[2] (Mortmain); while the merchant, the banker, and every
man engaged in secular concerns, does not, at all events, collect
his treasures so absolutely for himself as to withdraw them entirely from the general social system.   But if we see in the Sermon on the Mount a confidential discourse, in which Christ
communicates to His disciples the main outlines of His doctrine
and of His kingdom in opposition to the pharisaical system, we
shall understand how strongly He charged upon them as a sin
this amassing of treasure, and how this crimination itself might
arise from a presentiment of the corruption which, in future
times, the monkish and hierarchical covetousness would bring
into the Church.   He has warned His own people, particularly
in relation to their apostolic mission in the world, with peculiar
earnestness, of this tendency to suffocate men professing to renounce the world by dead monastic property,—the Protestant
Church, by immense endowments,—the ecclesiastical office, by
the management of small or perhaps gigantic and princely pas-
toral possessions, and altogether by striving after secular wealth.

The treasures which are accumulated on earth imperceptibly escape from their foolish collector; they are consumed or
taken away from him by moth, rust,[3] and thieves; therefore, by

---

[1] Matt. xxiii. 14.   [2] Manus mortua—The freedom from taxes, etc.

[3] It is doubtful whether the word βρῶσις is not to be taken in the more
general sense of eating, *gnawing*; although gold and silver in a literal sense
do not rust, yet in a higher sense they may rust for their possessors.

the vegeto-animal, by the chemical, and by the moral principle of destruction in the lower transitory world, or, on the one hand, because by the lapse of time the property wears itself out and becomes valueless, and, on the other hand, by worldly fraud, it is soon snatched away from the possessor. But the treasures in heaven are beyond the reach of the destroyers; these are what men ought to acquire. The treasure should correspond to the heart in the wants of its eternity; it must therefore be a treasure embracing eternity—the divine life itself. For by the treasure the heart is polarized, it is in the treasure by its aims and desires. The heart reposes, therefore, in the eternity of heaven when its treasure is in heaven; on the contrary, it always suffers the death-pang of transitoriness when it has its treasure on earth, in earthly things. But how can it come to pass that the heart of an immortal being cleaves to the transitory earth? By the deceit of the inner eye, the sight of the spirit. Just as the eye of the body is light, the organ of light in affinity to the sun, enlightening the body, the individual sunlight of the body,[1] transporting the body into the light of the world; so is the judgment of the spirit the inner light which mediates to the soul the light of God's eternal world, the knowledge of its ideality and holiness, or of the eternal relations, rules, and laws of its being. If now the eye is simply in close junction[2] with the soul, animated by the spirit and consciously directed to its proper object, then the whole body is luminous; it occupies its right place. But when the eye by inward thoughtlessness has lost its power of perception, and by a distracting vagrancy, so to speak, is become evil and false, the whole body is awfully darkened, it stands in night, and becomes a night-piece for others to contemplate. But this blindness of the spirit has a dreadful result. When the inner eye, the discernment of the soul, the understanding, becomes double-sighted and confused by the divided state of the heart, and thus a darkening power for the soul, how great then must be the darkness of all nature and the world in which the soul finds itself involved, not merely the sphere of its inclinations and desires, but also its experiences, means, and objects! The

[1] Tholuck, p. 377.

[2] ἀπλοῦς. The opposite, πονηρός, appears to me to correspond to this word and its meaning, and to denote a condition in which the eye deceives by seeing double.

whole of God's world becomes a midnight for one thus darkened,
so that, groping in the dark, he seizes on the perishable as if it
were the imperishable.   It is true, the covetous man does not
imagine that he is doing homage only to the earthly, but he
wishes to connect the two, the service of God and the service of
Mammon.[1] But he cannot persist in this divided allegiance,
but must neglect, hate, and despise one of the two masters, and
that will be the lawful one.   The servant of Mammon is therefore, as such, necessarily a despiser of God.   After this solemn
declaration, Christ lays open the fatal source of covetousness,
which consists in heathenish anxiety.   With the most glorious
expressions of filial confidence, He dissuades from giving way to
a baleful anxiety.   But this anxiety is a distinct, over-hasty, irregular, conjectural brooding over the possible necessities of the
future, by which the heart is disturbed in its distinct obligatory
consideration of the requirements of the present, since its aims
are divided.[2] Anxiety reckons falsely, for it is founded on a
false estimate of life.   In order to unlearn the pernicious reckoning of anxiety, men must reckon correctly according to the
thoughts of God; they must reckon in the following manner :
He who gives life that is so valuable, will also give the nourishment for it that is less valuable; He who gives the body, will
provide the clothing that is less important; He who feeds the
fowls of heaven that live in the open air of heaven, that neither
sow nor reap, will provide food for His human family, who yet,
with all their anxiety, cannot add to the essential measure of
their life, in any of its relations, so much as a cubit;[3] He who
so gloriously adorns the lilies that grow wild in the fields, that
neither toil nor spin, will much rather clothe men; He who so
urgently holds out to man the kingdom of God and His righteousness as the highest object, will give in addition to him, as he
may need, all lesser things which vanish in the comparison.
And as a man is certain of his existence to-day, in its full, clear,
sharp reality, with all the troubles of the day, so ought he still
more to commit himself confidently to God for the morrow,

[1] On the meaning of this word, see above, p. 215.
[2] 'As the etymology of μεριμνᾶν expresses it.'—Tholuck, p. 384.
[3] ἡλικία probably here denotes neither age nor stature, but the full unfolding in the nature of the individual in every relation; his matured
temporal appearance in general.

which rests entirely in the bosom of His providence, and the troubles of which he cannot and should not know. A man must expect that the following day will take care of its own, and will bring with it its peculiar earthly troubles and its peculiar heavenly aids. Thus he should reckon according to truth with the unlimited cheerfulness of trust, in God, and not gloomily according to an erroneous fancy, as the heathen are wont to reckon, because for them there is no treasure in heaven. But it ought to be the first care of the present day to seek first after the kingdom, and most decidedly to seek after the righteousness of this kingdom. Let the Christian thus seek to live according to righteousness, and it will be found that in doing so he provides for all the affairs of life, and that he will receive all the good things of life according to his need.

Along with the obscuration of man's vital energy towards God, which shows itself in anxiety, is ever more developed the last corruption of religious life in pharisaical righteousness, since on the one side it unfolds a fanaticism which always judges harshly of others, while on the other side it falls into an increasing carnal administration and waste of holy things. And as that monastic disposition has a polarized connection with anxious worldliness, so also this judicial fanaticism is connected with this desecration of holy things.[1]

The Lord opens His representation of that propensity to judge with the dehortation, 'Judge not, that ye be not judged!' God always lets man, in His administration, experience the consequences of his own principles, of his own doings.[2] As he judges, is he judged; therefore, for example, the Jew who has always condemned the heathen as a child of darkness, has been covered through all ages of the Church with the ban of contempt, and is now regarded by the converted heathen as an unenlightened half-heathen. And as a man attributes goodness to others, is it measured to him; therefore, for example, the secret order which has made Christian toleration from the first its watchword, has always enjoyed a decided toleration in the modern European States. But this is the way with the fanatic: he sees the splinter in his brother's eye, and is not aware of the beam in his own eye.

---

[1] The connection also here is by no means wanting.

[2] In God's moral government, the unrighteous blow which I aim at another falls back upon myself. Compare Tholuck, 397.

In the little faults of his brother which bedim his eye, he sees a dangerous hurt, he calls upon him to submit to his rude attempt at curing it, while he himself is in a far worse state of blindness. And this blindness is shown in the profanation and waste of sacred things. He gives what is holy, the priestly food, the sacrificial meat,[1] to the dogs; for example, the assurance of the forgiveness of sins, the Gospel, absolution to the most impure men,—he deals out what is holy without regulating it by the conditions of the law, of church discipline, and of repentance. He throws pearls, as if they were acorns,[2] before swine; before the most brutish, the most stupid men, sunk in sensuality, he casts the most precious pearls—perhaps the honourable distinctions of orthodoxy, good churchmanship, and a title to heaven, or the communication of the most glorious mysteries of the kingdom of heaven and of Christian experience; he distributes, therefore, Christ's noble treasures without protecting these goods by the instrumentality of the Spirit, of instruction, and of consecration.[3]

But when the adherents of pharisaical righteousness have gone such lengths, they have made the whole descent from the pure heights of the law to the very abyss of corrupt injunctions. And now judgment begins to break forth fearfully. The impure spirits and profligates, as scoffers at religion, tread the wasted treasures under their feet; at last they turn round malignantly upon their unspiritual and unintelligent leaders, they make a revolution ($\sigma\tau\rho\alpha\phi\acute{\epsilon}\nu\tau\epsilon\varsigma$), and in the fanaticism of unbelief they tear in pieces the depraved servants of the sanctuary. Just as the disciples of Jesus, in their mountain-ascent along the path of true righteousness, come at last by the inner ways of the spirit to the bright height of Christ, to the company of the prophets, to the vision of God; so these, in their descent to the valley along the way of false righteousness, in dead outward observances, at last reach the abyss among brutalized men, where the ruin of their disordered nature is completed.

[1] So Tholuck (p. 405) explains ἅγιον after Herm. von der Hardt.
[2] Tholuck has ingeniously remarked on the external resemblance between pearls and acorns.
[3] 'Dogs and swine were often classed together in antiquity as unclean beasts.'—Tholuck, p. 401. Dogs and swine taken together may represent what is savage and wild in common human nature—the dogs, more especially the untrustworthy-servile, the swine, the stupidly obstinate and savage.

After the Lord in these two divisions of His discourse had pointed out the great equalization which takes place in His kingdom, in the third part He gives instructions how to avoid the false way, and to proceed in the true way.

The first condition is a most decided striving of the spirit after true righteousness, especially in prayer. His disciples were to attain the right mark by asking, by seeking, by knocking; that is, by a progressive, continually more distinct, more urgent, and more humble craving for eternal righteousness with God. They could not possibly seek this righteousness with God in vain. Christ so expresses Himself on this subject, that we feel He could not sufficiently inculcate it on His disciples. It is invariably so, He means to say: he who asks receives, he who seeks finds, to him that knocks it will be opened, as a rule, because these strivers follow an internal motive; but how much more does this hold good in the striving of human souls upwards! This certainty the Lord illustrates by a comparison. No father would meet the request of his child with trickery, and hand him a stone for bread, a serpent for a fish; he gives him the good thing that he needs. So fatherhood does credit to itself among sinful men. How much more must the child on earth be certain that his Father in heaven will not disregard his holy importunity!

Then follows the exhortation: 'Therefore all things whatsoever ye would that men should do to you, do ye even so to them.'[1] These words appear not to stand in the right connection with the following. But this appearance is deceptive. It arises from this, that the exhortation forms a section by itself, and that its relation to the rest is so little developed. But it sketches the second means of attaining true righteousness, that it consists in right conduct towards men; while the first section represented the first means, in right conduct towards God. Hence the form of transition is explained, 'All things *therefore*' (πάντα οὖν). What man seeks with God, that he finds with Him. And so he

---

[1] On the relation of this maxim to similar expressions in heathen and philosophical writings, compare Tholuck, p. 412. Moreover, this precept of Christ is not so merely formal that every one can bring into it whatever he likes, and consequently the meaning would depend on the character of the person addressed. Whoever is induced to regulate his expectations on the part of mankind by his performances towards it, will be induced to abjure selfishness (*Egoismus*), and to live for mankind.

will at last find with men what he expects from them, if he
trusts them, and therefore attests and proves it. He trusts God
for divine things, and seeks them with Him in a divine life
through religion as a petitioner. He is to trust men for human
things, and must accordingly seek them with them by evincing
to them the pure human of humanity. He is to seek the peace
of God by praying, and the peace of his neighbour by bringing
his peace to his neighbour. In the former case he must feel
himself within the heart of God by the feeling of his own need ;
in the latter, within the heart of his neighbour, by the feeling of
his own wishes. If a man makes it the law of his life to hold
himself in living unity with his fellow-men, to transport himself
everywhere into their situation, to feel and advocate their interests in his heart, then he is under the attraction and on the path
of that love in which the law and the prophets have originated
on their human side, from which they set out, and in which they
meet.

True human noble-mindedness of this kind always stands in
intimate communion with that thirsting after holiness which is
manifested in importunate prayer. Thus is Christian endeavour
constituted in its polarity.

We are next taught the polarity of Christian *avoidance*, the
two means of right negative conduct, of right precaution against
the destructive path of error.

The first rule is, that we do not allow ourselves to be carried
away by the immense sympathetic attraction of the erring multitude, who are running to destruction through the wide gate
and on the broad way, but that we keep ourselves free from that
demoniac sympathy, and, sober-minded, free, and independent,
proceed to life with the comparatively small company through
the strait gate on the narrow way. The figurative exhortation
of the Lord is founded on the spectacle of the egress from a
city. The main body of the people go out by the principal gate
on the broad highway, and bear away with them whatever is
not independent. The wise, the independent man, finds a very
small door in the wall which leads him by a difficult steep path
to the heights where he finds the true enjoyment of life.[1] As
we are here first of all put on our guard against the mighty

---

[1] The door certainly stands at the head of the way, and marks the *decision*, while the way marks the carrying out the decision.

seductive influence which proceeds from the great crowds of the erring, so also by the second rule we are put on our guard against the company of false prophets, small, but operating with demoniacal powers. We may be easily deceived by them, since they come in sheep's clothing; since they present themselves with the appearance of a correct creed and Christian zeal as members of the Church, while inwardly they are ravening wolves, actuated by a selfishness (*Egoismus*) which could sacrifice the whole Church to its interests, and propagate principles which must destroy it, as the irruption of wolves destroys the flock. But the Lord gives a palpable mark by which they may be known, namely, their fruits. Men do not gather grapes of thorns, nor figs[1] of thistles; but as the plant, as the tree, so is the fruit. Thus, therefore, were the disciples to judge of the tree by the fruits, by the practice; that is, in this case especially, by the pretensions, doctrines, projects, and institutions of the false prophets, they were to judge of their *character* as well as of the *purity* of their knowledge. They were to judge by the sour, biting fruit of the sloe, by the unrefreshing, harsh dogma, of the thorn; by the tenaciously, bur-like clinging, the obtrusive proselyte-making, of the thistle. But deceptive marks might be confounded with the undeceptive. On this point Christ lays down the distinction: 'Not every one that saith unto Me, Lord! Lord! shall enter into the kingdom of heaven, but he that doeth the will of My Father which is in heaven.' Only the most prejudiced aversion to the genuine confession of Christ can adopt the interpretation, that Christ Himself intended here to depreciate such a confession. But the mere confession is not an infallible sign; and if it becomes formal and garrulous, if a man is lavish with his expressions of homage, *Lord! Lord!* he makes himself suspected, and forces observers to examine more narrowly how far the will of the Father in heaven is fulfilled by him. In truth, it is possible for a man to prophesy formally or with reference to the cause of Christ, to express in glowing language Christian sentiments and feelings, or on the other hand to cast out demons, to correct morbid states of mind in individual cases, or in num-

---

[1] ' "Ἄκανθαι or ἄκανθα is the generic term for all thorn-plants, the best of which is the buckthorn אָטָד, which bears small black berries similar to those of the vine; the τρίβολοι have a flower which might be likened to a fig.'—Tholuck, 426.

bers, by impassioned energetic words, and to perform other works of power, without his having really entered into communion with Christ's life, or made a decided surrender of himself to Him.   And many such ardent but impure operations will in the day of retribution be placed in the right light; Christ will declare to pretentious prophets and wonder-workers of this sort, ' I know you not! Depart from Me, ye who are prompted by lawlessness as your calling.'

The discourse delivered on the mountain-summit closes with a parabolic address, which depicts the decided opposition that exists between the true hearers of Christ's sayings who fulfil them, and the light-minded who let them slip.   This practical declaration, suited to the popular intelligence, formed probably the close of the plateau-discourse which Jesus addressed to the assembled multitude, and which we now have to consider.

The Lord now quitted with His disciples the lofty moun tain solitude where He had communicated to them the first principles of His doctrine and of His kingdom, and returned to the multitude who were waiting for Him on a plateau of the mountain-slope.   In this circle also He wished to announce the equalizing principles of the kingdom of heaven, and for that reason delivered an address which repeated the former discourse in a modified form, adapted to a popular audience.   The fundamental thought of the spiritual jubilee stands out in this discourse more forcibly than in the former.   His auditory represents to Him the ancient community, with its inversion of all the eternal relations of right in temporal as well as in spiritual things.   But in the spiritual foreground He finds His disciples in the poor, the hungry, the mourning, the despised, as they form the contrast to the rich, the full, those that laugh, those that men speak well of, who might also be then present.   But of the outwardly afflicted as such He does not speak, but of men who, for His name's sake, were hated, reviled, and excommunicated, specially for the Son of man's sake, after whom they called themselves (Luke vi. 22).   In this one suffering for Christ's sake, that threefold suffering has its climax which the Lord pronounces blessed, as in the Sermon on the Mount.   The seven beatitudes find their unity in the eighth, which is identical with the ninth.   That Christ could not bless the outwardly poor abstractly considered, even not in the apprehension of our Evangelists, must of itself be understood as reasonable. Or, ought He then to have seen the weeping in those that were actually defiling their faces with tears, and given them the consolation that a future hearty laughing in a literal sense would be their blessedness? There are, to be sure, critics who are on the look-out for such absurdities. But, on the other hand, Christ did not mean exclusively and simply, spiritually poor, hungry, and mourning. There are, indeed, spiritually poor persons who are outwardly rich and temporally poor, who stand before God in the self-deception of internal riches: both classes at once find themselves placed here, if we attribute a divine spirit to the discourse of Jesus, or to the account of the Evangelists; namely, the outwardly rich find themselves among the poor, and the outwardly poor among the rich of the Gospel. But there is also a region where this dualism vanishes, where the inward want coincides with the outward, the inward sorrow with the outward unhappiness, a region of holy unhappiness that will lead to the highest salvation, and this is the preparatory school—the seminary of Christianity. To this seminary of His disciples, in which the earlier agency of the unsearchable God, who breaks the hearts of His chosen ones, had prepared the way for the new work of the compassionate Redeemer, who was to heal just such hearts, Jesus turns Himself; and He knew that they immediately understood Him, since they had already eaten their bread in the tears of divine mourning, and were ripe for the Gospel. An Ebionitish poor man, who fancies that his poverty in this world gives him a right to the riches of the future world, is a spiritually proud beggar; such an one cannot be here intended. Nor the carnally-minded poor of any kind whatever, who are rich in resentment, envy, covetousness, and generally in the indulgence of their passions. But where distress of whatever kind is transformed into calm, gentle, pure longing before the throne of the divine fulness; where want does not produce rapacity, but has for its effect pure hunger, the painful feeling of destitution, inward and outward; where the weeper drops a true, genuine human tear, in which the eternal Sun is reflected and transforms it into a pearl,—there is Christ ready with the Gospel: and that such sufferers are ripe for Him is shown by this, that they willingly receive Him, adhere firmly to Him, and allow all men to hate, cast out, and reject them, for His name's sake.

They are blessed together, and are now to know, experience, and enjoy it from the lips of Christ. And as their distress was greatly hallowed, so also is their blessedness : to these poor is promised the kingdom of God,—to these hungry ones, fulness or satisfaction,—to those that weep, laughter.[1] In truth, although isolated, they are driven out from the world, under the heaviest burdens of the cross, into the night of shame and death for Christ's sake : it is they who immediately exult with heavenly delight, who already begin here the choral dance of a blessed community enclosed in God, and yonder, in the new world, celebrate the great jubilee with their associates, the prophets of the kingdom of God, who before them had experienced the same destiny. But opposite to them stand the fortunate ones of ancient time, who occupy a lower place by the equalization of the spiritual jubilee;—obtuse rich men, outwardly and inwardly at ease, comfortable in their superabundance, who enjoyed their comfort, and have changed it into discomfort; the overfilled, whose hunger reappears in a demoniacal surfeit; laughers, from whose merry jubilee already sounds forth the woe of an endless discord. These men form the class of those who are praised by all the world, the celebrities of the day, who are at once conceivable to the extremest superficiality of the worldly mind, and are intelligible from a distance; they are the heroes of the hour, celebrated as were formerly the false prophets, whose names are known no longer.

In these men Christ does not find His seminary, and the woe which He pronounces upon them is the authentication of a fact; it is one with their situation itself, a progressive inward and outward world of endless woe.

Yet His disciples are not to stand proudly aloof from that circle. In these relations they must rather show that they are Christians. Hence the Lord now proceeds to deliver exhortations which express the high demonstrations of love, particularly in the love of enemies, which the Christian spirit can render, and ought to render.

These exhortations the Lord has not here connected with an express criticism on the pharisaic maxims, for the people at large were not yet ripe to bear such an exposure. But a tacit criticism lies in the very words themselves. First of all, the Lord

[1] Compare Ps. cxxvi.

gives directions for right conduct in love. Love conquers all
enmity, since it encounters its evil weapons with the weapons of
light. It meets enmity in general as energetic love; and in
particular, deeds of hatred with deeds of beneficence, and so on.
Then follow directions how men are to endure, to exercise patience in love. The fundamental law is this: in the Christian
spirit of glory a divine power of endurance is to be unfolded,
which rises above and puts to shame all the persecuting power
of hatred. The two first directions we are also taught in the
former discourse; the third, 'Of him that taketh away thy
goods, ask them not again,' will indeed establish a Christian law
of superannuation which must put an end to the innumerable
contentions which proceed from lawful protestations against
inveterate and ancient wrongs in political, ecclesiastical, and civil
relations. Then follows the establishment of lofty precepts by
the canon, 'As ye would that men should do to you, do ye also
to them likewise.' But if a man knows himself, he must find
that, after all, he expects and requires from his neighbour those
high proofs of Christian love; consequently he ought to render
them. In this way, he must prove himself to be a child of the
Divine Spirit. For the canon, that we love those that love us,
already exists in the natural constitution of man. 'What thank
have ye?' the Lord asks,—what gain, what spiritual victory, what
blessing of God, is there in such a love which is to be found
even among sinners, the servants of sin? He does not here
hold up the publicans as an example; perhaps less out of regard
to the presence of publicans among His hearers, than to the
popular odium against them. Sinners also, He says, do good to
those who do good to them, and lend to those who return the
loan. On such grounds, therefore, they would always find themselves in the kingdom of natural selfishness, not in that kingdom
of love in which man overcomes himself.

When a man enters this kingdom, when his love begins to
embrace his enemy, and his lending begins to change itself into
a free gift, into a permanent benefit, then he becomes like God,
who evinces His goodness even to the unthankful and to the
evil, and his reward is great. It is his satisfaction that he has
favour (χάρις) from God. He will then find the highest blessedness in being one with God in His world-embracing love. His
chief characteristic is mercy, as the Father is merciful. He

judges not : he judges not the individual; and judges not absó-
lutely.   He condemns not : he establishes no tribunal of condemnation in his zeal for what is holy.   He leaves judging to
the judges and tribunals appointed by God, and condemnation
to the Judge of the world, whose justice is ever identical with
His mercy.   But not only in what he avoids, but in what he
does, he evinces this mercy.   He forgives, he cheerfully absolves, when he is injured in his personality, and has anything
to absolve.   He gives : he gives to his neighbour whenever he
has something to bestow, cheerfully in the most abundant measure ; and so everything comes back to him marvellously,—the
absolution as well as the gift ; and full measured returns fall into
his bosom, ' pressed down, shaken together, and running over.'
    Upon this the Lord closes His plateau-discourse with corre-
sponding parables.   The first shows so plainly with what caution
He treated the people on account of their submissive relation to
the Pharisees : ' Can the blind lead the blind ?   Shall they not
both fall into the ditch?'   That befell the Jews under the
guidance of the Pharisees and scribes, and the latter with the
former.   At the destruction of Jerusalem, they fell together
into the ditch of an unheard-of ignominy and misery, into the
foulest, deepest quagmire of the world.   Without doubt Christ
had these blind ones in His eye.   For ' the disciple is not above
his master,' He adds.   If he is perfect, he is exactly as his master ; the disciples of the Pharisees are Pharisees themselves.
The same subject is continued in the second parable.   The pharisaic spirit is precisely that judicial spirit which always busies
itself with the splinter in his brother's eye, while he never detects the beam in his own eye.   The third parable treats of the
tree, how it must be known by its fruit.   As the tree bears the
fruit which is peculiar to it from its own sap and pith, so man
brings forth the fruit of his life from his heart ; it comes forth
in the words of his mouth from the overflow ($\pi\epsilon\rho\iota\sigma\sigma\epsilon\nu\mu a$), the
over-pressure or spiritual productiveness, of his heart.   And
these ever acrid words of the Pharisees and scribes—these fault-
findings, and provisoes, and maxims, and conditions, and curses
—are they not as distasteful as the sloes on the thorn-bush ?
Who would take these fruits for the proper life-fruit of the
theocracy—for the figs, the choice traveller's food—for the grapes
that cheer the heart of man in the kingdom of love ?   The Lord

now impresses on the people, that if they would call Him Lord! Lord! they must also keep His words; in this way they must decide for Him.

This is enforced in the parabolic words with which Matthew's Sermon on the Mount is concluded, which exhibit the contrast of the wise man who built his house upon a rock, and of the foolish man who built his house upon the sand.

This prophetic parable is fulfilled everywhere in individual life, in the contrast between the true believer and the pseudo-believer or unbeliever. But it is fulfilled on the large scale in the contrast between the carnal and the spiritual Church, into which Israel was divided in reference to the words of Jesus; and without doubt Jesus consciously pointed here to the unfolding of this world-historical contrast. The true disciples of Jesus are represented by the wise man. They have dug deep, in order to lay the foundation of their house. They have laid it in the depths of bearing the cross and renunciation of the world, on the solid rock of God's faithfulness and Christ's conflict and victory. And the great world-storm has come with winds and torrents of rain, and in beating on the house has proved its stability: it is firmly fixed, a strong fortress. On the contrary, the foolish man built his house on a loose .unstable soil, on sand. Thus built the carnal community in Israel: they also heard the sayings of Christ, but kept them not. It was rendered evident by the critical storm that their house had no foundation. When the great world-storm beat upon it, and shook its foundation, immediately it fell; and the fall of that house was great, a world-appalling event.

Just as this similitude was fulfilled in the contrast of the spiritual and the carnal Israel, so must its fulfilment everywhere be repeated, where the contrast of a spiritual and a secularized church comes to maturity. But the similitude is fulfilled generally by individuals, either on its joyful or its dreadful side.

It is perhaps difficult to ascertain how far, by evangelical tradition, shorter passages have been transferred from the discourse in Matthew's Gospel to that in Luke's, or inversely. The possibility of such transferences is shown by the passages in which the second discourse agrees verbally with the first. But it is not to be overlooked, that not only has the second the peculiar colouring of Luke's mode of compiling and exhibiting the Gospel history, but that it also forms a complete unity—the unity, too, of a discourse which perfectly corresponds with its object. It is evidently a discourse to the people, in which the references to the Pharisees and publicans, as they are found in the former discourse, are with the highest wisdom couched in more general terms, as was suited to the spiritual standpoint of the people, without giving up a particle of the truth. The disciples of Jesus, therefore, received with the twofold discourse of the Lord at the same time a living specimen of His heavenly wisdom in teaching, which is one with the highest courage of the preacher, and which they so much needed in after times.

The discourse of Jesus also here again made a powerful impression on the people; for He taught them as one who had authority (the living power of teaching), and not as the scribes.

Having ended His discourse, He quitted the last declivity of the mountain, and the people streamed after Him. We cast a glance back at the consecrated height, and inquire what point it might have been which the Lord thus rendered illustrious. The Latin tradition has designated the 'Horns of Hattin,' between Mount Tabor and Tiberias, as the Mount of Beatitudes.' In respect of its position and configuration, this mountain may well represent the site of both discourses. It lies in a south-westerly direction about two German miles from Capernaum. As Jesus was now engaged in travelling through Galilee, He might easily come to this precise point on His way back to Capernaum. In its form, the mountain is a low ridge or saddle with two points or horns. The mental contemplation of that evangelical mountain-scene might easily transfer the confidential discourse of Jesus to one of those points, and the public discourse to a grassy spot on the mountain-ridge.[1] But

[1] 'The road passes down to Hattin on the west of the Tell; as we approached, we turned off from the path towards the right, in order to ascend the eastern horn. As seen on this side, the Tell or mountain is merely a low ridge some 30 or 40 feet in height, and not 10 minutes in length from E. to W. At its eastern end is an elevated point or horn, perhaps 60 feet above the plain, and at the western end another, not so high; these give to the ridge at a distance the appearance of a saddle, and are called Kurûn Hattin, " Horns of Hattin." But the singularity of this ridge is, that on reaching the top, you find that it lies along the very border of the great southern plain, where this latter sinks off at once by a precipitous offset to the lower plain of Hattin, from which the northern side of the Tell rises

Robinson has plainly shown that there is no evidence to support this tradition, which is found only in the Latin Church. The first written notice of it is by Brocardus, in the thirteenth century, who also mentions the same mountain as the scene of the feeding of the five thousand; which only renders it more obscure. Yet there are no positive reasons against the supposition that this mountain was the hallowed site where the two discourses were delivered. It would, indeed, be remarkable in the highest degree, if exactly on this spot Jesus had uttered the words, 'Blessed are the meek, for they shall inherit the earth (or land),'—the same spot, namely, where the power of the Christian Crusaders was broken by a terrible defeat inflicted upon them by the Sultan Saladin, in the battle of Hattin, on the fifth of July, A.D. 1187, so that in consequence of it they lost the Holy Land. Exactly at the last moment the combatants retreated to the summit of Mount Hattin; and here they were overpowered by the Saracens, after they had a short time before assembled round the cross.[1]

At all events, in this very district so many great battles, renowned in the history of the world, were fought, where Christ pronounced His true disciples blessed, as the meek, the merciful, and the peacemakers.

Neander supposes, without sufficient reason, that Jesus delivered this discourse on His return from one of His journeys to the feasts. And even then it is not sufficiently accounted for, when he supposes that the mountain was in the vicinity of Capernaum, and that Jesus, after passing a night on the mountain, and had given another discourse in the morning, returned thence to Capernaum. We might suppose this, according to Matthew's representation, though even Matthew places the healing of a leper between the Sermon on the Mount and the entrance of Jesus into Capernaum. But this incident is fully narrated by the other Evangelists, in a manner which we cannot fail to perceive is a complementary representation.

very steeply, not much less than 400 feet. . . . The summit of the eastern horn is a little circular plain, and the top of the lower ridge between the two horns is also flattened to a plain. The whole mountain is of limestone.' —Robinson, ii. 370.

[1] 'What a battle-field round about this mountain of Beatitudes and about Nazareth!'—K. v. Raumer, *Palest.* pp. 37, 41. In 1799 Bonaparte with 3000 men defeated 25,000 Turks in the plain of Jezreel.

442 PUBLIC MANIFESTATION OF CHRIST TO HIS PEOPLE.

On the way back from that Galilean mountain, Jesus (according to Luke v. 12) came to one of the cities which He intended to visit, and, though in its immediate vicinity, was solicited by a leper that He would heal him. The man was full of leprosy ($\pi\lambda\eta\rho\eta\varsigma$ $\lambda\epsilon\pi\rho\alpha\varsigma$), and according to the law dare not come near Him; he therefore cried to Him for relief from a distance, but then ran and fell on his knees before Him, exclaiming, 'Lord, if Thou wilt, Thou canst make me clean!' And Jesus had compassion upon him, and His compassion impelled Him to put out His hand and touch him with the kingly word, 'I will,—be thou clean!' And as He spoke, the leprosy was seen to depart from him. The white appearance of the leprosy broke out upon him, the sign of healing (Lev. xiii., xiv.). The man was cleansed; but Jesus in the fervour of His compassion had touched him, before he was cleansed; and this might be interpreted, according to the Levitical statute, as having defiled Himself. He ventured to take upon Himself this appearance; for thus He appeared to defile Himself on the great scale with sinful humanity by coming into the most intimate contact with it until it brought Him to death, while in fact He sanctified humanity by this communion. But because it might appear that He had become unclean according to the statute, while the leper had become pure, he must withdraw from Him. He sent him away from Himself with a strong emotion,[1] since He charged him to take care that he told no man [2] how he had been healed, but to go and show himself to the priest, and bring the offering of purification ordained by Moses, in order to obtain the legal attestation to his restored purity.[3] But the man violated the command when he left Him, and announced in the city what had happened to him. He proclaimed it far and

---

[1] $\epsilon\mu\beta\rho\iota\mu\eta\sigma\alpha\mu\epsilon\nu o\varsigma$ $\alpha\nu\tau\omega$ $\epsilon\nu\theta\epsilon\omega\varsigma$ $\epsilon\xi\epsilon\beta\alpha\lambda\epsilon\nu$ $\alpha\nu\tau o\nu$.

[2] $\mu\eta\delta\epsilon\nu\iota$ $\mu\eta\delta\epsilon\nu$, Mark i. 44. On the different occasions of similar prohibitions, see Olshausen. Olshausen thinks that in this instance the injunction had merely a pedagogical significance for the cured leper, 'since the healing was wrought in the presence of many.' But the connection seems rather to indicate that the act of healing was not wrought in the presence of many.

[3] See Lev. xiii. The expression $\epsilon\iota\varsigma$ $\mu\alpha\rho\tau\nu\rho\iota o\nu$ $\alpha\nu\tau o\iota\varsigma$ is so to be understood that the purified person, by the offering which he brought after his recognition on the part of the priest, obtained from the priesthood a legal attestation of his purity.

wide; probably he also mentioned his having been touched by
Jesus. The consequence of this publication of the cure was,
that the Lord could no longer carry out His intention of going
freely and publicly into that[1] city, since He felt Himself
bound to spare the legal spirit of the people. In order, therefore, to occasion no disturbance in the social relations of the
city by the Levitical scruples which the law of purification
brought with it, He turned back and sought a desert place,
perhaps in order to perform a sort of Levitical quarantine, not
according to the spirit of the law, but according to the interpretation which might be put upon it by Levitical casuists. He
devoted this time to solitary prayer. But while He on His part
paid respect to the morbid legal spirit of the people, the spirit
of His evangelical freedom continued to operate among them,
among whom the narrative of the leper, of the miraculous cure
he had experienced, was spread abroad. This was shown by
the result, that the sufferers did not trouble themselves about
the circumstance of His having touched the leper, but thronged
to Him from all quarters to seek His aid.

Thus the period of the retirement of Jesus passed away,
and He returned back to Capernaum.

NOTES.

1. In the above representation I believe that I have satisfactorily explained the original difference of the two Sermons
on the Mount in connection with their remarkable affinity.
This affinity is accounted for, (1) from the fact, that the announcement of the year of the spiritual jubilee is at the basis of
the two discourses; (2) from the inducement Jesus had to communicate to His disciples in a more restricted sense, as well as
to the wider circle of disciples, the main outlines of His kingdom in a similar form as far as possible; (3) from the blending
of some elements of the second discourse, particularly the conclusion, with the first, which takes place in Matthew's account.
That original difference, on the other hand, is explained from
the necessity which influenced the Lord, in the discourse to the
people, to have regard not only to the pharisaic element in the
larger circle of disciples, but also to the judaizing hearers who
were more estranged from His own spirit; and it is proved on

[1] ὥστε μηκέτι αὐτὸν δύνασθαι φανερῶς εἰς πόλιν εἰσελθεῖν.

this supposition by the fact, that the discourses, as pure, compact, organic structures, exactly correspond to these definite different objects. We see, therefore, in this relation of the affinity and diversity of the two discourses, not the repetitions of a 'poverty-struck' speaker, but the management of the most richly furnished and skilful master-spirit, to whom it might appear quite suitable to pour forth the fulness of His spirit in reiterated allied forms of speech, since He could not have the interest of a common speaker, to veil the proper measure of the actual amount of thought in its contractedness by the act of rhetorical transformation.

2. That a view of the world so inadequate, paltry, and external as the Ebionitish—of which the leading tenet was, that whoever had his position in this life would go destitute into the next, but whoever renounced earthly riches would thereby acquire heavenly treasures—must be foreign not only to Christianity, but to Judaism, and therefore likewise to the transition from Judaism to Christianity, ought to occur at once to every one who possesses some familiarity with the New and Old Testaments. The true Israelite could not adopt this tenet, since he regarded himself as the son of Abraham, his opulent and yet pious ancestor, not only in a bodily but in a spiritual respect, and since he held sacred the promises of temporal blessings which were given so abundantly to the pious in the Old Testament. But Christianity could still less begin its course with so paltry and preposterous a maxim, since from the first it came forward in diametric opposition to all sanctimonious performances, penances, monkish austerities, and misanthropic renunciation of the world, as meritorious in God's sight, and immediately numbered not only the poor but the rich among its professors. How an element so heterogeneous, originating in a totally different view of the world, could find its way into the centre of the transition of one religion into the other, is simply inconceivable. But, from the first, Ebionitism showed itself to be a barren border-land of expiring Judaism and Jewish Christianity, in which the theocratic religious feeling was mingled, as in the kindred Essenism, with the elements of a dualistic and pantheistic heathenish view of the world and asceticism. It has been also attempted to find in the Apostle James traces of that supposed Ebionitism which some have fancied they have discovered in the second Sermon

on the Mount especially. But this supposition is contradicted
by the passage in Jas. i. 10. Here the fact is recognised, that
the same person may be a Christian and a rich man; and such
an one is not exhorted to throw away his riches, but to humble
himself in spirit and to be rightly conscious of the transitoriness
of these outward possessions. It is evident, moreover, from the
passage in chap. ii. 1, etc., that in the Christian societies to which
James wrote, there was danger of giving preference to the non-
professing rich men who entered their assembly, and of slighting
the poor, which would not have been the case had these societies
adopted Ebionitish views. Or would any one suppose James
agreed in his view of the world with those societies whom yet he
corrected? But when he inveighs against that sinful preference
of the rich to the poor, it is throughout in an ethical, never in a
superstitious tone. He never reproaches the rich for being rich,
but that they are in general opposers of Christianity (ii. 7)—
that they placed their trust in riches—that they defrauded the
labourers—that they wasted in luxury what belonged to the poor,
but oppressed and despised the pious (v. 1). A similar 'Ebionitism' to this of James often lets its voice be heard again in
our times, though in general it does not appear with a religious
and moral purity of spirit like that of James; and very soon the
second Sermon on the Mount, like the Epistle of James, might
easily come into special honour, although grievously misinterpreted and abused. But this is evident, that the criticism in
question, with the protection with which it has favoured the rich
man in the parable, as generally with its hunting out Ebionitism
in the New Testament, has already perceptibly fallen behind the
progress of the spirit of the age. . Compare on this point the
admirable remarks of Schliemann, *die Clementinen*, etc., p. 377.
Also the general proof, that it has been charged most unjustly
on the ancient Church, and from the beginning was regarded
in the Church as heresy, p. 409, etc.

3. As to the relation of the parallel passages which occur to
the first Sermon on the Mount in Matthew, in the second in
Luke, and here and there in the latter, as well as in Mark, the
apparent confusion in which, to some, they are involved (see
Strauss, i. 614), is in part explained by the foregoing remarks,
and indeed (i.) by the difference pointed out in the two discourses, to which (ii.) the circumstance is owing, that Luke

could introduce in other places those exhortations of Jesus which belonged especially to the disciples. This is particularly the case with the Lord's Prayer, Luke xi. 1–4; with the exhortation to prayer, 9–13; with the parable, vers. 34–36; as well as with the warning against heathenish anxiety, xii. 22–31. It is, indeed, very conceivable that several of the sentences of the first Sermon on the Mount which recur in the other Evangelists, were repeated by the Lord in other connections; as, for example, the sayings in Mark ix. 50; Luke xii. 34, xiii. 24; xvi. 13, 17, and 18. But single passages might also be first brought by the Evangelist into another connection; as, for example, Luke xii. 58. As to the passages in question, particularly in relation to Strauss (i. 606) and Schneckenburger (*Beitrage*, p. 58), it will be seen how far this connection, even in a spiritual relation, can be marked as insufficient, or be placed partially under the category of 'lexical connection.'

4. The Sermon on the Mount, as the pure, spiritual, fundamental law of the New Testament kingdom of God, may be compared with other forms of religious and moral legislation. The comparison of this new form of the eternal law with the Mosaic, as well as with the pharisaic maxims, lies in the representation of it, therefore in the sermon itself. It appears, namely, as a harmonious development of the former (not as a correction of it, which would be altogether against Christ's express declaration); as a cutting, decided antagonism against the latter. On the relation of the statements of the Sermon on the Mount to heathen morals, Tholuck has adduced many illustrations in his excellent *Commentary*. Stier, in his *Words of the Lord Jesus* i. 172, has made some striking remarks on the false application of the Sermon on the Mount to political relations; as, for example, by the Quakers and other sects, and more lately in the evangelical Church, in reference to the political law of marriage.

5. It has been a controversy of long standing, how far the Lord's Prayer is an original creation of Jesus, or a composition from materials already known. Tholuck has discussed this question at length in his *Commentary*, under the title of 'Sources from which the Lord's Prayer may have been derived,' p. 322. According to Herder, Richter, Rhode, and others, the prayer must have been taken from the Zendavesta. This hy-

pothesis is regarded by Tholuck as exploded. It belongs, indeed, originally to the category of those hypotheses in which the difference of national mental character in the ancient world, and especially the characteristic differences of the religious systems, was utterly misunderstood. The case is different as to the derivation of this prayer from the old Jewish and rabbinical prayers of the synagogue. Tholuck himself remarks that the collections of prayers, of which the Jews still make use (called מחזור), contain striking prayers, borrowed both in thought and expression from the Old Testament. 'And why might not the Saviour have collected and combined the best petitions of those well-known prayers' (p. 323)? But he finds, in conclusion, that only similarities can be pointed out, which give no ground for supposing 'that the Lord's Prayer originated from the rabbinical prayers.' Von Ammon, in his *History of the Life of Jesus* (*Geschichte des Lebens Jesu* ii. 76), reverts to these similarities very fully. The address, *Father in Heaven*, he says, is frequently found in the Mishna. But it has been justly remarked that Christ needed not to take this address from the Mishna. As to the first petition, it is noticed that in the Kaddish, one of the oldest morning prayers of the ancient synagogue, it is said, *May Thy name be highly exalted and honoured* (hallowed). As to the second petition, the Kaddish has again ימליך מלכותיה *regnare faciat regnum suum*, followed by the words, *May His redemption bloom; may the Messiah appear.* Manifestly the first petition in the Lord's Prayer is reduced from an indefinite feeling to a clearly defined thought, and the second is essentially altered. This represents the kingdom of God as one still coming; the Jew, in his prayer, assumes that it is one already existing. The sentences adduced in reference to the third petition—*Let His name be glorified on earth as it is glorified in heaven; and fulfil Thy will above in heaven, and give Thy worshippers rest of spirit on earth*—are manifestly very different from the third petition. The analogy to the fourth petition taken from the Gemara is very interesting. *Thy people Israel need much, but their insight is little. Therefore, may it please Thee, O God, to give to every individual what he needs for life, and as much to every body as is necessary for it.* These words may certainly be applied to the exposition of the fourth petition. Had the Lord already found this formula, it might be said that the fourth

petition bore the same relation to it as a finished creation to
a world in process of formation.   For the fifth petition the
author has only quoted this sentence from the Mishna : *May God
blot the sins against his neighbour only when the transgressor has
reconciled himself with his neighbour ;* also the petition from a
Jewish liturgy of an undetermined date, *Forgive us, O Father,
for all have sinned.*   As to the sixth and seventh petitions it is
said, ' In the seventh and tenth petitions of the eighteen blessings, the subject spoken of is expressly the many afflictions and
scatterings of the Jews in their dispersion, and then the hope of
their near redemption, when the trumpet shall sound to bring
them back to their own land.'   This manifestly presents no
definite analogy.   Also an ascription of praise similar to the
doxology is found, according to the author, ' not only in other
Jewish prayers, but also in the eighteen blessings.'   He looks
upon this as a reason why the critical examination respecting
the doxology in Matthew should not be considered as finally
settled.   In the relation of the prayer of Jesus to the rabbinical
similarities adduced, we see at least the common participation of
the two forms in a theocratic religion.   Moreover, the Lord's
Prayer is related to these similarities, in their scattered state,
as a piece of pure gold to a piece of ore containing gold but
in very small quantities.   We cannot here speak of a mere
collection, nor of a mere composition, nor indeed of a mere
reproduction.   For, apart from the scattered state of these
similarities, definite parallels are altogether wanting to some
petitions, and even the more definite analogies are here found
in a new form.   But we see from the comparison that the
fundamental thoughts of the ancient Jewish devotion are concentrated in the purest gold form in the devotions of Jesus,
while in the rabbinical synagogues they are lost in discursive
expressions, so that the Lord's Prayer is exactly related to
these similarities as Christianity itself in general is related to
Talmudism.

6. ' Legally, fasting among the Jews on the great festival of
Atonement was from evening to evening (Lev. xvi. 29), and
traditionally (*Taanit.* iii. § 8) in autumn, when the rainy season
had not begun and the sowing seemed in danger.   But since
the conservatives (*Stabilitatsmänner*) or rigorists held it to be
meritorious, they fasted twice (Luke xviii. 12), or even four

times in the week (*Taanit.* c. iv. § 3); they appeared in the synagogue negligently dressed, pale, and gloomy, in order to make the meritoriousness of their maceration visible to every one.'—Von Ammon, p. 81.

7. On the disease of leprosy, compare the article relating to it in Winer's *R. W. B.* 8. Since the bad tree, δενδρον σαπρον (ver. 17), had been already characterized by thorns and thistles as plants which belong to that class, we cannot understand by it either a tree that bears no fruit, or an old half-dead tree which often bears good fruit, but rather a degenerate or wild-growing tree. See V. Ammon, ii. 103. According to this, the expression is significant, and testifies that Christ recognised a depravation in nature (corresponding to the ethical evil in the world) which showed itself specially in the nature of thorns and thistles.

END OF VOLUME II.

CPSIA information can be obtained
at www.ICGtesting.com
Printed in the USA
LVHW101340160422
716387LV00003B/108

9 783752 591576